PRAISE FOR *BETWEEN LOVE AND HONOR:*

"This is a beautiful book based on strong research, illuminated with very successful novelized touches." —Jean Soublin, *Le Monde*

"Built as an adventure novel, but based on rigorous work of research, this book tells the true story of a noble and powerful man torn between two cultures and two loyalties...The result is a fascinating epic." —Robert-Yves Quiriconi, *Associated Press*

"This powerful novel is the result of colossal research serving an exalted plot." —Nathalie Six, *Le Figaro Littéraire*

"Those who love sagas will have everything they can hope for! One cannot help but think about Alexandre Dumas, and also—and mostly—about the movie this fabulous story should become!" —Elodie Marillier, *Le Point*

"With this novel written the bit between her teeth, Alexandra Lapierre—sovereign and galloping—proves to be the true riding heiress of Joseph Kessel." —Raphaël Stainville, *Le Figaro Magazine*

"Alexandra Lapierre's book reads like an adventure story, an epic, a universal tale." —Christelle Lefebvre, *Var Matin*

"Though it looks like a novel, Alexandra Lapierre's book is a true and exemplary piece of history." —*Direct soir*

"A gripping historical novel written by an authentic pro." —*Version Fémina*

"You are overwhelmed by the power of the writing." —*Télé 2 semaines*

"A novel in the grand style of Alexandre Dumas, where the magic of the story blends with love, war, religion...A total success!" —Philippe Vallet, *France Info*

"The shattered destiny of this Chechnyan prince is worth all the screenplays in Hollywood! Everything here is true, from the daggers, the horses, the diamonds...to the blood, the tears...With a light hand, Alexandra Lapierre achieves the union of history and epic...she offers us this rebel, his love and his honor, heartrending certainly, but glorious in the end." —Jean-Francois Kervean, *Gala*

• ALSO BY ALEXANDRA LAPIERRE •

AVAILABLE IN ENGLISH:

Artemisia

Fanny Stevenson: A Romance of Destiny

Women Travelers: A Century of Trailblazing Adventures 1850–1950 (in collaboration with Christel Mouchard)

AVAILABLE IN FRENCH:

La Lionne du Boulevard

Un homme fatal

L'absent

Artemisia

Fanny Stevenson

Le salon des petites vertus

Le voleur d'éternité

Elles ont conquis le monde. Les grandes aventurières, 1850–1950 (in collaboration with Christel Mouchard)

Tout l'honneur des Hommes

L'excessive

Between Love and Honor

ALEXANDRA LAPIERRE

• TRANSLATED BY JANE LIZOP •

amazon crossing

Printed in the United States of America.

Between Love and Honor was first published in 2008 by Plon as *Tout l'honneur des Hommes : Dans la Russie des Tsars, le destin du fils de l'imam de Tchétchénie.* Translated from French by Jane Lizop. Published in English by AmazonCrossing in 2012.

Cover portrait of Jamal Eddin by Andrea Fortina, private collection, France, reprinted here by permission of the artist.

Published by AmazonCrossing
P.O. Box 400818
Las Vegas, NV 89140

ISBN-13: 9781611091458
ISBN-10: 1611091454
Library of Congress Control Number: 2011963463

"He felt as though he carried within himself
all that remained of the honor of men."

–Joseph Kessel, *La Règle de l'Homme*

• CONTENTS •

RUSSIA AND THE CAUCASUS
IN THE TIME OF JAMAL EDDIN

CHECHNYA, DAGESTAN, AND GEORGIA IN THE TIME OF JAMAL EDDIN

• TO THE READER •

The story of Jamal Eddin Shamil, eldest son of the third imam of Dagestan and Chechnya, a man caught between two cultures, two faiths, and two loyalties, is true. I have chosen to write it as a novel in order to more fully flesh out—in dialogue, action, and sequence—the fruits of my three years of research in Russia and the Caucasus. The reader can be certain that the dates, the sequence of events, and the actions of the main characters cleave to the facts and closely follow the sources that I uncovered in the archives.

At the end of the text, the reader will find a small glossary of Caucasian terms, a list of main characters and place names, and a short bibliography.

A. L.

PROLOGUE

Not Ours, Nor Theirs

A Plain in Greater Chechnya
Thursday, March 10, 1855

As the coffin of Czar Nicholas I descends into the crypt of the Romanovs in Saint Petersburg, two groups of horsemen gather on the banks of the Mitchik River, in Chechnya.

On one side of the river stand the warriors of the imam Shamil, the Lion of Dagestan, who has been resisting the Russian invader and decimating his immense Christian army for the past thirty years. The sounds of the horses' pawing and the clicks of loaded rifles are the only signs of his troops, most of whom are hiding among the trees of the forest, which ends abruptly at the riverbank. The imam's personal guard stands in a row along the shore. With their long beards, shaved heads, and lambskin hats and black coats, sabers slung bandolier-style across their shoulders, and banners held at arm's length, they are the warriors of Allah. They surround four heavy canvas-covered wagons, which reveal no sign of life within. A splendid white stallion in silver-trimmed tack, riderless, paws the gravel at the riverbank nervously. Beyond the thoroughbred and the wagons, the Caucasus Mountains rise, massively and majestically, along the horizon, toward the sky.

On the opposite bank stand the Russians. With considerable effort, their three regiments have just finished dragging their cannons to the summit of the only hillock on the plain. All of them, soldiers and officers alike, are aware that they will be advancing shortly with no cover at all. There are no bushes, not even any shadows on this side of the river, only an empty plain that descends gently to the water.

Shamil's Muslims are in a position to fire at them at will. Indeed, the Chechen horsemen are the ones who chose this spot for the meeting, mercilessly exposing the Russian troops. In the event of an incident, they are prepared to cross the Mitchik and massacre the flower of the army of infidels.

Three generals of the Russian army—all Georgian princes—sit tall and still in their saddles on the facing hill, a fourth officer, a young lieutenant wearing the blue of the Vladimirsky Lancers, at their side. Like the three princes, the young man is looking through his binoculars to zero in on the warriors on the opposite bank, the other world. He searches for the master of this strange ceremony, the imam Shamil. The Montagnard is waiting farther up, away from his troops, seated beneath a huge black parasol. The young lieutenant sees only his shadow.

An unseasonably hot sun shines on the ragged branches of a dead fir tree, a lone tree on the Russian shore, halfway between the Muslim and Christian camps. This is where the exchange will take place.

Both armies are still. No one moves, but all are tense, ready to attack.

This morning, though, no blood must flow.

On the other side of the river, thirty-five Dagestani and Chechen Montagnards begin to ford the river, flanking the four wagons with their mysterious loads. The wagons teeter, threatening to overturn, as the wheels sink into the rocks and mud of the riverbed.

But from sandbank to islet, they manage to get across. The first wagon reaches the dead tree.

One of the imam's horsemen breaks ranks, waving a banner to signal that the meeting may now proceed.

The princes and the young man ride down the hill.

Four abreast, they make their way across the plain, followed by their aides-de-camp and thirty-five soldiers. And by a convoy of four other wagons carrying forty thousand rubles and sixteen Chechen prisoners.

The ransom.

The two enemy groups are face-to-face, each warily watching the other's every move.

As the princes reach the tree, they can barely make out the figures of the twenty-three women and children huddled inside before the Chechens close ranks around the enemy wagons.

They will not allow the Russians to approach the hostages. These are the princes' wives, sisters, sons, daughters, and nieces, whom Shamil kidnapped the previous summer and has held in captivity for over eight months.

Bargaining chips.

One of the imam's sons, a formidable warrior of twenty, pale and nervous, greets the princes with a hand held over his heart. He delivers an interminable speech in a language none of the four understand: Avar. The interpreter translates only the bits and pieces he finds essential.

"My father wants you to know that your women return to you as pure as lilies, protected from all eyes like gazelles of the desert."

Joy, anger, and a burning desire for vengeance cross the faces of the princes, who stiffen. They nod without comment.

The lieutenant slowly leaves the Russian contingent. He guides his mount forward and bows to the imam's son, his brother.

Without a flicker of recognition in either of their faces, Shamil's two sons embrace. They have not seen each other in sixteen years. This cold greeting leaves them both trembling.

The Chechen horseman holding the banner presents the lieutenant with a *cherkeska*, the traditional uniform of the Caucasus, and asks him to put it on. The puzzled young man, who has forgotten his mother tongue, turns to the interpreter.

"The imam wants to see his eldest son dressed only in the clothing of his country," the interpreter explains.

Dismayed, the young man protests, "How can I get undressed here, in front of everyone?"

"The wishes of the imam are law. You will learn that no one disobeys your father. No one."

He dismounts. The Chechens press around him, forming a dense circle that hides him from the view of the others.

He cannot, must not, keep anything of his Russian past; nothing. Not his boots or spurs or epaulets. No more bright colors, no more purple and gold. One by one he undoes the buttons of his uniform and unbuckles his belt. He unties the decorative silk cords, whose copper tips glint in the sun.

The circle opens and he emerges. His transformation into a Chechen warrior is complete.

The young man is now identical to the horsemen who surround him: he wears a black knee-length coat with cartridge belts across his chest and soft leather boots; his slim waist is cinched tightly with a leather strap, and a dagger is tucked into the waist. They recognize him as one of their own. Well-built like them, he has their noble bearing, their agility, and probably their stamina too.

But beneath the heavy lambskin hat, the former lieutenant's face is pale, his features more drawn than ever.

His regimental companions, his boyhood friends, the comrades he grew up with at the Russian court, gather round him one last time.

One of them unbuckles his baldric and hands him his own saber.

"Take it, as a remembrance."

Choked with emotion, the lieutenant's friend tries to joke, "But please, don't kill any of ours with it!"

"Not ours," the young man replies, his expression serious. Devastated by this farewell that he knows is definitive, he repeats, "Not ours, nor theirs."

He leaps into the saddle on the white horse that was brought for him, the purebred that had been pawing the ground at the riverbank, the mount that will take him to the shadows where Shamil awaits him.

Far from this spot, the imam trembles too, with love and fear and impatience. His beloved son was torn from him by his enemies so long ago. How had the Russians brought up his son, the proud little eight-year-old boy he had been forced to surrender as a hostage? Has the eldest son of the imam Shamil become a *giaour*? A dog of an infidel? A renegade? A traitor?

Before going to prostrate himself at his father's feet, in keeping with Muslim custom, the young man looks at the wagons carrying the captive princesses. Standing there in silence, the women seem to have been transformed into statues. All are dressed in rags and veils.

Through the long foulards that cover them, they look intensely at their liberator. They know him. They danced the mazurka with him at the court balls of the Winter Palace. Beneath the layers of fabric, their faces are streaked with tears of relief, gratitude, admiration, and pity.

They know how he was torn from his people and brought to Saint Petersburg by force. They know he has built a life for himself in Russia, that he is now a well-read officer, fond of the music of Glinka and French poetry. They know the czar considers him a favored son, a member of the imperial family, a lieutenant in the Russian army, to which he belongs completely.

They know that his renunciation of this world whose values are now his own is the only thing that has saved their lives.

They know as well that Czar Nicholas left him to choose freely. The young man could have refused this exchange. And that at this very hour, the imam's son is sacrificing his very existence for them.

One of the three princesses knows other things as well. She knows that once, long ago, he loved her.

Watching him approach, she remembers the whispered secrets they once shared, when they were together.

The image of this horseman in black, running toward a destiny he rejects, reminds the princess of another, of the little boy fate had thrown into a universe he never should have known. It was sixteen years ago. A Chechen child rode down a mountain path, through the boulders, between his father's eyrie and the Russian army camp. Behind him, the cadavers of his tortured people rotted, unburied, among the ash-colored rocks. He did not cry. He had kept his dagger and his saber. He would kill them all. Full of pride, hatred, and fear, the little boy had reached the camp of his executioners.

And now, today, he must return upon the same path. He must go back to his childhood, his reluctant steps forward taking him back. All he has lived for the past sixteen years, all he has learned at the hands of the invaders, he must forget.

He must unlearn everything, again.

He rides before the captives, and for a fleeting moment, their two worlds are one. The women are indistinguishable from one another. And nothing distinguishes him, a Chechen horseman, from their captors. Except that he is searching among the veiled women for his first love. His eyes finally come to rest upon the one he instinctively knows, beneath the shawls, is her.

He passes next to her and reins in his horse.

No words can express what the long look they exchange does: the adieu of Varenka, hostage of the imam Shamil and daughter of a Georgian prince, and Jamal Eddin, hostage of the czar and son of the imam.

Book One

The Years of Apprenticeship Among the Horsemen of the Caucasus 1834–1839

La ilaha illa Allah
There is no god but Allah

"Oh, savage are the tribes that haunt these gorges.
Liberty is their god, and War their only law!
Loyal in friendship, even more loyal in vengeance
[…] For them, Hatred is as boundless as Love."

– Lermontov, *Ismaïl Bey*

CHAPTER I

Without Limits

Ghimri, a fortified village in Dagestan
September 18, 1834

For those unfamiliar with the mountain, the path was impassable. The dogs, the sheep, even the goats hesitated to venture out on it. But old Bahou-Messadou traveled it back and forth between the village and the spring several times a day. She had gotten into the habit of going to fetch water before dawn, before the call of the muezzin, before the other women were up, when no one was around to witness the difficulty she suffered moving around in the early morning.

With a jug on her head and her veil held between her teeth, she walked into the darkness, feeling her way along with uncertain steps and a shaky distress that had filled her entire being ever since her son had left again, a visible sign of her emotional state. She knew from habit that her ankles might loosen up halfway down the path, but that her hips and knees would feel stiff all the way to the well. Only when she leaned over the coping to get hold of the rope, stretching her sore muscles to catch the bucket and, finally, hung over the coping with all her weight to bring the water up, would her joints loosen up. Concentrating on her chore would take her mind off her thoughts—the snatches of sentences, the accusations overheard or dreamed, the memories, the plans, even the prayers.

On the way back, head held high, the weight of the huge copper ewer compressing her spine, her limbs relaxed, she would walk with her back straight. No one would ever guess that Shamil's mother carried a heavy heart full of apprehension.

Bahou-Messadou couldn't put a finger on this unnamable burden. It had started a few days before, with the news that the second imam had been murdered, his assassins punished by a vengeful Shamil. She should have felt proud, even light-headed with joy. Her only son, born sickly and puny, had emerged as the spiritual guide and military chief of all the Caucasian Muslims, and all this thanks to his own valor, the fervor of his faith, his superior mind, nobility, and beauty. Today Allah had conferred upon him the supreme honor, the most sacred of powers. At this very moment at the mosque of Ashilta, Bahou-Messadou's village, home of her ancestors, Shamil was being consecrated imam. The third imam of Dagestan and Chechnya.

The first had been killed here during a Russian attack two years ago. The second, yesterday, by renegade Muslims. This morning, Shamil would take their place as the shadow of God on earth. Why wasn't she beaming with pride and joy? Any semblance of either was so mitigated that she felt guilty. Allah permitted—indeed Allah *ordained*—her to rejoice on this day. What was wrong with her, that her feelings were so unusually reserved?

Perhaps it was because of what she heard and sensed here in Shamil's absence, in the elders' attitude toward him, in things she had heard around the well. She would deal with the women's gossip later.

For the time being, she needed to be alone in the silence of the night.

Bahou-Messadou knew that Shamil's most ferocious adversaries were here at Ghimri, the *aul*, or mountain village, where he had been born, grown up, and gotten married. She knew that his community had voted against him when all the others had selected him as imam, and that his peers would have blocked his path had he wanted the consecration to take place here. She knew also that Shamil had broken their resistance with iron and fire. Was that why her son had emptied his own village of the faithful, dragging his troops four hours' journey away to Ashilta, his chosen rallying point? Was it to avoid another bloodbath at Ghimri? Was that the reason?

Or was it because he was waiting for the men of Ghimri to openly betray him? Then he could break them, bring them to their knees, and force them over to his side. Was it a test? If so, Bahou-Messadou feared the consequences. She glanced around her.

It was a black, starless night, though she could see the reflection of the moon on the eternal snows across the mountain chain. The mountains. Their mass pressed into the tiny figure of Bahou-Messadou, closing in on every side but the left.

On the left was a drop into the void.

She heard the roar of the Avar Koysu, the raging river that rushed through the bottom of the chasm, and the soft, familiar sound of the pebbles that rolled beneath her thin soles and fell straight to the bottom of the gorge. Shamil was a good son who looked out for her, and he disapproved of her trips to the well in the black of night. But she did not need the daylight to know the number of steps between the ledges that hung over the path, which hung so low that the women had to bend over beneath the rock face to creep past. Bahou could smell the humidity of the rocks where the cliff face jutted out, she could feel the wind blowing about her feet, and she could hear the dull, muted roar of the river. She would slide the jug down from shoulder to belly and crouch down, holding the water close to her.

Nonetheless, had one of her grandchildren ventured out before the call of the muezzin to follow her here, she would have pinned his ears back.

Her thoughts returned to the village. When all was said and done, Bahou-Messadou was wary of Ghimri, even though she had lived there for forty-five years. She looked up to see the dawn piercing through the clouds that hung over the terraces of the aul.

Even though Ghimri was in the south, perhaps even farther south than Ashilta, the sun would not reach the hamlet, even on this clear September day. What Bahou-Messadou disliked most about Ghimri was the cold. How would they keep warm this winter, when Shamil had forbidden cutting down a single tree from the forest below? Not so much as a branch or the trunk of a beech tree or an oak, not even the bark of a chestnut tree. He saw the forest as vital, the best rampart to stave off a Russian assault. Bogged down in the branches, the Russian soldiers would become easy prey. As long as the forest was there, he said, the warriors of the Caucasus would be invincible, so he had issued strict orders that it be preserved everywhere. Anyone who touched it, even to gather wood to build a house or make a fire, would be punished. A felled tree would cost the offender a cow; two, his life. That was yet another source of discontent.

She paused a moment to catch her breath on the uphill climb. The village was so high up the mountain that the air was thin. She slid the jug over to her other shoulder, an action she never would have undertaken in public, and for good reason. Twisting the small of her back caused a flash of such sharp pain that she could not suppress a grimace. She continued up the path now, grumbling in her placid, quiet way. She groused about her body, which was no longer able to contain its suffering. The fear that someone would discover this made her avoid people's gazes in Ghimri.

But why hadn't Shamil taken the whole family to Ashilta? Why not move there once and for all? Because Ashilta was too far down the mountain? Too close to the Russian lines, too easily accessible? Regardless, he had still chosen the mosque of Ashilta for the ceremony of investiture. She herself had grown up in the shadow of its walls, and she believed what they said: the mosque at Ashilta was the greatest, the most beautiful, and the only one left standing. The mosque at Ghimri had been beautiful too, but the Russians had razed it to the foundations after desecrating the place with their excrement.

She glanced anxiously up at the overhanging rock. All she could see was a slab, barely distinguishable by its color, slightly darker than the uniform ash gray of the mountain. On this dark September morning, Bahou-Messadou imagined the village as it had been two years ago. She thought she could see the tiny one-story houses, like cubes with flat roofs, that served as the thresholds of the houses above them, piled one upon the other like boxes, arranged in an open circle like an amphitheater.

The first and largest row of buildings hung on the cliff, facing the void. The last was tucked up against the summit of the mountain. In between was a jumble of balconies and terraces, with a minaret and a few doorless, windowless lookout towers, a labyrinth so tightly constructed no stranger would ever venture in.

Everything, even the steep, narrow, tortuous alleys too narrow for two horsemen to pass, seemed designed to discourage the visitor and drive back the invader. In fact, with every fortresslike house defending the one just above it, the village could only be taken by assault.

Shamil had left nothing to chance. He had had the ramparts reinforced and had towers and redoubts built. Conscious of Russian artillery power, his choices were all motivated by a single question: despite all his preparations, could the infidels' cannons reach his eagle's nest? His chief, Khazi Mullah, the first imam, had reassured him. How could the Russians drag their heavy cannons up to these heights? How could they hoist so much weight up paths made for guerrilla warfare, trails so vertiginous that even the animals avoided them?

Of course, the Russians had taken these questions into consideration as well. Unfortunately for the men of Ghimri, they had found answers.

As the sun rose, Bahou-Messadou looked out upon a landscape she knew all too well: a field of ruins, charred rocks and squat tree stumps. It had been two years ago yesterday, or perhaps tomorrow. What would happen if these pigs descended on the village again while Shamil was gone?

She had no illusions. If the Russians took the second path, high above the river and just as dangerous, there would be no sharpshooters or horsemen waiting to ambush them. They would find only the silver river of the Avar Koysu at the bottom of the abyss; the gray, overhanging cliffs; and the birds of prey hovering over the invisible herds. No one would block their path. They could take over the wells, the towers, and the tiny fields they had already burned to the ground. They could make themselves right at home. The family chiefs who had not followed Shamil to Ashilta would pay them allegiance. No holy war would take place at Ghimri.

And yet once, not so long ago, the men of the Caucasus had loved their freedom so fiercely that no young woman would have accepted a husband who had not laid at her feet the heads of a dozen infidels, their hands nailed to her father's door.

Bahou-Messadou despised her neighbors' cowardice. In her clan, those who favored peace were called the hypocrites. Somewhere deep inside, though, she pitied their weakness.

How could the survivors resist the invaders when, two years ago, such valiant warriors as Khazi Mullah, the first imam, and Shamil, who was then his lieutenant, had not been able to?

The Russians had decimated their ranks with weapons unknown to the village. They had blown up the mountain, dug into the cliffs with explosives, and climbed vertically from one ledge to the next, hoisting their cannons with pulleys and winches from one level to the next. Their soldiers had dropped like flies under fire from Shamil's troops, and they had suffered great losses, but no matter. As the casualties fell, others took their places. The Russian army had an unlimited reserve of officers, soldiers, and serfs. Shamil said they had tens of millions of slaves.

So the war was lost before it had ever even started, the hypocrites argued today, and for a dreadful reason: it violated the Koranic proscription to combat an enemy superior in number. Shamil and his men were four hundred against thirty thousand. Thirty thousand Russians had swept down upon these boulders, spreading death and devastation. And since then, the corn and the barley no longer grew in the small fields and the children cried with hunger. The rocks had turned the color of ashes, and no wind or rain washed them clean. The soot that coated everything formed a dark, greasy layer over the snow. Was this the victory God conferred upon those who served Him?

Day by day the rumors swelled. Shamil was not one of the chosen. He was weakening Islam. He displeased God.

In the silence of the night, Bahou-Messadou could no longer ignore their words, and she wondered. To her son, resisting the Russians was all about crushing everyone who opposed the holy war. But wasn't this fight against the teachings of the Koran?

Allah have pity on Bahou-Messadou's presumptuousness! How could she, an old, ignorant woman, dare to think such thoughts when Shamil was opening the path to Salvation?

And yet, she was incessantly tortured by doubt. She prayed for the pardon of her son and the pardon of Allah; she did penitence by carrying burdens that crushed her body and spirit. She brought the water from the ravine and pushed and dragged loads of earth and stones far too heavy for her for the reconstruction of Ghimri. She worked in the fields and did all the domestic chores that the men of the clan would not lower themselves to do, repeating the gestures for which Allah had created her. The men had their weapons; their role was to live up to the honor of fighting and killing and dying courageously. Hers was to lighten their woes and support them on their journey through life.

Bahou-Messadou walked past the ruins of the old well that the Russians had poisoned by throwing carrion and cadavers down it, past the watchtowers and the first courtyard. As always when she neared the village, she held her head high. She tried to straighten up fully, and God punished her for her pride. She bumped into a rock. The jug slid from her shoulder, and she hadn't the strength to hang on to it. The ewer clattered onto the ground, the copper clanking over the rocks. She rushed to pick it up and stood listening for a moment, afraid a dog's barking might wake up the women of the village.

But no, the shepherds' dogs were out prowling around on the mountain. And the others, those that had guarded the meager store of fruit and the chickens, had been killed. All was still silent. She patted the ground to measure the extent of her mistake.

The water trickled down in thin rivulets. In her mind's eye, she watched the tiny streams of lost purity rush down the incline.

It reminded her of a vision even more disturbing, of thousands of dribbles of purple trickling down to her feet, bathing them in a bloody puddle. The memory washed over her with a wave of nausea. But it hadn't been blood that had stained her pants to the ankle; blood would have been purer, more noble than this vile poison. It was wine, all the stores of wine that Shamil had forced his people to spill, entire casks of it, denouncing each other and repenting the sin they had committed by making alcohol as they poured it down the hillside.

How long ago was that? Seven years, eight? In any case, it was long before the Russians attacked the village and burned the arable land. At the time, Shamil wasn't yet thirty. Bahou-Messadou approved his actions wholeheartedly—her husband had been a drunk, like his father before him. But the vineyards, why had he destroyed the vineyards? The most beautiful vines in all the Caucasus grew in Ghimri. Shamil had ripped them up by the roots, removing even the temptation to offend God. Nothing was left, not a single stock, not even a shoot.

She could see him, standing there in the midst of the terraced plots. She saw him, splendid and colossal, digging in the soil with his sword, the soil that had been carried up here, plot by plot, on the backs of women. Her mother, her grandmothers, her ancestors, all of them had labored to accomplish this, at pains only Bahou herself could appreciate. She had been shocked by the destruction of the fruit of such great effort, repeated generation after generation.

She understood that it was a symbolic gesture. And she knew what it signified: the replacement of the old order, the order of men, with the new order of the *Sharia,* the law of God, which demanded the purification of souls and unbridled war against the infidels.

Her mind returned to the question that nagged her incessantly: what if the inhabitants of Ghimri chose to reject a spiritual guide they had not elected?

They held him responsible for all their misfortunes. It was Shamil's raids, and those of the like-minded first imam, also from Ghimri, that had provoked the fury of the Russians. Other auls, infinitely easier prey, had not known such massacres for a simple reason: Shamil had not lived there.

What if they sold him to the infidels? Why not? There was a price on his head.

By the evening of the attack in 1832 when the first imam had been pronounced dead, Shamil's worth had increased tenfold. Today, on the morning of his consecration, the price on his head had multiplied a hundredfold. Unlike the others in her camp, Bahou-Messadou was not proud of the fact. She blocked out the thought of how pleased the Russians would be to capture the man who had slipped through their fingers two years ago, only to resurface and set fire to all the villages that had gone over to the Great White Czar.

Her thoughts wandered, going over all the potential pitfalls of the future.

If they couldn't get their hands on Shamil himself, the hypocrites of Ghimri could give the infidels his family—his mother, his sister, his wife, and his two sons—in exchange for peace.

As soon as the muezzin called them for prayer, the elders would certainly meet to discuss the possibility. Bahou-Messadou had no illusions about the fate that awaited her, and Fatima, and especially little Jamal Eddin, the eldest of Shamil's children and his heir, if the villagers should decide to hand them over. Worse than capital punishment, they would be forced into exile. And perpetual bondage.

Slavery in the midst of the giaours? The thought of such a betrayal filled her with revulsion. If there was one state no Muslim man, woman, or child could tolerate, it was slavery.

"God does not listen to the prayers of slaves," Shamil roared. "No one can allow himself to be taken alive by the infidels."

Bahou knew he was not haranguing his horsemen. It went without saying that none of them would ever surrender. These orders were destined for the ears of his mother, his wife, and his sister. When they could no longer resist, they must kill their children before killing themselves. Death was preferable to captivity, the greatest of all disgraces.

But first, he fully expected them to prove their worth by taking as many of those pigs as possible with them.

Bahou-Messadou ran her free hand lightly over the handle of the small dagger that she carried hidden beneath her tunic. It was nothing unusual; all the women of Dagestan wore a *kinjal* tucked into their belts.

She was not afraid. Her fate was written, and what would be would be. She had no fear for herself. She only worried about protecting her grandsons and all those dear to Shamil. Losing the water this morning was a bad omen.

She set off again down the path to the well, with the same measured steps, thanking Allah in his mercy that not a soul in Ghimri had witnessed her weakness and her mistake. She had known that this day would be difficult, but her journeys back and forth gave her a sense of peace. She felt at home here, on the path to the river.

The night and these desolately rocky surroundings—the peaks that loomed, somber and threatening, the raging river at the bottom of the ravine, these abysses so black that bats flew there in the middle of the day—this was all she knew. She loved the impassable massifs that had shaped the men here for so many centuries, even if their immensity made unity among the different villages impossible. How many times had she heard Shamil repeat that Allah desired the union of the "believers" of the Caucasus, and that their union could only be achieved through their faith in God and respect for his law. He said that there were hundreds of thousands of Muslims in the mountains, most of them in Chechnya and here in Dagestan. Of the thirty tribes of Dagestan, 125,000 people were Avars, like themselves. But among the Avars, the Darghis, the Laks, the Lesgiens, the Chechens, and the Inguches, no one spoke the same language. There were forty languages in Dagestan alone. How could they ever come to an understanding?

There was always Arabic, but only the mullahs and the religious leaders spoke it. She herself did not understand it. She knew how to listen, though, and she was interested in the people who lived in the villages around her. When Shamil returned, whether from battle or after delivering a sermon, he always came to see her, because he knew he would find an attentive ear. How could they achieve union, he pondered, how could they unify for freedom and the glory of God, if not by marching together in the service of Allah?

On this point, he had convinced her. The believers could not revive their power, their influence, their prestige, or the grandeur of their past and resist the infidels unless they returned rapidly to their faith and its original principles, the laws dictated by God in the *Sharia.* The Muslims had no choice. Catastrophe was imminent unless they reestablished the laws of God everywhere. The coming of the Russians and the propagation of their corrupt ways threatened all with defilement and extinction.

Shamil's confidence in the wisdom of his old mother flattered Bahou-Messadou. But what advice could she give him? She knew the holy war began with oneself, within oneself, with the reconquest of purity and the return to God. There was no other way. Through sermon and example, Shamil must convince those who remained unconvinced on this point. And if his eloquence was not enough, he must use force.

It was this war that Bahou feared above all. The terror her son bred within his own ranks, the death and destruction he wrought among his brothers against all who did not follow him—could that war ever end?

This was the price of freedom, in Ghimri, in Ashilta, and in all the villages of the Caucasus.

And now?

Dawn was about to break, and Bahou was still on the mountain path.

And now? What was happening in the mosque at Ashilta? Had Shamil succeeded in asserting himself as the supreme leader of the entire Caucasus? Had the tribes joined together under the authority of the Montagnard, whose stronghold had been razed by the Russians? Had he triumphed over the powerful Chechen Hadj Tasho, who had made the pilgrimage to Mecca and considered himself more worthy of the title of imam? Bahou-Messadou was counting on the influence of Shamil's spiritual mentors, the courage of the faithful, and Shamil's own deft handling of the situation.

But would he be able to return to Ghimri to save his family?

She set down the jug carefully, and propping it solidly upright with a handful of stones, she sprinkled a few drops of water on her henna-tinted right hand, then on her forehead and her face.

Then, steadying herself, her right side, shoulder, and knee jutting out slightly over the void, she knelt on the incline, facing southwest.

Forehead against the rock, eyes closed, the old woman listened to the echo of her prayer, the one that she had repeated all her life. She murmured fervently,

I bear witness that there is only one God

I bear witness that Mohammed is the messenger of God

God is Great, God is Great

There is no other god but Allah.

Far above her, the cry of the muezzin awakened the believers.

"Neither Russian cannon, nor the imam's saber! Death to the heretic! Death to false prophets!"

As she reached her home, the spectacle before her confirmed Bahou's fears. In the courtyard, children circled around her daughter-in-law, chanting the words they had probably heard in the madrassa, their Islamic school. Fatima, dumbfounded, had not had time to react. Draped in a brown veil, her water jug tied to her back, she had just stepped out to go to the well.

Her two little boys followed her. Barefoot and in rags like the other children, they had close-cropped hair and wore old, rust-colored shirts that fell to their ankles. She could count on the feistiness of Jamal Eddin, her eldest son. He shouted louder than all the others and kicked and punched anyone within reach.

He looked about six, but he was actually much younger. Tall, slender, and dark-haired like his mother, he wouldn't let anyone give him a hard time. Behind him stood his little brother, a toddler who copied his sibling's shouts like an echo.

Bahou was struck to the core. Her sense of foreboding was confirmed. She knew danger was imminent.

She hesitated, trying futilely to measure the gravity of the situation. The upheaval of the last few days had made it impossible for her to get her bearings, leaving her in a state of confusion.

A few pushes and shoves were probably all that her grandsons were in danger of receiving this morning. But tomorrow? Or even later today?

She knew that she didn't need to go to her daughter-in-law's rescue; Fatima was quite capable of taking care of things herself. Though she looked soft and frail and unassuming, anyone who dared to criticize her husband or touch her children soon discovered another side of her character. Shamil had chosen his spouse judiciously. Bahou would have preferred a girl from Ashilta, but he had chosen the eldest daughter of the surgeon in the neighboring village of Untsukul. He had not been mistaken. Fatima gave him sons and worshipped him, supporting all his actions. She was such a good wife that he wanted no other. Though he always made a point of coming to see his mother before returning to his wife, Bahou knew how deeply he loved Fatima. Bringing him joy and peace, she was the incarnation of happiness in his life. Bahou understood the significance of the insults directed at her and at Jamal Eddin.

In the two years since the mothers and grandmothers of Ghimri had returned to the village, jealousy had sprung up among the women in the seraglios. Why were their sons, daughters, and husbands dead? Why was the imam Khazi Mullah dead? Why had they all been murdered during the attack? All except Shamil?

He should have perished with them. His family too.

Of course, no one dared deny that he was courageous. The strength and bravery of Bahou-Messadou's son was legendary. He had resisted until the very end, killing more infidels than even the bravest of Ghimri's defenders. Pierced by a hundred blows, he had fought to the end. And so? What difference did that make? He had not died a martyr, like their own loved ones, so he had contravened the precepts of Allah that promised paradise to those who truly served Him. The dead were the brave ones, not Shamil. His partisans could sing of his prowess and tell of his last-minute escape—a spectacular leap over the heads of the Russian soldiers. What his followers persisted in calling his "Death Leap" did not constitute divine intervention. On the contrary, the villagers interpreted his survival, when his 399 warriors had been slaughtered, as a pact with Satan. The faithful elsewhere in Dagestan considered the miraculous preservation of his home, when all the other homes of Ghimri had been burned to the ground, to be further proof of Allah's protection. The inhabitants of Ghimri knew otherwise.

The old women remembered that, when Shamil was a child, he would often disappear into the mountains, to the back of the caverns with the giants, to meditate upon the loss of the believers. Only the devil's disciple would have dared to wander near the sulfur fields of Arakhanee, where tongues of fire welled up between the rocks and wreaths of smoke rose from hell along with the stench of sulfur.

They told of Bahou-Messadou's son, born left-handed, sickly, and scrawny. In those days, his name was not Shamil but Ali, Ali the Southpaw, Ali the Impure, and he was a sad sight indeed. Frequently susceptible to fever and evil spirits, he did not learn to ride or shoot or participate in games like the other children. Poor Bahou, these hypocrites moaned, poor thing, between a drunk for a husband and a sickly child, luck certainly hadn't smiled upon her. And then one day when Ali was seven, she wrapped him up, naked, in the pelt of a sheep she had skinned herself. She left him lying in this bloody sheepskin for seven days and seven nights. Then, among the hundred names of Allah, she chose a new one for him: Shamil, he who embraces all. Though still left-handed, when Shamil changed his name, his nature changed as well. He began to grow like a weed and secretly trained to develop the skills of an athlete. But God was not responsible for this transformation. No, it was the giants who had fashioned him in their own image—a colossus.

Bahou didn't care about the jealous old ladies and their silly stories that blended the outrageously false with a grain of truth. Nonetheless, she was wary when such gossip was echoed in the conversations of the men in the council of elders. If Shamil had been here, they wouldn't have dared speak that way!

More children came running down the hill toward Shamil's house. Squat and unexceptional, it was in the middle of the village and had remained intact, with its ground floor stable, its mud walls that had flaked off in places, and its ladder. Its wooden balcony was supported by two pillars that had been scorched black by the flames. The fire had gone right over the roof, sparing the family's few possessions—the big cushions on the benches, the carpets decorating the walls, all of Shamil's books, and the precious manuscripts of his Sufi mentors. Even Muessa, his beloved cat, named after Mohammed's, had been spared, not a hair singed. Surely this was proof that Allah watched over them.

Bahou hesitated. Amid the chickens, the firewood, the nuts and little bouquets of herbs drying on the terraces, the crowd of angry matrons was growing. Ghimri was like a huge stairway she would have to climb against the tide. She had a few words for the elders, and those words could wait no longer.

The village sages were stunned when Bahou-Messadou barged through the council door. No woman had ever dared force her way in.

A dozen men with trimmed medium-long beards sat cross-legged on the narrow platform that ran along three walls, facing the mountain. On the remaining side, the room opened out onto a wooden balcony, a sort of open loggia supported by thin pillars planted in the boulders overhanging the void. Bahou had known them all for nearly half a century, but she defied all custom by bursting in on them. Her behavior was inexcusable. She uttered the words that, in the Caucasus as in the Orient, were the equivalent of a talisman. *Azh dje ouazhek*: I am your guest.

This phrase, which every traveler pronounced when asking for hospitality, placed her under their protection. As long as Bahou was in their dwelling, each member of the council must guarantee her safety. The moment she left to go home, she would cross the threshold of their domain and her fate would be in God's hands. They could slit her throat or shoot her in the back. But she would have said what she had come to say.

Eagle-nosed, gray-bearded, his lower lip split by an old wound whose scar extended all the way down his neck, the tall and noble patriarch Urus-Datu sat in the center.

"*Salam Alaïkoum*," he replied in Arabic to her request for hospitality. Peace be with you.

The old man touched his forehead, lips, and heart as Bahou-Messadou answered him with the same words and gestures. A murmur of discontent went round as she advanced to the center of the circle.

Bahou-Messadou was blinded by the daylight that struck her full in the face. It took her a few seconds to identify the old men who sat before her. There was Saïd Mohammed, the *qadi* who lost all his sons in the massacre at Ghimri. And Kural Mohammed Ali, the muezzin, her own nephew, who might take her side.

Bahou-Messadou was in no hurry now, and acted as though no urgent danger threatened her. Time seemed suspended as she silently scrutinized these austere horsemen with their craggy faces and sparkling eyes, her relatives. She knew they were all brave. Noses broken at the bridges and the scars of blows on their brows, across their cheekbones, and down their cheeks were proof of the violent combat that each had experienced in the past. Why were these men ready to make peace with the enemy? Did the yoke of Shamil weigh that heavily upon them?

Their expressions were far from amiable. She sensed the resentment of these men, some of whom she had played with as a child. At the time, boys and girls had not been so strictly separated. They had been forbidden to mingle beginning only a decade before, under the rule of Khazi Mullah, the first imam. It was he, her son's friend and mentor, who had outlawed dancing and music and all the secular gatherings where men and women could meet, and he who had demanded the sequestration of the weaker sex in seraglios and the wearing of the veil when they went out. Barely ten years. Bahou-Messadou respected Khazi Mullah's teachings to the letter.

Frankly, the imam's imposition of another veil hadn't made much difference. It was just a scarf, a sort of handkerchief that covered the mouth up to the nose, knotted at the back of the head. All it took was a dip of the chin to put it on or take it off. For the rest, she had kept her mother's long, straight shirt that revealed the bottom of her pants. It had been white in her youth, then red, the color for married women. Now that she was old and a widow, it was blue. It had no pockets. Pockets had always been forbidden.

In addition to Khazi Mullah's kerchief, she wore another scarf, which covered her forehead down to her eyebrows, and, on her head, a long white shawl draped over her entire body, covering her to her ankles.

Nonetheless, the moment she walked in the door, everyone recognized her. Even draped from head to foot, the familiar figure of Bahou-Messadou had not changed. Her posture was still noble and erect, her manner dignified.

Of course, time had made her a bit rounder, perhaps a little stooped, but she had put on no discernable weight as was often the case with age. And if she was imposing, it was not due to her height or her weight, as was the case with her daughter. It was something else. Her eyes. All one saw was her eyes.

Instinctively she tried to hide their brilliance, blinking slowly like a cat and softening their flame beneath a coat of tears. But Bahou-Messadou's eyes flashed. Joy could make them sparkle, anger or attention darken them to almost black. The members of the council knew this predatory look, this fixed stare, the eyes' clear but indefinable color somewhere between green and gray. The look of Shamil.

With a habitual gesture of her chin, she dropped the kerchief that covered her mouth. One of the few privileges of her age, Bahou-Messadou did not have to hide her beauty or avoid tempting the devil. She was permitted to reveal herself, unveiled, before the hypocrites. One privilege she did not enjoy was that of the first word.

She stood there silently, waiting for them to ask why she had come. Fed by surprise and hostility, the silence went on and on.

She noticed that they rolled their amber prayer beads between their fingers, like all good Muslims. Their shaven heads were covered, as the prophet wished, as a sign of respect for God. All of them wore the *papakha*—a tall hat of black sheepskin. Not a single one wore the turban of the followers of Shamil.

The very fact that none of them had tied a white sash around his papakha made the biggest statement of all: their opposition to the consecration of Shamil as supreme leader. It was also a means of preventing the Russian spies, who understood the significance of the turban, from mistaking them for the disciples of the imam, his *murids.*

For the Sufis of the Naqshbandi order, the word "murid" designated the pupil of a spiritual guide. The Russians, however, had broadened it to mean rebel, warrior, and fanatic. Since the arrival of the first imam, the Murid Wars were, for the Russians, simply synonymous with *gazavat,* the holy war.

Every head of family took special care to avoid confusing "murid" with "Montagnard," well knowing the danger any mix-up might cause. The Russians couldn't tell one from the other—or didn't bother to do so. The turban was the only mark that distinguished the warriors of Shamil from the other men of the Caucasus.

They wore identical hats of black sheepskin and the same long, collarless coat, one lapel crossed in a V over the other, the cherkeska. Tightly cinched at the waist, it fell in folds to their boots. They all wore rows of cartridge belts, *ghizirs,* across the breast, which held powder and simplified reloading the pistols they carried at their waists. All were armed with kinjals.

They valued the dagger in particular and wielded it like a saber. It was a straight knife about two feet long with a double-edged blade that was striated with grooves for the blood to run down. Bahou-Messadou used it to cut the throats of stray dogs, slicing their necks elegantly, without transpiercing them, in contrast to the giaours, who stabbed their victims in the belly with bayonets.

The Montagnards also carried *shashkas,* slightly curved scimitars, and on their backs, muskets that obliged them to stand up straight.

None of them would have considered parting with a single piece of this heavy arsenal, not even for an hour sitting at the council. An unarmed man was not a dead man; he was a man without honor.

Sitting with their legs tucked under them, their prayer beads around their wrists, they were ready to attack, so it was a relief when the head of the council, Urus-Datu, pointed at Bahou's bare face.

"Immodest woman, is this how you obey your son's commandments?"

"My son commands only what the Koran dictates: that believers respect their elders, and that you listen to what they have to say."

Ullou Bek, whose sharp tongue she had feared from the first second, interrupted her.

"Shamil does not respect the elders. Shamil respects nothing."

Bahou particularly disliked him. She sensed that whatever vestiges of prestige she retained were worthless in his eyes. He did not come from the village. Richer, younger, and more oriental, he had slightly slanted eyes and full lips beneath his moustache. A quick glance at his splendid white papakha and the chasing on the silver cartridges decorating his cherkeska distinguished him clearly from the others.

He had the same emaciated face, the same aquiline nose and high cheekbones, the same height and slender build of the Montagnards. A neighbor from the East, he had been invited to sit with the council. Since he hadn't the power to throw her out, he simply ignored her. This woman counted for nothing. He took up his discourse at the precise point where her unexpected arrival had interrupted him.

"Shamil cares nothing for our laws, Shamil does not respect tradition. What right has he to scorn the *adats,* our laws of the elders, which have settled our conflicts since the beginning of the world? What right allows him to keep us from respecting the law of blood and vengeance, the *kanly* that commands us to avenge our insults and our dead privately, without the intervention of the qadi? He declares that our debts of blood decimate our families, our communities, and our tribes, and prevent us from uniting as Muslims. Lies! Honor dictates that we take a life for a life, but Shamil wants them all. All for him alone, not for the glory of God, but in the service of Shamil."

Ullou Bek knew how to influence his audience. *Your lives, Shamil wants them all, he wants them all for himself.* At Ghimri, this was a sensitive point. Here the inhabitants were born free and equal; their sole governing authority was this annually elected council. Even the infidels called some of the mountain communities "democracies" or "republics." Ullou Bek, however, was a khan who governed in sovereignty over his province. His title and his prerogatives had bought him the support of the Russians, who pretended they sought to deal only with a noble. They had immediately dubbed him a "prince" and conferred upon him the rank of major in their army. He was a sellout.

Bahou-Messadou hadn't been mistaken. The presence of Ullou Bek was proof of the enormity of what was at stake at this meeting.

Suddenly addressing her presence here, he looked her squarely in the eye.

"Your son does not order us to act according to the commands of the prophet. Your son takes himself for the prophet!"

This phrase provoked such an outcry that Bahou knew she had lost. She was not up to dealing with such a dreadful accusation of sacrilege and impiety.

Ullou Bek waited for things to calm down before going on.

"Shamil named his cat after Mohammed's cat. He divulges his proclamations on little bits of paper, like Mohammed. Shamil wants to think he is the reincarnation of Mohammed on earth."

Bahou-Messadou had no answer.

"Ullou Bek is right," the men all cried out at once. "Shamil's election at Ashilta is illegal!"

She was overcome with emotion. She could no longer follow the discussion or even register the meaning of their comments.

"Several different living imams cannot coexist in Islam. The only spiritual chief of Islam is the Ottoman sultan."

Ullou Bek. She should listen only to Ullou Bek, to his arguments, his deductions and conclusions. They were the real source of danger.

"The Ottoman sultan, the only imam we recognize, signed a peace with the Russians. If we continue to fight the Russians, we are flouting the authority of the legitimate imam, the sultan."

"My son respects the authority of the Ottoman sultan," Bahou insisted heatedly. "He worships him."

Her clear, metallic voice, distinct from all the others and trembling with emotion, cut through the melee. For a moment, all were silent.

The head of the council pointed at her again.

"Speak," he ordered her.

Bahou, once again speaking in her usual measured tones, seized the occasion to prevail. Outwardly calm, she repeated, "My son worships the authority of the sultan. But Sheik Jamaluddin, his revered guide, told him that the sultan's authority cannot extend to our lands. He said that the sultan's authority can no longer be felt in our mountains, for the infidels have cut us off from the rest of Islam."

She chose her words carefully, measuring their influence and subtly shifting the attention to someone everyone in the room respected, the major figure absent at this assembly.

Sheik Jamaluddin al-Ghumuqi al-Husayni, Shamil's guide in the apprenticeship of knowledge, passed for a direct descendant of the prophet. He spoke fifteen languages, including Arabic, and forty mountain dialects. He could recite the entire Koran as well as the four hundred adats Ullou Bek had referred to earlier that constituted the social code of the communities. He was the incarnation of the highest religious authority of Dagestan, the greatest spiritual guide, or *murchide*, of the Naqshbandi order. Bahou had not lied; Shamil worshipped him. He worshipped his wisdom and knowledge, heeded his advice, and listened to all he said.

The elders could rage all they liked. But at this very moment in the mosque of Ashilta, the approval of Sheik Jamaluddin confirmed the legitimacy of the election of his pupil, as chosen by the troops.

Bahou-Messadou drove her point home.

"You should elect a third imam so you won't be left to yourselves, without a spiritual guide. That is what Sheik Jamaluddin said."

"There was a time when Sheik Jamaluddin held an entirely different point of view!" Ullou Bek exclaimed.

The head of the council intervened.

"What do you know of Sheik Jamaluddin, woman, other than the fact that the first of your descendants bears his illustrious name? I myself heard him forbid your son to take up arms. Back then he said that, even if we were prepared to fight the infidels, a religious leader who preached the *Tariqa* in a mosque should not do so."

"Sheik Jamaluddin changed his mind," Bahou insisted.

"And do you know why?"

"Yes, I do."

"We're listening."

"Because the believers owe allegiance to no one. To no one!" She enunciated each word explicitly, looking Ullou Bek directly in the eye, a breach of propriety that, in such extraordinary circumstances, all the men ignored. "No one but the faithful who are favored by Allah."

"That is to say," Ullou Bek countered, his words dripping with sarcasm, "to your son."

"To the mullah who possesses both the wisdom of the religious science of the Tariqa and the military talents of a warrior chieftain," she corrected him.

"Shamil is not that man! Shamil is not favored by Allah. He wants absolute power so that he can take our property. Look what he did with the treasure of the khans of Avaria!"

At last.

Bahou-Messadou took a deep breath. Finally they had broached the subject that had been on all their minds, the object of all their worries: the treasure of the khans of Avaria. Now they would evoke the real reason for this discussion, the reason that made them fear Russian reprisals and gave rise to this urgent need to make a decision. The events of the last month justified their questions. The upheaval of the past two days demanded they find an answer.

Today, September twenty-fifth, the muezzin would call the faithful to the second prayer of the morning.

Four weeks ago, on August twenty-fourth, Shamil had left Ghimri with all of his men to join Hamzat Bek, the leader and second imam, who had taken the place of Khazi Mullah, slain during the attack. They had left to conquer Kunzakh, the capital of Avaria, a community under Russian subjugation, six hours away on horseback.

Hamzat and Shamil had taken the city and all the property of the ruling family. They had decapitated the khanum, the widow of the khan, who had been the infidels' ally. They had executed all of his followers and massacred his three sons.

Hamzat Bek had then moved into the palace, with all their treasure. Shamil had returned home to Ghimri. That was five days ago, on September twentieth.

The same evening, a messenger came to Ghimri to tell Shamil that Hamzat Bek had been murdered by Hadji Murat, the foster brother of the heir of one of the khans. He had stabbed Hamzat in broad daylight in front of the mosque of Kunzakh, then fled.

Within the hour, Shamil had called a meeting of Hamzat Bek's warriors to elect a new imam.

"But Shamil," they had said, "we already have a leader. It's you."

He had refused their offer twice, but twice more they voted for him. Time was short, and vengeance could not wait.

Shamil had finally accepted their choice, but not without demanding that each of them make a solemn oath to obey him, in blind faith and absolute submission. He then gathered his murids together and galloped off toward Kunzakh.

There, he sacrificed all the prisoners, confiscated the treasure, and kidnapped the last child of the khans, a boy of eight. The ruling house of Avaria, once the realm of the Russians, seemed to have been definitively wiped out.

The plunder and the child had been loaded on mules and sent to Ghimri, where the boy had been strangled in public, his body thrown from the bridge over the Avar Koysu. The coffers of booty had been carried to Bahou-Messadou's home. This had all taken place the day before yesterday.

Shamil had immediately left for his investiture and the official consecration by the heads of all the tribes of the Caucasus at the mosque in Ashilta. Just yesterday.

And tomorrow the Russians would attack with a vengeance and try to recover the treasure.

How could they deal with this threat? Perhaps by taking the imam's nearest as hostages?

They could be used as barter.

Either in negotiations with the Russians or, later on, in negotiations with Shamil himself.

No matter, as long as Ghimri was able to keep the wealth of the ancient capital of Avaria.

That was what Bahou-Messadou had come to talk to them about, the treasure that Shamil's Polish soldiers, deserters from the czar's army who had converted to Islam, were guarding at this very moment in the outbuildings of her apartment.

As it happened, she did not have time.

All of them could hear the clamor in the village below as a breathless messenger burst into the room where the council was meeting.

"The Russians are coming!"

CHAPTER II

Sabers in the Torrent

Ghimri
September 25, 1834, at midday

The Russians. The members of the council greeted the news in stony silence.

They made not a move and uttered not a question, which was unusual for these fierce and vivacious old men, so adept at eloquence and irony. Discipline of body and mind prevailed as they demonstrated the impassive dissimulation of long habit.

They barely shifted their backs from the wall. Their heads held high, their palms remained at their knees. No one moved a muscle. The black line of their hats seemed to have been traced upon the red background of the carpet. The looks in their eyes revealed nothing. Not agitation nor contemplation of danger, nor the excitement of imminent combat. Even the expression in Bahou-Messadou's eyes, now glassy and half-closed, had become vague.

Everything seemed so serene that the messenger was suddenly ashamed of his own precipitation. He took a deep breath and decided to deliver the most urgent information deliberately and calmly.

"They have crossed the Avar Koysu at the Devil's Bridge. They are taking the lower path. There are a hundred of them and they are four hours from here. They are burning every aul in their path."

Urus-Datu thanked him with a nod.

Then Urus-Datu turned to the muezzin and, in a single concession to the danger at hand, asked him to issue the call to the second prayer of the day. This was a ploy learned from Shamil, who had not hesitated to advance the ritual time for prayer by a few dozen minutes during difficult negotiations in order to gain time. The decision of the elders, to resist or surrender, could only be made after turning to Allah.

The pale September sun was far from its zenith when the muezzin appeared on the balcony. But invoking the name of the Lord brought neither relief nor serenity this time. No one in Ghimri listened, except for the council.

The women ran all over the place, yelling as they gathered their possessions, rounded up their children, and grabbed their chickens. Experience had taught them that they had no choice but to flee. To escape with their meager possessions by the peaks and the steep slopes that led down to the river and hide deep in the forest, where they would listen and wait. The giaours were afraid of being ambushed in the woods, and perhaps this would discourage any chase. Maybe this time they would decline to die from the single shot of an invisible assassin, especially when the prize was so unappealing—a few chickens and women who were so worn out by successive pregnancies, back-breaking fieldwork, and daily chores that, at twenty-five, they looked twice their age.

* * *

The same turmoil reigned in Shamil's seraglio. Bahou-Messadou's daughter, the heftily built Patimat, rushed back and forth, stringing on her bracelets and necklaces, hiding the rest of her jewelry and the silver plate beneath the loose floorboards, at the bottom of a hole where they had been safe two years ago when she had fled to the forest.

That was all she had salvaged from the first attack. Her husband and son had both been killed.

The five Polish deserters who guarded the treasure at Bahou's home loaded the khans' chests on mules from the stables. Like the women, they knew what the advent of the Russians meant. They knew what followed submission to the czar and the annexation of a country to the empire, for less than four years ago, they had seen how the Russian army had reestablished order in Warsaw. They knew all too well how Nicholas I smothered revolts and treated the vanquished.

All former officers, they had been humiliated, stripped of their ranks, and deported to the Caucasus, where the peasant-soldiers starved them and forced them to take on the most degrading tasks, treating them worse than serfs. Thus they paid for their taste for liberty in the service of the conquerors, dying courageously for a cause they viscerally rejected, the triumph of the Russian Empire. Until the day when, with nothing to lose, they had gone over to the enemy.

The Dagestani imams could count on their hatred. Every one of these men would consider it a joy and an honor to massacre those who had tortured them. Knowing as they did the fate that awaited them if captured, they never allowed themselves to be taken alive.

Shamil's assignment of the Polish soldiers to his mother's house had been a carefully calculated move.

"Where is Bahou-Messadou?"

Fatima, ready to leave, ran up the terraces of Ghimri toward the assembly room, the youngest of her two sons strapped to her back.

"Have you seen Bahou?" she asked the panicked women anxiously, one after another. "Is Jamal Eddin with her?"

At the muezzin's call to prayer, the council members rose to perform their ablutions and pray. God would tell them how to behave toward the invaders. They left together and headed toward the mosque.

It was then that Bahou-Messadou committed her second mistake of the day. She left with them.

She had scarcely crossed the threshold when Ullou Bek turned to Urus-Datu, the head of the council.

"Now's the moment. Take her," he said. It was a suggestion more than an order.

Bahou was astounded.

"No servant of Mohammed would show such a lack of respect toward someone who is old and poor."

"You're not as old and poor as you pretend to be, Bahou-Messadou."

"And you're not a true Muslim, Ullou Bek. The infidels pay you, and you serve them like the dog you are," she snapped back.

"Yes, they pay me. And they'll pay all of you, if you take a step toward them. The first to do so will receive the best treatment and the finest gifts. Those who linger will receive less. Go welcome them at the gates of the village, go with your women and children, go to them freely. They'll ask nothing of you, except that you live in peace with the Great White Czar. What do you have to lose?"

Bahou-Messadou straightened up to her full height and threatened the men of Ghimri. She knew why they hesitated.

"The vengeance of Shamil! Remember what he did to the khans of Avaria and the people of Untsukul, and all those who surrendered to the Russians."

"The Russians will defend you. If you are protected by the power of the Russian cannons, Shamil cannot harm you."

"Will they defend you the way they defended Kunzakh and protected the khans there?" Bahou answered, with more than a little irony.

"As they are avenging the khans of Avaria at this very moment, taking back the lands that belong to them. As they burned the villages of Arakhanee, Irganai, and Akulgo as a reprisal for Shamil's actions at Kunzakh. As they will burn Ghimri and kill you all."

"Don't listen to Ullou Bek. The Russians have sent him here to lull you with his words. They'll kill you anyway. Since there aren't enough of you to defend the village, you should burn it yourselves, run with what remains of the harvest, and join Shamil. Then the giaours will find nothing to eat, drink, or steal here."

Old Urus-Datu was still skeptical.

"What about the treasure?"

"The Poles will take it into the forest with us."

Ullou Bek shook his head back and forth in disapproval with a low whistle.

"In the forest," he said with scorn. "The Russians will follow you, and believe me, they'll catch you. But if you offer them something amounting to a bargaining chip"—he gestured offhandedly toward Bahou-Messadou—"something they're interested in, then they'll offer you something in compensation. If not..."

He raised a hand toward the ruins of the mosque and the charred watchtowers.

Bahou-Messadou spit on the ground at his feet.

"If you're afraid, Ullou Bek, give your saber to the women and hide beneath our veils."

In a lightning gesture, the head of the council blocked the khan's kinjal in midair in its trajectory to behead her.

"Take her away," he ordered. "Throw her in the pit with the other hostages."

The pit, which the giaours called "Shamil's well," was just outside the village. It consisted of a hole that had been dug vertically into the rock face, with an entry hatch. It had been the titanic work of Russian prisoners, whom Shamil considered his slaves. He forced the hardest of tasks upon them, with the ultimate purpose of exchanging the wealthier ones, the officers, for exorbitant ransom.

These captured men from raids on the Russian forts and the villages that had surrendered to the infidels, hostage taking, horse thieving, and the theft of arms and livestock—all this made up the treasure of Shamil's war chest.

Shamil despised luxury and ostentation and was not interested in acquiring wealth for himself. His life was based upon piety, discipline, and austerity. Though he was keen to acquire, personal interest was not an element of his greed. Unlike most of his fellow citizens, he had never intended that the treasure of Kunzakh serve his personal needs or desires. The booty was a tool, nothing more, a means to resist. He counted on using it to buy the favor of the tribal chiefs and to pay his spies, the Armenian merchants, and the Polish soldiers he recruited in the forts. He planned to use it to acquire the rifles that the English adventurers, determined to impede the czar's march toward India, had offered to the Chechens and the Cherkesses—for a price. He wanted to bargain for horses in Kabarda, a city famous for its swift and hardy stallions, so that he could establish a network of intertribal messengers. And he wanted to have a medal struck to honor the heroism of his murids and compensate them for their feats of courage. He wanted to take care of the families of the wounded and the dead. And much more. From the least significant decisions he made to the most brutal cruelties he committed, all were motivated and justified by his dream of a strong and free Muslim state.

The Russian prisoners languished on the straw of Shamil's well with eight hostages from Untsukul, the neighboring community he had punished for treason. These prisoners' fathers had been decapitated, and following the traditional treatment of friends and relatives of traitors, the executioner had gouged out their eyes. As for the infidels, blinded by years of reclusion in the tomb, they dug each day a little deeper; their hunger, thirst, and exhaustion were such that they could barely stand up. This was the little group Bahou-Messadou was to join in the stinking obscurity of the pit. She well knew the fate reserved for enemy families.

To add to her pain, she was informed that her daughter-in-law, who had looked everywhere for her and finally come to the mosque, had been taken too.

Fatima followed her down the long ladder, the toddler still strapped to her back. The little boy wiggled, furious at being bound up like a baby.

Face-to-face in the dark, the two women peered at each other in the obscurity, crying out as one, "Jamal Eddin is not with you?"

"Calm down," Bahou soothed, "he probably ran away with Patimat."

The Russian prisoners, excited at the prospect of imminent freedom, paid no attention to them. But the blind captives of Untsukul, the village where Fatima had grown up, recognized her voice. They crowded forward to chase the two women, eager to get their revenge for Shamil's cruelty. They rushed at them, their hands feeling for the one who carried the baby. She flung them off and backed away. As they groped for the child, two of them felt something warm and wet on their palms. It was their own trickling blood. They had grabbed two blades with their hands.

No one had thought to take away the women's kinjals, and they used them now against the men, who were not armed.

Suddenly the thunder of hooves above them vibrated through the air of the cavern, and they heard gunshots. Everyone stood still and listened. Nothing. There was not another sound. Once again they were cut off from the world.

Then once again they heard cries, this time what sounded like orders. The trap opened and the ladder was thrown down.

"Descend."

The sudden brightness prevented them from distinguishing who stood at the edge of the hatch. A stocky, veiled figure struggled above them. It was Patimat, Shamil's sister. She fought them all, calling the hypocrites traitors, swearing that Allah would not let their crimes go unpunished.

Bahou was afraid the elders would throw her daughter into the pit.

"Descend!" she cried.

Patimat's foot had barely touched the straw when Fatima accosted her.

"Jamal Eddin?"

"He was with the Poles."

"They took him with them?"

"The Poles don't know the mountain. As if they could cross the Avar Koysu on mules!" Patimat's lip curled scornfully. She had never understood why her brother kept renegade Christians under his roof and let his son play with them.

"Ullou Bek captured them."

"All five?"

Patimat nodded. "All of them, with the treasure."

Everyone here knew what that meant. By now, their heads were swinging from the pommel of the bey's saddle.

"The council decided that no one is to leave Ghimri," Patimat continued, breathless. "Urus-Datu is preparing to meet the Russians. He is going to negotiate with them, with Ullou Bek as intermediary. The women and children are to stay behind, to welcome them to the village.

"As for Jamal Eddin, I don't know," Patimat said, her tone sharp with fury and anxiety. Her voice was hoarse, with the guttural inflections of the women of Ghimri. Unlike the other women, though, Patimat was tall like her brother. She shared his ardor, his piety, and his authority. Since her husband's death, she had ruled over Shamil's seraglio. Her passion for him was limitless, and she only differed with him—and only in the intimacy of their private quarters—on one point: his insistence on austerity. If it had been up to her, she would have established the power of the house of Shamil through the possession of fine arms and beautiful clothes. So she devoted a good deal of energy to adding to her collection of fine fabrics and kinjals with chased handles, squirreling away all the spoils she could find under her bed. As for her brother's enemies, her hatred for them guaranteed her family's safety here in the pit, at least for the time being. The punishment of the Untsukul traitors struck her as far too lenient. They deserved much worse for having made peace with the infidels. Patimat had also kept her dagger and fully intended to use it.

The three women sat down. More than by the stench of the place, they felt sullied by the proximity of the Russians.

Bahou-Messadou had taken her grandson on her lap and cradled him softly. She rocked him to and fro, chanting a variation of the "Ballad of Shamil," the war song his horsemen sang as they left for battle, in the metallic voice that was hers alone.

Awake, people of the mountains,
Bid farewell to sleep,
Unsheathe young sabers and draw your kinjals,
I call you in the name of God.

She invented new verses out of old lyrics, varying the rhythm and droning away.

Patimat rocked beside her, her eyes closed. As her mother's threnody went on and on, she relived the dark days in 1832 when cannon fire had destroyed Ghimri. From the forest where she hid, by the river, she had imagined what was happening in the aul above as she listened to the death chants of the last survivors.

In their gutted home, her husband and their very young son had stood with the rest of the warriors, sabers drawn, ready to fight the enemy hand-to-hand. Following tradition, each murid had taken his belt and tied his thigh to that of the man next to him, forming one body, a bastion of flesh. They would fight together and die together as one. Praying in unison, they asked God to forgive their sins, chanting the *shahada* as Bahou was just now: *There is no other god but Allah.*

La ilaha illa Allah.
The earth will be consumed by the fire of the sun,
The mountains will have melted,
Before we shall lose our honor in combat.
There is no other god but Allah.

When the infidels finally surrounded them, they leaped upon them, howling in vengeance, and cut them to pieces.

Patimat, Bahou-Messadou, Fatima, and all the other women standing on the ruined ramparts of Ghimri had watched them fight the Russians, hand-to-hand. They saw their men force them back to the ledge, grab them, and throw themselves into the abyss, taking the enemy with them in a final, fatal embrace. They had seen them fighting even in midair, falling in a slow spiral with the infidels in their arms before all were crushed, with a dull thud, on the boulders of the torrent below.

We were born the night the wolf howled, Bahou-Messadou continued to sing softly.

We grew up in the eagle's nest,
We owe our dignity to our people and our mountains,
There is no other god but Allah.

That evening, Patimat remembered, the village had been taken. Only two refuges remained.

She recognized in her mother's song the call that had resounded through Ghimri that evening, a raucous cry that had come from the forest. It was Khazi Mohammed Mullah, the first imam, rallying his murids.

Shamil had so respected this man, his friend and mentor, that he had named his second son, the boy now drowsing in Bahou's arms, Mohammed Ghazi in memory of him.

Of all four hundred warriors, only a dozen were left to answer his cry. But the battle had continued. Someone was still firing from one of the refuges. The Russians tried to take the house, but they fell like flies, one after another. Their officers ordered them to clear it out with the cannon.

The explosion reverberated throughout the forest. At last, calm reigned over Ghimri.

From the river below, the women could smell the acrid odor of fire and hear the crackling of flames and the cries of vultures, already come to hover over the mutilated bodies.

And then.

Sitting in the straw next to her mother, Patimat never tired of listening to Bahou-Messadou's litany of legends. Recited even in the forts of the Russian lines below, the images themselves were so familiar to the Montagnards that they had the feeling they had all lived through the events.

And then the last of the warriors, a colossus with a piercing stare, his beard tinted red with henna, had sprung from the heart of the inferno. He stood immobile for a moment on the threshold, as though giving the infidels time to aim, and then, bounding suddenly like a wild animal, he leaped over the heads of the soldiers who were ready to slaughter him. In the same motion, he beheaded three of them with the saber in his left hand just as a fourth ran him through with a bayonet. The blade penetrated his chest to the hilt. He seized it, tore it from his breast, and killed the soldier. In another gravity-defying leap, he bounded over the wall and disappeared into the shadows.

This warrior, the sole survivor, was Shamil.

Listening to Bahou chant the ballad of her son in a low murmur, Patimat's courage, faith, and hatred were renewed.

Oblivious to her surroundings, Fatima saw and heard nothing. Anguish pressed upon her heart and turned it to ice. She thought only of her lost child. She longed only for the warmth of Jamal Eddin against her breast.

* * *

The little boy, squeezed into an opening in the rocks, watched the long line of figures in white threading their way arduously up to the promontory, pulling their mounts behind them. Fascinated, he looked at the saddles laden with equipment as they scraped against the rock surface of the ledges and the animals who refused to advance. He watched as horses fell into the abyss, taking their loads with them. Like his father, Jamal Eddin loved horses and weapons. He inspected the rifles, sabers, bayonets, and grenades that hung from the soldiers' belts as the disembodied boots tramped by his hideout at the level of his nose.

He saw Urus-Datu and the khan approach the entrance to the village, accompanied by the muezzin and carrying a white flag.

He listened attentively to their long discourse, the interpreter's translation, the discussions and answers in a foreign tongue. Nothing escaped him, not old Urus-Datu going back and forth between the army and the village, not the soldiers who set up their tents and lit fires. He was intrigued by a golden object placed upon the fire. It was round and shiny and seemed heavy. A samovar. Inhaling the perfume of the tea that they poured into their glasses, Jamal Eddin was suddenly thirsty.

Instinct told him to stay put. He was not afraid. He was used to going without and to sleeping alone. For nearly a year now, since he had begun to ride, he no longer lived with his mother. Custom dictated that a boy not be softened by women, so he lived in the house next door with Yunus, his father's companion at arms. Yunus, also his tutor, was at this very moment at Ashilta.

No, Jamal Eddin was not afraid. But Yunus had warned him that if the Russians took him, they would scalp him, as was standard practice. They scalped the shaved heads of both the dead and the wounded. Jamal Eddin had seen cadavers his father had bought from the infidels to bury in the cemetery here. The foreheads of all the murids had been cut, the scalp stripped to the crown with a knife.

Their skins swung at the end of a banner, there in the camp, a standard for the Christians. Like the severed heads of the Poles that the khan had waved in his face before Jamal Eddin managed to escape from him a short while ago.

The child fell asleep.

On this evening of September 25, 1834, he was the only one to sleep. In the officers' tent and in the council room, the heated discussions went on until dawn.

By morning, the elders had agreed upon their duties and their demands. At ten, the Russians ratified the commitments of the two parties. At noon, the interpreters drafted a treaty with the following terms:

1. Each of you may practice your religion, and no one may object to your rites.

2. You will not be conscripted into the army by force, and no one will turn you over to the law.
3. All the lands of Avaria, situated on the plateau where you lived before the rebellion of 1832, will be returned to you.
4. You will govern Ghimri yourselves, according to your adats and the Sharia.

In exchange:

1. You will swear by Allah never to break the peace you are signing today.
2. You will give us three of your sons as hostages, and you will give us back all the Russians you are holding as prisoners.
3. You will return the treasure of the khans of Avaria to us.
4. You will hand over the imam Shamil and his entire family.

These two last points preoccupied the elders, who continued to discuss the terms of the contract in the privacy of the council. Some mentioned, not without concern, that they were not holding Shamil, only his women. As for the bounty—it was out of the question to give it to these dogs!

Urus-Datu pointed out that the infidels had no idea what was included in the treasure of the khans of Avaria. It would be easy to keep a portion of it. The most pressing thing was to save the harvest and ensure the immediate survival of the aul. As for the rest, patience and craftiness would get their due.

A promise from these pigs was not to be taken seriously.

To the Russians, the eight clauses seemed satisfactory, all the more so since, among all the officers, none was authorized to sign such an accord.

General Klüge von Klugenau, one of the two generals who had destroyed Ghimri before, was busy with skirmishes around Kunzakh and had no intention of coming here. He had only dispatched this contingent to facilitate the passage of his superior, Major General Lanskoy, who was on his way from the fort at Temir-Khan-Chura, the Russian base twenty-six miles from here. Lanskoy planned to bring his cannons along the path across the mountain ridges.

So much the better if the skill of the scouts resulted in the pacification of these "savages," as the general staff called the Montagnards with arrogance and contempt. If little Lieutenant Rostkov's empty promises led to their unopposed surrender, the capture of the imam, and the recuperation of the booty, perfect.

And if not, no matter. The piece of paper was worth nothing.

Nonetheless, there remained one last detail to settle, one about which Lieutenant Rostkov remained intransigent. The villagers must come to his territory, outside the village, and lay down their weapons. All their arms, without exception, must be handed over to the officers. Then they would proceed with signing the treaty.

It was not the light of day that woke Jamal Eddin but the cries and insults of the infidels as they yelled orders at the elders. An army of Montagnards, a formidable mass, was marching straight toward their camp.

The elders had put on their longest cherkeskas and softest leather boots, and proudly wore their heavy, black sheepskin hats pulled down over their foreheads. Their chests shone with silver cartridge belts they had filled with powder. Along with their kinjals, some wore several pistols in their belts and carried their sabers as bandoliers and their muskets on their backs. They presented themselves not as the vanquished, but as warriors, equal to equal.

The Russians continued to bellow their strident orders, but the child no longer paid any attention to them. They seemed unreal, like puppets. He could not understand what they said, nor what was going on. He recognized the gray beard of Urus-Datu, the emaciated figure of the muezzin, the score of men who had not followed his father. What were they doing? Had they come to give themselves up? Or were they here to defend the village, as Shamil had ordered?

He looked toward the village gates, where the women and children stood silently. His playmates, his enemies, their sisters, the mass of veiled girls and babies, the entire population observed the scene from afar, as he did. He could not pick out his mother and his little brother in the crowd. Crestfallen, he searched for Bahou-Messadou, whose presence always reassured him. She was nowhere to be found.

The wave of anxiety that washed over him made him catch his breath. For the first time since the khan had killed the Poles and he had run for cover, he wished Shamil were here. His inner voice begged him to come. He knew instinctively that he hadn't the right—a Montagnard should cope by himself. Better than any other child, Jamal Eddin knew how Shamil's son, the son of a Dagestan horseman, should behave.

The Montagnards had stopped a few feet away from the soldiers. The boy watched the Russians maneuver about to encircle them. He glanced at one group, then the other, then back at the village, hoping to see his mother and grandmother appear between the two watchtowers.

Powerless, his throat dry, clutched by a sense of foreboding he could neither define nor control, he watched the khan Ullou Bek translate the harangue of the lieutenant in the flat cap. When he had finished, old Urus-Datu answered the officer, proudly and directly.

"A man without arms is not a man. We have come to make peace, but we shall remain armed."

No interpreter was necessary to understand the pantomime that followed. The lieutenant ordered all the Montagnards to throw down their kinjals, sabers, and pistols, here, at his feet.

"Come on," he pleaded, "be reasonable. Give us your arms and no one will be harmed."

The Montagnards hesitated. The muezzin was the first to come forward, silently offering his kinjal to the officer closest to him. Two, three, four others did the same, containing their rage and hatred.

One of the officers leaned over to whisper cockily in his comrade's ear, "When we're done disarming them, all we'll have to do is take off their women's pants."

"When we've relieved them of their trousers, everything will be just fine," his friend chuckled softly.

Did Urus-Datu, the head of the council, understand the gist of the insult from the expressions on their faces? He had been one of the most fervent partisans of submission. But when it was his turn, he refused to give up his pistols.

"To allow oneself to be disarmed is to allow oneself to be dishonored," he said firmly.

The exasperated lieutenant launched into a new speech, explaining that it would be fruitless for them, for anyone, to resist the power of Russia.

"We know that Russia is strong," the patriarch countered. "We know it is impossible to oppose Russia, we know that Russia will exterminate us with no trouble in the event of a revolt. We even know that one day or the next you will kill

Shamil. We know all of that. But we cannot give you our arms."

He hammered out the last phrase, word by word, as though this would make its import sink in, "We cannot do it!"

Jamal Eddin saw the Russians take aim at the old man. He turned halfway around to look at their rifles.

"Or else, yes, we can," he concluded, raising his gun to aim at the forehead of the soldier who had made the tasteless joke, "like this!"

He shot the man at point-blank range, then casually threw his smoking weapon at the lieutenant's feet.

What happened next made Jamal Eddin crouch lower in his hiding place.

A hail of bullets ricocheted off the rocks, all the way to his hole.

When the fusillade was over, he crept forward to take a look. The elders were lying about on the rocks where they had fallen. Ullou Bek lay among them, bathed in his own blood. Not a single Montagnard remained standing.

The women cried out. A second deafening salvo eclipsed their cries as they fell to the ground between the two watchtowers. Those who fled toward the mountain were shot in the back. The others were chased through the village. Their hatred, fear, and horror of the giaours intact, they defended themselves, pitifully, with handfuls of pebbles. They would not let themselves be taken.

When they could find no more rocks, they grabbed the blades of the bayonets aimed at them, pulling them off to slit the throats of their children. Then, using the bodies of their dead children as the ultimate weapon, they hit their assailants with them before stabbing themselves too.

Jamal Eddin heard the wails of the villagers in agony, the cries of the babies and the old people in the alleyways, broken by the explosions of rifle shots as soldiers shot blindly at anything that still moved.

* * *

"Who's shooting?"

At the bottom of the pit, they heard the gunfire.

"Who's shooting?"

The crackling of the fusillade spread hope and panic among the prisoners.

The Russian prisoners shouted, their faces turned up toward the hatch, trying to get the attention of their compatriots, whose voices they heard above.

Fatima, Bahou, and Patimat, hands pressed against their hearts to keep them from pounding, did not cry out. But they too peered up at the rays of light that filtered through the planks of the trap. Who was shooting? Shamil?

On the mountain ridge path, General Lanskoy's soldiers, arriving at a forced march from the fort of Temir-Khan-Chura, were listening too. They, too, stopped and wondered who was shooting at Ghimri. Had the detachment of scouts General Klugenau sent to meet them been attacked? Every day spies had confirmed and reconfirmed that Shamil was not at home. Had he returned?

The men picked up the pace, hoping to arrive in time to relieve their comrades. They advanced on foot but had great difficulty restraining their horses and their cannons on the steep inclines.

Ahead, they saw that the aul was in flames.

The troop finished its vertiginous descent on the double.

Looking over the piles of corpses, General Lanskoy was quite relieved to learn that the carnage had cost the life of only one officer.

A veteran of Russia's army in Poland, he had little experience with this kind of war. But he had read the reports of his predecessors and concluded, just as they had, that the Montagnards of Dagestan and Chechnya were incapable of listening to reason. The only way to civilize them was through terror. The law of strength was the only one that they were capable of understanding or respecting. The Russians had to act on this premise and then, applying the precepts of old General Yermolov, conqueror of Napoleon and first viceroy of the Caucasus: "Destroy the harvest. Kill the livestock. Burn the homes. Kill the women and children. Take hostages." For the past twenty years, this tactic had proven effective.

Lieutenant Rostkov had no difficulty justifying the gun battle and the ensuing fire. The elders had more than deserved their fate. In place of the treasure of Avaria, they had proffered a few baubles. As for their imam, whom they had feigned to have in captivity, ready to deliver into Russian hands, they had lied. Shamil was nowhere to be found. These Montagnards were incorrigible, forever inventing ruses to rob and cheat the conqueror.

The general ordered his troops to recuperate the coffers of bounty and destroy what was left of the village with mortar fire. Then they would go on to Kunzakh, which he planned to take back from the fanatics.

Hardly three hours passed between the massacre and breaking camp.

The army started off, led by the general, with the lieutenant bringing up the rear. Both were satisfied with the current state of things. The frost that threatened now would probably make their return impossible before spring. No matter. At this altitude, corpses took a long while to decompose, and this was ideal. Even if Shamil's murids took several weeks to return, they would still recognize the faces of those they had lost. Before such evidence, they would be forced to admit that there was no other path than the laws of civilization that were being offered to them.

As they rode past the remains of the watchtowers, the soldiers in the rear guard heard the cries of prisoners in the well, outside the village gates. They hastily pulled the Russian captives from the hole, leaving the others. But the indigenous militia that had guided General Lanskoy this far—the "pacified," as they were referred to at the forts—insisted that the rear guard liberate their own relatives, who had also been imprisoned by Shamil.

It was they, the blind of Untsukul, who brought the three women left at the bottom of the pit to their attention.

Jamal Eddin instantly recognized the figure they dragged up from the pit. His grandmother. He lunged toward the opening of his hideout in an instinctive desire to go to her. His gesture caught the attention of Bahou-Messadou, who spied his refuge with an eagle eye and shot her grandson a piercing look. She was fully aware of the location of his favorite hiding place, having pulled him out of it by his ear more than once. He was on the brink of leaping out, but her look suddenly stopped him. The order was clear, her expression dark: better to kill yourself than be captured! He understood and drew back. He saw them haul his aunt out. As always,

Patimat screeched, keeping the giaours from approaching her or touching her, shouting insults at the men of the indigenous militia, spitting in the faces of the pacified. He saw his mother bent over Mohammed Ghazi as she held him in her arms, trying to protect him. They were thrown at the feet of the lieutenant and his soldiers who were bringing up the rear.

They didn't even have a chance to appreciate the value of the captives just delivered to them.

A new salvo of gunfire mowed down all the men standing on the plateau. This time, it was the Russians who would not rise again.

Hundreds of horsemen sprang from the boulders, shouting the name of Allah in an immense roar. They thundered down from the ledges, clambered up from the ravine, appearing out of nowhere and firing into the crowd. Bahou-Messadou, fascinated, paid no attention to the men around her, dropping like marionettes with their strings cut. Her eyes were everywhere, seeking Shamil.

Her daughter grabbed her by the elbow and dragged her into the shelter of the ruins by the watchtowers. Fatima followed them at a run, her child clutched to her. Jamal Eddin saw their veils disappear among the boulders. Already his attention was elsewhere.

The horsemen ran straight across the rock planes, ignoring the trails, jumping over crevasses and precipices. The horses; the child stared at their horses.

Barrel-breasted, with hooves grinding rock and pebble and sparks shooting from their iron shoes, the horses' beauty and power was stunning. Their manes were long, their tails silken, their coats lustrous, their nostrils on fire.

He felt their warm, damp breath above him and inhaled the mingled odors of sweat, dust, and leather as they passed over his hiding place. Their round flanks were covered with froth.

Charging with sabers drawn and pistols raised, the horsemen swept through the crowd, shattering the rifles the soldiers hastened to load, slicing the officers from crown to saddle with a vertical blow. In a single charge they reached the towers, then turned around to take the Russians from the rear. Standing in their stirrups or crouched over their horses' necks, the men were seized by a hatred so fierce that it not only inspired their combat but was somehow akin to joy.

Their love of arms was entwined with a passion for these equestrian games as they rivaled each other in skill, speed, and ardor.

To Jamal Eddin, nothing distinguished this cavalcade from others he had witnessed, for man and beast had trained together on this ridge for generations. They knew all the traps, every rock and hole. They knew how to leap into their saddles and take off at a full gallop, how to cross the walls of the enclosure and the watchtower in one jump, how to hang down from the saddle, head at the belly of one's mount, jump a precipice, get back in the saddle on the other side, and leap over the torrent once again. Jamal Eddin had grown up with one dream: to one day become such an amazing horseman, capable of the impossible, in unendurable climates and for unlimited distances. To become a *djighit.*

What could this cumbersome army of invaders do, stuck between the gorges of the Avar Koysu and the peaks of the Eperlee? How could they possibly fend off these hordes of centaurs?

Lithe, fervent, and quick, the natives could withstand the rigor of long marches and the intensity of attacks. Unlike the cumbersome convoys of Russian columns, they traveled light, without stocks of food, tents, samovars, or cannons. Even on long journeys across vast distances, they carried no supplies. Extremely frugal, they ate just what they needed to keep them going—a drink of water, a few greens, a little cheese. Raid after raid, they had a single purpose: to kill the most enemies, steal the most livestock, kidnap the most hostages. The terrain, the time, and the season were all immaterial. One rule and one only governed their choices: surprise the adversary.

They were never where the enemy expected them to be. When the Russians thought they were at Ashilta, they were at Kunzakh. When they thought they were at Kunzakh, they were at Ghimri. Speed, endurance, and ruse were the backbone of their skill. Their attacks were as brief as they were unpredictable, never lasting more than two or three hours. An electrifying charge. A sudden retreat. They disappeared as one body, leaving all in their wake breathless and terrified.

This was the state of General Lanskoy's troops at the moment. Of the seven hundred troops that had accompanied him from the fort at Temir-Khan-Chura, two-thirds lay decapitated, their right hands already cut off. The few survivors, under the command of a wounded, inexperienced leader untutored in the technique of raids, scattered far and wide. The Chechen horsemen made a game of chasing them, letting their unbearable terror build before their kinjals sliced through the air, decapitating them midflight.

This time, the butchery was endless. The assailants did not retreat. After all, they were home. The Russians had no choice but to escape by clambering up the mountain to the ridge path, leaving the treasure, their cannons, and all their supplies below. To flee at all costs. They had not counted on the relentlessness of the most furious of the Montagnards, the one who struck with his left hand.

He had heard the echo of the fusillade earlier and wondered who was firing at Ghimri. He felt a pang of anguish as he recognized the sound of Russian rifles. Now that he was here, he would decimate these swine, down to the very last one.

With his pale gray eyes, translucent skin, and copper-colored beard, the horseman looked like a man of the North. This was no longer a young djighit eager to race but a wild animal of thirty-five, in full possession of all his faculties and talents. Taller than the other horsemen, more lithe and more powerful, he wore the same long, black coat cinched at the waist, the same purple boots that hugged calf and ankle. And on his head he wore the black sheepskin hat, draped with an immaculate, pleated turban, a panel of which trailed down his back and blew in the wind.

All were stunned by his elegance, his nobility, and his ferocity. Jamal Eddin had picked him out from afar. He loomed all the larger as he was riding a small horse the boy did not recognize, swift, rapid, and gray like his father's eyes.

This time Bahou and Fatima wouldn't stop him. Bounding forth from his hole, the little boy ran across the battlefield as fast as his legs would carry him. Barefoot beneath his long, rust-colored shirt, he zigzagged like a fox between the cadavers and the horsemen, running toward the one he called, deep down inside, by the same legendary name as the others: Shamil.

The horseman had seen him. Leaving the victim at hand to the vengeance of another, he turned and galloped toward the child. Without reining in his horse, he bent over to grab him, holding him tight as he placed him before him.

No one else would have dared to do such a thing. No one.

In a world where demonstrations of affection were a sign of weakness, a man's kindness toward his progeny was considered undignified. Simply taking a baby in one's arms to play with him was interpreted as a lack of virility, a dishonor only women could permit themselves to commit. In such a harsh world, Shamil's patience with little ones and his love for children and cats remained a great mystery to those who were faithful to him.

Facing his father in the saddle, Jamal Eddin glowed with pleasure as he answered the questions Shamil murmured in his ear.

Intimately entwined, father and son raced toward the towers, blindly pursuing their path, to the surprise of all on the battlefield.

Yet no one would have thought to criticize the mullah's behavior. He was the guide, the religious and military chief, the third imam of Dagestan and Chechnya. It was he who had led them to victory. He was, above all, the only one here to have found his loved ones alive and unharmed. Allah had spared his family. For the second time. This was clear proof that Shamil was favored by God. For the chosen one of the Almighty, anything was possible.

Even tenderness.

Ghimri
September 27, 1834, at daybreak

The odor of rotting flesh made her want to gag. Bahou-Messadou walked down the path to the water, this path that, for the first time in her life, she had not taken the day before.

A blackish liquid streamed across the ledge, making it sticky, and her steps were uncertain as she navigated her way through the oozing muck. Flies landed on her forehead and buzzed around the jug, settling on her veil, her hands, and the hem of her pants. Their agitation unnerved her, causing her to watch her steps carefully. If she had felt sick at the sight of the wine that had trickled over the ridge long ago, it was nothing in comparison to this nauseating slime that trickled between the rocks now. The blood of the beheaded infidels, the blood of the hypocrites, the blood of the elders, of women and children and all the innocents of Ghimri seeped into the striations of the rocks, flowing down to the riverbanks where it stagnated in great pools. Even the river was turning purple. Even the spring seemed cloudy and impure, not fit for ablutions.

The night of the massacres—just last night—her son's first act had been to pray. His second was to honor the dead. His third, to punish. The gorges of the Avar Koysu resounded with the cries of the hypocrites and the pacified who had led the Russians here. Their horribly mutilated corpses rotted, unburied, between the two watchtowers, an abject lesson to those tempted to go over to the infidels.

General Lanskoy, one of the few who escaped the massacre, had returned to the fort at Temir-Khan-Chura, more dead than alive. The spies later declared he died of fright, succumbing not to his wounds but to jaundice. The others lay at the bottom of the abyss, among the bats that flew through the obscurity of the chasm below Ghimri. Shamil had had nearly a hundred of the dogs thrown off the cliff, delivering them to the eagles and vultures below.

Men from the neighboring communities, women and children of Arakhanee, Irganai, and all the auls that the scouts had razed on their way to Ghimri, had arrived en masse to help dig graves and join the murids. They participated in the funeral ceremonies with chants and dances that lasted through the night on the roof of Shamil's house. It was another miracle: his house was still standing, perfectly intact. The cannons and the flames had not touched it.

The shouts of the believers blended with the wailing of the mourners and made the few survivors in the pit shiver in fear. Prisoners of the Caucasus, the new Russian captives were perhaps the only ones who understood how little their Christian arrogance had convinced the local population. On the evening following the massacre, Shamil could thank the invaders. Their brutality had served the holy war, driving the last waverers into his arms.

Compelled to choose between two parties, both capable of decimating their ranks, the Montagnards much preferred men of their own blood and faith. There was nothing to be gained by befriending the infidels. The Russians tried to buy their submission, but they never kept their promises and they never paid. In twenty years, they had proven their duplicity, paying both rebels and pacified in the same way, murdering even their own partisans. They had even shot the khan, Ullou Bek.

Terror for terror, in the eyes of the people, the yoke of Shamil was the more worthy. Serving God and fighting for their freedom epitomized all that remained of Muslim honor. The imam was right.

In her mind's eye, Bahou saw him as she had yesterday evening, standing on the roof at his full height of six foot two, facing the mountain as he led the mourning and addressed the crowd.

"I have come to you with the Koran and the sword, and I will lead you. Take comfort, the day of deliverance is at hand. This world is a carcass, and he who would win it is a dog, but we shall rid it of the infidels for good, as it is written."

After the horrors of the day before, she finally allowed herself a mother's pride. Never given to vanity or coquetry, she nonetheless reveled in his beauty. She admired Shamil's naturally noble carriage and the elegance of his clothing, as she had last night at the funeral ceremonies. She liked the lighter coat he wore, which was a deep black. She loved to see his white turban shine in the night, his arsenal glinting at his belt. Her son's weapons were such sacred objects that not even Fatima was allowed to touch them. He took pleasure in cleaning them himself. But on those rare evenings when he was at her house, he left the privilege to Bahou.

A vague smile crossing her lips, she relived the moment when the murids had cheered him. The time of bad omens, when she had spilled the water and feared that Shamil might not be able to return to save them, that morning seemed long ago. Today she was confident. Allah watched over them. She no longer doubted that her son enjoyed divine protection. She saw as proof the ultimate and unexpected resistance of Urus-Datu, which had saved them from the worst fate. Had the Russians not slaughtered the elders, Shamil would have been compelled to avenge their betrayal of his children, his wife, his sister, and his mother. He would have had to strike the elders in the flesh, along with all of their descendants, their sons and grandsons—even those who had opposed the hypocrisy of their fathers by following him to Ashilta, the bravest of the brave. The families of the elders would then have sought vengeance, taking a life for a life, pursuing the blood relatives of Shamil from one generation to the next, extending their reprisals far beyond Ghimri. It was the law of kanly. This was the evil that Shamil feared and fought everywhere, the vendetta that was capable of tearing his Muslim brothers apart.

Bahou knew that her son's real battle was not the one he led against the Russian invaders, but the struggle against disaffection among the believers. They had elected him. What had he to fear in the future? She imagined the echo of the chant she had heard in the night, one voice, in unison, crying "Shamil, imam!" And his answer, ringing out in all its power over their voices.

"Be strong," he thundered. "Be vigilant. Prepare your weapons, fortify your villages, and mortify your flesh, for soon you will mortify that of your enemies. We shall nail their hands to our doors, their heads will roll down our mountain slopes, and the rivers will run red with their blood."

Fatima followed her mother-in-law down the path to the water. She too was replaying in her mind the scene she had witnessed the previous evening.

Like Bahou-Messadou and the other women of Ghimri, she did not usually attend any public gatherings, not even the *djighitovkas,* the famous equestrian games held outside the town gates. She had never seen her husband's remarkable litheness as he nudged his horse into an instant gallop beneath the posterns, nor had she ever heard him harangue the crowds. Until the day before, she had only known of his reputation for powerful eloquence.

Yesterday had been the first time, and it still struck her like a revelation. True, she knew that students from Koranic schools far away came to listen to him preach at the mosque. Like them, no doubt, she was impressed by his passion, his authority, and the fire of his conviction. But at home, Shamil was given to silence and rarely raised his voice. By nature he was a man of few words, but in the privacy of their room, she could scarcely shut him up. She never tired of hearing him whisper the tales of his adventures in her ear, as he had that night when he returned from battle. Fatima knew the words relieved his tension. He told her of his admiration for the imam Khazi Mullah, his dead friend, the story of their first victories and defeats, his hesitations about the future and his doubts about decisions he must make. He always ended with the same question.

"What do you think?"

She was too humble and too clever not to sense the direction in which his instincts were leading him. She tried to follow him along the paths he had already outlined, confirming her approval of decisions he had already made.

"Fatima, what do you think?"

The very few times she had hesitated or expressed doubt or disagreement, he had asked her to explain her reasons. She dared to do so, revealing her concerns. He teased her about her fears, but he always listened.

But yesterday, when she had seen him on the roof like a gigantic dark shadow hovering over his murids, she had been taken aback. It was the shadow of God on earth. This morning, this strange impression lingered, one that Bahou absorbed as well with the same surprise and pride.

* * *

As they reached the courtyard, the two women found Patimat plucking the chickens found beneath the rubble with exaggerated vigor, obviously fuming with ire.

Her stoutness was a sign of her status; it also kept her from having to go down the mountain to draw water or work in the fields. Instead she was mistress of all domestic chores, a distribution of roles that no one dared to challenge. Shamil's return necessitated a thorough housekeeping. She must reopen the reception rooms and prepare big meals for visitors from neighboring villages and the *naïbs,* the leaders of his army. But the Russians had slit all the sheep's throats and burned all the stores of barley.

This morning, though, Patimat was not grousing about the material problems of the household. Her brother had just ordered her to pack up everything for a move from Ghimri. They would leave the village tomorrow. To go where? No answer. She knew where this new caprice came from. Really, Shamil was far too receptive to his wife's influence. A man like him! For years now, Patimat had been encouraging him to take a second wife—advice that did nothing to improve relations with her sister-in-law.

Absorbed in her thoughts, Patimat said nothing to the peasants whose villages had been destroyed; anonymous figures, slumped beneath their veils, they silently gutted the chickens at her feet.

To leave Ghimri, the burial place of their ancestors, the cemetery where her own husband rested? Winter was coming, and the Russians would not return for a while. Why go into exile with no threat on the horizon? Bahou would be all for it; she had always hated Ghimri. The prospect of this maternal betrayal was the ultimate irritation. Yes, of course the old lady talked about marrying her off to a man of Ashilta. And negotiations with his relatives, the visits it would require of Bahou, and the preparations for a wedding could not be carried out from here. No matter, Patimat could wait. She was in no hurry. Her brother still needed her, more than ever, in fact. Fatima let her children run all over the place. She would be incapable of overseeing the organization of the seraglio and the apartments of the new imam. What would happen to Shamil's precious manuscripts, his speeches, and his weapons, to all that he treasured, without Patimat? What would happen to the Koran that he had inherited from Khazi Mullah, whose iron fittings she polished, and that she wrapped up in the finest material every night?

Her legs spread wide, her head in a cloud of feathers, Patimat relived the spectacle she had witnessed yesterday. She too had seen Shamil on the roof and listened to his impassioned words, equally impressed by his wisdom, his power, and his beauty.

"We are the refuge and the protectors of the true believers, the terror of the infidels and of irresolute minds. Obey our law and heaven will endow you with all its beneficence. Your worldly goods will be respected, your safety ensured. I say to the hypocrites who persist in their obstinacy, I shall obtain by force what they have refused me in good grace. My warriors will descend upon their auls like black clouds. We shall leave fear and destruction and bloody footprints in our wake. My words may carry little weight in their hearts; my acts, however, will convince them."

Remembering this speech, Patimat smiled to herself. If the murids acclaiming her brother had known his faults and weaknesses as she did, they would have been too surprised to believe them.

She knew what the legend did not say, what the words to the "Hymn to Shamil" left out. She could have told them how the story of the "Death Leap" ended, and of the hero's flight into the mountains the day after the first attack on Ghimri.

Forgetting the ordeals of the believers and the service of God, the third imam of Dagestan had fallen asleep in a conjugal embrace, cradled in the loving arms of his wife. And that was the secret of the disappearance he had never wished to explain. His wife had held him captive in a shepherds' hut for six months.

Fatima could go on all she liked, the hypocrite, about the shepherds who had come to get her at the home of her father, the surgeon of Untsukul. She could tell how they had brought her to Shamil, who lay hidden and wounded in their little hovel. She could talk about the sores that covered his body as he spit blood from the lung that had been pierced by bayonets. She could go on about how her father had nursed him back to strength. Fatima was still from Untsukul. And the people of Untsukul were still traitors and sellouts. By their charms and their drugs, they had sought to bewitch the man known everywhere as the Lion of Dagestan. Patimat preferred to pardon with a smile today, but the thought that the great Shamil had barely escaped infamy by abandoning the fight still made her burn. It was she, poor little Patimat, a widow, who had found the strength to make him hear the call of duty.

"Just imagine," she sighed, "if I hadn't been there."

With this sigh she greeted her mother and her sister-in-law, who had just put down their ewers against the two thin posts that supported the roof. She tossed the last plucked chicken into the copper pot and got up, dusted off her tunic, and, in case no one had heard, asserted, "Yes, what if I hadn't gotten involved!"

The look she exchanged with Fatima confirmed that they understood one another. It was the same look that had passed between them on the terrace the night before. It expressed the same pride, the same joy in belonging to this man—and the same provocative expression. Each was convinced that she had saved Shamil from the other.

Patimat's incessant insinuations always hinted at the episode at the shepherds' hut, and her veiled references filled Fatima with anger and fear.

"If this harpy had not interfered," she thought, "perhaps Shamil would have had some peace of mind."

When the shepherds had led her to the pitiful body of her husband, Fatima had had to fight the spirits who sought to push him over the edge. Day and night she had battled the spirits of evil, trying to pull him back to her, to life. And Allah had allowed the miracle to happen. The fever broke, and Shamil lived. The nightmare of almost losing him was followed by three weeks of blissful convalescence, a period suspended in time and space. She had never felt that Shamil was afraid of offending God by cherishing her so. In fact, his narrow brush with death had made him more peaceful and softened his character; he no longer worried about the future and felt newly free to love her.

Then, in a great flap of veils and clinking of bracelets and earrings, Patimat had appeared out of nowhere. Beating her breast, tearing her veils, wailing loudly, she had made a scene before her brother that Fatima would never forgive.

Patimat had dared to say that it was Shamil's fault that their people had lost everything. She had lost everything, her husband, her son, her home, everything. And what was he doing about it? He was lounging around, playing sick. You could see the ruins of Ghimri smoking from the opposite bank of the Avar Koysu, Khazi Mullah was dead, their mother was holed up in a grotto, and the Russians were searching everywhere, shouting, "Where is Shamil?"

And what was he doing? Nothing. The great Shamil was doing absolutely nothing.

Leaning on one elbow, livid, with a flicker of madness in his eyes, he allowed Patimat to go on and on. She knew the violence of his wrath. Contradictors beware, Shamil could not stand being criticized. She continued to spit her accusations in his face. Shamil wasn't worthy of carrying arms, because he had to rely on his own sister to teach him what service to God and the honor of men demanded. He heard her out, fascinated, without interruption. By the time Fatima finally pushed her out the door, the damage was already done.

The fever returned, and with it hallucinations. With his visions came the myriad anxieties that had already pushed him to the edge of the grave once. Shamil did not return as he had before. This time he returned from hell, stripped of all serenity and joy.

Fatima knew of the wounded man's questions for Allah, of his fear at not being able to perform his ritual ablutions, of his terror at not being able to say his prayers, of the dreadful guilt he felt at having betrayed and lost the confidence of Allah. He let himself believe that the Almighty had reopened his wounds merely to protest the ostentatious wealth of his sister, the silver bracelets and necklaces of precious stones that she always wore. He could think that Patimat's immodest vanity was the source of God's displeasure. But the truth was something else altogether.

And when it came to this truth, Fatima and Patimat both agreed.

In discovering such happiness in the shepherds' hut, Shamil had found in himself the weakness he punished in others. He had felt the desire that so endangered the survival of Muslims, a desire so dangerous that he tried to eradicate it wherever it was found.

The day before, when he had addressed the faithful, he had done just that. He had censured his own tastes and his own demands, struggling against the two tendencies that had nearly been his undoing a few years before: the temptation of peace and the temptation to forget.

"The Russians flatter you by inviting you to make peace. Do not believe them! Do not give up! Be steadfast and patient. Remember what happened when the infidels tried to confiscate your weapons in 1804. Thirty years ago, ten years ago, yesterday. And if God had not enlightened the elders in time, today they would be soldiers of the czar, marching far away from our mountains, fighting with their bayonets instead of our daggers. If God had not armed the hand of Urus-Datu, the Russians would have unveiled our women and dishonored them, and you yourselves would be forever dishonored. May the past serve as a lesson for the future. Better to die fighting the infidels than to live with them. Think about this. I forbid you not only to surrender, but to even contemplate surrender."

His incantation was graven on the heart of each of them. Even that of little Jamal Eddin. Listening to his father, the child imagined Shamil spoke to him and him alone, looking directly into his eyes. He wanted to return this look, unblinking.

During the entire ceremony, Jamal Eddin had stared at Shamil until tears had welled up in his eyes; he had nodded his support and approval as he listened to the rhythm of his father's voice.

"You may consider yourselves good Muslims. All your alms, all your prayers, all your ablutions, all your pilgrimages to Mecca will be for naught if the eye of the infidel witnesses them. As long as one Russian remains in your country, your mosques will be sullied. As long as there is one Russian on this earth, your marriages will be null and void, your wives illegitimate, and your sons bastards!"

Sitting with his legs tucked under him at his father's feet, his small face upturned, Jamal Eddin gleaned from his fascination one certainty. This speech was directed at him, and him alone.

And in case he had misunderstood the meaning of the message, the words repeated themselves in a singsong in his mind. As long as one Russian is left, your sons will be bastards!

This last phrase he would be careful never to forget.

"Come quickly! A fight is taking place at your house!"

Abruptly ending the brewing storm between his mother and his aunt, the little boy rushed in, caught Bahou by the pant leg, and tried to drag her home in one motion.

"At my house?" she said, not moving. "Who?"

"All of them!"

"Your father?"

"Mirza Kaziaho, Yunus, Surkhaï, the others," he panted. "They're fighting about the khans' treasure."

Pulling her veil over her brow and the scarf around her neck up over her nose, the old woman hurried for home.

* * *

It was a one-room apartment with a central pillar that supported the roof beams. The walls were bare. Rugs covered the floor, and a few cushions were stacked in a corner. Eight or ten rolled-up mattresses were stored along the walls. The door was the only opening. A thick coating of soot, the result of a chimney that did not draw well, made the room look all the more dingy. Bahou had cooked here for years, for her neighbors, her relatives, and the wives of the naïbs who came from distant villages. Sometimes the guests, as many as fifteen or twenty of them, stayed for months, sleeping at Bahou's house the entire time. The room was well situated since it led to the back courtyard that was reserved for the women of the household. When she had no guests, Bahou-Messadou used the room for storage. All kinds of things ended up here—the executioner's axe, an old cradle, assorted bridles and saddles, pots. And the two chests of treasure from Kunzakh.

Coveted by the elders, stolen by the Russians, they rested in obscurity in this windowless room, a sanctuary that no man except Shamil, not even Jamal Eddin, had the right to enter. It was the harem of the imam.

There they were, a band of pillagers, including some of Shamil's closest friends, standing, sitting, and kneeling, and rifling through a collection of objects that lay scattered about them on the floor.

Standing in the doorway, blocking the light, Bahou scolded them in a loud voice.

"What right do you have?"

They paused only briefly in surprise before returning to their haggling. The heads of all the clans of Chechnya and Dagestan continued to divide the treasure of Avaria among themselves, claiming this golden sheath or that silver dagger, this sword or those bracelets, by bargain or threat. Jamal

Eddin was astonished at such splendors from another world. He had never seen anything like them. The khans' amber cups and gem-studded jewelry lay amid the gleaming plunder taken from the Russian soldiers: their medals and epaulets, their belts, caps, and boots and, most important, their weapons. All were there before him.

Wide-eyed, the little boy shivered with a yearning to touch, to possess.

"Who gave you the right?" Bahou repeated angrily.

"I did."

Shamil's voice. Jamal Eddin, hiding in his grandmother's veils, had not seen him. Neither had Patimat, who had come running after them and now stood in the doorway. Shamil leaned against the far wall in the shadows, his head down and arms crossed. He was watching the distribution. The two women stood there, paralyzed. Shamil had authorized the presence of his generals in his harem? Shamil had sanctioned the pillaging of his war treasure?

"The imam will have his part," scolded the Chechen mullah Hadj Tasho, who had rivaled Shamil for the supreme title at his investiture at Ashilta.

His beard was long and full, and he wore a high papakha draped with the white turban and a long green coat, the color of Islam. With a jerk of his chin, he pointed to the second chest, which remained sealed and intact.

"The best part."

The best part. Really? A dubious Patimat was about to demand what the chest contained.

The unequivocal message in the look her brother shot her stopped her from opening her mouth. The two lines between his eyebrows had deepened, and his frown was more severe and downright threatening. His cheekbones were more salient, his cheeks hollow, and his lips pursed. His steel-gray, almond-shaped eyes narrowed like blades. When Shamil's gaze struck upon someone this way, it was best to shut up and disappear. The two women did so immediately, taking the child with them.

The following day's exodus resembled Shamil's habitual maneuvers only in the secret of the destination and the silence of the troops. Otherwise the procession looked like the interminable Russian columns that were sometimes visible on the horizon, a pantomime of shadows moving across the crests of the ridges.

Doubled over by immense bundles of firewood, Fatima, Bahou, Patimat, and the other wives made their way down the incline to the water. They carried most of their supplies and household goods on their heads and backs. Like ants, all they left behind were small piles that blended with the ashen rocks. Even the ruins no longer resembled dwellings but were merely rocks, no different from any of the others that studded the mountain. It was hard to imagine that only yesterday the remains of a village had existed on this ridge.

Patimat was against this exile, but she knew very well that they would have to abandon Ghimri before the snow fell.

The Russians had done their job in slaughtering the herds and burning the harvest. The survivors of Ghimri would starve if they remained there this winter. But here, and everywhere, the problem remained: how to stay warm and cook without felling a single tree? All night she had led Jamal Eddin and the few children from the other auls around the village to collect every precious stick of wood. They had dismantled the houses, cut up the beams and roofing, gathered logs and twigs, and recuperated the nails. On the terraces of

Ghimri, on every level of the vast amphitheater, squabbles broke out over utensils, tools, and anything else that might come in handy. And at Shamil's home, the heated discussion had continued late into the night.

Jamal Eddin returned frequently to the window of his father's house to listen from afar to the angry voices of the naïbs coming from the guest room. They were still quarreling when it was time to leave. Unlike his mother and grandmother, he found the turbulent atmosphere exciting, the promise of action to come. What took place at dawn did not measure up to his expectations.

After the last few frenzied hours, the column formed calmly. Not another sound was uttered, not an insult, not a baby's cry, not even a neigh from any of the horses. All that could be heard was the dull roar of the torrent below, which grew louder as they neared the river.

With their bundles of wood, some of which were so long that the branches trailed after them, Fatima and the women advanced carefully, one after the other, in the tracks of the three cannons that the Russians had abandoned.

The murids rode before the cannons, their whips at their wrists, carrying their standards with extended arms, in a long, black line that zigzagged over the narrow trail. Jamal Eddin, severed forever from the world of women since Yunus's tutelage, sat astride in front of the youngest of the horsemen. Like the others, he was dressed in black, proudly wearing his sole cherkeska, his heavy sheepskin hat, and his boots. For a weapon, he carried a baton at the waist. The horse lowered his head as he slipped and slid down the steep incline. The child gripped his mane to keep from sliding onto his neck.

Before them paraded the naïbs, Shamil's inner guard consisting of Yunus and the ten tribal chiefs, whose saddlebags bulged with treasure. Their disgruntled expressions showed that the altercations of the previous evening were far from settled. Each felt cheated by the division of the spoils and resentful toward his peers, a feeling exacerbated by the sight of Shamil's share, which was so heavy that it had to be carried separately on the back of a mule.

Indifferent to their hostility, Shamil led them all, the mule following behind, tied to the saddle of his prancing gray mare.

It was true that he had kept the best part for himself.

When he reached the bridge over the Avar Koysu, the bridge where he had once strangled the last child of the khans, a boy scarcely older than his son, he signaled to the men to stop. He dismounted.

Suspended on the steep incline, the column came to a vertical halt behind him. All the men and women could see what was happening on the riverbank.

Jamal Eddin saw his father approach the mule, then stop and turn around. He advanced to the river, dipped his hands in the water and splashed it on his face. The naïbs, who had stopped on the shingles, dismounted as well and came to kneel at his side. Piously they turned their faces toward the Lord to render him grace together. The murids and the women who had stopped on their way down the rock face shared their prayer, giving themselves over to Allah's protection in the secret of their hearts.

Jamal Eddin saw his father rise and return to the mule. He seized the coffer and lifted it off the beast's back in one sharp tug, and carried it to the middle of the bridge. With a blow of his kinjal, he broke the lock. The astounded crowd stared at the jumble of metal and precious stone, the source of the elders' betrayal and last night's disputes. All of these wonderful things, carried by caravan from Persia and Turkey, the presents of the shah to the khanum of Avaria, the sultan's gifts to the noble *beks* of Kunzakh, now belonged to their imam. Jamal Eddin was pleased to recognize the daggers that had left him open-mouthed with wonder the day before, as well as the Russians' weapons. The best part.

Shamil allowed the murids to absorb the magnitude of this prize. His treasure would enrich his army and finance the holy war for a long time to come.

Then he took out the first object, a superb golden mirror, chased in turquoise. He held it high over his head for all to admire before flinging it with full force into the rapids. The object floated for a while, then, caught in the eddies of the current, disappeared. The women, the murids, and the naïbs stood there, breathless. They did not understand. Nor did Jamal Eddin.

By the armful, his father flung plates, bracelets, sheaths and swords, even kinjals into the swirling water. No, the little boy could not understand. Finally Shamil threw the coffer over the bridge, and all of them watched as it crashed on the rocks.

Rid of it all, Shamil walked toward his generals' horses.

With a word, spoken so softly that no one heard, he forced them to detach their saddlebags and bring them to the river. One by one, each of the ten naïbs had to open his sack and empty it over the guardrail, shaking it over the rushing river.

A few pieces of an alabaster cup floated for a moment, as white as the foaming water, before the swirling current dragged them to the river bottom.

* * *

When Yunus, head down, returned to his horse, he found the little boy in his charge seated in the place his share of the treasure had occupied.

Jamal Eddin had managed to put his foot in one of the stirrups and lift himself up to the pommel. The look on his face showed that he was perplexed. His eyes looked questioningly at his tutor. Why had they thrown away the sabers, whose beauty he had learned to worship?

Yunus's sole response was to chant the shahada, the hymn of the murids, and to let Jamal Eddin climb behind him to ride pillion.

"La ilaha illa Allah. There is no other god but Allah."

The rest of the horsemen took up the chant, singing at the tops of their voices, drowning out the roar of the river and making the mountain air tremble. The echo rippled down the narrow gorge and reverberated from valley to valley down the immense chain of the Caucasus. It went on forever, and with it the lesson of the imam Shamil, reaching even the most isolated auls. Unity in the service of God was the most precious treasure of the Muslims. Unity was the incarnation of absolute good that justified all sacrifices. No sword, no cup, no treasure in the world was worth risking the disunity of the servants of Allah.

But the image of the sabers in the torrent continued to haunt Jamal Eddin, leaving a great question mark in his mind.

CHAPTER III

The Shadow of God on Earth

Dagestan, three years later,
in the mountains around the aul of Chirquata
September 1837

"Yunus," Shamil said after his usual polite greeting, "tell me about my son."

"Mohammed is the first prophet of Allah, Shamil is the second," Yunus said, avoiding the question.

The phrase was common among the men of Dagestan, who used it as a greeting, a prayer, and a rallying cry. Declared with hand over heart, it acknowledged the divine mission of the imam and proclaimed the union of his people under his authority. Coming from Yunus, it summed up Shamil's glory and his successes: the shadow of God spread across the earth.

Nonetheless, Shamil's spectacular gesture on the bridge at Ghimri had ruined them all.

While his actions had reinforced his image as a saintly man, they had hindered the liberation of the Caucasus. How could one finance a holy war without gold? How could they buy horses, guns, and cannons?

Shamil had nothing.

Avoiding any direct confrontation with the Russians for the time being, he concentrated upon community affairs.

Armed with the axe of justice, flanked by the sabers of his executioners and the muskets of his well-trained troops, he traveled from village to village, preaching the Sharia and keeping his promises to the hypocrites. His injunctions to repent, if they went unheeded, were followed by punishment, as he executed those who disobeyed his laws, the law of God, or the laws of men. He levied heavy fines on those who committed lesser transgressions, filling his coffers anew. In three years, through rigor and terror, he had instituted a system of taxation to which all were subject and imposed a religious, political, and moral code that excluded corruption and formed the basis for a state.

One essential task remained: to drive out the infidels and let liberty triumph.

On this late September day in 1837, Shamil and Yunus rode together, reins slack, avoiding the usual trails as they slowly circled the village of Chirquata. Tucked into the mountainside, the fortified aul of dilapidated hovels with terraced roofs spread over the hillside. Heavy storm clouds hung over the houses where their families awaited them. Shamil had scarcely had time to watch his children grow up these past three years. He had spent all his time on horseback, like a nomad, leaving his wife and sons in the protection of one community chief or another for weeks, even months, at a time. These long stopovers had permitted Bahou-Messadou to remarry Patimat to the mullah Akbirdil Mohammed al-Kunzakhi, one of the only natives of Kunzakh to have rallied to the murid cause. Shamil's sister had given her new husband two sons. The eldest was named Hamzat, the name of the imam assassinated by Hadji Murat.

This last separation, the longest, had gone on for eight months. Yunus, who had galloped from village to village to meet the imam, knew at this very moment that Shamil was trying hard to control his impatience. His face was a mask.

Heads lowered, their flanks dark with sweat, the horses nibbled at the rare blades of grass they found between the rocks. The horsemen would let them dry off before taking them to the fountain to drink. They had a good deal to say to each other but spoke sparingly, embarrassed by the soft intimacy of the evening light. Yet they knew each other so well. They had shared everything, from nights of camping out on the banks of raging mountain streams to solitary rides through the snow, the adrenaline-infused waiting period before an attack and the long hours of watch duty beneath a leaden sun outside the Russian forts. Theirs was the communion born of men facing death.

But in forty years of friendship, they had never taken this sort of leisurely ride in the quiet of dusk.

They had matured at the same time, both filled with the same love of liberty and a thirst for God. They were equally attached to those close to them. Yunus's young wife Zeinab was as precious to him as Fatima was to Shamil. Both of them loved to come home to their wives, and both were equally capable of sacrificing them. Beyond that, they were very different. Black-eyed Yunus had swarthy skin and a long, thin face like the blade of a knife. His pointed beard made it look even thinner. Of medium build, his wiry body projected not power, but a stamina and agility that resulted from years of training himself to push beyond his limits. He seemed as nervous, nimble, and irascible as Shamil seemed leonine, placid, and calm. It was a distribution of roles that gave them an advantage over strangers. Shamil had not chosen Yunus to serve as his eldest son's tutor, or *atalik*, by chance. He was a man of honor and a steadfast companion.

Today, as naïb and administrator of Chirquata, Yunus had a matter of importance to discuss with Shamil. Their spies at the nearby fort of Temir-Khan-Chura had just informed him that the *padishah* Nicholas, the "Great White Czar of the Infidels," was expected to arrive in these mountains at the end of September. He planned to travel from far-off Saint Petersburg to Tiflis, the capital of Georgia and the seat of the Russian viceroyalty of the Caucasus. During his tour of inspection, he might very well stay at one of the forts along the line. If that were the case, should they resume hostilities? Harass the dogs everywhere? Stage a grand coup? Or profit from this extraordinary visit to negotiate?

That was the subject of their conversation. What game should the humble Shamil of Ghimri employ to conquer the emperor of all the Russias?

"First of all, tell me about him," murmured the imam, finally breaking the silence.

"Their padishah—"

"No, Jamal Eddin. How do you find him?"

"Almost like you at the same age," Yunus replied reluctantly.

He could not understand how Shamil, whose wisdom and judgment he admired, could keep asking about his son. A man should never mention his wife or children before a third party. He must not even refer to their existence.

"Almost like me?" Shamil insisted mischievously.

Yunus had no sense of humor. He tried to explain himself seriously.

"Your son is training himself to run long distances, with a pebble in his mouth to force himself to breathe regularly."

"You're the one who gave him the pebble?"

"No need, your son knows. He imitates you all the time, in every possible way. He walks barefoot, bare-chested, and on an empty stomach. Like you. He wrestles and practices with the saber, he swims and high jumps. Like you. But he's still—" Yunus hesitated, searching for the right words.

"Still what?" Shamil repeated, smiling.

Yunus scratched the back of his neck. He was going to say, "still green," but he restrained himself, thinking that the boy's father would take it as a reproach or an insult.

"Young."

"Young? Well, of course he's young. What do you mean by that? That he's weak or lacking in courage?"

"Your son is not weak. Sheik Jamaluddin al-Ghumuqi, your own mentor, who is instructing him in the Koran, can tell you about his progress better than I."

Shamil wouldn't let it go.

"But you're the one who's educating him. I'm listening."

Yunus sensed Shamil's dismay at his embarrassment and was afraid that this would lead to a misunderstanding. He decided to speak frankly.

"The imam Shamil should have fifty sons like Jamal Eddin."

Relieved, Shamil nodded. "And Mohammed Ghazi?"

"The youngest promises to have all his brother's attributes."

Shamil savored the information. The subject was closed, and Yunus knew it would not come up again. Finally he worked up the nerve to say, "Two sons are not enough to ensure your lineage. Allah protects them, but if either of them came to harm, what would happen to the imamat?"

Shamil scowled but said nothing. He feared disunion too much not to have considered making his position hereditary. He vividly remembered the power struggles that followed the deaths of the first two imams.

He patted his horse on the neck to make sure his coat was dry. The gentle slap of his palm resonated in the mountain air.

Yunus wanted to get this over with. He felt that what he was about to say was immodest and crude, and he tackled the subject only with extreme reluctance.

"Take another wife," he said in a rush of words, "among the daughters of the Chechen chiefs, and a third and a fourth, since Mohammed permits it. You should form alliances everywhere, ties to all the peoples and all the tribes of the Caucasus. I'm telling you so on my own behalf, and on behalf of all your naïbs."

"Enough! You're talking like a woman."

Shamil pretended to be angry, but he shared the same intuition that only blood ties could seal the union of the Caucasian tribes, with him as their leader. He should marry into the most powerful families and leave many successors in the service of God. He would need several sons to create a dynasty that would perpetuate his work. It was another wise piece of advice from Yunus. Beneath the red beard that hid his expression, a smile crept over his lips. All these circumvolutions to explain to him that he should procreate. Poor Yunus, he could not possibly know that his advice was late in coming. With his baggage, Shamil was bringing home a young girl of sixteen whom he had married last month. Her name was Jawarat. Born in Ghimri, she was the daughter of the khan of Irganai and the niece of the late Ullou Bek, who had corrupted the elders. In her belly she carried a third heir. Tomorrow she would arrive at Chirquata to take her place next to Bahou-Messadou.

Shamil had asked the witnesses at his marriage to say nothing until he had the chance to announce the news to his mother and the mother of his sons himself. Yunus's words reassured him that the secret had been properly kept. His nights with the very young Jawarat changed none of his feelings for Fatima. She was still the beloved, and his fear of hurting her had not a little to do with his desire to meet his lieutenant outside the village before he returned there. Decisions of state must be made before he saw her or talked to her. In any case, his sister, who had been nagging him for years to take a second wife, would be satisfied. Well, no, she would not, for he had committed an unforgivable act against Patimat.

Four months earlier, the giaours had burned the mosque at Ashilta, symbol of his power, and recaptured Kunzakh. The leader of the hypocrites, Mohammed Mirza Khan—a puppet the Russians had placed on the throne of Avaria to do their bidding—had surrounded the murids in the aul of Tiliq. The siege had gone on for weeks, but the khan still had not taken the village. Negotiation was the only means open to Shamil to extricate himself from this stalemate. Before the negotiations, the khan had demanded hostages, as was customary, an unavoidable condition that Shamil was not in a position to reject.

It was customary for the party suing for peace to send its children to the enemy as a gage. Called *amanats* in the Caucasus, these human guarantees had to be the sons of influential families between two and eighteen years old, proof in the flesh of good faith. If negotiations fell apart, they could be executed or taken captive, but only breaking one's word or an act of high treason justified such treatment. And that was rare. Once the accords were sealed and the peace concluded, the amanats returned home.

The regent of Kunzakh's demands at Tiliq were extravagant. He wanted Shamil's two sons as amanats. The khan himself did not believe his enemies would respond to such excess, but the murids, still in control of the village, were strong enough to make a counter-proposition. The imam offered the khan not two but three prestigious hostages: the sons of his two allies here in the aul and his own nephew, the first-born of his only sister. The khan was pressed for time and accepted. On July eighteenth, Shamil had taken little Hamzat from Patimat's arms and given him to the hypocrites. This was the price of liberty.

Never could he have imagined that Mohammed Mirza would keep the child. When the peace had been agreed upon, he had returned the two other children, but not Hamzat. The khan had given the imam's nephew to the infidels, and even the Polish spies could not find out what had happened to the boy. Had the Russians killed him?

This betrayal haunted both Shamil and Yunus. Two sons are not enough to ensure your lineage. If anything should happen to them…

A glacial wind was rising, and nightfall was near. It was time to let their horses drink and address the issue that Yunus could not resolve without his chief's approval. What message of their reaction should he give the messenger, who awaited a response at this very moment in the village? The urgent decision of what stance to assume was sufficient reason for Shamil to return to Chirquata.

"Their man, the Russian emissary, did he bring news of my nephew?" he asked somberly.

Yunus shook his head no.

Shamil repressed a gesture of anger and nudged his horse in the direction of the fountain. It stood on a narrow strip of land that was part of the cliff, facing the abyss.

"Not a word about Hamzat in their letter," Yunus added.

Hiding his disappointment, Shamil let his horse dip his nose into the fountain. The two mounts drank in long gulps, the water whistling through their teeth.

"The letter was from the commander of the fort at Temir-Khan-Chura," Yunus went on. "He wants to meet you personally."

Shamil expressed no surprise, rejection, or triumph. He waited for the rest.

"He proposes a one-on-one conversation, at whatever meeting place you find appropriate. You pick the day and the hour, but the sooner the better."

"General Klüge von Klugenau is inviting me?" he said with irony.

The request was indeed a first. It was a tacit official recognition of the imam Shamil as the religious authority and military chief of all the tribes of Dagestan and the only individual to be addressed in a procedurally correct exchange. The offer was worth taking into consideration.

"He'll probably try to buy you off," Yunus grumbled.

"Coming from anyone else but General Klüge von Klugenau, the proposal of a meeting would be unacceptable."

"It still is. Even from him."

Shamil listened to his instinct and his past experience. Among the infidels, this swarming vermin they had to crush everywhere, Klugenau was the only one who was not entirely contemptible.

After the first destruction of Ghimri, when the population was starving to death in the grottos and he was off somewhere, delirious, in a shepherds' hut, Klugenau had taken the trouble to have three mules carrying three heavy sacks of flour sent to the survivors. This gesture, unprecedented in the Caucasus, had earned him the surprise, gratitude, and even a kind of respect among the Montagnards. The initiative had also earned him the ire of his superior, General and Chief of Staff Karl Karlovitch Fézé. The butcher of Ghimri and Ashilta, nicknamed Fazi the Louse by the local population due to his small stature and his despicable acts, was hated by all. Since the matter of the three sacks of flour, Fézé and Klugenau had been continually at loggerheads, especially concerning the general strategy of "pacification." Fézé maintained that the natives understood only violence and vowed to show them that he was "more ferocious than they were." Klugenau, who had the reputation of being as bad-tempered and vulgar as he was honest and generous, believed other means could be effective.

Both of foreign origin—Fézé was Swiss, Klugenau, Austrian—they each sought to please their master, the czar. Each one accused the other of incompetence. Shamil's spies at Temir-Khan-Chura regularly brought back stories of their petty little tricks and major confrontations.

The spies also revealed that ever since the Russians had taken Ghimri and recaptured Kunzakh, the giaours had behaved as though the holy war were over. These filthy liars even went so far as to congratulate their Great White Czar for his dazzling victory. The network of Polish informers intercepted their reports to Saint Petersburg and translated them. They described the imam as a vanquished rebel, in chains and begging on his knees for the czar's mercy. Shamil relished the portrait. These dogs were fooling each other now, comforting each other. As for his chains and his cage, he was still at large.

"Do you recall, Yunus, which of these pigs was bragging about my capture?"

"The Louse."

Shamil chuckled. "His padishah's arrival has left him sleepless, fretting about how to negotiate an arrangement. Now that he's pressed for time, he's even willing to let his rival engage in discussions with me."

"They're weaving the ropes to hang themselves with. Well, let them put them around their necks."

"All the same, let's see what Klugenau proposes."

For a moment, the two friends were lost in their own thoughts. Yunus had no doubts whatsoever: the imam should refuse the offer.

"Lies, nothing but lies," he said. "They're still trying to fool us. The Russians are just like lice that sneak in and crawl all over; they infiltrate and multiply, as poisonous as the serpents that slither through the deserts of Muhan. We must destroy them wherever we find them."

Remembering these words, taken directly from one of Shamil's sermons, reinforced Yunus's bellicose feelings and further convinced him that any contact with the Russians was pointless. He continued, citing with feeling, almost word for word, what he had heard from Shamil's own lips at the mosque.

"We must destroy them in their homes, in their fields, by force and by ruse, so that they will cease to proliferate and disappear from the face of the earth."

"You know how to listen," Shamil said with approval.

"And to remember. I haven't forgotten how those traitors took your nephew."

"It's worth it to try to make peace with Klugenau."

Yunus was taken aback. Mystified, he turned to his friend and looked him in the eyes.

"You want peace?"

Shamil's gray eyes were glassy, impenetrable. He blinked twice, as he did when he sought inner solitude to listen to the voice of Allah. He said nothing.

This time Yunus needed an answer. "You want peace?" he repeated, incredulous.

"I want the word of God to reign everywhere in these mountains."

"But you said there's no peace possible with Satan. You said that the devil speaks through all those who settle with evil and promote sacrilegious compromise. You said we must behead the hydra of submission."

"I said I want the infidels out of here, forever. Yes, we could crush them today, give them a lesson here and there. But exterminate them?"

Shamil looked sadly at the jumble of dilapidated hovels that clung to one side of the valley.

"If they could raze Ghimri and Ashilta with a mere three cannons," he sighed, "then, Chirquata! We're not ready, Yunus. Not yet. We have to build a city in the heart of these mountains, an unassailable fortress where our murids from across the region can gather. A capital."

"Dealing with these jackals will bring you nothing," Yunus said stonily.

"Yes it will. Time."

The call of the muezzin, coming from the little mosque below, interrupted their conversation. In a very short while, their thoughts and words had strayed far from the voice of the Lord. They dismounted.

"Allah will decide."

Looping their reins around the pommels, they took the prayer rugs that were rolled up behind their saddles and let the horses go. They couldn't stray far, for the promontory was too narrow. They would stay there, drinking at the fountain behind them.

As the sun set between the chasms of the Caucasus, they performed their ablutions at the fountain and knelt on their rugs, touching the ground with their foreheads. The shadow of the cliff behind them grew longer. The silence was broken only by the clink of the bridles, the murmur of the stream, and the rush of the damp wind from the gorge of Ghimri, which struck them head-on and made them sway. Miniscule figures in the heart of this immensity, they prayed fervently.

When Yunus got up, he was certain of one thing.

"Even Klugenau is a hypocrite. Especially Klugenau!"

"Therefore tell him to meet me here on this ledge. Two days from now, here at the fountain of Chirquata."

Stunned at this conclusion, Yunus could not help protesting, "It's a trap!"

"Insha'allah."

* * *

"The knowledge of 'All' is what allows you to tell the difference between what is only passing and the eternal. Jamal Eddin, are you listening to me?"

No, the child had heard nothing. In the two days since his father had come home, he had been in a constant state of excitement. He was determined to accompany Shamil to the fountain; it was a desire that had become an obsession. He wanted to see the Russians.

On the terrace of the humble mosque, a cube of beaten mud like all the others, Sheik Jamaluddin al-Ghumuqi was distracted from his instruction of the imam's heir. See the Russians? Should he give in to Jamal Eddin? The sheik, who had not always known the infidels to be as cruel as they had become today, could fully understand the boy's desire. The repulsion of those close to him for these beasts who lurked in the shadows, the look of horror on his mother's face at the very mention of their name had turned his curiosity into fascination. And with good reason. Even Shamil's voice trembled with disgust when he spoke of the giaours.

See the Russians? Why not? But certain precautions were necessary. The presence of Shamil's son should not give them any ideas. But there was little risk of this tomorrow, since the entire army would be there, and the one-on-one meeting would be transformed into field maneuvers. No one would notice the child among all the other horsemen.

Of all Shamil's advisors, the sheik was the only one who had not totally disapproved of Shamil's decision to meet with Klugenau. He shared the conviction of the naïbs that a holy war was inevitable, a necessity to which he must devote his intelligence and knowledge. But he did not like the idea. If the infidels, finally enlightened, could allow the Montagnards to govern themselves freely in their own territory and worship their God as they chose, Jamaluddin al-Ghumuqi would be favorable to negotiation. Peace for the Muslims of the Caucasus was his deepest desire. And his greatest hope.

The others, like Yunus, were wary of an ambush. Shaken by their conviction, Shamil prepared for that eventuality. The Russians could only reach the fountain by the narrow gorge of Ghimri; in the event of a problem, Shamil's men could cut off their retreat. The naïbs could retreat to Akulgo, which was naturally defended by its location at the summit of the peak. The plan was to move in there for the winter. Whatever happened, the army would evacuate Chirquata, which was too accessible to reprisal, and the population would follow. See the Russians? Well, Jamal Eddin would see them soon enough.

The teacher was touched by the small boy, with his dark eyes and long lashes, his alert, mischievous expression, and a child's body that he tried hard to control. The scratches on his cherkeska, whose sleeves only reached his elbows, and his scraped-up arms and legs were proof that the child was growing up too fast, trying too hard to emulate his father.

Jamal Eddin was by nature less sensitive, less somber and tormented, than Shamil, but he shared his father's thirst for the absolute and his strong will. When he decided to do something, he would go on trying until he had overcome his fears and obtained his objective. Or been proven right. At seven, he could be as tenacious as he could be tiring.

Squatting oriental-style on the terrace, the old teacher tried to pick up the thread of the lesson.

"Sit down here in front of me, and answer. What is Islam made of?"

The boy tried to escape his quizzing by asking another question, but the mullah persisted.

"What are the three distinct, interrelated elements that make up the chain of the Naqshbandi order? I'm listening!"

His teacher's tone was adamant. Jamal Eddin settled down, crossing his legs obediently. It was in his interest to be patient. Apart from the fact that he liked the old man, he needed his support. It would be no easy task to obtain it, since he rarely had occasion to be alone with him. Usually he studied at the *madrassa,* the Islamic school, with his little brother and the other boys of the village. Shamil intended to interrogate his son about al-Fatiha, the first *surat,* or chapter, of the Koran, and the sheik was going over the lesson with him.

Jamal Eddin knew that despite his long white beard the sheik was scarcely a decade older than his father, and that he also had several wives, who were said to be very attractive. But Shamil worshipped the wisdom so evident in his words. His voice could be patient and kind, but it could also cut to the quick, like Bahou-Messadou's. Jamal Eddin wiggled with discomfort thinking of his grandmother. She had forbidden him to go to the fountain to see the Russians. Usually Bahou was kind and good to him, acceding to all he asked. But she was a woman, and she was frightened.

If the sheik was in favor, his father would take him to the fountain.

He recited docilely, "The three elements are the Sharia, the law; the Tariqa, the way; and the Hakika, the truth."

"And what is the Tariqa?"

"The direct relation between the source of the river and its tributaries."

"That is to say?"

"The relation between the teachings of the prophet and the teachings of his followers, the Sufi masters who enrich the river."

"And the Hakika?"

The child was a bit less sure about this element. He fidgeted again, searching for the answer.

"Be still! What is the Hakika?"

"The truth. Union with the divine spirit."

"And?"

Jamal Eddin hesitated. "The capacity to know the infinite."

"And what is the name for this state of meditation that liberates the mind?"

This time Jamal Eddin could no longer resist. Abruptly changing the subject, he returned to the problem that preoccupied him.

"Why did Hamzat disappear with the Russians?"

Jamal Eddin had only a vague memory of his sole encounter with the Russians, of white caps, golden objects, and rocks sticky with blood. But now that he was big, he no longer rode pillion like Mohammed Ghazi. He rode his own pony and he carried a kinjal. What should he think of his cousin being held captive by the infidels?

"My aunt Patimat says that even if they give Hamzat back, she doesn't want him anymore."

"Your aunt doesn't really believe what she says."

"Yes, she does! She says that since the Russians have touched him, Hamzat is impure. He stinks."

"Allah is much more merciful than your aunt Patimat."

"She says it's the same thing as for the birds. When an eaglet falls from the nest, you mustn't touch him or his mother won't recognize his smell any more. She says Hamzat has been sullied by contact with them. That he should accept nothing from their hands, not a raisin, not a scrap of bread, not pilaf, no food. She says he should let himself starve to death."

The sheik frowned.

"For Hamzat, there are many other choices besides death."

"She says no, there's no other way."

"Neither Patimat nor anyone else on this earth can presume the ways of the Lord. As for the dishonor of Hamzat's captivity, the infidel your father plans to meet tomorrow has always been loyal and courageous in combat. If his integrity deserves Shamil's trust, contact with him cannot dishonor your cousin."

Jamal Eddin looked doubtful as he digested the sheik's words, then he said mischievously, enunciating his words one by one, "That I'd like to see."

* * *

The imam and his naïbs rode at the head. Now there were thirty of them instead of ten. Behind them was a unit of monk-soldiers dressed in black, who had renounced conjugal ties and chosen a life of abstinence. They were followed by most of the army, dressed in brown; the murids carried banners, a forest of flags and lances all crowned with the same metal ornament, the crescent of Islam. The rest of the troops were composed of *murtaghazets,* village fighters. One out of every ten families in each hamlet had contributed a horse, a warrior, and his arms. Shamil had transformed this obligation into a glorious privilege, and all had sworn on the Koran to die for their imam. All of them wore the white turban of Shamil. Those who had made the pilgrimage to Mecca wore green, the others brown. Only the youngsters, who, like Jamal Eddin, were not yet knowledgeable enough in religious science, wore no drape of white on their sheepskin hats.

In all, hundreds of horsemen strode forward, their sabers in bandolier, daggers at the waist. Over their shoulders, they wore the *burka,* a broad black goatskin cape impermeable to wind, rain, or snow, so stiff and wide it fell in heavy folds over the horses' rumps.

Jamal Eddin's pony pranced amid the troops. Standing up in the stirrups, all his senses alert, he was discovering the joy of belonging to the greatest army on earth, the one fighting for the triumph of God. He was giddy with this feeling of belonging. With bravery and devotion, he and his brothers would fill the void between man and God. All Sheik Jamaluddin's lessons were intended to render him capable of crossing the chasm between human existence and divine existence to reach union with God. He knew that he was part of a long chain that ran from Allah to his faithful, from Mohammed to Shamil.

He stopped with the others at the narrow groove in the earth that formed a recess between the cliffs. There was no one in the rocky corridor; the Russians had not arrived. The wind howled, carrying the faint whistles of the sentinels Shamil had posted above the gorge, signaling the enemy's approach. Jamal Eddin's heart beat faster.

He wouldn't miss a second of this adventure, and this time he would understand.

Jamal Eddin saw the first Russian advance. A murmur rippled through the crowd of horsemen. Klugenau. He was riding a bay horse, bigger than most. He rode alone, a colossal figure on the ledge, nearly as imposing as Shamil. His arms were hidden beneath the burka that covered him like a shell, blacker than their own, with longer, shinier hair that curled with the humidity in the air. He wore a blue cap, gloves, and boots. His chin was clean-shaven, but the odor emanating from his thick gray moustache was perceptible all the way to their lines. A vile stench. He was smoking! Tobacco was a sin that merited corporal punishment, like wine or alcohol in general. The Sharia forbade smoking. And here he was, chewing on a cigar. A Russian through and through. He carried a crutch across his saddle. A second officer followed, wearing a blue coat that matched his cap instead of a burka. He was young and slender, and his cheek was marked by a fresh scar.

Behind them rode fifteen Cossacks wearing cherkeskas and papakhas, like the Montagnards. These Russians were difficult to tell apart from the Kiranis tribe, a neutral tribe whose men served as intermediaries and interpreters.

Jamal Eddin waited for the rest. But no, there were no more, just these thirty horsemen. Shamil did not move as he watched them approach. He waited.

He turned to his naïbs and issued brief orders that Jamal Eddin did not catch. Word traveled down the lines. Do not move, do not follow. Be prepared, but remain at a distance. Shamil would advance alone.

The Russian had undoubtedly given similar orders, for his troops gathered at the entrance to the corridor.

The Russian and Shamil nudged their horses toward each other. Each kept two men with him—the aide-de-camp with the scar and the Kirani interpreter accompanied the Russian, Yunus and the naïb Akbirdil, Patimat's husband, escorted Shamil. The six horsemen met at the fountain and dismounted. The Russian, still smoking, set himself down on one leg, hopping in place as he reached for his crutch. His limping caused Shamil to wonder whether one of his boots was empty. It must be an old wound, in any case, since he handled the crutch adroitly.

The naïbs and the aide-de-camp spread out their burkas at the foot of the fountain. Shamil and the Russian sat down cross-legged with the interpreter. Yunus and Akbirdil Mohammed sat down behind Shamil, while the young officer remained standing a little way away.

Jamal Eddin took advantage of the moment to dismount from his pony too. He threw the reins to his neighbor and rapidly made his way to the front row, heedless of the remonstrances and the firm hands that tried to prevent him from doing so.

Even this close, he could only hear snatches of conversation; the rest was lost to the wind.

Turning to Shamil, the interpreter translated the Russian's long introduction.

"I have come in peace. I have never broken my word, and you can count on it for your personal security. Look around us. Only thirty soldiers accompany me, while you, you have come with three hundred horsemen. Which of us is the most fair? Which of us has not lived up to his honor, you or me? But I know you are a man of integrity, and I have confidence in your noble intent, as you must have confidence in mine. Do you remember the three sacks of flour I sent you, when your people needed them so badly? You know that I have always supported you and offered good advice. Now I would like to help you obtain prosperity, and this is what I want to discuss with you."

Shamil listened phlegmatically.

The Russian's cigar stunk up the air. He smoked nonstop and talked on and on and on.

The interpreter used all his eloquence to persuade Shamil to come to Tiflis, in Georgia, to meet the Great White Czar. It would be a meeting between chiefs. Though not equals, they could at least engage in a friendly meeting between two sovereigns. Klugenau guaranteed the clemency of his padishah. He would grant pardon, liberty, and peace, to say nothing of untold wealth for the imam and his sons, gifts for his people, and the numerous advantages of an honorable and pacific surrender.

Shamil heard him out politely.

Jamal Eddin's eyes were glued to his father, whose actions interested him as much as those of the Russian, whose odor turned his stomach. Inscrutable beneath his beard, Shamil said nothing. Eyes half-closed and looking inward, this was the look he assumed on his nights of prayer and fasting.

Klugenau seemed to be growing irritated and spoke more loudly, more rapidly, and more passionately as time passed. The cigar he had just lit kept going out. Fighting the wind, he relit it with difficulty.

Jamal Eddin heard the naïbs grumbling behind him. Enough of this playacting. It's all hot air.

The horses pawed the ground impatiently as the army fidgeted restlessly. Everyone sensed the negotiations were going nowhere.

Still energetic and lively, Klugenau pulled out all the stops. At every one of his exhortations, Shamil nodded his head in assent and replied with extreme courtesy. He was not at liberty to commit himself; it was not in his power. He would have to consult with his naïbs and his council. He would not fail to do so.

With one last drag on his cigar, Klugenau rose awkwardly to his feet, grabbing the crutch to put under his left arm. Shamil followed suit. Then, cordially, in a gesture of conclusion and farewell, Klugenau held out his hand. Shamil did the same. At that instant, Jamal Eddin saw his uncle Akbirdil throw himself between them, dramatically interrupting the handshake. He shouted in Klugenau's face, his words full of hatred.

"Giaour! The imam cannot touch the hand of a dog of an infidel!"

Livid with rage, the Russian brandished his crutch, waving it in the air in an attempt to knock Akbirdil's turban off his head. Jamal Eddin instantly comprehended the magnitude of the insult he tried to express with this most outrageous of offenses. To uncover one's head before Allah was to insult God. A Muslim must remain covered. Shamil caught the crutch in midair with one hand. With the other, he held back the kinjals of Akbirdil and Yunus. He shouted to his men to put back their sabers and back off.

Pushed by the threatening mass of murids, Jamal Eddin was thrown forward, landing between his father's legs. With the back of his hand, Shamil pushed the boy behind his back. He continued to yell, his voice finally dominating the tumult.

By this time, the Cossacks had marched forward to come to the aid of the Russian. The murids continued to advance. It was their turn now. Three hundred against thirty, here was their opportunity to avenge the massacres of Ghimri and Ashilta.

Arresting a blood bath, in a toneless voice, Shamil urged Klugenau to retreat. Akbirdil and Yunus, daggers drawn, prepared to leap at his throat and restore their honor. He couldn't hold his horsemen in check much longer.

Beside himself with anger, Klugenau did not move. He yelled a torrent of abuse at Akbirdil, every foul word in his vast vocabulary, enriched by fifty years of military life. The young aide-de-camp did his best to shut the general up and pull him back. Finally, still spewing wrath, Klugenau allowed himself to be led to his horse.

Shamil stood still as he watched Klugenau sling the crutch over his saddle and put his good foot in the stirrup to mount. The general tugged on the bridle to turn the horse around. His Cossacks followed.

Standing in the middle of the corridor to protect their retreat, Shamil watched the figure as he gestured in the direction of the fort at Temir-Khan-Chura. He did not move until Klugenau and the last of his men had left the ridge.

Jamal Eddin decided it was time to clear out. He disappeared into the group of horsemen, running back to jump on his pony. He hoped Shamil would forget that he had been there.

Nothing in his father's behavior could have warned him of the violence of his anger, nor the scope of it. With the Russian gone, Shamil set off on the path to Akulgo, as planned, without a word for his son or a glance at his men.

No one could miss his displeasure, though, and all of them feared the severity of the punishment awaiting them. Akbirdil would pay dearly for his insubordination, as would Yunus and the other naïbs who had ignored his order to put away their kinjals. As for the presence of Jamal Eddin underfoot, the boy had no illusions about what he was in for. The trip seemed as short as it was clouded with threat. The switch or the whip? How many blows?

To everyone's surprise, there was no tongue-lashing for Akbirdil or Yunus or the rest of the naïbs when they had reached the plateau of Akulgo. Even Jamal Eddin was not whipped. Shamil made no reference to his meeting with Klugenau. What had the general wanted? He was silent about the substance of their exchange.

Fatima the Beloved was probably the only one who grasped the extent of his anger that night. The insult he had just suffered was immeasurable. The Russians had summoned him for that? They had dared propose an arrangement that even the lowest and most cowardly of men could not have accepted? In return for promises and gifts? It was like throwing scraps to the pigs to lure them into the slaughterhouse. What they were demanding was capitulation, pure and simple.

The Russians took them for fools, Shamil and all the rest of the Caucasian Muslims. Evidently they had no idea who they were dealing with.

In the morning, Shamil had the prisoners, the hostages, the amanats, and those whose fathers, uncles, families, and villages had surrendered to the Russians or were prepared to do so gather on the village square. All the men in these mountains who, at one time or another, had dared speak to him of peace. All the men who had, even once, pronounced the word "surrender." He had their eyes gouged out and their tongues torn out. And then he set them free, ordering them to go home and spread the message. The following day, a horseman left with his response for Klugenau:

"Even if I am to be cut up in little pieces for this refusal, I will not come to Tiflis to meet your padishah, for I have experienced your treachery far too many times."

The insult was like a slap in the face to the czar, and his reaction was immediate. He replaced Fazi the Louse with a general said to be even more brutal, multiplied by ten the contingents of his army, and ordered total war. He wanted Shamil, dead or alive. The conquest of Chechnya and Dagestan became his first priority. The fight was now personal.

In the same spirit, Shamil set himself to the task of fortifying Akulgo.

Jamal Eddin finally had his answers.

First of all, he judged that he had behaved rather bravely. He hadn't even been afraid during the incident with the crutch. Well, almost not. After that, he concluded that the Russians were vulgar beings, noisy and so impure that one could not even touch their hands. They lacked manners. What's more, they smelled bad. Patimat was right. Hamzat's captivity in the company of the Russians had sullied and dishonored him. The question was settled. That left one last problem: why had Shamil protected them when he had had them at his mercy?

Why had Shamil spared them?

Neither Yunus nor the sheik, not even Bahou-Messadou nor anyone he asked would—or could—explain this enigma to his satisfaction. The solution was a function of a principle so fundamental that even alluding to it was not considered proper.

So Jamal Eddin decided to consult the source.

He approached the imam just as he was coming from the mosque on Friday. Carrying the Koran, dressed in his green ceremonial robe, he was crossing the courtyard in the direction of his apartments. The child accosted him and, without formalities, went straight to the heart of the matter.

"Why did you protect Klugenau from Yunus's and Akbirdil's kinjals?"

Shamil stopped. But instead of answering, he asked him a question.

"Why do you think I did?"

Searching his thoughts, Jamal Eddin contemplated the question for a moment. He looked up at his father when he decided he had found the answer.

"For…"

He hesitated for a long moment, searching his father's face with large, dark eyes. He began again, carefully.

"For…"

Shamil's gaze was impenetrable.

With great precaution and respect and infinite pride, Jamal Eddin pronounced that glorious word, the word that was as sacred as the name of the Lord.

"For honor."

Akulgo, a year later
September 1838

"I understand," Bahou-Messadou sighed, "but it will be difficult, very difficult."

Jamal Eddin lay on one of the cushions in the little room reserved for him. Bahou had tied his arm to his belly and his body to the mattress. He could not move. And not being able to move drove him crazy. It had been four months already!

Last spring, when he was playing at acrobatics on the waterwheel, he had slipped between the planks. The wheel had continued to turn, crushing him in the stream and smashing him against the rocks. The result was three months at death's door and a return to the realm of the women.

Of his multiple injuries, only one, an open fracture from shoulder to elbow, refused to heal. But he was doing well, and Shamil had just allowed him to leave the harem, where he had been smothered by the tyranny of Patimat all summer long.

So Bahou had brought him to the only room that opened out onto the upstairs gallery, between the den of the women and the imam's apartments. The location of the room allowed Shamil to stop by to see his son whenever he had a spare moment. Mohammed Ghazi and their friends, their teacher, Jamaluddin, the atalik Yunus, and visitors of both sexes could come here too. Fatima could continue to bring healers to his bedside to sprinkle him with nail clippings, burn herbs on his chest, and swab him with ointments to chase away the evil spirits. And the surgeon Abdul Aziz, his grandfather from Untsukul, could throw the ants he carried in a pot on his wound.

"Remarkable ants, for their size and their ferocity," he said. "When they have bitten into the flesh, I cut them in two so the pincers of their mandibles will continue to hold it together and suture the wound."

Some of the visitors and some of the treatments tried Jamal Eddin's patience, but he absolutely adored this great family fuss over him. Brothers in blood, word, and the service of God, he loved their presence, their noise, and their warmth. He loved this solid house where his relatives, his friends, and his friends' friends gathered around him. He loved this suite of interior courtyards whose walls and towers sheltered the thirty naïbs, their wives, and their horses, this stone citadel with crenellated roofs that no one could enter except from the mountain. It was an impregnable fortress, like the peak village of Akulgo. Even on the bad days, when the spirits invaded his mind, he was not afraid that the demons would carry him off. No force of evil could tear him away from here, Bahou-Messadou had told him so. His adoration for her did the rest. She watched over him, and she was capable of anything.

Squatting with her back to him, she was serving tea to three strangers.

This morning, when she was crossing the first courtyard, Mohammed Ghazi had brought her a message from three Chechens who had stopped him on the village square. They begged an audience with the khanum Bahou-Messadou. The old woman's heart skipped a beat. Still hoping for news of Hamzat, she invited them to Jamal Eddin's room.

They gave off the acrid odor of the suint that soaked the wool of their hats. They reeked of sweat, leather, and the steam that rose from the boots and burkas they had left at the door. These men had come from a long way off.

Sitting in a semicircle before the brazier that Bahou-Messadou had moved to the back of the room for them, they drank the hot, black liquid in long, grateful gulps, without uttering a word. When they had all set their bowls down, they spoke, one after the other.

Jamal Eddin listened absently to their consultations. He was dreaming of the day, the hour he could leave. He turned his face toward the door and life outside.

Akulgo was a beehive, a Tower of Babel of all languages, all castes, all peoples: Polish officers, Russian serfs, Georgian peasants, Dagestani horsemen, Chechen warriors, Lesgiens, Inguches, Ossetians, Circassians. Free and captive, Muslim and Christian, deserters and renegades. Shamil listened to those who taught him what he needed to know: the great art of military fortification. Arsenals, garrisons, shelters, and trenches. They cut into the rock, bored tunnels, dug wells, and mapped out canals. They hollowed out the mountain, digging an underground defense network in its depths, a system that would allow them to face the longest attack and the most brutal charge. Jamal Eddin heard the sound of the pickaxes on stone, the hammers on wood, the bustle of an entire people preparing for combat. Without him.

Exasperated by his weakness, he turned his attention to his grandmother, who had come to his bedside. The ordeals of the past few years and the anxieties of recent months had made her thinner and broken her frail figure. Even Jamal Eddin realized that she was now a very old woman. He knew as well that her dignity, her will to live, and a desire to fulfill her duty were what kept her going. She still carried her head high and looked straight ahead; nothing diminished the liveliness in her eyes or the gentleness of her smile. Bahou-Messadou went about her business with her usual energy, coming and going from sickroom to kitchen, from well to fields, receiving the guests her age and rank attracted here in the new capital, for the time being in her grandson's room.

All Jamal Eddin saw was the look that she gave her guests, her gray eyes shining and attentive above her veil as she listened to their requests. He could tell that she was not smiling; on the contrary, she grew more serious and sober. What news had they brought her that was so grave?

They were poor and dirty. Their cartridge belts and the sheaths of their sabers and kinjals were plain, enhanced by no silver. What did they want? Jamal Eddin heard only a breathless murmur.

Only the customary compliments praising the khanum Bahou-Messadou's wisdom, spoken loudly in Arabic, had been intelligible. They had heard of the goodness of Shamil's mother, they said, and of her son's respect for her, as far off as their little village. This had given them hope she might understand the horror of their situation.

Their command of Kumik being limited, they spoke in Chechen. Jamal Eddin understood only one word out of two. Each of the three men said more or less the same thing, and little by little he grasped the situation. At home, the hardships of war had become close to unbearable. Since the grand padishah's tour of the region, the infidels had returned with a vengeance. Three times they had burned the village to the ground, raping their women and taking their children as slaves. They had followed the imam's orders. No one had surrendered, and the men had managed to flee to the forest. Three times they had rebuilt their villages from the ruins. Three times the Russians had contaminated their wells, burned their harvests, polluted their mosques with filth, killed their sheep and goats—everything. The village had resisted, three times. Following Shamil's law, no one had surrendered.

But even the most courageous could not face the famine that was sure to come with winter. Dysentery had done the rest, and with the summer, the Russians would return. The only ones left to fight them were the sick and the wounded, a few old men and some women. The village needed some relief. The village must make peace with the infidels, even for just a few weeks, a few months. But how could they make peace? The murids were everywhere, punishing even the thought of surrender. Between their cruelty and the czar's, between mutilation and hunger, there was no choice—and no hope of survival. Could the khanum talk to the imam, tell him personally of their situation? Ask his consent for a temporary capitulation, allow them to lay down their arms for just a few days? The time to take a deep breath?

"This will be difficult. Very difficult."

The child stopped listening. He turned his face toward the door, dreaming of the moment he would jump on Koura the Proud, gallop through the three gates of the enclave, and ride off down the mountain.

After she had fed and bandaged her grandson for the evening, Bahou sent a servant to Shamil asking permission for a visit. She waited in her own apartment in the harem instead of Jamal Eddin's room. The invitation came at a bad time; Shamil, his naïbs, and Yunus were deep in consultation. Bent over a map of Chechnya, Shamil listed the communities that were ready to betray him. It was unusual for his mother to disturb him at this hour. Surprised, almost apprehensive, he interrupted the session and went immediately to her home.

Witnesses said later that the imam stayed for a long while, leaving Bahou-Messadou's apartments only at about midnight.

He left the harem with heavy steps, walking along the gallery past his son's room without even looking in. He strode into the room where his counselors were still waiting for him, walked past them, crossed the courtyard, entered the mosque, and shut the door.

Alone.

It was broad daylight when Jamal Eddin woke up. The door to his room was wide open, and the slate gray light of a storm hung over the gallery, the courtyard, and the ramparts. There was no sound at all, none of the ordinary noises of rocks being pounded to make powder, or the bawling of the buffalo when they were let out at dawn. No clamor of the newly arrived, forced to dismount before the walls of Akulgo because of the narrow alleyways. Even the muezzin was silent, and there was no call to prayer. Fatima, Jawarat, and Patimat were nowhere to be seen. He could not hear Mohammed Ghazi and Saïd, Jawarat's son, playing in the courtyard of the seraglio. Yunus's three children and Sheik Jamaluddin's were not crying. There was no noise, no movement, not a breath of air, not a sign of life. Absolute silence had fallen on the house, and the city. Only Muessa, Shamil's cat, locked in his master's house, meowed pitifully, his cries filling the emptiness. No servant came to feed him or set him free.

Jamal Eddin wiggled, trying to sit up, trying to understand. His arm hurt, but his concern was of another nature. Where was Bahou? What had she told the men yesterday?

"I'll try." That was all. "I'll try. It will be difficult, very difficult. But I'll try."

He remembered that the Chechens had thanked her profusely, and that she had discouraged their thanks.

"I can't promise you anything. Come back tomorrow after the second prayer."

That was all. Was it really all? Jamal Eddin searched his thoughts.

"I'll try."

And since then, she had disappeared.

He stayed there, tied up, all morning long.

Around noon, the three Chechens returned to the room just as Bahou arrived. With an anxious look, she nervously pulled her veil down over her forehead.

"The imam cannot give you his authorization," she muttered. "The imam cannot decide, it is Allah who commands. My son is at the mosque, praying, fasting, and listening to the voice of God."

Avoiding the light and muttering unintelligible comments, she returned to the corner, where the Chechens had left her the day before.

"Shamil orders the people of Akulgo to join him," she said rapidly, continuing in the same breath, "wait there, wait with him, pray, repent, and wait for the will of Allah."

She added a few confused words and fell silent.

The three Chechens left hurriedly. Jamal Eddin heard Yunus stop them at the end of the gallery. What were they doing in Shamil's house? Who had invited them?

Bahou-Messadou answered no questions. She was praying.

Outside, the morning silence had changed to a dull grumble, announcing the coming storm.

* * *

Blind and deaf to the world, she rocked back and forth, reciting her prayers softly. But Bahou's chanting did not rise to God in his heaven, and it brought her no peace. What premonitions, what signs, what omens did she sense? What had she asked Shamil yesterday, and what business of hers was it? What had she said, and what had she done?

His heart going out to her, Jamal Eddin watched her shrink from one hour to the next, becoming a little old woman who moaned and droned just like other little old women. The child felt her anguish.

All day long, she did not move from the shadow at the back of the room. No one came to pay them any attention. It was as though neither one of them existed.

"Come to me," he begged. "Bahou-Messadou, do you hear me? Come, set me free."

By dusk, he no longer begged but snarled like a wolf, "Come here."

She hesitated then. Humble and unsteady on her feet, she rose.

"Closer!" he insisted.

"Take your kinjal and cut my bonds," he ordered.

The brutality of his tone made her conscious of her surroundings.

"Cut them!"

She obeyed.

What was left of his grandmother's dignity now? She set about awkwardly changing his bandages in a disordered fashion, like a servant.

When she had taken them off, a pain shot through his arm, so sharp that he thought he would faint. But what was his suffering in comparison to Bahou-Messadou's terror?

He clenched his teeth harder, stood up, and took her by the elbow, leading her out the door.

The house was empty.

The waves of people streaming through the alleyways carried the boy and his grandmother along toward the mosque. A huge crowd had gathered before the flat-roofed building to which the imam had retreated in solitude. The men had spread their prayer rugs on the square. The women stood, arms reaching toward the sky, uttering prayers and moaning softly.

The crowd fell silent as the khanum appeared, bent over beneath her veils. The tide of faithful parted before the old woman and the child.

It was a low-built mosque, with neither a minaret nor a dome. Funeral ceremonies were held upon the terracelike roof. The muezzin issued his call to prayer from an overhanging wooden ledge, supported by solid pillars. Jamal Eddin tried to lead Bahou beneath this little balcony, which served as an awning of sorts for the building. The slightest brush against his arm revived the pain and struck him to the quick. Pale as guilt-stricken criminals, the pair made their way through the mass of people to the closed door.

Fatima, Jawarat, Patimat, the wives of the *naïbs,* and the professional mourners knelt in the dust in a row directly before the door. All begged for pardon, sobbing and lamenting their faults.

Bahou knelt just before the doors, between her daughter and her daughters-in-law. The moaning that had ceased at her passage began anew, more loudly this time. Mohammed Ghazi, the children, and the babies added their tears to those of their mothers. Jamal Eddin remained beside them.

* * *

For two days and two nights, the murmur of groan and supplication carried on unceasingly. The crowd camped on the square, praying and fasting among the horses, cows, and goats. No one dared leave. Everyone waited, and their prayers filled the blank skies of Akulgo with a menacing rumble.

On the third morning, the sudden creak of the hinges signaled the opening of the double doors. The crowd fell still as Shamil appeared upon the threshold, arms open.

Blinded by the light of day, his livid countenance framed by the stray whiskers of his bushy red beard, he stood still for a long moment before the prostrate crowd.

Supported by Yunus and Akbirdil, Bahou-Messadou dragged herself toward him. She kissed the ground and knelt there at his feet, her forehead touching the dust. The imam's eyes were swollen, as though he had been weeping. He studied her in silence. Then he climbed the few steps up the ladder to the terrace, which was scarcely higher than he was.

On the roof, Shamil raised his right hand and turned his eyes to the south.

"Oh, Mohammed, thy will be done, thy judgment fulfilled," he proclaimed. "Would that thy just sentence serve as an example to all true believers. For thy commandments are unchanging and sacred!"

He turned to face the crowd.

"Murids of Akulgo, hear now the message of the prophet."

Jamal Eddin had never seen that look, nor heard that voice. Normally he loved nothing more than Shamil's eloquence. His father's passion, the fervor of his fearsome harangues, which inspired in him a love of God and the ardor to serve Him, normally filled him with delight.

But his father's tone today was utterly foreign to him.

"The Chechen people, forgetting their vow, are ready to submit to the will of the Russians and obey their laws. Their emissaries, too craven to tell me of their dishonorable proposals, addressed themselves to my mother. Playing upon her great kindness and her weakness as a woman, they convinced her to appeal to me in their stead. Her insistence in pleading their cause, her tears for them, and my infinite love and respect for her gave me the strength and the boldness to seek the will of Allah through Mohammed. With the strength of your devotion and your prayers to sustain me, I have thus begged the favor of the prophet, that he should deign to hear my presumptuous question. This morning, after three days of fasting and prayers, Mohammed gave me a response. And I was stricken by the thunder of His voice."

The crowd held its breath. Shamil drew himself up to his full height.

"Allah has ordained that the person who first spoke to me of submission should be punished with a hundred lashes. And the first one who spoke, that first person, is my mother!"

Bahou-Messadou uttered a cry. A moan rose from the people. Jamal Eddin felt himself trembling. He searched his father's eyes, but Shamil's stare was fixed and veiled. Yunus and Akbirdil, holding up the old woman, bowed before him in silent supplication. Everyone knew that a Muslim was not permitted to strike his parents. All were aware that Shamil worshipped his mother. And they knew that a hundred lashes meant death. Surely the imam would commute the sentence.

"Bring her up here and tie her up."

At his words, the mourners broke into a strident clamor of ritual keening, the lamentation of a funeral ceremony. They followed the executioner as he dragged Bahou-Messadou up the ladder.

Jamal Eddin wanted to scramble in front of his mother, Patimat, the *naïbs,* all of them. Whereas before he had been trembling, now he was shaking violently.

He was the last one on the roof. The executioner had already tied Bahou-Messadou's arms behind her back. She was weeping.

Jamal Eddin saw the executioner hesitate. How could he dare to rip the tunic and reveal the flesh of the imam's mother? The crowd felt a surge of relief and hope.

Shamil was already snatching the whip from the executioner. He was going to commute the sentence. Jamal Eddin took heart. Shamil would grant her mercy.

And then he saw his father rip Bahou's tunic, raise his arm high, and strike her himself with all his strength. She howled in pain. Before the child's horrified eyes, the whip stung her back and slashed at her shoulders and sides. He watched the leather strips tear into her bony back. Two blows. Three. Bahou's cries became weaker.

By the fifth blow, Bahou-Messadou was silent. She had fainted.

Jamal Eddin saw his father throw himself upon her and untie her. What else would he subject her to, what further torture and torment? As he watched, his father fell, weeping, to his knees upon the prostrate figure.

Shamil's tears, the tears of his father, filled him with terror. Jamal Eddin had never seen a man cry. He suddenly sensed Shamil's unspeakable despair.

And Shamil's despair was that of God.

But the imam was already on his feet. He turned his burning gaze to his son, his wife, his *naïbs,* to all of them.

"There is no other god but Allah, and Mohammed is his prophet!"

Towering over the people of Akulgo, he raised his face again to the sky.

"Oh you, who dwell in paradise, you the blessed and the chosen who rejoice in the eternal beatitude of the gardens of Allah, you have heard my prayer! You allow me to submit to the rest of the punishment to which my poor mother has been condemned. I accept these blows with joy, they are the gift of your love and your infinite mercy!"

He unbuttoned his cherkeska, took off his shirt, and knelt beside his mother's still body.

"Executioner," he ordered, "give me the ninety-five lashes yet to come."

The executioner still hesitated. How could one whip the imam?

"Disobey the will of Mohammed and I will kill you with my own hands! Strike me!"

The lash descended.

Jamal Eddin could no longer control his face, his body, his soul. Everything within him had turned wobbly and unsteady. He tried to pull himself together, counting the lashes with the executioner. But he heard the crack of the whip and its slashing descent from somewhere far away. Whistling through the air, it took his breath away, and he felt it burn to his very marrow.

The leather strips dug into his father's shoulders. The lacerated flesh fell away, its scarified layers swelling like the leaves of a book consumed by flames.

By the ninety-fifth lash, Shamil's back was nothing but a black, shredded mass, a magma of muscle, flesh, and blood. He rose slowly, picked up his tunic, and covered his wounds.

And then, he turned again to his people, who knelt before him.

"Where are the cowards?"

He leapt from the roof in a single bound.

He scrutinized the crowd of faces frozen in terror.

"Where are the traitors?"

Striding through their ranks, he stopped before each bowed head and repeated, "Where are the hypocrites who brought this punishment upon my mother?"

Yunus and Akbirdil dragged the three Chechens forward and threw them at his feet. They scrabbled in the dust, their faces to the ground. None of them offered excuses or explanations or thought to beg for mercy. The best they could hope for was that the end might come quickly. They murmured their prayers.

Everyone waited for Shamil's verdict. He leaned toward the three men preparing themselves for death. The executioner drew his saber and waited expectantly.

Standing on the roof above their heads, a petrified Jamal Eddin closed his eyes.

If only. To see nothing, hear nothing. Disappear with them.

"Take courage…"

Shamil made the Chechens stand.

"Return to your village and tell your people what you have heard at Akulgo. Tell everyone at home, in your auls and your forests, of the word and the will of God. Spread the word everywhere, of what you have seen here. May Allah be with you always. Go in peace."

For the child, this spectacular pardon, this mercy that defied all the traditional codes, all the laws of Shamil, was the ultimate upheaval.

He swayed on his feet and vomited.

* * *

After the guilty men had set out again upon the mountain path, blessing the imam for his wisdom and mercy, Shamil returned to his mother's side. Leaning over her, he took her in his arms with infinite tenderness and carried her home, still unconscious.

His demonstration before his people had cost him dearly.

Like all who had witnessed the drama, Jamal Eddin understood the lesson. By ordering his servant to strike his own mother—when the authority of the elders was sacred and inviolable—the imam had offered proof of the boundless wrath of Allah before the Chechens' weakness. As clear as it was effective, the message spread throughout the Caucasus. Of all sins, peace with the infidel was the fault that Allah could not pardon, the crime He would punish most harshly.

No one, ever again, should pronounce the words of damnation. No one, ever again, should speak of surrendering to the Russians.

In the depths of his being, Jamal Eddin absorbed the obvious message: Shamil lived in union with God. Jamal Eddin's own destiny was to live and to die for Shamil. And yet he discovered that, contrary to all his experience, in contradiction of all appearances and his own convictions, his father was not omnipotent. A power infinitely superior to Shamil's will dictated his conduct, constrained him, and tormented him as He tormented all men. It was then that a profound mistrust of this mysterious force that was stronger than his father was born in Jamal Eddin, a wariness that knew no bounds. The boy was not afraid of the Russians. He had never been afraid of them. But the wrath of God that had commanded his father to beat Bahou-Messadou filled him with terror. It took root in the heart of the child, as it had once grown in the soul of the old woman.

His grandmother did not regain consciousness until the evening. Jamal Eddin never left her side. She died in his arms a few days later, paralyzed and unable to speak. For Jamal, all the sweetness of life disappeared. Nothing certain existed for him anymore. Not even the love and the protection of Shamil. As she left this world, Bahou-Messadou took with her her grandson's innocence.

CHAPTER IV

You, the Imam, You, My Father

Akulgo, nine months later
The siege of eighty days
June–August, 1839

On this evening of June 24, 1839, the attack was imminent.

"They're down there!" cried the little boy, his eye glued to the arrow slit. "There! They're down there!"

Far off in the distance, three Russian battalions emerged from the depths of the boulders and spread out over the right bank of the river. Of course, they were only the relief troops for the regiments already bivouacked at the foot of the promontory. But the two army corps together had invaded the entire valley. Hundreds of tents flecked the ground as far as the eye could see, white like the foam of the river that broke on the lava-colored rocks. A tide of men, horses, mules, and cannons spilled out over the shore.

This time, war was at the gates of Akulgo.

Shamil and his men were ready. Among the natural fortresses of Dagestan, they had not chosen this one by chance. Like a rocky island rising out of the sea, the peak of Akulgo stood at the heart of a desert of stones, an immense piton broken in the middle by two unequally high plateaus encircled on three sides by the loop of a raging river. Twin auls clung to the summit, separated by a deep, narrow canyon with a rushing mountain torrent at its floor. The two villages were joined by a suspension bridge that crossed the gorge.

Old Akulgo was located on the lower part. Once bombarded by Fazi the Louse, it had been reconstructed and fortified under the supervision of Polish deserters. The narrow alleyways and the jumble of houses, stacked one atop another, their successive flat roofs like miradors, had transformed the whole into a compact bastion. New Akulgo was higher up, its back to the mountain, with only the tower of Surkhaï, a terrible keep that protected the rear of the village and dominated the entire valley, above it. Shamil's house was on the front line, overhanging the abyss and blocking any attack. There, through the only arrow slit in the family redoubt, an excited Jamal Eddin watched the operations in the giaour camp behind his father and Yunus.

For the past three months, Shamil had tried to avoid a siege. He had raided the enemy at the rear and practiced scorched-earth tactics, burning his own fields, rendering his own trails impassable, leaving the houses in his path in ruins. Sweeping down on the villages around them, the infidels found no people, no livestock, no chickens, nothing to eat or pillage. Only ashes. General Pavel Khristoforovitch Grabbe, Fazi the Louse's replacement at the head of the army, had no choice. If he did not want his troops to starve, he would have to retreat to the forts in the rear. But that was impossible. The czar's orders were to advance, advance, advance, despite losses and shrinking food supplies, advance. Nicholas I had been humiliated by the imam's snub during his imperial voyage to Tiflis, and the czar was not one to forget an insult. He demanded a definitive victory at any price. Attack this nest of fanatics, take Shamil dead or alive, wipe out the murids, and crush any semblance of resistance in the Caucasus. Forever.

From the arrow slit, Jamal Eddin watched the column of refugees on the mountain, a stream of men and beasts fleeing before the infidels and trying desperately to reach the fortress. Yunus said they were more useless mouths to feed and should be turned away, but Shamil demanded that they be welcomed and protected. The flow of beings seemed to act accordingly, as though aware of the debate between the imam and his deputy. They sped up, jumping over the holes and obstacles placed as deterrents on the path, then stopped as though those blocks were suddenly insurmountable. Among the donkeys, sheep, and goats, Jamal Eddin saw the occasional figure of a horse, the hat of a rider. But most of them were old people on foot, children so young that their heads scarcely rose above the sea of animals, and women bent over under sacks of provisions.

Their advance caused small landslides here and there. Pebbles rolled down the hill, boulders tumbled down to the river, and patches of rock toppled, carrying with them man and beast. The caravan stopped and watched silently when that happened. Strange forms floated in the river now. The swift current carried balls of black, hooves in the air, with bloated bellies, down past the rows of immaculate tents. Sometimes long panels of fabric caught on the buffalo horns or the legs of cows floating on their backs. Brown, white, and blue, they were the veils of girls who had drowned. Like sails, they filled with air before being sucked to the river bottom by the swirling current. The caravan continued.

At this point in their misfortune, the men of the Caucasus had nothing left to lose but their dignity and the hope of finding protection behind the ramparts of Akulgo. They all knew the peak was impregnable. How could the Russians come this far? Even they, even the Russians knew it.

From dawn until nightfall, the giaours watched the movements on the ground, the cliffs, and the ridges. They seemed to be perpetually looking up, with binoculars and the telescopic spyglasses that fascinated Jamal Eddin, faraway specks of reflected silver along the black shelf of the river bank. But this evening, the fading twilight played instead upon the bayonets of the fresh troops parading down the shore. Their blades gleamed and flashed like a thousand lightning bolts, capturing the sun in a forest of steel.

The arrival of supplies that had broken through Shamil's blockade forced him to rethink his strategy. Now that these dogs had full stomachs, it would be impossible to attack them without huge losses. Raiding the camp, destroying their saps, and burning their footbridges were no longer viable tactics.

Worse still, the defeat of the tribes of the northeast, on whom Shamil had counted to trap the assailants in a pincer action, was a major loss of support for Akulgo. And to add to that, the defeat of the Chechen allies had freed the czar's army to converge upon Dagestan with its artillery.

The cries of relieved soldiers, already drunk, rose all the way to the austere bastion, filling Jamal Eddin with impatient excitement for the battle to come. He listened to the cheers that greeted the arrival of pieces of high-caliber ordnance, three campaign cannons, and several cases of munitions. Though he could not measure the consequences, he sensed the gravity of the moment. All the details of this eve of combat became firmly fixed in his memory. He could have cited the number of white flecks on the field below, recognized the breed of the horses and the ranks of the officers by their stripes, described the colors of the regiments and their drums that marked the hour. He could have described the smoky odor of Yunus, standing beside him, the odor of leather and sweat. Yunus had just returned from a tour of inspection of their defenses at Old Akulgo. He remembered the green robe Shamil wore as he harangued his followers one last time at the mosque. Jamal Eddin was aware of the variations in their voices, the smallest nuances in their tones, the intensity of the emotions behind the ostensible calm.

For the first time he recognized in his father, his tutor, and all the men this tension that had not left him since the death of Bahou-Messadou, this blend of joyous apprehension before the demands of God, this exaltation at the prospect of serving Him.

"Yunus, take care to have goatskins brought up from the river, as many as you can, to fill jars and jars. Store them in the grottos behind the village. Don't forget about firewood and fodder, or about the livestock. We have enough food supplies to hold out for three months, but not enough water in the wells to make it through the summer. And there's not much time left to finish preparations, less than three days. After that—"

"After that," said Yunus, casting an accusing eye over the line of refugees. "After that, there will be four thousand of us at Akulgo. And of the four thousand, how many warriors old enough to fight?"

"A quarter."

Yunus motioned toward the Russians with his chin.

"And them?"

"Around eleven thousand. Without counting the militia of the traitors who have gone over to them—about four thousand hypocrites.

"Total?"

"Fifteen thousand of them, a thousand of us."

"A thousand against fifteen thousand?" the child asked, amazed. "And we're going to fight them?"

He regretted the words the moment they had left his mouth. In no circumstances were the young permitted to take part in conversations. They were to stand off to the side and remain silent in the presence of their elders. Expecting to be punished and dismissed, the little boy faltered under his father's stare.

"Don't believe that God is with the greatest number, Jamal Eddin," he replied. "God is with the good, and the good are always less numerous than the evil."

"But all the same, down there, they're swarming by the thousands. When we—"

"Look around you. Aren't there more bad horses than good, more weeds than roses? If there are more weeds than roses, does that mean we shouldn't pull them out, but let them proliferate until they smother the flowers? And if the enemy is more numerous than we are, does that mean that, instead of fighting them, we should let them proliferate until they strangle us? Don't ask me why the nonbelievers thrive and multiply, why they send fresh troops and replacements as fast as we kill them. For millions of poisonous mushrooms in the forest, how many trees grow? How many, Jamal Eddin? Just one. Just one beautiful tree that grows and spreads. I am the roots of the tree of liberty, our naïbs are the trunk, our murids the branches. Go shut the gates of the city with Yunus. The siege of Akulgo can begin. Even at ten, even at two against fifteen thousand, God willing, we shall win!"

July 1–August 4

A deluge of fire rained down. The Russians bombarded nonstop, pouring hellfire on the handful of defenders who clung to the summit. Their strategy was clear: surround the piton and cover their advances with cannon fire.

After a month of shelling, they had reached the narrow gorge between the two villages, invaded the river, and cut off the Montagnards' water supply. Now they were trying to scale the canyon.

Their telescopes swept over the peak tirelessly. The shelters, caves, and grottos of the subterranean network that protected the people were invisible, but they picked out the ledges that their own shells had carved out of the mountain and began to plan how to scale the rocks. A hundred and twenty feet separated each of the three breaches, which the Montagnards had immediately invested. The Russians in the valley sought a way to blow them out, but the angle and the distance of the vertical shots diminished their capacity for accuracy. A stroke of luck eliminated the problem as the boulders above came crashing down, crushing the Montagnards in one blow.

There was no sign of life above, not a breath of air or a movement.

Suspended by long ropes along the rock face, the sappers resumed their ascent from rock spur to rock landing, all the way to the tower of Surkhaï.

It looked like a deceptively simple task, but though the besieged knew how to die, they were born again from the ashes.

Above the sappers' heads, a band of children pelted them with rocks. Their shrill voices penetrating the air, they used sticks as levers and forced the broken boulders over the cliff onto their attackers. The youngest ones, Jamal Eddin and Mohammed Ghazi, picked up the small stones the boulders had crushed and lapidated the invaders with them. The sweat that dripped into the boys' eyes and the swarms of flies and mosquitos swirling around them scarcely diminished the accuracy of their aim, which was sharpened by hatred. Behind them, hordes of women, disguised as warriors to fool the enemy, rushed forward in successive waves, brandishing their kinjals. They cut the ropes and massacred the men hanging onto them with pitiless fury. Slashing their hands and drawing deep gashes across their faces, they slit their throats and sent them plummeting to the bottom of the canyon. Young and old, they fought like wildcats, imbued with the same battle fever and passion as their sons and little brothers. A deafening new salvo eclipsed the sound of their cries. The cannon fire swept over the ridge, indiscriminately mowing down Christian sappers and Muslim fighters. As usual, the children simply disappeared, crawling into their holes until the next assault.

Forty days and forty nights of bombardment had made this butchery an ordinary daily occurrence. The cannon smoke that blocked out the clouds and the sound of explosions, like artificial thunder, were now part of the landscape of Akulgo.

Down below, in the harsh light, the smashed cadavers rotted in piles, stuck in the twists and turns and puddles of the river. So far, the Russians had suffered over a thousand casualties. In his tent, the obstinate General Grabbe paced up and down as he went over his plan: take the jutting ledges that the cannons had cut in the rock face, no matter what the cost, and from there the donjon that protected the two villages. He knew, as did Shamil and the hundred warriors enclosed by the thick walls, that if he could take the tower of Sukhaï, the upper city would have no rear defenses. He would be able to shell Akulgo from the summit and from all sides.

But Grabbe's companies advanced, one after the other, and died in vain. Those fine days of the torrid summer of 1839 cost the Russians dearly.

But they cost Shamil even more dearly.

The double line of ramparts had been broken. Only a few fetid drops of water remained in the wells. The fallen lay dead in the ruins or under small piles of pebbles. Even the earth and the sand had disappeared from Akulgo, and burying the corpses became impossible. No one even considered throwing them into the ravine. Though the men, women, and children were not afraid of dying on the battlefield, they were appalled at the thought of their bodies being abandoned dishonorably, without a grave, left to the beasts by their brothers and sons. At the moment, only the wives were there to protect the deceased from the vultures.

A hot, red sun burned the coarse-grained rock until it was incandescent, and the putrid stink of decomposing bodies became unbearable. The nights brought no cool air and no rest. The exhausted naïbs descended to the river in relays, bringing up water under the cover of the sentinels' fire, while the women wore themselves ragged repairing the fortifications damaged during the day.

Exposed to gunfire by these tasks, those who had survived the siege so far fell by the dozens. At least they had ceased to suffer. There was no more water, no more food, not even firewood to cook the soles of their boots. Dysentery and typhus had finished off the wounded and struck down the survivors with colic and fever. But of all their afflictions, the pestilent stench of rotting flesh was the worst.

The stench, the vermin, and the thirst.

August 5

It was 104 degrees in the shade.

On the burning piton, the clefts, the ledges, and the landings, the rocks no longer reflected the changing colors of daylight. The entire peak was streaked with the purple and black of blood and flies.

Three battalions struggled to take the tower.

Impeccable in his summer whites, his cap jammed down tight over his bald head, his telescope stuck to his eye, General Grabbe surveyed the operations from the camp. Thick beads of sweat stood out on the tufts of gray whiskers that adorned his cheeks at the corners of his mouth. This cursed tower that he had been shelling for weeks should have long since fallen—and buried all its occupants in the ruins. But day after day, the same war cries, the same resistance, the same hail of rocks, and the same volleys of gunfire greeted his battalions. Stumbling over the cadavers of comrades that blocked the way before and behind them, they could neither advance nor retreat on the steep, narrow trail. They couldn't even take cover. And they were being decimated.

The general listened carefully to the clamor rising over and over from the donjon. A great opera lover, he concentrated on counting the voices. Of a hundred combatants, there couldn't be more than a dozen left in there. With each attempt, the howling became more tenuous and shrill. Patience.

Sponging his sideburns, he stubbornly repeated his orders to shell with high-caliber ordnance and to send fresh troops in to relieve those that had been massacred.

He had all the time in the world.

August 9

On this night by a full moon, Jamal Eddin tried desperately to sleep. Lack of food, water, and rest had reduced him to a trancelike state that he could not control. The howls of Ali Bek, the last defender of the tower, the last survivor, rang in his ears, a bitter, strident wail that went on and on. In throwing himself from the summit, the naïb had taken ten of the enemy with him to his death. His enraged call forever defied their false gods, the idol of the infidels, and all the demons of the Caucasus. His death cry, a cry of triumph, echoed in the child's mind, making him deaf to the other cries of agony, to the babies' cries, to the explosion of cannon fire that ripped into the mountain. Since the fall of the tower, the cannonballs had rained down in such quantity and violence that everyone had abandoned Shamil's bastion and retreated to the grottos. Jamal Eddin had made a place for himself on an overhanging rock in the family cave, about six feet above the ground. His stomach empty, his eyes burning, his limbs exhausted by the day's efforts, he tried to rest there for a few hours. But sleep would not come. Sleep never came.

Unless the reverse was true. Perhaps he was sleeping, never to wake up. The borders between dreaming and waking, his body and the real world, the visible and the invisible, were no longer clear. He had ceased to be hungry or thirsty. He wasn't even afraid anymore. He felt empty inside, absent from himself.

In his thoughts, he spoke to himself as to a stranger. An inexperienced newcomer to Akulgo, the other eldest son of the imam, the other Jamal Eddin. He would have to take this one by the hand, lead him and advise him. You climb up here with me, away from all these moaning and groaning people. Climb in as close as you can to the wall. Lie down on your side and draw up your legs, there, like that. Pretty soon you won't hear the wailing of the wounded around you or smell the stink of the dead. You won't see or feel anything, not even the rock jabbing into your side. There, sleep.

But the real Jamal Eddin felt the rock, like a bayonet stabbing him in the small of the back. In his mind, the vision of the blue eyes of the flaxen-haired soldiers that he and Patimat had stoned to death played over and over like a hallucination. He heard the cracks of their splitting skulls as the rocks reached their marks, forcing them to let go. He felt a wild joy when one rock, by some miracle, annihilated several of them at once.

But he shuddered at the dull sound of their backs breaking on the boulders, the sound of bones exploding against the shingles.

The stalactites of the cave's vault pricked him like the sting of the ants in his wound long ago. They touched the scar and reawakened the old pain. Bahou-Messadou, if only Bahou-Messadou had been there.

"Bahou, come!" he sobbed in his dream.

Maybe it would be better to get down from this ledge and lie on the ground. The rough patches wouldn't be as rocky. But he did not move. In the shadows, he saw a bowl of lamb and rice, swimming in grease. He threw himself on it, hitting his head on a rock. The bowl had disappeared. Stunned, he no longer thought of food or of cuddling up at his mother's side.

Fatima was eight months pregnant. She struggled for air with Jawarat, Patimat, Mohammed Ghazi, and Saïd, but what little there was to breathe was thick with the dust of ashes that hung suspended in the still heat. At the beginning of the siege, they had all returned to camp in the ruins of Shamil's home at dusk. The naïbs' daughters had still taken care of the livestock and scrubbed the steel blades of the kinjals, crusted with giaour blood. The old women had cooked flatbread on the braziers and tried to make life seem easier, as it once had been, in the evenings. That seemed like a long time ago. But earlier today, General Grabbe's troops had bombarded the aul from the rear, and they could no longer take shelter there.

Was Fatima asleep? She was exhausted by the heat. In her state, she could not take part in combat. But the next day, when there was a period of calm, she would leave this hole and sneak out to the horses' cadavers. She would deftly quarter them before the birds picked their carcasses clean. Mohammed Ghazi, smaller and more agile, invisible to any sniper, would help her.

On other nights, when the moon was not full, Jamal Eddin would go through the cadavers of the Russians who had been shot down by Akbirdil's muskets beneath the tower. He would strip them of weapons and boots, and his older comrades would slit the throats of any who might have sounded the alarm.

While the little ones took care of the dead, the men made dangerous forays, crawling out to the ridges the infidels had taken. Those dogs were hoisting their cannons up here with pulleys. They hauled the artillery up in wicker baskets, the men in vessels of armored wood. Every night Shamil, Yunus, and a few others slithered over to the pulleys and cut the lines and cables, trying to overturn the vessels full of men so that they would fall into the depths of the canyon, their cries muffled by the rushing river.

Jamal Eddin knew that at this very moment his father was engaged in hand-to-hand combat somewhere in the moonlight and his heart beat faster. A thousand stings pricked his body. Lice. These filthy vermin multiplied as fast as the Russians, and he scratched himself bloody trying to relieve the itching. He knew how to get rid of them by burying every item of clothing separately in the ground, with only a scrap of material sticking out of the dirt. The lice would gather on this scrap, and then he had only to burn them. Burn all the lice—and the giaours with them. But where was there a corner in Akulgo where he could burn them?

Nights like this seemed to go on forever. Actually, he didn't want to sleep. He was afraid of falling asleep and dreaming the same dreadful dream, always the same one, and far more terrifying than any of the daytime battles. At the beginning of the nightmare, he was happy. He thought he saw Shamil entering the grotto and walking toward him in the long green robe he wore for preaching on Fridays. In his extended arms, the imam carried the Book, wrapped in golden fabric. He shone like a flame above the sleeping women, his feet not touching the ground. He approached the stone table where Jamal Eddin was waiting for him. His face no longer looked like a clay mask as it had for weeks now, his beard covered with dust, an opaque veil clouding his gray eyes.

He smiled and said, "We have announced good news to the prophet, the birth of a boy of gentle character."

Then it was God who spoke through the voice of the imam, "When the boy was old enough to accompany him, his father said, 'Oh my son, I saw myself in a dream, and I was immolating you.' "

Shamil leaned down to him and asked, "What do you think of this?"

Looking into his father's inquisitive eyes, those infinitely tender, amiable, and kind eyes, Jamal Eddin felt his heart stop, and he would wake up with a start, terrified.

He was seized with apprehension, a stark fear of the future. He wasn't afraid of dying here with all his people. What made him tremble was the thought of being abandoned, alone in a deserted aul, with the giaours coming.

No one saw the little boy's tears or heard him cry. Shamil, Yunus, and Akbirdil all knew it, and he knew it too. Akulgo would fall. They were vanquished, nearly vanquished.

August 10

The day's attack ended as it had every day for the past two months. For the enemy, the results were dismaying. Nine hundred killed the day before, another five hundred today. There was not an officer left among the Russian scouts.

The only naïbs left to Shamil were Akbirdil and Yunus. The others—Surkhaï, Ali Bek, his ninety companions of the first hour—were all dead. Yes, the survivors could kill another few hundred giaours before perishing like martyrs on this rock. But would their sacrifice be a service to the holy war?

In the grotto where the council met, a heated discussion was taking place among the eight remaining members. The seventy days of siege had reduced these most faithful among the faithful to a state of skeletal emaciation. Sitting cross-legged, they kept their hats on and each rested a hand on the handle of one of the two kinjals crossed at his belt. Their eyes burned with fever above their black beards. Next to each sat a young boy, a son or nephew, who acted as aide-de-camp. This evening, there were only three child soldiers still fit enough to serve them, among them Jamal Eddin. He waited for his orders, standing a few steps behind his seated father. Shamil presided over the circle, with Yunus on his right and Akbirdil on his left. Neither said a word, but the others still had the strength to argue. Their guttural voices rang out beneath the vault of the grotto.

Shamil, impassive, let them say what he had heard whispered for days now, "What good does it do for all of us to disappear?"

Wasn't it precisely the giaours' mission to empty the Caucasus of all Muslims, wipe them off the face of the earth, annihilate them so that not one would remain? The imam should not give them this satisfaction. He should negotiate, not to surrender, but to survive, to go on. So that one day they could again resume the holy war and conquer the infidels.

Shamil tried hard to hide his indignation. How could the men of his own clan speak of such a thing? Even old Barti Khan, Bahou-Messadou's twin brother, brought up the idea of opening negotiations. Even cousin Hadj Ibrahim, the muezzin of Akulgo, was in favor of speaking with the enemy.

Observing his father's trembling shoulders, Jamal Eddin could sense Shamil's efforts at self-control. Sheer exhaustion might cause him to burst into anger too soon. He must choose the right moment.

Though narrow-shouldered, with spindly legs that scarcely made him the ideal fighter, Hadj Ibrahim had the right to speak first. His green turban, proof of his pilgrimage to Mecca, indicated that his status was higher than the others'.

"With the tower, they've taken the left bank of the river. We're completely surrounded," cousin Ibrahim pointed out.

"There's not a single drop of water left in the wells, not even for ablutions," Uncle Barti added.

"I went down to the river last night," Shamil interrupted, tight-lipped, as though saving his breath. "I brought up two goatskins."

"That's not enough to quench the thirst of five hundred people."

"It will have to be."

"Five hundred," Shamil's uncle said soberly, "out of four thousand in June. There are too many infidels, and they are too well armed and equipped. We know how this is going to end."

Coming from anyone else, this kind of talk would have cost the upstart his life.

"Shut up or I'll cut out your tongue, like all the others who spoke of capitulation."

Shamil had once respected the courage of Barti Khan, but the hardships of the siege had transformed the old man into someone he no longer knew. The thin, white, unruly beard that covered the tip of his chin gave his face a vindictive expression. Beneath his eyelids, which were half-glued together by an infection, his gummy eyes, clear gray like Bahou-Messadou's, shone with spiteful bitterness. His gaze was direct, but void of affability or wisdom.

This disagreement with the last of his forebears troubled Shamil.

"Nothing is written in the book of destiny that Allah has not decided," he said with restraint. "We must play for time and wait for Chechen reinforcements to come."

"But the Chechens are blocked on the plain, by that dog of a Klugenau that you spared!"

The memory of this missed opportunity caused a rumble of discontent and more than one bitter remark. They should have slit his throat, against Shamil's will, they should have slit that pig's throat at Chirquata. It would have been so easy.

"Once, you were willing to talk to the Russians, Imam. Let us open negotiations."

"That's useless. They will not give us peace and freedom."

"If you don't negotiate with them now, when they want to talk too, they will kill all our men, dishonor our women, and turn our children into slaves."

"If we negotiate with them now, they will bring every Caucasian Muslim to his knees, you said so yourself, Barti Khan. They'll make all of us, you and him and me, their serfs. They will throw the servants of God in the dust and keep them bent under their yoke. I'd rather kill my three sons, slit their throats with my own hand, down to the very last, than let them live in slavery. Purify yourselves. Burn the spirit of servitude that has shackled you from your souls."

He leaped to his feet and stared down at them all.

"He who serves Allah cannot serve the Russians at the same time," he said severely. "Will you renounce the promises of heaven for these dogs? Here, our hours are measured by the day. But up there, our lives will be eternal. Our native land is in paradise, and each of us has a home prepared for him there. But listening to your words, I'm sure none of them will be inhabited!"

He turned on his heel and left the grotto abruptly.

The waning moon had swept away the cloud of heat. Shamil felt so tired, so fatigued and so alone that the trials of this world left him close to despair. Was he mistaken? Had God ordered him to make peace? Should he dispatch an intermediary to the camp below? Should he send Yunus to negotiate in his name?

His sorrow mingling with envy, Shamil thought of his dead friends who had already entered the Gardens of Allah. Water as pure as diamonds flowed from the fountains where they had all of eternity to slake their thirst and rest in the shade of the cypress trees. Beautiful virgins with shining eyes and arms as round as swans' necks waited for them in their homes. And he was here, watching the birds of prey hop between the stones to peck at the cadavers of his people. Was it he, Shamil, the shadow of God on earth? Or these black birds that hovered like a cloud over Akulgo that Jamal Eddin chased with stones?

The child had not left his side for nearly a week. He followed him everywhere, walking a few steps behind, alert to his every need, aware of his doubt and dismay. The boy relieved him of his weapons, took his messages to other survivors in the grottos, and cared for his horse when he returned from combat. Shamil let him do all this without a look, without a word, accepting his presence as a gift from God. This evening, for the first time, he looked at the rags hanging from the boy's emaciated frame. The oval of the small face was so thin that it seemed to have changed shape, and the high cheekbones and once almond-shaped eyes had turned to slits beneath his puffy eyelids. He noted the boy's fixed stare, the long lashes no longer able to hide his feverish look. His son, his disciple, his comfort.

The stifling night weighed upon his shoulders.

Continue the war and perish tomorrow? Capitulate tomorrow and save the children of Akulgo? He could find no answer within himself. Had Allah abandoned him? What did he ordain? Shamil no longer heard the voice of God.

He walked down across the roofs to the entrance of the village, passing slowly from terrace to terrace, striding across the interstices of the narrow alleyways, avoiding the holes in the structures. He walked from one end of New Akulgo to the other, all the way to the terrace of his former fort. He walked up the ruined crenels and sat down on the parapet overlooking the chasm. Jamal Eddin sat down on his lap, one leg dangling over the abyss. There they sat, immobile, as exposed to enemy fire as possible. From down below, they must be all the Russians could see, the imam with his white turban gleaming in the moonlight and the bare-headed boy. Why were they waiting to shoot? From here or in the back if they liked, from the distant tower above.

Unconscious of or indifferent to danger, Jamal Eddin leaned back slightly against his father's chest. Shamil put his arms around him and held him as he had once held him long ago, when he had whisked him away from the battlefield, seating him on his horse's withers. Jamal Eddin snuggled up to his father's breast, feeling his warmth and his strength. Eyes half-closed, he looked at the river, the rows of white tents, and the chain of mountains rising unevenly beyond the Russian camp. The blue mountains of the Caucasus, their mountains. He closed his eyes, still seeing the image of the mountains, distinct and luminous, in his mind's eye. He felt his father praying, reaching toward God, and he let himself go, sinking back against him.

"O Lord," Shamil murmured, "this child is the soul most precious to me on this earth. If you take me with a bullet in the forehead, do the same for my child."

Jamal Eddin was still. He knew that, at this instant, his father was testing the will of the Almighty.

Did Allah want them both to die?

August 11

"Allah be with you."

"The Lord be with you."

"General Grabbe replied to our overtures," Yunus said as he bent over to slip into the grotto where the council was meeting.

He carried a piece of paper in his hand.

"What kind of a Russian is he," Shamil growled with disdain, "this Pavel Khristoforovitch Grabbe?"

"What can one say about a chief who doesn't take part in combat? A coward."

"And what else?"

"An enemy without honor. He lies like all the others."

Shamil slowly breathed in the hot, muggy air, as though to absorb all this. His lieutenants had forced him to compromise, to feign a desire for peace in order to gain time and put off the final attack. They would simulate an overture for discussions, act as though they were debating the possibilities, and drag out the negotiations.

Until the Chechens got there.

"Four propositions."

"I'm listening."

"All of them unacceptable," Yunus added calmly.

"Read aloud, so everyone can hear."

"First, the imam will offer his son as a hostage, an amanat."

Jamal Eddin could not help but start. Shamil was impassive.

"Go on."

"Second, the imam and all the inhabitants of Akulgo will give up their arms to the officers before leaving the village and coming to surrender. They and their families will be safe, under house arrest in a location that General Grabbe reserves the right to choose. The rest—"

Shamil motioned for him to stop there.

"The rest we know. The massacre of the elders they disarmed at Ghimri, the disappearance of my nephew, taken as an amanat at Tiliq."

"The rest," Yunus continued to read, "is up to the magnanimity of the czar."

"Send them an emissary with other propositions," Barti Khan suggested.

This time, Yunus was not received. General Grabbe was waiting for new cannons. He too knew how to be crafty, to drag things out, to "negotiate oriental style," he said.

He needed no reports from his spies, imagining with little effort the horror of the situation on the piton. The smell was enough. Even down here in the camp, the stench was such that the poor sentinels passed out on the riverbank, handkerchiefs to their noses. They had to be relayed every half hour. His soldiers, either conscripted peasants or serfs of the empire, had seen as much in Russia, yet nothing compared to the vile odor of Akulgo.

The general stalled, on the pretext that he would not open talks until the imam sent his son.

"Never will I give Jamal Eddin to the Russians."

"You're going to let all your people be massacred, just to spare your son?" Akbirdil said, astonished.

Hadn't he sacrificed his own firstborn, Hamzat, without a word of hesitation? And the others, the eight naïbs present, hadn't they sacrificed their own children?

"Your thinking is off, Imam, your judgment colored, and how can it be otherwise?" Barti Khan suggested. "You are both judge and defendant in this affair."

The moment the rumor of peace spread, Fatima sensed danger. The infidels always demanded hostages in their talks with the Montagnards. People said they let their amanats starve to death in their forts, that they poisoned them.

She could not share the imam's bed, for she was pregnant. She couldn't even touch him, approach him, speak to him, or listen to him. But she did not let him out of her sight. When Shamil left the council den, when he went off by himself to pray or prepare for battle, he found her there, in her veils, kneeling in his pathway. Her eyes looked up into his in a silent appeal. With all her heart, the beloved begged for grace for their son.

Shamil fled from her presence.

August 13

Sitting on a rock at the entrance to the family grotto, Jamal Eddin felt vaguely bothered by the looks people gave him. In no way did he seize their significance. Picking lice off him, Patimat peered at him as though she were seeing him for the last time. She said nothing. She did not scold him. She just kept fussing over him, taking advantage of the calm to hunt the lice and shave his head meticulously. Her dedication to her task was scarcely typical.

But Patimat's silly moods didn't matter. If only she would get on with it and let him go!

It was his little brother, Mohammed Ghazi, who explained the meaning of this mixture of pity, accusation, impatience, and nostalgia that he read on the faces of the women. Toddling over to the stone where their aunt was sharpening his kinjal, he brought Jamal Eddin a stunning piece of news. The naïbs had decided to send him to the Russian camp. The suffering of Akulgo would soon end, thanks to him!

Jamal Eddin shrugged his shoulders. He didn't believe a word of it. None of his father's naïbs had ever let himself be taken alive. From his very birth, he had been conscious of their example. "Better death than the dishonor of captivity with the giaours." All his father's teachings rested on this principle: "Better to die than make peace with the infidels." Hadn't Bahou-Messadou paid with a hundred lashes for the sin of having spoken of surrender? The wrath of Allah would descend on the hypocrites guilty of dealing with the Russians.

But when Jamal Eddin looked into Shamil's eyes, the look that met his was blank. He received no confirmation, no support, no certainty. His father's eyes, so sure, so hard, met his only fleetingly.

The anguish the child glimpsed in them filled him with terror.

August 15

There was a new ultimatum from General Grabbe. If the imam's son had not come down to the camp by sundown, he would raze Akulgo to the ground. Tomorrow he would take no quarter. It was up to the murids to decide the fate of their families. He gave them twenty-four hours.

Jamal Eddin was no longer allowed to listen to the council's discussions. He waited outside. This isolation, which excluded him as though he had already suffered the contamination of the infidels, added to his anguished apprehension. He could stand being afraid, without question or complaint. He took pride in remaining silent. If he could prove his own valor, he thought, if he could show himself to be useful, docile, and brave, braver than the bravest, Shamil would find him indispensable and would save him.

Grateful and hopeful, he listened to his father fervently pleading his cause down in the grotto.

"These dogs won't offer you peace, even if they hold my son. I am telling you now, sending my son as a hostage will in no way prove advantageous to us."

"The Russians won't harm him. When they've concluded an agreement with us, they'll suspend combat and leave Akulgo, and they'll send him back. They swore they would. But if you don't give them Jamal Eddin, he'll die with you in the attack, Imam. And if you leave your other sons unprotected, they will become their slaves. You said so yourself. The giaours will make them serfs and soldiers and send them far from our mountains to be killed in their service. Not to mention our wives, who will be thrown to their battalions. Allah does not order you to give up the fight, he ordains you to continue. Listen to him, as you always have. Live, Shamil, and save your people!"

A tormented Shamil fell to his knees among the stones. He had sent his guide and mentor, Sheik Jamaluddin al-Ghumuqi, to stir the loyalty of the Chechen reinforcements with his eloquence. Now he was alone and isolated in his doubt.

His face in the dust, he prayed fervently, "Almighty God, you asked Abraham for his firstborn, and when he was ready to sacrifice him, you spared him."

But he was already wavering, and his thoughts turned from Abraham to the prophet who had grown up far from God, the child captured by pagans.

"Almighty God, you delivered Moses from the pharaoh and his dogs, bringing him back to you. If I give Jamal Eddin to the infidels, take him under Your protection. You are the best of all guardians."

Jamal Eddin watched his father from afar, not moving a muscle. He did not dare approach him. He did not dare question him. He did not even dare to offer his help anymore.

The guide of all the believers of the Caucasus was suffering because of him. This was more terrifying than his nightmares, when the imam leaned over him to question him with a kindly look. Jamal Eddin searched within himself for a way to ease his father's pain.

He wanted to cry out, in the words of Isaac, "Do what has been asked of you." But the words stuck in his throat.

He felt guilty.

August 15, in the evening

"You've said nothing, Yunus. What do you think of the advice they've given me? Should I give up my son?"

Asked in public, here before the council, the answer to his question had the weight of a verdict. Yunus was the most pious of all the naïbs, and the most loyal. His peers respected his word.

Up until now, Shamil had intentionally avoided asking his opinion. He knew that his friend was not particularly articulate, and he feared that the weight of Yunus's judgment might be weakened by interminable and vain discussion. He had saved his question for the end.

Deliver the son of Allah's prophet into the hands of the giaours? Yunus could only be revolted by the very thought of such infamy.

In addition, his meeting with General Grabbe had given him the opportunity to judge the man. It was clear to him that the Russians didn't give a damn about making peace with the inhabitants of Akulgo. Peace? What a joke! A peace that had cost them three thousand soldiers was far too bitter a pill to swallow. They had no intention of retreating. What the general had wanted from the outset was the head of the imam, the heads of his naïbs, and the heads of all who were close to him. To be done with the murids, once and for all.

Offering Jamal Eddin to General Grabbe would be not only stupid, but dangerous as well.

Shamil repeated his question, "What do you think?"

His son's tutor answered with another question. "Who will take him down to the camp?"

The question was like a knife in Shamil's heart. The sacrifice, then, was certain. He rose without a word.

"If you want me to accompany him to the camp of the infidels, I will. And I'll stay with him, to take care of him there," Yunus concluded somberly.

"I want only what God dictates."

"It would be preferable for us to carry out the will of the Lord together, instead of you doing it all alone, as you seem ready to do!" Barti Khan interjected furiously.

"Then prepare yourselves to die with me tomorrow. We will withstand the attack and fight until Allah decides the outcome of the battle."

August 16

With his back to the cliff, Akbirdil caught his aggressor by the hair and beheaded him in one stroke. The Russian's body scarcely wobbled; he stood there straight for an instant before collapsing on top of the pile of headless cadavers. The buttons and stripes of the uniforms shone like blots of sun, golden accents glinting against the white of cartilage and vertebrae in the lake of blood.

Akbirdil sent the head rolling down among the legs of the soldiers attacking him. They tripped on the incline, sliding on the blood-soaked stones.

Despite his disapproval of this new carnage, old Barti Khan went about it methodically and with a vengeance. His musket wedged between the forked branches of a staff, he was holding the suspension bridge by himself. He waited for the Russians to cross the abyss, arriving at his level one by one. Economizing his powder, he aimed directly at a spot between the navel and the genitals. Of all wounds, this was the most painful and the most humiliating. Hit in the lower abdomen, the Russians fell back.

Over a thousand fresh cadavers were strewn over the two promontories.

Standing on the ramparts, Yunus pushed back the enemy with his lance. His blows seemed haphazard, but he mutilated the infidels with carefully aimed thrusts. He sent the pike deep into the ear, then pulled it out like a siphon to perforate the spleen or the bladder. The throbbing of a young recruit's viscera left the shaft of his weapon vibrating. He jerked it free from the entrails.

Bugles blew everywhere as officers gave the command to charge. The soldiers, paralyzed, the blood drained from their faces, refused to budge. In these last months of siege, they had seen too many of their comrades fall on this trail in futile attacks. Too many dead, too much effort to take this pile of rocks. They had lost faith.

Looking up to the promontory far above, they saw a group of children helping a colossus of a man—Shamil in person!—turn three high-caliber pieces of ordnance to aim them in their direction. Three immense mouths of fire, taken from the gunners whose throats they had slit. They watched as the balls were loaded and the fuses lit—and they understood. The remnants of General Grabbe's army felt no compunction whatsoever as they scattered far and wide.

Evening was not far off. Akulgo held. Akulgo would hang on.

Until the next attack. Until tomorrow.

Grabbe would attack at the first light of dawn.

Shamil strode down to the village in long steps.

"Allah did not want us to be defeated today. Allah is with us."

An immense sensation of relief lifted his spirits. "The murids did not fail," he thought to himself with pride. "The naïbs fought valiantly."

His joy was short-lived.

When they had taken the cannons a while ago, a thought had crossed his mind, one he now had the calm and silence to consider at length. The Russian artillery could not have come this far up without the complicity—no, the betrayal!—of the Caucasian tribes.

Not for a moment did he doubt his counselors, Barti Khan, Hadj Ibrahim, or any of his companions. Despite any disagreements they might have, he knew they were incorruptible. He believed in the loyalty of the Christian deserters too. The Poles would rather be cut up into little pieces than be retaken by the Russians. No, he did not question the honor of the inhabitants of Akulgo.

But the Montagnards of the neighboring auls, the believers of Irganai, Untsukul, Ashilta, and Ansal, those he had counted on to bar the way before the cannons, they hadn't lifted a finger. Worse still, it was the Montagnards of Ghimri who had led Grabbe's mortars over the trails. Ghimri had facilitated his passage through the mountain passes and the rivers, Ghimri had shown him all the secret shortcuts.

The cravenness of his own village, after the opposition of his own clan and the discord within his own family, opened a breach in Shamil's soul, one wide enough for despair to enter. Even his own formidable pride could not fill the void. Yes, Akulgo had held. But the holy war was lost.

Defeat. But the defeat wasn't due to the Russians' power or their numerical superiority. Nor to Grabbe's obstinacy, his indifference to his troops, or his basic negligence, based on a fundamental ignorance of Dagestan that had made him blind and deaf to all difficulties. No, Shamil did not owe his defeat to the infidels. It wasn't due to the spirits either, or the evil eye or this unprecedented heat wave that had turned Akulgo into a furnace. The defeat of the holy war was due only to his Muslim brothers' lack of faith.

A great bitterness toward them rose in his soul. They were not fit to have been born. Their conduct was shameful. The destiny that lay in store for them was ugly and base. Let them be lost, let them all be damned in surrendering.

He couldn't save them from themselves or keep them from slavery in this world and eternal damnation in the next. He begged the Almighty for forgiveness. The shadow of God had not been up to the task. He had not been able to unify them. Let them go feed from the Russians' hands, let them go beg for a cease-fire and accept all their conditions.

They were out of ammunition. The tunnels and caves were collapsing. The survivors amounted to a poor little group of women and children. And the Chechens weren't coming.

It made no sense to continue this carnage.

The fight for the triumph of Allah wasn't over, though. Now the imam's task was to keep the flame of God burning. Save the faithful warriors, save the children.

"In order to spare your son, you are going to sacrifice all your people?"

Shamil had his answer. He had lost this battle. The Almighty commanded him to accept the deal. He must follow the advice of naïbs who were wiser and more pious than he. Play for time. Send up the white flag.

Tomorrow at daybreak, he would send Jamal Eddin to the Russians.

Night found the child in the stable. Among the few scrawny horses that had survived the siege were the little gray mare his father rode in the campaign; Tsaol—Solitude—the splendid white stallion Shamil reserved for the charge and equestrian games; and Koura, Jamal Eddin's beloved pony. Koura was hardy and playful. Shamil had given him the pony at the feast of the sacrifice, when Jamal Eddin had immolated the lamb with his own hands for the first time. Thus at age seven he had become a man, a horseman, and a servant of Allah.

The pony greeted him with a friendly neigh. The child pressed his cheek against Koura's, put an arm under his neck, and held him close, running his fingers through his rough mane.

"Remember, my proud one, when we galloped down the slopes, bolting like the devil down to the river? That was before the Russians came to camp at the foot of Akulgo. Before I broke my arm, before—"

Before Bahou-Messadou's death, he almost said. But he preferred the memory of their rides together.

"And when I grabbed the stones in the puddles, and you, you pretended to dip your head low before I did."

Had they really attempted these acrobatic feats, hoping to perform them before Shamil one day as part of the djighits' show?

He breathed in the smell of the horse, and with it the smell of their cavalcades. He felt the pony's jugular, swollen with the heat, beating against the inside of his arm, the carotid just under the skin.

Pressed against each other, the child and the animal stood very still, unperturbed even by the horseflies and the flies that tortured them both. Only the occasional tapping of the other horses' hooves on the stone floor and of their tails whipping through the still air broke the silence. Catching hold of Koura's ear, Jamal Eddin murmured, "Should I kill you too, to keep the enemy from capturing you? My brother, I bid you farewell. Tonight I shall die."

He drew his kinjal, then hesitated. He knew how to slit the throat of a sheep. He could find the courage to slit his own throat. But Koura?

"Put that back!"

Shamil stood very straight beneath the sloping roof, his colossal figure blocking the light.

"Your life does not belong to you. Your life belongs to God!"

Even in his dirty robe, his face blackened by powder, his beard dusted with gray and the folds of his turban undone, he spoke to the child with merciless authority.

One look told Jamal Eddin that this was not his father speaking. It was the imam. The man who preached at the mosque, who was capable of tearing out the tongues of the hypocrites and raising a hand against his own mother.

"Thank the Almighty for all that you do not know. For all that you cannot understand. For all His mercy may allow you to learn. Thank Him for your fate. And ask His pardon, here, now, for not having seen, for not having understood what He has decided for you. Repeat after me, 'Lord, I beg You, give me the strength to do what You wish me to do.' "

"The strength to do what You wish me to do," the child murmured.

Jamal Eddin raised his head. For the first and only time, Shamil clearly read defiance in his look.

"How will I know what He wants me to do?" Jamal Eddin said bitterly. "God doesn't listen to the prayers of slaves."

"He doesn't listen unless the slaves pray for deliverance. The strength of their arms may compensate for their weaknesses."

This response seemed to calm the child.

"Down there. Can I keep my weapons?"

Hunger had made him hallucinate. He imagined the camp below like a dark pit swarming with serpents, worms, and a thousand nameless beasts. The thought of being swallowed up by these reptiles overwhelmed him with a sense of disgust that bordered on terror.

"Can I wear my kinjal?" he insisted. "Can I use it against them?"

A fleeting glimmer of compassion broke through the harshness of Shamil's expression.

"God willing, you will not stay long in the Russian camp. Not long enough to use your dagger."

"But how must I act with them?"

He remembered what Patimat had said. Even if the infidels had given Hamzat back to her, his odor would have changed and she wouldn't have recognized him. Jamal Eddin, too, would change odors. Never let them touch you. Never accept even the least thing to eat.

"With the infidels, as everywhere in this world, you must live by holding on to the memory of the presence of God," Shamil replied. "Live, my son, and show them that you have preserved your most precious asset, the fortune no one can take from you: the faith of your ancestors."

Jamal Eddin was silent as he contemplated these words. He raised his eyes again and looked directly into his father's. He was suffocating with incomprehension, anger, and fear.

"But tomorrow," he said haltingly, "on your orders, I shall betray the faith of my ancestors."

His emotions and his efforts to control them made him short of breath.

"I shall betray God."

His voice broke and he started over. His voice higher this time, he spoke rapidly.

"Tomorrow, on your orders, I shall commit what the Almighty forbids. Why?"

"Pick up nine pebbles here, and then follow me outside."

Burning with rebellion, trembling with anger, Jamal Eddin did not obey. "Why are you making me unworthy of you? Of Him?"

Raising his voice, Jamal Eddin repeated, "Why are you making me unclean, instead of letting me die?"

Choking on his words, he took a deep breath.

"Why you, my father, you, the imam? You!"

It was no longer a question, but an accusation.

"Why are you taking away my honor?" he cried.

Shamil caught him by the collar and grabbed a handful of pebbles himself. He tightened his grip and dragged the child toward the ruins of the mosque.

He forced his son to sit astride what was left of a low wall and sat down with him, as they had on the terrace of the old house. But this time, father and son faced each other.

"Your master, Sheik Jamaluddin al-Ghumuqi, taught you about *zikr*, didn't he? The 'Memory of God,' attained by finding solitude in a crowd, through internal breathing and concentration. I'm going to teach you another technique that will help you hold on firmly to the cord of Allah," he said, placing the nine pebbles in a horizontal line between them. "Look. Listen. And repeat. There is no other god but Allah. La ilaha illa Allah."

Eyes half-closed, Shamil took the pebbles and placed them, rapidly and precisely, one on top of the other. As he ecstatically pronounced the name of Allah, his breaths became a communication with the divine breath. He breathed in deeply, exhaled, and inhaled again, powerfully and rhythmically, in syncopated time with his monotonous chanting.

Jamal Eddin knew the throbbing cadence. This was the litany that accompanied departure for battle, actions of grace—the life of his people since the dawn of time.

Instinctively he began to follow the familiar rhythm, rocking back and forth, breathing in time with his father, concentrating on the movement of the nine pebbles. Pick up, set down, pick up again, set down again. La ilaha illa Allah. In a state bordering on a trance, he murmured the incantation. Little by little, he joined in the recitation, incessantly repeating the ritual phrase out loud.

Chanting in time, with the same panting breaths blending with infinity, the voices of the man and the boy rose above Akulgo. Ever stronger, louder, and huskier, they echoed throughout the mountains above. Their chanting filled the air, embracing the universe and rising toward God until it became one with God.

When this mystical ecstasy was at its peak, they fell silent, both in a state of bliss. For a long while, they sat completely still.

At the first light of dawn, Shamil murmured in the child's ear, "Wherever you are, you can always return to these mountains through the zikr. The Memory of God will bring you back. Practice it mentally, in silence, without moving, in the depths of your soul. And never forget, Jamal Eddin, that liberty is found in the Memory of God. Now go say good-bye to your mother. It is time."

August 17

The murmur of a crowd rose from the valley floor. The Russians raced through the camp, grabbing their weapons in haste before running to the river. The wave of excitement was caused not by panic, but by impatience and curiosity. The officers lined up along the banks of the Andi Koysu in tight ranks. The guards encamped at the foot of the promontory pressed forward like an audience before a stage. All eyes looked up toward the fortress, observing an unprecedented scene. Instead of their sappers zigzagging from one plateau to the next, two enemy horses picked their way down to the trenches. The first was a bay pony, one of those little Kabarda stallions they had all come to recognize, whose vigor justified their worth. Astride the stallion was a child of about ten who gracefully guided his mount down the steep incline as though the two were one. His white linen coat, tightly cinched at the waist, fell in folds onto his boots, and the superb white lamb *papakha* on his head was so high and so full that it looked like a crown. Accustomed to the cries of warriors swooping down in hordes like a flock of crows in flight from a ledge, General Grabbe's soldiers were stunned by the silence, the solitude, and the gravitas that emanated from this approaching vision. The murids' standards were always black, black like their beards and their *long cloaks.* How could these barbarians have preserved this immaculate costume amid the stench, the filth, and the dust up there? A *dagger* with a silver pommel hung from the child's belt and a long saber gleamed at his side.

The message was clear: this was not a hostage but a prince. The imam had sent his son not as one of the vanquished but as a warrior chief to deal with the Russians as their equal. Dignified and elegant, the young horseman embodied that message to perfection. Heedless of his horse's steps, he ignored the cracks and holes in the ground, the rocks and any other obstacles on the treacherously steep path. Not once did his gaze turn to the winding river that lay below, nor to the crowd of strangers smoking and exchanging noisy banter as they commented on his descent. He stared beyond the trenches and the tents, beyond the mountain range, straight ahead at the faraway line of the ridge.

The boy was accompanied by the *naïb* Yunus, whom the interpreters and officers had met during the negotiations. His face, sharp as a blade and as proud, distant, and closed as his protégé's, expressed a mixture of defiance and anxiety. His bearing was rigid, his tension apparent in the way he gripped the white flag close to his body rather than letting it unfurl from his extended arm as was customary.

The young boy's stallion had barely touched the shingles of the bank when Yunus spurred his mount forward, passing him and covering him with his entire body.

One behind the other, they crossed the trenches that bordered the camp. The officers shared a moment of consternation as the pair arrived at the Russian lines. Should they disarm them?

They thought to take it slowly, beginning with the boy's saber. Jamal Eddin started, then drew back violently when a soldier began to reach for his sword. Confronted with such vehement resistance, the officers understood the potential consequences of insisting. Better to let it go.

As for the other—the snarl on Yunus's face discouraged any further impulse.

Escorted by soldiers, followed by the interpreters, they were led to General Grabbe's tent.

Jamal Eddin stared straight ahead, jaw clenched. Oblivious to everything around him, he moved forward.

General Grabbe was seated beneath the canopy, savoring his breakfast on this first day of truce. The samovar of tea purred on its golden burner.

The arrival of the hostage he had demanded for weeks, this precious guarantee, whom he had made a condition *sine qua non* for peace talks, aroused in him little more than a vague curiosity, barely a flash of satisfaction.

Yunus dismounted. Grabbe did not bother to look at him, much less extend a greeting, but commented casually in the *naïb*'s direction.

"You there, you go back up to your village and tell your imam that if he wants to see his progeny again, he'll have to come here. In person. Go on now! After that, we'll talk about making peace."

Yunus trembled with humiliation and rage. The Russians had toyed with him. The Russians had tricked him. They couldn't have cared less about him or the imam or his son. Most important, they didn't care about making peace. Shamil was right. They wanted the imam himself. Dead. The murids, dead. Fatima, Jawarat, and all the children, dead. The sacrifice of Jamal Eddin was in vain. The infidels would attack, no matter what.

With the same lazy indifference, the general ordered that the *hostage* be led to his headquarters. If the child was hungry, he added grandly, they could feed him.

Yunus's hand was at his dagger. Jump Grabbe, slit his throat. But the boy stood next to him, and he knew what would happen to Jamal Eddin—what would happen that very moment—if he killed Grabbe.

One of the interpreters, an Armenian veteran of the Caucasian army with whom Yunus had dealt during the negotiations, saw Yunus's face twist with hatred and feared the worst. The Armenian slapped him on the back casually and spoke to him in the Avar vernacular.

"Don't worry, old man, not to worry. You're a man of faith, Allah is your friend, he's watching over you. He'll protect you all, you, your Shamil, and his kid."

Jamal Eddin involuntarily recoiled at the man's vulgarity and his overly familiar tone. This reaction, his first since the officers had tried to take his saber, jolted him back to the horror of reality.

He could not restrain himself from doing what he had sworn to himself he wouldn't do; he turned in his saddle and looked back at the village.

It was then that he saw the dark figure of his mother, leaning over the ramparts, apart from the other women. It was she who had dressed him in this bright costume a short while ago. She wanted him to be handsome, to do them honor. She had sworn that their separation would last only a few days, that soon they would be together again. He had held back his tears as he nodded. He sensed the courage and effort it cost her to make her words persuasive, to convince herself that they were true.

She had clasped him in her arms. And then, in a low voice, she had blessed him. Around his neck he wore what the infidels could not see, his most precious possession: a small silver tube containing a verse from the Koran, an amulet to protect him from the evil eye, which she had strung on a leather cord.

He thought he could hear her sobbing up there, all alone. Hidden in her veils, leaning over the chasm, Fatima called to him. She could no longer hold back her tears, he knew it. He could not bear her pain and glanced away, looking for Shamil.

The imam had accompanied him to the outer limit of their lines. Astride his white charger, Tsoal, the best of all his stallions, his colossal figure filled the sky. Barti Khan, Akbirdil, and three of his other companions stood behind him on horseback—the guard of the prophet, the guard now so pitifully reduced. The shaft of their pennant pointing to the ground, the flag dipping low toward the earth as a sign of farewell, the *naïbs* paid their respects to the imam's son.

From the moment of their parting, Shamil had not moved from this spot. Nor would he.

Jamal Eddin could clearly make out his turban, his long red beard, the sparkling gleam of his weapons. But he could not distinguish his father's features.

Up to the very last second, he had thought Shamil would change his mind, that he would keep him back, that he would save him. But as the two trudged through the piles of rotting, unburied cadavers, among his comrades infested with worms and flies, whom no mother, no sister could protect any longer from the vultures, Jamal Eddin had understood. What choice had they left, both of them, but to believe in the honor of the infidels?

In exchange, the Russians would allow the survivors to go home. The women, the children, and the elders would be able to leave Akulgo and return to their villages. General Grabbe had given his word.

Shamil had stood immobile on the brink of the abyss that separated the murid forces from the army of the czar. Falling into line, Jamal Eddin had halted beside him.

The moment he had dreaded, the instant of separation, had come.

His heart leaden, fighting back his tears, Jamal Eddin had reached for his father in a gesture of love. Shamil had stopped him with words no father in the Caucasus had ever uttered.

"Do not embrace me, I am not worthy of it. My son, I beg you to forgive me."

Jamal Eddin had wanted to throw himself at his feet.

"With the help of God, I will bring you out of the camp," Shamil had continued, as overcome with emotion as his son. "You will not stay long with the infidels. I swear to you," he had added solemnly, "never will I abandon you."

Shamil made no further gesture toward the small boy who looked up at him. But his father followed him with his eyes and accompanied him in his soul.

Was he already regretting having listened to the advice of his men?

Beneath his father's unflinching gaze, a look at once hard and full of tenderness, Jamal Eddin straightened up.

Swallowing his tears, he sat up in the saddle and kicked his pony lightly, guiding Koura slowly forward between the tents.

He plunged on among the horses, the cannons, and the soldiers. For an instant he seemed to float above the swarm of giaours.

Then suddenly, as though swallowed up by the multitude, he disappeared.

Book Two

The Other Side of the Mirror
In the Splendor of the Russian Court
1839–1855

"For God and for the Czar!"

—Nicholas I

CHAPTER V

An Unexpected Discovery

1839–1840

Saint Petersburg, four months later
December 1839

"Pretty name, your Akulgo. A victory that has a nice ring to it. Akulgo, like Borodino and Waterloo."

The *kibitka* flew over the snow. The sound of the runners gliding over the ice-covered ground, the harness bells, even the horses' heavy breathing as they galloped in rhythm was muted in the winter air. Only the officers' voices broke the stillness as they crossed the vast hollow that led from Tsarskoye Sielo, "the czar's village," to Saint Petersburg. Thirty versts in a straight line. At this rapid speed, the sleigh would be there in a few hours. Thirty versts, in addition to the three thousand that one of the two passengers had just traveled.

He was coming from the Caucasus. It had taken four months to travel across the empire, four months of unbridled racing, from the famous Akulgo that his companion had just mentioned to the Alexandrovsky orphanage at the edge of the imperial domain.

The circumstances of the war had made this twenty-three-year-old lieutenant the abductor and jailer of a child he had been forced to snatch from his mountain home and bring here, to this institution reserved for wards of the state.

Mission accomplished.

The child was alone now, without bearings whatsoever, at the other end of the earth. Far, so far away from his own world.

The lieutenant had just handed him over to the doctors and teachers who, at this very moment, were trying to get the boy to undress so that they could examine him and judge his physical state and his reflexes. A Muslim boy, stark naked in front of women? A Muslim boy, poked and palpated by the hands of giaours? How would he survive such humiliation? How could he possibly survive in such an alien world?

The lieutenant imagined so well the helplessness and confusion of the child that he could not bear to think of it. Any more than he wanted to remember the series of degrading acts his superiors had forced him to commit.

Jamal Eddin had been taken from his people and concealed from his father in an act of betrayal—and on the explicit orders of General Grabbe, commander of the armies of the Caucasus.

By order of the czar.

Abducted with complete disregard for all custom, for their word, and for their code of honor.

With scorn for the glory and grandeur of Holy Russia.

Strapped tightly in their parade uniforms, the two officers sat next to each other, stiff and straight, behind the coachman.

Their conversation was reduced to an occasional word, cut short by the biting cold. They shivered under the sable blanket they shared, cocked hats pulled down tightly on their heads against the cold, their sabers clutched between their knees. The wind blew through the white plumes on their hats, the lustrous hair of their furs, and the gold braid at their collars and cuffs, which sparkled in the pale light of winter.

The older of the two was Count Pavel Dmitrievitch Kiselyev. Nearly fifty, he had a receding hairline and his once-abundant locks were turning gray. But the hairstyle made popular by the czar, with short curls combed forward at forehead and temples, neatly trimmed sideburns, and a full, waxed moustache, emphasized the oval shape of his face in a becoming fashion. Tall and broad-shouldered, with a neat waist, Count Kiselyev was still considered one of the handsomest men in Russia. Hero of the Napoleonic wars, veteran of the Congress of Vienna, former governor of the provinces of the Danube, Wallachia, and Moldavia, today he was a member of the Council of State. Among Nicholas I's favorites, he was the incarnation of the court's ideal of intelligence, integrity, and power. An exception. A miracle. For beneath the arrogant exterior was a vivacious personality, full of warmth.

The other man was somewhat less imbued with the honor of his class. He lacked neither distinction nor looks, but the worn traits that marked his otherwise youthful face betrayed his extreme fatigue. Pale and thin from a long journey, on this January afternoon he had the look of an adolescent who had grown up too quickly. Nothing about him was gauche or careless, but it was evident that he had dressed hastily, shaved and combed his hair in a hurry. His hair, parted on the side, fell in unruly ash-blond waves to the nape of his neck. The sideburns that framed his weary face were bushy and undisciplined; he could not remember when they had last been trimmed. His listless exhaustion had emptied his heart of emotion and his head of thoughts. Normally energetic, he found his inability to overcome this malaise distressing and humiliating. His name was Dmitri Alexeyevitch Milyutin, and he was the count's nephew.

Both of them were career officers in the military, officers by chance or necessity rather than vocation. The army was the czar's great passion. He was mistrustful of civilians, people who did not know the meaning of the word "obedience." His capital of Saint Petersburg was like an immense barracks, a garrison town, inhabited solely by uniforms. A military career was the sole possibility, the only future for a self-respecting Russian from a good family. But from that to requesting a transfer to Dagestan and Chechnya, as Dmitri Alexeyevitch had done last spring—whatever could have possessed him to behave so uncharacteristically and so impulsively?

Was it a reaction to his immense sorrow at his mother's death last February? Boredom with his studies at the military academy? A youthful desire for risk? Or glory? Whatever it was, it was an absurd gesture for a young man who had nothing to atone for. The Caucasus was known as a land of exile, a place where one was sent as punishment, "our sweet Siberia," as the emperor called it. It was there that he sent the undesirables, the agitators, and Pushkin and Lermontoff, the poets in disgrace.

The "wars of pacification" gave demoted lieutenants and disgraced generals a chance to redeem themselves. They could win back their stripes and return as heroes. If others observed them closely, the eyes of those who were lucky enough to come back betrayed something both wild and somber. It was the shadow of "the mark of the mountains," a nostalgia for the grandeur of nature, for their adventures among the rebels, and for the freedom from the empire that they had enjoyed even within the empire. They became arrogant and contentious and adopted the affectation of wearing only the cherkeska, the papakha, and the sacrosanct kinjal when in civilian dress.

These veterans were known as "the Caucasians."

Though his nephew appeared to be immune to this kind of behavior, the count was nonetheless surprised to find him remote and sullen, their reunion scarcely up to his expectations. After all, the uncle had taken the trouble to go fetch him personally, south of Petersburg, at the very place where he was to report for his mission, this much-talked-of mission that had required Lieutenant Dmitri Alexeyevitch Milyutin's return to Russia.

Once through the initial greetings, Dmitri barely thanked him. His mind seemed to be elsewhere; he spoke little and asked no questions, not even regarding the honor he was about to receive. It was an honor of some magnitude: on this December afternoon, the count would escort his nephew to the Winter Palace. He had succeeded in having his nephew invited to dinner with the imperial family in their private apartments. This was no ordinary feat, since only the czar's most intimate friends were invited to the legendary four o'clock dinner. Of course, Dmitri had already been presented to the czar, along with hundreds of other officers, during official ceremonies at court, but never as part of a select group at a small get-together. The count had high expectations for this meeting.

As luck would have it, the invitation was for the very evening of the day the boy arrived, after an extensive campaign and a journey of several thousand versts across the country. And so? This was such a rare privilege, such a precious favor, that no one would even have considered postponing.

The uncle shot a puzzled look at his protégé. His own disappointment so annoyed him that he could find no adequate way to break the silence.

He had no children of his own. His sister had married beneath her station, her spouse a local squire from the Moscow area. They hadn't the means to give their children an adequate education, so he had seen to the progress of the boys, the third one of whom was not yet ten. He made sure they were admitted to the best lycées and introduced to the higher circles of society. His affection for the eldest, Dmitri Alexeyevitch, now went far beyond any family obligation toward a poor relative. Despite the boy's uncompromising character, he saw in him a reflection of his own character, a patience, a level-headedness and cleverness that excluded neither tenacity nor passion. And he knew that Dmitri admired him and returned his affection.

Dmitri had been wounded twice during the siege of Akulgo. Perhaps the scars were deeper than the young man cared to admit.

A diplomat by nature and a courtier by trade, the count tried other means, short of blatant flattery, to lighten the atmosphere and rescue the conversation.

"Akulgo," he repeated. "Now that was some baptism by fire! You never do things halfway, do you? Typical of you, my boy, and quite a feat of arms. I'm proud of you. General Grabbe wrote to tell me that your conduct was impeccable."

The shadow of a smile played about the lieutenant's lips.

"General Grabbe gives me too much credit," he replied.

It was impossible to tell whether his tone expressed modesty or bitterness. But at least he had responded.

"You've begun your career under the orders of a great general, and you've lived through a historic moment," the count insisted.

"Nonetheless, the siege cost us three thousand men."

The uncle sensed, if not criticism, then at least a certain reticence. He deftly changed sides.

"Three thousand, as many as that?"

"Three thousand Russians in two months. Dead or mutilated."

"What a slaughter for a pile of rocks!"

"And the carnage isn't over down there."

Kiselyev began to smile beneath his moustache. Fine, the conversation had taken off again. All he had to do was let it ramble on.

"What? Not over?" he exclaimed. "The Caucasus has been pacified; it's a complete success."

Dmitri restrained himself from showing his impatience. "Who says so?"

"Grabbe himself, in his report to the emperor. He wiped them off the map, you wiped them off the map, all the rebels!"

"With all due respect for General Grabbe, I think he is mistaken. And if His Majesty does not take necessary measures, very rapidly—"

This time it was the count's turn to frown.

"The czar knows the situation in the Caucasus, down to the finest details. He is better informed than you or anyone else as to what is going on there. He knows everything. 'The necessary measures'—what kind of a phrase is that?"

"General Grabbe needs more resources and his officers more intelligence."

Kiselyev recognized his own dynamism in his nephew, but this time did not admire it.

"I'd advise you not speak in these terms later on."

"Uncle, if you only knew what shortcomings I've seen with my own eyes, the ignorance and stupidity of some of our own captains!"

"It is not your place to judge your superiors."

"Our troops are poorly trained, poorly organized, poorly fed, and poorly equipped."

"What are you talking about? The Russian army is the most powerful in the world. The emperor takes care of his soldiers, he gives them his time, his energy, and his love! He loves you—you, the young—because you are faithful, disciplined, and handsome."

"Handsome, yes, on the parade ground, no doubt," Dmitri cut him off. "But this is no parade, and it's not an ordinary war, but a holy war."

The count softened. He had gone through the same kind of crisis Dmitri was experiencing. This contrast between the horror of war and the placidity of home. He never should have arranged to bring the boy to see the czar so soon after being in the throes of action. It was his mistake, an error in judgment.

"His Majesty is perfectly conscious of the difficulties you have had to face," he said soothingly. "He considers all the complications. And as a matter of fact, that is why I managed to have you invited here this evening, as the victor of Akulgo."

Dmitri was no longer listening.

"And there's something else. We're so sure of our own superiority that we don't take the Montagnards seriously. We aren't remotely curious about their culture, their tribal structures, their politics, or their religion. We can't even fathom the possibility that we could learn something from them, if only from the way they fight. Yet if we knew them, it would help us to defeat them."

"They're already defeated," the count muttered sternly. "The war is over. They've given up. They've even given us their children so that we can make good little Russians of them. This mission you just completed, at Tsarskoye Sielo, this boy, the rebel's son you brought there—that is striking proof. Finally they understand what's good for them!"

Milyutin chose not to follow this unexpected turn in the conversation. Yes, he had just delivered the small prisoner in his care to the Alexandrovsky Cadet Corps at Tsarskoye Sielo. So?

It was precisely this, this last journey, that he still couldn't stomach.

Four months earlier, during the peace negotiations with the Montagnards, he had seen how General Grabbe had treated his hostage. How he had had him imprisoned in the camp. How he had had him sent to the fort at Temir-Khan-Chura. And from there, how, with violence—

He tried to chase the images from his mind and returned to strategic considerations.

"For the past fifty years, Uncle, ever since the reign of Catherine the Great, all of our generals have been crying victory. All of them, one after another, General Fézé, General von Klugenau, and now General Grabbe. One day, their arrogance and their blindness will cost the empire dearly."

"The wars of pacification have put enough of a strain on the treasury and weighed too heavily on the crown and on the czar," the count snapped, losing what remained of his patience, "for you to come here this evening and explain to us that they were poorly conducted and, what's more, that they're not over. Anyway, why should they continue? As you pointed out, there is no gold in the Caucasus, no silver, no iron—nothing. If the Montagnards are as poor as you say they are, why don't we leave them alone so they can fight it out among themselves? Why are we knocking ourselves out?"

"Why?" Dmitri stared at the count. Could a man so well read really be asking such a naïve question?

"Because we have no choice, Uncle! The chain of the Caucasus is a fortress that cuts the empire in two. It runs all the way across the country, from the Black Sea to the Caspian, barring our path along a thousand versts. We cannot permit an enclave inhabited by hostile Muslims to separate us from our people, the Orthodox Christians in the south. How can we accept the fact that the routes leading to our own territories—the roads to Georgia and to Armenia—are constantly subject to the raids of a bunch of fanatics whose goal it is to extend the power of Islam? How can we abandon our western ports that look to Constantinople and to Europe, and the eastern ones facing Asia, without sacrificing the fleet and giving up trade? As for the security of our frontiers, protecting ourselves from the invading Turks, from Persian incursions, and from England's designs on Afghanistan and India depends entirely upon holding the Caucasus. We have no choice but to conquer the tribes and colonize the land. Pacify. But how?"

"To hear you tell it, that, indeed, is the question."

"In any case, not the way we're going about it now, by massacring the population. Do you want to know the truth? Our brutality serves only the imam Shamil."

"The imam Shamil is dead."

"The only man we should have killed," the young man muttered angrily, "the one we allowed to get away, out of sheer stupidity, is not dead."

"Dead or on the run, it's all the same, now he's worth nothing. Grabbe says he's just a miserable wretch sneaking from cave to cave, defenseless and without resources, abandoned by his people there in the mountains. We'll catch him sooner or later."

"He is alive. He is free."

"He has been defeated, Dmitri!"

"But he's kept what is essential: his honor, his weapons, and something more. After the miracle of his escape from Ghimri eight years ago, the miracle of his flight from Akulgo has transformed him into an indestructible figure. He has become a legend in his own eyes, and in the eyes of the Dagestanis and the Chechens too. Now they're all as convinced as he is that he's God's Chosen One. The death of all his companions, of his sister, of his second wife, even of his youngest son in atrocious conditions—all that changes nothing. As for kidnapping his heir, his desire for revenge—which has now become very personal—dictates that he must survive. For the Russians, the nightmare is just beginning."

"You're exaggerating, Dmitri Alexeyevitch."

The young man restrained himself only with great effort.

"I'm exaggerating nothing. Grabbe's report is a tissue of half-truths. I'm sure they'll be worth a cross of the Order of Saint Alexander Nevsky for him. And for me, this splendid silver medal that I value above all others, with the inscription:

'For the assault on Akulgo, 22 August 1839.' I wear it with pride, like all of my comrades who took part in the siege. As for 'Akulgo, 22 August,' you should know that things didn't happen exactly the way—"

"I thought I told you to be quiet."

"Don't worry, I won't say a word in front of the czar when we get there."

"I should hope not, not in the presence of the empress and the children."

"I'll shut up, I give you my word. I will not talk about the things I saw happen there at the dinner table. How the siege really ended. But you, my uncle, you who are close to the czar, you to whom he listens, you my benefactor, whom I love and respect, you should hear what we did during the last assault."

"I suppose that, in your present worked-up state, no argument will stop you. All right, I'm listening. But hurry up. I'll give you three minutes. What did you see at Akulgo that is worth my telling the czar?"

* * *

As the kibitka covered the last four versts of the Nevsky Prospect, the beginning and the end of all journeys for those who served the empire, Count Pavel Dmitrievitch Kiselyev was still contemplating what he had just heard. As he drove under the triumphal arch, past the Alexandrine column, across the square, and along the side of the massive red Winter Palace, and all the way up to the main entrance, the images turned over and over again in his mind.

Could a massacre of such proportions have consequences in the future?

And, contrary to what he had thought earlier, should he let Dmitri tell this story? This opportunity would not present itself again. But should he seize the moment? He knew his nephew well enough to be certain that he would not step beyond the limits of propriety. But, in speaking freely, the young man would be taking a huge risk. Should he hold him back or encourage him to do so? He had asked himself these questions all his life. Intervene in affairs of state or let things take their course? How to act—and when to act—for the honor of Russia?

He had thought about this at length in 1837, when he had presented Czar Nicholas with his proposal for reform, which included the emancipation of the serfs. It was the only proposal to date that had dared to suggest such a thing. True, His Majesty himself had commissioned the report on the condition of the peasants. But the uproar in the aristocracy that had ensued had made him fear for the fall of all the Kiselyevs. The emperor, relieved at the reaction of the nobility, had immediately dismissed the report—and understandably so. The emperor hated change and disorder. He hated reforms and constitutions. And ever since the revolt of the Decembrists had nearly cost him the throne, he particularly hated liberals. How the count had managed to remain in favor all these years was a mystery. Far from banishing him after the scandalous report, Czar Nicholas had appointed him minister of domains. He, Pavel Dmitrievitch Kiselyev, who had granted constitutions to the two provinces under his administration, who was considered at court to be a worthless democrat!

"Strange weaknesses of the tyrants who govern us," the count sighed to himself.

His thoughts implied no reproach, no criticism of his master, only a sort of self-mockery. His loyalty to the czar was total, his admiration sincere. He loved him. As for His Majesty, he considered Kiselyev a charming idealist, an old courtier who knew how to choose his moment and sugarcoat his message.

But regarding Akulgo, should he speak up or not?

The count patted the gloved hand of his protégé and whispered in his ear, not without irony, "Insha'Allah!"

* * *

The moment his polished boot crossed the step to the landing, Kiselyev's doubts evaporated.

"Ah, Milyutin, there you are!"

Cigar clenched in his teeth, an immense greyhound at his heels, the bulky figure of Grand Duke Mikhaïl Pavlovitch, the czar's youngest brother, was already bounding up the stairs.

"I'm just going up to see my niece for a second," he shouted, "and I'll be right with you. Wait for me in the little office."

His Imperial Highness the Grand Duke Mikhaïl Pavlovitch always reserved a warm welcome for his soldiers. At forty-one, he behaved with officers, especially the young ones who had distinguished themselves in combat, like a paternal generalissimo. It fit with his stentorian voice and his penchant for regimental camaraderie. Even so, the count's casual greeting to an officer of minor nobility—"Ah, Milyutin, there you are!"—without addressing him by his full patronymic or his rank was highly unusual. In this case, it simply indicated that His Highness knew him well and was fond of him.

Count Kiselyev had been misleading himself in thinking that his nephew's invitation to the Winter Palace was a prize won through his tireless efforts. Dmitri Alexeyevitch was expected there. Naturally. And that was why the young man had not commented on the honor his visit implied. He was a member of General Grabbe's staff. He had just returned from a mission in the Caucasus. This was not so much a privilege as a duty: he had been summoned to give a report.

The count discerned the extent of his misperception. He immediately sensed that there was a strange atmosphere of agitation in the White Hall, a brouhaha marked by murmurs of dismay. He looked at the courtiers—not a sign of black, not a tailcoat in sight. The men were in uniform, according to the czar's orders, the women in national dress and *kokoshnik,* the ancient Russian headdress in the form of a diadem. Tradition, autocracy, orthodoxy.

But the groups that normally remained stationed in their appointed positions at the palace were scattered all over the place. The silver-helmeted Chevaliers-Gardes, the maids of honor with their azure trains gathered in the crooks of their arms, the chamber gentlemen outfitted in green and gold, the pages in purple, and the small black boys in yellow glided to and fro between the rooms, the rainbow of their costumes reflected in the huge mirrors that reached all the way to the balconies of the galleries. This ballet was a far cry from the palace's habitual staid processions.

The arrival of the master of ceremonies and two chamberlains striding over the polished parquet created even further disorder, as everyone rushed toward them, hoping to catch any snippet of news that might be distilled in hushed voices.

The trio walked directly toward Kiselyev.

“Ah, Count, there you are. We’ve been looking everywhere for you, to warn you—at your home, at the circle, at your dacha—but you were nowhere to be found. Her Majesty the Empress cannot receive you. The four o’clock dinner has been canceled. Their Majesties are at the bedside of Grand Duchess Maria.”

“My God! Nothing serious, I hope.”

“The grand duchess had a malaise in the chapel, an indisposition that may presage a happy event. The czar joins the empress in begging you to please excuse them. They hope this complication has not inconvenienced you too much.”

The count bowed.

“I recognize the habit of exquisite courtesy on the part of Their Majesties, the great generosity that is characteristic of them both. They always have a thought for the well-being of their subjects, even though they themselves must be very worried.”

He stepped back slightly to take his leave; the master of ceremonies accompanied him politely to the landing.

“Good evening, Count, take care of yourself, we look forward to seeing you tomorrow. Cover yourself well.”

He turned to the lieutenant who stood stock still, cocked hat in hand.

“Lieutenant Milyutin, if you will be so good as to follow me to the little office.”

* * *

The “little office,” an annex to Grand Duke Mikhaïl Pavlovitch’s residence, was little in name only. In contrast to the czar’s two offices of spartan simplicity, the room was comparable in opulence and scale to the interconnecting salons.

It was nonetheless a distinctly male space, with no plants, flowers, or mirrors. The velvet drapes, the leather chairs, the marble floor, and the jasper on the colonnades were all bottle green. Gilded copper insignias—imperial eagles and sheaves of arms, lances, battle-axes, and standards—shone on the green earthenware stoves, the candelabra, the wall lamps, the arms and the feet of the chairs. The thick cashmere carpet of green and gold repeated the motif of bicephalous eagles and sheaves of arms. Three great chandeliers holding hundreds of candles were lowered over tables scattered with maps, quills, and papers. The grand duke was fond of comfort.

On the walls, the portraits of his two brothers, the late Czar Alexander, who had defeated Napoleon, and Czar Nicholas, shared a striking family resemblance. Both tall and robust in stature, with well-formed round heads, short hair, moustaches, and sideburns, they shared a certain martial appeal. In contrast, Mikhaïl Pavlovitch seemed redder, rounder, stockier, and totally lacking in his older brothers' grace. In short, he was more of a caricature.

Boots resting on the table, a cigar in his mouth, he motioned to the lieutenant, still standing at attention, to take a chair.

"At ease. Sit down. You've done your duty, and you have served me well."

Duty. Service. At the Winter Palace, these words were sacred. Indeed, service and duty were the pillars of the throne. When Nicholas I spoke these two words, they were ennobling. In Mikhaïl Pavlovitch's mouth, they sounded a bit like a parody.

Like the emperor, the grand duke's great passion was the army. And like the emperor, he was capable of cruelty toward his soldiers, of being merciless and vicious when punishing any dereliction of discipline. Yet he was considered a good comrade, more proud of his rank than of his position. And even though he smoked and drank, collected mistresses, and had a fondness for salacious jokes, his puritanical family adored him—with the exception of his wife, who had spent her wedding night alone since he preferred the company of the girls and the squadron chiefs.

Nicholas I found his vulgarity shocking, but he still loved "Micky's" gaiety, energy, and devotion. Fourteen years ago, when he had acceded to the throne, he had even appointed him to several major posts, including head of the council of education of the military schools, an organism of utmost importance to both of them.

Intelligent despite his boorish ways, capable of subtlety in the accomplishment of his task, Mikhaïl Pavlovitch was devoted to his work. He considered himself omniscient, perhaps in part because he studied his dossiers carefully too.

He was personally involved in the recruitment of students, presided over the commissions in charge of admissions, and decided himself who should be assigned to which post, based on birth, wealth, and the influential contacts of his future officers. As a matter of fact, it was in this context, as administrator of the Pages' Corps and inspector general of the Cadet Corps, that Mikhaïl Pavlovitch had summoned Lieutenant Dmitri Alexeyevitch.

"Well, Milyutin, what's new? Oh, by the way, before I forget, the emperor sends his thanks. The personal effects of your Montagnard arrived. Superb, this kinjal! How do those savages manage to find such splendid arms?"

"Their confiscation was very humiliating for the child, Your Imperial Highness."

"What, did he think we'd let him keep them? So he could murder you? They're amazing, they continue to take us for imbeciles. Does he at least like it at the cadets'?"

"We just arrived at the Corps Alexandrovsky this afternoon, Your Highness."

"And you, how do you find the kid?"

"Better, Your Highness."

The grand duke arched an eyebrow in question.

"Better?"

"He was wounded, quite seriously."

The grand duke, who liked to think he knew everything, had not been aware of this detail.

"In a skirmish as we were leaving Akulgo," Milyutin explained. "We were attacked as we were taking him to the fort at Temir-Khan-Chura, by his father and a few of his men. They tried to take him back. The child was wounded, his arm pierced straight through by a lance. A nasty wound. And the trip didn't help it heal; it was long and difficult."

"All the same, Kharkov, Rostov, those must have impressed the lad, to say nothing of Moscow."

"He was delirious for several weeks. The fever cut him off from the world outside. In reality, that may be what saved him."

"And now, is he happy?"

"I think he's disoriented, Your Highness."

Dmitri reflected and chose his words carefully before continuing.

"He's completely overwhelmed."

"But what do you think, can we make something of him? Is it worth the effort?"

"He's intelligent, courageous, and proud. For the rest, I couldn't say."

"Have you been able to interrogate him? Find out any information that might interest us?"

"He is silent, obstinately silent. I think he has begun to understand a little Russian. But he has no desire to communicate and says nothing. He accepts nothing—not from me, anyway. Not even his food. My interpreter, one of the Muslims in the militia, is the only one so far who can get him to eat anything."

"They're all the same. They think they'll be sullied by contact with us. Is he religious?"

"Even when he was very ill, he found a way to say his prayers five times a day."

"You know what I think, Milyutin?"

The grand duke reflected for a moment, pulling on his cigar. He watched the smoke rings rise, took his boots off the table, and stretched his legs out beneath it.

"If we want to use these fanatics, we mustn't try to convert them. On the contrary, they should be raised in their faith and never allowed to forget their mother tongue. I wrote Chernychev to tell him this. Have you read my letter?"

The grand duke alluded to a note he had written to Count Chernychev, Minister of War, on the sixteenth of that month.

"I have had the honor of reading it, Your Highness."

"I informed him that the cadets' school of Moscow, where he had planned on sending your Montagnard, was not the place for him at all. There is no mullah in Moscow to instruct him in the Koran, guide his theological studies, help him follow the rites of his religion. Whereas, here—"

Dmitri knew that the grand duke had ordered the transfer of the "rebel's son" to the boarding school at Tsarskoye

Sielo, an institution reserved for wards of the state where he would find other "Cherkesses." The minister had simply approved the order and commanded the officer accompanying the child—himself—to continue their journey.

"I believe it is a wise decision, Your Highness. It will help him."

"Help him what? To be of service to us? I should hope so! Has he asked any questions about what kind of future we have planned for him?"

"None at all."

"Does he think we're going to kill him? Is he afraid?"

"He has already seen the worst. He is not afraid."

"Does he know what happened in his village, after Grabbe sent him out of the camp?"

"Your Highness's orders were obeyed. He knows nothing. He doesn't even know if his family is still alive."

"Perfect."

Milyutin refrained from expressing that, of all the acts he had been ordered to execute, the imposition of this blackout was by far the most painful. This absence of any explanation, this silence before the child's obvious anxiety every time he heard his father's name mentioned—the only emotion he could not control—was unbearable. He despised his own cruelty at leaving the boy to live in fear and doubt for four months. But the orders had been explicit and unequivocal. He was forbidden to tell the boy anything.

The grand duke stubbed out his cigar in the ashtray with little jabs.

"He'll know what he wants to know soon enough. He is to attend New Year celebrations on Monday. The czar has reserved for himself the pleasure of giving him news. Until then, His Majesty wants him to be taken round to see everything here. And for him to take a good look. We're going to show this savage what civilization is and how the true faithful celebrate the name of God."

Mikhaïl Pavlovitch stood up. Dmitri stood at attention. The interview was over.

The Winter Palace
January 1, 1840

Petersburg was up before dawn. In the candlelit boudoirs of the English Quay, the barracks of Chpalernaïa Street, and the garrets of the imperial buildings, everyone donned their ceremonial costumes. The morning's first event would take place at ten o'clock. That gave them just enough time to prepare, especially since, on New Year's Day, the palace was open to everyone, just as it was on the czar's saint's day, December sixth, and the empress's birthday, July first. Well, not to the little people, but open at least to prominent members of society. The lowest of the aristocracy, even those furthest from power, would be received. Nearly ten thousand visitors were expected.

The customary celebration of the New Year had begun with Peter the Great, who had proclaimed it by *ukase.* Catherine II, with her penchant for German traditions, had decreed that the symbol should take the form of a huge fir tree, laden with thousands of nuts, red apples, and brightly wrapped bonbons. Hundreds of candles on the tree would be lit at midnight the night before. Now, each of the grand dukes—brothers, sisters, sons, daughters, and grandchildren of the czar—had his own personal tree in his apartments or in the nursery.

But at the dawn of the year 1840, the tree for the whole Romanov family had been placed, not in the czarina's salons, but in the Throne Room. It was taller and more handsome than all the others, a tree such as one would never find in the mountains of Europe, one that embodied the expansion of the empire: a tree from the forests of the Caucasus. To commemorate the recent victory at Akulgo, its black branches had been transformed to shimmering light and gold, a symbol that all could understand. The chief of police's last hymn of praise expressed the allegory: "Russia's past is admirable, her present…beyond all magnificence. As for her future, it exceeds the wildest imagination." Court and city prepared to revel in this truth, dazzled by their own power.

A hard, icy frost covered the ground before sunrise. The sleighs discharged their passengers at the foot of the stairway of honor, then went to park in a circle around the Alexandrine Column. A huge bonfire burned there in the middle of the snow to warm the coachmen and horses. There was no disorder, no pushing or shoving among the teams. Outside as well as in, each knew his place.

The White Hall, the only one open for the moment, was already crowded. Streams of people strolled back and forth, zigzagging between the gilded furniture, the malachite tables, the porphyry candelabra, and the lapis lazuli vases. Like moths around a flame, the visitors pressed beneath the incandescent round balls of the crystal chandeliers. Some stood in the galleries, between the candlelit pillars of the long colonnade. The light sparkled and glanced off the sabers, the epaulets, the decorative cords, the gardes' helmets, and the demure crosses at the ladies' throats. It scintillated in the tiny pendants that dangled from their ears, the rows of pearls at gloved wrists, the blood-red rubies that rested against white-powdered breasts.

Nearly a thousand ladies of honor packed the balconies. Their sumptuous traditional costumes, in keeping with Nicholas I's wishes, subtly announced each woman's respective duty, age, wealth, and rank.

The most titled among them, the empress's attendants, wore the imperial monogram pinned to their shoulders. The older women in charge of the czarina's toilette, the *dames à portraits*, wore diamond-framed miniatures of her pinned to their bodices. Younger and more numerous, the maids of honor assigned to the service of the five grand duchesses all wore satin tiaras of azure, trimmed with swan feathers. Forbidden from wearing the colors of the imperial attendants' trains—purple or green trimmed with gold, or plain blue—the other ladies of the court wore colors that harmonized with the blue of their sapphires and the green of their emeralds. The feathered fans they waved in the stuffy, crowded premises lifted the veils of their crownlike kokoshniks, and the sweet, heady scents of their hair wafted into the air.

These blended with the perfume of lilies and tuberoses from the window boxes and the incense from cassoulets that burned near the stoves. Scents of the Orient, the heavy fragrance of Russia.

The foreign dignitaries, also in dress uniforms covered with gold, plumes, metal, and gems, breathed in this potpourri as they listened and observed the scene before them. Never before had they encountered such a spectacle of colors, fabrics, and perfumes. Not at the courts of Paris or Vienna, nor at the sumptuous ceremonies of the Vatican. Even the princes of the reigning royal houses were hypnotized, breathless with wonder. Few things could compare to the magnificence and solemnity of the Russian court.

There was nonetheless one element of this vibrantly colored crowd that particularly intrigued the foreign guests, one touch of black in their midst, an incongruous figure who looked entirely out of place.

It was a child of about nine or ten, dressed in a cherkeska that was too long for him, obviously a hand-me-down, with his left arm in a sling.

"Who is he?" the visitors asked. "What's he doing here?"

No one answered their questions.

The child was, of course, not the only one of his age to attend the ceremony. At the four doors of the White Hall, the cadets of the First Corps, dressed in green and red, stood at attention in formations of twenty square. But the austerity of this little one, the coldness of his expression, and the solitude that emanated from his entire being, made him stand out among all the others.

He appeared to be accompanied—or rather, watched over—by a young lieutenant who leaned down to whisper things in his ear from time to time. But every time the officer tried to catch his attention, the child moved perceptibly away, straining to distance himself from the voice of his guardian. Perhaps because of all the noise around him, or because Milyutin did not speak his language well, the boy did not even pretend to listen or to look in the direction of whatever the lieutenant was describing. His expression haughty, his faced closed and impenetrable, he remained at whatever distance he could, as though he had seen, heard, and understood nothing. The spectacle was probably too new for him to be touched or impressed by it all. What event in his past could possibly compare to all this? There was absolutely no common point of reference between his past and what he saw before him, no link whatsoever that would have offered him a means to compare and judge what was taking place.

The crowd and the noise made him feel confused; he was blinded by the vivid colors and light-headed from the violent onslaught of all the various perfumes. In sum, none of it particularly pleased him. On the contrary, the disorder of all these sensations made him dizzy. He concentrated on concealing his feelings and behaving with all the politeness one should show when under another's roof, without expressing any sign of rejection or surprise. No curiosity, really? To all outward appearances, this seemed to be the case.

Ten shots of cannon fire marked the hour. All the double doors clacked as they opened in unison. A murmur passed through the crowd of courtiers who pressed forward excitedly toward the connecting rooms, the majordomos holding them back behind the cordons. These signs, like battle preparations, made the boy nonetheless lift his head attentively. From the back, a boot step resounded on the parquet.

A shiver of impatient expectation rippled through the crowd, and he understood. The Great White Czar was coming. In spite of his efforts, his curiosity got the better of him. No longer able to stand still, he leaned forward with the others.

His view was blocked by a line of soldiers standing at attention along the connecting rooms. But already a procession of harbingers, pages, and gentlemen was arriving at the White Hall. A voice silenced the crowd.

"Messieurs, the czar!"

The women curtsied deeply, and the men bowed.

Above all the respectfully lowered heads, Jamal Eddin at first saw only one thing: the high, black papakha of his countrymen.

This was a shock, one that went straight to his heart.

The Great White Czar was not wearing the traditional Russian uniform, with its epaulets, gold-tipped silk cords, military decorations, and golden crucifix. Instead, a gleaming ghizir covered his breast, the row of cartridge belts festooned with silver. He wore the tightly cinched cherkeska of the Caucasian Montagnards, with his pants tucked into his boots and a pair of splendid crossed kinjals slipped into his belt, as was customary. The severe expression of his heavy-lidded steel-gray eyes was impenetrable. The high forehead, the beauty, the nobility, and authority of this face—in fact, everything about this individual—was the incarnation of Jamal Eddin's idea of a commander. His unusual height—gigantic in comparison to most of the other men at court—made him immediately stand out. A colossus. His gait, the way he held his head, his adamantly imposing presence—the child recognized it all.

Milyutin observed the child's reaction and immediately understood. The illusion was almost complete. The idea had never occurred to him, the comparison had never entered his head, but today, standing next to this child dressed in what appeared to be a costume matching the emperor's, the likeness struck him for the first time. Because of his age, his size, his complexion, and his look, the czar could not help but evoke the image of his father, the imam Shamil. The same majesty and the same austerity governed his features, the same sense of theater. And, as the crowning detail, the same escort.

Following in his steps marched not the harbingers and pages who had preceded him, but Lesghiens, Avars, and Chechens. A detachment of twenty Montagnards, all of them splendid in their red cherkeskas, rich sheepskin hats, and leather boots, armed with kinjals, sabers, and crops, served as his praetorian guard.

"The bravest warriors of the empire," Milyutin whispered in Jamal Eddin's ear, "the fiercest and the most loyal. The emperor places all his pride and his confidence in these men. They alone are chosen to serve him and to protect and defend him."

Milyutin chose to omit one crucial detail of his otherwise appealing discourse. The men, hand-picked for their handsome looks, did indeed accompany the czar wherever he traveled. However, he had failed to mention that Nicholas I was not wearing the costume of the murids, as Jamal Eddin might have thought, but rather the uniform of the Terek Cossacks, the "Christian settlers" of the Caucasus. In fact, he was dressed as the ataman of the Cossacks, the generalissimo of the troops that fought the Montagnards.

Why tell him?

Having lived so long among the Montagnards, fighting them and hating them and fearing them, the Cossacks had eventually adopted their dress, their customs, their arms, even their horses and equestrian exploits. They differed in only one respect, thought Milyutin, but it was the most important one—religion. In any case, ever since Akulgo, the Montagnards had belonged to the same people as the Cossacks. They were all Russians.

The young officer drove this last point home by concluding, "That, Jamal Eddin, that is the empire!"

Even if the boy had understood his words, the lieutenant could see that they scarcely inspired the reaction he had expected. Glancing at the child's face, he was surprised to see what a transformation the vision of these wealthy, powerful Muslims, submissive to the infidels and serving the czar, had wrought.

In four months, Jamal Eddin had never allowed Milyutin even a glimpse of his feelings. Through silence and reserve, he had steadily expressed his disdain for the giaour. But now his features were suddenly contorted with contempt, indignation, and anger at his own people. This time, he lost control of himself.

His eyes flashed, his face flushing dark with fury as he watched these believers who had abandoned the inhabitants of Akulgo and deserted his father.

Cowards. Pacifists. Hypocrites. The words, all those words he had not said for months, crowded into his head and filled him with murderous indignation. The words swirled in his mind.

To the hypocrites, I make it known that I will obtain by brute force what they refused me in my kindness. My warriors will descend like black clouds on their auls.

His hatred was so obvious that his guardian was taken aback.

Traitors to the imam Shamil, traitors to the Almighty.

Though the child said nothing, the officer was sure the child would spit his anger and disgust out before everyone. In the Caucasus, Milyutin had seen how the defeated branded the traitors—not their flesh, but their honor—by spitting spectacular and copious jets of saliva in their faces. He wouldn't give his prisoner the chance to do this. Grabbing him by the elbow—their first physical contact since the child had been kidnapped and wounded—he pulled the child along behind the others in the cortège.

The procession of courtiers followed the emperor, leaving the White Hall, crossed the Marshals' Room, its walls hung with the portraits of the three hundred generals who had defeated Napoleon, and arrived in the Throne Room.

The sight of the Montagnards had so enraged Jamal Eddin that he had paid no attention to the ladies around him in their feathers and finery, nor had he noticed that the czar had offered his arm to someone as they walked on. Now he was in for a new shock.

He did not see the throne. He did not see the tree. All he saw was the empress, standing in the middle of the room as she accepted the good wishes of the court for the New Year. Incandescent beneath her tiara and diamonds, fluttering in her veils, she shone like the bird-woman of the Dagestani legend. Her face set with stones, wearing a necklace of golden fruits, she was like a fiery creature rising with beating wings out of the flames. But in contrast to the monsters of the mountain, this bird-woman did not seem evil at all. She stood in the middle of an immense carpet, more splendid than any he had ever seen, even at the mosque, a carpet of flowers that was like a garden of paradise.

Slim in her radiant gown, with a supple waist and fine wrists, she embodied all the canons of Caucasian beauty as she stood there greeting her guests. Her pale, sweet face, a bit melancholy in repose, lit up with each compliment. Behind her were two girls whose only ornaments were roses. Roses everywhere—in their hair, at belt and bodice. They were the freshest and most beautiful creatures Jamal Eddin had ever seen. Even Milyutin was visibly full of admiration. Behind the princesses were other girls, who were equally modest and well-behaved, if not as pretty.

The members of the council who had gathered in the antechambers entered one by one, followed by the members of the senate, the aides-de-camp, and the generals. All came to kiss the empress's hand and to pay their respects to the children. At the end of this interminable chain, Lieutenant Milyutin and Jamal Eddin would take their turn. They would cross the Throne Room, advance, bow and kiss the hand of—

The child shot a terrified look at his guardian, one of panic that held, beneath it, a veiled threat. Not them, not him! With a barely perceptible gesture, his stance became defensive. It was the boy's second visibly emotional response of the day. Milyutin smothered a smile.

"Let's say Grand Duke Mikhaïl Pavlovitch demanded his presence here to impress him or, better still, to stir his emotions," the lieutenant said to himself. "Well, his method worked, at least better than any of my paltry efforts."

Poor Lieutenant Milyutin, he thought, with an inner chuckle. For four long months, he had been confronted with the placid fatalism of the Orient. It was clear that he had no idea what he was doing, that he was ill-matched for the role. And now? Would he drag Jamal Eddin to the middle of the room, force him to bow with a hand on his head, oblige him to publicly kiss the glove of the idol? He knew the child well enough to know how stubborn he could be. Jamal Eddin would not stand for it, and given the fuss that would ensue, it was scarcely worth the trouble.

So the inauguration of the festivities was over. The participants lined up to enter the chapel. With his protégé, Milyutin ducked into the shadow of the antechamber and let the procession pass.

Nearly a kilometer long, it passed through the interconnecting salons. The visitors never tired of admiring the magnificent furnishings and décor. It took almost two hours for them to reach the chapel.

From afar, a blank sky of snow illuminated the cupola. The sun's rays pierced the dull daylight through the four fenestrae and were reflected by the candles of the chandelier. The emperor and the empress stood together in a box next to the choir, with their seven children and other family members behind them. Farther down were the faithful, who were separated from the sanctuary by a balustrade. The women, whose jewels now seemed a mere echo of the gilt that dripped from pillar, cornice, and vault, stood on one side, the men on the other.

The crowd was quiet and staid. The stoves from the antechambers made the chapel stiflingly hot, and the service went on interminably. The members of the court were so numerous and the chapel so comparatively small that some of the maids of honor could not stand it. Strapped into their corsets since dawn, having fasted before mass, a few of them collapsed without a sound and remained unconscious until the end. Some vomited discreetly into their handkerchiefs, remaining immobile so as not to disturb the service. The doyenne of the *dames de portraits* whispered, in French, "Poor little kitten, she's spurting." Those who found the steam room stuffiness unbearable backed into the last antechamber. There they fanned themselves, exchanged smelling salts, and loosened each other's corsets.

Jamal Eddin and Milyutin, among the last to arrive, observed the mass from this room full of half-undressed women. The spectacle was a sharp contrast to the typical modesty of the feminine world, whose qualities of dignity and propriety the child had witnessed a short while ago while observing the empress.

The boy's face was once again closed and inscrutable, revealing no trace of curiosity.

How to get him out of here? Milyutin searched for a way out of this predicament. He did not dare imagine what a Muslim must think of this display of nudity, these décolletés, these half-bare breasts, this general indecency, unprecedented in his experience. The shock of it all, the shame, must be intolerable. And all of this going on right next to a religious service. Pushing aside a group of maids of honor who were trying to reach the windows, he looked down at the child and realized that his concern was misplaced.

Jamal Eddin was not looking at the sea of uncovered décolletés that surrounded him; he was oblivious to the perfumes, the vinegar, and the smelling salts. Another kind of storm raged beneath his mask of studied indifference. For the third time today, he was overcome with emotion.

He listened.

He listened to the choirs, whose chants made the icons vibrate. There, beneath the cupola, this music was familiar—he recognized the voices of men. They were singing as they did at home, without any instruments accompanying them, since Shamil had forbidden flutes and drums. But at home, when the muezzin called everyone to prayer, it was in a monotone. And when the naïbs prepared for war, they modulated the same sound. There, when the men sang together, they sang the same thing, in rhythmic unison. Here, with the basses providing a steady background, a thousand other melodies combined and contrasted to form an echo that emanated from everywhere.

He listened without daring to move or breathe. It was not just the beauty—the deep, polyphonic harmony—that transfixed him. In an undefined, inarticulate, sensual way, he felt what Milyutin had tried so hard to express to him earlier that day: the empire, the hundreds of thousands of voices of the empire. It gave him goose bumps and brought him close to tears. Though he did not understand it, he listened, and the feeling that the music inspired was like a small flame that reverberated into infinity in an endless series of mirrors.

The choir had begun to sing the *Te Deum.*

The iconostasis opened. The priests, in gleaming tiaras, with their full beards standing out against their long, golden chasubles, paced toward the czar in single file. The monarch descended from his pedestal and walked toward the oldest, the most hunched-over, the weakest of God's representatives, and bowed deeply and respectfully before the elder, kissing his hand.

Jamal Eddin understood this language, and he instantly comprehended its meaning. The Great White Czar was bowing before a principle more powerful than himself. He bowed before God. With this gesture, he set the example of submission for his subjects. He bowed as all the peoples of the universe should bow before him, the shadow of God on earth.

The child understood the symbolism and rejected the message. The power of the infidels was an illusion. Their god was a false god and the czar a vile giaour.

The service was over. Now the entire entourage would go home in their sleighs to rest for a few hours before returning for dinner, the ball, and supper.

With the exception of Lieutenant Milyutin and the "rebel's son," who were to wait here.

In the study of Nicholas I
January 1, 1840

"Well," the czar said, visibly irritated, "is he ready?"

His heart racing with emotion, Milyutin was flustered. He looked at the profile of his master, backlit by the daylight, but could not discern his expression. He recognized only the tall figure, standing there poring over his dossiers, a dozen or so files marked and arranged in a fan on a separate table.

"The son of the Dagestani rebel is awaiting your orders in the antechamber, Your Imperial Majesty."

The czar turned to look at Milyutin, his gaze gray, neutral, devoid of expression.

"I have a great deal of affection for your uncle, Kiselyev. He's a good man. And I have great respect as well for the medal you wear; the pacification of an entire people was an impressive work. My only regret—my profound regret, as a matter of fact—is that Shamil escaped us. Your uncle tells me you too share my concern. We'll see, we'll see."

How had Milyutin dared to compare the czar to the imam earlier? With his high forehead, Greek profile, straight nose, oval face framed by a few short curls combed forward at the temples, and two long, brown sideburns, at forty-three, Nicholas seemed the incarnation of classical beauty and absolute power. The incarnation of the emperor.

The nobility of his features, the coldness of his eyes, something stiff and martial in his demeanor all contributed to his incomparable perfection. He sat down with solemnity, as though being seated on his throne.

He had already changed for the ball and was wearing the uniform of the Gardes-à-Cheval, the most sumptuous of all his costumes.

But even more impressive than his natural bearing and the richness of his costume—a gold-trimmed white tunic on which he wore the respective crosses of the Orders of Saint Andrew, Saint Alexander Nevsky, Saint Vladimir, Saint George, and the Order of the Eagle—was the décor of his surroundings. The room held a single couch, three armchairs, and a flat desk upon which a portrait of the empress and seven miniature pastels of their children were displayed. That was all. The only decorations on the walls were a few engravings and a large icon that had accompanied Peter the Great to the Battle of Poltava. For Milyutin, nothing amid all the splendor of the Winter Palace was nearly as touching as the fact that this man who made the earth tremble in his wake, who could give or take away everything—fortune, liberty, honor, even life—had chosen a simple camp bed with a straw-filled mattress and an old plaid blanket. This sobriety inspired the lieutenant's admiration and love.

"I have here the report of my brother, His Highness the Grand Duke Mikhaïl Pavlovitch, concerning your mission. I have a few comments for you," he said severely. "Let me finish the director of cadets' report, and we'll discuss this calmly."

Indefatigably energetic, as meticulous in nature as he was calculating, hard on others and demanding of himself, the czar had a well-known reputation for attention to detail. He indulged his taste for responsibility and his sense of duty by controlling even the most minor aspects of his administration.

"The emperor of Russia is commander in chief," he liked to say, "and every day of his life is a day of battle. Even the first of the year."

He was taking advantage of this break between the mass and the ball to settle some affairs.

Twilight had fallen. In this narrow room, where the fate of sixty million subjects was decided daily, the only luxury was a vast window that covered an entire wall. The quay of the Neva was dark with crowds, onlookers and passersby who had paused to watch the czar perusing his dossiers on this festive evening. The lights of his ground-floor study would be on until midnight. Everyone knew that the "little father" worked late for the good of his people. And that he would return after the last cotillion.

Nicholas turned to Milyutin again with a distracted look that indicated he had worries other than the one at hand.

"Well?" he repeated. "Did you take him where you were supposed to?"

Milyutin blinked, not sure what he meant.

"I don't know, Your Majesty. I hope so."

"Have him come in. You speak his language, you can serve as interpreter."

"Your Majesty, I spent only six months in the Caucasus, and I—"

"And he, four in Russia," the sovereign interrupted. "Go fetch him, we should be able to understand one another."

In less than a minute, the lieutenant reappeared with Jamal Eddin.

The interview, customarily brief, was over in less than a quarter of an hour.

But twenty-five years later, His Excellency Dmitri Alexeyevitch Milyutin, at that point minister of war, would clearly remember the exchange to which he had been witness and accomplice. In his memoirs, he described the first encounter between the czar and the child as one of searing intensity.

"How are you, my little one? And how is your arm? I've been told it's not healing well. You must let a doctor see the wound. You don't want me to send you back to your father in bits and pieces?"

The boy had looked up. No one dared look the czar in the eye that way. Was it his voice that had affected him, the deep, sonorous voice that his soldiers found so engaging, the voice so accustomed to a commanding tone? Or was it the words that Milyutin tried valiantly to translate, "…send you back to your father?"

"Sit down, there."

Another exception. Only members of the imperial family, intimate friends, and a few ministers were permitted to listen to the emperor expound from an armchair.

The child obeyed and sat down in front of the desk.

"I have some news for you."

One could almost hear Jamal Eddin's heart beating beneath the cartridge belts of his ghizir.

"Some very good news."

He listened, straining to understand. His eyes shone beneath his long lashes, which made them seem even darker as they met the impassive gaze of the Great White Czar in anxious expectation. Soulful and attentive, they questioned him with infinite hope.

"I want you to know that your mama is very well. She gave birth to a baby, a little boy, and his name is Mohammed Sheffi. I'll confirm his name for you when I receive more precise information. Your little brother is fine too. As for your father, he is a great warrior, your father, of a courage and skill one can be proud of."

After having kept the child in heartbreaking ignorance, the czar had just performed a miracle. All at once, he had swept away all his anxiety, reassured him, saved him.

"He even managed to escape from Akulgo. Of course, I'm not surprised. I'm well aware of his reputation for bravery. Had we been able to meet, your father and I, had we been able to discuss things, we would have understood each other. He would have realized that I am not his enemy. But he mistrusts us. I do not blame him. So many iniquitous acts have been committed in my name, so many unspeakable betrayals. In his place, I would have behaved in the same way."

Of any speech he could have imagined, this was the last Milyutin expected. He translated with considerable difficulty, cutting to the essential.

"Now, Jamal Eddin, you must understand one thing: I loathe betrayal and I loathe laziness. At the Alexandrovsky Cadet Corps, you will study under the direction of a very learned mullah. I am expecting great advances in your knowledge of God. The faith of your forbears is your treasure, one you must preserve and prove yourself worthy of. Never forget that it is God who brought you here. You must obey and follow the path He has chosen for you. God is your protector, as He is mine, as He is for each one of us. Nothing can be done here on earth unless He has decided it will be so. You are responsible for your acts before Him. Just as I am responsible before Him for everything that happens in my kingdom. You must conduct yourself here as you would at home, in keeping the memory of His presence. I have confidence in you in this respect, and in many others. And I will give you proof..."

The emperor opened his desk drawer.

Milyutin instantly recognized the object he took out.

"...by returning what belongs to you."

Jamal Eddin paled when he saw what the czar held in his hand.

"I give you back your arms."

Even if Jamal Eddin had been able to speak Russian, this rush of emotion would have left him breathless.

"I am simply asking you not to use it, not against yourself and not against your comrades. Here is your kinjal, you may have it back now."

Jamal Eddin stood up, incredulous. He held out his right hand and took the dagger, nodding his respectful thanks, not daring to sit down again.

Nicholas was touched by the restrained dignity of his gesture, even more so by the expression of boundless gratitude that transfigured the little boy's face. The czar looked down at him kindly.

The czar loved animals. He loved horses and dogs. And he loved his children. He took an active and personal role in their upbringing, treating them with a rigor that was by no means lacking in tenderness. Every day he questioned them about their activities. He was interested in what they were reading and how they were progressing, and he was the one who meted out punishment and rewards. He had just allowed the eldest of his daughters to marry for love, as he himself had done twenty-two years before when he wed the empress. He still considered his wife to be the most remarkable of women. As for his four sons, though he raised them with strict discipline and let them get away with nothing, he was also well aware of the individual merits of each one. The child before him was between his last two sons in age. Perhaps they could grow up together? This boy was noble. He was beautiful. And he was alone and vulnerable. He must be guided and protected.

"You won't try to escape, and you won't hurt anyone. Will you give me your word?"

A faint sign of reproach flickered in Jamal Eddin's eyes.

Did he need anyone to tell him that, if given back his arms, he could neither use them nor take back his freedom? It went without saying. He had been given back his honor. The rest, obviously, followed.

He nodded his agreement with a haughty look.

The czar did not miss the look of remonstrance and changed his tone.

"The next time, Jamal Eddin," he said sternly, "the next time, I expect you to reply 'Yes, Your Imperial Majesty.' Now I shall bid you good evening and ask you to leave. I have a few words for Lieutenant Milyutin."

Jamal Eddin hesitated, unsure of how to take his leave and how to express his gratitude. He bowed deeply, hugging the kinjal to his heart, against the arm that was in a sling, and returned obediently to the waiting room.

He passed in front of the valets in livery and went to perch on the chair he had occupied before his audience with the czar. He sat there, spellbound, alone and immobile, indifferent to the aides-de-camp who came and went, the visitors who would be granted an audience next.

What he felt was so new. Floating in the antechamber, he saw the sweet face of his mother, whom he had feared was dead. Just as he had feared Mohammed Ghazi was dead. During the long journey, he had misunderstood what the giaours had said when they spoke of the massacre of Jawarat and of Saïd. Of so many others.

He pitied his own, but he could no longer feel as sad.

Fatima looked at him with the same faint smile full of love and courage she had shown on the boulder of Akulgo as she had dressed him in white and pulled tight the strap that would hold his kinjal. Shamil had saved her. His father, invulnerable, watched over her, watched over him, watched over all of them. His happiness and his sense of peace were boundless. The Great White Czar had given him back not only his honor, but his hope.

Such was not the case for Milyutin, on the other side of the door.

He had scarcely shut it behind him before he received the first unexpected warning shot across the bow.

"What is that outfit?"

The czar no longer seemed merely irritated. He was furious.

"Where did that costume come from?"

Milyutin glanced down at his uniform in dismay. A missing button or poorly shined boots could send him to Siberia.

"This is the last time I want to see that boy in a Montagnard getup. I never want to see him again in a cherkeska! You will transmit my wishes to the director of the Alexandrovsky institution: this very evening, I want the rebel's son to put on the tunic of the youngest cadets. In no way will he be distinguishable from the others. He may be brought up with all the superstitions of Islam—fine. I am tolerant when it comes to religion. It may actually be of service to us for him to retain his mother tongue and remain the spiritual heir of his father. If trouble arises in the Caucasus again—God help us!—we will make this Muslim our spokesman. The most precious of our intermediaries. And ultimately, who knows, the legitimate successor of the imam? In any case, if, eventually, perhaps one day, we choose to send him back to the mountains, he should return like all his classmates in the corps, like you, like me, like all of us, in the service of Russia. I want him to become the best Russian possible, Russian in body and soul," the czar insisted, "above all, a Russian. Keep me informed as to further developments.

"And the boy must give his dagger back to you. He's just a child, unhappy and lost. I wanted to calm him down, give him a little peace of mind. He will have had time to play with his knife in the antechamber, under the watchful eye of the guards. That will do. In Russia, a child as young as that does not possess a weapon, especially a child like this one, who is scarcely reliable and who has already killed others. Imagine, if he gets into fights with his companions, the risk we'd be taking with the others! Do you understand me? Take back this kinjal immediately.

"You are dismissed."

The tumultuous sounds he heard as he was leaving the Cadet Corps of Tsarskoye Sielo, where he had handed Jamal Eddin over to the teachers, would ring in Milyutin's ears long afterward. The boarding school, which accepted only young children, was run by women: nursemaids, supervisors, and schoolmistresses. The lieutenant had given them his instructions, and then he had fled.

At the foot of the steps, in the snow, he listened to the shouts of the women struggling with the little boy and Jamal Eddin's cries as he tried to explain, in Avar, "The czar gave it back to me! You must not, you have no right, the czar is the one who gave it to me. The czar gave me permission! It's the czar!"

The young officer felt guilty. But what choice did he have? What other order should he have obeyed? Honor commanded him to obey orders.

Obey? He had seen too much at Akulgo. But what could he do? Leave the army? Travel?

Lost in his troubled thoughts, Milyutin picked up the reins of the sleigh.

He sat there, incapable of making the horses move, listening to the protests of Shamil's son. What did honor dictate that Jamal Eddin do? That he give up his kinjal without a fight, as he had promised? Or that he use it to defend himself, as he was trying to do? What laws should he respect from now on?

Once again robbed of what was essential to him, abandoned in a world he did not understand, the child sputtered his first words in Russian and hung on to the only person who had spoken his language.

"It's the czar." He repeated those three words, incontestable proof of what he was trying to explain, three words whose power, on that morning, he could not imagine.

And he was crying, as he had never cried before in his entire life.

CHAPTER VI

Doubt and Heartache

1841–1845

Tsarskoye Sielo
The Alexandrovsky Cadet Corps
The Cemetery and Hospice for Horses at Alexander Park,
a year and a half later
June 1841

It was the hour of the nighttime prayer, the last prayer of the day. The child stood at the dormitory window, his face lifted toward the sky. He was looking for the stars that would indicate the direction of Mecca. But there weren't any stars here, just the moon. How could one glorify God in the shadows, as the Book said? Here, the shadows were white. How could he say the name of the Almighty at dawn or prostrate himself before Him at twilight? Here, the sun never set. And how could he sneak out, under cover of darkness? You could see everything as though it were daylight! This was, indeed, an inconvenience, but it didn't prevent him from escaping, as he did every night.

All the same, there was one advantage to the summer. The heat forced the supervisors to leave open all the windows of the huge wooden building that housed the school. Most of the supervisors were old and deaf and snored in their sleep. He would have no trouble creeping along the eaves, slipping through the hole in the fence, and scampering as fast as his legs could carry him across the silvery plain.

In his full uniform shirt, buttoned at the side Russian-style, he ran barefoot through the pastures. The fog floating over the river in the distance formed white ribbons that reminded him of the mountain streams back home and of the torrents that escaped from the gorges like metallic serpents.

The scent of the prairies was intoxicating, the air full of the perfume of the earth and the heat of the animals. The foliage smelled like the Chechen forests. He knew the way. He kept his eye on the high brick tower he could see over the treetops and headed straight for it. In the midst of the green mass of branches, the red tower shone like fire. He knew it rested on top of another building.

Soon he had reached the corner of the crenellated roof.

The outline of the building's crenel-tiled border against the pearl-colored sky made him think of the terrace of his father's house at Akulgo. A fleeting thought, it was quickly overtaken by another, for here were the stables. These were not the magnificent imperial stables of the Catherine Palace, but a retirement home for old horses, built by the czar just north of his summer residence at the Alexander Palace. The courtiers staying at Tsarskoye Sielo had baptized this new establishment "Les Invalides."

"After the orphanage, the hospice," joked those less fortunate, who rented dachas in the meadows between the

Alexandrovsky Cadet Corps school and Les Invalides of Alexander Park.

Jamal Eddin could not remember which of his classmates had first mentioned the presence of this haven for noble horses less than a verst from the dormitory. On these June nights, Czar Nicholas's Orlovs, the stallions and mares and geldings that had been sent to end their days here, enjoyed the air literally in his own backyard. All these horses that had carried members of the royal family roamed about freely in the vast fields, which His Majesty had had planted with rich grass and clover.

He never tried to enter the building; there was no point. He had peeked through the window and seen that the stalls were empty. But over the stalls lived the caretaker and the grooms. Unlike the teachers at school, they were all young and less inclined to sleep. They had already chased him, and one night, they had nearly caught him.

In the opalescent light, twenty animals crossed the meadow at a leisurely pace, one behind the other. Jamal Eddin watched their dark silhouettes, which cast no shadow on the plain, and was struck once again by their power and beauty. He had never seen anything like them. With their round hindquarters, which shone in the moonlight, their broad breasts, their long necks, and their thick manes, they appeared gigantic.

In fact, everything here seemed gigantic—the carpets, the cupolas, and the crosses, the arrows, the men, the dogs, the animals. And the horses of Tsarskoye Sielo.

In his eyes, the world had exploded and multiplied. He did not consider all that he discovered to be "magnificent," as the giaours always tried to make him admit. The universe of the infidels did not seem more beautiful or more prosperous or even all that different. But big, yes, infinitely vast. He had known the chains of the Caucasus, the interlacing mountains that rose to the sky, barring the horizon, immense mountains whose rose-colored peaks seemed to break through the sun. But they had never crushed him as the massiveness of Russia did. He had known wind and storms, but the wind here made him breathless. It made him feel as though he were being swept away, swallowed up, drowned.

He found this omnipresent sense of oppression exhausting. It took away his spirit. It deprived him of desire and of his will to escape. Nothing attracted him here, not in the fields or anywhere else. The imperious call of the horses was the only thing that brightened his dull spirit and made it respond.

The horses were here. When he spit on his hands and caressed their nostrils, grabbed them gently by the nose and pulled their heads down to his shoulder and murmured his endless litanies in their ears, he was speaking their language. The horses obeyed his voice—just as they had at home.

Among all these magnificent animals was a sorrel mare who was his favorite. She would see him coming from a distance, flatten her ears and charge him from across the field, head down like a bull. He knew this game. She wanted to show him that she was beautiful and still fearsome. He stood his ground. She would stop just before him, turning around him, trying to nip him. But she never actually tore his shirt, and eventually she would turn her back in feigned indifference and trot away. When she had reached just the right distance, she would spin around abruptly and gallop forward to charge him anew. Chestnut coat gleaming and large, black, liquid eyes shining, she would stop just short of him like a streak of fire, rearing and pawing the ground. A display of honor. Her dance over, she would let him approach. He moved slowly, his hand reaching no higher than her muzzle, touching only her mouth. Their saliva blended in his open palm, and he spoke to her in a singsong voice.

"You are proud. Where do you come from? Did you fight in the Caucasus, do you know my mountains? Have you heard of the imam Shamil? At home, we don't ride big horses like you into battle. We prefer little Tartar mares for war. We can jump from one to the other, dismount and remount at a gallop. Otherwise they're like you, noble and faithful. When their riders are wounded and there's nothing they can do, they lie down and serve as a shield for them. They are the first to die. Did you ever lie down to protect your master? You must be very brave if the czar granted you both peace and liberty. He can't be all bad, if he takes care of you even though you no longer serve him. Koura, my horse, has never had clover to eat, not even in the summer, in the clearings in Chechnya. But he had fine legs and his eyes were as beautiful as yours. He could cover fifty versts without a pause, and I'm not exaggerating. Were they the czar's friends too, the ones who are buried among the trees? What wonderful feats did they accomplish? Will you go and sleep with them one day, in this garden?"

He gazed toward the large white slabs aligned along the lane, a little way away. Like the scholars, the ancients, and the saints, the horses in this country were buried in tombs. Their names, forever united with their riders', their dates of birth and of death, and the history of their exploits were all engraved in stone, so that posterity would honor their memory. Jamal Eddin understood. At home, too, the djighits sang of the valiant deeds of their faithful mounts. They mourned their dead companions and honored them. He wouldn't have thought of forcing the little gate that marked the entry to the sanctuary in the shadow of the stables or of climbing over it. Not for any lack of desire or curiosity, but precisely because his intrusion would have amounted to a profanation.

"When you're no longer here, I'll come and visit you in your cemetery. It won't be a sacrilege, because we know and respect each other. But I'm talking nonsense. In a few days, the parade marks the end of the school year, and then, it will be over for me. I'm old, like you. I'm ten years old, and that's the age limit at the orphanage of Tsarskoye Sielo. It looks like they'll send me far away from here, maybe to Saint Petersburg, maybe somewhere else. I don't want to leave you," he murmured with passion, "abandon you the way I had to abandon Koura. How old are you? Let me see your teeth. You're much older than I thought you were. We'll never see each other again."

He had placed his hand lightly on her withers, moved it slowly all along her back to the beginning of her hindquarters. Eyes half-closed, his nose in her mane, he could see the colorless, flat countryside beyond the trees.

"I know you're not strong enough anymore. I know you shouldn't."

With the sure fingertips of a connoisseur, he pressed lightly on the muscles where her rump began. The mare's ears perked up, she snorted a deep breath and turned toward him with her large, black eyes.

"But do you want to? Do you?"

Consumed, like him, with a desire to melt into the plain, she stretched her neck in anticipation.

"One last time?"

He grabbed a clump of mane at her withers, stepped back, and leaped on her back. She took off like a shot. They crossed the field beneath the moon at a silent gallop, a dazzling farewell.

When they reached the fence that separated the field from the cadets' courtyard, he leaned back as though pulling on invisible reins, took his weight off one side, and dug a heel into the other, making her pivot.

"I know, you would have liked to have jumped. And died, perhaps. I understand."

Against her will, he slowed her gait to a walk as they headed back to the stables. He spoke to her softly.

"Don't be afraid of what's going to happen. For the past two years, I've decided I'm already dead. Don't be scared. Imagine, like me, that you're going off to battle, but you're already dead. If you live for one more day, take it as a gift from God. And don't ask for one minute more.

"Yes, you're old, but you're wise too. So tell me something. What should I think of the Great White Czar?"

The First Cadet Corps of Saint Petersburg August 1841–September 1845 "We, the Cadets of the 1840s" By Alexander Alexeyevitch Milyutin

Extracts of an article from a
Moscow military journal from June 1904

"[...] I have been asked to collect my memories and describe our life in the First Cadet Corps of Saint Petersburg in the 1840s, when I shared a room with Jamal Eddin Shamil, the son of the famous imam. I don't feel any particular need to do so, but since I am one of the last surviving members of the class, I acquiesced, and I shall begin.

"My name is Alexander Alexeyevitch Milyutin. I am the youngest of the Milyutins, who gave Russia the reforms we all know. But, unlike my older brothers, I have accomplished nothing that justifies my taking up the pen as I have been asked to do. I did not reorganize the army, like my brother Dmitri Alexeyevitch, nor did I work for the emancipation of the serfs, like my brother Nicholas Alexeyevitch. I wasn't even a childhood friend of Leo Tolstoy, like my brother Vladimir Alexeyevitch.

"A short while after the death of my mother, when I was about ten, our uncle, Count Pavel Dmitrievitch Kiselyev, succeeded in obtaining for me what he had failed to obtain for the others. He convinced the Grand Duke Mikhaïl Pavlovitch to have me accepted as a cadet in the First Corps, the most prestigious military school in the Empire, and the most difficult to be admitted to after the Pages' Corps. The First Cadet Corps only accepted the offspring of the most illustrious families, whose ancestors had been cadets themselves. We stayed there for eight years. When we left, we became officers in one of the imperial family's regiments. The Czar was so fond of this institution that he had his own sons educated there. As for me, I belonged to the minor nobility and I was poor. That Count Kiselyev's patronage should extend to my humble person was a miracle. I was drunk with joy.

"The cadets, friends of my older brothers who often came to my uncle's home, tried to temper my enthusiasm with a few warnings. It was no use, I was swept up in the honor of having been admitted to such a company. For example, they insisted that I should prepare to be beaten by the older cadets. That even if they broke my bones, even if I bled like an ox, I would have to defend myself alone and without complaint. They also told me that, if anyone asked me who had done this to me, I must reply, 'I don't know.' If a superior should punish me for not having answered his question, even if he should beat me, starve me, and put me in solitary confinement, I should still reply, 'I don't know.' In short, they initiated me into what they called 'the rules of Corps life' and assured me that I would suffer at first.

"The school was housed in the Menchikov Palace, just as it is today, next to the Beaux Arts Academy on Vassilievsky Island. It consisted of a complex of austere buildings with several courtyards, stables, an equestrian ring, and huge rooms for fencing and gymnastics. Although it seemed immense at first, I soon found it cramped.

"I was placed in what was called a 'company without specialty,' reserved for those who had not yet decided whether they would serve in the infantry, the artillery, or the cavalry. When I presented myself before this company, there wasn't a single bed available, and all the other companies' dormitories were full as well. For this reason, I was put up in a big separate bedroom that was reserved for the Cherkess students, about twenty of them. The bed I was assigned was next to that of Shamil's son. I had heard his story from my brother Dmitri, who had told me about the siege of Akulgo.

"Jamal Eddin Shamil had just arrived from the Alexandrovsky Cadet Corps where he had been for almost two years. He had been admitted here at the Czar's expense, out of his own purse, with two other orphans (whose names I still remember: Pavel Kolosov and Alexi Kirdan), either due to their excellent academic results or their superiority at physical exercises. I suspect the latter was the case for Jamal Eddin, for his classmates took great pleasure in describing how he distinguished himself on his first day at the Alexandrovsky Corps by refusing to be undressed by any of the teachers or to be touched or even approached by a doctor. And that, despite his recurring problems with discipline, he had become the glory of the school, unbeatable in the long jump, leapfrog, mountain races, and rope climbing. To hear them tell it, his exploits surpassed all the records of all the cadets of every age since the creation of the orphanage. As for equitation, at the year-end review in the big ring at Tsarskoye Sielo, Czar Nicholas, who prided himself on being the best horseman of his generation, saw him in the saddle. A glance at Jamal Eddin was enough to make him understand that this was not a ten-year-old on a horse but a magnificent centaur, straight out of mythology—and in the future, an incomparable cavalry officer.

"The three new cadets from the Alexandrovsky Corps had arrived in Saint Petersburg a few weeks before me. Though I felt far inferior to the other cadets, by wealth and by birth, I felt close to these three.

"Our great preoccupation was the 'uniform question.' As long as we weren't wearing a uniform, we weren't considered cadets. My uncle had neglected this detail. As for my three friends, their uniforms had been sent back to their old school so that the Director could hand them down to other orphans. The administration gave Pavel Kolosov and Alexi Kirdan old jackets to wear during the time it took for the tailor to make them new ones. As for Jamal Eddin Shamil, the administration returned his Circassian costume to him. He was dressed as a Cherkess, placed in the Cherkess dormitory, and treated like a Cherkess. The very fact of being able to wear his cherkeska again made Jamal Eddin fervently grateful. It almost made him happy.

"He now spoke Russian without any accent and his years at Tsarskoye Sielo had inured him to the 'rules of Corps life': lie to one's superiors, defend one's friends, never denounce another cadet. He had mastered these rules to perfection and took me under his wing.

"Some of the hazing was really out of line, but the supervisors did nothing to stop it. As long as a new boy did not explicitly complain and reveal the names of his aggressors, they looked the other way. As first years, we couldn't go out for the first six months anyway, as that was the period before our first examination. During those six months, we had time to get ourselves in shape. Those who didn't, those who died from the harsh treatment and those who were crippled for life, weren't made for the Russian army anyway.

"Jamal Eddin and I were the same age, but he was more mature, taller and slimmer and much more agile. It wasn't just that he was as lithe as a cat; in addition to being supple, he was swifter than anyone I'd ever seen, even more so than his compatriots. He never let anyone hurt me and sent anyone who expressed any inclination to pick a quarrel with me to the devil. He knew how to fight, how to kick and fight with his fists, but when his adversaries ganged up on him—he was, after all, young in comparison to the twenty-year-old cadets—the other Cherkesses came to his rescue.

"The Cherkesses in our dorm room got along well among themselves, and all of them liked to wrestle. I often participated in their fights [...].

"I admired Jamal Eddin so much, and I was so grateful to him that, one day, I decided I wanted to show him that I knew how to defend myself if anyone ever bothered me. So I intentionally elbowed a cadet who happened to be passing in the hall. The cadet turned around and called me a 'Dutchman,' an insult reserved for those of us who didn't have uniforms yet. In response, I punched him in the nose. He started to bleed and went to the supervisor to tell on me. When the supervisor came to find me, I got scared. I didn't know what to say. That was when Jamal Eddin intervened. He said it wasn't my fault, that the older boy had pinched me and hit me and that I had only shoved him to defend myself. The older boy was unjustly given a caning. Jamal Eddin, judging him guilty of having complained to a superior, let the punishment take its course.

"To our surprise, the older boy didn't hold it against us; thanks to us, he was promoted to 'corporal.' You see, the cadets did not consider those who had never been whipped to be real cadets. Only the first caning conferred the title of cadet. The second enabled one to move on to corporal, and the third to noncommissioned officer. And so on.

"Six months after arriving, Jamal Eddin was already a Field Marshal, which signified that he had been beaten eighteen times. I remember a certain Count Buxhöwden, a long-time Field Marshal, who was beaten every week. This was a problem, because there was no higher rank of the army to promote him to. So we invented children for him, entire generations that could continue to rise through the ranks in his place. Every time Buxhöwden was caned, we imagined for example that it was his son who was promoted to first cadet, then NCO, and so on. When Buxhöwden's son had made Field Marshal, it was his grandson's turn to take over. After fifty-four beatings, Buxhöwden gave birth to a great-grandson who began a new career with us.

"Buxhöwden was two or three years older than we were and belonged to an illustrious family from the Baltics. He became Jamal Eddin's friend and remained so throughout our studies. I don't know what became of him, but if he is still alive today, he would surely have memories to share with our readers about daily life at the Cadet Corps.

"After a while—readers will forgive an old head like mine if I mix up the years a bit—when I finally had my uniform jacket, to my great dismay, they placed another bed in between Jamal Eddin's and mine. This bed was assigned to a boy named Youssouf, who was the son of a wealthy khan who had allied himself with the Czar. His father had presented Youssouf at the Russian Court with great pomp, in hopes that the Czar would take him under his protection. Youssouf and Jamal Eddin despised each other immediately.

"Several months after Youssouf had settled in—probably a year or so after our arrival, in 1842 or 1843—Czar Nicholas made one of his surprise lightning visits to the school. These unexpected visits terrified the director, who always had a guard posted at the Isakievsky Bridge to warn him. The problem was that the Emperor came into town every day, alone or with a few aides-de-camp, to 'breathe the air of his capital.' He drove in in his summer carriage or his little sleigh in the winter, and generally made a quick loop. When the sentinel arrived, breathless, with the terrible news that the Czar was headed in this direction, we had only a few minutes to prepare ourselves.

"The Czar's arrival filled everyone with dread. Even the cadets who had done nothing wrong felt guilty. The smallest transgression could incur the severest of sanctions. There was no such thing as a venial sin. He visited each class, interrupting the courses with irrelevant questions that we answered, terrified, with nonsense.

" 'Don't disturb the order of the day,' he'd say. 'Just go on as if I weren't here.'

"I remember his rage at the conduct of Cadet Buxhöwden—our Field Marshal with the long line of descendants—who forgot himself in His August Presence and leaned his elbow on the desk during a lesson. As a result, the Czar immediately demanded that his teacher be sacked. As for Count Buxhöwden, he earned another great-great-great-grandson.

"This time, after having visited the house, His Majesty came to our room, the dormitory of the Cherkesses. He walked up to Youssouf and asked him amiably how he was, and had he received any letters from home?

" 'No,' replied Youssouf.

"The Czar turned to the director, furious, and barked, 'Teach him how to speak correctly!'

"Then he turned to Jamal Eddin and put his hand on his shoulder.

" 'If you would like to write to your father, you may do so, my boy. I grant you authorization and will personally see to it that your letters reach him.'

" 'I am happy to thank Your Imperial Majesty,' Jamal Eddin replied, politely and spontaneously.

" 'You have learned how to express yourself suitably. Bravo, my boy. And your arm, is it better? Show me.'

"Jamal Eddin quickly pushed up the sleeve of his cherkeska and revealed his scar, between the wrist and elbow of his left arm, which had healed well.

" 'That's perfect. Continue on this path. I'll be back soon to have a look at your progress and collect your letters.'

"Then His Majesty left, leaving us all breathless.

"Jamal Eddin did not revel in the Czar's favor, but acted instead as though he found it perfectly natural. He refused to take part in any of our games from then until the next imperial visit. Instead, he holed up in a corner and wrote frenetically, covering sheet after sheet of stationery. He was probably afraid that the Czar would return before he had finished his letter to his father.

"Jamal Eddin remained a mystery to me. He never confided in me. All I knew of him was what my brother Dmitri had told me. I don't think he even revealed his feelings to Buxhöwden, his best friend, of whom I was jealous.

"He was fiercely sensitive, and dignified, in a haughty way that sometimes made him aggressive—and dangerous to anyone who insulted him or was suspected of doing so. But he knew how to laugh and have a good time, too. He had an instinctive curiosity about everything around him and was always game for pranks and mischief. A great teaser, and an excellent comrade. In other circumstances, I believe he really would have been full of joie de vivre. He liked to clown around, especially on horseback, when he became downright impish and droll.

"But his own lightheartedness seemed to shock and displease him, and he tried to contain it. When he found he was enjoying something too much, as was often the case, when he was learning how to draw, for example, or how to dance—he was the best dancer, the most agile of all of us—sooner or later he would become annoyed with himself and tone it down. He stifled his own impulses and, in the end, he always tried to break himself.

"As for his arm, though he had scars all over both of his arms, this wound that the Czar knew about had attracted our curiosity. As usual, he was very discreet about it, and we had to worm it out of him. He told us, with great reserve and difficulty, that a Cossack of the Don had wounded him with a lance when his family was escaping from Akulgo. His family had managed to get away when he, Jamal Eddin, had fallen from his horse. That was when he had been captured and made a prisoner.

"I think he doctored the truth a little and mixed up several incidents, because he couldn't admit that his own people had given him up. He still couldn't bear the idea.

"But I did not understand that until later, in our room, when Youssouf, humiliated by the Emperor's remarks and probably envious, started shouting that, if Jamal Eddin was in Russia, it wasn't because he had been captured when he was running away, but because he had been betrayed and given away by his father.

"The fight that followed cost them both dearly.

"As luck would have it, after the Czar left, our company had been assigned a new captain—Captain Argamakov, also known as The Beast—who loved the sight of blood. The usual punishment for insubordination was twenty-five lashes with the cane. But twenty-five lashes from Argamakov were like the knout used in public beatings of true delinquents. In this case, the punishment was forty lashes for each of the two Muslims.

"The problem with Argamakov's thrashings wasn't so much the pain as the splinters they left all over you. He chose birch sticks covered with short, dry shoots three or four centimeters in length, and these cut deeply into the flesh during the flogging. If we did not remove the splinters immediately, they would get infected, and then we could do nothing—they would only emerge on their own, with the pus. But by that time, they could have made a person very sick. The doctor had advised the proctors to make Argamakov's switches more flexible by soaking them in water. So they did the easiest thing and left them on the floor in the toilets. As a result, the infections caused by the filthy canes were even more serious. The only way to limit the damage was to bribe the guard to let us into the shed where The Beast kept his damned switches. Then, with utensils stolen from the refectory, we could cut off all the shoots to make what Jamal Eddin called 'velvet canes.' He could make a hatchet out of a spoon and knew better than anyone how to sharpen knives. Before exams, we got very busy with this task, because we knew our bad grades would inevitably lead to more beatings. Jamal Eddin called these secret sessions of honing the canes 'cramming.' Unfortunately for him and for Youssouf, we didn't have a chance to hone or prepare anything, since their punishment was carried out on the spot.

"This was unusual. Monday was caning day for the youngest cadets, Saturday for the oldest. The administration had not chosen these days by chance. The wounds of those who had been caned on Monday had a whole week to heal before they went home on Sunday. Saturday's canings meant being restricted on Sunday, so those cadets would have time to rest before the beginning of the week. The director's goal was obviously to send the cadets back to their illustrious families in acceptable condition. However, this thinking did not apply to the Cherkesses. If they ever left the Corps at all, it was only on the rare occasions when they were invited to the barracks of the Montagnards of His Majesty's Personal Guard. Usually, the Montagnards came to the school to pay obligatory visits. The Grand Duke Mikhaïl Pavlovitch had instituted a weekly visit from the Muslim officers, so that the children would not forget their native dialects.

"So Jamal Eddin took off his cherkeska and was the first to lie down flat on the bench, his torso bare. Argamakov had picked three older students known for their strength to beat him.

" 'Go for it, but not just on the back and the buttocks, hit him between the legs too. As hard as possible—with the end of the canes—there, between the thighs!'

"The canes whistled through the air, delivering their splinters to the most sensitive places. His pants were soon soaked with blood. When the older boys didn't strike him with enough energy, or when Jamal Eddin closed his legs too tightly for the switches to reach his bottom, Argamakov bellowed, 'On his privates! Harder! Come on! Anybody else object? Silence, or else you'll all get it. Go on, hit him on his privates!'

"Jamal Eddin did not cry out. He did not make a sound, and he did not even flinch as the blows rained down on him. I suppose he'd seen worse in the Caucasus. The Beast's switches probably seemed like small stuff compared to the imam's whip. This ultimate act of bravado, his silence, cost him two more points on his grade for discipline. He didn't care though—he'd already endured the worst at that point.

"Youssouf, though, couldn't stand the shock. Like so many before him, he howled with pain until he passed out.

Argamakov's canes made him so sick that they had to send him to the infirmary. There he caught cold. The climate of Saint Petersburg didn't agree with the Cherkesses. A lot of them caught pneumonia, some of them consumption. That was probably what happened to Youssouf. They told us he had been sent home, and that he died shortly thereafter.

"Jamal Eddin was more somber than I had ever seen him. I guess he blamed himself for having brought misfortune to a Muslim, a boy who was one of his own people, even though Youssouf had been the incarnation of the traitor, because he belonged to the clan of the pacified who opposed the imam Shamil.

"And speaking of treason, I may be wrong, but I think he was obsessed by the idea, the fear of his own betrayal, of being a traitor. Fear of forgetting all that his father had taught him, fear of forgetting the past and the laws of his religion. This confused feeling of guilt, far from fading with time, grew greater the more and the better he adapted to the world around him.

"After Youssouf left, a certain incident bothered him for a long time. He was asked to turn in his cherkeska—the costume he had worn for over a year—and to wear the cadets' jacket again. He asked for an explanation and resisted as best he could, but to no avail. The worst, for him, was that the uniform suited him perfectly. He really looked like a Russian, and we told him so without irony. In his green tunic and cap, with silver buttons, a red officer's collar and shoulder straps, he was magnificent. And I was thrilled! Now there were two of us in the dorm, two cadets among the Circassians. He didn't understand the reason for this change, though, and it annoyed him and made him touchy.

"I finally discovered why he was asked to give up his cherkeska when I was researching this article. I came across a note, preserved in our archives, from the director of the Alexandrovsky Corps to our director. It is dated August 22, 1842, and it goes without saying that Jamal Eddin was never aware of this correspondence concerning him. The reader will no doubt understand:

" *'During my last visit to Your Excellency's establishment, on August 17th, the day of the distribution of gifts, I noted, as I passed through the halls, that former Alexandrovsky Corps student Jamal Eddin Shamil was wearing the costume of the Cherkess Montagnards. I should inform you that I made inquiries to the hierarchy regarding what dress the Dagestani rebel's son should wear at my school. I was made aware of a precise order from His Majesty on the matter, an order from January 1, 1840, indicating that the boy should wear the uniform of the cadets. This order was respected at my establishment, but it is not being followed at yours. I am therefore warning you of this serious breach of orders so that you may remedy it and dress the rebel's son according to His Majesty's will.'*

"Even though Jamal Eddin had been dressed like a Montagnard when the Czar had come to visit—and the Czar had made no comment about his dress at that time—our director was quick to obey the monarch, who punished any and all with the same adage: 'I cannot permit an individual, whoever he is, to dare to oppose my wishes once he is aware of them.'

"As for our studies, what is there to say? Jamal Eddin always managed to pass from one class to the next and never had any difficulties with his studies, as far as I know. His grades were average, except in gymnastics and all the martial arts, in which, of course, he excelled. They were terrible in discipline, and quite good in mathematics. I remember he was fascinated by physics, especially anything that had to do with electrical phenomena. Like all the Cherkesses in the dormitory, he was instructed in the Muslim faith and in the drawing of General Staff maps. I wondered why maps and plans were so important for the people in my dorm. I understood only much later, when I realized that one of the purposes of educating the Montagnards was to turn them into informers who would be capable of giving us precise information as to the disposition of rebel strongholds.

"As for our teachers, there were perhaps ten out of sixty who were of any use at all. The worst were the French, nicknamed 'The Drums,' and the Germans, whom we called 'The Butchers.' Even the cadets who spoke one of their languages when they arrived at the school managed to forget it in their presence. Our masters taught us the art of strategy with a strangely nationalistic bent. They informed us that our arms were the most sophisticated in all of Europe and that our uniforms were suitable for the North Pole as well as an equatorial climate. And that the Emperor's long greatcoat—that famous gray tunic His Majesty wore all the time—offered equally adequate protection from the sun and the cold. In sum, every element of our army had been so perfectly and intelligently planned, down to the last detail, that a Russian soldier could travel the world without ever enduring any discomfort.

"Our days began at six with the bugle sounding reveille and ended at ten with a group prayer. The cafeteria food was disgusting and the schedule inordinately heavy. Our courses included military history, the art of fortification, geography, topography, horsemanship, mechanics, chemistry, and on and on. And that doesn't even include art, music, and dance, or fencing, equitation, and maneuvers.

"In spite of this impressive curriculum, we learned nothing. Our only real interest was a close study of our masters' weaknesses and how to exploit them. Apart from the first-year hazing, we were very united as a group, a solid bloc against the adversary. I don't know if the famous motto of Alexander Dumas was inspired by ours, but if I were to sum up my youth, it would be with those words that were carved on every step of the stairway: *All for one, and one for all.* We, the First Corps cadets every one of us, were occasionally bad sons, sometimes bad brothers, perhaps bad fathers and husbands, but we were never bad comrades. In this respect, I daresay that Jamal Eddin was an exemplary cadet. He placed the honor of the Corps above personal considerations, and there were no limits to his capacity for self-sacrifice in the name of friendship.

"As for vices, we didn't drink and we didn't gamble much, which suited him. But we gave blow for blow and insult for insult, and that suited him too. And we knew that we could get rid of an instructor by bungling our exercises on the parade ground, knowing it would result in his demotion.

"When Argamakov unjustly punished Buxhöwden one time too many, we decided the time had come to exact revenge. It was springtime, and the grass in the fields was high. We split up into two groups. One group ripped out the grass by the handful, and the others used the bunches of grass to write on the school wall: ARGAMAKOV, BASTARD. This inscription in bright green, which could be seen from one end of the garden to the other, upset our superiors. You never knew when the Czar might show up, and he would have immediately observed that the letters were not the work of a single culprit. He would have noted that we would have had to have climbed by the dozens, one on top of another's shoulders, tufts of grass in hand, to write those words so high up. It was obvious that this huge BASTARD, visible from all over, was the work of the entire Corps.

"The incident reached the ears of our inspector, the Grand Duke Mikhaïl Pavlovitch, who in turn told his brother, the Czar. A few days later, His Majesty arrived and called the entire Corps into the yard. He had us do a few exercises, which we accomplished to perfection, as usual. His reaction was to shout, 'Terrible! Unacceptable! Get them out of here.'

"He was furious and immediately went to see the director. He had barely crossed the threshold of his office before raging at the director, 'Things are not going well at all here! Laxity is rampant! It's time for them to shape up, and it's up to you to see that they do!'

"Shaping up began immediately. Our teachers made the transition from harsh to cruel, and there was no reprieve. But when Argamakov made the mistake of calling one of the cadets an imbecile, the insult shook the entire company. All the cadets, on all sides, began shouting, 'Imbecile yourself! Out with The Beast!'

"We started tapping the floor with our stools and shaking the tables. And when he cried, 'Attention!', we answered him with whistles of disapproval. In short, the word the Czar dreaded most—revolution—seemed to be materializing.

"Word of the incident spread throughout Saint Petersburg. Soon there were rumors that the First Corps cadets had thrown stools at an officer's head, that they had broken his arm, beaten him on the head, and all kinds of other wild tales.

The Czar demoted all of us, forbade us from going out on Sundays, and from receiving visitors for the remainder of the school year. The Grand Duke Mikhaïl Pavlovitch hurried to the school. He had the Corps line up in three rows in the courtyard.

" 'Rebels, you have forgotten your discipline. Do you want to become soldiers? On your knees!'

"A murmur rippled through the lines, 'Not on our knees! Not on our knees!'

"For the cadets of the First Corps, being forced to kneel was the pinnacle of shame. One brave cadet had recently opted to be beaten to death rather than go down on his knees. Another had agreed to serve as a soldier for twenty-five years rather than to kneel. It was a rule of honor. Those among our superiors who had been cadets themselves never inflicted this abject punishment; it was an indignity that no cadet could accept without dying of shame. Didn't the Grand Duke Mikhaïl Pavlovitch know this?

"He continued to shout the order, the only one we could not obey. 'On the ground before me, band of traitors! On your knees, all of you!'

"Thank heavens, he saved the day himself. He demonstrated by example, falling to his knees and crossing himself, as though he were kneeling before an icon. Before God, we gladly debased ourselves. Before God, we could kneel with humility. The entire Corps, including the Cherkesses, knelt submissively around the Grand Duke.

" 'Only God can help you obtain the pardon of the Emperor now. Pray to the Lord that the Czar will pardon you.'

"After praying, he ordered us to get up and gather around him for a sincere discussion. We knew that this was a trap designed to ferret out the leaders and that we should not enter into any kind of discussion with him. Mikhaïl Pavlovitch had a horror of any disorder or lack of discipline. Even more than the Czar, his contempt for anything resembling criticism or resistance was boundless. Anyone who attempted to justify our conduct would be subjected to the severest punishment. In his eyes, we were guilty of the ultimate crime: insubordination.

"Jamal Eddin stepped forward. With his usual poise and courtesy, he assured His Imperial Highness that we were not rebels. He knew he was taking a great risk. He knew that we all feared what might happen to him, that he might be expelled and, in his case, subjected to even further sanction. He explained that there had been no conspiracy on our part, that this was not a revolt but a spontaneous protest against the cruelty of the officers, whose harassment the cadets had been putting up with for many long years. He pointed out that the honor of the Cadet Corps was continuously scorned by our uncouth, ill-bred officers. He, a man of normally so few words, pleaded our case so eloquently that the Grand Duke listened to him. Jamal Eddin ended his discourse brilliantly by begging the Grand Duke to please tell the Czar that the cadets were praying to the Almighty that His Majesty might forgive them.

"A month later, the Czar appeared again. He inspected the school and seemed satisfied with the order of things. Officially, nothing had changed. But as a result of Jamal Eddin's speech, the officers were ordered to temper their zeal and behave in a more civilized fashion. A few months after the Czar's visit, we were forgiven. Our demotions were lifted and we regained our original ranks. The story of the grass-painted letters was forgotten.

"But for Jamal Eddin, the opportunity to present his precious letter to the Czar never occurred again. He kept writing nevertheless. Did he really think that the Emperor would have it delivered to his father, when Shamil had made his reappearance in Chechnya and was massacring our soldiers with unprecedented efficiency? The order had come from higher up to hush up news of our enormous losses in the Caucasus, so we knew nothing of what was taking place down there. Not yet.

"I spent nearly three years as Jamal Eddin's roommate in the Cherkess dormitory. Though he said little during the day, he was a real chatterbox at night. He dreamed out loud, and his muttering, in Russian, with Avar mixed in, often kept me awake. I never wanted to tell him that. And I never, never dared to ask him the meaning of the word that kept recurring in his dreams, that he kept repeating over and over. He wouldn't have answered me, and I know that he would scarcely have slept after that had I done so. When I tried to repeat the word to my brother Dmitri, he didn't understand it. I confess, I did not look any further. Today, sixty years later, I present it to our readers, the way I believe I heard it. I'd be grateful if someone could tell me what it means.

"The word was *bachou* [...]."

The First Cadet Corps of Saint Petersburg March 1845

"Bahou, Bahou-Messadou, are you the mountain torrent that I dream of every night?

"No day passes without my heart crying out your name. Every time the cane whistles through the air, every time the lash cuts into the skin of one of my comrades, it is your back that takes the blows, your flesh they gash. Every time blood spurts from those wounds, I see you in my mind's eye, kneeling beneath the pillory at Akulgo. I hear you weep and my lost soul sobs with you.

"But at night, is it really you, Bahou? Is it you who sends me these visions, like the saints of the believers who pray and fall asleep on their tombs? Where are you now? Do you come down from the gardens of paradise to visit me in my dreams?

"In my dreams, you are no longer there in body and voice. You are the river that flows beneath the bridge at Ghimri, you are the Andi Koysu that roils and rumbles and breaks against the boulders. You are not deserted, you are not empty. Mirrors of gold, plates, bracelets, sabers and their sheaths rise from your depths. The crests of your waves carry alabaster dishes, as white and pure as the foam. The most beautiful kinjals are swept along with the flow. They drift and swirl between the rocks. But you, the river of Ghimri, instead of sending them to disappear at the bottom, you throw them at my feet, on the riverbank. Then you recede, leaving me alone with this treasure that sparkles blindingly, and you forget about me. You have given me the lost sabers of the khans but you continue on your way, pure and limpid. What are you trying to tell me? I searched in the Book, but I found no answer. I asked the mullah, also in vain.

"Compared to Sheik Jamaluddin al Ghumuqi, he knows nothing, and I don't trust him. When I asked him why music is forbidden for the true believers, why I should not listen to the song of a piano, why I should not learn how to play, he told me that, on the contrary, music is the creaking of the hinges that open the doors to paradise. But if that were true, my father would not have pierced all the drums. So he tells me that there are different sorts of music. That some can excite the soul and lead it to places it shouldn't go. That what may seem right in the Caucasus, what we feel is good, isn't necessarily so in Saint Petersburg. How can this be? There is only one law, the Sharia—and the Sharia forbids music and dance.

"According to him, life is so hard in our mountains and time so precious that men cannot permit themselves to be softened, their attention to God distracted, by music. But here in Petersburg, where time isn't quite so dear, where the day goes on all through the night, where war is far away, music opens the heart and elevates it. He says that music here is a hymn to the Almighty, a way of thanking Allah for the life he has granted us. He says that all of the wonderful things that surround us here are a gift of the Lord, and that by naming his son Jamal, which means 'beauty,' and Eddin, which signifies 'religion,' my father agrees with him.

"I don't believe it. He's lying. He serves the infidels. And that is why the infidels have made him our guide. So he will trick us, mislead us, and send us down the wrong path.

"When he says that the Russians here are not like the Russians at home, on this point, he's right. If my father were to meet the czar, I am sure that he would love him and respect him. The czar is noble and just and generous. Look at the way he treats his prisoners. See how he treats me. The giaours are not all as worthless as we think, Bahou. Yes, their women dance, they wear perfume and décolletés. And yet the empress conducts herself with the utmost modesty and dignity. She behaves honorably, and her sons respect her.

"Is this an illusion? An artifice of the devil? Should I despise her and all the other giaours? Buxhöwden's friendship, and Milyutin's, are they a trap? Should I not trust them? Bahou, answer me, tell me how to act. All this treasure at my feet, the gold borne on the waves, should I throw it back into the Andi Koysu or should I pick it up and keep it? Tell me, what do you ask of me?"

The Palace of Count Kiselyev in Saint Petersburg on the day of the feast of Saint Dmitri September 21, 1845

"This place is a regular boarding house," Count Pavel Dmitrievitch Kiselyev commented as he watched the flames of the smoking room ceiling light flicker with the resounding cavalcade upstairs.

The pink-and-white reflection of the sumptuous Zurova-Kiselyev Palace on the Moïka Quay shimmered in the water of the canal. This year, the feast of Saint Dmitri had taken on a special luster, and with good reason. For Count Pavel Dmitrievitch, this twenty-first of September, 1845, there was more to celebrate than just the memory of the family's patron saint. Tonight he was welcoming home his beloved nephew, who had just returned from his second campaign in the Caucasus. Dmitri Alexeyevitch came home as perplexed as the first time, but now he was also in love, married, and full of plans for the future.

Two years earlier, he had fallen for Natalia, the daughter of General Poncet, and they had hastily married just before he was called back to his post. Their newlywed bliss had been ephemeral. His young wife had stayed in Saint Petersburg, while he had been forced to leave her for a solitary and tragic reunion with the mountains of Dagestan. But those dark days were over, and Dmitri was alive.

Although seasoned by hardship, at twenty-nine, Dmitri still had the candid gaze of a much younger man. His thick, ash-blond curls had scarcely darkened and remained as unruly as ever, a neat part on the side and brilliantine notwithstanding. It was a bit too long at the nape of the neck for the count's taste, but that was of no importance. Dmitri was there, seated beside him in the smoking room before the hearth. And this evening, Kiselyev was giving a big party in his honor.

There would be a dinner, a ball, and supper, festivities that all the generations could enjoy. On this occasion, the youngest of the Milyutin brothers, the fourteen-year-old Alexander Alexeyevitch—Sacha—had been given permission to invite one or two of his schoolmates from the First Cadet Corps. He had begged to extend the invitation to two more of his closest friends, pleading that Saint Dmitri's fell on a Sunday and that, because their illustrious families were far away, these boys were consigned to remain at the corps every weekend of the year. It would only be charitable, kind Christian charity, to invite them to the celebration. Cleverly skirting the whole truth, he named only two of his guests: Grand Duke Mikhaïl Nicolaïevitch, who was his age, and Grand Duke Nicholas Nicolaïevitch, who was a year younger. Their dear mama, the empress, had gone to Italy for her health at the beginning of the summer and their father, Czar Nicholas, unable to do without her, had followed. Czarevitch Alexander, who was filling in for the emperor as head of state during his absence, scarcely had time to take care of his little brothers.

The excellent company Sacha kept no doubt influenced the count. He did not ask for the names of the other two boys but simply signed his name, authorizing leave for all four of them.

Another rumble shook the ceiling light.

"What on earth are they doing up there? At fourteen, one should know how to behave! If they keep this up, they'll make the candles fall and set the place on fire."

"Sacha is so excited this evening," Kiselyev said gaily, reassuming the tone that matched his mood, "I suppose he can't wait to welcome you home."

A smile played about the count's lips.

"Unless it's the prospect of being around all these demoiselles that has them all in such a state of excitement. I have invited a few girls their age. I've been told they're as lovely as can be."

Now it was Dmitri's turn to smile. Women, his uncle's great weakness. He had dreamed of them so and loved them so. Clearly he could imagine the excitement of the five adolescents getting ready upstairs, combing their hair in front of the mirror. The count would probably feel the same way when he dressed for the evening a short while later.

"You can go up and see your little brother in a little while. I told him to stay upstairs with his buddies and not to come down until the girls arrive. We can still enjoy a few hours of peace and quiet. My dear child, I've thought of you so much. I wanted to set aside a little time to have you all to myself. You were right, weren't you? Things aren't going well down there."

In the past week since his return, Dmitri had avoided talking about the war, reluctant to bore his entourage with his tales. But the count had appealed to his patriotic feelings in an intimate conversation between officers, and he couldn't resist the need to confide in him for long.

"Shamil has taken most of the mountain passes between Dagestan and Chechnya. He and his troops circulate freely between the two regions."

Sitting on the couch behind the card tables that were already set for games, the count pulled on his big cigar. With his legs comfortably crossed, he listened attentively.

He knew that Dmitri was thinking of leaving the army, but he thought that would be a mistake. A folly, especially when the young man's career was just taking off. His courageous actions in the Chechen forests had earned him a promotion to captain, and he was being considered for the Cross of Saint George. Dmitri might criticize his superiors, but they appreciated him. Now he was toying with the idea of resigning from the army and finishing the work he had begun on those long nights of watch duty in his tent in Chechnya: a book on the Caucasus. Well, why not? With time, Dmitri had come to know the region well, both its geography and its customs. After every battle, when every massacre was over, he had recorded what he had seen, continuing with the reflections that he had begun after the siege of Akulgo. But his personal experience was not enough, and with his usual enthusiasm, he had begun to research the subject thoroughly, delving into documentary sources. He dreamed of offering his suggestions to the czar and helping Russia to end this war. His greatest hope was to conclude a lasting peace. Yes, why not?

But there was no point in abandoning the service. Dmitri could just as well write his report—his book, if you will—without leaving the regiment. The count was ready to facilitate his task. His guests this evening had been chosen with precisely this project in mind. He had invited the relatives, the acquaintances, and all the friends who had ties in one way or another to the history of the Caucasus and who could provide Dmitri with information. The grand aristocrats of the Bagration dynasty, who had joined the ranks of the Russian army and fought the Muslims ever since Georgia had been annexed by Czar Alexander forty-five years before, would be coming. The members of the general staff of the new viceroy who had just been posted to Tiflis, Count Mikhaïl Vorontsov, would be there too. And he was expecting the officers of the regiments on the line, who were on leave. There would be plenty of "Caucasian youth" on hand.

The count had extended the evening's theme to the female guests as well. The princesses of the Georgian royal family, granddaughters of the last king, George XII, would be chaperoned by their mother, Princess Anastasia, who was an old friend. Born Princess Anastasia Grigorïevna Obolenskaïa, the princess had once been a great beauty. Now forty years old, she had thirteen children—eight girls and five boys—a gold mine for adolescent balls. Although her husband, Prince Ilya of Georgia, held the rank of Serene Highness and lived in Moscow, their three eldest daughters attended the Smolny Institute, which was reserved in principle for the daughters of the impecunious aristocracy of Saint Petersburg. Said to be even more breathtaking than her mother had been, Anna, at seventeen the eldest, had just been received at court as a maid of honor to the empress. Of course, all that was of no interest to Dmitri, who had already met his soul mate. But his second brother, the handsome twenty-seven-year-old Nicholas Alexeyevitch Milyutin, preferring a civilian career to the army, had chosen a more difficult path. And Volodia, the third, was at the university, supposedly studying philosophy. Perhaps Nicholas and Volodia would find an advantageous match among this evening's guests, one that far exceeded their expectations. One could always dream.

Encouraged by the count's questions, the guest of honor was not mulling over any of these urbane considerations.

"We're losing ground and retreating everywhere," Dmitri sighed. "In a single year, Shamil's bands have taken fifteen fortified towns and twenty-seven cannons."

"A disaster, I know, I know. And the czar is at the end of his patience. Every Monday, at the council meeting, he explodes, demanding that we have done with it. In this respect, you should note that the czar has taken what you once termed the 'necessary measures.' His Majesty dismissed Grabbe. He replaced all the generals and doubled your troops. This time you can't possibly claim that you lack means."

"No, I wouldn't dare. The emperor has also sent money, a great deal of money, to bribe those closest to the imam. We tried to have him assassinated; we even provided the killers with poison. They took the vials and the funds and laid all of it at the feet of their victim."

"And you seem to find that normal."

"The only choice we've left the Montagnards is to remain faithful to the imam Shamil."

"Faithful? That close to treason? That kind of loyalty hardly seems commendable."

"On that point—Russian loyalty, our own loyalty—we have a curious way of treating the indigenes who back us up and serve us. On the one hand, we spare no expense persuading the renegades to join our ranks. But once we have won them over, we pay no more attention to them and turn them over to the vengeance of their own without batting an eye. As a result, we reinforce their conviction that it is preferable to fight us, so we will try to buy them off, than to join us, only to be abandoned to a cruel death at the hands of the murids."

"The arrival of Count Vorontsov will change all that. He's been granted full powers. I know him. He's very intelligent and shrewd. A formidable strategist, one of the great conquerors of Napoleon."

"But what does a battlefield in the Napoleonic wars have to do with the war of ambush Shamil is waging?" Dmitri flushed with anger and slapped his knee, emphasizing each word with indignation. "Except perhaps that in Napoleon's time, the Russians were defending their own liberty, their own territory against the invader. Whereas now, we've taken on the opposite role."

The count uncrossed his legs and furiously crushed out his cigar, then hurled the contents of the ashtray into the fire in the hearth.

"I strongly suggest that you refrain from writing this sort of thing in your book, my dear. You risk finding the climate in Siberia much harsher than that of your much vaunted Caucasus."

Genuinely sorry to have provoked the ire of the man he owed so much, the young man calmed down before continuing.

"But Count Vorontsov is moving too quickly, Uncle, and the czar is urging him on. He operates at double time. When he orders his entire army to plunge into the Chechen forest without taking the time to cut down even a single tree or clear out a single thicket, he's committing an error that not even the most humble veteran of the Chechen regiments would be guilty of. He would know there are Montagnards hiding behind every tree trunk. He would be prepared for the barricades at every path, set to trap the middle of a column between several heaps of branches and isolate our soldiers in small groups—with men ready to decimate our troops once they are helpless to advance, retreat, or defend themselves. All that would be obvious.

"As for the horrors of the spectacle the imam regales us with, those of us who have managed to force our way through the obstacles and survive, they're included in every report. Barbarities that make your blood run cold, a foretaste of what awaits us. The heads of our comrades planted among the branches, their mutilated bodies—hands, feet, and genitals chopped off—draped over the barricades, their bloody remains that must be removed before we can advance. I don't want to upset you with such visions, Uncle. But I must tell you that just last month, Shamil massacred four thousand Russians. In three days."

"That fanatic is a monster!"

"Indeed, that's what he's becoming."

"What do you mean, what he's becoming? It's what he's always been. For the past twenty years, he's spread carnage and death."

"For the past twenty years, he's been fighting for the survival of his people. But now he wants something else."

The count shrugged his shoulders.

"Of course, gold."

"No, his son."

"The kid you brought back?"

"The child I kidnapped. Shamil will do anything to obtain his return. He's ready to murder, blackmail, even take hostages to exchange."

"A wide-ranging program," said the count with bitter irony.

Another thunderous commotion from upstairs shook the room, and the fifty candles of the ceiling light went out.

"Now they've gone too far up there! This is the last time I let these vandals come here, they've got some nerve! Go see what the hell Sacha is doing and tell him what I think of his behavior. As for the imam's son, all you have to do is give him back. We don't need the offspring of monsters and madmen here."

Dmitri had scarcely reached the top of the stairs before Sacha threw himself into his arms. As he glanced at the other "vandals" standing on the landing, he immediately recognized the tall, slender figure of Jamal Eddin Shamil.

Milyutin was so taken aback that it did not occur to him to mask his surprise and emotion.

Jamal Eddin greeted him with a nod that the captain acknowledged. Standing stock still, they exchanged a long look of mutual anxiety and curiosity. Both felt a catch in their throats as memories of the past flashed through their minds.

Of the two, the younger one seemed the least troubled. He had been waiting for this encounter, wishing for it and seeking the opportunity to make it happen. He knew that Sacha's brother had returned from the Caucasus. It was this that had motivated him to accept this invitation, not his friends' excited chatter about getting away from the school, dancing with real partners, and finally, finally, meeting some girls. If only he could approach the captain to ask him about what was happening in Dagestan and Chechnya. His knowledge of his father's triumphs was limited to rumors circulating in the Cherkess dormitory, all of them contradictory, ambiguous, and deformed by the pacifieds' mistrust of the growing power of the imam. Would Dmitri Alexeyevitch be willing to give him some real news?

Despite his impatience, Jamal Eddin did not move and asked no questions. The boy hadn't changed in that respect, Milyutin thought. With his characteristic reserve, this blend of restraint and assurance, he waited politely for the captain to speak. He kept the same distance from his former jailer as before, but this time his expression was devoid of all aggression and scorn.

The captain even thought he saw a certain softness, a hint of kindness, in the boy's serious face.

In five years, the "hostage" had changed. He had become a sleek adolescent, extremely elegant in his red and green cadet's uniform, cap in hand, saber at his side. A Russian aristocrat of the First Cadet Corps of Petersburg. He seemed only slightly less crazy than the two grand dukes, Count Buxhöwden, and the youngest of the Milyutins, who were racing up and down the corridor, doing handstands and myriad other acrobatic antics.

Dmitri hadn't time to pursue his reflections further. The crystal of the torchères vibrated, and he heard a heavy step behind him.

The count had emerged from the wing that served as his apartment and approached the little group. He had come to pay his respects to the emperor's sons and to thank them for honoring his home. It was also an opportunity for the others to be presented to him.

"This Muslim can't sit at this table with our guests!"

Kiselyev paced between the columns of one of the two rotundas on either side of the white banquet room.

The horseshoe-shaped table was set for two hundred, the candles of the three overhanging chandeliers not yet lit. On the immaculate tablecloths, a long line of silver candelabra shimmered in the mirrors, reflecting into infinity the image of the fine china plates, the gold-rimmed crystal carafes, the goblets and flutes.

"Do you hear me, Dmitri?" the count stormed. "He will stay upstairs. I do not want him to come down here. I forbid him to appear. His presence here would be an insult to the men who have fought in the Caucasus, an affront to the memory of those who died there."

When standing before the boy in question, Kiselyev had shown more skill at dissimulating his sentiments than his nephew. Old courtier that he was, he had masked his surprise and dismay.

However, his fury was all the more violent upon his return to the ground floor, disrupting the hostess's final preparations.

"Just to make sure, have him taken back to the Cadet Corps immediately. As for your brother, he has no idea what he's in for. He hasn't seen the likes of the caning that's in store for him. I'll have him whipped publicly here, this evening. How dare he invite this rebel to mingle with my guests?"

"This rebel, Uncle, is the classmate of the grand dukes and a ward of the emperor."

"The emperor is magnanimous. But we, Dmitri Alexeyevitch, we cannot welcome him here, among us. I have told you, and I will repeat once again, that it would be a slap in the face, an unacceptable humiliation for the victor of Akulgo."

Milyutin was petrified with horror at the allusion. "You have invited General Grabbe? This evening? Whatever possessed you?"

His uncle sensed his disapproval and swept it aside.

"You wanted the Caucasus? I give you the Caucasus, my boy!"

Dmitri refrained from further discussion on this wobbly ground. The proximity of Grabbe nonetheless perplexed him. He turned his thoughts over in his mind for a few moments before returning to the subject at hand—how to handle the presence of Jamal Eddin Shamil.

"To offend him without reason, shut him in upstairs, send him away, or in any way treat him as an enemy would be to diametrically oppose the education the emperor has chosen to give him and contravene His Majesty's wishes. This boy now belongs to a better world, and that is the czar's decision."

His argument was a convincing one.

"Well then, have a second table set up, in your aunt's dining room or the crimson salon or the blue one or the green one. Wherever you want, but way the devil away from here. The house is big enough. Organize festivities reserved for the children at the other end of the palace."

"And who, among their young Imperial Highnesses and the little Serene Highnesses will you exile to 'the other end' of the palace, Uncle? The Georgian princesses can only be seated here in the banquet room, at your right and next to their mother. As for sending the grand dukes way the devil away, that would be a first of some magnitude. You'd beat all records in terms of snubs and humiliation."

"So, as you tell it, the problem is insoluble? Really, really, really," the count exploded, "your imam has caused me no end of trouble, down to the very seating plan for my dinner!"

Dmitri smothered a smile.

"For the seating plan, I fear that the only thing we can do is follow the rules and leave the rest up to God."

Milyutin feigned all the more gaiety because he realized just how serious the situation was.

Sacha had pulled off a masterstroke inviting Jamal Eddin to the Kiselyevs' and consequently presenting him to the higher spheres of the court. Here he was, the son of the "monster" who had cut off the hands, feet, and genitals of relatives of all the guests. The evening promised to be lively.

"Unless—Uncle, just a little while ago, you told young Count Buxhöwden that you had met his father in Bucharest, right?"

"I've known several Buxhöwdens in my life, his father, his brothers, his grandfather. All of them strapping lads, hotheads, daredevils, and swashbucklers. But all had pure hearts and gallant souls. Why do you ask?"

"Because, from what Sacha tells me, the son is made of the same stuff. He's the oldest and probably the only one of the little band who's capable of measuring the consequences of a scandal for Jamal Eddin's future."

"The boy's future, my dear, is scarcely my concern."

"Nonetheless, I'll warn Buxhöwden of the reactions his friend's presence might provoke. So he can stick close to him, see to it that he stays as far away as possible from the officers, and keep an eye out for trouble."

As for the potential trouble in question, Dmitri refrained from voicing his true concern. He did not admit that the sensitivity of the "Petersburg Caucasians" worried him less than that of the only real Cherkess at the soirée. The danger lay in the violence of Jamal Eddin's feelings. What would he be able to endure as he listened to the conversation around the dinner table?

The violence of his feelings was one source of concern, but he also worried about the speed of his reactions.

Having experienced it before, Milyutin was already familiar with Jamal Eddin's pride. And he knew that he was both quick to defend it and easily offended.

The things he was in danger of hearing about his people could not fail to hurt him. All that he held precious—his religion, his flesh and blood, his very honor—would be subject to attack.

As for the presence of General Grabbe under the same roof, how could Jamal Eddin behave with restraint and dignity toward the man who had betrayed him and had him kidnapped?

It was insoluble. The count was right.

The moment Dmitri heard the rustle of petticoats and skirts and crystalline feminine voices in the vestibule, he realized he had forgotten the most important thing—the presence of girls. With luck, the evening would not play out the way he had imagined. With luck, the party would be frivolous and gay. Jamal Eddin could not carry the weight of the world on his shoulders or single-handedly solve the tragic situation of his people. The time had come for the boy to be what he always should have been: a child who acted his own age, an adolescent lad just like all the others.

"Well, even the worst," Dmitri thought to himself, scoffing at his own gloomy apprehension, "even the worst scenario is by no means a sure thing."

First breach of propriety: Sacha and his band did not come downstairs to greet any of the guests. Although the count had given them permission to descend, the five cadets remained glued to the steps midway down the staircase until dinner. They probably found it more interesting to watch, unseen, as the girls took off their wraps in the vast antechamber, arranged their hair in the mirrors, and smoothed the wrinkles of their skirts with fans. Though the boys' conduct would normally have been considered unacceptable, in this case, it was perfect. This way Jamal Eddin would not be introduced to the families. Dmitri had no intention whatsoever of reprimanding his little brother.

Perched on the steps, they whispered and giggled and exchanged witty comments in low voices. At fourteen, Nicholas Nicolaïevitch—Nicky—the elder of the two grand dukes, already had a reputation as a connoisseur of horses, dogs, and women. He and Buxhöwden agreed that small hands and tiny feet were absolutely ravishing. For once Sacha had not exaggerated when he bragged of the charms of the Georgian princesses (on whom, of course, he had never before laid eyes).

Sisters and cousins continued to arrive, representing different generations. George XII, the last king of Georgia, had had twenty children, and the eldest of his progeny were dowagers. They were dressed in their sumptuous national costume, with a headband worn like a crown and a long, diaphanous veil trailing down the back. Their dresses, hemmed just above the ankle, were richly embroidered. The ensemble recalled the chatelaines of the Middle Ages from Sir Walter Scott's novels. They were too old-fashioned for the young people, who scarcely noticed them.

But the young ones were something else entirely. They wore crinolines of pink, blue, or white satin, in the latest Parisian style, with fresh flowers on their belts. They had large, dark eyes and long, lustrous black curls that framed their delicate features. With olive complexions, oval faces, and a similarly light step, the family resemblance was striking. According to the grand duke, ladies always fit into two entirely distinct categories. One group, His Highness pontificated, had a sort of languor about them, a faraway look of melancholy softness in the eyes. The others were intense and voluptuous, the incarnation of a promising sensuality.

Though Sacha did not understand all of these subtle distinctions, he did notice two girls his own age. Their governess was just helping them remove their wraps. Scarcely on the other side of childhood, they probably would not stay up for the ball and the midnight supper. But in their short, full-skirted dresses and their lace pantalets, they struck him as accessible, graceful, and worthy of conquest. Without informing anyone, he rushed down the steps, clicked his heels smartly, and presented himself as entertainment director of the junior class.

Indeed, Sacha was in fine form tonight. Everything was turning out for the best.

Dmitri was thinking the same thing as he sat down in the banquet room. Everything was turning out for the best.

Only the adults, the young people between sixteen and twenty, and the adolescents of the imperial family had been placed at the table. The rest of the children were seated at the two extremities of the horseshoe, the boys with their tutors, the girls with their teachers.

Due to the random order of the procession through the reception suite—the random order, or the skill of Buxhöwden, who had been confidentially informed of the potential difficulties of the evening—Sacha, his friends, and the sons of some of the guests entered the dining room last. Count Kiselyev already presided at the center table, with the two grand dukes, the princes of the Bagration family, and the generals seated next to him. Countess Kiselyev, née Princess Potocka, was seated at the center of the right wing, with the Georgian princesses and the other ladies across from her. Dmitri presided over the left wing of the table, surrounded by the dignitaries and officers. On the men's side, the table was nearly full, so the dozen or so last to arrive sat on the other side, with the readers, chaperones, and governesses.

Dmitri sat back in his chair, satisfied with the arrangements. Yes, it had worked out fine to leave things to chance; in fact, it could not have been better if it had all been planned. Sacha's band was directly in his line of vision, so he could easily keep an eye on Jamal Eddin. Even better, the group of chaperones separated the boys from the rest of the guests. It would be impossible for "the rebel," as his uncle insisted on calling him, to hear any conversation other than that of his friends. No one had noticed the boy during the greetings and the procession. He had blended into the mass of uniforms. And no one would single him out now, seated on the other side of the world, two hundred place settings away from General Grabbe. The problems he had foreseen had simply disappeared.

One could even suppose that the boy would do his best not to attract attention. Wasn't this reception his first, his introduction to society? His first formal dinner, his first ball? Dmitri recalled his own state of mind in the same circumstances. He had been fourteen and in mortal fear of appearing ridiculous, gauche, or awkward. His most fervent wish had been that no one should look at him or notice his presence.

And as he watched him, Jamal Eddin did not say a word. With his usual reserve, he seemed to want to disappear, sitting back slightly in his chair so that his neighbors could fully observe Sacha's antics.

Sacha, on the other hand, was too much. He was going too far with his clowning. Dmitri knew that his little brother was trying to impress his rivals—in fact, all the boys at the party—because he thought he was ugly. Or at least he did not think he was as handsome as Their Imperial Highnesses who, with their blond hair and blue eyes, looked more German than Russian. They were the incarnation of all he wanted to be. But they were seated too far away for him to compete with them. Buxhöwden? Sacha definitely considered himself to be less masculine than Buxhöwden, who was a strapping, well-built, somewhat enigmatic lad. Jamal Eddin? Sacha undoubtedly knew that he was less attractive than Jamal Eddin, with his high cheekbones and large, almond-shaped cat eyes. Well, the devil with looks. With his turned-up nose and freckles, and the cowlicks he was forever trying to paste down, he was determined to be as witty as could be. So he exaggerated his comic side, overcoming his shyness by speaking loudly and gesticulating wildly.

Dmitri saw him address the two girls he had greeted in the vestibule, speaking over their governess's head. They laughed unrestrainedly at his clever comments.

They were the younger sisters of the beautiful young woman sitting next to her mother at Countess Kiselyev's right. Dmitri thought, deep down, that had he not been so happily married, the lovely Princess Anna of Georgia... In any case, Sacha's conquests were named Varenka and Gayana. Varenka was fourteen, Gayana a year younger. Endowed with a delicate constitution, Varenka was slender and frail, with immense dark eyes and well-shaped, arched eyebrows. Gayana was a brunette like her sisters, but chubbier and livelier, and every bit as impudent as Sacha.

Placed on either side of their teachers, the girls wheedled their two chaperones into exchanging places with them, allowing them to sit next to the boys. They had just won their case and were sitting down between Jamal Eddin and another boy, who wore the prestigious gold-buttoned blue uniform of the Lycée Impérial, where Pushkin had studied. A smile crossed Dmitri's lips. They were having a much better time at their end of the table than he was here, in the company of the minister of war.

Finally reassured, he ceased to pay attention to the goings-on around his little brother. The game had been won.

However, on this score, he was mistaken. The student from the Lycée Impérial, who was talking even more loudly than Sacha, was making him dangerously excited. As for Jamal Eddin, he was struggling to control a violence well beyond what Dmitri could have imagined a short while ago when he tried to put himself in the boy's place.

What was so oppressive? The solemnity of the décor, the heaviness of the twenty-four white pillars, the Corinthian columns that supported the enormous vault above? What was it? The light? The heat? The shimmering flames reflecting off the crystal of the chandeliers and dancing in the mirrors like fragments of a rainbow? Whatever it was, Jamal Eddin felt trapped, caught by the throat, close to panic.

Tonight he was capable of measuring what had escaped him five years ago during the New Year celebrations at the Winter Palace. He could judge the splendor of all these objects, let himself be dazzled by the refinement of each detail and fascinated by so much richness and radiance.

He knew both too much and not enough about the world around him.

Though he had learned how to navigate in the realm of the cadets, he suddenly understood the great distance he still had to go. Yes, of course, he knew how to recognize an officer's rank at a glance and how to salute according to protocol. His table manners were impeccable. But for the rest? His masters had not shown him how to click his heels before a girl or revealed how to flirt with her. And when it came to mastering the correct dinner utensils before him, all these knives and glasses, he was at a loss. Dmitri had been right in supposing that Jamal Eddin felt awkward and ashamed. But added to his adolescent emotions was another kind of malaise, a moral one that multiplied and complicated his discomfort.

He didn't even need to touch the wine that sparkled red, white, and golden before him, the wine his father had poured out by the cask—the odor was enough to inebriate him and fill him with guilt.

In coming so close to what he never should have approached, in discovering the opulent beauty of women he should never even have imagined, in running his eyes over their plunging décolletés and their bare shoulders, he was playing a dangerous game with temptation. And he sensed this.

He wished he had never accepted Sacha's invitation. He was angry with himself for taking part in it. He was angry with himself for being at this table, in this room, in this palace, in this country. He was angry with himself for everything.

He looked for an opportunity to disappear discreetly, but it was too late.

"Jamal Eddin," Sacha cried, "you who know the region, the Caucasus belongs to Georgia, right? So Her Highness the Princess Varenka Ilyinitchna and Her Highness the Princess Gayana Ilyinitchna are at once Russian, Georgian, and Caucasian, no?"

Given his present state, Jamal Eddin did not understand the question at all.

"Monsieur maintains that that's not the case," Sacha insisted, indicating the student seated across the table from him. "Monsieur declares that Orthodox Georgia and the Muslim Caucasus have nothing in common."

"I never said that!" the boy cried.

His voice was changing. Sharp and shrill, it carried a long way.

"Oh, really? Then what did you say?"

"I said that only part of the Caucasus Mountains are in Georgia. And that in this sense, the Georgian people are more Russian than Caucasian."

The sententious student liked giving lessons.

"That's totally idiotic!" Sacha burst out, ready to say anything in order to have the last word.

"All of the Caucasus is Russian," said his adversary, developing his rationale.

"All the Caucasus is not Russian," Varenka corrected him.

This intervention put a damper on the heated conversation, and a moment of silence ensued. Buxhöwden squirmed in his chair, sensing the danger. Jamal Eddin did not move. He listened intently to the girl's words.

"The proof," Gayana simpered, "is that Varenka's sweetheart was Shamil's prisoner for eight months in the Caucasus."

"He's not my sweetheart!"

"Maybe. But anyway, he was Shamil's hostage for eight months."

"Shamil?" smirked Sacha's rival. "My father had him under his boot."

The color drained from Jamal Eddin's face. He was so visibly upset that Buxhöwden was afraid he would completely lose his composure.

"Our relative, Varenka's fiancé, lived with him in his village, in his house," Gayana professed insistently. "He says that Shamil is not at all the way everyone imagines him. He says that he is a great warrior, and he admires him."

"Your relative," the boy said condescendingly, "probably belongs to the branch of the Georgian royal family that chose to serve the shah of Persia rather than the Russian czar."

Varenka turned almost as red as Jamal Eddin was pale. The student had struck a nerve.

Certain members of the Georgian aristocracy had plotted against the Russian occupation, and though they were Christians, they had fought in alliance with the Muslims. At the beginning of the century, when Russia definitively annexed Georgia, Queen Miriam, the widow of George XII, had stabbed the Russian general who had come to arrest her in her bed, with a kinjal. Her youngest son, little Ilya, who was only nine at the time, had helped her murder him. Ilya was Varenka's own father.

The criminal queen had been shut up in the monastery of Voronets for seven years before being allowed to live in Moscow on probation. To some, she was a heroine of the resistance. To others, she was the incarnation of all that was barbarous, shocking, and vulgar.

Forty years later, Emperor Nicholas had granted her his pardon. The girls' grandmother was now received at court, and the privileges, titles, and ranks of the entire family had been restored. The Georgian princes had been integrated into the Russian aristocracy and now counted among the most influential members of the empire.

In suggesting that Varenka's "sweetheart" belonged to the enemy camp, the student had unwittingly attacked her loyalty. Even he did not realize the extent to which his comment was insulting.

Varenka managed to contain her anger, but she trembled with indignation and was close to tears.

"Our father fought Napoleon at Borodino, sir," she said, her voice quivering. "Our uncles fought the Persians at Yerevan. The father of Prince Elico Orbeliani, our relative whom you have just denigrated, took the city of Poti back from the Turks. His brother distinguished himself in every battle against Shamil. The prince himself was taken prisoner at Dargo when he was fighting Shamil."

"Of course, of course. I'm just surprised that he could have escaped from the clutches of the imam alive. Everyone knows how cruel he is."

Varenka calmed down a bit.

"It's true that he spent some very difficult periods in the pit where the imam kept his captives."

Buxhöwden shot Sacha several urgent dark looks that warned of imminent disaster. Sacha understood that they had ventured out onto a minefield, but he could not find a way to cut the conversation short.

"The imam wanted to exchange him for his heir," Gayana explained.

How could Buxhöwden drag Jamal Eddin away from all this? He tried to catch his friend's eye, while Sacha attempted to distract him with subtle gestures and kicks under the table. It was all in vain.

Jamal Eddin hung on every word the girls said. He saw and felt nothing, nothing but the violence of the images and emotions their words evoked.

"The imam," Gayana continued, all too pleased to be center stage, "had only one thing in mind when he captured our relative. He wanted to force him to write to the czar, to oblige him to beg His Majesty to give him back his son."

"But the prince resisted," Varenka cut in, with pride. "He refused to write the letter; he could not ask such a thing of his emperor."

"So Shamil had him brought from the pit to be executed."

"And the prince prepared to die. But the imam was so touched by his courage and his dignity that he pardoned him and spared his life. He even gave him free run of the village, as long as he promised not to try to escape. And that is how our relative lived with him for several months."

"And that's why he says he's not cruel," Gayana lisped.

"All that sounds too good to be true," the boy scoffed.

"Well, you're wrong," Varenka murmured softly, "it is true."

"Allow me, if you will, Your Highness, to express my surprise that the imam pardoned your relative without asking for anything in return."

"Shamil finally exchanged him for several of his captains."

"Your relative must have rendered some important service to the Montagnards for them to spare him and set him free," the student insisted. "They're very greedy, these people, as rapacious as they are corrupt. They in no way resemble the noble lords you're describing."

Varenka frowned. Exasperated this time, she lost her temper. "That, however, is the way things happen between men of honor! And that is how they did happen."

"Please stop, sir."

Jamal Eddin's voice, like a knife slicing in one clean blow, cut into the conversation, its coldness matched only by its natural authority.

"You are insulting the princesses and questioning their word."

"I don't doubt their word, not for a second! That's not what I wished to say."

"I asked you to be quiet."

He did not make the slightest gesture. He did not even raise his voice. It was worse. His entire person breathed contempt.

"On my honor, I never—"

"Do not use words whose meaning escapes you completely."

His terse words expressed such pent-up anger that Buxhöwden was afraid he would grab the other boy and throttle him. However, Jamal Eddin did not move a muscle. The student, worried that he had offended Varenka Ilyinitchna, chose to ignore the interruption.

"I swear to you, Your Highness, that—"

"Be quiet. The subject is closed."

"Yes, let's all be quiet, shall we," Varenka agreed, gracing the boy with a conciliatory look. "The war in the Caucasus is too painful and controversial a subject. Let's all talk about something else."

She gave her opponent such an encouraging smile that he was sure he had won her over, which was actually the intent of all his quibbling in the first place. Swallowing his humiliation, he complied. He was content to seek proof of her pardon by asking Her Highness for the *honor*—he emphasized the word pretentiously—of granting him the first waltz.

"Who is that cretin?" Buxhöwden whispered in Sacha's ear as they were leaving the room.

"Tell me about it!" he exclaimed under his breath. "How could my brother have let that fool horn in at our table?

Dmitri hit the bull's-eye, giving us that son of an imbecile. We need to avoid him at all costs."

"Jamal Eddin put him in his place."

"That's nothing. Just think what he would have done had he known he was talking to Nicholas Pavlovitch Grabbe!"

Everyone was waiting for the ball to begin. The women strolled in small groups through the adjoining receiving rooms while the men played whist in the smoking room. The young people played ambassadors and other games under the watchful eyes of their governesses. Behind the closed doors, they could hear the violins tuning up.

Suddenly, in an explosion of brass, the first measures of a polonaise resounded throughout the halls, a veritable thunderclap that instantly emptied the salons. Jamal Eddin found himself alone in the small rotunda known as the Hercules Rotunda.

Situated at the end of a gallery of paintings, the room was considered by many to be less than congenial. Decorated only with palms, potted plants, and four monumental statues of Hercules leaning on his club, it struck the ladies as cold and uninviting. Even those who were curious to see the entire palace turned around before entering this room. This was where Jamal Eddin had sought refuge when dinner was over.

He stood in the shadows of one of the alcoves, hidden by the palms and ferns. Varenka and Gayana had obtained permission from their mother to stay up until ten, until the mazurka, but he wouldn't go watch them dance. He did not want to see them again; in fact, he was waiting for them to leave. It was not that he hadn't found them attractive. On the contrary, he could think only of them and hoped that the evening would never end. Or else that the soirée would conclude then and there, while he was still reveling in this feeling of security and peace.

He was happy.

He thought about what he had just heard, about the message they had transmitted.

The girls had said that Shamil was a great warrior, a generous and noble man, so noble that even his enemies admired him. And they had told him other things that were even more gratifying to hear.

They had said that Shamil was keeping the promise he had made when he had been forced to surrender him at Akulgo. "Never will I abandon you."

They had told him that his father remembered him, and that he loved him.

All this time, these five long years without news, Jamal Eddin had feared that Shamil had forgotten him. He thought perhaps that his father had denied him, rejected him, the same way they had rejected his cousin Hamzat, whose own mother would have nothing to do with him, declaring that he stank and that he had been sullied.

Suddenly this constant, throbbing anxiety had vanished.

A knot inside him had unraveled this evening, leaving him confident and content. He was proud of the present, proud of the past, proud of Shamil and of his own origins. His faith in his love of his own people made him feel light, almost free, as he had been as a child. Hope had conquered his fear.

"Oh, are you there?"

Even before her full skirt and lace pantalets emerged from the forest of plants, he recognized her voice. Soft and sweet and a bit husky, Varenka's voice belonged to the voices of his past and rose from the murmur of his memories. Of all the voices that sang in the back of his mind, hers was already the clearest.

The girl now stood before him, her dress a bright stain of pink among the leaves.

"We're leaving," she said awkwardly.

She seemed a bit out of breath, as though she had crossed the gallery at a run. She was wrapped in a warm shawl that covered her hair and shoulders, à la Russe. Covered like this, she reminded him of the silhouettes of the women who went to fetch the water in the mountains at home. The princess of Georgia was every bit Caucasian.

Her presence seemed friendly and familiar. Unlike Sacha, who would have been struck silly by her sudden appearance, he wasn't surprised. Yes, of course he found those arched eyebrows and big, dark eyes lifted toward his unsettling. But the girl's face, which had looked so serious when she had spoken of the honor of men, now seemed a part of the peace he had finally found.

She did not share his serenity. He could see that she was embarrassed and didn't know what to say.

"We're leaving," she repeated. "And we wanted to—a little while ago, I didn't tell you."

She stopped and began again, slowly and steadily.

"A little while ago, at the end of our discussion, my sister and I were worried about making things worse with the...well, we're very grateful. But before leaving, both of us wanted to thank you for having defended us."

Her words went straight to his heart. For a moment he said nothing. The moist breath of the plants bathed his burning cheeks.

"Don't say anything about gratitude. You have no idea, I am the one who is grateful."

"Who is that cadet who's talking to one of our Anastasia Grigorievna's cute little things, at the foot of the Hercules Farnèse?" Tatiana Borissovna Potemkina inquired, squinting through her lorgnette at the statue among the palms.

The imposing Princess Potemkina stood several meters from them, two-thirds of the way down the gallery, with her husband and three of their contemporaries.

Her nickname at court, "La Potemkina," à l'Italien, was exclusively hers and signified neither the overly familiar nor the pejorative. She was the wife of a marshal of Saint Petersburg nobility and self-appointed guardian of the temple. She considered it her duty to ensure the proper conduct and respect for tradition of nearly everyone, and boys and girls had to be presented to her before they made their début in the world. After a visit to La Potemkina and a dozen other powerful old ladies, one was considered to have completed the "dowager tour," a condition *sine qua non* to being received at any party. Of all the young people present, not one had failed to pay his respects by calling on La Potemkina.

"I asked Count Kiselyev the same question," replied her companion. "He's going deaf, poor dear, he didn't even hear me. The boy is remarkably beautiful."

"Yes, ravishing. But at this age, cadets of the First Corps don't have private conversations with girls, they play hunt the thimble with them in the nursery. Or else ask them to dance. Sacha, come here for a moment."

The sturdy arm of La Potemkina had stopped him in midflight and now held his own arm firmly. Who would ever have imagined that Tatiana Borissovna had once had the figure of a sylph? Her friends had called her a liana, whose stylishly cut dresses with empire waistlines had emphasized her slenderness.

All that remained today of the nymph with the face of a Madonna was her long, straight nose and the pursed lips that accompanied her ponderous stare. At forty-eight, she had gained as much weight as she had confidence. Despite her full skirts, fluted bonnets, and the mass of curls framing her face, these days she resembled nothing so much as a man, all the more so because of her energy and pugnacity.

"You know your little comrade there, I suppose. What's his name?"

Sacha clicked his heels and bowed before the four ladies, greeting them politely and paying a small compliment to each, as he tried to play for time. It was no use. Dmitri, engrossed in conversation ten steps away, would never come to his rescue. He would have to reply, and he couldn't think of anything to say but the truth.

Good Lord! La Potemkina—of all powers, the most fearsome—La Potemkina had spotted Jamal Eddin. The worst had finally happened.

"He's a friend of Their Imperial Highnesses the Grand Dukes," he hedged, "His Majesty's personal protégé. One of his wards from the Caucasus. His favorite ward."

"The son of a khan. I thought so. I'd recognize a Cherkess anywhere."

For several years, Tatiana Borissovna had been head of the ladies' prison committee, and in this capacity, she had visited Montagnards who were being held in the empire's jails.

She had met so many that now she was indeed capable of picking one out in a crowd.

La Potemkina had strong ties to the most influential members of the Orthodox clergy and was active in church life. She had devoted her immense fortune to the conversion of "pagans" and had financed several missions to the Caucasus and to Kamchatka. She had also founded a home for Jews whom she was preparing for baptism. But her specialty remained the conversion of Muslims. During her long career as lady catechist, she had converted over a thousand, or so she said. She organized the baptisms with great pomp in the chapel of her palace in Saint Petersburg or during her huge parties at Gostilitsy, her country home. She always invited her friend the empress Alexandra Feodorovna to the mass and the celebration that followed on such occasions. During the summer, the czarina stayed at her domain of Peterhof-Alexandria, only a few versts from Gostilitsy.

Tatiana Borissovna was widely respected by her entourage for her generosity and her religious zeal. Her husband, however, a little bald man, found her sanctimoniousness and her proselytizing exasperating and often teased her about both.

"Well, hurry up, my dear, go invite the emperor's favorite to spend his vacation with us. By rights he's yours, and you'd better act quickly before someone else grabs him and saves his soul."

She shrugged her shoulders and rushed to the rotunda where Varenka had just disappeared through the rear door.

"Ah," he said in mock horror, "if this ravishing young man is not only the czar's ward but a Muslim, I'm done for. My wife will have him come to stay, feed him, take care of him, and practically adopt him. Poor boy, he doesn't know what he's in for."

CHAPTER VII

In Search of Inner Peace

1847

The pleasures of palace life
at the cottage of Peterhof-Alexandria
on the outskirts of Saint Petersburg,
two years later
Summer, 1847

As he often did after his evening prayers, Jamal Eddin retreated to his favorite spot, a refuge he had found in a little glade carved out of one of the hillocks of the park at Peterhof. He had found this open place among the summer pavilions and work sheds, far from the cottage where the imperial family had settled in. The imperial family. His family. At the far end, between two marble benches that faced each other like fireside armchairs, was the sculpted bust of a young woman. Her hair, parted in the middle and looped back on the sides in a braided chignon that exposed the nape of her neck and the perfect oval of her face—everything about this delicate little head of marble reminded him of Varenka of Georgia.

The scent of the roses and lilies cascading from the four basins above the benches reinforced a feeling of almost feminine religiosity in this isolated spot. The peaceful stillness he had discovered here had been his alone since the beginning of his vacation.

Between the end of the year and August exams, he savored a mere ten days of happiness, which were too intense to be honestly deserved. The boundless joy of living in this paradise made him feel almost guilty, as though he should temper his feelings or hold himself back in some way. So every morning and every evening, he came here to talk to his father, as though Shamil were seated on the bench facing him. He imagined his father, calm and sober, sitting there in his long imam's robe. Only at these moments could he summon the presence of the man as he remembered him. Despite all his efforts, Shamil's face had faded with the years, and he could recall nothing more than a shadowy figure.

He resented this silence. Since the czar had allowed them to correspond, why had Shamil never answered his letters? He had stopped asking that question and so many others. His faraway guide, his cherished master, obstinately refused to show him the way, and so he asked no more. But he told him everything, describing what he saw and mulling over the events of the past few years with him. He constantly tried to convince his father that he and Czar Nicholas were very much alike. Both were charitable to the poor, both honored their ancestors' memories, and both looked after the honor of their progeny. The czar prayed and fasted and praised his god too.

Jamal Eddin went into great detail in these ongoing monologues, explaining to his father that the much-feared czar was kind and tender to defenseless beings. Like Shamil, he played with the children for hours, letting them climb all over him. He ate frugally, drank only water, did not smoke, and detested the odor of tobacco so much that it was banned from the streets of the capital.

Jamal Eddin didn't dare push the comparison further by suggesting that perhaps, without realizing it, the czar practiced the precepts of the Koran. That would be going too far; it would be both absurd and blasphemous.

In any case, he had reached his own conclusions about the Great White Czar. No one was so solicitous of the welfare of the poor and more merciful to those he conquered. He was incapable of corrupting anyone with whom he had daily contact.

For Jamal Eddin and his fellow cadets, knowledge of the reality of Russia was confined to their limited experience as the sons of aristocrats.

In the rarefied atmosphere of court and army society—the only one he knew—his masters, his officers, and his comrades repeated day and night that Czar Nicholas was a great and wise man, almost a saint.

He himself had experienced the czar's imperial generosity, and so he shared their opinion and could not imagine how the same man could pass for a monster in other circles. Those circles had dubbed him "the Iron Czar" and considered him a despot as stubborn as he was cruel, who silenced the voices of those who had the courage—and the misfortune—to express an opposing point of view.

Jamal Eddin longed for his own people to comprehend his gratitude to his benefactor, to whom he had become so attached.

His own people?

He shared Shamil's view of the Muslims he had encountered in Russia, his disgust for the renegades and hypocrites, whom he failed to differentiate from other "converts." Jamal Eddin's judgment concerning them remained unchanged, he told his father. He despised those parasitic Cherkesses who adopted the religion of the infidels and complied with Princess Potemkina's insistent demands out of sheer self-interest.

His violent rejection of members of his own community explained his apprehension at the thought of the Georgian princesses' imminent arrival at the cottage of Peterhof-Alexandria. La Potemkina would be here tomorrow. What more would she ask of him? What further pressures would she subject him to?

For the past two years, he had resisted her demands and refused to attend mass at Gostilitsy. But he had accepted the invitations to the children's balls at her Million Street palace. She had paraded him in her salons and presented him to the mothers of "her little friends," boasting that he was "the best equerry in all of Petersburg, a capital the finest horsemen in the world call home." She gushed to any and all, even in front of him, that he was as handsome as a Chevalier-Garde and had the presence of an Imperial Guard, alluding to the empire's most prestigious cavalry regiments.

He detested La Potemkina's florid compliments concerning horses, the beasts he loved so, but what could he do? She attended all the drills at the cadets' stables, the parades and dressage, the charges and the carousels, behaving as though his virtuoso performances before the emperor were her own personal triumphs. And he was inundated with invitations to her home. During the school year, he could beg off with protests of studies, rules, and disciplinary actions forbidding him to go out. Last winter he had intentionally sought punishment and restriction several Sundays in a row. A lot of good it did him—the princess wrangled dispensations for her protégé. It was becoming increasingly difficult for him to resist the friendly overtures of the marshal's wife.

Personally, he felt no antipathy for her. Impatience, yes, irritation and annoyance as well. But she was so solicitous of his well-being, considering herself his guide and mentor, that, in the end, he found the indefatigably warm and energetic old lady quite touching.

As for those Muslims who committed the supreme act of betrayal—daring to justify their crimes against God as a mere façade—they earned his profound contempt. They were only kissing her hand because they could not cut it off, the Gostilitsy converts told him confidentially, just like the peace seekers of Ghimri long ago. They were traitors who deserved death and weren't even worth the rope it would take to hang them.

He condemned them irrevocably.

Then he compared them to the czar.

Yes, the czar was mistaken. He prayed to idols and false deities. But this absolute master that his enemies called a tyrant allowed the faithful to worship the true God. They were free to pray to the true God, free to believe in the truth, free to accept that there was no god but Allah and that Mohammed was his prophet.

Freedom for the Caucasian Muslims—wasn't that what the imam Shamil was fighting for? Freedom to obey the laws of Sharia.

Sensing his father's judgment, Jamal Eddin admitted that it was hard to fulfill his religious duties in imperial society. Harder, in any case, than it had been in the Cadet Corps, with his Cherkess roommates. Here, in the summer, there was no mullah to teach him. He could still perform his ablutions at the fountains in the garden and isolate himself for a few minutes at dawn, at dusk, and in the evening to say his prayers. As long as he attracted no attention and his disappearance did not interrupt the activities, no one cared. Better still, everyone pretended not to notice. As for his dietary restrictions, he had managed to stick to his regimen by declining certain dishes. It didn't come up often, as the czar's chefs rarely served pork, and only his guests were served wine.

Jamal Eddin was making a spirited effort to convince his father that he should meet this particular infidel.

His friends, accustomed to his habitual reserve, would have been surprised at his eloquence and determination. He readily confronted every possible argument to convince Shamil that if he spoke with the czar, he would understand and respect him. Then their peoples could live in peace, perhaps even in unity.

He was obsessed with this certainty that Russia and the Caucasus could be united, a dream that applied to his love life as well. But he never told Shamil of his dreams of that kind of union.

* * *

That morning, as the sovereigns started off on their walk through the forest of Peterhof, they noticed the sun's waning warmth on the cottage. Summer was almost over.

"The plums should be picked tomorrow," the empress murmured. "It's time. I'll go have a look at the trees later on."

At almost fifty, Czarina Alexandra Feodorovna's taste had scarcely changed since her youth. She still preferred white gowns to colored ones and voile, silk, organdy, and chiffon to heavy velvet. Tall and slim, she was still elegant and stylish, and her passion for music and dance hadn't faded at all. It was said that her step was so light that she seemed to glide, and her melodious voice still enchanted all whom she met.

However, upon closer observation, one could detect a nervous tic that made her nod her head at emotional moments, and her graying hair, her thinness, and a fleeting look of uncertainty in her eyes betrayed a profound fatigue.

The czar towered at her side as they walked toward a grove of trees. He wore the uniform of the Chevaliers-Gardes, as was his custom, and his erect posture added to his perfection. The years were taking their toll, though. A toupée hid his baldness, and his budding paunch was restrained by a corset.

Before them, the garden sloped gently down to the sea. The maritime breeze carried the scent of the gillyflowers from the empress's mixed-border flower beds up to the cottage. With its gray gables, broad bay windows, and a combination of gothic and Victorian architecture, the house resembled a great English country home. The cottage had been lovingly built by Mouffy and Nicks—Empress Alexandra's and Czar Nicholas's nicknames for each other—with comfort in mind, as they envisioned a life of peace and harmony together. Like a well-matched bourgeois couple, they looked forward to years of conjugal happiness, surrounded by their children and their grandchildren.

This extraordinary setting was as amazing as the splendor of the court, as exotic as a ball at the Winter Palace. The hostess of the manor always offered the same description to the wives of those diplomats who had applied the necessary energy and determination to be granted the rare privilege of a visit.

"This domain is named after me because it was my wedding present, the wonderful gift of our late and beloved Czar Alexander to his little sister-in-law. I had just arrived from Prussia, and I was feeling a bit lost. But when I discovered the sparkling sea, these ancient trees so close to the water, this magnificent view of the Gulf of Finland, Petersburg, and Kronstadt, I was filled with joy. Everything here was conceived with one thing in mind: happiness.

"And so my husband commissioned an English architect to build us a little cottage, just big enough for the two of us and the children we would have, and I've never been happier than I have been in this house. Its simplicity is a respite from all the gilt décor. Really," she insisted, "I find the magnificent palace at Peterhof, with its grand fountains and thousands of statues and acres gold leaf, tiring to look at. Whereas here—come see my apartments. You'll see that my bedroom is on the ground floor and looks out over the lawn."

The visitors, charmed by such intimacy, returned to London or Paris to gush over the exquisite taste of every detail, the walls decorated with personal memorabilia, the portraits of the girls, the busts of the children, and the charming pastels and aquarelles.

"And do you know what all my sons tell me now?" the czarina continued. "Do you know what Constantine told me the other day as he prepared to leave Russia for several months?

" 'If I find a single place abroad as beautiful as our cottage, dearest Mama, I will consider my trip worthwhile.' "

She was scarcely exaggerating when she described the house as a "little cottage." She had merely neglected to mention that her close friends stayed at pavilions scattered over the fifteen hectares of surrounding parkland and that an army of cooks and servants occupied cabins deep in the woods. And that she could receive prestigious guests and the emperor's counselors at the immense Peterhof Palace, less than a verst from her domain. She had forgotten as well that her flamboyant gothic chapel towered like a cathedral amid the greenery of the garden. And that in addition to the cavalry house, the stables and kennels of her four boys, an annex had been built next to the cottage for her three daughters. Here, at what the clan modestly called "The Farm," they could learn cooking and housekeeping. Having served first as a playroom, then as a classroom, The Farm was now the private residence of twenty-eight-year-old Czarevitch Alexander, who was married and had a family of his own.

Who would have guessed that this was the Romanovs' nest? The bicephalous eagle—the emperor's emblem—was absent from the gates. A poet had designed a second crest for Nicholas and Alexandra's familial village, a saber encircled by a crown of flowers, an allegory for power wrapped in softness, the arms of courtly love. Graven on an escutcheon over the porch, carved on the medieval-styled furniture and chests, painted on the china and the bibelots, the saber and roses were visible everywhere. Even the spidery woodwork of the high-backed chairs and the filigree of the voile curtains at the bow windows were marked with variations on this symbol of imperial tenderness.

The emperor led his wife beneath the pine trees that shaded the lane, satisfied with his home and the impression of simplicity it presented to the world.

* * *

"This garden is so charming," Princess Tatiana Borissovna Potemkina exclaimed as she descended from her carriage and stepped tentatively onto the lawn. "Absolutely breathtaking."

In her absence, the czarina had asked her youngest son, Nicholas Nicolaïevitch—Nicky—and his favorite maid of honor, Anna of Georgia, to welcome Princess Potemkina and take her round the cottage until she returned.

The moment he saw the carriage, Nicky went running off in search of Jamal Eddin.

"Since my father is always saying he should feel at home here, the least he could do is come out and fill in for me, play the son of the household," he groused as he strode through the park. "Look after La Potemkina, take my place and receive the old witch and her dwarves."

That was the last thing Jamal Eddin intended to do.

Anna, on the contrary, went running down the lawn to greet the party the moment the dowager arrived, primarily because her mother, Princess Anastasia of Georgia, and seven of her brothers and sisters accompanied La Potemkina. They were staying at Gostilitsy Palace, a few hours from the imperial domain.

The two princesses, lifelong friends and both close to the imperial family, were paying a neighborly visit. They would stay for lunch and spend the afternoon here. The czar was fond of both and liked to tease them, calling Anastasia "my fertile Ceres" in reference to her prolificacy and dubbing the holier-than-thou Potemkina "my good nun." Both took his teasing as a mark of affection, and rightly so. Rarely did he appear as relaxed as he was in their company. He found La Potemkina, with her Bible in hand and a thousand projects in mind, amusing. She read to him from the Gospels before lunch and they discussed the day's lesson at siesta time. At teatime, she would beg for subsidies for her unfortunate charges. Ever the good prince, the emperor would always comply with her requests. And then the empress would insist she stay for dinner.

Grand Duke Nicky knew from experience that La Potemkina would end up spending the night. Everyone said her own palace was filled with hangers-on and converts. Even here, she arrived with a gaggle of children and nannies who followed her coach in a train of three carriages. This tribe was all too content to escape the caravanserai at Gostilitsy and looked forward to their summer break in the country.

"Isn't he lucky, our handsome Cherkess, to live in such a setting," the dowager remarked as she leaned with her full weight on Anna's arm.

The young woman's mother, who had ballooned to nearly the size of their friend after the recent delivery of her last baby, took her other arm. Their skirts blending in a rustle of silk, the three walked up the lawn arm in arm toward the house.

Behind them, the horde of siblings—Varenka, Gayana, Gregory, Georgi, Lili, Piotr, and Dmitri, who had stepped down at the foot of the hillock—weaved their way slowly through the flower beds.

"And how is he getting on, here in this Eden?" La Potemkina persisted, her eyes searching the shadows beneath the trees.

"Is he here?" Gayana asked breathlessly, rushing forward and falling into step with them.

Anna smiled. The older woman's glance toward the woods had not escaped her, but she pretended to address only her little sister.

"Are you looking for him, galloping with your nose to the ground through the bushes?" she teased. "Of course he's here, Gayana. He's spending the summer with us, just like last year. And like Christmas and Easter too. But I doubt you'll run into him before lunch. Between the boats and the horses, he has plenty to keep him busy."

"Such magnanimous hospitality is so typical of our angels," La Potemkina sighed. "On the pretext that this orphan has no place to go during vacation, they invite him to paradise. All the same, the lad would be more in his place at Gostilitsy with the Muslims under Father Alexis's instruction. He has so little time to learn all he does not know."

"He already knows quite a lot," Anna smiled. "He draws, he's taking piano lessons with the empress, and he's a much better musician than His Highness the Grand Duke Nicholas Nicolaïevitch. Which, of course, is no great achievement," she giggled.

Anna did not like the grand duke. Worse, she was afraid of him, even though he was three years her junior. He followed her everywhere and persisted in his attentions, oblivious to her rebuffs.

This was a long-standing obsession for Nicky. Ever since he had turned ten, he had had crushes on all of his mother's maids of honor. He had a vast choice since there were nearly a hundred debutantes every winter who offered their services to the empress. And during the season of balls in Saint Petersburg, their ranks swelled with her sisters', aunts', and cousins' attendants. In total, over three hundred ingénues of seventeen to twenty, all aristocratic damsels of Russia, Poland, Georgia, Lithuania, and all the conquered and annexed states, would be part of the intimate imperial circle, leaving court in a year, or two, or four, to marry.

They were an inexhaustible source of intrigue and passion. Nicky's brothers, Czarevitch Alexander and Grand Duke Constantine, had sampled their charms abundantly before him, often to the ire of indignant parents. For the Romanov boys—at least the older ones—always tempted their conquests with the promise of marriage. These scandals always ended in travel. The broken-hearted young lady was sent home. The irresponsible young prince was sent abroad, and the uncles in Prussia or Austria were asked to find among the crowned heads of Europe a spouse better suited to his station.

But at sixteen—Nicky and Jamal Eddin's age—a little crush on one or another of the girls they had grown up with was a perfectly harmless, almost childish sentiment. Or so the empress thought.

For the young people, falling in love in the summer was infinitely more dangerous and exciting than the lighthearted gallantries they indulged in at the palace. In this setting, their dreams became such an obsession that they colored every other aspect of life. The young people's passions for horses and dogs, for sailing and the sea heightened their sense of romance. Love was as much a part of cottage life as sled races on the quays of the Neva were part of Christmas and lights in the forest were part of the czarina's birthday celebrations in July.

And this August 1847, the graceful Anna of Georgia was the incarnation of love. Favorite reader and secretary, accommodating bearer of parasol and pruning shears, the carefully selected maid of honor was kept in Olympian seclusion for her virtue. With tresses as black and shining as a bird's plumage, dark eyes, and red lips set in a perfectly oval face, she enchanted the entire family. Even the czar cast long looks at her and invented strange and elaborate compliments for her. Even the brooding Jamal Eddin readily gave up his solitude for her company. At siesta time, they would go off to some corner or the gazebo in the garden to recite *The Prisoner of the Caucasus* or Pushkin's verses in praise of their mountains. As for the empress, she gardened, embroidered, painted on porcelain, and went for strolls with her chosen demoiselle.

"For Anna and me, our atelier is our own little world," she would smile. "When we're working there together, we're so content that we don't like to stop, not even for a moment."

In this respect, as in others, Alexandra Feodorovna's behavior was guided by her beloved husband's tastes and convictions. Nicholas detested idleness in those close to him; laziness, he said, led to daydreams, which led to trouble. He himself was physically indefatigable and morally irreproachable—which he considered to be equal virtues. He constantly encouraged summer projects for his entourage. Of course, at Peterhof-Alexandria, the children were on vacation and daily life was free of etiquette and protocol. The guards did not present arms when their imperial highnesses passed, nor did they note the names of all who came and went through the different rooms. However, punctuality was a must, and each was expected to respect the schedule and order of daily tasks. It was up to each of them not to waste a minute of these precious days together.

At dawn, the bugle signaled the beginning of one of the military parades that both the sovereigns adored. Held in a clearing behind the house, the parade ended at ten. Their majesties then went inside to change for their morning stroll. Every morning at eleven on the dot, rain or shine, whether guests were expected (as was the case today) or not, the couple took off across the park, without an escort, like lovers, for an intimate walk and a chat. Whether on foot, on horseback, or in a landau, after thirty years of marriage they still treasured these moments alone together.

And it was precisely at those moments that Anna would find herself in an uncomfortable tête-à-tête at the cottage, alone with Grand Duke Nicholas Nicolaïevitch. She was aware of her own beauty. During the long stays with relatives and friends at the great houses of Tiflis, in Georgia, she could not help but realize the extent of her power. She understood what the men's looks and smiles conveyed. But the grand duke wasn't content to just sigh like the others, dreaming of her charms as any well-bred prince would. His experience with other young women and the certainty that Anna, out of sheer modesty, would never complain—to whom?—made him bold. He would wait for her in the corridor and grab her in passing, forcing his embrace upon her. Nothing she did—vehement protests, slaps across the face, even indifference—discouraged him in the least. He always came back for more. His greedy appetite and brutal nature compelled him to act.

So in the absence of the imperial couple, the young girl desperately sought the protection of someone else, anyone who was not a servant. Where on earth had Jamal Eddin gone? Every morning was the same. Oblivious to Nicky's imminent assaults, blinded by his own happiness, he was doing whatever he pleased. But where? In the boat house? The gazebo? The atelier? Was he busy breaking in his little Kirgese mare, the czar's exquisite gift to him on his sixteenth birthday? Was he riding her in the corral, as he often did? The beach, the garden, the telegraph tower, the library—he could be anywhere. He never rested in the summer; he lived at the cottage as though every day were his last.

"Who among us," La Potemkina paused to collect her words, then continued, addressing her two interlocutors and the group of children. "Of all men, who would refuse to punish the son of his enemy and treat him instead like his own son? One, and one only. The father of us all, who lives in Our Lord Jesus Christ."

She paused in meaningful silence for a moment before uttering the sovereign's name. Like the czar's sixty million subjects, she claimed to have no will of her own, no personal judgment. She was solely an instrument of His will, the will of the Almighty, creator of the emperor as well.

Today her story of Jamal Eddin's destiny in Russia was marked by even more pregnant pauses. She pretended to be so overwhelmed by the enormity of the czar's imperial kindness that she literally had to catch her breath. And in this respect, the wife of the imperial marshal reflected the attitude of all the aristocracy. The portrait she drew was that of a just and benevolent guide.

Nicholas took great care to propagate the myth and publish the accomplishments of this irreproachable master and valiant knight, a legendary figure in whom he sincerely believed. The tale of the mercy he had shown his prisoner was peddled far and wide and had served him well in the hearts of all.

The young people gathered on the grass behind La Potemkina understood that her stance was indicative of her infinite devotion and reverence to the house of Romanov.

"They live to do good, be useful, and spread progress everywhere," the dowager continued as she walked through the hydrangea bushes and the beds of roses. "They are so close to God, our angels, that they fail to realize that a pagan who is ignorant of the truth—"

There. She had said it. Now she could zero in on her main point and express what had become her newest obsession, which she did with great emotional fervor.

"—that a pagan who has not received the word, who does not know the Lord, has developed bad habits here. He has lost all sense of discipline, and he is being corrupted and spoiled."

"But the example of Their Majesties is the very best model," Anna of Georgia protested. "He's receiving an incomparably excellent education."

Sensing that the young woman had taken her observations as criticism, La Potemkina toned her comments down a bit.

"He's not studying what he should, my dove, I'm just saying…what does he read?"

"Goethe, Schiller."

"And the French writers," she interrupted triumphantly, "who talk of nothing but liberty and revolution."

"The empress doesn't fancy French novelists. We read Walter Scott and Fenimore Cooper."

"*The Last of the Mohicans,* I'll bet," Gayana interjected, "which just happens to be Varenka's favorite book."

She shot her two older sisters a waggish look.

"Is Jamal Eddin in love with you too, Anna? Have you turned his head like all the others? Is he flirting with you?"

"That's all we need!" exclaimed their mother, who had never accepted the presence of a Chechen bandit's son in Their Majesties' midst.

She had experienced firsthand the terror that Shamil's men had spread when they swept down upon her husband's lands and attacked the villages on the plain—raids, kidnappings, and ransom had been rampant. At home in Georgia, the Muslim threat was real and close, and with it loomed the shadow of carnage and death. And the sale of kidnapped Christians in the slave markets of Persia and Turkey.

"One good thing about the Cherkesses is that they don't drink or gamble," La Potemkina pontificated.

"And that they would make great sons-in-law?" Anna teased impertinently. "Then why do you want to convert them?"

"Ask Varenka what she thinks," Gayana said snidely. "Hmm? She's so pious, our little Varenka."

Her sister blushed perceptibly but said nothing.

* * *

Late in the morning, returning from their walk, the imperial couple stopped for the second time near their cottage. From afar, they could see the group of young people running down the steps of the perron, the girls in pink dresses, the boys in white uniforms. A searching glance told them that Nicky and Jamal Eddin, the young men of the house, were nowhere to be seen. They stopped talking, sharing their unspoken sadness over the fact that none of the youngsters on the lawn were theirs.

Their second daughter, Grand Duchess Olga—Ollie—had gotten married the summer before, and a year ago she had left Russia to live with her husband in Wurttemburg. Her brother Constantine had accompanied her as far as her new kingdom, then continued his travels. He was sorely missed at the cottage. Even Mikhaïl—Mischa—the youngest at fifteen, was spending the month of August elsewhere. Yes, children always grow up, and inevitably they leave. Of the seven, only Nicky was presently at home. They had recalled all these departures during their long walk and agreed to invite plenty of friends to the domain so that Nicky would have plenty of other young people around.

They avoided mentioning their biggest sorrow, the loss of their youngest daughter, Alexandra, three summers before. It was an emptiness they tried to fill in vain, and neither of them had been able to surmount their pain. She had died just months after getting married, at nineteen, while giving birth to a premature son who did not survive her. The empress's great affection for Anna of Georgia was no doubt influenced by the resemblance of her maid of honor to her lost child. The family kept up appearances, surrounding themselves with young people and entertaining often, but they had never gotten over this loss.

"I'm glad Jamal Eddin is here with us," Alexandra Feodorovna sighed, leaning on her husband's arm as they turned into the lane that led to the back of the house. "There's something reassuring about his presence."

"Reassuring? Mouffy, that's a funny way of putting it."

"And yet I choose my words carefully," she smiled apologetically.

"If, as you put it, this boy is reassuring, where do you suppose that comes from?"

"Why, from you, Nicks. You are the one who has made him the prince he is becoming. You taught him everything."

"True, I wish I received letters from Constantine like the ones he writes to his father. From all our sons, for that matter."

"What does he tell him?"

"Oh, he thanks Almighty God for his life. And he thanks Mohammed the prophet. And he thanks his father."

"He thanks the imam Shamil? Whatever for, for heaven's sake?"

"For being allowed to learn all that he is learning here with us. He tells him that the infidels have shown him incomparable generosity, that no one humiliates him in Russia. That he's grateful for his destiny."

"I'd expect nothing less from such a noble nature. And what does the imam answer?"

"Nothing. You don't think I'd send a single word back there! All the letters land in my desk drawer, and when I'm done reading them, they end up at the war minister's. Good old Chernychev says there are so many that he doesn't know where to file them all. But then, he gripes about everything."

"But then," she said, a bit surprised, "why do you tell this child to write? Why do you encourage him?"

"So that he will remember."

"Oh, Nicks. If you only knew how he longs for an answer, how much he hopes for one."

The emperor frowned, sensing the shadow of a reproach.

"Hope never killed anyone," he said curtly. "I do not want him to forget his origins, at least not completely. Speaking of which, I'd like you to have a little talk with La Potemkina soon. Our good nun needs to temper her zeal. She must stop pestering him with sermons and invitations to attend mass at Gostilitsy. I need this Muslim to remain as he is, a Muslim. Do you understand? I forbid her to convert him."

"But he belongs to our world now. He is part of us."

"You're right, but then again, you're wrong. I want him to be both Russian and Cherkess. Completely Russian and just a little Cherkess—that's what I'm aiming for with this boy."

"I can't imagine him any other place," she persisted, "or any other way. What if he falls in love one day? What if he should want to marry, to start a family?"

"Mouffy, whatever are you talking about? He's only sixteen."

"And you were only twenty when you married me."

"What does one have to do with the other?"

"What would happen if he were taken with a young girl in our entourage? In his entourage, I should say. One of the maids of honor, for example? Like Constantine, like Nicky, like Mischa, and all their friends, like every one of you here."

By alluding to the czar's conduct, Alexandra Feodorovna was venturing out on shaky ground. Three years ago, when their daughter had died, he had taken a mistress, one of the maids of honor at the palace. He had fallen in love with her and pursued her mercilessly, and she had finally consented.

The empress had accepted this liaison, just as she accepted everything about him.

Her many pregnancies and the exhausting pace that the emperor demanded of her when they were not at the cottage had taken their toll upon her health. She had already suffered several cardiac alerts. The doctors, fearing that the next one would be fatal, had forbidden her from indulging in her conjugal duties. Nicks, full of energy and in constant need of activity, had no choice but to form other ties, elsewhere. She forgave him.

The emperor of Russia was so good, so just. So perfect.

Nonetheless, her jealousy was palpable. The proximity of the young woman, whom the czar had installed in a pavilion in the park and whom he insisted be present at every meal, caused the empress unbearable suffering.

In a sense, her marked preference for other young women, for Anna, for all the youngsters of the Georgian family who would serve her one day, was a means of distancing the czar's chosen one from her own intimate circle.

"I understand Jamal Eddin has a penchant for one of the princesses," she continued.

"What normal, healthy young man wouldn't have a weakness for Anna? I'm glad he knows enough to appreciate all the beauty around us, Mouffy. The beauty that you yourself incarnate."

"So do they," said the empress pensively, nodding toward Varenka and Gayana, who stood among the hydrangea blooms. "So do they, Nicks, they are beautiful."

Alexandra Feodorovna hurried down the slope to greet her guests.

The curtains fluttered, white and diaphanous, and floral scents from the garden floated in with the breeze. Light streamed into the dining room. Jamal Eddin loved nothing more than these meals with the entire family gathered around the long table. He loved the sonorous voice of the czar commenting on military reviews and the empress's soft, melodious inflections. He anticipated the rustle of Anna's petticoats before she even appeared. He loved her sparkle and how passionate she was when she spoke of the Georgia of her forbears. He even liked Nicky's asides when he leaned close to Jamal's ear to point out the young girl's charms. He loved the delicate clarity of the glass in the bay windows and the streaks of sunlight on the pastel-painted walls, the warmth of the parquets and the shouts of the imperial grandchildren—Grand Duchess Maria's four sons and the czarevitch's two—

as they played at his feet. Everything felt so familiar to him now.

And now, this miracle, the long-dreamed-of appearance of Varenka. His friendship with her sister and their bond of complicity within the circle of the imperial family had strengthened the tie and kept his memory of her alive.

Every night since he had met Varenka at Sacha Milyutin's, he had relived that moment in the Hercules Rotunda, that face, as he drifted off to sleep. Varenka's presence made this new day at the cottage perfect. Dazzling.

* * *

Calm down, Jamal Eddin told himself. Control the turmoil inside for a moment. Stop and think. Varenka was here. And he was going mad.

Sitting on the bench in the shadow of the sculpted bust, he breathed deeply.

At the cottage, an impromptu ball was about to begin, a country dance on the lawn in honor of the visitors. And he was possessed by a desire to join the festivities, perhaps even dance with her.

Get a hold of yourself.

A rumble of unusual activity from the Peterhof Palace nearby signaled that the carriages were coming for the guests. A line of teams clip-clopped down the lanes leading to Alexandria, and he could make out lights beyond the trees. In the glade behind the house, he knew they were setting up a buffet and stringing Chinese lanterns between the trees. But he would respect his spiritual meeting with Shamil. He would force himself to stay seated in this quiet place longer this evening than on other evenings after prayers.

Excited bats traced endless circles above the green outdoor room. Though he could find nothing to say to his father, he refused to give in to his own impatience. He would stay here in his company for as long as it took him to regain control of himself.

"What do young people dream of on a moonless night like this?"

The emperor's voice.

Jamal Eddin started.

"Don't get up. I'm pleased that this place is still alive, that of all the benches in the garden, you have chosen this one."

Instantly recognizable, the czar's deep voice conveyed its usual authority but lacked its usual composure. He hesitated.

"This is where my daughter loved to come."

Jamal Eddin was embarrassed by his own ignorance and lack of tact as he suddenly understood: the bust of the young beauty between the benches was a memorial to the dead girl. How could he ask forgiveness for sitting in so sacred a place? He stood up, immobile before the powerful mass of a man who sat down in his place. The shadows were so deep that he could not make out the czar's features, not even the shape of his face.

"She used to read here, she—"

His voice broke.

Jamal Eddin had known him only in strength and triumph. The sorrow of this capable and powerful man upset and intimidated him.

It was the same as long ago at Akulgo, when he had seen Shamil suffer, hesitate, then crumple in pain when he was to surrender his son. He would have liked to have relieved him of his burden, taken on his suffering on his behalf.

He wanted to express his love to the czar.

However, he dared not and said nothing.

"You never met her?"

Jamal Eddin shook his head. It was not entirely true; as a child, he had seen the grand duchess several times. He remembered her as a wonderful, distant vision. But he sensed that the emperor expected only the briefest of answers.

"Unfortunately, no, Your Imperial Majesty."

"Alexandra. Her brothers called her Adini. Adini said that, from here—" The czar stopped, inundated by memories. "She said that the view from here—"

Overwhelmed by sadness, he could not go on.

Powerless and unhappy, Jamal Eddin stood still before him, the bust of the young woman barely brushing his shoulder. He was afraid to move and disturb the czar. For a long while, neither one of them spoke.

The emperor finally broke the silence, his voice full of sorrow and regret.

"She was an incomparable singer, such a musician. Of all my daughters she was the one who most resembled her mother. And she so loved—" He choked on his words, regained his composure, and repeated, "so loved life."

At these words, the czar finally broke down.

It was then that Jamal Eddin made an incredible gesture. In a surge of sympathy, he knelt on one knee, clutching his benefactor's hand in his own, and embraced him.

They clasped each other for a long moment.

The older man finally let go with a sigh, tapping him lightly on the shoulder.

"We are all in God's hands. Our souls are not our own. He makes use of us according to His will."

Finding consolation in this thought, the czar repeated, "I am the means he has chosen, that His will be done.

"And you?" he asked briskly, the tone and register of his voice changing abruptly. "What's new with you? I've heard that the princess Potemkina is planning a big party in your honor at Gostilitsy?"

The warmth of his tone suggested that the news pleased him.

Disconcerted, Jamal Eddin did not know what to think or feel. At a loss for words, he rose to his feet.

The czar was well known for his mercurial changes, this manner of passing from one emotion to quite another in the same conversation, without any transition or warning. His interlocutors always found themselves baffled as he plunged them into another of a series of contradictory states. Some—the opponents he sent to Siberia—said Nicholas changed moods the way one would a mask; his contrasting expressions were merely the grimaces and poses of an unfeeling manipulator. Others—his loyal subjects—maintained that Czar Nicholas had such self-control that he prevailed in every situation, through his intelligence and moral strength.

"So, she has performed a new miracle, our good nun?" he exclaimed. "It's true, she knows how to guide the most impenetrable souls to the path of love. I'm glad she succeeded in touching your heart, better than I, better than all of us."

Jamal Eddin withdrew slightly. He stepped backward toward the bench.

"I respect the princess Potemkina's faith, Your Imperial Majesty," he said politely.

He could see it coming. He would stand up to the czar and incur the displeasure of the one man whose will no one opposed. The prospect terrified him.

With all the poise he could summon, he continued, his voice trembling slightly with apprehension. "I admire the princess's generosity toward me, and I am grateful to her, but—"

"And so you should, my boy, for you owe her your salvation."

The czar pretended not to understand where all this was leading.

A short while ago, the empress had spoken of Jamal Eddin's future, his crushes, and the need for him to be baptized if he wanted to pursue a career, eventually marry, and settle in Russia. The czar found such prospects disturbing. He admired his protégé's exceptional faculty of adaptation and realized better than anyone the extent of his intellectual acumen. He even thought, without bitterness, that Jamal Eddin might outshine Nicky or Mischa to become a more brilliant and better-read officer. But to imagine that this Cherkess would exceed the objectives for which he had been educated for the past eight years, deny his origins, renounce his religion, and become a Russian soldier, identical to thousands of other Russian soldiers? It was out of the question.

He knew the mind of his "brave nun." The princess was not only a mystic, but a great romantic, the keenest matchmaker in Petersburg. Many, many aristocratic unions had budded under her auspices. For the good of the families, of course. Whether divine love or human love, love was her primary concern. She was so wealthy and generous that she would even provide a dowry for young girls who confided in her so that they could marry their chosen suitors. Or rather, the suitors that she herself had chosen, in her salons, having ensured that they measured up to the highest standards. Once, and only once, she had dared to provoke imperial fury by arranging the marriage of two of her protégés at her parish of the Holy Trinity, at Gostilitsy, without parental consent. The czar had made sure she would not do it again.

But when she had a heathen in her sights, he knew that she could be tenacious. Who could tell? She might even succeed with Jamal Eddin.

Under other circumstances, he would have been pleased that this child, to whom he was sincerely attached, should find the truth. Unfortunately, the situation demanded that this heart be prevented from seeking the path of light. Nicholas was sounding him out, preaching falsely to discover the truth.

"Only in answering the call of God, of what He expects of you, can you do what is right."

"I beg your pardon, Your Imperial Majesty, but—" the adolescent began to insist more vehemently, only to be interrupted again.

"All your happiness today, Jamal Eddin, your future here on earth and in eternal life depends upon your positive answer to the call of Our Lord Jesus Christ."

This time, the young man could no longer contain himself. Defensive and almost threatening, his words were also full of pain.

"I would give my life for you, but this you must not ask of me."

"I demand nothing, my boy, I simply thank the heavens for the grace you have been granted."

"Do not force me."

"Have I ever forced you to do anything?"

As though surprised and wounded by what he had discovered, the czar scrutinized his protégé.

"Have I ever forced you, Jamal Eddin Shamil?" he repeated, raising his voice. "Answer me!"

"Never, Your Imperial Majesty."

"We were under the impression, the empress and I, that you wished to be baptized," he explained curtly. "I was happy for you, and I gave you my blessing. However, given the violence of your reaction, your unspeakable rudeness, I see I was mistaken. The subject is closed. Since you haven't enough love for God, for the czar, and for Russia, let us speak no more of it."

"I love Russia, Your Imperial Majesty. I love the czar. I owe them everything." His voice quivered with love and rebellion. "But I cannot serve them without honor. I cannot serve them by betraying my God and my people."

The passion of his words left Jamal Eddin's entire body trembling.

"Calm down."

In the shadows, the czar smiled. For the very first time, the young man had lost his composure. When he abandoned his reserve, when he opened up, his feelings were quite transparent.

The czar had his answer.

"Calm down, please. And sit down there," he added softly.

He pointed to the bench facing him. Jamal Eddin was reluctant to sit down.

He remained standing.

"You have already disappointed me," the czar thundered. "Are you going to disobey me? I said sit down!"

Jamal Eddin sat down.

The czar seemed to be thinking. He measured his words.

"Of course you can remain a Montagnard and become Russian—who would tell you otherwise? The empire is vast.

The empire is generous. Look at our friends, the little princesses from Georgia. They will all go home and live their lives. They will all leave, to be married in the Caucasus. The two eldest are already promised to Georgian princes. But their marriages will not change the fact that they are still Russian princesses. And you, when you go home to your father, you will be the imam's heir. God willing, you will become his successor. And you will marry a Muslim princess, several even, since your religion permits it. But you will always be the child of the czar. I love you, Jamal Eddin. Like my own child. Do you know that?"

Distraught, Jamal Eddin rose to his feet again. The czar read his expression and understood that he had won. The boy had passed to the other side—his side—without even realizing it. Nicholas's affection for him was boundless. This child was truly his son, a Russian prince who was worthy of him and worthy of the empire. He hadn't been mistaken about Jamal Eddin. He was noble, devoted, and full of integrity—and still so young and so pure.

He began again, his voice full of kindness.

"I forgive your outburst just now, this stubbornness that is your worst fault. But in exchange, you must promise me one thing. We'll make a pact, the two of us. When you return to the Caucasus, you will convince your father to come and see me. No matter what happens there, you and I will secure peace."

This request corresponded so perfectly to Jamal Eddin's inner feelings that he exclaimed, "I shall devote myself to the task with all my strength, Your Majesty!"

"And I know that you will not disappoint me. Now listen to what I have decided for you. In two years, you will be a standard-bearing cavalry officer in the Russian army.

You will join one of my regiments; we can choose which one together. You will start your military career in Poland or on the Western frontier. When you have had enough experience and have become an excellent officer, then, Jamal Eddin, you will pay back a hundredfold what Russia, your country, has given you. You will work alongside your father to put an end to this fratricidal war forever. And in the meantime, my boy, take advantage of what your country has to offer, profit from all that Russia can teach you. Continue your studies, practice your English, your French, and your German, as well as the Avar language, Chechen, and the dialects of the mountain people. Keep up with your mathematics and physics, since you love those subjects. Accept all the blessings of providence with a mind free of concern. I authorize you to do so. Indeed, I encourage you.

"Go to Princess Potemkina's balls when she invites you. There you will encounter enlightened minds, the best of Petersburg aristocracy. In her salons, you will meet the Muslim officers of my personal guard. They are the sons of khans and Cherkess princes, with whom you should develop ties of friendship, so that you can rely on them when the time comes. This elite will be precious to you. But in the meantime, in the meantime, my child, live! Live, I beg you, take advantage of all that you can. Now return to the terrace and tell the ladies I am coming. And leave me alone for a moment. Please, go back now."

Jamal Eddin took long strides across the woodland grass. He could scarcely believe it. All that he had waited for, all these years, had just happened. The emperor had told him what he expected of him. Finally! And he had finally told him why he was here, in Russia, and how to repay his debt. Of course, during their first encounter in the Winter Palace, the czar had given him to understand the reasons for his abduction from Akulgo and his education in Petersburg. But at the time he had been too young to understand their meaning and too wary to believe him. Today, eight years later, he subscribed wholeheartedly to his benefactor's plans.

Gone was the anguish that had prevented him from belonging completely to the Russian world, from accepting and approving its values. The guilt, the fear of betraying his past, the fear of forgetting his people—it had all vanished. The incredible announcement that he would soon return to his mountains endowed him with the one thing whose lack had always kept him from fitting in: confidence.

All at once, His Majesty's explicit consent, their agreement that he was free to choose his own religion, and their pact for the future destroyed the last bastions of his resistance and swept away all his doubts and conflicting feelings.

Now everything was possible. Well, almost everything.

When it came to the Georgian princesses, he now knew that he was chasing rainbows and that his dreams of love were hopeless. But then, hadn't he always known it? He had never expected his feelings to be reciprocated; he had never wanted anything from them. Because of their shared Caucasian origins, the homesickness they all felt for the mountains, the familiar common memories he read deep in their eyes, he had thought he could reconcile their different worlds through his passion for the young women. But he had been wrong. Anna and Varenka could not be the unifying link between two worlds. The czar had been clear on this point as well. Their destiny was not to be joined with his.

Knowing this, understanding it, even accepting it was one thing; feeling it, of course, quite another. He quickened his pace.

As he approached the cottage, his desire to be with Varenka grew stronger. His heart had sunk when the czar had said that she would belong to another, that the matter was settled. He thought he had overcome his twinge of sadness at the news, but now it returned, suddenly transformed into a raging storm. What did they expect of him? That he should sacrifice his feelings on the pretext that separation was inevitable? That was absurd! His complicity with Varenka was now free of the burden of the future, liberated from any ambiguity whatsoever, and could only become lighter, more innocent, and more joyous. He seethed in revolt against the voice that told him to let her go.

How was he supposed to conduct himself? Should he disappear among the plants, hiding in the shadow of the Hercules Rotunda, as he had the first time? Should he hide his attraction to her, feign coldness, and pretend to be indifferent to her? Should he invite all the other girls to dance, all except the one he loved? Why? Why should he behave in such a stupid manner? Because she was Christian, the granddaughter of a king, and promised to a Georgian prince? So what? The others were Christians too; the others were engaged as well. Why sacrifice his affection for her to his fear of suffering? Or friendship to caution? Tenderness to reason? His entire being rejected that way of thinking. Since life had offered him this glorious gift of freedom, why should he not take walks with Varenka, talk to her, laugh with her, even love her? Nothing else mattered. She was there, under these trees, just footsteps away.

He began to run. She was there tonight. She was waiting for him tonight. Who could tell what tomorrow would bring? Tomorrow he would lose her. But in the meantime…*In the meantime, my child, live! Live, I beg you, take advantage of all that you can.*

Yes, all the happiness in the world was still possible. Tonight.

Overjoyed and burning with gratitude toward the czar, he joined the group on the terrace.

The bay windows of the salon were wide open. The crown prince, his wife and sister, their maids of honor and the children, Count Kiselyev, and other guests among the close friends staying at the palace had just arrived for the empress's impromptu party.

The musicians were already seated in a semicircle on the lawn. After tuning their instruments, they launched into a Glinka polonaise and a few rousing quadrilles to open the ball. Then it would be Alexandra Feodorovna's turn to play their favorite waltzes and popular mazurkas. Her piano had been brought out and stood on the parquet that had been installed at the center of the dance floor.

Everyone was going back and forth between the hall and the perron, waiting for the czar, who was to accompany his wife on the flageolet and the cornet. It would be lovely.

Leaning against the doorpost, Nicky watched Anna as she passed back and forth before him, carrying the sheet music, the stool, the lectern, the candles and candelabra.

"Walk on, mademoiselle, walk on," Nicky said in French, "you're awfully pretty this evening."

He was careful not to brush against his mother's second maid of honor, the one who lived in the pavilion of the park.

Instinctively he sensed she was already spoken for and off limits.

Pretending, like Nicky, to be unaware of the presence of "this person," Alexandra Feodorovna was supervising the final preparations. Jamal Eddin watched her flutter about. He found the empress beautiful this evening, lively and gay, the way he liked to see her. He noticed every detail: the nosegay of red mignonettes she had slipped into her belt and the filmy gown of white chiffon that she wore. He noticed Anna's white dress too, which was not quite so bright and softened with gray-beige stripes, and that Varenka and Gayana wore matching skirts. They were pink, as was customary at fifteen, but they were long now, hiding their pantalets and ankle boots.

Jamal Eddin's conversation with the czar had made him receptive to other impressions as well. He appreciated the beauty of some of the married women and the opulence of their décolletés, proof to their admirers that time and successive pregnancies had robbed them of none of their charms. He even admired the ample shoulders of Princess Anastasia of Georgia. As for La Potemkina…Ah, La Potemkina. Ensconced in her plum-colored flounces, dripping with jet and braid, her black curls springing from her white headdress, she was simply amusing. He watched her bustling back and forth, checking on the party arrangements, and losing her patience. There was something touching about seeing such energy in someone of such a mature age, and her spontaneity and high spirits were contagious.

"It isn't hard to be happy tonight, is it?" Anna remarked, eyes sparkling, as Jamal Eddin walked up to where she was standing beneath the trees.

The Chinese lanterns hung among the branches, just as he had imagined them earlier. The young people stood together in a halo of light.

"There's a party in the air," she mused. "Just breathing, it feels like a party."

"Anna! Where did you leave my fan a while ago?" exclaimed La Potemkina, seated at the edge of the dance floor.

The young girl rolled her eyes toward the sky.

"Oh, she's always losing something, that one."

"And while you're at it, get me my shawl too, will you? Anna."

"Coming, coming."

Varenka made a vague gesture to follow her.

"You're not going to leave?" he said, half mocking, half serious. "Not right away, not yet. Not like the last time?"

She understood the allusion and smiled at him.

"Then everything is fine," he said gaily, "and I'll be able to make the speech I've been preparing for the past two years."

He bowed deeply.

"Will you do me the *honor*"—he emphasized the word ironically, as the obtuse student had done long ago at Count Kiselyev's dinner table—"the honor of granting me the first waltz? The first, and all the others?"

Princess Potemkina and the Georgian princess sat back in their armchairs and fanned themselves as they watched the young people.

The ball began, as planned, with the contra dances.

Jamal Eddin led the quadrilles tirelessly, taking the dancers up and down the steps of the perron, making each couple execute bows and curtsies, then leading them toward the garden only to draw the farandole back along the paths all the way to the sovereigns. Everyone laughed at the figures he imposed upon his poor quadrillers.

When everyone had tired of prancing about in bands of eight, a sudden stillness filled the air. Both dressed in white, the czar and the czarina rose, crossed the dance floor hand in hand, and bowed to the assembly like two strolling players. The wild applause made the Chinese lanterns sway, casting glimmers of red, yellow, and blue deep into the foliage.

They sat down next to each other among the great trees, whispered in consultation, smiled, then broke into a waltz. The emperor set the tempo, playing his cornet with lively enthusiasm.

The young people hesitated shyly. No one dared to be the first.

"Well now?" Nicholas exclaimed as he changed from trumpet to flute, in between breaths. "Are you going to dance?"

Since it was an intimate party, young men were permitted to ask the girls to dance without seeking permission from their mothers. Nicky grabbed Anna, Jamal Eddin, Varenka. And the others followed.

"It's exceptionally hot for this time of year," Princess Anastasia of Georgia lamented as she fanned herself more vigorously.

"Their Majesties are the best musicians in the world," La Potemkina burbled. "And just look at the young people. I must say this is a show that is worth coming for. Our Jamal Eddin—"

"Indeed, the Dagestani twirls around quite agilely," the Georgian princess agreed.

"You mean, he waltzes like a god. I've seen him ride, and I knew he was an extraordinary horseman, but I wasn't expecting this. He is the best dancer in all of Petersburg. Look at the other girls. Look how they tap their feet when he passes. They're waiting for only one thing. Our dear, handsome Nicky is really a magnificent waltzer. But Jamal's dancing—it's something else entirely. Even in His Imperial Highness's arms, Anna is trying to catch his eye. You can see she's hoping for the next dance. But at this age, a boy is faithful to a girl, and he only has eyes for one."

"Yes, it's rather selfish of him to always choose the same partner."

"Ah, the exclusivity of puppy love, my dear."

"He's going to end up compromising her."

"Compromise Varenka? In whose eyes, my dear? We are among our own here."

"Among our own? This boy has neither family nor fortune nor title. If it were not for Their Majesties' magnanimity, and your protection, my dear—"

"Among our own," La Potemkina interrupted, "such support is indicative of one thing: his own merit. Do you think Their Majesties, in their infinite mercy, would grant their august protection if they did not think he deserved it? When a young man with his presence takes over the mazurka, leads the cotillion, dances the French quadrilles."

"Precisely. Such an excellent dancer has obligations. He does not consider himself the appointed partner of only one young girl; he dances with all of them, one after the other."

As he turned around the dance floor, Jamal Eddin heard their comments. He felt heady with success. It was delightful to sense the music coursing through his veins, the piano lending its rhythm, and the flute beating time. He felt the music with Varenka's every quickening breath. Something golden lit up and faded in her, in time with the waltz.

"Live," the emperor's flute repeated to him joyously. "Live, Jamal Eddin!"

CHAPTER VIII

That Day May Dawn and Night Perish
The Taste of Happiness
1848–1853

The training field for maneuvers at the camp of Krasnoye Sielo, near Saint Petersburg
The military academies parade, a year later
May 1848

There was a roll of drums and a clash of cymbals. Jamal Eddin and his comrades stood impatiently behind the barriers at the edge of the field. The eleven brass bands of eleven regiments converged before them, saluting each other as they entered the parade ground. With each company playing its own theme, all eleven military marches burst into tune at the same time. While anyone else would have been stunned by the noise, the deafening racket lifted their spirits with pride and joy.

Today marked the justification and the apotheosis of eight long years of training.

Dressed in a white gown, the empress was enthroned in the first row of a sumptuous green box built for her at the edge of the field, surrounded by her daughter, daughters-in-law, ladies-in-waiting, and grandchildren. In the grandstands next to the imperial box on the same side of the field, the high society ladies flitted about, escorted by foreign officers, travelers, and visitors of rank rather than their husbands. The men of Saint Petersburg would serve in the arena. The highest dignitaries, Czarevitch Alexander, the grand dukes, and General Count Kiselyev, would lead their regiments in the parade. Even the cadets of the academies, who normally did not participate in military reviews at Krasnoye Sielo, would parade today. The special circumstances of this May 1848 justified the presence of the empire's entire corps.

As a result of the revolution that had taken place in Paris the February before, Holy Russia had been forced to protect herself from the contagion of liberal ideas by preparing for war. Entertaining yet symbolic, today's magnificent performance was a showcase designed to display the perfect training of the young recruits and the crushing power of the czar's army. France, the constitutional republics of Europe, and other republics throughout the world were the intended audience. When the ambassadors left the grandstands shortly after the show, they would return home convinced that thousands of men stood as one behind God's representative on earth. And that this amazingly cohesive and powerful bloc was the guarantor of universal order.

* * *

In the saddle since dawn, the cadets waited their turn. All of them searched the grandstands for the familiar faces of mothers, sisters, and their favorite girls. Like the others, Jamal Eddin scanned the crowd. There in the second row, gesticulating extravagantly, was La Potemkina, who loved the excitement of military parades and the odor of gunpowder. She was accompanied by her usual retinue, the patronesses of the prison committee and a gaggle of nieces and protégés. Most importantly, he noticed, the Georgian princesses were missing. The entire Georgian family was absent. Of course this was no surprise to him. This very month, Anna was to marry a Georgian prince of the illustrious Chavchavadze line of Kakhetia, and Varenka was part of the wedding party. He so yearned to parade before her, and up to the very last moment, he had held out some hope of seeing her. Fate had decided otherwise, and he accepted it, crestfallen. But even his disappointment could not entirely spoil his pleasure today.

The colors, smells, and sounds of war—the clarion of the bugles, the cannon fire, the pungent scent of leather and horse manure, the taste of gunpowder and dust—were intoxicating.

His eyes were riveted upon His Majesty's guards as they crossed the field, parading in columns, as they had during the Napoleonic wars. He knew, as they all did, that each of these horsemen had been chosen because of his looks. Long legs, broad chests, splendid complexions, suitable eye color, and lustrous hair were the predominant criteria for joining this exclusive group.

The magnificent Preobrajensky Guards wore their famous green uniforms. All of them were exceptionally tall, like the czar. Broad-shouldered, regular-featured, slim-waisted, with sturdy calves, and mounted on identical chargers, they sought to evoke the reincarnation of the heroes of antiquity.

The green sea of Preobrajensky Guards gave way to the blue lines of the Semenovsky Regiment, followed by a white wave of Izmaïlovsky uniforms. The Pavlovsky Regiment, with their conical helmets and sabers drawn, a tradition fiercely won during the battles of the last century, brought up the rear. Then came the artillery, its first batteries of cannons on caissons drawn by teams of six bay horses. The second were drawn by sorrels, the third by gray barbs, and the last by black geldings.

The atamans of the Cossacks of the Don followed, riding little Kirgese mares. Then came the Uhlans, dressed in red-trimmed blue, a forest of lances broken occasionally by standards wrested from the Turks. Thousands of horsemen brought up the rear, and the cadets of the military academies closed the parade.

At the foot of the tribune, in the arena, the czar rode astride a prancing stallion, escorted simply by his brother, Grand Duke Mikhaïl Pavlovitch, and a bugler who trumpeted his orders. He directed the drills.

Jamal Eddin missed the gesture that silenced the crowd, but suddenly all eleven brass bands fell silent, and the thousands of horses came to a standstill, their riders waiting expectantly.

The grand duke galloped off to the edge of the field with the bugler. The czar remained alone, facing his troops. It was absolutely silent. Not so much as a neigh, the creak of a harness, the click of a bit, or the spin of a spur wheel broke the quiet. A powerful silence and stillness reigned over all, in the grandstands and on the field alike.

Then the czar gave a mighty cry, one word that echoed as far back as the ranks of the First Corps cadets:

"Charge!"

In one fluid movement, Jamal Eddin and his comrades, all the men, horses, cannons, and mounts, bounded forward.

Waves of green, blue, and white swept across the camp at lightning speed, the thunder of pounding hooves eclipsing the women's cheers.

The czar stood stock-still before the tide of horsemen. His horse pawed the ground, startled by the approaching spectacle. Ten thousand horsemen charged toward the imperial box, headed straight for the emperor.

The distance shrank by the second, and it looked as though the mass would trample the stallion and the grandstands full of women. But the instant they reached the box, the ten thousand horsemen stopped as abruptly as they had started, as a single body.

The horses' breasts formed a single line, their hooves aligned along an invisible mark that went on for several versts. Row after row, the ranks repeated their original order.

The only sounds were the bated gasps of the men and the snuffled panting of the horses. Their delicate nostrils quivered, some bleeding, less than a meter from the pale, distraught face of Czarina Alexandra and half that distance from the satisfied countenance of Czar Nicholas.

The sheer intoxication of participating in such a ballet, the excitement of executing such perfection, was inexpressible. Boot to boot, elbow to elbow, Jamal Eddin and his comrades—Sacha Milyutin, Buxhöwden, and all his comrades of the corps—had triumphed at this complex exercise, and their pride was boundless.

The feeling echoed Jamal Eddin's long-ago memory of galloping among the murids, his brothers-in-arms. At the time, he had felt that he was part of the greatest army in the world, Shamil's army.

More perhaps than all the other horsemen loping across the training field at Krasnoye Sielo, he was carried away with the headiness of that joy he had known long ago—a joy brought on by the sensation of belonging.

"My children, I am pleased with you."

His Majesty uttered the ritual phrase that honored their work and crowned their exploits.

As one voice, they answered with a spirited, "At your service, Little Father!", the ritual words of an equally sacred response.

The opening of the grand opera was over. The regiments headed toward their assigned corners of the maneuver grounds.

It was time for the performances of the Cadet Corps. Grand Duke Mikhaïl Pavlovitch had informed their master of the program of drills to be accomplished, and the cadets had practiced for months. And they would practice again today, as many times as necessary.

Their maneuvers before the czar could go on for an hour or two, or six, or eight, until the horses were exhausted or their riders dead. No matter, the corps would continue to practice until it achieved the unity of divine Russian cohesion. But to do that perfectly with absolute precision was nearly impossible on this hilly, unfamiliar terrain full of bumps and holes.

One of the drills was the formation of an immense "8," done at a gallop. At the intersection of the 8 were two low walls that the cadets coming from both directions had to jump. The challenge lay in jumping the wall in synchronicity with the rider arriving from the opposite direction, all while maintaining speed. The problem no one had taken into account was the dust. The earth had already been hammered by thousands of hooves, and hundreds of riders charging across the dry ground had stirred up a great deal of sand. Jamal Eddin, Sacha, and Buxhöwden could scarcely make out the rumps of the horses in front of them, and the obstacles loomed, gigantic, before their eyes at the last moment. Worse still, it was impossible to judge the remaining distance before the rider to the right or the left would crouch low in the saddle to clear the obstacle a few seconds before them or after.

With horses colliding in midflight, head-on crashes, thrashing horses, and trampled riders, a considerable number of men and beasts were lost that day.

The brutality of the falls and the gravity of the accidents did not prevent Grand Duke Mikhaïl Pavlovitch from galloping up to the leader to bark in his face, "In your fourth squadron, first platoon, the first cadet's curb chain has not been cleaned. Disciplinary action for the entire corps!"

The leader galloped down to the cadet in question. And there it was, to Buxhöwden's horror—a spot of rust on the horse's bit.

As a result, all the cadets would be forbidden to leave camp for a month. And Buxhöwden would be under arrest until further orders. But what did it matter to be punished, as long as the entire corps was in it together? They were there to live and die together. And the grand duke, with his eagle eye and his demanding nature, inspired more admiration than fear. Nothing counted but solidarity among comrades and admiration for their leaders. And love for the czar, of course.

* * *

Covered with dust, staggering with fatigue at the end of this long day, Jamal Eddin took the path along the river to return to camp. He had stayed at the stables longer than the others, and evening had begun to fall.

As he walked among the first rows of white tents, headed toward the lane where he and his companions were billeted, he had the sudden impression that he had seen this place before.

Puzzled, he stopped and looked around.

There was no doubt about it, he knew this place—the cordoned-off alleys, the tents like whitecaps as far as the eye could see. Of course. The camp at Akulgo.

The image was from long ago. From high up on the ramparts, he had gazed out over a sea of men, horses, mules, and cannons that spilled over the banks of the Andi Koysu. The light of the setting sun had played off the bayonets of the troops bivouacked along the river, just as it did here at the river of Krasnoye Sielo. The glinting blades had caught the sun's rays in a forest of steel. Just as they did this evening. He had heard the shouts of greeting to the latecomers around the campfire. Just as he heard them this evening.

He suddenly realized that he had already lived through this scene, but on the other bank, the other side of the river.

He had stepped through the mirror. He had changed sides.

He was moved by his discovery, but not sorry. On the contrary, now he knew where the Most Merciful had placed him in the game of reflections and appearances. His place on the chessboard of destiny seemed clear, and he knew it was natural and just, because it had been designated by God.

He strode forward again, gaily reciting the last verse of Pushkin's "Bacchanalian Song":

That day may dawn
And the night perish.

Between Saint Petersburg and Warsaw
1849–1852

The exhilaration that Jamal Eddin had felt the first time he waltzed around a dance floor and galloped across the training grounds was repeated—and just as intensely felt—many times in the years that followed. Be they balls at the Winter Palace, receptions at La Potemkina's, suppers at the barracks, parades, or hunts, Jamal Eddin was present for them all. And although he neither drank nor smoked nor gambled, his comrades always welcomed him as a boon companion they knew they could count on for high spirits and a little mischief. He finished his studies with execrable marks in the two subjects that counted for the czar: an average of six in routine drills, including the sacrosanct goose step, and four in discipline.

These mitigated failures did not prevent him from being named to his legal guardian's regiment, the Uhlan Lancers of His Imperial Highness the Grand Duke Mikhaïl Pavlovitch, the strictest of the generals. He entered as an officer of the seventh division of the Vladimirsky Lancers and was immediately posted to Poland, to help protect the Russian border.

The miracle of his integration into a prestigious regiment despite his mediocre grades and the haste of his departure for Warsaw were both a consequence of the bellicose atmosphere that had sprung up in 1849.

That winter, the fall of King Louis-Philippe of France had been rapidly followed by the Hungarian revolt against the Emperor Franz-Joseph. Overwhelmed by the magnitude of the uprising, Austria had asked for the czar's help, and he had seized the occasion to invade Hungary. His army crushed the rebels and reestablished order throughout the country. The need for recruits among students old enough for military service increased considerably.

The emperor's choice of post for Jamal Eddin suited his skills perfectly. He was now part of the light cavalry, prized for its capacity to move rapidly. Tall, slender, dark-haired, and elegant, he fit the typical Uhlan physical type as well.

The first steps of Jamal Eddin's military career were exceptionally brilliant. Though Russia's lightning victory in Hungary scarcely lent the Uhlans of Poland the opportunity to distinguish themselves, Jamal Eddin's superiors were quick to recognize in him the qualities of an outstanding officer: bravery, authority, and a sense of honor. While Buxhöwden was still a junker and Milyutin a cornet, Jamal Eddin was promoted to lieutenant. It was quite an achievement, a record even, for officers of Montagnard origin had to show uncommon diligence to advance in rank. His military talents were not his only advantage; his popularity, the affection and respect of his men, and the friendship of his comrades also contributed to his rapid advance.

Moreover, it happened that the lancers' fearsome commanding officer, Grand Duke Mikhaïl Pavlovitch, was felled by a fatal heart attack in Warsaw and subsequently replaced by his nephew, Grand Duke Mikhaïl Nicolaïevitch, Jamal Eddin's former comrade in the Cadet Corps. The small group of friends that had so often gathered at Count Kiselyev's home were together once again. Only His Highness Nicky, now a colonel of the guard, was absent. But Nicky had other matters to attend to or, more precisely, other skirts to chase in Petersburg, with his fellow lancers. Since Anna, the eldest Georgian princess, had married, the following year he had fallen for Varenka, who had replaced her sister as the czarina's reader. But Varenka had then followed in her sister's footsteps.

In May 1851, she married a Georgian prince, General Elico Orbeliani, who had been the imam Shamil's hostage a decade before.

And so Nicky moved on to the third Georgian princess, Gayana. She was an easier target than her sisters and soon succumbed to his advances. Both families were scandalized to learn that she had become his official mistress, and the subject of Nicholas Nicolaïevitch's liaison with one of the little Georgian princesses dominated court gossip for some time.

"That's it, it's done," La Potemkina wrote to Jamal Eddin with her habitual elegance in a letter announcing the marriage of one and the fall of the other. The knowledge that he had definitively lost Varenka saddened Jamal Eddin, but he had not seen the love of his childhood since he had joined the army. He had long known that her marriage was inevitable.

During those two years, he had been involved with other women and had other affairs. At Kovno, where the Uhlans were stationed, he had become the favorite in a circle of several married women who competed in their efforts to seduce him with an onslaught of charm. The handsome, mysterious, elusive Jamal Eddin was indeed considered a catch.

The orgies and visits to the brothels that his fellow officers enjoyed did not tempt him, but he enjoyed the fact that he was attractive to women. No woman ever left him feeling indifferent. He gave in to their advances readily and without fuss, but neither his friends nor his mistresses could count his conquests. Although he formed an emotional attachment to a few, he could not imagine a more serious relationship with any of them.

The former cadets remembered those years of inaction at Kovno as a carefree existence of concerts at the châteaus of the aristocracy, regimental dinners, and balls at the viceroy's palace. It was *la belle vie* for the czar's officers in Poland.

In the eyes of all, Jamal Eddin was now perfectly integrated and assimilated—more Russian than a Russian.

The soldier Jamal Eddin Shamil's official acceptance into the occupation army had initially posed a problem for the seventh division military administration: what were they to inscribe on his passport?

Just before his departure in 1849, the emperor received an urgent and disturbing note from Jamal Eddin's captain concerning the official civil status of the recruit. Should he write down the words habitually penned on his scholastic records: son of a rebel?

The czar had penciled in his response in the margin of Jamal's military records. "Since the boy is not responsible for the acts of his father, and the word 'rebel' does not indicate his country of origin, the expression 'son of a rebel' is not appropriate. Moreover, it could negatively influence the character of the soldier in question. Consequently, his first name, his last name, and the notation 'of Montagnard origin' will suffice."

The question of his identity resolved, the captain was faced with another, one that the authorities were already familiar with: what uniform should Jamal wear? The papakha, cherkeska, ghizir, and kinjal of the Montagnard regiments? Or the imperial eagle-emblazoned shako, royal blue tunic with its red plastron and double-breasted button closures, wide silver-threaded belt, and lance of the Uhlans?

Exasperated by the errors of his predecessors, all of whom were going off on the wrong tangent, the captain composed a second note to the czar, this time concerning "Shamil's uniform."

Again in the margin of Shamil's military records, His Majesty scribbled his reply: "The dress he prefers."

Beneath this comment, Jamal Eddin's decision would be noted.

But what would he choose?

This question became the subject of a guessing game the following day when the czar posed the question to the empress, Count Kiselyev, and the rest of their intimate circle at their "four o'clock dinner."

"Mouffy, you know him well. What do you think, will he wear the cherkeska or the blue tunic? Which one has he chosen, the uniform of the Caucasian Montagnards or that of the Vladimirsky Lancers?"

His tone was triumphant. He did not wait for her reply.

"Well, no, you're wrong, you're all wrong. Jamal Eddin did not make the choice you all expected. He is faithful to his past, to his father and to his origins. He didn't hesitate for an instant. In a gesture from the heart, he chose the symbol of his people of the Caucasus."

The czar was jubilant.

Why would he be so pleased that his chosen son, his protégé, his favorite, had preferred the cherkeska? The empress and their guests were mystified. The czar was the only one who understood the significance of this ultimate act of loyalty, this gesture of faithfulness and affection that confirmed all his own acts and intentions. In choosing the cherkeska, Jamal Eddin demonstrated respect for his ancestors and for his commitment to the czar. He had, in effect, sealed the pact they had made that evening on the marble bench at Peterhof. He remained what he was always had been: a Caucasian.

Wasn't this what they had agreed upon?

Both Russian and Montagnard, the boy was continuing to embrace the path of dual loyalty.

But did he think—as His Majesty feigned to believe—did he really believe he could reconcile the two? Without renouncing one or the other? Without betraying who he was?

Loyal to the czar and loyal to the imam, Jamal Eddin was trying to meet that challenge and make good on his word.

Keen to lend him support, the emperor immediately dispatched a Chechen aide to serve as his orderly at Kovno. He had no doubt that his envoy would prove both useful and pleasant. This servant would help Jamal Eddin perfect his knowledge of the language, the people, and the customs of the Caucasus. Jamal Eddin must progress considerably on this path before he could send him back to the mountains. And this Shibshiev was fluent in over thirty dialects.

He didn't know it at the time, but the actions of this individual would prove fatal to the czar's plans.

* * *

"A Muslim like you, Jamal Eddin, a Muslim who sleeps with his feet pointing toward Mecca, a Muslim who shaves his beard, a Muslim who wears scent, who kisses the hands of women, a Muslim who does not get up to pray in the middle of the night. A Muslim like you is no longer a Muslim, but a dog."

With great difficulty, Jamal Eddin refrained from slapping the man across the face. Shibshiev was driving him crazy and had pushed him to the limit.

Shibshiev wasn't much to look at. Small and stooped, he had an unhealthy gray complexion, and his cherkeska was always dirty. He lacked any of the elegance and physical courage that marked the mountain men and did not even wear the traditional Montagnard weapon tucked into his belt—a telling detail. He wore a long beard, which made him stand out among the Cherkesses of Saint Petersburg. How he had managed to get the czar's stamp of approval was a mystery. Czar Nicholas execrated bearded men and had ordained that all at court, in the army, and in the city should be clean-shaven. He tolerated beards only among the Jews, the muzjiks, and certain indigenous regiments, with whom Shibshiev had never served. In fact, he wasn't Chechen at all, but Uzbek, from the Kipchak tribe—a detail that escaped the notice of the Russians, who, in their contempt and ignorance of all other peoples, had failed to make the distinction. He had grown up in Dagestan and joined the imperial army as a "child of language." General Fézé, whom he had served as an interpreter, had highly recommended him to communicate with the sons of khans studying at the military academies.

He had come to Petersburg a few years before Jamal Eddin, at the age of thirty-five. At the time, he had been very friendly to the infidels, especially to the young Circassians he sometimes visited. Jamal Eddin had known him for a long time and remembered him clearly. As a child, he had given Shibshiev a letter for his father, hoping to secretly bypass the authorities. The letter had ended up on the emperor's desk, like all the others, and his efforts had earned Jamal Eddin a stern scolding and strict orders that he write only through the intermediary of the director. This incident had convinced Jamal Eddin that Shibshiev worked for the police as an informer charged with surveillance of the Cherkesses of the Cadet Corps, including himself. He had cut off any contact with Shibshiev immediately.

However, Shibshiev had changed over the past twelve years. He had taken a different path, in precisely the opposite direction of Jamal Eddin's trajectory.

He was neither impressed nor attracted by the Christian lifestyle. In fact, his experience in the empire's capital had transformed Shibshiev into something he had never been in his Dagestan village: a good Muslim. In Russia, he stopped smoking, drinking, and gambling. He learned to recite from the Koran and knew Sheik Al-Buhari's *Book of Hadiths* by heart. This late-in-life return to the Sharia had made him all the more rigorously devoted to his religion. Now he obeyed all the precepts of the imam Shamil and concentrated his efforts on fighting the holy war, furtively and from afar.

Among the exiles of the Caucasus, Shibshiev was not the only admirer of Shamil. In the early 1850s, the imam's victories had become legendary. Even his old enemies, even the hypocrites and the sons of the khans, had to admit that Shamil had brought honor to the Muslims. His network of spies now reached far beyond the line of Russian forts along the Caucasus. He received information from all over the empire, even the Saint Petersburg papers, which he had translated by his prisoners at the eagle's nest of Dargo-Veden. He was so well informed that he had written to Queen Victoria, pointing out that his combat, and his alone, here in the mountains with his warriors, had prevented the czar's armies from threatening the interests of the British as they advanced toward Afghanistan and India. Since, as he pointed out, the holy war was such a boon to the queen, he had asked her for arms. In London, in absolute secret, her ministers discussed whether or not to send rifles to the imam. And Shibshiev knew that he was a link in this chain, a cog in the wheel, and a relay in the organization of this formidable head of state.

When the czar had chosen him to serve Jamal Eddin, the eldest son of his guide and master, Shibshiev could scarcely contain his joy. He had galloped off for Kovno right away.

His disappointment was as immense as his hopes had been.

He understood instantly what the Russians had done to this boy. They had corrupted him, perverted him, and turned him against his father.

"Your forehead is as smooth as a woman's," he sneered, observing the absence of the *zabtba,* the blue callus that marked the faithful, above Jamal Eddin's brow. He considered this to be ample proof that the boy did not pray as he should. Shibshiev did not even bother to look at his pants. He already knew that the knees were not worn out, as they should be if he knelt in prayer seven times a day as the faithful did. He could well imagine the rest. This Jamal Eddin was vain, soft, accustomed to luxury, his every action an affront to the law of God. He danced, he played music, he touched women and petted dogs. He used both hands at table and consumed food that the dietary laws forbade. He was even more impure than a giaour.

Profoundly shocked, Shibshiev pelted Jamal Eddin with threats and curses. He stuck to him like a shadow, relentless in his abuse. Jamal Eddin, who could not stand a confrontation or a row, considered Shibshiev's behavior highly uncivilized. His crudeness and vulgarity were appalling. Shibshiev's reproaches were so constant and so merciless that they exasperated him before he had even bothered to understand or register their substance. Most importantly, they were so excessive that they didn't elicit in Jamal Eddin the least doubt or worry concerning his own conduct.

Since Jamal Eddin could not dismiss him without the czar's approval, he simply tried to stay calm and tune him out—in short, put up with him. Only once did Shibshiev manage to shake his resolve, striking a nerve that touched Jamal Eddin so profoundly that he flew into a rage.

One evening the young lieutenant returned to his quarters to find that Shibshiev had fresh news from the Caucasus, information that seemed to have dropped from the sky. He announced that Jamal's mother had died seven years ago and that the imam had chosen the eldest daughter of Sheik Jamaluddin Al-Ghumuqi as her replacement. He had taken other wives as well, who had borne him more sons. But that was nothing compared to the next piece of news. Shibshiev coddled his revenge triumphantly. No, it was nothing.

A year ago, Shamil had named Jamal Eddin's younger brother, Mohammed Ghazi, as his spiritual heir and successor. The eighteen-year-old had legally taken his older brother's place in a ceremony attended by all the naïbs.

Jamal Eddin listened to all this calmly and asked only one question—in Russian.

"Where did you get this information?"

"I know it," Shibshiev replied, in Chechen.

"How?"

"I know it," the servant repeated smugly.

"Who told you this?" Jamal Eddin exploded.

Jamal Eddin grabbed him by the collar. Shibshiev made no move to defend himself. He was not armed and would not engage in a fistfight.

Jamal Eddin let go of him. "Get out of my sight!"

He did not have to tell Shibshiev twice. The servant took the lieutenant's coat, saber, and kinjals and left.

Stunned and enraged, Jamal Eddin could not believe the news. What? For the past thirteen years, he had written faithfully to his father, without ever receiving so much as a word of response. Never had the imam deigned to answer even one of his letters. He was so upset that he could not even find words for the exact reason for his anger. How could he have been stripped of all his rights of primogeniture when his father knew that Jamal was alive? The fact that Shamil had chosen this savage, this accursed shadow, Shibshiev, to deliver his message only added to the disgrace.

This kind of renunciation contravened all the laws of the kanly, as well as those of the Sharia, both the laws of blood and the laws of Islam. Such a repudiation signified the dishonor of the eldest son—and his death in the heart of his father. Shibshiev had delivered his message with full knowledge of these facts.

It would be his last.

Shibshiev's smug disclosure of the imam's relationships with his heirs had rendered him so hateful to Jamal Eddin that he ordered his aide to swallow his tongue. There were to be no more sermons or speeches. He assured Shibshiev that if he opened his mouth to utter so much as one word of criticism, he would live to regret it. At the merest hint of an accusation or an insult, Shibshiev would pay.

* * *

Shibshiev failed to comprehend the significance of this command from an officer like Lieutenant Shamil. He was too obtuse to realize that beneath Jamal Eddin's calm exterior lay an untapped reservoir of passionate feeling. He learned the extent of his poor judgment when he dared to begin reiterating his insults. It was to his extreme detriment. The beating he took left him panting in terror at the violence of his master.

Anyone but Shibshiev would have planned vengeance for such humiliation and stabbed the officer in his bed. And in fact, Jamal Eddin was counting on an act of attempted murder to finally send Shibshiev back to Saint Petersburg. Or, quite simply, to get rid of him for good.

But Shibshiev did not budge.

He cowered in submission, kissed the hand he could not cut off, and ceased to call the imam's son a dog or a woman.

His master demanded nothing more of him.

* * *

If the czar's purpose had been to familiarize his protégé with Caucasian customs, the endeavor was a rousing success. By the time the Uhlans returned to Russia in June 1851, Jamal Eddin and Shibshiev were no longer on speaking terms.

Each waited for the opportunity to pursue his hatred to its inevitable conclusion.

Each, in his own way, did all he could to destroy the evil incarnate in the other.

Russia
At the Torjok garrison, in the province of Tver
September 1851

The scent of ripened wheat and lucerne rose in waves from the damp earth. It was wonderful to slip into the open country at daybreak, when the air was still, before the buzz of bees and insects filled the linden trees of Torjok. Banks of mist hovered low over the prairies, creeping toward the lakes, the ponds, and the thousand streams that dotted the countryside of Tver, then formed a thick blanket above the woods.

"Not far to the forest," Jamal Eddin thought.

The game was to keep his horse in check until they reached the first pines, then to suddenly give him his head. Impatient to break into a gallop, Jamal Eddin turned off at one of the paths. The vast mass of trees, blue in the light of the summer dawn, stretched as far as the eye could see. He spurred his horse gently into a trot. Crushed beneath the horse's hooves, the first pines needles released their tantalizing scent of resin. Applying firm pressure with his legs, Jamal Eddin directed his mount to bound forward. He crouched over the horse's neck to avoid the low-hanging conifer branches, covered with gray barbs, as he took off into the cluster of tall trees. The croaking frogs on the banks of the streams fell silent. A woodcock fluttered away. The deer disappeared. But he knew that the animals were there, and the thrill of their presence made him forget Shamil, the czar, and Shibshiev. He forgot about his anger and the sense of injustice that loomed over him always. Without a doubt, that savage's accusations had finally borne fruit.

If sometimes, in his innermost thoughts, he still spoke to his father, it was to tell him that never once had he faltered, that he had always fulfilled his religious duties, that he had always said his prayers and observed Ramadan, that he was still a Montagnard. In the midst of all the Uhlans, he had worn the national dress, the cherkess. He did not go beyond that in his silent monologues. He did not speak of his violent struggle within or of all the restraint and effort his loyalty to the Caucasus had cost him. He did not mention that his memory of the mountains was becoming increasingly vague and—worse still—that his sparse memories were painful, that the images Shibshiev evoked disturbed him. How could he have expressed the truth and admit that the problem was not that he felt different from his comrades but—on the contrary—that he felt neither different nor in any way excluded from the world around him? The difficulty lay in belonging to a lost world that was no longer relevant to his existence but to which his sense of honor demanded he remain loyal. And he was no longer even certain of that.

Oh, the hell with all these confusing thoughts. Gallop in a straight line, gallop over the immense flat stretch of Russian forest. The appeal of the endless, compelling plain defied the call of the Caucasus. Everything played out before him, rushing by thick and dense, the past, the future, all of it—life suddenly seemed simple.

He threaded his way swiftly among the black tree trunks, streaked now by the morning sun, whose light penetrated everywhere as he crossed the forest floor. He was flying, free, alive.

As he rode wildly on, he occasionally heard the echo of another set of pounding hooves. It was then that he caught a fleeting glimpse of his double, galloping through the foliage as the sunlight streamed through the trees. Far off in the distance was another horseman—no, it was a young woman, blonde, bareheaded, riding sidesaddle and dressed in a green habit. Her grace was enchanting. Now there was someone who knew how to ride. She held herself in the saddle with such natural elegance that even her mare seemed to sense it as she galloped on, limbs contained, head lowered. A magnificent beast, she reminded him of his friend from the horse cemetery, the sorrel mare from his first Russian summer, who played at charging him in the sleepless nights at Tsarskoye Sielo. In different circumstances, he would have pursued them. But this fugitive vision was so completely part of his pleasure, along with the pungent perfume of the earth, the images of the clearings, the croaking frogs, the light, the sun and the forest, and all that was Russia, that chasing them would have seemed not only futile but an utter sacrilege.

It was only in autumn, when the green-clad Amazon no longer appeared, that he realized he had been listening expectantly for the dull pound of hooves in the sand, just as he had counted on hearing them all summer. The strident cry of the black grouse mating in the branches above him now made him shiver with impatient anxiety. Somehow, in the midst of the triumphant radiance of nature, he sensed that he was waiting for something.

Something that did not come.

In his mind, he contemplated the face of Varenka and the eyes of all the women he had been attracted to at Covensk, all the women he had had to renounce. When he thought of his Polish mistresses—whom he had invariably chosen among the older and married women in order to discourage any illusions of a future or even a hint of a shared destiny—those with whom his religion forbade him to form any bonds, he felt a restlessness that cost him many sleepless nights.

A few dance steps, the whirl of a waltz—were those all he could ever share with these women? A turn around the dance floor. It all amounted to nothing. Even now, when he was known as a heartbreaker, he had no choice but to keep his own heart at a respectful distance; he could not allow himself to become attached to anyone. Could he ever marry a young woman of Torjok? Certainly not.

He had no choice but to curb his inclinations. Contain his instincts. Maintain his distance.

The forbidden pursuit of the Amazon in the forest embodied his sacrifice.

But he had reached his limit of insatiable dreams and crushed impulses. He could not stand any more impossible loves or chaste embraces. He needed air; he was suffocating among the green plants and love affairs nipped in the bud. In six, eight, ten months, he would return to the Caucasus. And bid a final farewell to passion. He regarded this return, this farewell, as inevitable, a source of neither revulsion nor pleasure, a necessity that he did not dream of eluding. But before then, he wanted to live! The devil with reserve and prudence! He was twenty, and he wanted to take a chance, to dare, finally, to love!

So when the mating season burst around him, when the cry of a bird made him look up and hear the echoing desire of the female, he imagined the celebration of consummation.

And in his mind, he returned incessantly to the image of the horsewoman. He sensed that the vision was not a dream, a mere chimera caught in the summer sunlight. There was nothing evanescent about the strength and haleness he had seen in the figure on horseback. The curve of the small of her back, her skirt sweeping through the hawthorns, her golden hair streaking through the sunlight—he was obsessed by it all. Everything about the young woman attracted him, down to her determination to cross his path, then cut him off. It was a game that had instantly threatened what little remained of his self-control.

And yet he had resisted the urge to respond and let life slip away.

The thought of this lost chance at a rendezvous represented the only real terror of his existence: the fear of dying without ever having loved, of meeting death without ever having lived.

In the shadow of Torjok's onion domes and linden trees, six months later May 1852

Leaning out the window of her carriage, as was her habit, La Potemkina spotted the rider far off in the forest. Ah, the cherkeska. Not the long, black one, but a cherkeska of azure blue, with an officer's collar of green velvet and the silver epaulets she so fancied. On each side of the breast was a ghizir, not with seven-cartridge belts but Russian-style ghizirs of fourteen cartridges circled with rings that gleamed in the sun. It was superb and represented everything that she admired. The ladies of the prison committee could say what they wished, but this costume, when worn as it should be, was still the most dashing of all uniforms.

The horseman trotted toward her, passing near the fences of the last houses on the outskirts of Torjok. She was blinded by the morning light and the little clouds of dust stirred up by his horse's hooves. She would wait until he came alongside the carriage to flag him down and ask him for a favor. It was a stroke of good luck to have run into this strapping lad, who could help her get through a change of horses at the relay post of Torjok.

She had missed the turn-off to Machouk, the domain of her Olenin nephews. Now she would have to continue into the city, leave her own team, turn around and go back. Her doctor, her priest, her reader, and her two maids were all ready to give up and stop here for the night. Well, too bad. She was not one for putting off until tomorrow what could be done today. The trip promised to be full of inconveniences, and they might as well get on with it. She wanted to arrive at her nephews' place today. So what if they didn't expect her to arrive before the weekend? All the better for them, for the sooner she got there, the sooner she would leave. It was indeed a piece of luck to have happened upon a lieutenant in the lancers of His Imperial Highness's guard (as she had discerned from the color of the trimming on his epaulets, as well as his rank, regiment, and the number of his division), one who had galloped through the forest and was coming home before the heat of midday. Unless of course the reverse was true, and he was leaving the city. She had been wandering through the forest for so long, and, having gotten lost and turned around several times, she was no longer sure in which direction she was going. Imagine that. Arriving here, in this God-forsaken outpost, only to run into a Cherkess—no doubt a Muslim—of this rank and distinction. The Lord always showed her the path, leading her evermore in the direction of His lost lambs.

"I say, Lieutenant?"

He stopped and leaned politely toward the door of the coach.

"Would you be so good as to—What? It's you! You're not in Poland? I thought you were in Covensk."

With her lace cap and ribbons fluttering in the window frame and her two clusters of black ringlets that hadn't yet gone limp from the journey, La Potemkina seemed to have sprung forth from another world.

"What on earth are you doing in this hole, my poor friend?" she continued.

The "hole" in question spread across the two banks of a wide river. It counted over thirty chapels, ten churches, a cathedral, and a monastery of incredible wealth. The virtuosity of the spinners of Torjok had made its gold thread famous throughout all of Russia. Most of the gold-embroidered court robes and church vestments came from Torjok, as well as the sacerdotal tiaras and chasubles. A hole? More like a hive. The hum of spinning wheels filled the air in every house, bells rang the hour from every campanile, and the "smell of Dame Daria's meatballs," whose recipe Pushkin had immortalized in one of his poems, wafted from every kitchen. The sleepy banks of the river that flowed into the Volga a few versts from Torjok were dotted with long barracks that could be spotted through the linden trees. For over half a century, the light cavalry had been stationed here. And for the past three years, in the absence of the soldiers currently bivouacked in Poland and Hungary, the military administration had been building new barracks and an entire camp for the garrison.

The officers rented apartments in the city or outbuildings of the nearby manors. Jamal Eddin, who lived off his pay, hadn't the means to afford one or the other and lived with his men. But his comrades, officers belonging to the nobility who were posted at the garrison of Torjok, enjoyed a wide selection. Most of the domains surrounding the city belonged to one or another branch of their relatives. They could live at Mytino, the domain of the Lvov princes, with the Poltoratsky princes of Grousino, or with the Olenins of Boristovo, who would house them at Machouk. All of the aristocratic families, both from Saint Petersburg and Moscow, possessed at least one manor in the area. And with good reason. The region was situated on the Sovereign's Road, the royal path that linked the two capitals. Four hundred versts from the Winter Palace and three hundred from the Kremlin, Torjok was an unavoidable relay post. The entire empire passed through its courtyard. Even the czar changed horses at the relay post of Torjok; even he dined and slept here.

So when La Potemkina implied that she was setting forth into a desert, she was simply demonstrating her usual disingenuousness with regard to anything that annoyed her. She had only reluctantly abandoned her dear Gostilitsy and the prospect of festivities at Peterhof and intimate soirées at Alexandria cottage. Among the many properties she possessed was a country home at Torjok (along with several thousand souls there, for whom she was responsible). For over fifteen years, she had put off coming to have the roof repaired and the church restored—in short, to look after her affairs here in person. She had finally decided to do so. During the work, she would stay with her closest neighbor, the son of her late sister, the painter Piotr Alexeyevitch Olenin.

"Will you come keep me company there, Jama?" she simpered, employing a diminutive she had never used before. "They're nice, my nephew's family, but so very provincial. Do you know them? Yes, of course you know them."

Her urbane prattle took him by surprise. He had forgotten this chatty tone. Amazing, wasn't it, how La Potemkina's voice was enough to evoke the air of Petersburg, a breath of court air right here under the pine trees. It took him a few moments to get in tune with her.

"I won't ask you to ride with me, as the carriage is full."

Behind her in the carriage he saw the haggard, crumpled faces of her five or six traveling companions. A second rattling and shuddering carriage followed with difficulty in the wake of the first. Who else but this old woman would have dared to make the trip without stopping? She might protest that she could only breathe the rarefied air of kings and emperors, but she still had more energy and impatience than most. She hadn't changed at all. Jamal Eddin found her vitality amusing and endearing, just as he always had.

He had turned back and dismounted and was now slowly backtracking through town in her company. He would gladly have accompanied her all the way to Machouk, but he was on duty today, and the captain required his presence. He would take her as far as the relay post and ensure that she would be able to start off again as she wished.

The indefatigable Potemkina nattered on at the coach door window, listening to nothing, looking at nothing, paying no attention whatsoever to her companion, nor to the monuments along the path. She did not see the neoclassical pediments, the colonnades, the porticos, or the domes that perched, white and monumental, between the isbas and the wooden churches. What could it possibly matter to her that "this village" was dripping with history, that it had been burned by the Mongols, captured by the Polish, retaken by the Slavs, and finally rebuilt by her relative, the very wealthy Prince Lvov, an inspired architect enamored of antiquity and benefactor of the city?

"Yes, of course they receive the gazettes at Machouk," she continued, obsessed by the prospect of her forthcoming stay. "They translate Byron and transcribe Scarlatti, they compose and paint and hunt and dance, but they simply know nothing of social graces. When I think of the stature the Olenins once enjoyed in society—their relations, their fortune. Do you remember Alexis Nicolaïevitch Olenin? Do you have any idea what a man of character he was?"

No, he didn't remember. Truth be told, he had never known.

"The founder of the National Library, director of the Academy of Beaux Arts, a friend of Pushkin, of Krylov, of Briullov. Alexis Olenin's salon at Priutino was altogether different from his son Piotr's circle at Machouk. Guess what he had the audacity to tell me this winter—that ninny Piotr! Just guess! After I had arranged a position for his eldest daughter with the empress. 'My Lisa, at court? Never. She's much too good for that.' I thought I was dreaming. And the poor girl, in the carriage just behind us, pretended not to be disappointed to go home, pretended to prefer the charms of her Machouk to the pleasure of serving the empress. Well, you'll soon see for yourself. Just don't expect much. Of course you know the Olenin girls. You met them at my home. I gave a ball for Lisa when she made her début, along with the young Lvovs. You remember, it was four years ago. A group of sisters, cousins, and aunts, all more or less the same age. A tribe much like our Georgian princesses. Less illustrious, less exotic, but more numerous. This winter, eighteen of them came to spend the ball season at the house; it was absolutely exhausting. And now that it's over, they're heading back to Machouk. I'm bringing ten of them home all at once."

Seated on a bale of hay in the courtyard of the post house, La Potemkina chattered on.

The lieutenant came and went around her as he selected the horses, negotiated the price, and found two men to drive her to her nephew's home, bring back the team, and return the one she was leaving behind now.

It was only when they were about to leave that he saw her, the figure of a small and delicate young woman among the animals. He was taken aback. She had alighted from her carriage with her companions and was leaning against one of the arches, among the horses tied up to the iron rings. The trip had left her chignon in some disarray, and a few locks of blonde curls had escaped from it. He noticed that, contrary to custom, she was bareheaded. She wore no hat, not even a head scarf. Two diamond teardrops scintillated from her earlobes, catching the sunlight. She had been observing him for some time and did not try to hide the fact. She seemed to find Jamal Eddin's ballet before La Potemkina—his politeness and diligence, his efforts to please her—highly amusing. Nice show, her eyes said. How gracious and competent! He frowned, feeling ridiculous. Such open curiosity on the part of one of her sex and age surprised him. Young women did not usually scrutinize men, or if they did, it was only from behind the cover of the feathers of their fans. She was challenging him. He walked toward her.

"Lisa, come over here," La Potemkina quickly interjected.

She dipped under the horses' necks and strode forward among the animals.

"Have you met Lieutenant Shamil?"

"Yes, of course, Aunt. But don't ask him the same question, he'll tell you no."

No, Elizaveta Petrovna Olenina? He hasn't had the honor. She shot him an impudent look, her eyes black and lively. "We were introduced at your home in Gostilitsy and at your home in Petersburg. And once again here at Uncle Lvov's, in Torjok, last summer. He never recognizes me."

"I beg your pardon. Even at a distance, in a green riding habit, you are unforgettable."

She was taken by surprise, and her astonished expression was even more genuine than her insolence. He was flustered. How could he have uttered this imbecilic compliment, pronounced those idiotic words? Moreover, he hadn't any proof that this young woman was the rider in the forest. Except that she was blonde. And that she stood up straight. And seemed to like horses. Had he already been introduced to Lisa Petrovna? It was impossible. She was teasing him. At

Gostilitsy? His memory was a blank. At one of the Lvovs' many balls in Torjok? Disaster. Nothing rang a bell there either.

La Potemkina cut things short, sending all the travelers in her entourage back to their carriages.

"Come to see me, Jama, come soon," she said plaintively, leaning on his arm. "You know, it's going to be just dreadful for me there."

He promised he would, helped her into the carriage, and shut the door. Lisa had taken her seat at the back of the second carriage.

"You know," the dowager stressed even more loudly, "Machouk—"

The young woman pressed her face close to the window. They were talking about her home, and so she listened.

"It's everything I detest."

He glanced at the girl at the window. She had heard everything.

"The little flowers, the nightingales' songs, the old neighbors, the ancient cousins, the entire summer, without anyone—my God, what a bore!"

Embarrassed, he flashed her an apologetic look, asking the young woman to excuse this lack of tact, begging her not to take these insulting remarks to heart. The princess didn't really mean what she was saying. Lisa understood and acquiesced with the same look she had given him earlier.

He was once again struck by this strange blend of good sense and sparkle, of sweetness and irony. She shrugged her shoulders, a twinkle in her dark eyes, as if to say, "Yes, I know, the princess is like that; she always goes overboard. What can we do?"

He smiled at her. "Strangle her. Or forget it."

The carriages shuddered as they started off.

As the old lady passed the porch, she leaned out the window of the door again.

"Don't leave me!" she wailed in a tragic voice, in case Jamal Eddin had not fully understood her distress.

This time, he and the girl both raised their eyes to the heavens and laughed out loud.

He did not wait for the proper period of time to pass, not a week, not even a day. After a sleepless night, he started off on the road to Machouk.

At Machouk
May 1852

Riding along the edges of the ponds, he already knew. He had no doubts or worries. He just tried not to give in too soon. Ordinarily he might notice that no forest seemed more ideal for hunting, that none of the four hundred lakes in the district looked so suitable for fishing. He could talk himself silly with observations and obvious facts. But no matter what he said or did, on the road to Machouk, he was consumed with something other than fish and game. The mystery of this aquatic landscape, the great trees that swayed languidly between water and sky, the rustle of game, and the birds' cries all contributed to his state of mind, suspended somewhere between wakefulness and dreaming. All around him he felt intense forces at play; he sensed the cause of all his sleepless nights the September before, when he had waited, hoped, and searched in vain for the return of the Amazon. He would not let her escape a second time.

He needed no proof that the young woman at the relay post was the woodland rider. He didn't even think about it. No more than he thought of those big, dark eyes, the blonde tendrils at the nape of her neck, the curls that fell from her temples, her laugh, and all the other details that possessed his mind. Her face was already such an intimate part of him that its individual traits no longer mattered. Its passion and freedom were a part of him, and he carried the softness of the way she looked at him deep within himself. Lisa's very self haunted him body and soul.

However, he was not prepared for the universe he would discover at Machouk.

Turning in beneath an arbor of trees, at the end of the lane he saw a wooden manor house that entirely blocked the lawn. It was a low white house situated at ground level, with a veranda that wrapped around it on all sides. He hesitated, his heart racing.

All his senses alert, he came forward almost solemnly, intuitively sensing the importance of this moment. The most minute details were inscribed in his memory. He noticed, for example, that the entire house was bathed in light, inundated by the sun's rays streaming through the French doors that opened wide onto the terrace. Unobstructed by blinds or curtains, the light spilled out over the lawn on the other side. The garden behind the house was aflame with peonies, and several people were playing badminton beneath the chestnut trees near a long white table. Far beyond them, below the park, a winding river sparkled in the sunlight like a silver serpent.

As he came nearer, he realized that he had been mistaken. A muslin curtain veiled one of the casements on the right side of the façade and fluttered in the breeze. Pausing in the springtime heat, he could hear through the window the sound of a piano playing a lively Glinka variation on an Italian theme. It was a piece Jamal Eddin knew and loved, and it made him feel all the more keyed up.

He jumped down from the horse and handed the reins to the groom, then waited at the bottom of the steps as a servant disappeared inside the house to announce his arrival. He tried to smother his timidity by distracting himself with other sensations—memories of the cottage at Peterhof-Alexandria, the feelings the Glinka divertimento evoked, the colors, the sounds, and the scents all around him. He breathed in the perfume of the orange trees, which were aligned in large planters along the guardrail of the veranda above him. Everything—the clutter of furniture on the veranda, the buttercup-yellow satin that covered the chairs, even the yellow tablecloth on the pedestal table—seemed to be soaked in sunshine.

The wasps buzzed in the lilacs.

The piano was still.

Now he saw the ruffles of a gown rapidly approaching. He wished the Glinka melody would go on and that the rustling skirt would never reach the perron.

Expecting Lisa Petrovna to suddenly appear before him, he was disappointed.

The woman who stood at the top of the steps had gray hair. She was beautiful, with a round face and black eyes, and she looked down into his face with the same gaiety and self-confidence that Jamal Eddin had found so captivating in the young woman at the relay post.

"You're Lieutenant Shamil, aren't you?"

She smiled at him kindly.

"We've been expecting your visit."

So here was the woman who ruled over this marvelous domain. He did not know the heritage of her past, or that Machouk came from her first name, Macha. Initially built on other grounds by her illustrious forbears, the Lvov princes, the house had been her wedding gift when she married the painter Piotr Olenin. It was she, Princess Maria Nicolaïevna Lvova, who had had the house transported and reassembled here, board by board, enthroned in light above the ponds and the meadows. Her five children had been born at Machouk and their home had witnessed twenty years of untroubled conjugal bliss. The kindness in the eyes that met Jamal Eddin's at this moment was a good indication that this woman had a gift for happiness, one that she shared freely everywhere she went.

He felt immediately at ease in her presence. And the instantaneous fondness was reciprocated.

"You are most welcome here. Our aunt can't stop talking about your surprise encounter. Come in, come in."

He strode after her across the salon.

From between the branches of the chestnut trees that bowed low over her chaise longue, Lisa Petrovna saw the young man she was waiting for suddenly appear on the terrace with her mother. Lieutenant Shamil at Machouk? A flush of joy enveloped her entire being. At last. She did not move, savoring the vision of Jamal Eddin as he walked toward the table where all her loved ones were seated. He greeted her father, her sister, her two brothers, her nanny, the Lvov cousins, even Coutin, her grandparents' old governess. He even kissed Aunt Tatiana Borissovna, who had risen to embrace him, addressing him in French, as "my darling, my heart, my favorite," rolling the "r's" in her loud, lilting voice. Lisa did not get up. She would wait for him to come over to the chestnut trees. It had taken four long years to arrive at this point.

She had by no means exaggerated the day before when she said that they had been introduced on numerous occasions. What she had not mentioned were the consecutive maneuvers she had employed to arrange this series of encounters. The first time? She remembered the gown of white tulle she had worn that evening, the rose in her hair, her ribbons and slippers. She had never felt so pretty, and she was surprised at having been so invisible. True, she had only been fourteen at Count Kiselyev's party honoring Captain Dmitri Milyutin's second return from Chechnya. La Potemkina had arranged for her to be invited to the children's ball that the count gave for his youngest nephews. But Lisa could only listen to Sacha and his friends' discourse from afar. Seated at the table surrounded by governesses, she had so envied the Georgian princesses who seemed to be having such fun in the company of the cadets. She had even heard their argument about the Caucasus and the honor of the Montagnards and the harsh exchange that ensued between the student from the Lycée Impérial and the most dignified of all the young men, until then the most silent and most reserved of the group. This boy's bearing had appealed to her. She had decided to reward him by choosing him as her partner to dance what would be her very first waltz with a real suitor. But he had disappeared.

Much, much later, when she had spotted his tall figure in the salons, she had felt the same flush of pleasure and was met with the same disappointment. In an effort to get to know him, she had placed herself in his path. Afraid that he might be put off by a direct approach, she had always managed to meet him in the company of her cousins, her aunts, and a gaggle of chaperones who would draw no special attention to her. But in this last ploy she had been all too successful. Her name, her face, her entire person were lost in the mass, drowned in a sea of vague relations. He had greeted her as he had all the others, bowing with the same courtesy and aloof politeness that he had accorded all the ladies. He had looked right through her—and with good reason. He was utterly blinded by another and had eyes only for his love, the princess Varenka of Georgia.

Last year, Lisa had learned that Jamal Eddin's regiment was stationed in town. By this time she knew the story of his origins—and she knew of his fondness for horses. She herself was a horsewoman of such unparalleled excellence that last winter, during the season of balls at her aunt's, the czar had allowed her to train on the obstacle course of the imperial stables. To this day, she was the only young woman to have enjoyed such a privilege, even though she was not a member of the court.

Those long gallops through the forest of Torjok had never been a matter of chance.

* * *

She had imagined this moment so many times, dreamed of it so often, that she was suddenly paralyzed, incapable of rising from the chaise lounge to greet him.

If he should cross the distance that separated him from the chestnut trees, he could not help but notice—of this she was certain—the beating of her heart, plainly discernable beneath her blouse.

She placed her hand on her breast and pressed with all her strength to still the pounding. To no avail.

Nothing calmed the feeling that was becoming more violent with each passing second.

Machouk
May 1852–April 1853

In that moment, Jamal Eddin succumbed to another kind of charm. Entranced with the entire family, he opened his heart to an immediate and total affection, an impulse akin to love at first sight, that included every member of the tribe.

There could not be a warmer, more welcoming, more whimsically imaginative clan than the Olenins of Machouk. There was nothing conventional or narrow-minded about them.

Life at Machouk brought back the enchantment of his days at Peterhof-Alexandria, the spell of summers with the czar's family and the princesses of Georgia. Yes, Machouk had all the magic of the cottage—without the penchant for appearances, obligations of power, or ostentatious simplicity of the stage-managed events of the imperial household.

Singing, drawing, poetry, and theater were all an integral part of daily life at the manor. Jamal Eddin's beloved Pushkin was the object of a unanimous passion, the very soul of the circle, the god and protector, and all of them knew *Eugene Onegin* by heart. But each one spent his time and efforts according to his own tastes and talents. Princess Macha practiced the piano for several hours a day in the salon. Piotr, the painter, engraved portraits of his friends and illustrated the frontispieces of their books in his studio at the far end of the garden. The young people declaimed Corneillian tragedies and spouted Marivaux beneath the vaulted roof of the gazebo in the glow of the Chinese lanterns. Even Princess Potemkina had to concede that her previous offhand comments that "her nephew received the gazettes" and translated Byron were a bit thin. In reality, the household was the incarnation of all that artistic and literary Russia revered.

The environment suited him so perfectly, and he moved in it with such grace, that all at Machouk were as taken with him as he was with them. Alyosha, the eldest of the boys, cornet in the Army of the Caucasus, swore by him. The sixteen-year-old Tatiana, twelve-year-old Maria, the Lvov cousins and their entire entourage, who lived in the surrounding manors, unanimously agreed that no performance, no ball, no hunting party was complete without Jamal Eddin's presence.

All of them concurred.

With a few exceptions.

"I'm in the dark as to Lieutenant Shamil's upbringing," old Mademoiselle Coutin said in French, giving the thread of her embroidery a sharp tug. "No one knows his family; we really don't know where he comes from."

Seated in a row in the shade of the veranda, the four governesses and two readers—senior among the several generations of chaperones and duennas who guarded the honor of the young ladies of Machouk—were busy with their needlework. A gigantic silver samovar, "Pushkin's samovar," sat on the pedestal table before them. A veritable institution, it had a spout in the form of an eagle's beak, which had leaked for the past thirty years, but no one would even have considered having it repaired. Legend had it that Pushkin had asked for the hand of the sister of the master of the house, the famous Anna Olenina, before this samovar. And that, also before this samovar, he had fallen in love with another of their relatives, the equally beautiful Anna Kern.

La Potemkina shrugged her shoulders.

"Who could have transformed this boy into such a marvel," she said, with a hint of mock wonder.

Seated near the embroiderers and absorbed in a game of solitaire, the princess fussed over her bad cards. Never lifting her nose, incessantly turning over one, then another, she heaved a deep sigh and muttered, "I wonder too, Coutin. An officer of the highest merit, a mathematician, a pianist, a poet," she ticked off his qualities with her customary exaggeration. "A man from the best of circles, whose many talents outshine even those of your charges."

Sensing an imminent critical remark, La Potemkina restrained herself, with some difficulty, from uttering further hyperbole. She didn't mention the inanities she confided to her maid concerning her hopes for "her" Muslim—that Jamal Eddin was of royal blood and destined to inherit an empire, that he would become governor of the Caucasus—but she did make one point:

"To whom do you suppose this great *seigneur* owes his perfect education, Coutin? If not to the master of us all."

"The czar?"

La Potemkina deemed no further comment necessary.

However, she did find it necessary to remind them that the young man navigated in the highest circles and that she would not have introduced him had he not been a welcome favorite at the Winter Palace with close ties to the court, the chosen son of the emperor himself.

All these details were superfluous at Machouk, except to the guardians of the temple, who were more particular, more conservative, and more suspicious about the pedigree of visitors than the proprietors of the domain themselves.

Enjoying long strolls, picnics, and teas, La Potemkina was overwhelmed by the surfeit of pleasures and her datebook was full. Between fishing parties and rounds of whist, she was constantly coming and going. And to think she had worried about being bored.

In a sign of her changing mood, she had come to the conclusion that the two young ladies of the household, the twenty-year-old Lisa and Tatiana (her namesake), actually resembled her. There was no doubt about it, they had inherited her energy. Lisa hunted, shot, and danced with all the enthusiasm that La Potemkina had had in her youth.

"Indeed, far too good for the court," Jamal Eddin teased her.

Lisa's free spirit made Jamal Eddin feel restless, even violently agitated at times.

What he experienced when she galloped at his side could only be called ecstasy. He loved the proud way she carried herself, the clear, clean profile of her head. He loved her supple wrists at the rein, the way she sat straight in the saddle, the graceful movement of the small of her back, which naturally followed the animal's rhythm. And her hands, which were so gentle at the horse's mouth. Yes, it was a form of ecstasy to watch her tapered fingers, slim and strong and skillful, as she gently reined in her spirited mare without the least hint of violence in her gestures.

Lisa's confidence and open manner kindled his senses and illuminated his imagination. Conscious of his feelings, he was always careful to treat her with respect, or at least never to compromise her by revealing his desire. He could not bear the thought of offending her.

He had known so little tenderness in his life that he could not even imagine how tenderly he was loved.

Atop a haystack, on the grounds of Machouk August 1853

"She is a goddess. With this kind of woman, it was inevitable. Something had to happen," said Sacha Milyutin. He continued, without any irony, "Something dreadful, terrible, irremediable—like marriage."

Buxhöwden and Jamal Eddin were so used to Sacha's ranting about women and conjugal ties that they hadn't paid any serious attention to him in ages.

With their hands behind their heads and eyes gazing up at the sky above, each of them was dreaming of his own love. Lying in the hay, they were waiting for the appropriate time to present themselves at Machouk. There, Lisa, Tatiana, and all the young ladies were resting beneath the mosquito nets. The men would join them after their siesta for the evening's entertainment.

They were not the only ones waiting there at midday. Behind a nearby haystack, Shibshiev was spying on them. Jamal Eddin's attentiveness to the giaours at Machouk had revived his old worries, and a sense of foreboding had taken shape in the back of his mind.

Though the memory of his beating had made Shibshiev more prudent, he had nonetheless returned to his former ways as a spy.

Indifferent to this hostile presence, the three friends lay still in the sun. Though they shared the same hopes and dreams, the similarities among them ended there. Despite the broad red moustache that dominated his face, Sacha still looked like a child. With close-cropped hair and a square, clean-shaven jaw, Buxhöwden—"Bux"—had become a blond giant whose imposing stature belied a more gentle soul than one might have imagined. The two comrades had followed Jamal Eddin down the same romantic path and found themselves, like him, at the mercy of their feelings.

Bux was smitten with the youngest of the Lvov cousins. "In love, absolutely cooked," in the words of Sacha, who admitted that he loved young Tatiana "more than life itself." As for Jamal Eddin, his fascination with the eldest of the Olenin daughters was no secret—except, perhaps, to the young lady in question.

That August, the girls seemed to have bewitched the Uhlans of Torjok. The officers of the seventh division rivaled for the hearts of Lisa, Tatiana, Marina, and the others. Rumors of a conflict with Turkey, which had been threatening to break out since April, only added to the urgency of their sentiments. The brief separation they had just suffered due to the rites of the grand maneuvers had merely fanned the flames of their respective passions.

Not that springtime at the camp at Krasnoye Sielo had been a failure. On the contrary, it had been a great success. That year, even more so than in 1848, the emperor had sought to discourage any foreigners' inclinations to enter into an alliance against him. The show had been particularly brilliant. With the simulated battles performed before the Persian ambassador, the parades for the American senator, and the drills and charges done before the European diplomatic corps, the lancers had outdone themselves. In addition to their heartache, strict discipline, tension, and exhaustion made Jamal Eddin and his comrades eager to return to Machouk. Each one set out on the path to the manor with renewed fervor.

As for La Potemkina, she would not have missed the Indian summer season at her nephew's for anything in the world. The speed of the train that carried her to the new station of Tver on the recently inaugurated railway line joining the two capitals had definitively converted her to celerity and modernity.

But summer was almost over, and time was short.

"Yes or no, did Tatiana miss me while we were gone?" Sacha wanted to know.

"Who cares?" grumbled Buxhöwden, a man of few words. "As long as she loves you today."

"But tell me frankly, do you think she's too young for me?"

"For you? No."

"For me to marry her?"

"You're not the one who should get married. He is."

These few words—uttered in Buxhöwden's typically offhand way—resounded for an instant in the leaden heat.

Sacha, always ready for a counterpunch, yelped, " 'He,' meaning whom?"

"Him," Buxhöwden replied, with a slight gesture of the chin in Jamal Eddin's direction. "He's the one who should be getting married," he repeated.

Jamal Eddin had closed his eyes and remained perfectly still.

Sacha looked at him for a moment, then announced, "Bux is right. Marry her, old man. Propose now, the sooner the better."

The piece of straw that Jamal Eddin had been absently chewing on was suddenly still.

Scarcely unclenching his teeth, he muttered, "Impossible."

"Why impossible?"

"Because."

"Why impossible?" Sacha repeated insistently.

Jamal Eddin said nothing.

"Is it that fanatic?" murmured Buxhöwden, gesturing toward the shadow of Shibshiev behind the haystack. "Is he the one who has poisoned your blood and driven you crazy, to the point of preventing you from living?"

At this, Jamal Eddin opened his eyes. Explicitly formulated criticism was not generally Bux's style. His judgments—and Buxhöwden's frequent disapproval of his superiors seriously threatened his military career—were normally expressed with innuendo, contempt, and the force of inertia.

Jamal Eddin did not move but continued simply to gaze at the sun.

"Do you want my advice?" Milyutin cut in pompously. "Marry her, my friend, marry her. Without a doubt, you will never find a finer girl than Elizaveta Petrovna."

"He knows that," Buxhöwden snorted. "He's persuaded that this woman is the companion destined for him by God or the devil. Just look at him, he's burning with love, he's drying up and withering away. And she, poor thing, is literally dying of hunger and thirst right next to him. If this imbecile keeps this up, he'll end up instilling doubts in her mind, and then he'll lose her. And it will serve him right."

"I agree with Bux, hurry up. She loves you, she'll say yes, it's obvious."

Jamal Eddin abandoned any pretext of composure.

"A woman like Elizaveta Petrovna cannot accept a man without a birthright. Without a name, without a title. Without wealth."

"That's what you think," Buxhöwden countered sourly.

"You're forgetting your own merit," Milyutin seconded him.

"What future could I offer her?" Jamal Eddin's features hardened. "What destiny? Just stop!"

He softened his tone. "Quiet, Bux, you don't know what you're talking about."

"And you, Jamal Eddin, you're talking about destiny, but you're still vacillating, a prisoner of yourself and paralyzed with fear. As long as you are incapable of choosing your camp, of risking everything for what you feel, that is what you will remain: a man without freedom, a pawn caught between two worlds and two loyalties, a hostage to both Shamil and the czar. And he who has not dared all is a man of little substance."

Jamal-Eddin paled at Buxhöwden's attack.

"Do you think her father would give her to a Muslim?" he shot back vehemently.

He was silent for a moment before adding, "The subject is closed."

Sacha shrugged his shoulders.

"I don't see the problem: you love her, she loves you, her parents love you, the czar loves you. It's your move, old man, convert."

"The subject is closed," he repeated, his tone final.

But he was mistaken. The subject was not closed.

The conversation had opened a chasm he could not close.

Buoyed by a wave of fragile hope, he was overwhelmed by conflicting thoughts and feelings.

Impossible. Impossible, but why? Sacha's questions and Buxhöwden's words ran endlessly through his mind.

He was caught between two worlds and two loyalties, each of which excluded the other. The choice he had always refused to make, between the Caucasus and Russia, was now an imperative. How could one belong to two universes at once? What would happen if he dared to ask for Lisa's hand, if he dared to marry her? He could not even find the words to express his thoughts.

Choose. Dare. A man is of little substance unless he has done his utmost to live in harmony with himself.

And in response to such high-minded eloquence, he recalled the suras of the Koran that condemned to death one who denied Islam: God would not tolerate another divinity sharing His place.

He went over his reasoning again. What if he should go all the way and truly embrace what he had become: a Russian, who belonged to the Russian army, in love with a Russian girl—and married to a Russian woman? He would have to renounce the task for which Allah had created him and the emperor had educated him. He would not be able return to the Caucasus and serve his people.

His people? Who exactly were they—Shibshiev?

He who denies the Almighty after having believed in Him, he who deliberately opens his heart to nonbelief, has provoked the wrath of God. For he will have chosen a life in this world over a future life.

Was this what it meant to dare all? To commit the act of supreme betrayal?

A traitor before God. A traitor to his father, a traitor to the czar.

He abruptly ended his visits to Machouk.

What now?

* * *

"Everything happened very quickly," Elizaveta Petrovna recounted in her memoirs, written over half a century later at the age of eighty-seven. "I have forgotten nothing of the events that transpired in late August, 1853. By that point, we knew Jamal Eddin well, and my parents had a great deal of respect for him. He had been coming to see us all year, he had become an attentive companion to Tatania and myself, and he didn't seem to differentiate between the two of us. His conduct was irreproachable, he treated us both exactly the same way. In all sincerity, I never once suspected that Jamal Eddin had been coming to see me. No one would have guessed it.

"But then, one morning I was sitting in the salon, trying to sew by the light streaming through the French doors, when he suddenly appeared on the terrace. A morning visit was unusual. He had not come to Machouk for the past several days, and I had been very worried about his absence. When I got up, my sewing box fell to the floor and the spools of thread rolled away around me. He was as pale as death. He looked like a madman. I knew that something had happened, that he hadn't eaten or slept during all that time. He strode across the room, his eyes ablaze, took me by the hand, and said, without introduction or explanation, in a flood of words, 'I love you, Lisa, I love you, I love you!'

"His eyes brimmed with tears and his lips were trembling.

" 'If it's yes, if you love me too, I'll go talk to your father immediately.'

" 'Yes, yes, yes, I agree!' I stammered. 'To everything, yes, yes!'

"He took me in his arms. Together, we went to knock on the door of the studio at the far end of the garden."

* * *

“Good Lord, what’s going on?” La Potemkina said to herself as she came charging out onto the terrace.

Her instincts had alerted her. The governesses, the children, and the servants, all of them, were standing, petrified, amid the garden furniture in disarray. The readers and the nursemaids, standing before the little shelf that held the votive candle to the Virgin, were crying and praying. Old Coutin, forgetting her former Roman Catholic habits, crossed herself incessantly. She swayed before the icon, bending to kiss it as she droned on.

La Potemkina paled beneath her rouge and powder.

“What has happened?”

Even the young people, even Alyosha and the Lvov cousins gazed in a state of expectation that bordered on the trancelike. She noticed the absence of several family members in the group.

“Where is Lisa? Where is your mother, where is Piotr?”

“In the studio,” Tatiana replied. Although visibly moved, the young woman spoke in a normal voice. “They’re talking. They have some things to discuss. He has asked for her hand in marriage.”

“He—” La Potemkina instantly understood. “Lord, oh Lord, protect him!”

“It’s done. Papa consented. Papa says Lisa is fortunate to marry a man of his character. He summoned Mama, and she joined them at the far end of the garden. When Mama learned the news, she nearly fainted. But once she had recovered, she seemed very, very happy for them too. Papa has said they may marry on two conditions. That Jamal Eddin be baptized. And with the consent of His Majesty and his blessing of their union.”

La Potemkina clasped her hands together.

"Praise be to thee, my God, who has illuminated the soul of your child in granting him Grace. He is saved."

La Potemkina, however, had gotten a little ahead of herself. Saved? She was forgetting that her own efforts to lead Jamal Eddin toward the light, along the path of the "true faith," had earned her the sharpest warning of her life: an imperial reprimand, very close to complete disgrace.

Saved? There was still the sizeable challenge of attaining the czar's blessing, which would entail his sacrificing the political project that had motivated the boy's kidnapping in the first place. The czar would have to forget all that he had invested in Jamal Eddin's education, all of the strategies he had employed to gain his confidence, seduce him, and shape him in accord with his own plans for the past fourteen years. To defy the will of Czar Nicholas and make him change course was no small endeavor. Would Jamal Eddin manage to wrench approval from the emperor? He preferred to avoid asking himself that question.

* * *

Wild with joy, he gazed at Lisa as she walked in the light. At long last, he felt a deep sense of harmony within himself. All traces of anxiety and doubt had fled. After months of agonizing heartache, Jamal Eddin had finally discovered peace.

He requested a few days' leave and took off at a gallop the next morning along the Sovereign's Road, which led to the Winter Palace.

CHAPTER IX

The Choice

1853–1855

The Winter Palace
September 1853

Standing before the massive red palace, Jamal Eddin felt a moment's hesitation that strongly resembled panic.

Between Torjok and Petersburg, he had had time to contemplate what he was about to ask. He was preparing to commit the unthinkable, the act he had always refused. The step he was about to take contradicted everything he had been for the past fourteen years. It denied his own will and refuted all his former choices. It renounced the child he had been. It defied all of his own reasoning and betrayed his pact with the czar.

How could he present the emperor with such an insane request?

His destiny hung in the balance. He knew it. He could win or lose everything. Double or nothing. He could lose

Lisa. The terror of such a thought made him forget all the others.

He dashed up the stairs of the entrance to Saltykov. The sentinel recognized him and he walked on through. However, he noticed a strange confusion among the soldiers, a disorder that increased at each landing as he rushed, unsuspecting, up the stairs. He was nearly out of breath when he reached the White Hall. The chamber attendants who greeted him let him cross through the adjoining salons without asking him the nature of his visit. Their uncharacteristically lax attitude and lack of curiosity surprised him. But it was just as well. He descended the steps toward the imperial office.

He knew the way. He had been received here several times when he was younger. It was here, in this modest room on the ground floor, that he had first met the "Great White Czar." The camp bed, the portrait of the empress on the table, and the pastels painted by his seven children all remained engraved upon his memory, forever linked to the moment when His Majesty had returned his kinjal to him. Every time he found himself alone with the czar, he remembered that compassionate gesture. Though he only thought of it fleetingly, he had never forgotten it. And each time the memory evoked within him the same surge of admiration and gratitude for his kindness.

He thought of it today as he rushed toward the office, his confidence renewed as he recollected the incident.

The door was closed.

None of the attendants had bothered to inform him that the emperor no longer received visitors here, nor in his immense office on the second floor. He now met with his audiences in the former headquarters of his late brother,

Grand Duke Mikhaïl, the gold and green salon with its Kashmir carpet and its earthenware stoves emblazoned with the battle-ax and the lictor's fasces.

As he retraced his steps, he was struck this time by the strange atmosphere.

The embassy attachés, orderly officers, administrative personnel, and secretaries all seemed to be in a state of agitated turmoil that he hadn't noticed on his way in.

They seemed unusually numerous and rushed, all headed in the same direction he was going. It was impossible to pass them, so he followed the flow.

"The outcome is certain," said one of the courtiers, "since God is with us!"

He listened attentively now, catching snatches of conversation among the small groups walking alongside him, all of whom were saying the same thing.

"Russia is not fighting for any material gain."

"She is embarking on a crusade."

The word rang in his ears. It had never been used at Uhlan headquarters in reference to the previous six months' preparations for a conflict with Turkey. At Torjok, they had said that the czar was arming for war, not that he was leaving on a crusade.

"We are waging a holy war," a young girl insisted.

His blood turned to ice.

He was familiar enough with the ways of the Winter Palace to know that this was not an idea that any of them had come up with, but one dictated by the emperor. What was the czar thinking? He had better find out fast.

"We are fighting for the triumph of the eternal faith."

"That's why everyone is against us," one of the maids of honor nodded. "Monumental and contradictory forces are pitted against each other, the East against the West, the Slavic world against the Latin one."

He stopped to take stock. He must forget his own feelings, his passion, even forget about Lisa—and calm down. What on earth were they talking about?

The affair—the crusade—had begun a few years ago in Jerusalem, Turkish territory, with a quarrel between Christians. This he knew. He recalled that the czar had been livid to discover that the Muslims had allowed the Roman Catholics to be in charge of the holy places, when the honor had belonged to the Orthodox Church since time immemorial. And Russia was the protector of the Orthodox Church throughout the sultan's territory. Catherine II had even signed a treaty to this effect with the Sublime Porte. It was an official pact. For the sultan to have broken his word, granting Napoleon III's Catholics all the privileges that the Orthodox Church and Czar Nicholas were due, was an outright betrayal. Ambassadors and diplomats had hastened to make the Turks admit their duplicity. But the sultan, backed up by the French and encouraged by the schemes of the British, refused to budge.

That much Jamal Eddin knew. He also knew that the czar had suggested that Russia and Europe share the scraps of the Ottoman Empire, whose demise seemed imminent.

The only detail Jamal Eddin had not picked up on at Torjok was that the European powers were extremely wary of Russia's expansion into the Balkans and the Black Sea. That proposition had been accepted on the condition that the czar (representing Russia) be excluded when it came time to divide up the remnants of the Ottoman Empire. The czar had protested the snub, insisting that he had never intended to seize Constantinople. But it was to no avail. Europe feared his appetite for conquest too much to believe him. The result would be war—war with Turkey, of course, but also with France, England, maybe Austria, and perhaps even Russia's long faithful ally, Prussia. Now Jamal Eddin understood.

His timing could not have been worse. What did his destiny matter when the entire country was threatened? It was utterly mad! He wanted to turn back, but something pushed him inexorably toward the antechamber of the green salon with the rest of the supplicants.

The room was crawling with dignitaries, ministers, and members of the council, who had come to discuss current affairs, quite separate from military matters. Like Jamal, each had mentally practiced the speech he would present to the czar, backed up by a thousand arguments and reasons, all the way here. It was best to be prepared and to be brief; the czar never received anyone for more than ten minutes. As a result, he saw a regular parade of visitors.

The imperial schedule was further complicated by the czar's imminent departure for Olmütz, where he planned to meet the emperor Franz-Joseph in a last-ditch effort to keep the peace.

Jamal Eddin stepped back. What good was his energy, his eloquence, his love for Lisa in such circumstances? It was mad. He should wait for a more opportune moment. Rapidly and a little awkwardly, he turned to press against the tide and make his exit. Too late.

The orderly officer opened one side of the double doors to the czar's office and summoned him.

"If you will be so kind as to follow me, His Imperial Majesty will receive you now."

From the back of the salon, the emperor's resonant voice boomed jovially.

"Come in, my boy, come in! It's always a pleasure to see you. Come protect me from all these sharks!"

The office was crowded too. A swarm of officers huddled around maps that were spread across several tables. The décor had changed, as well as the atmosphere. The looming figure of the czar across the room was the only thing that remained as it always had been. Clad in an impressive white uniform, he was standing erect, backlit by the sunlight from the window, absorbed in the files he was poring over. Jamal Eddin was familiar with his habits and knew he would maintain this pose until the last minute. An old tactic, it was a way of making his visitors slightly nervous before he surged forth out of the shadows in all his splendor. Or in all his wrath. Over time this act had become a ritual of the imperial audience.

Jamal Eddin could not see the czar's features clearly, but he sensed his tension and fatigue. His self-control was usually evident. Today, however, he seemed to have difficulty concentrating. He handled the dossiers absently, opening this one or that without really reading them.

"Let me just finish what I was doing, my lad. It's good to see you. You'll tell me all about your life in Torjok. Frankly, I'd like to be in your place, with the path laid out before me. You at least know where you're going. I," he said to the room at large, "I seem to endure one betrayal after another. And to try to remain faithful to what I consider my duty.

"Russia shall remain faithful to her honor," he continued, "faithful to all she is committed to."

The czar was no longer addressing Jamal Eddin but haranguing the assembly of officers. He chose his words carefully. He wanted everyone here to remember them and to spread them far and wide. He spoke forcefully, mistaking his adoring audience for the judgment of posterity.

"Russia will defend Christianity against all the countries fighting on the side of the crescent."

Now he turned to Jamal Eddin, who stood at attention before the unoccupied desk.

"For you see, my boy, among the traitors and hypocrites, the Turks are not the worst. No, the worst are not those who advise the sultan and his hordes of fanatics. The worst are the faithful who betray God."

The czar's words made Jamal Eddin uneasy. This invective against hypocrites and the traitors, these words so familiar to him, upset him deeply.

"Actually, the worst ones are the Christians."

Now was clearly not the moment to ask to convert to Christianity.

The czar was so perturbed at the mention of this European alliance with the Muslims, this monstrous and incomprehensible choice—against him—that he dropped one of his dossiers.

Petrified, Jamal Eddin did not move. He remained standing, heels together, arms at his sides. His heart was beating as though it would burst.

All the aides-de-camp scrambled to their knees to gather up the sheets of paper scattered on the floor.

After a brief silence, the emperor returned to the question that obsessed him.

"Is it conceivable that Russia can find no allies among her Christian brothers? That the king of Prussia and the emperor of Austria are capable of adopting Mohammed's cause as their own?"

He straightened his shoulders and roared again, "If they dare to do that, then so be it! I place my hope in God and in the justice of the cause I defend. Russia alone will raise the holy cross, and Russia alone will follow its commandments."

He turned back to Jamal Eddin and repeated, "I'll be with you in a moment, just let me finish what I've begun."

But he broke off again, leaving the window to walk to the chair behind his desk, where he sat down heavily.

"At ease, my boy, sit down, sit down. I'm glad to see you. You, my dear children, are my consolation and joy. What brings you here, my lad, what can I do for you? You would like to join the army of the Caucasus, to go and fight the Turks, is that it? You would like to take the occasion of this war to see the mountains again? Unless—"

A glimmer of bitterness flashed in the czar's eyes.

"Unless you have come to ask me to send you back to your father? To take up arms against me, like all the others. You're all the same. You come to walk all over Russia before stabbing her in the back without regret!"

This last wounded Jamal Eddin so deeply that he replied in nearly the same tone, with anger and disdain.

"My father does not need me to fight you, Your Imperial Majesty. He has designated a successor more to his liking to command all his naïbs—my younger brother, who is much more capable of serving him than I."

The czar frowned.

In the confusion of recent months, he had only glanced at his captains' reports concerning Shamil. He vaguely recollected having read a few sentences about a transfer of power in Dagestan. It came back to him now. The "heir," who would become the fourth imam, was said to be made of the same stern stuff as the father. An incomparably courageous djighit, a magnificent horseman and a formidable warrior, he was a fervent partisan of the holy war and as religious and violently anti-Russian as Shamil. The designation of this twenty-year-old chieftain, much loved and admired by the Montagnards, had complicated the czar's projects for the Caucasus. Though the plan to install Lieutenant Shamil as the legitimate successor may not be totally nullified, it would be, at the very least, much more difficult to achieve.

The czar chose to dismiss this new annoyance.

"What are you talking about?" he said curtly.

"About my loyalty to Russia, Your Imperial Majesty!" Jamal Eddin answered passionately. "Nothing more stands in the way of my love for her. My father's choice has freed me from"—he took a deep breath, searching for words to express what he had felt as a fundamental deliverance—"from the conflict that has been tearing me apart."

He weighed his words carefully and repeated, "My father's choice has released me from the duty of answering your kindness with hatred."

A torrent of words followed.

Jamal Eddin confessed that, at last, he could love his country without reservation, that this sense of belonging was so real and so deep that he was asking his benefactor, to whom he owed everything, permission to adopt his faith, to convert and to marry a Russian.

The czar deciphered the meaning of his words instantly. Conversion, marriage. Why, the young man was in love! The empress's fears, during all those summers that Jamal Eddin had spent at the cottage, had been confirmed. He was smitten with some lovely creature in his entourage. It was entirely predictable. La Potemkina had finally achieved her objective.

Did that matchmaker have anything to do with this? Yes, quite probably. Baptism and marriage. Bravo!

The czar gave him a blank look, as though he had not heard or understood. His silence plunged Jamal Eddin into a state of anguish. Perhaps he hadn't explained himself clearly enough. But how could he clarify himself now if His Majesty did not grant him permission to speak?

Impassively, the czar summoned the orderly officer and asked him to escort the other men out, dismissing him as well. The officers left the salon.

When the door had closed behind them, the czar leaned forward on his desk and said severely, "Is it up to me, Jamal Eddin Shamil, is it up to me to remind you of the meaning of apostasy for a Muslim?" He exploded in anger. "I was under the impression that I had provided you with a religious education from the mullahs! In Islam, apostasy means death! If you were to convert, it would be the duty of the first Montagnard who crossed your path to kill you."

"As it would be to kill any Russian, Your Majesty."

"No, Jamal Eddin, not any Russian, and not any giaour. A renegade! Do you understand the gravity of the act you are asking me to approve? You would be useless in any negotiations for peace. On the contrary, the worst possible interlocutor! You speak of serving me. Of what use is an intermediary who can only inspire hatred and mistrust among his own people? I could never send you back to the Caucasus!"

"Send me to the Caucasus, Your Majesty, and I will serve you. Send me to Turkey, and I will serve you. I am not afraid of death."

"But you are afraid to live without love, is that it?"

"Yes, Your Imperial Majesty. I love a young woman."

"Her name?"

"Elizaveta Petrovna Olenina."

"Piotr Alexeyevitch's daughter?"

"The same, Your Imperial Majesty. When I met Elizaveta Petrovna, when I fell in love with her, I thought of you and your family." He lowered his gaze. "I thought of you and the empress."

"Good God, what does that have to do with it?"

"Because of your example, Your Imperial Majesty. You taught me the meaning of happiness."

Jamal Eddin went on to describe Lisa, her grace and her virtues, the kindness of her parents, and his own feelings. He confided in the czar, admitting everything. He said that Lisa was the wife God had chosen for him, and that with her by his side, he could accomplish his duty and face any trial.

The czar had professed nothing less, felt nothing less toward Mouffy, throughout their entire life together. In a startling flash of intuition, he had known she was his soul mate the very first time they had looked at each other.

And even now, when he felt alone and abandoned by all the kings of Christendom, he still found peace when he was with his wife, despite his liaisons with younger women. Without his wife, where would he be today? She had given him so much joy. With her, he had been content to be "Lord of the Cottage," the title he had once used to travel incognito in England. It suited him better than "Emperor of Russia." If God had not put him on the throne, he was sure he could have lived a simple bourgeois existence, as long as he had Mouffy and the children by his side. The children. The very thought of them amid all this chaos raining down on him made him sentimental. What kind of a world would he bequeath the czarevitch Alexander, a world where Christians allied with Muslims to fight Christians? Thank God his daughter Alexandra would never see this, his beloved lost daughter, who was in heaven now with the angels. The memory of Alexandra, Adini, who had not been able to live out her earthly existence, saddened him. Emotion began to color his reasoning. What right had he to rob Jamal Eddin of his happiness, to deprive him of salvation? What right had he to prevent him from saving his soul by being baptized?

The boy's return to the Caucasus had become problematic. And if, moreover, he no longer wished to return—

The czar was not crazy enough to send him back to this father against his will. That would be a monumental wrong. Without the young man's love for his people, he would be useless to Russia there. It was certain to be a disaster. The fact that he preferred civilization to barbarity could be seen as a triumph.

That today he should choose Russia, of his own free will—yes, it was a victory! And far more brilliant than any military victory.

Once the idea took root, it had obvious appeal, and the emperor began to see its advantages.

This much was clear: Jamal Eddin's choice embodied the triumph of the Russians over the Chechens. The triumph of the czar over the imam. Nicholas's personal triumph over Shamil.

The voluntary conversion of the imam's son proved to these savages, and to the entire world, that no one could resist the Orthodox faith and the truth that was incarnate in Holy Russia.

The voluntary conversion of the imam's son was proof of the triumph of light over the forces of evil.

It proclaimed to the whole world that Christ was King.

Jamal Eddin's mind was characterized by such integrity and his heart had resisted for so long. Such a call could only come from God.

The czar renounced his earlier plans entirely. He accepted the fact that his protégé would never become an imam at his service.

But he was still worried, not about carrying out his plans, but about Jamal Eddin's affections. The boy was so sincere—was he sure he wasn't making a mistake? He knew Jamal Eddin was passionate by nature, his character and his actions wholehearted. He was probably the most passionate of lovers as well. Overcome with adoration for this young girl, he was perhaps blinded by love.

The czar sounded him out one last time.

"You understand that if you marry a Christian, you will never be able to go home to your father?"

"But you are my father!"

A cry from the heart.

The czar was so touched, tears welled up in his eyes.

Kings may have abandoned him, but this child remained loyal and loved him. He reacted by making a decision that was completely irrelevant to the matter at hand.

"You will be named an officer in my own Chevaliers-Gardes!"

"Thank you, Your Imperial Majesty," Jamal Eddin stammered, this incongruous order jolting him back into the world of practical decisions. "But I cannot accept such an order—"

"Because you haven't the means? Don't worry about a thing, my lad. My treasury is now yours. In all the great changes your future holds, I will always be at your side. Come here, my son, come closer, Prince Jamal Eddin, so that I can embrace you."

Deeply moved, Jamal Eddin stood up. The czar rose too.

"Come here, let me bless you."

Jamal Eddin obeyed and walked around the desk.

Trembling with emotion, the two men looked into each other's eyes for a long moment. Then they clasped each other in a heartfelt embrace.

As he had six years ago, sitting on his daughter Alexandra's favorite bench at Peterhof, the czar was the first to pull away. His face was wet with tears.

"I want to be godfather at your baptism," he said with infinite tenderness. "And I shall be best man at your wedding. Take this cross."

The czar unbuttoned his collar and removed the crucifix he wore under his uniform. He placed it around Jamal Eddin's neck. As the gold chain touched Jamal's skin, it caught for an instant on the leather cord he wore beneath his cherkeska. The inlaid precious stones of the cross clicked against the little silver tube he had never removed, not since the day on the ramparts of Akulgo when his mother had rolled up the sura of *Men* and placed it inside to protect him from the temptation of evil. The last sura of the Koran.

"Take this crucifix as a token of my love and of the immense love of Our Lord Jesus Christ. His will be done. Go now, my child. I consent to all for your happiness."

Machouk
October 1853–April 1854

"No other story could have begun so inauspiciously," La Potemkina prattled on before her audience of governesses and fellow embroiderers, "and ended in such an apotheosis!"

She reveled in this success as though she had been personally responsible for it.

Her priest, accustomed to the conversion of Muslims, was already giving Jamal Eddin religious instruction, and she followed his progress with her usual zeal. Her nephew's family was too far removed from the affairs of aristocratic society to organize this kind of a ceremony, so La Potemkina was planning the two masses that would take place at her Church of the Holy Trinity at Gostilitsy.

"His Imperial Majesty as godfather! His Imperial Majesty as best man! Such an honor!"

She scarcely took a breath before enumerating the countless privileges "such an honor" implied. Godfather, best man. In assuming these roles, the czar was not only symbolically taking part in the destiny of the young couple, he was ensuring the social and financial future of their household as well.

"The prerogatives of the czar's godsons can extend to their progeny as well," the wife of the marshal of the aristocracy explained to the women of Machouk, who were deplorably unsophisticated in her opinion. "The crown pays for their education, they are granted an honorary function as a career, and their fortunes are assured with gifts and substantial emoluments. At every parade and official ceremony, they are in the front row."

La Potemkina was equally quick to point out that Jamal Eddin's admission to the regiment of the Chevaliers-Gardes elevated him to the rank of a Russian prince. To belong to the Chevaliers-Gardes, a young man had to count so many noble forbears that relatively few cadets were eligible for the honor, even among those of the First Corps. Quite apart from his blue-blooded lineage, a candidate had to count at least one former general of the Gardes among his grandfathers. Not to mention a colossal fortune to be invested in equipment, the purchase of several uniforms, and the maintenance of several dozen horses and as many servants. The czar's generosity would provide for all of this.

"If anyone stands to gain from this marriage, it is surely the Olenins," she insisted, with her usual habit of stretching the truth. "Ah, she can congratulate herself on her conquest of Jamal Eddin, our little darling. A veritable triumph over fate!"

In the eyes of the lovers, there was no talk or triumph, destiny, or fate. For them, the universe opened up. Each dawn was the beginning of the first day of the world, and the sun rose over an immemorially radiant present.

Even Shibshiev seemed to have vanished from sight.

Of course, his services were no longer of any use. But overwhelmed by emotion at his meeting at the Winter Palace, Jamal Eddin had forgotten to ask that Shibshiev be dismissed. If the latter had had any suspicions regarding the purpose of Jamal's trip to Petersburg, they were confirmed by the gold chain that glittered around his neck upon his return. In addition to the fact that no Montagnard was allowed to wear an ornament of gold next to the skin, Shibshiev had immediately guessed the significance of the medal that dangled there, hidden beneath Jamal's collar.

The engagement dinner at Machouk, officially confirming the czar's approval, left no doubt in his mind as to what was to come. This unspeakable disgrace inspired in him a single reaction—the desire to kill.

His choice and his duty were now clear. He must assassinate the son of his imam.

Knowing this, Jamal Eddin was constantly on his guard and extremely attentive where Lisa's security was concerned in the weeks that followed the announcement of their marriage.

But Shibshiev did nothing.

Unpredictable to the very end, he was unusually silent. He made no threats, no speeches, no scenes. Nothing. Outraged, and probably terrified by the act that Shamil's son was about to commit, he melted into the landscape and fled.

"Good riddance!" thought Buxhöwden, who had always strongly disapproved of Shibshiev's presence in the regiment of lancers at Torjok.

No one would see his shadow skulking around after Jamal Eddin in the forest of Machouk anymore.

But one day, when it was nearly autumn and the sun had dipped low between the distant mountain peaks, Jamal Eddin sensed a threatening presence as he rode through the woods with Lisa. They dismounted. Lisa was leaning against the tree where he had just tied up the horses. He bent over to take her hands and kissed them one by one. She smiled, her eyes sparkling. He bowed before her, and she looked down at the nape of his neck. He stood up straight; she did not resist when he took her in his arms. He felt her go limp in his embrace as he slowly kissed her eyes and mouth. Her blonde curls cascaded over her shoulders, and for a moment he held her head, with its golden hair and pale face, in the crook of his arm. She raised her lips to his, and Jamal Eddin was carried away, consumed, burning within.

Suddenly he started, and his eyes flew open.

She raised her head.

"Don't move," he whispered.

He drew his weapon and bounded forward. There was no trace of Shibshiev in the surrounding thicket.

He hurried back to her with long strides. He looked about sharply, his kinjal still poised, on his guard and ready to protect her. Something inscrutable about his intensity stirred her deeply. His eyes were narrowed, his black hair pushed back off his forehead, and he moved like a slender and nimble animal in the wild. She was dazzled, not by any danger at hand, but by his beauty and by the miracle of being loved by this man. She chose to make light of this rush of emotion and laughed.

"Did you see Satan?" she teased him.

"I saw nothing."

"And for good reason. He's not crazy, this devil, he knows he's lost all his power. He must have left Torjok by now."

Jamal Eddin was still worried.

"Come on," he said, "let's go home."

The warning in the forest was the last.

Jamal Eddin was experiencing a period of joy too perfect, a degree of happiness too intense to allow any anxiety to enter his mind. He had overcome wrenching indecision; his contradictory feelings were a thing of the past.

He forgot about Shibshiev.

The two ceremonies would take place when the czar was available. His schedule was heavy and complicated, and he was not especially in the mood for festivities. Jamal Eddin sensed this and searched for a way to speed up the plans for his wedding day.

His usual reserve, the calm he expressed when he was away from Lisa, gave way to agonizing impatience. When he leaned down to take this slight young woman in his arms, when he carried her to a green clearing in the shade of the trees and laid her on the moss, when she pulled him close, their bodies enlaced, he could no longer contain his passion, and their pleasure became a torment. They had dreamed so long of the moment when they could love each other that desire was turning into torture.

"This is becoming unbearable," he murmured, his face pale as he untangled himself from her embrace.

She said nothing but understood completely. If her parents' trust in Jamal Eddin was such that they had promised her to him, he could not take her from them before they were married. He would have to wait. Like them, he must have faith in life, in this promise of happiness, in the czar, and in God.

She sensed the violence of the restraint he imposed upon himself in order to respect his word, implicitly given to the Olenins, and how he suffered in refusing what Lisa held out to him. She loved him all the more for his scruples, his force of will, even his sense of honor.

"Hold me," she murmured, "hold me back."

He clasped her tightly against him.

At the double declaration of war—against Turkey in October, and France and England in March—La Potemkina was obliged to postpone the date for the festivities. With the signature of a defensive alliance between Prussia and Austria and the consequent conscription of the Army of the West, to which Jamal Eddin belonged, she put it off a second time.

The czar was convinced that the main attack would come through the Balkans and Poland rather than the Crimea, so he sent his elite troops to protect the Western frontier against a Hapsburg invasion. The Uhlans' departure for Warsaw and, from there, for Lublin became imminent.

In the little wood at Machouk, all the couples who had been floating on air descended abruptly back to earth. Buxhöwden and Marina, Milyutin and Tatiana whispered a thousand vows and embraced a thousand times. There were no farewells and no tears, just a very tender and serene au revoir. Yes, tomorrow the Torjok lancers would leave for war. But they would be back the day after. The Ottoman fleet had already been sent to the bottom of the Black Sea. The army in the Caucasus—the troops normally engaged in fighting Shamil—would soon crush the forces of Mustafa Sherif Pasha. On every front, victory over the Turks seemed assured, so much so that the Persians sought to protect themselves from the Russians by signing a treaty of neutrality. As for the French and the English, the czar's troops had already planned a heavily armed reception for them if they attempted to land in Crimea. That left the Austrians, but the Uhlans could take care of them.

Like the Hungarian conflict five years ago, this war would be as short as it would be glorious.

Jamal Eddin and Lisa walked arm in arm beneath the tall trees. They felt so inextricably tied that it seemed that the blood of each beat in the other's veins.

"I want to take you away with me now, this very instant."

He stopped and took the young woman's face in his hands. She did not move. His voice trembled with passion.

"Next time."

The little diamond teardrops hanging from Lisa's ears sparkled between his fingers.

"The next time I hold you this way, it will be for the rest of our lives."

* * *

Jamal Eddin had no sense of flashback when he departed for the Polish border. On the contrary, everything had changed; the world looked entirely different to him. He was leaving as a Russian officer, engaged to a Russian girl. For the first time, he knew the future belonged to him. He felt at peace with himself as he never had. He was twenty-three years old, he was happy, and he was in love.

Because he was defending his country, Lieutenant Shamil had exchanged the cherkeska of the Montagnards for the red, blue, and gold uniform of the Vladimirsky Lancers.

The Cottage of Peterhof-Alexandria, six months later Late September 1854

"Odessa bombed. Bomarsund under siege. How are such disasters possible, Major General Milyutin?" the czar roared, pacing up and down in the spacious room, which, built to look like a ship's cabin, took up the entire attic of the cottage.

Dmitri, the eldest of the Milyutin boys and Jamal Eddin's former guardian, stood up straight in the center of the room, miserably watching His Majesty come and go before him.

The czar wore a simple tunic; the only touch of color was its gold epaulets. The light that flooded in from the balcony played on the frescoes of the wall murals and the ceiling, a décor of trompe l'oeil draperies that evoked a war chief's tent at the Field of the Cloth of Gold.

The two men had known each other for a long time. Major General Milyutin had accompanied the czar to Olmütz and to Potsdam during the most recent negotiations with the Austrians and the Prussians.

Nearly forty years old by this time, Dmitri had filled out considerably. His blond curls, though still a little too long, had touches of gray now. But he had maintained a youthful figure reminiscent of an adolescent who had grown too quickly, and his shoulders stooped only slightly. His capacity for work, his enthusiasm, frankness, energy, and integrity—qualities all too rare in this administration—had earned him the resentment of powerful enemies. He had not been spared the opposition of various aristocrats, particularly the adversaries of his uncle Kiselyev, but they had failed to affect what had been a splendid career. Today Dmitri was among the emperor's closest military advisors.

As first secretary to the minister of war, he had been assigned to elaborate strategies of defense in the Baltic Sea, but Major General Milyutin's field of specialization remained the wars in the Caucasus. His Majesty hadn't gotten around to reading his report, the fruit of ten years of research on the Muslim peoples of the mountains, nor had he yet deigned to hear the major general's conclusions on how to achieve a lasting peace in this mysterious region of the world. Nonetheless, Milyutin did not despair of one day capturing his interest. The czar had chosen him as his privileged advisor and sounding board on all questions relating to Chechnya. But for the moment, those questions had been pushed to the back of the sovereign's mind.

"The English fleet here, beneath this balcony, the English fleet in Russian waters, daring to thumb their noses at me all the way here, at my home, at the cottage!"

In June, the shadow of war in Europe had indeed descended over the czar and his family at Peterhof-Alexandria. The enemy had sailed into the Gulf of Finland, just a few cables' lengths from Petersburg. For several days, you could spot the British admiral's sails from the windows of the czar's office. The courtiers at Peterhof had found the nautical show amusing, but the czar was beside himself. Milyutin found him so changed that he didn't dare bring up the new disaster he had come to discuss, the taking of hostages on his lands in Georgia.

"And now France!" the czar ranted on. "Europe sold out and the French are disembarking on the beaches of the Crimea! How is this possible?"

He struck one of the shelves with his palm and repeated, "How is this possible? I accepted without protest our defeat on the Alma River, since that was God's will. But what pain,

Milyutin, what utter humiliation it is to know that this defeat is due only to a lack of courage on the part of my troops. You, Milyutin, you who know how to fight. Think of Akulgo. Taking the promontory of Akulgo was infinitely more difficult than merely defending the Alma! I ask you, what has become of our glorious army? What happened to this army that vanquished Napoleon, crushed the Turks, took Warsaw, and saved the Hapsburg Empire?"

"The Russian army hasn't changed since 1812, Your Imperial Majesty. The Russian army is still the bravest and the most faithful of all armies. But our rifles, Your Imperial Majesty, haven't a quarter of the range of the French rifles."

"What are you talking about?" the czar snapped. "Our soldiers are so well equipped that they could go around the world and back and still lack for nothing."

Milyutin had been hearing this phrase in schools and ministries for twenty years and always found it exasperating. However, he thought it best not to mention this and returned to his central preoccupation.

"I'm only telling you the truth, Your Imperial Majesty. Even in the Caucasus, we are sometimes issued rifles without any triggers, without bullets and munitions. They send us cartridges that are too small. Or too big for the breeches. Or cartridges filled with millet dust instead of gunpowder. The imam Shamil's muskets are even older and in worse shape than ours, but—"

"But that doesn't prevent him from committing atrocities. Let's discuss that then, Milyutin, since that is why I summoned you. Your minister's reports about this affair are confusing, though I suppose that he, like all of us at this difficult time, has other pressing worries on his mind. But the empress can't sleep for thinking of it."

Indeed, Czarina Alexandra Feodorovna hadn't slept for months. The conflict pitting the czar against her brother, the Prussian king, had upset her to the point of making her ill. Like her husband, she could not understand Europe's attitude. Her surprise at the hatred of powers she had always considered friendly, her disgust and anguish, were wearing her down. There was too much injustice, too much ingratitude. The slight nod, a nervous tic that she had developed when she was upset, had become a continuous trembling. She was fifty-six, but she looked twenty years older. Her two youngest sons were leaving for the front the next day, Nicky for the Crimea and Mischa for Poland. And now, as if the danger threatening her children were not enough, her old friend Princess Anastasia of Georgia had thrown herself weeping at her feet with a dreadful tale of the imam's latest abomination.

Anastasia's daughters, once her own maids of honor, beautiful Anna and sweet Varenka, had been kidnapped by the hordes of the imam Shamil. Anna and Varenka were now hostages of the Chechens! The empress lacked both imagination and experience of the world, but she had no difficulty conceiving what this kind of captivity implied. The heartbroken mother had told her how the young women had been attacked at their country home. How they had been robbed, stripped of their clothing, and forced by blows of the lash to leave their manor house. Half-naked, they had been dragged to the mountains on foot, barefoot, with their children and all their servants riding pillion behind the murid horsemen. How they had galloped for a month, hanging onto their kidnappers, even though Anna was still breast-feeding her new baby. She described how all their little ones, from two months to six years old—all of Princess

Anastasia's grandchildren—had been separated from them, and how Lydie, Anna's infant, had slipped from the arms of her exhausted mother during a chase and been stabbed and trampled by the Montagnards. The czarina was horrified by such terrifying images. She knew she must speak to the emperor and force him to do something. He alone could save Anna and Varenka.

But Nicks had other worries on his mind, things far more pressing than the kidnapping of twenty-three women and children. There were so many dead in the Crimea. Poor Nicks. He was so good and so generous; he did not deserve this.

"The empress is begging me to intervene and negotiate with the imam," Nicholas continued, frowning. "The czar of Russia doesn't talk to bandits! Dealing with Shamil would make all the Muslim fanatics think that they can get what they want simply by attacking defenseless victims. One cannot give in, one can never give in to blackmail; it's a question of honor. But then, what does honor mean now, when Christians are betraying each other?

"However, I'm not like those traitors, like the emperor of Austria and the king of Prussia and all those other ingrates who abandon their friends in the face of adversity. The family of Georgia has always served me faithfully, and the princesses' mother is very dear to us all. Right now she is waiting in tears in the salon. This dreadful business has been going on for nearly three months. I owe her an answer."

His Majesty could not contain his rage.

"I had hoped that in the space of three months, you might have found a way out of this matter without my intervention!" he exploded. "Now what is your opinion? Can we still save the girls?"

"Yes, Your Imperial Majesty. They are imprisoned in the imam's seraglio. Although they lack everything, they seem to be well treated. But time is short."

"I'll give you five minutes, Milyutin. Be brief. What the hell has been going on in the Caucasus while we have been fighting a war on the Turkish front?"

"An old story, Your Imperial Majesty, a very old story. Your Majesty is no doubt aware that Shamil has been demanding the return of his son for the past fifteen years? In all the peace overtures that we have extended to him, the return of Jamal Eddin has always been a condition *sine qua non.* How did he learn his son was about to marry a Christian? How did this news reach him so quickly? I suppose the imam has always feared that his son would be converted and placed informers in his entourage. Shamil's network of spies is as effective as ours in the Caucasus and far superior to those of all the European powers. He knows everything. According to our sources, he was devastated at the news of his son's forthcoming marriage. No doubt judging that he could not allow his son to be lost in this world and damned in the next, he reacted with all the determination that we already well know is part of his character. He took advantage of the fact that so many of our troops have been transferred to the Turkish front and are spread thin elsewhere to dare to do what he had never attempted before: a hostage raid on the plain, far from his eagle's nest in Chechnya. We never would have imagined him capable of such audacity."

"You should have expected it. The Montagnards' raids on Georgian villages have been terrorizing the population for ages."

"No murid band had ever dared to venture that far, Your Imperial Majesty. The expedition had been carefully planned.

It was led by his younger son, a warrior named Mohammed Ghazi, the future imam. This Mohammed Ghazi swooped down from the mountains with an army of three thousand horsemen to attack the manor of Princess Anna."

"Sinandali?" the czar interrupted.

"The same, Your Imperial Majesty."

The czar was referring to the property of the Chavchavadze princes, a mansion nestled among the vineyards at the base of the high, snowy mountains of the Caucasus, three hundred versts from Tiflis. A domain blessed by the gods, it had a charm and sensuality that was matched only by the intellectual climate provided by the hosts. Griboyedov, the famous ambassador who had married the sister of one of the owners, had lived at Sinandali. Lermontov enjoyed long stays there as a guest. Even the emperor had chosen to spend a few hours in this paradise, in the company of the most eminent members of the Georgian aristocracy, during a trip to the Caucasus twenty years ago.

"I remember the vast terrace and an exotic garden with flowers everywhere. A chapel, too, on the riverbank."

"They climbed up that way, from the riverbank, Your Majesty, and they burned everything—the chapel and all the rest. There's nothing left. And as for the family—"

"I know. The empress shed every tear in her body describing what they did to them. I know, I know. And what is the state of negotiations now?"

"They are at a standstill, Your Imperial Majesty."

"Who is talking to the Chechens right now?"

"The hostages' family, Your Majesty, Prince David Chavchavadze, who is Princess Anna's husband and the master of Sinandali. He wasn't captured."

"Where the devil was he?"

"At his post, Your Imperial Majesty, commanding the fort where he was stationed, on the other side of the river. He was fighting for Russia, not protecting his property. His relative, Prince Grigol Orbeliani, is negotiating for the princess Varenka Orbeliani on behalf of his brother, the princess's late husband."

"I didn't know little Varenka was already a widow."

"Her husband, Prince Elico Orbeliani, was killed by the Turks in December."

"He had also once been the hostage of Shamil, if I'm not mistaken."

"Your Majesty is correct. Prince Orbeliani was taken prisoner by Shamil about eleven years ago. Apparently the idea of exchanging an important captive for his son has been on his mind for some time. But fate has been cruel to the poor Orbeliani family. Varenka lost her husband during the siege of Oguzlu, at nearly the same time that one of her sons took ill and died in Tiflis. Her other child, a boy of eight, is being held prisoner with her in Shamil's seraglio, along with her sister's surviving children."

"What does Shamil demand in exchange for their freedom?"

"Hostages for hostages. He wants his son, of course, and his nephew Hamzat, whom he believes is still alive. Third, he wants the son of his old friend, Ali Bek. And a hundred forty-eight other prisoners. As well as a ransom of a million rubles."

"A million rubles! Does that savage have any idea what a million rubles represents? That's my entire budget for the war ministry!"

"That's what Prince Chavchavadze and Prince Orbeliani told him, Your Majesty, that his demands were so exorbitant that they made it impossible to continue the negotiations. They explained that this was an affair between families, theirs and the imam Shamil's, and that they were dealing person-to-person, not state-to-state."

"Well said. And how did Shamil react?"

"By threatening to sell their sons on the slave market in Constantinople and to divide up their wives, sisters, and daughters among his naïbs before the end of the month."

"Will he do it?"

"He's done much worse, Your Majesty. This is the kind of promise he keeps. The princes wrote back immediately, explaining that his son is not a hostage or a prisoner but an officer in the Russian army, and that they could not force him to return to the Caucasus. They added that no one would ever dare to request that the emperor send him back to his father. However, if Jamal Eddin wished to return to his family and asked for the czar's permission to do so, then perhaps it would be granted. But such a request could come only from him."

The czar sat down at his desk to think, his head bent over his clasped hands. If he surrendered Jamal Eddin to Shamil, all of Europe would believe that the imam of Chechnya had brought the emperor of Russia to his knees, that he had sold out to the crescent. He could just picture the headlines in London and Paris: "The will of the humble Shamil prevailed over that of the powerful Nicholas." In these terrible times, this new humiliation would be one more slap in the face.

On the other hand, it was possible that complying with Jamal Eddin's wishes and permitting him to marry had not been a wise move.

Had God allowed Shamil to seize the princesses so that the czar might reconsider the situation? Did the Lord actually want him to return to his initial plan, the idea that had motivated his educating the boy in the first place? He was still a Muslim and still fully able to fulfill the mission for which the czar had always intended him. His return to the Caucasus was still possible.

In the end, was this the best solution for Russia? To send Jamal Eddin back to his own people, to work for peace, as he had always planned?

The emperor mulled all this over for a long time.

"Despite Shamil's despicable methods," he said decisively, "I don't see any political obstacle to returning his son to him."

Milyutin then rapidly conveyed the message that the war minister had entrusted to him.

"In the case that His Imperial Majesty has no objections—this is from our headquarters at Tiflis—the princes humbly request that His Imperial Majesty obtain a response as quickly as possible. In only three weeks, the princesses are to be distributed to the naïbs, in their auls. Even a definitive refusal is preferable to silence. A refusal would leave room for the slim hope of reopening negotiations on new terms. But in the absence of a clear response regarding the return—or not—of the imam's son, Prince Chavchavadze has no choice but to bid farewell to his wife and children, forever."

"Good. Jamal Eddin should be informed of the kidnapping and given the choice to stay in Russia or return to his father's home. It is up to him. I'm not going to say, like Pontius Pilate, that I wash my hands of the affair, but personally I'm neither for nor against his return. Therefore I will make no decision in this matter. He must express his wishes. The choice is his. I leave him free to make it."

Report of the commander-in-chief of forces in Poland Warsaw November 8, 1854

From: Count Nicholas Mikhaïlevitch Muravyev,
General of the Armies of the West

To: Major General Dmitri Alexeyevitch Milyutin,
First Secretary, Ministry of War

"[…] A week ago, on the 30th of October, I received a letter from His Imperial Highness the Czarevitch Alexander commanding me in the name of the Emperor to urgently summon Lieutenant Shamil to my headquarters.

"The Vladimirsky Lancers are bivouacked two hundred versts from Warsaw, near Lublin. Lieutenant Shamil made haste and reported to my office this morning, November 8. He had ridden all night, and I received him within the hour. Since he did not know the reason for his urgent recall, he was concerned about those close to him. He asked after the health of Her Imperial Majesty the Empress, whom he knows to be ill, and that of the family of the painter Piotr Alexeyevitch Olenin at Torjok. I reassured him on both counts with a simple question that amounted to, 'Would you be willing to return to your home in exchange for the princesses who have been kidnapped by your father?' He seemed astonished, I would even say stunned, by my question. He turned very pale. When he had recovered a bit from his surprise, he questioned me about the kidnapping. I gave him all the details he asked for. I did not hide the threat to the honor and the lives of the hostages, but I emphasized the fact that His Majesty had left him entirely free to decide. He could not hide his dismay. I told him that he could take his time to think things over and give me his answer; the mail for Saint Petersburg did not leave until late morning, and all he had to do was to knock on my door when he was ready.

"He left the antechamber. I had several visits this morning. He did not seem to notice. Every time I received someone, I saw him there, standing very still against the wall in the shadow of a corner, oblivious to everyone coming and going around him.

"Although he remained standing, perfectly straight, he seemed devastated, as though stricken."

In the antechamber of
General Muravyev's office
Warsaw
November 8, 1854

Prisoners in a Caucasian village.

His mind raced; he could not get hold of himself. What, exactly, did the general say? That Anna and Varenka, their children and their servants were being held captive on the promontory of Akulgo. No, wait, the general had not mentioned Akulgo.

An abyss yawned before him. He felt dizzy, as though he were on the edge of a precipice. He felt nauseous as his mouth filled with the taste of blood and dust and he breathed in the odor of rotting flesh—the taste, the stench of Akulgo. What other name had the general mentioned? Prisoners at Veden. The seraglio of Dargo-Veden. He said the words over to himself. Varenka was Shamil's hostage. Jumping from one detail to the next, drawing his mind back to the objective facts, he tried to penetrate the reality, understand the meaning, and measure the consequences. But in his turmoil, he was unable to identify the nature of the shock that had struck him. He could not express the actual pain. He clung to a kind of generalized suffering, an overall view, and to snatches of the conversation that came back to him. The princesses were to be distributed. The princesses were to be sold. Varenka would become the servant of a naïb. Varenka, the slave of a Shibshiev! The reality of that image appeared before his mind's eye in all its horror, and he could follow it no further. Varenka, the prey of a vermin such as Shibshiev. Yes, of course it was Shibshiev who was behind the whole plot—the kidnapping and the blackmail. That sneak hadn't wasted a minute informing his master.

"I should have crushed him like a cockroach on that first day in Poland. I should have chased him and slit his throat in the forest, with Lisa, the last time."

Lisa, the last time? Until this moment, he hadn't dared contemplate the link between Varenka and Lisa. Of course he knew, he had instantly made the connection: returning to his father's side meant losing Lisa. Going home meant giving up love, happiness, and the future, everything he had once believed was possible.

But not returning meant killing the princesses.

Whether he stayed or left, there was no solution.

He was caught in a vise, torn between two impossible choices.

"If I obey my father, maybe he will free his hostages. And then what? I will take my place beside him among the warriors of Allah. Just as before."

He dared not imagine what his life would be like in the Caucasus. He had come such a long way in Russia.

How could he go back?

"How do I unlearn all that I have learned here? How do I unlearn the books and physics and mathematics, unlearn the music? Destiny is so strange. At the very moment I accepted all the advantages of studies and civilization, at the precise moment I was preparing to devote myself to them, fate throws me back into the heart of ignorance. I shall probably have to forget all that I have known and walk backward, like a crab.

"But what does it matter? Without Lisa, what does anything matter? Without Lisa, the rest is immaterial. How can I unlearn loving her? Happiness with her seemed so close. Her parents had consented, the czar had consented. Nothing stood in our way. Who is forcing me to sacrifice her today? Who is making me sever myself from her? No one. The czar has left me to be master of my own destiny. Who is forcing me to leave Lisa? Who is forcing me to abandon my regiment, leave my friends, disown Russia? No one. Why should I sacrifice Lisa for the princesses, if no one asks it of me? Why should I break the heart of the woman I love in the name of hatred? Out of duty? Come, now. What duty? Filial duty? I can recognize no sense of duty toward a father who turned his son over to his enemies. For the son that the imam supposedly claims today was not *captured* by the infidels at Akulgo. He was *given* to them. He was abandoned for fifteen years without any news, even though Shamil was evidently powerful enough to place informers in his midst to spy on him. Of all the traitors and hypocrites, my father is the greatest; he speaks of love, but his acts express only vengeance and hatred. My only duty today is to Czar Nicholas, my benefactor. And to Lisa, my wife. Why should I sacrifice her to the cruelty of men? Why should I sacrifice her to the conflicts of the past and the uncertainties of the future? What can that possibly accomplish? She has nothing whatever to do with the tragedy of the princesses. If the imam has the audacity to carry out his threats, then he alone is responsible. I have no part whatsoever in his brutality. I am free to make my own choices, free to choose my destiny. I am a free agent."

An immense strength surged through him and buoyed him with hope and elation. He had his answer. He could stay in Russia, share his life with Lisa, and be happy with her. Yes, he had the answer.

"I shall marry Lisa. Shamil can sell the princesses and kill them. I disavow all of his crimes and disown him for his barbarity. He is nothing to me."

But the victory of love, the triumph of hope over fate, was ephemeral.

"But then, how will we ever find peace after that? How can we construct our own happiness—a family, children—upon the deaths of twenty-three people?

"Honor demands that I deny all that I feel, renounce all I desire, to save the captives. I have no alternative. The czar knows it. He knows that Lisa cannot love a man who has built his life upon an act of cowardice. He knows that I shall lose her either way. What would my wife think if I refused to return to my father and spare his victims? What would I think of myself?

"Yes, I will lose her. *Les jeux sont faits*, and were from the very beginning. I have no choice, though they let me believe that I did. It's all been an illusion. No matter whether I stay or go, our life is over, and our happiness is dead. At the very least, we can save the princesses."

Follow-up of General Muravyev's report to General Milyutin November 8, 1854

"[…] Late this morning, Lieutenant Shamil entered my office. He brought me his response. I suppose he had done some difficult soul searching.

"At the conclusion of his reflections, the sentiment of filial love prevailed, and his immense respect for his father ultimately convinced him. He was serious and pensive when he announced to me that he was ready to join him. I asked him to confirm his decision in writing, immediately, on the sheet of paper I handed him. He deigned to write a single sentence: 'I accept returning to my father, according to his wishes and with the permission of His Majesty.'

"He had nothing more to say once he had agreed, and that was sufficient. I hope that the Ministry will find these few words adequate. I have sent him back to the Vladimirsky Lancers until further notice. I beg Your Excellency to inform me of the Emperor's wishes concerning him.

"Should I send him to Saint Petersburg?

"Please find enclosed with this letter the accord signed by Lieutenant Shamil. […]"

The Winter Palace
Saint Petersburg
December 31, 1854

Just as he had fifteen years ago at Christmastime, Dmitri Milyutin escorted Jamal Eddin through the salons. The two men were the same height now. They wore similar uniforms and walked at the same pace.

Tomorrow Petersburg would rise before dawn to celebrate the first day of the new year with a visit to the Winter Palace, as was customary. The candles on the Christmas trees of the grand dukes' apartments would be lit at midnight the night before, and garlands of tinsel would decorate the immense Christmas tree in the Throne Room. It was there already, glittering with shiny red apples and bonbons, pathetic and solitary in the twilight of the czar's reign. The two officers detoured around it without so much as a pause or a glance.

With their spurs jangling and their sabers clicking and scraping the parquet, the men's boot steps echoed down the corridors. The sounds broke the silence like a knell. The days when the police chief had sung of the future of Russia, comparing the new year to a fireworks display whose splendor illuminated the world, seemed long ago. The drawn curtains in the middle of the day, the veiled mirrors, the emptiness and shadows—everything here spoke of death and disaster.

The few courtiers who mingled in the White Hall voiced their thoughts out loud, and no chamberlain silenced them. They said that the czar was at the end of his tether, exhausted and worn out. He had been in power too long—just think, thirty years—and his judgment had suffered. How else could one explain this string of defeats, if not to attribute them to his own errors and indecision? How could one explain the thousands of wounded at Sebastopol and the siege that promised to worsen as the city became bogged down by winter?

Absorbed in his thoughts, Jamal Eddin did not even hear them. He lifted the end of his saber, conscious of the racket that their martial pace made in the stairway leading to the small study.

His Majesty had moved back to his office on the ground floor, which still contained its familiar objects, its camp bed, and its old English lap rug. This was the narrow study where they had first met.

Outside the snow was falling in big flakes, just as it had that first time.

And like the first time, Jamal Eddin was chilled to the bone, overcome with sadness, anxiety, and fear of the future.

Back to the beginning.

Milyutin stopped in the waiting room. Lieutenant Shamil would see the czar alone.

Jamal Eddin stared at the familiar figure, standing in the alcove at the window in his usual pose, but he scarcely recognized him. No one had taken the trouble to warn him. Stooped, much thinner, his complexion leaden, and tottering on his feet, the czar was a ghost of his former self. He did not bother with dramatic effect and paused only briefly in the backlight before approaching the young man with that robotic step Jamal Eddin had noticed when they had met last year. The czar hugged him briefly. He seemed distracted, his mind elsewhere. He nonetheless made an effort to summon his habitually warm paternal tone.

"I expected you. I'm glad to see you, my child, very glad. We have so much to talk about. Sit down. I've brought you here so we could talk about your future, face to face. I understand you want to go home. Are you very sure?"

The czar said what he had to say, and his voice was affectionate. But there was no light in his eyes, no warmth in his words. He did not appear to differentiate his separation from Jamal Eddin from any of the others; he had seen too much tragedy, and for too long. The grand emotional displays that he usually enjoyed, the tears and embraces and effusions, were absent.

"I haven't answered Prince Orbeliani and Prince Chavchavadze. I was waiting for you to confirm your intentions to me. You can still change your mind."

Why was he putting on this show? The czar had given his consent long ago. Jamal Eddin had received letters from the two families thanking him for his agreement and begging him to hurry. Even Shamil knew he was planning to return.

The czar's disingenuousness was obvious and added to the young man's confusion, destroying what was left of his composure.

He stiffened.

"Your father has asked for the authorization to send emissaries to speak with you on his behalf. Would you like to talk to them and reserve your decision until after you have heard what they have to say?"

"I have no need to meet my father's emissaries to be convinced, Your Imperial Majesty."

"You do not wish to see them?"

"No, Your Imperial Majesty."

"Your decision is final, you are returning? It's irrevocable?"

"Yes, Your Imperial Majesty."

"Have you informed the parents of your fiancée of your departure?"

"Yes, Your Majesty."

"And have you told her?"

"Yes, Your Majesty."

"So she knows what you have chosen. And she accepts this? She understands?"

"For both of us, it is neither a matter of choice nor of acceptance."

"But of duty. You are right. I would not have expected less of you, my child. We are alike, you know, and you are every bit my son. No doubt you think I am the most powerful man on earth. To all outward appearances, I can do anything I want. However, the truth is precisely the opposite: I've never done what I wanted to. If you asked the reason for this strange state of affairs, there would be only one possible answer: duty. For example, I did not want to ascend the throne. I was happy with my wife and my children. I didn't want any other life. And yet, for thirty years, I have been obliged to reign."

How many times had Jamal Eddin heard this speech? He'd listened to the czar tell it at intimate family gatherings, at formal balls, in moments of emotion and eloquence, to soldiers, ministers, children, and his wife. "The czar reigned reluctantly, the czar demonstrated the good example, the czar obeyed the will of God." He used to adapt the speech to the circumstances. Today he hadn't even the strength to modify it for the occasion. Sincere and sentimental, the words spoke themselves automatically, like the chorus of an old and often-repeated song. All that was left was the words—and the melancholy.

"Duty. For you and me, duty is sacred, and we are instinctively compelled to respect it. We must both sacrifice ourselves to duty to the death. That is what I have done all my life and what you are doing now. I want you to know, my boy, that I'm proud of you. And since I know you are courageous, I shall ask for an ultimate sacrifice on your part. I want you to give me your word of honor that you will not attempt to see Elizaveta Petrovna Olenina before you leave for the Caucasus."

Jamal Eddin remained impassive.

"I will not give you my word on this point, Your Majesty," he said firmly.

"Nonetheless, I am asking for it."

"I have pledged my faith to Lisa Petrovna. I refuse to leave her without having exchanged a spoken word, ending it all with just a letter."

He was not trying to convince the czar or to obtain his permission. He was not pleading his cause; he was flatly refusing to obey.

"But you must," the emperor said softly.

"Her parents welcomed me as a son, Your Majesty. I must take my leave of the family that was to become my family in person."

"I will convey your greetings to Piotr Alexeyevitch, in your name."

"Your Majesty, I love Lisa Petrovna. She gave me her trust and her tenderness. I owe her an explanation. Do not deny me this moment with her."

"I am denying you nothing. I am protecting you from yourself. Do you remember our agreement, in the glade at Peterhof? That evening, on the stone bench, you promised me you would return home and try to convince your father to make peace with me. Then you changed your mind and decided to stay in Russia. And now you've changed it again, and you have decided to go home. If you see your fiancée again, how do I know you won't change it a third time? I am simply trying to spare you both needless suffering. I know how painful it is for you to give up this young woman. But God will ensure that your sacrifice is not in vain. In the Caucasus, you will accomplish the mission the Almighty created you for. You will end this fratricidal war between our two peoples and save thousands of lives by making peace. Do not give up hope, never give up. The Lord moves in mysterious ways. Who's to say that one day you might not marry your Lisa?

"Come here, my child, let me bless you, let me embrace you. I shall not say farewell, but only au revoir for now. Send in General Milyutin. Then the two of you will go to see the empress. She has been very ill, you know, and she's still in shock at this series of events. She wants to see you, but don't stay long. Please spare her. And don't forget to stop by the Potemkin manor as you leave the palace. Our brave nun is quite upset at the news of your departure. Now go outside and wait for a few moments, my son. May God protect you."

Their parting embrace was as brief as their greeting had been.

He found the general seated among the secretaries waiting for an audience, cocked hat on his knees.

Milyutin occupied the same little gilt-trimmed chair that the amanat Shamil had perched upon so long ago. Jamal Eddin remembered sitting here in this antechamber, feeling almost happy, fifteen years ago. The Great White Czar had revived the sweet-faced image of his mother, Fatima, and it had floated in his mind's eye, her expression carefree and full of love. At the time, he had been won over, overcome with gratitude toward the man who had returned his kinjal to him. This gesture of trust had marked the beginning of his Russian adventure. Now, in this same antechamber, the menacing specter of the imam Shamil, with his long, henna-tinted beard and his unforgiving eyes, loomed before him.

He thought of the mournful, glassy stare of Czar Nicholas, and the echo of his pompous voice uttering those same hackneyed phrases over and over rang in his mind. A puppet pulling the strings of all the other puppets, he was still trying to manipulate the marionette Jamal Eddin as he did all the other marionettes at his court. Had the emperor ever understood the meaning of his words?

Even their leave-taking today had been a setup. Why hadn't the czar simply told him the truth?

Why hadn't he admitted that he had to return to the Caucasus because there was no other way to save the princesses? Why this farce of choices made, this talk of fake freedom, these silly questions and this entire masquerade? It all served to bend him to his will and bind him to this decision. "I understand you want to go home. Are you very sure, my child?"

Did the czar think he was a fool?

Jamal Eddin flushed in anger and disgust.

Although there wasn't a shadow of a doubt, even for a moment, that he must return to his father as soon as possible so that Varenka would be spared, he had plenty of doubts about everything else. He no longer trusted the czar, or his love, or his motives, or even the moments they had shared during the past fifteen years. He questioned his former impressions and even his own memories.

Had the emperor ever been honest with him?

Had the emperor ever done anything but mislead him?

* * *

Jamal Eddin sat down in Milyutin's empty chair.

Milyutin took Jamal Eddin's place in the study. The order he heard was not what he expected.

"Place him under arrest."

Milyutin chose not to understand.

Too much responsibility weighed on the czar's shoulders on the eve of this new year. He had endured too much strain and humiliation, and the vision of the world he had believed in all his life was about to crumble. Even he felt that he had failed in his mission on earth and was leaving a crumbling empire to his son. He knew he would have to answer for this before his creator.

"Did you hear me, General? Take him to see the empress, and then place him under arrest!"

His Majesty may have still had his wits about him, but his emotions had obviously spun out of control and he didn't know what he was saying. Milyutin played dumb.

"Who should I have arrested, Your Imperial Majesty?"

"The rebel's son. He's going to disobey me. He's going to go see the little Olenin girl in Torjok, even though I forbade him to do just that. He refused to give me his word. I can't take such a risk. If he sees his love again, he'll certainly falter."

"If Lieutenant Shamil has said he will return to his father, he will do it, Your Imperial Majesty," Milyutin replied heatedly. "All I know of him, everything I have seen for the past fifteen years, makes me certain that he will."

"This boy is lovesick. Who knows what his fiancée will tell him, who knows what she'll do to convince him not to leave her? If he doesn't return, or if he even delays his journey, the hostages are done for. I repeat, we cannot put the princesses' lives at such risk."

Milyutin stared at his master. Was it possible that he felt nothing?

Or were his pride and his affections so wounded that he could not bear to face the necessity of sending Jamal Eddin back? This entire affair had forced him to bend to a will that was not his own: the law of Shamil. It reinforced the feeling of impotence that had become a constant in his life, driving him to despair.

"I do not mean that Jamal Eddin should be ill-treated, of course," the czar added wearily. "On the contrary, I'm counting on you personally to look out for his well-being. He should be given books, maps, instruments for physics experiments, a paint box, sheet music. I'm granting him unlimited credit on my own personal treasury. Tell the war minister to set aside three hundred rubles to outfit him completely with uniforms, arms, and horses. I want him to put on a good show when he returns to the Caucasus. Once he's back with his father, he won't have anything. He should return like a prince, laden with gifts and accompanied by a retinue of young people his own age. If I didn't need you so badly here, I would tell you to accompany him. Choose the most trustworthy of his companions in the regiment to escort him."

"Does Your Majesty mean, to keep an eye on him?"

"I mean nothing but what I said, General Milyutin!"

"Will he be sent there as a prisoner," Milyutin countered bitterly, "just as he came here?"

He recalled that terrible journey through the snowstorms of the Russian winter, with this child who had retreated into silence, whom he himself had torn from his people.

"On the contrary, I wish for Jamal Eddin to return in as comfortable circumstances as possible. I mean it, in the manner that will be the least painful for him. It is your responsibility to see to it that he is in the company of his friends. Your younger brother, for example—I understand they are very close. And one or two other Vladimirsky Lancers, according to his preferences.

"But I forbid him to see Elizaveta Petrovna Olenina! Make sure that the young woman is warned and that her parents are warned as well. That is an order. I forbid it. Have I made myself clear? To be safe, take him immediately to Stavropol. General Muravyev, whom I've just appointed commander of the Armies of the Caucasus and governor of the region, will join him there with his friends, the Uhlans from Poland that you will have carefully selected."

* * *

Jamal Eddin did not wonder what the two men were discussing behind closed doors. He did not imagine that it had taken all this time just to decide what to do with him.

He contemplated this realization that the man he called his "benefactor" was not who he thought he was—not entirely, at least, not completely.

He nonetheless could not help but remain attached to the czar. Today he felt a kind of tenderness for the old man, this defeated emperor who had become a shadow of his former self and for whom the appearance of power still counted so much.

His manipulations and his duplicity didn't matter. So what if this father, who pretended to possess the truth and thought himself morally irreproachable, who considered himself a man of honor, was perhaps only a brute and a phony. In spite of it all, he still loved him.

But their last conversation, far from reassuring him, had left him feeling totally helpless and confused. He had the feeling that a wall had grown up between himself and the czar, a wall he would never be able to scale.

He suddenly felt certain that they would never see each other again—and that they had both bungled their last encounter.

* * *

Jamal Eddin's kibitka, escorted by two other sleighs, slid through the snow along the Sovereign's Road, taking him south toward Moscow.

"How can I do this again, deny a world I have grown to love? How can I rebecome the spiritual heir of the imam Shamil? How can I take this long journey back to my childhood?" he wrote to Lisa on January 15, 1855.

The three hundred rubles that the war minister had supplied were spent on bribes and messengers, and he managed to correspond with Lisa. Though they exchanged a thousand letters, Jamal Eddin was never able to return to the Olenins'.

The czar had taken every precaution to make such a visit impossible.

Snow sprayed from the horses' hooves as the sleighs slid through the silence. The quiet of the forest was broken only by the jingling of the harness bells, the coachmen's shouts, and the gentle hiss of the runners cutting through the snow.

"Come on, my beauties," they sang out as they cracked the whip, "courage, my darlings! We're in a hurry, speed it up!"

"No," thought Jamal Eddin, "keep going, but don't ever get there."

He differed in this respect from all the other voyagers traversing the empire just then. He would have wished for a vast and endless Russia, spaces that went on to infinity. He wished it would take all eternity to cross the country.

But between the trees, little black-and-white signposts capped with the imperial eagle at regular intervals told him how many versts they had just covered and of the distance pulling him farther and farther away from happiness.

With all the lanterns dimmed and escorted under guard by two other sleighs, his sleigh flew through the snow. They had passed the little woods at Machouk and had already plunged into the forest at Tver. The coachmen had not stopped to change horses at the relay post of Torjok.

"Without you, Lisa, I shall die in the Caucasus."

Book Three

The Return:
Keep on Going and Never Get There
The Caucasus
1855–1858

CHAPTER X

The Exchange Will Not Take Place

1855

Fort Khassav-Yurt
Frontier post
between Chechen and Russian territory
February 1855

Their peaks covered in eternal snow, the mountains loomed, black and gigantic, a massive chain that blocked the sky and eclipsed the horizon. As the sun set, the glaciers changed from white to pink to violet to purple. The dull murmur of the waterfalls sounded like the beating of a heart. The air was filled with the pungent odor of wood fires, leather, saltpeter, goats, pilaf, and curdled milk, and, sharper than the rest, the stench of suint that rose from the papakhas and burkas. Jamal Eddin thought that he had forgotten the sights and smells of his past, but they surfaced again, intact. The sounds, the colors, and the odors were all still vivid. The only exception was the Caucasus themselves, which seemed infinitely more vast and powerful than anything he could remember from his childhood.

The Russian camp was located on the stony plateau.

Situated on a soil embankment, the square fort had four miradors. A hedge of bushes reinforced a high, wooden stockade that was dotted with holes to accommodate the mouths of cannons. Several entry gates were guarded by sharpshooters in watchtowers. Inside, the artillery was posted along the length of the enclosure. The cavalry was positioned in the center.

There were stone cottages for the officers and isbas for the Cossack families, wooden barracks for the soldiers, and barns with lofts, cowsheds, and stables. A few streets crisscrossed the square, and the commander's quarters were situated in the center. Tied to the top of a roughly squared fir trunk, the purple and gold imperial flag snapped in the wind. All this was pompously baptized Fort Khassav-Yurt.

It was not even a village.

Jamal Eddin spent over three weeks behind the walls of this frontier outpost a few versts from the Chechen forests. He shared meals, quarters, and even a room with Prince David Chavchavadze, Anna's husband, master of the now-ruined Sinandali and leader of the negotiations with Shamil.

The soldiers who saw them drink, smoke, play cards, and joke in Russian and French had no idea that Prince David and the hostage—as they referred to Jamal Eddin, who was once again "the rebel's son"—had known each other for a long time. The two men exchanged books that came by the caseload from Saint Petersburg and lent each other musical instruments, painting supplies, and other items, all gifts of the czar. From all appearances, it seemed that they got on famously.

The reality was rather less rosy. Together, in a state of strained anxiety, they awaited the imam's instructions.

Of medium height, slender, and with light-colored eyes, Prince David Chavchavadze was thirty-eight, fourteen years older than Lieutenant Shamil. He had begun to lose his hair and wore it combed forward, like the emperor Napoleon. His thick moustache was short and clipped in a straight line.

A man of honor, Chavchavadze came from one of the oldest families of the Georgian aristocracy and had made the military his career. Though his father had been exiled to Russia for resisting the annexation of his country and plotting against the occupying forces, the Chavchavadze clan had finally accepted the situation. Now the prince served the czar faithfully.

His superior, General Muravyev, had handed the lieutenant over to him the moment the young man had arrived from Poland with his friends. Leaving Sacha Milyutin and Buxhöwden to follow them, Chavchavadze had been careful to keep his prize in his own carriage. The prince could not risk the escape of his bargaining chip.

For the past nine months, he had been living a waking nightmare whose only constant feature was the uncertainty about the fate of his family. His wife, four of his children, his sister-in-law, his niece, the nannies who had cared for the Chavchavadze children for generations—in short, his entire household—were in the hands of Shamil. And so he had traveled all the way to the city of Vladikavkaz, the last town before the forts on the line, to fetch the precious "rebel's son" and bring him back to Khassav-Yurt.

During this trip across the Caucasus, a strange friendship had developed between Prince David and Lieutenant

Shamil. Sitting at the back of the sleigh that brought the former toward hope and pulled the latter into the past, they had shared their childhood memories of the Winter Palace. Together they remembered the magic of the Chinese lanterns in the wood at Peterhof, and they discovered that they shared similar tastes in poetry and music. Two men of the world, they chatted as though they were resting among potted plants in the corner of a salon.

Later Chavchavadze would describe his surprise at discovering that his traveling companion was a well-read officer of lively character and uncommon intelligence and energy. In addition, he found in Jamal Eddin another virtue: kindness. Though they had discussed all kinds of subjects during those long, intimate hours in the sleigh, they had carefully avoided the one that most concerned them both: the exchange. Where, when, and how would the lieutenant be exchanged for the princesses? Both pretended not to be thinking of how inextricably their respective fates were entangled or that David's happiness depended entirely upon Jamal Eddin's misery.

The prince was also struck by Jamal Eddin's modesty, dignity, and self-control. He emphasized later that the younger man refused to play the hero or the victim. Only once during their long journey together did he express his distress, and even then, he did so with self-mocking black humor.

When they arrived before the sentinels of Khassav-Yurt and presented arms, Jamal Eddin wondered aloud how he could go back to killing Russian soldiers. He immediately erased the sadness of this thought with irony, explaining that—what a stroke of luck!—the honor his filial duty imposed upon him would surely inspire him to overcome his scruples. Thanks to "honor," he would soon be able to justify slitting the throats of those who had been his friends.

On the evening of his arrival at the fort, Jamal Eddin had written to his father. He asked him to forgive his late arrival, explaining that the blizzards and avalanches of the last month had hindered his return, but that now he was here and awaited his orders.

He could not know that this letter, among the scores of others he had sent over the last sixteen years, was the only one that would ever reach its destination.

Shamil had known for a long time that his son was on his way home. He had known it ever since Jamal Eddin had left Warsaw the previous November.

At Christmas, Chavchavadze's negotiators had even been received in the aul of Dargo-Veden, the eagle's nest where the imam held the princesses captive, with these supposedly prophetic words:

"I had a dream. I saw the princes' messengers bringing me good news of my child. My eyes followed his path. But is he really coming back to me?"

The note signed *Jamal Eddin* confirmed the reports of all his spies that his son was less than two days away on foot. The entire aul—even his wives and the princesses sequestered in the seraglio—heard the imam's cries of joy.

Nonetheless, Shamil had plenty of reasons to be wary. How could he forget the duplicity of the Russians? What if the Great White Czar had kept the real Jamal Eddin and sent an imposter?

Among his naïbs, he chose four men who had known Jamal Eddin well as a child and sent them to identify the hostage.

Waving a white flag of truce, the four horsemen descended in broad daylight and presented themselves before the stockade.

It was early in the afternoon on February 20, 1855.

The no-man's-land between two worlds
Monday, February 20–Wednesday, March 9, 1855

Obeying the commander's orders, the sentinels made no move to disarm them this time.

Prince Chavchavadze and the "rebel's son" had been waiting for this visit for days.

The messenger dispatched to give them the news had found them having lunch in the prince's modest quarters in the company of Cornet Milyutin and Junker Buxhöwden, their usual dining companions.

Conforming to the code of honor that dictated that no Russian officer should let the whistle of a bullet interrupt his conversation, the four men pretended to ignore the salvos of gunfire that the Chechens seemed to enjoy firing every now and then, day and night. It was an old Caucasian tradition: the Montagnards would creep up to the edge of the camp like cats, shoot at the sentinels, and melt back into the mountain.

But this time the commotion was a signal for action.

The soldiers got rid of the remains of their meal, the empty bottles, the champagne flutes, and glasses of vodka, and emptied the ashtrays where their cigars still smoldered.

Outside, they were playing for time. The four murids were requested to dismount and leave their horses at the camp gates. Carefully guarded, they were led to the center of the fort on foot. There they were asked to wait, guarded by about fifty soldiers, while the officers and the interpreter rushed into the house.

The ground floor consisted of only one room, which was divided by a central pillar. A long dining table stood in the light from the only window. A pedestal table with a reading lamp had been arranged at the back of the room, where the light was dim.

Two fires were barely enough to warm the place during the glacial winter of Khassav-Yurt. Four chairs were placed between the fireplace and the stove. Then Chavchavadze instructed his subordinates.

"All of you leave, except the Uhlans, the interpreter, and the two orderlies. You," he addressed the Vladimirsky Lancers, "each of you stand against a wall, and do not sit down, even if I invite the Chechens to do so. You too, Lieutenant Shamil. Remain standing, no matter what happens. Draw your weapons if the Montagnards try to use theirs."

David stood majestically, nonchalantly leaning an elbow on the mantelpiece of the fireplace.

He turned slightly to inspect his reflection in the mirror. He smoothed his moustache and adjusted his jacket, straightening his decorations and his officer's cap. He knew how much elegance, dignity, and an aura of calm impressed the Montagnards.

The color drained from his face, and his heart beat wildly. He glanced at the reflection of Shamil's son and saw that he too was pale.

Jamal Eddin stood opposite him, leaning on the mantel of the stove with one arm. His head uncovered, his face inscrutable, he gazed intently before him. He wore the indigo uniform of the Vladimirsky Lancers, with the waist tightly cinched into his silver belt and his saber at his side. His appearance was impressive, but his efforts to breathe normally were transparent proof of his struggle to control his emotions.

They exchanged a look, and Jamal Eddin nodded slightly to him. He was ready.

"Send in the emissaries," David ordered.

The four murids, lean and gaunt in their dark cherkeskas, walked into the room in single file. Their medals—silver discs that Shamil conferred upon his naïbs in recognition of courageous or murderous acts—gleamed beneath their rows of cartridges.

All had almond eyes, hooked noses, and high cheekbones. All of them wore the same headdress of black lambskin crowned with a white turban, pushed back slightly from their foreheads, Chechen style. Their muskets and sabers were slung across their shoulders as bandoliers, and each wore pistols tucked in his belt and two kinjals crossed at the waist. Though all of them were at least twenty years older than any of the soldiers in the room, not a single white hair was visible in their long beards.

Jamal Eddin didn't recognize any of them.

They did not look around and showed no curiosity as to which of the Russians was the son of the imam.

Their backs to Jamal Eddin, they bowed before Chavchavadze. He responded with an even more ceremonious salute. The guests introduced themselves, one by one. The interpreter translated.

The first was Khadji, Shamil's steward. The naïb of Dargo and the brother of the imam's first wife, who was deceased, he was the maternal uncle of Jamal Eddin.

He was followed by Shamil's brother-in-law, the naïb Akbirdil, spouse of the late Aunt Patimat.

Then came the interpreter, Shah-Abbas, who had negotiated the surrender of the amanats at Akulgo with General Grabbe.

Finally there was Yunus, the naïb of Chirquata, the atalik of the imam's son, his former tutor. This was the man who had accompanied Jamal Eddin to the Russian camp so long ago.

Yunus. Jamal Eddin could not help but react at the sound of the name, which he had not heard uttered for sixteen years. He leaned forward to look at him. He could only see the man's craggy profile, the nose like an eagle's beak, the beard shaped to a point.

When the interpreter had finished the introductions and Chavchavadze's guests had declined his offer to be seated, all of them moved to the center of the room.

Then Yunus took a bunch of grapes from his haversack and turned to the three young Vladimirsky Lancers standing together. He offered them to Sacha, the short redhead, to colossal, blond Bux, and—not hesitating for a moment—to Jamal Eddin. Had Yunus recognized him from the start? But how? Jamal Eddin could scarcely hide his surprise.

The grapes were dirty and withered. Jamal Eddin took them politely, but—his first faux pas—he did not understand a word of the speech that accompanied the gift.

He had tried not to forget his native tongue, but he had not spoken it for a long time. None of the Cherkesses in the Cadet Corps had spoken Avar, and Yunus's accent in no way resembled Shibshiev's. He turned to the interpreter.

Yunus had explained that this was a gift from his stepmother, Zaïdet, the daughter of Shamil's old mentor, Sheik Jamaluddin. She was now the first wife of the imam and wished to welcome him.

Jamal Eddin thanked Yunus in Russian, asking him to express his gratitude to his father's wife for this kind gesture. But he seemed encumbered rather than impressed by the bunch of grapes. What should he do with them? This was his second mistake. The emissaries were disappointed by his lack of grace. Their offering had been subtle and carefully conceived, a generous concession to Jamal Eddin's Russian customs. Hadn't the imam forbidden wine, hadn't he had all the grape vines torn out and destroyed?

And finally, he made the ultimate gaffe. Instead of sharing the bunch of grapes with his guests and tasting them then and there, he gave them to one of his orderlies to be rinsed. This gesture was taken not as ignorance of custom or a hygienic measure, but as a gross insult. The imam's son mistrusted his naïbs and was afraid of being poisoned by his own people.

Yunus made mental notes of all these faults but expressed no disapproval. He did not even look askance.

Turning back to the prince, he said, with great dignity, "The purpose of my visit is to make sure that this young man is the son of the imam. My mission does not extend beyond that."

David nodded in agreement. He moved to the back of the room, motioning to Buxhöwden, Milyutin, and the other Russians to follow him and gather around the pedestal table.

Jamal Eddin remained alone with the Montagnards. Still leaning on the mantel of the stove, he did not move as they scrutinized him.

His uncles, his tutor, his peers—the men of his family—consulted each other as they studied him closely. He felt no affection or even liking for these strangers, who felt entitled to do what he would not have tolerated under normal circumstances. Their wary and expectant stares made him feel as though he had been stripped naked.

He caught a few words of the emissaries' conversation. They remarked on how tall he was and commented on his striking resemblance to his younger brother, Mohammed

Ghazi; how he had the same stature, the same powerful build, the same expression.

Yunus asked him a direct question.

Again he did not understand. Again the interpreter had to translate for him.

Yunus asked if he remembered his childhood, the names of the defenders of Akulgo, of his father's naïbs.

Jamal Eddin hesitated. Yes, he remembered one name.

"Which one?"

"Bahou-Messadou."

"That's all?"

"My grandmother. That's a lot," he said brusquely and bitterly. "The khanum Bahou-Messadou, who was punished by the imam."

"No one, nothing else?" Yunus insisted.

He made an effort to remember, sifting through the vague images that flashed through his mind. He had a vision of sabers swallowed up in the rushing mountain stream, the silver kinjals and plates of gold bobbing up from the depths and whirling in the river's strong current. He hadn't had this dream, he hadn't thought of these images since—since he had met Varenka. They had faded as his life had become busy with balls with Anna and Varenka.

With some difficulty, he described the few sparse details he had retained: the position of the aul of Akulgo, at the summit of a peak; the grotto hollowed out in the cliff; the water they had had to go all the way to the bottom of a ravine to draw.

"Do you remember the color of the horse your father was riding the day you left?"

This time his response was immediate and sure.

"My father usually rode a gray mare. But that day, he stood on the ramparts riding a white stallion."

The emissaries seemed satisfied.

Yunus wanted further proof.

"Would you be so kind as to show us your right arm?" the interpreter translated.

Slowly Jamal Eddin unbuttoned his sleeve and pushed it as far up as he could, holding his arm out to Yunus. A slightly raised scar was visible from his shoulder to his elbow, the trace of an old injury. Yunus touched the scar and asked if he remembered how he had gotten it.

"Falling off a water wheel."

For the first time, the two men looked each other in the eye intensely for a long moment, both of them deeply moved, but for entirely different reasons.

Yunus turned toward the Russians and smiled.

"Since you have warmed our hearts by arranging the return of our great imam's son, so we shall warm yours by reassuring you that your family will return to you." He beamed.

The Russians and the Chechens bowed to each other.

"We will return in three days with instructions for the exchange."

Their mission complete, Shamil's four emissaries took their leave and disappeared into the mountains.

They returned home fully convinced that the tall, dark-haired officer was indeed Jamal Eddin. But they were horrified as well. His beautiful indigo blue uniform reeked of cigar smoke and alcohol. The son of their imam drank and smoked. The son of their imam broke the law. He was a giaour in every way!

Their visit caused them great consternation, which was equal only to Jamal Eddin's dismay and dejection. This first contact had made his blood run cold. The encounter with Yunus had confirmed all his worst fears. What could he possibly still have in common with these four men?

Prince David eagerly and impatiently awaited their return.

Thursday, February 23

Three days later, the four horsemen returned as promised. This time they were escorted to Chavchavadze's quarters immediately. They brought a letter, penned in Shamil's handwriting. Prince David read it out loud:

"Thank you for having kept your word in making possible the return of my son. But do not think that the negotiations end with his return. Remember that in addition to my son, I asked for a million rubles and the liberation of one hundred fifty prisoners. These conditions must be fulfilled before I can permit the return of your family."

This completely unexpected note left Chavchavadze and Jamal Eddin thunderstruck. Both were appalled, and the grim look they exchanged said as much.

Judging any discussion with the intermediaries pointless, the prince asked them to return with a message for their imam. He retreated to the back of the room to consult with Jamal Eddin.

Both in an agitated state, they sat down at the pedestal table to discuss what to write. Even the smallest concession now would only debase them in the eyes of the Montagnards and encourage them to make further demands. Finally Prince David penned a brief letter.

"Having considered the affair to be settled, we are stupefied by your new demands," he wrote. "We did not think you capable of going back on your word once you had given it. We, however, are in the habit of keeping our promises. And today I, Prince David Alexandrovitch Chavchavadze, will keep mine. At the very beginning of negotiations, I informed you that I was capable of raising a ransom of forty thousand rubles. When I obtained a loan for this astronomical sum—despite the fact that, thanks to your actions, I no longer have a home or any other personal resources—when I decided to borrow, it was because I could not allow myself to count on the emperor's gracious permission authorizing your son to return to his country. Had I known this permission would be granted, I would not have offered you even a quarter of this sum.

"I await your response."

Upon reading the letter, Shamil reacted as violently as its contents. Wild with fury, he announced to his people that he was breaking off negotiations. The princesses would be parceled out as slaves among his naïbs before the week's end. They would be free to use them as concubines, to sell them, or to execute them.

Tuesday, March 1

The emissaries returned a third time, carrying messages from Anna and Varenka that confirmed the imminence of the fate he threatened.

With their cries of distress came a last word from the imam:

"You are very far from having met my expectations. I have thus decided to distribute your family to my naïbs, in their auls. I already would have done so but for the intervention of my son, Mohammed Ghazi, who persuaded me to send you one last message, to convince you to add the necessary amount to the sum you have offered us."

As David read these words of vulgar bartering, Jamal Eddin blushed with shame. He was overcome with rage and indignation. He had come back to live with a father who was as greedy as he was lying and treacherous, a man whose word was worth nothing.

He had sacrificed Lisa, his happiness, his future, for this?

Prince David turned to Yunus.

"I shall not write to your imam again," he said icily. "But you can tell him this for me. If, by Saturday, you do not bring word that my offer has been accepted, I swear before my creator that I will leave Khassav-Yurt that day, and I will take Jamal Eddin with me. You can follow us for twenty, a hundred, a thousand versts, and beg me to return with him. I will not even bother to look at you. Then you can do what you like with my family.

"Tell your imam that I have always been grateful for the care he has afforded my loved ones. But tell him as well that if he dares to carry out his threats by sending my wife and my children to the auls, they are no longer mine. I will renounce them the very moment they cross the threshold of his seraglio. I want them to return here, now, because I know that no one has violated their honor. But if they were to become the slaves of your naïbs, know that I would no longer recognize my wife as my wife, my sister as my sister, or my children as my children. I am telling you one last time: I will give you until Saturday. As sure as I stand before you now, Sunday you won't find me here. I will be gone, and so will Jamal Eddin. After that, Shamil can offer to return my wife to me for nothing, he can send her back to me laden with treasure, I swear before God I will never look at her again. And that he will never see his son."

With these closing words, the prince intended to leave the room, but a last remark from Yunus held him back.

"There is another reason for delaying the conclusion of this affair."

"And what is that?" the prince bellowed.

"The imam proposes that the princess Chavchavadze and her children be freed in exchange for the forty thousand rubles and his son. And that the princess Orbeliani and her child remain his captives until her ransom is paid by the prince Grigol Orbeliani."

The prince strode toward Yunus with a threatening gesture and might well have committed an irreparable act had Jamal Eddin not lunged forward to block his way.

The prince had lost all semblance of poise.

"Not only will I not leave my wife's sister a prisoner," he roared, "but I will not abandon a single one of my servants!"

Yunus ignored him and turned to Jamal Eddin.

"Don't worry. This is just the way we Montagnards do things. There's absolutely nothing to fear, everything will turn out as we wish."

His words were meant to be reassuring, but Jamal Eddin replied bitterly, "Worry? There's nothing to worry about." His voice trembled with rage. "If I had something to worry about, it would be that things will turn out exactly as you wish. What else should I be worried about?"

"Be quiet," the prince murmured, devastated.

This time it was David who tried to calm his comrade, but it was no use.

Indignant, disgusted, overwhelmed by the antipathy and repugnance this haggling stirred in the depths of his being, Jamal Eddin could no longer contain his feelings. His anger, his revulsion, his contempt, and his disappointment exploded in a bitter tirade.

"I forgot you, every single one of you. You know very well how old I was when I was taken, because you yourselves gave me away!" he continued violently. "I had forgotten this land, and I return here without joy. And if I had to go back to Russia, believe me, I would do so tomorrow, immediately and without regret!"

"Quiet!"

The prince tried to restrain him, but Jamal Eddin struggled free.

"Why should I be polite to them? Why shouldn't I tell these liars the truth?"

"Shut up!"

"Traitors and hypocrites—they can go to hell!"

"Your words could have terrible consequences for the fate of my wife and my sister-in-law."

The weight of David's words finally registered in Jamal Eddin's mind. He calmed down and remained silent for the rest of the interview.

Wednesday, March 2 • Thursday, March 3 • Friday, March 4

No news from Shamil. Nor from the princesses. Chavchavadze and Jamal Eddin were under unbearable strain.

Had Anna and Varenka been sold?

Saturday, March 5, 11:00

A sentinel ran to tell them that the four emissaries were on their way.

Prince David jumped to his feet. He was so nervous that he paced to the doorstep, turned round and came back three times. Jamal Eddin sat in a chair watching the prince, so obviously beside himself, stride back and forth.

He knew that any excessive haste would make a bad impression and that Yunus would respect only calm and serenity.

The prince took up his pose at the fireplace mantel and waited. Milyutin and Buxhöwden stood beside him. Jamal Eddin stood at the far end of the room, in the shadows.

The envoys arrived and were greeted curtly. This time when offered a chair, they bowed and accepted the invitation. The four Russians sat facing them. No one said a word.

The silence went on for an eternity, at least several minutes. Finally Yunus spoke.

"If the prince will permit me, I will say a few words."

"If you have come to say that Shamil accepts all my conditions and has chosen the time and the place for the exchange, then, yes, you may speak. If not, I must ask you to get up and leave my quarters immediately."

Yunus and his three companions rose as one.

It was all over. The prince wavered, as though the blow had been physical. The princesses had been distributed to the naïbs; they had been sold or dishonored. Jamal Eddin was horrified. A wave of hatred and disgust washed over him like nausea. But beneath his dread, despite himself, an atrocious joy, a feeling of immense relief, rose instinctively from deep within. He suddenly realized he had never stopped hoping that the exchange would never happen, never ceased to deny his own will in forcing himself to do all he could to make it possible. From the outset, he had burned with the desire to leave, to get away from this country, to escape from these mountains.

Yunus bowed to the prince. David no longer had the strength to react, to speak, even to throw him out.

"In the eyes of our grand imam, money is like grass. Money grows, it dries out, and it disappears."

This was beyond Shah-Abbas the interpreter's talents. Neither Chavchavadze nor Jamal Eddin understood the meaning of the words he translated into bad Russian.

Unperturbed, Yunus went on.

"Shamil does not serve money. Shamil serves God. He has asked me to congratulate you; the bargain is concluded on your own terms."

Silence. No reaction.

"You are aware that our grand imam cares for his people and hopes for their well-being. His people are poor. His people have served him; some even died for him when they captured the princesses, and they demand money in return for their liberation. Without the consent of his people and his naïbs, Shamil can do nothing, nor does he wish to. When we gave him your message, he gathered all the elders and informed them of your words. 'If you do not accept the prince Chavchavadze's final conditions,' he said, 'then you must take his family and guard them in captivity yourselves. I do not want to see these women and children in my home any longer.' The naïbs and the elders answered unanimously, 'How can we leave your son in the hands of the infidels? We will agree to anything, as long as your son is returned to you. Send the captives back, take the forty thousand rubles, and bring your son home.' "

Prince Chavchavadze was flooded with joy as he listened to this speech. And Jamal Eddin with dread. The exchange would take place. Both of them maintained an appearance of calm. David asked for the date and location of the encounter.

"On this point, Shamil has said he will speak with you directly," his agent replied.

They bowed and left the prince's quarters.

But they did not leave the camp.

Saturday, March 5 • Sunday, March 6 • Monday, March 7 • Tuesday, March 8

They spent that night and the following days and nights counting the ransom. Khadji, the steward, soon realized he could never have counted a million rubles in pieces of silver.

Jamal avoided all contact with him and with Yunus and the others. He divorced himself from their preparations, Chechen and Russian alike, leaving them to work things out among themselves.

For all of them, he was merely a pawn. A toy. A token. A marble, to be shot back and forth. That was what he had always been, a piece on a chessboard. He refused to play anymore. He had come to the end of that road.

He even avoided David and his boyhood friends. Buxhöwden and Milyutin watched as he widened the distance between them, keeping to himself, silent and solitary. They were at a loss. What could they do or say to bring him back?

The counting was finished by Tuesday evening.

The imam's emissaries left Khassav-Yurt, accompanied by the prince's interpreter, who had conducted the negotiations since the kidnapping. Shamil would instruct him on the practical details of the exchange in person.

The night of Tuesday, March 8 to Wednesday, March 9

The imam received the interpreter beneath his canopy, shortly before dawn on Wednesday, without waiting for the first light of day. Shamil and his entire army were camping a day away on foot from the Mitchik River, the location he had chosen for the rendezvous.

In the nine months since they had first met, Shamil and the interpreter had come to know each other well.

The imam welcomed him, reclining on the cushions splayed over the carpet before the fire in his tent. His impeccably trimmed beard was still red, dyed with henna. He wore the same high, black papakha crowned with a white turban, the trail of one of its folds falling down his back, and the same green robe, with kinjals crossed at the belt.

Despite sorrow, fatigue, battles, and cavalcades, time had left no mark on him. In war and peace, prayer, solitude, and waiting, he remained very much the man he had always been. A sober, towering figure, he seemed much younger than his fifty-eight years.

Deep in thought, he fingered his string of amber prayer beads.

After their usual greetings, the imam cut to the heart of the matter, speaking in a low voice.

"I wanted to see you, first of all, to thank you for all your service. And to tell you that tomorrow will be a great day. Tomorrow, hatred will cease to exist between our two peoples. Tomorrow, Montagnards and Russians shall meet in peace.

"According to our laws, a father must never go out to meet his son; it is the son who must come to the father. But tomorrow I will break this rule in order to prevent any incident that might occur in the course of the exchange. Tomorrow I shall inform all my naïbs that none must go beyond the limit I shall indicate to you. And you must swear to me, on your honor, that you will do the same. And that, on your side, this rule will not be broken."

"You may be assured, Imam, that everything will happen according to your wishes and that we shall respect our word."

A short silence ensued.

"And my son, tell me about my son. Is he well?"

"He is very well, thank God."

"I have been told he no longer understands our language."

"That is correct. But it is perfectly natural. He spent such a long time in Russia. You cannot blame him for having forgotten his Avar."

"I will let him live as he likes in our mountains."

"After a few months with you, he will become accustomed to your ways again. And I'm sure he will find it more interesting to command tens of thousands of horsemen here than a few hundred soldiers in Russia."

Shamil, eyes half-closed, looked into the fire, lost in thought.

"Make sure this affair takes place without any treachery tomorrow."

"Prince Chavchavadze shares your wishes. He has nothing to gain by trying to deceive you. He is just as anxious to recuperate his family as you are to find Jamal Eddin safe and sound, and just as happy at the prospect."

"I admit, I'm terribly impatient. So impatient that, as you can see, I haven't been able to sleep tonight for thinking of him."

"Speaking of which, I'd like to transmit a message from Prince Chavchavadze. He knows that it is customary here to express high spirits with shouts and gunshots into the air. The prince begs you to order that nothing of the kind should happen tomorrow, in an effort to avoid any confusion on the part of our soldiers and any possibility of disorder among all of them."

"I will respect this wish. Now listen to my instructions."

The Same Day

On Wednesday, March 9, on the eve of the date chosen by Shamil, with the ransom in the sacks, the wagons loaded, and all the details arranged, the convoy was ready to leave the fort. Suddenly a sentinel announced the arrival of a horseman galloping toward Khassav-Yurt.

The men rushed to the camp gates, Jamal Eddin and David among them.

"Could they possibly want to change things again?" David said, his voice toneless.

"Why not?"

Jamal Eddin managed a wry smile. "Last night, they gave us their word, swearing on the Sharia, but this morning, the code of the adats takes precedence. They obey the law of God or the law of man depending on what suits their interests. That way they can break their promises and ignore their honor with a clear conscience," he said sarcastically.

The cloud of dust cleared. From the mirador, the sentinel shouted that the horseman was not a Chechen but a courier from Saint Petersburg.

Jamal Eddin's heart skipped a beat. A courier from the emperor?

The czar had spared him. The czar was saving him. The czar had found another solution. Something else to barter. Nothing was impossible for the emperor of Russia!

The messenger handed the missive not to Prince Chavchavadze but to his superior, the commander of the fort—a sign that this was an order from Petersburg.

Jamal Eddin was filled with irrational and uncontrollable hope. He watched the commander break the imperial seal, unfold the letter, and read. The czar was sending him back to Lisa, he was giving him back his happiness.

The commander refolded the letter and turned to the troops.

"Gentlemen, I have news."

He had to compose himself before going on.

"His Imperial Majesty the Czar Nicholas is no longer with us. The Lord God has recalled him in peace. All the regiments shall gather on the main square and immediately take the oath of loyalty to his son and successor, the emperor Alexander."

Pale, his eyes red and brimming with tears, Jamal Eddin listened to the account of the death of the man he had loved and could not help but grieve. Apparently the czar had gone out without a coat, when it was twenty degrees celsius below zero. Hatless, he had reviewed the troops, and he had caught a cold that had rapidly turned into pulmonary congestion. At the end of a night of agony, he had motioned for his son to come close. The distraught Czarevitch Alexander had stood at the foot of the camp bed in the little study where His Majesty lay.

"Hold on," he murmured, breathing laboriously. "Hold on to everything."

With all the strength he had left, Nicholas had clenched his fist, as though holding the empire in his hand, and repeated, "Hold on to everything!"

Those were his last words.

His last thoughts, his very last words were for the grandeur of Russia.

He died like a saint, praying God's forgiveness for all his sins.

After the official account, Jamal Eddin heard rumors. Far from the charmed circle of the court, far from the dazzled Princess Potemkina and the upper aristocracy, Jamal Eddin knew how unpopular the czar had become. It was especially evident here among the soldiers of the Caucasus: Polish resisters, torn from their lands and deported to the mountains; free-thinking, enlightened, and liberal Russian officers; men who had been broken, deprived of their rights, and exiled by Nicholas, all sent here to be massacred by the Chechens. Nicholas the Knout, Nicholas the Flogger, merciless to those who did not worship him, cruel to those who criticized or resisted him. The Iron Czar.

His was a thirty-year-long reign of terror. He isolated Russia from the rest of Europe and shut himself off from the reality of his own people.

In his overwhelming desire to control, direct, and manipulate everything, he had ultimately corrupted and lost it all.

It was even whispered that his death was self-inflicted, that he could not face the humiliating defeat of his armies in the Crimea. There were even wild rumors of his doctor providing him with poison.

Jamal Eddin was close enough to the emperor to know he could not have committed suicide. But he sensed that, haunted by the judgment of history, which he knew would be merciless, the czar had done all he could to shorten his life.

* * *

The bells of the little church at Khassav-Yurt tolled mournfully. The brass bands played gloomy dirges. The flags floated at half-mast. And the hundred horsemen accompanying two wagons loaded with sacks of silver and two full of prisoners seemed very much like a funeral procession as they left the gates of Khassav-Yurt.

Jamal Eddin marched at the head of the convoy with Chavchavadze and the other officers. No one had thought to urge him to participate in the ceremony of allegiance that had been held a few minutes earlier on the square. He had come spontaneously, of his own volition.

This ceremony was his last act as a Russian officer, the final gesture of love and loyalty of Lieutenant Shamil of the seventh division of the Vladimirsky Lancers to his emperor.

Now he would try to become again what he should never have ceased to be, a djighit, the best horseman of all the mountain men, a proper son to the Lion of Dagestan who had been decimating the ranks of the infidels for the past thirty years.

Now he would fight to make the sacrifice of his life worthwhile.

He would try to convince the two worlds to make peace.

CHAPTER XI

The Sacrificial Ceremony

On opposite banks of the Mitchik River
Thursday, March 10, 1855

At the very hour that Czar Nicholas's coffin was being lifted into the crypt of the Romanovs in Saint Petersburg, five thousand murid horsemen amassed on one bank of the Mitchik River in Grand Chechnya.

Except for the crunching of hooves upon the shingles of the beach, all was silent.

Behind the warriors lined up on the beach, one could hear the distant sound of occasional falling rocks and earth, the click of cocked guns, and the pawing of other horses. Another army waited, hidden in the forest.

It was impossible to judge how many were in there.

Higher up and far beyond the treetops, smoke from the auls drifted above the crags and boulders.

An immense red sun rose over the chasm, passing between the ice fields and the snowy peaks to hover over the horsemen.

A warm wind, a breath of spring, swept the sky, leaving it cloudless and blue.

The first dawn of the world was rising over the Caucasus, these mountains that both believers and infidels considered closest to God and agreed were the most magnificent of all His creations.

Lost among the horsemen, four heavy covered wagons were parked on the riverbank. No sound came from them either, not a sign of life, not so much as a whisper. Even the six geldings that drew the wagons were as still as statues.

At the foot of the teams of horses, a few slaves knelt to complete the path they were building to facilitate the wagons' descent to the riverbed. The Mitchik was nearly dry. The backfill would allow them to cross from deep puddle to puddle over the gray sandbanks and the little islands of gravel.

The only luminous spot to break up the ashen line along the riverbank was a splendid white stallion nervously pawing the ground, his scarlet saddle blanket as bright as the silverwork of his tack. One of the naïbs held him firmly by the bridle. The horse awaited his master, the djighit who would know how to ride him.

Thursday, March 10, 1855. Shamil had not chosen this date by chance. Thursday was his lucky day.

Recalling allegories, symbols, and strategies, he had carefully considered every detail of this glorious morning. Everything, today, must have significance.

The imam had taken even further precautions for the success of this day that was just beginning.

The opposite bank of the Mitchik was Russian territory. It was a vast plain without so much as a single tree or bush—it offered no shade from the sun that streamed down, nor any place to take cover. It rose in a gentle slope from the riverbank and ended at the foot of a hill.

Both sides of the riverbank were deserted at this hour, as was the plain.

But at the summit of the hill overlooking the river, the giaours had just finished setting up their artillery; their cannons were ready to bombard the enemy in the event of the least incident.

Prince David was wary of the Chechens and fully expected some treacherous move on their part. His troops were ready to charge, his infantry and cavalry lined up and ready to tear through the valley and cross the Mitchik.

Their orders were clear: they were not to move and not to fire, under any circumstances, unless ordered to do so by Prince Chavchavadze.

On the hill, the officers took out their binoculars.

Accompanying his fellow officers, sitting up straight in his saddle, Jamal Eddin looked down over the valley. For the moment he felt nothing. He had thought of this scene too many times, dreaded this moment for too long, to be surprised. He must take in his surroundings and understand—quickly—what awaited him.

On the Russian side, five hundred paces from the river, he saw a black spot. A dead tree whose twisted trunk was clearly visible above the high grass. Shamil had chosen this solitary, lightning-struck tree as the site of the rendezvous. Its five twisted branches reached toward the sky like an open hand.

Fine. He had located where the exchange was to take place.

Now he looked through his binoculars to the opposite bank.

Straight ahead of him, above the bank, a mountain path led to a platform, a promontory much like the hill he was standing on.

There, a circle of huge dark flags embroidered with half-moons and Koranic verses whipped in the wind. These were Shamil's standards, flying above his camp.

Through the binoculars, Jamal Eddin watched the men ride down the path and dismount on the platform before a broad, black parasol, the same color as the banners and the horsemen's cherkeskas. A Montagnard held the canopy over a seated figure.

Jamal Eddin could make out the large red rectangle of a carpet on the stone plateau. The figure did not move. At this distance, he could not distinguish the man's features or even his costume. Only his white turban and a shadow, the shadow of the imam himself.

Jamal Eddin squinted through the lens, his eyes never leaving the figure. Shamil gestured briefly and leaned on his elbow to look through a telescope fixed upon a tripod before him. He pointed the glass toward the Russians gathered on the opposite hill.

The telescope swept over the line of officers and came to rest for an instant upon Jamal Eddin. But how could the imam recognize his son among all these lancers in uniform?

The young man's heart beat faster as he zeroed in on his father through the incandescent lens.

Neither of them could see anything more than these shadows.

Each was searching for the other.

Standing next to Jamal Eddin, the Russian interpreter commented on the scene as he watched.

"Their weapons are magnificent," he remarked. "Look at the pommels of their kinjals, the saber hilts, the pistol grips—they look like they're all chased in gold! And even—look—even inset with precious stones. They're so much richer than usual. And the fabrics, the carpet, and the canopy are all infinitely more sumptuous! Shamil has obviously gone all out to welcome his eldest son home. It's so unlike his usual austerity measures and the murid laws that stress renunciation and abstinence."

The interpreter pointed out the most physically imposing of the naïbs, a tall murid whose mount danced around the canopy. Dressed in white, riding a bay stallion, Mohammed Ghazi, the younger brother—and the heir—stood out among the mass of black-clad horsemen.

Near him was an adolescent dressed in an indigo cherkeska that shone brightly as his horse pranced back and forth in the sunlight. It was Mohammed Sheffi, the youngest of the three brothers. Born in the forest of Akulgo as his parents fled, just days after Jamal Eddin was kidnapped, he was nearly sixteen now. He was said to be a lightweight, as scatterbrained and generous as Mohammed Ghazi was fearless, religious, and disciplined.

Yunus stood to the right of Shamil, and behind him waited the rest of the cavalry, five thousand men. To say nothing of those hidden in the forest.

On Chavchavadze's order, and according to the agreement concluded with Shamil, the interpreter left Jamal Eddin's side.

Carrying a white flag, he rode down the slope, past the dead tree and across the river, around the wagons, then strode up the hill to take his place a few steps from Shamil.

The Russians watched and tried to imagine what he was saying.

Everything in this strange ballet had been planned during the night, down to the last word. The ceremony must follow its course according to the established formalities.

"Imam, what are your orders?" the Russian said.

"Take my two sons, Mohammed Ghazi and Mohammed Sheffi, thirty-five of my men, and the wagons with you. Lead them across the river to the dead tree and signal me when you have arrived. Thirty-five Russian soldiers will then descend from the hill on your side, with the wagons carrying the money and your sixteen prisoners, along with my son. The two groups shall meet at the tree and each will take back what the other has brought."

"You have no further wishes?"

"When the exchange has taken place, return to me here with my son."

Jamal Eddin watched the interpreter make his way back to the riverbank.

The four wagons shuddered to a start, accompanied by the thirty-five horsemen, led by the rider in white.

Jamal Eddin's gaze was riveted to the convoy as it approached the riverbed. The wagons paused, sucked into the mud. For a moment it seemed that they might get stuck there and overturn, but they rattled on unsteadily to the other bank.

They continued a short distance across the plain and came at last to the dead tree. The first of the wagons stopped.

One of the murids—Khadji, the steward—waved a banner, the signal for the exchange.

The interpreter left the group and galloped toward Jamal Eddin.

As agreed, Lieutenant Shamil was accompanied by thirty-five lancers—including Sacha Milyutin and Buxhöwden—the four wagons containing gifts from the czar and his own books, the forty thousand rubles, and the Chechen prisoners the Russians had promised to release.

The convoy descended the hill with some difficulty. Jamal Eddin rode at the head, like Mohammed Ghazi.

The sun shone brightly, as though it were summertime. Shamil had calculated that, weather permitting, the giaours might be blinded by it. There were stagnant puddles on their side of the riverbank, attracting horseflies that would annoy and excite their mounts.

The Russian horses shook their heads, and their tails swatted their hindquarters furiously. The officers perspired beneath their caps.

Jamal Eddin felt nothing. Not the heat. Not his own sadness, not even fear.

Though he felt nothing, his mind was active, concentrating on the adversary's every move, and the tension of a body ready to fight. He sensed a profound, almost physical wariness of the natural setting and the men he was about to meet.

He advanced without cover onto the plain with Chavchavadze.

They were flanked by two Russian army captains: Baron Nicholas, David's second brother-in-law and representative of the empire, and Prince Bagration, Prince Orbeliani's aide-de-camp and representative of the royal family of Georgia to which Anna and Varenka belonged. Prince Grigol Orbeliani, who had negotiated Varenka's liberation, was not there. He was holding down the fort at Temir-Khan-Chura with the rear guard of the army, in case Shamil had lured the czar's forces into a vast trap.

The four officers rode at the same gait and seemed bound together by the same thought: did the four wagons really contain the captives?

There was no sign of movement from the wagons, other than that of the fat blue flies that alighted on the canvas exterior then flew away to land again on another spot.

When the four men had reached the dead tree, Mohammed Ghazi's horsemen closed ranks. The four wagons were hidden from the Russians by their bodies, their horses, their high black papakhas, and their banners.

David and Jamal Eddin exchanged a dubious look, both reining in their mounts to slow down slightly. What did this mean?

They saw that one of the Chechens held a toddler in front of him on the saddle. The murid kept him centered before him, like a shield. David recognized Alexander, his son who was not yet two.

What was this new blackmail?

The murid broke away from the group. What was he going to do with the child?

Hearts pounding, Jamal Eddin and David came to a halt and waited for the Chechen to approach.

Amazingly and unexpectedly, the horseman spontaneously handed the little boy over to his father and retreated.

David clasped his son in his arms and hugged him to his chest.

At the same moment, three little girls jumped out of the wagons. They ran between the horses' limbs toward their father. The prince leaped from his horse to embrace his children.

Jamal Eddin could not bear to watch this touching scene of a family reunited.

He continued riding toward the wagons, heading off to the side to avoid the rider in white.

The ranks of the murids parted to let him pass. He reached the first wagon.

He waved a hand across the canvas, chasing away the flies, and pushed back the cover. His stomach churned with anxiety. What would he find? For the first time, he gave words to his fear: were the princesses still alive?

He pulled back one of the canvas flaps.

In the dim light, he could barely make out the figures of two women, veiled and dressed in rags, sitting on opposite benches. They seemed petrified. Had they been saved? Were they free? They did not dare believe it and continued to pray in muffled, breathless voices.

The princesses were unrecognizable under the layers of shawls that covered them from head to foot. He bowed politely and apologized for having been so long in coming.

He handed them a letter that their mother, Princess Anastasia, had written them when he had visited her shortly before leaving Russia. One of the phantoms took it from his hand without a word. Anna? Varenka? The form remained silent.

She would have liked to thank him, but the stress of captivity, the anxiety, the terror leading up to this day, and the apprehension that had filled these last hours had robbed her of her faculties.

She managed only to say, "My sister is in the second wagon."

He nodded, left her, and approached the second wagon.

A figure was standing among the other seated ghosts. The princess Orbeliani. He knew her with absolute certainty, even smothered in these rags. Varenka, the love of his youth, his first love.

Though he could not read her expression, she saw his face clearly through the weave of her veil. She had recognized him instantly, and no wonder. Jamal Eddin, her dancing partner of so long ago, had been the primary subject of conversation for the many months of her captivity at Dargo-Veden.

Jamal Eddin, the eldest son, the kidnapped son, the cherished son of the imam.

Shamil's three wives, his daughters, and their governesses—in fact, all the women in the seraglio—had listened avidly for rumors, stories, and spies' reports that circulated in the village. They had followed Jamal Eddin's path to his father's fortress, from Poland to Saint Petersburg, Moscow to Vladikavkaz, Khassav-Yurt to the Mitchik.

For every one of them, his return was a personal victory, the triumph of their beloved master over the infidels, the triumph of God's chosen over the treacherous giaours, a victory over the will, the wealth, and the power of the Great White Czar.

The princesses, too, had thought of the imam's son every day of their captivity, even more than the other women. They had hoped and prayed for Jamal Eddin, anxiously awaiting his arrival every day.

Today they owed him their lives, and Varenka Ilyinitchna, Princess Orbeliani, knew it. And many other things as well.

She knew that, waltzing in his arms at the Peterhof-Alexandria cottage, her heart had been in his keeping. She had loved Jamal Eddin when she had been very young, loved him secretly, passionately, despite her own natural reserve and the calm her own shyness imposed, despite the outward appearance of chastity she had maintained.

She was still aware that back then, had he been more insistent and less sensitive, he could have dishonored her.

She knew that Shamil had considered keeping one of the prisoners to offer his son as a bride. He had chosen Princess Nina Baratachvili, the penniless niece of the Orbelianis and the Chavchavadzes. Of all the hostages, she was the only one who had never been married or had children. When Princess Nina, a virgin of eighteen, found out, she was horrified at the prospect of being abandoned by her aunts here in the mountains and handed over to a Chechen like chattel. She had flown into a rage, insulting the imam, and Varenka had avoided the potentially serious consequences of her tirade by offering herself in the princess's place. One or the other of the prisoners, it was all the same to Shamil. He simply wanted to save a Russian princess for his son, and his own wives had assured him that she was young and pretty. The violence of David Chavchavadze's outrage at the mere suggestion of delaying the liberation of the princess Orbeliani had prompted him to drop the idea.

However, Varenka knew that she had been widowed, that she was free now, and that, perhaps, it was still a possibility.

But now, she knew it was all over.

It was not just seeing Jamal Eddin again, here, in these circumstances, that rendered her speechless, but a thousand other emotions that filled her heart as well.

They looked at each other, both incapable of saying a word.

Suddenly the horseman in white, on foot now, appeared out of nowhere. With a brutal tug, he silently pulled down the canvas flap, and Varenka disappeared from sight.

It was not yet time for the two brothers to proceed with the exchange or even to acknowledge each other. Custom dictated that Prince Chavchavadze and the imam's heir greet each other first.

Mohammed Ghazi, pale and tense, spoke only to David. He began a long and solemn speech, of which the interpreter translated bits and pieces.

"My father has ordered me to tell you that, if your women suffered during their stay with us, their pain was not inflicted intentionally, but out of lack of means and our own lack of familiarity with the way they should be treated. My father wishes you to know they are being returned to you today worthy in every respect, pure as lilies and protected from all eyes, like the gazelles of the desert."

The prince bowed and replied with equal ceremony.

"I have been informed for some time, in my wife's letters and those of my sister-in-law, of the respect the imam has shown toward my family. In writing to your father myself, I have had several occasions to express my gratitude in this regard. Now I beg you to present to him my most sincere thanks."

The formalities had been observed down to the last detail. Mohammed Ghazi could now turn to Jamal Eddin.

They stood politely, face to face.

One wearing the blue, purple, and gold uniform of the lancers, the other a cherkeska, they were the same height, with the same youth and elegance, and the same nobility. Two sides of the same coin.

Their eyes locked, each finding in the other the reflection of himself. Nothing in their exchange betrayed their feelings; nothing in their respective expressions revealed the storm of conflicting emotions both felt.

They saluted each other with a simple nod of the head, and then they embraced.

The murids lowered their rifles and cried, "La ilaha illa Allah"—there is no god but Allah.

In the eyes of the Russians, the brothers' embrace was glacial.

It was time to leave.

Jamal Eddin turned toward Baron Nicholas, Prince Bagration, and the other officers.

All of them removed their caps to salute him.

He turned to Prince Chavchavadze.

David stood there, surrounded by his children. He still had not seen his wife. But judging from Jamal Eddin's body language when he looked inside the wagons, he had guessed that she was there and that she was alive.

The prince shook his hand warmly, assuring him that if he should ever need anything, there in the mountains, a book, or anything—

Chavchavadze paused. What could he add except the most obvious of words.

"Thank you."

The two men embraced.

The farewell of these two brothers in no way resembled the icy greeting of the previous pair.

Jamal Eddin leaped into the saddle.

Milyutin and Buxhöwden, who had been ordered by the late czar to accompany their friend all the way to his father, came forward and spurred their horses toward the murid ranks. The naïb Khadji, who had given the signal for the exchange, approached the Russian lines.

He held out the package he carried to Jamal Eddin, who turned to the interpreter, puzzled.

"The imam wishes to receive his son in the dress of his country."

Jamal Eddin recoiled involuntarily.

"How can I change here, in front of all these people?"

"The wishes of the imam are law. You will learn that no one disobeys your father. No one."

"We're in plain view of everyone, even from the other bank," Jamal Eddin protested.

"That presents no problem. We'll go behind the dead tree."

Jamal Eddin paled. This demand—a change of costume in public, before his peers, before the Russian officers, even before the princesses—was the ultimate humiliation.

"Let's go behind the dead tree," the interpreter insisted.

His tone was anxious. He dreaded the thought of an "incident," any little slip that both the Russians and murids had worried about since the beginning of the exchange.

Jamal Eddin read the dismay in the eyes of everyone around him.

What would happen if, in the middle of this plain, he refused to go through with it? He had no choice but to swallow his disgust and comply.

He rode toward the branches and dismounted. Khadji, Buxhöwden, Milyutin, and the thirty-five murids followed and dismounted too. They formed a circle around him, hiding him from view.

Jamal Eddin unbuttoned his tunic.

In his short life, he thought bitterly, all he had done was change from one costume to another. From the cherkeska to the uniform, from the uniform to the cherkeska. How many times had he done this?

How many times during his youth had he been forced to deny the symbols of his heritage?

And now, with a lump in his throat, he was giving them up, one final time.

He was renouncing his officer's stripes, his epaulets, and his decorative silk cords, his Russian cap, his Russian tunic, and his Russian arms.

He was stripped of his past, of his future, of Lisa, of all he held dear.

He emerged from the circle.

In other circumstances, Sacha would have let out a whistle and shouted, "Splendid, old man!" And Bux, making some choice comments, would have enjoyed the show.

Dressed in black, with a high papakha crowned with his father's immaculate white turban on his head, a whip at his wrist, and his waist cinched by the straps that held his daggers, Jamal Eddin was a djighit who had stepped straight out of Russian literature, a lyric hero of Pushkin.

He was truly splendid.

But Buxhöwden was too sensitive to the tragedy beneath the perfection of his appearance to laugh.

Undoing his baldric, Bux handed his own saber to his friend.

"Take it, as a remembrance. But please," he tried hard to make light of the situation with irony, "don't kill any of ours with it!"

Jamal Eddin accepted the gift.

"Not ours," he replied, his eyes brimming with tears, "nor theirs."

He quickly tied the baldric around his cherkeska. Buxhöwden's saber clinked against Shamil's kinjals.

At that moment, an adolescent boy broke through the crowd of murids and ran into his arms. It was his little brother, Mohammed Sheffi. Surprised and touched, Jamal Eddin hugged him close in an embrace quite different from the one he had shared with their brother.

Jamal Eddin jumped on the white horse, the fine stallion with the scarlet saddle blanket that someone had led over for his new master.

The horseman in black passed next to the wagons.

The women had not dared to remove their veils in front of the murids, but they had pulled back the canvas and stood there, all of them, in the sunlight.

He nodded to them in farewell and rode off.

One of them watched, the tears trickling down her cheeks beneath her veil. She was crying with relief and gratitude, regret and pity. She cried for him, and for herself.

Varenka knew what awaited Jamal Eddin and all the difficulties he would face trying to adapt to this world that was so new and so different, that she had discovered and was now leaving.

The imam's three sons crossed the river side by side.

Followed by the interpreter, the two Vladimirsky Lancers, the thirty-five murids, the wagons, and the baggage of Jamal Eddin, they made it unhindered to the other bank of the river.

No sooner had they reached the strand than they were surrounded by a horde of deliriously joyful Montagnards. All of them wanted to see, to touch, to feel, to kiss the hand, the leg, the boots of the eldest son of the imam, their guide.

Jamal Eddin, the beloved.

Nearly swept away by the jubilant crowd, Buxhöwden and Milyutin were suddenly cut off from their comrade and the rest of the troop. The crowd's welcome did not extend to the two Russians, the infidels, the giaours. Threats and insults rained down on them from all sides.

Jamal Eddin tried with difficulty to advance toward his father. He too was isolated as the crowd separated him from Mohammed Ghazi and Mohammed Sheffi.

All around him—men on foot, simple villagers from the auls in ragged cherkeskas and shaggy papakhas—shouted with joy at the sight of him.

But to Jamal Eddin, their elation sounded menacing.

On the narrow mountain path that led to the black parasol, the crowd became increasingly dense and excited. It was impossible to move forward.

Jamal Eddin stopped and turned around.

He saw that the Montagnards had grabbed the bridles of Buxhöwden's and Milyutin's mounts, and were shoving and jostling the horses in an attempt to make them fall off the path. The two lancers saw that they were about to be knocked down, but they were defenseless against the hostile crowd.

Suddenly afraid they would be lynched, Jamal Eddin yelled at them, demanding that they clear the path for Buxhöwden and Milyutin to join him and remain by his side. No one understood his orders.

His stallion reared.

The interpreter, too far away, could not translate his words.

Jamal Eddin conveyed through gestures that he would not take one more step forward if the crowd did not let his escort pass. With a good deal of pushing and shoving, Bux and Milyutin finally reached him. He caught each one by the sleeve and hung on so that they would not be swept away again. With a light kick, his horse continued up the path, and the three men went forward, Jamal Eddin still hanging on to both of his friends.

A few steps from the canopy where the enthroned Shamil awaited him, a murid dismounted and started toward Jamal Eddin, clearing the crowd in front of him with his crop. Yunus.

He walked up to Jamal Eddin. But Jamal Eddin, still encumbered by the crowd hastening to touch him, kiss him, catch his leg, all the while yelping and shouting, did not greet him.

Once again he demanded that the crowd step back, yelling at those near him in Russian. His voice carried over the tumult.

His composure and tolerance were stretched perilously thin.

Without comprehending the reason for his anger, the crowd stepped back, amassing a little way away, kept in line by Yunus.

Jamal Eddin began riding forward again toward the imam, once again joined by his brothers on either side. Bux and Milyutin followed close by.

A dozen or so steps before reaching Shamil, Jamal Eddin and the others dismounted.

Jamal Eddin trembled with emotion. He could not even look at his father.

After all these years of waiting, he was no longer able to see him.

He approached with halting steps and bowed.

Shamil grabbed him with open arms, drawing his child against him. Tears ran down the imam's cheeks onto his beard. He could not stop weeping.

Father and son remained locked in each other's arms for a long moment, both conscious of the beating of the other's heart.

Not a sound broke their silence; it was respected by all around them.

Then the imam lifted his eyes to those around them and said fervently, "I thank God for having kept my son safe. I thank the czar for having permitted his return, and I thank the princes for having contributed to it."

Then he noticed Milyutin and Buxhöwden standing beside his other two sons.

He turned to ask the interpreter, "Who are they?"

"Your son's boyhood friends, who wanted to pay you their respects," the interpreter explained.

"I thank them," said Shamil.

Jamal Eddin disengaged himself from his father's embrace and stood up.

His friends asked if they could bid him farewell, Russian style.

"Why not?" Jamal Eddin replied.

With spirit and élan, each one embraced him and kissed him three times.

Shamil was worried that seeing Jamal Eddin in the arms of the giaours would make a very bad impression upon his people. In an effort to justify their behavior, he explained loudly to those around them, "These three boys grew up together!"

The imam then rose to greet Milyutin and Bux politely. He ordered Mohammed Ghazi to accompany them back to the other bank, with the protection of a hundred murid warriors.

This time, the three friends' farewells were final.

Jamal Eddin embraced his companions one last time and asked them not to forget him. He also asked them to send Prince Orbeliani his regrets at not having made his acquaintance.

Courteous and gallant to the last.

The interpreter and the officers rode back across the river and returned to the Russian contingent on the hill.

Now that the Russians were gone, an unrestrained volley of gunshots and whoops of celebration at the return of the imam's son broke out.

The echo of exploding guns and the clamor of men would ring in Bux's and Milyutin's ears for a long, long while.

They turned back, searching for the horseman in black more noble and elegant than all the rest. They saw only his back.

Riding next to Shamil, Jamal Eddin climbed the boulder in the direction of the woods. They zigzagged between crews of men, who were busy uprooting the shafts of banners, gathering the standards and carpets, and rolling up the tents. The army was packing up.

Father and son rode off toward the forest.

They were of equal strength and height. The older man rode a gray mare, the younger a big white stallion. The panels of their turbans fell in straight lines to the small of their backs.

For a moment, Jamal Eddin seemed to float above the abandoned parasol, above the teeming crowd.

Then suddenly, as though the mountain had swallowed him up, he disappeared.

* * *

Neither Sacha Milyutin nor Count Buxhöwden nor Prince Chavchavadze nor any of the other officers in their company at the exchange ceremony would ever see the "rebel's son" again.

But they would tell of that intense moment, of watching Jamal Eddin disappear down the mountain path into the vastness of the Caucasus, carrying within him all that remained of the honor of men.

EPILOGUE

All That Remained of the Honor of Men

Dagestan and Chechnya

1855–1858

"At first, we received letters from him," Elizaveta Petrovna Olenina wrote in 1919, at the age of eighty-seven. "I learned that he had tried to escape three times, and that three times he had been recaptured by his brother Mohammed Ghazi, whose prisoner he had become.

"It was my own brother, Alyosha, then stationed at the garrison at Stavropol, who transmitted the messages that Jamal Eddin had managed to pass through his father's lines.

"At the beginning, we had news from him fairly regularly through Alyosha, and he passed on what was being said in the forts of the Caucasus about what was happening to my fiancé."

Rumor had it that Jamal Eddin had set about his task the very day after his return. He explored the mountains of Dagestan and the forests of Chechnya, visited all of his father's mountain eyries, studied the state of his fortifications, passed his troops in review, and methodically examined arms and equipment.

The conclusions of his investigation were scarcely surprising and confirmed what he had feared. The Montagnards were too few in number. Their weapons were old, worn out, and defective. The population was splintered by interclan squabbles, and the villages were ready to betray Shamil at the least sign of weakness.

Over the long term, the murid resistance was doomed to fail.

He sat down with his father for a serious discussion about all this. He tried to describe the immense wealth of the new czar, the power of his armies, and the sheer size of his empire.

The current succession of Russian defeats in the Crimea, however, did not help his cause.

Jamal Eddin's argument only reinforced Shamil's conviction that victory was imminent and that, more than ever, he should continue to harass the infidels. The holy war must go on.

The young man tried again, leaving aside the power of the Russians and concentrating on the unfortunate state of the Montagnards. Soon there would not be a single fighter left in the Caucasus—no more men, young or old. No more men at all.

Years of bloodbaths had decimated the population, and every new massacre weakened them further. The ranks of cavalry were too sparse, and their muskets were not powerful enough. If Shamil wanted his people to survive, he must seek peace with the enemy.

It was exactly the same thing that the imam had heard so long ago, at Akulgo: "If we don't negotiate with them now, when this is what they want, they will kill all our men, abuse our women, and enslave our children. Give your son to the Russians, since that is what they ask. And play for time."

Negotiate now. Jamal Eddin's words echoed the past. Negotiate now, right away, when the invaders are busy elsewhere and in a difficult position themselves. Negotiate with them now, when they're still clamoring for negotiations.

Afterward, it will be too late.

The siege of Sebastopol was over. Yes, the Russians had lost the war against the Europeans. But they had learned a great deal from their contact with modern and powerful troops. And now they would be free to concentrate on another front.

Prince Bariatinsky, the new commander-in-chief of the Armies of the Caucasus, was a personal friend of Alexander II. He would have every means at his disposal to bring this conflict to a positive end. And he was of an entirely different mettle than Grabbe and most of his predecessors.

Jamal Eddin emphasized that the situation was urgent. If he negotiated today, his father could still obtain the essential conditions he desired: religious freedom and possession of the land. As for the rest, he should let it go.

It was said that his words broke Shamil's heart.

They wounded him to the core, and then they sent him into a mad rage.

His son was an agent, in the pay of the infidels!

The giaours' henchman!

This is what his son had become? A hypocrite? A traitor?

This was probably the only reason the Russians had agreed to send him back to the Caucasus—to spy, to lead them astray, to corrupt his own people!

Wasn't that the objective of the Great White Czar's entire plan? Wasn't that why he had kidnapped his son, kept him, and educated him?

He had succeeded in turning the son against the father, in alienating his child and defiling him.

Profoundly hurt, disappointed by his efforts, his love betrayed, Shamil suffered anew because of Jamal Eddin.

He began to avoid spending time with his son and soon became suspicious of his influence.

When young Mohammed Sheffi, fascinated by his older brother, also began to speak of the necessity of peace, their father's wrath knew no limits.

Fearing contagion, the imam took away every vestige of Jamal Eddin's Russian past, every impure object he had brought with him from the land of the infidels. He had thought it would be possible to let his son live as he liked here in the mountains. He had been wrong.

Shamil burned his books, his novels, his poetry, his maps, and his works of grammar. He burned the instruments he used to study physics, his sheet music, and his painting supplies.

The imam invited his son to concentrate on reading the Koran, exploring Sheik al-Buhari's *Book of Hadiths*, and learning Arabic. He asked him to take instruction with the mullahs Shamil had chosen and not to leave the madrassa until his masters deemed him worthy and ready. He gave his son extensive access to his own library, which was replete with the knowledgeable works of his own masters and precious manuscripts that he himself had collected.

In Tiflis, it was rumored that Shamil wanted Jamal Eddin to marry. He had chosen for him the daughter of the naïb Talguike. She was said to be young, beautiful, and submissive. His purpose, no doubt, was to make his son an integral part of the life of his people and the future of Dagestan.

But Jamal Eddin said that he did not love the woman who had been chosen for him and that he would not live with her. He publicly refused to live under the same roof with his wife or even to touch her.

Infuriated at his son's recalcitrance, which not only insulted the young woman's family but humiliated him by flatly disobeying his orders, Shamil turned cruel.

His heart was already broken. Now it filled with hatred.

He had Jamal Eddin arrested and exiled to the fief of Mohammed Ghazi, at Karata.

So the eldest son became the captive of his younger brother.

Mohammed Ghazi was no torturer. He did not throw his prisoner into the bottom of a pit or mistreat him.

But he professed thorough contempt for what Jamal Eddin had become—a Russian.

Mohammed Ghazi, the horseman in white, was pure and sincere.

He was appalled by everything about Jamal Eddin—his tastes, his instincts, and his habits.

Jamal Eddin's discourse was identical to that of the sellouts of Ghimri, Untsukul, and Arakhanee. Because of their cowardice or their own interests or for money, they let themselves be corrupted by the infidels and allowed their own brothers to be massacred.

He hated Jamal Eddin.

How could he not?

Other things contributed to Mohammed Ghazi's insurmountable antipathy for his brother.

Hadn't Jamal Eddin deserted their camp for sixteen years? And yet, because he was the eldest, he remained the true successor to the imam, the legitimate heir.

At least, that's what the hypocrites and those who favored peace negotiations began to think—and to say.

After Jamal Eddin tried to escape from Karata a third time, Shamil exiled him to an even more remote place, farther up the mountain.

Farther from the inhabited auls.

And farther, most importantly, from the Russian lines.

Robbed of his books, completely helpless and isolated, Jamal Eddin fell ill. At least that was the rumor that was going around Tiflis.

In the forts along the line, it was said that he had caught cold in the glacial solitude of the high mountains where he had been banished and that the cold had rapidly degenerated into pneumonia. But no one really knew the actual causes of his illness nor its symptoms.

The murids spread the rumor that the giaours had poisoned him before turning him over to them.

For several months, there was no news of Jamal Eddin's condition.

Baron Nicholas's headquarters, Prince Orbeliani, and Prince Chavchavadze hounded their spies for information about the imam's son. None was forthcoming.

On February 15, 1858, three years after the exchange ceremony, a Montagnard bearing a white flag rode down from Dargo-Veden, the aul where Shamil lived, and presented himself at Fort Khassav-Yurt. He carried a message from the imam asking for medicine for his son, Jamal Eddin.

The commander took in the significance of such a gesture.

Shamil's willingness to lower himself to beg for assistance from the infidels was an extraordinary indication of his love for Jamal Eddin.

This humiliating request had obviously come from the young man and spoke volumes about the imam's distress. It was an admission before all, the Russians and his own people, that he had never ceased to love his child. It proved to Jamal Eddin the immensity of his affection.

The commander did not miss the chance to accept the hand that reached out to him. He immediately told the messenger he would do all he could.

He called in his own personal physician, who listened to the description, such as it was, of the patient's symptoms and provided a few vials of medicine that might correspond to the illness.

The commander sent word to the imam that if his son needed medical attention, he was ready to send a doctor.

Four months later, on June 10, 1858, the same messenger returned to Khassav-Yurt. The imam asked whether the doctor the commander had mentioned in February could visit Jamal Eddin.

The commander sent Doctor Piotrovsky in exchange for an amanat.

Shamil had foreseen this possibility and had sent five of his naïbs, five murids who were waiting in the woods. They were his offering as hostages.

The commander retained three.

Doctor Piotrovsky set out from Khassav-Yurt the following morning.

Jamal Eddin lived in the small, extremely remote village of Soul-Kadi, near the source of the Andi Koysu. Even the Montagnards considered it virtually inaccessible.

The doctor's journey took over four days and was, as he described it, a harrowing experience. He descended into chasms on trails whose stones slipped and crumbled beneath his feet and experienced nearly six hours of vertigo on precipices that, looking down, offered a sheer drop and, looking up, offered no path at all. Worse still, Shamil's own messenger and their guide had to hide them from the local inhabitants, who would have massacred all three of them had they discovered a Russian in their mountains.

The doctor arrived in Soul-Kadi late in the night on June fourteenth. The aul appeared particularly mean and desolate to him.

The house where Jamal Eddin lived was guarded by a sentinel. The patient was living in captivity.

Sacks of grain lay everywhere, and fruit had been left to dry among heaps of clothing at the entrance.

Jamal Eddin's room was sparsely furnished. A rifle and a saber hung on the wall.

The young man was lying on an iron bed.

He awoke at the arrival of his visitor. Deathly pale, his eyes hollow, Jamal Eddin coughed incessantly.

The doctor tried to ask him a few questions.

But Jamal Eddin realized that the man was completely spent and invited him to sleep first. A mattress had been prepared on the floor next to him. Exhausted, the Russian collapsed on it.

In the morning, the doctor noticed that Jamal Eddin had persuaded his jailers to accept some rather bizarre habits.

While he lacked everything and lived in utter poverty, he insisted that his meager meals be served with the silverware that had been stolen from the princesses, on what was left of their fine china—knives embossed with the family's coat of arms, fine white gold-rimmed porcelain plates, all the plunder of Sinandali—the ultimate symbols of a lost past.

All signs of wealth and luxury were forbidden by Shamil, and the naïbs and partisans of his brother took Jamal Eddin's attachment to worldly goods as further proof of his corruption.

Such whims only confirmed their contempt for him.

Although he was surrounded by spies and guarded by men the Russian doctor described as "fanatics," the patient appeared to be adored by the women who cared for him, the inhabitants of Soul-Kadi, and everyone who came into contact with him.

But he was already so weak and ill that he could no longer walk.

The doctor understood that his pitiful state was due to despair, an acute case of depression that no medicine could cure.

He diagnosed tuberculosis as well.

He found Jamal Eddin "dignified, calm, reasonable," and fully aware of the gravity of his condition.

The young man was letting himself die. What else could he do?

Doctor Piotrovsky stayed at his bedside for two days.

He was increasingly struck by the fact that the people's adoration, even adulation, of Jamal Eddin was as strong as the naïbs' hatred for him was absolute. The dignitaries maligned him incessantly, depicting him as a degenerate to anyone who would listen—especially those who did not know him.

Shamil's naïbs were the ones who had forbidden him to read the Russian press, the newspapers of Petersburg that

Shamil himself had translated for his own information. It was just one more deprivation, added to a long list of others.

Jamal Eddin explained that the imam had had no choice; he had been forced to break him and silence his voice to preserve the love and confidence of his captains.

To the doctor's way of thinking, this forgiveness made no sense at all. Perhaps Shamil had been forced by circumstance, by public opinion, to behave this way. But the consequences of his actions were before his eyes. He had killed his son.

And local cures were finishing him off.

Jamal Eddin was fed saltpeter scraped from the rocks around the aul together with a variety of fermented plants and minerals, all of which was mixed with donkey's milk. The concoction had disastrous effects upon the patient.

"I could not cure Jamal Eddin," the doctor wrote in his report to the commander of the fort at Khassav-Yurt. "I could not even prevent the disease from progressing. I simply tried to assuage his suffering.

"Unfortunately, I am certain that he will not survive beyond another two or three months. At the very most.

"I should add that, instead of preparing himself for this grand and final event that is death, this sensitive young man of such fine character spends his time contemplating the jewels that were stolen from the princesses in July 1854.

"He considers the earrings in particular to be his personal property and hides them very carefully under his mattress.

"But at nightfall, he delicately takes two tiny diamond pendants from their case.

"He holds them in his hand, turning them over in his palm. He never seems to tire of admiring these little teardrops of precious stone.

"Doubtless this occupation distracts him from the specter of Death standing at the foot of his pallet.

"Ah! God, how strange and full of contradictions is the human condition. Who would have imagined that this apparently civilized being is, in the end, interested only in a pair of stolen diamonds? And that on his deathbed, he should never cease to be fascinated by all that glitters, just like all savages?"

The doctor was clearly lacking in imagination.

Perhaps a woman would have understood the secret behind this fascination.

Lisa.

When they had first met, at the relay of Torjok, hidden in the locks of hair that fell from her temples, Jamal Eddin had glimpsed the sparkle of two diamond teardrops that caught the sun.

That was the first time he had laid eyes on the young blonde woman, and the same day he was dazzled—thunderstruck—by love at first sight.

It had been the first promise of happiness.

"The next time I hold you this way," he had murmured.

He had taken his fiancée's face in his hands.

"The next time..."

The next time these tiny drops of light dancing at Lisa's ears trembled between his fingers again, it would be for the rest of their lives.

He never saw her again.

"My brother Alyosha received Jamal Eddin's last letter, dated June 25, 1858.

"I'm dying slowly, and with great suffering, he wrote. *I beg you, try to come and see me, and try to bring another Russian doctor*

with you. I refuse to let the local doctors treat me any longer. I beg you, bring especially a little note written by Lisa, so that I may see her handwriting one last time. Hurry, or you may get here too late. Kiss Lisa for me. So she knows that I have not forgotten her. So she knows I love her.

"My brother started off right away.

"But when he arrived in the mountains, less than three versts from Soul-Kadi, one of Jamal Eddin's friends ran to meet him, blocked his path, and gave him the following message from my fiancé: *Hurry back to your regiment, Alyosha. I found out that they have let you come to me in order to capture you. Run away, leave, I cannot see you, I do not want to. In any case, I am lost.*

"As usual, Jamal Eddin told the truth.

"He died a few days later, on July 12, 1858.

"He was twenty-seven years old.

"They say he is buried on one of the village terraces, looking out over the immensity of the Caucasus.

"As for me, more than sixty years later, I continue to carry within me the living memory of his love. Jamal Eddin's tenderness, like all of his passions, was limitless.

"He had written to me, 'Lisa, I shall die without you in the Caucasus.'

"Our story ended with these words.

"I dare to declare, on the eve of my own death, that I would have been happy to marry a man of such character.

"To my sorrow, almighty destiny decided otherwise."

APPENDIX

What Became of Them

ELIZAVETA PETROVNA OLENINA

Lisa was married twice, the first time to Hippolite Alexandrovitch Dmitriev-Marmonov, the second time to the son of Baron Alexander Engelhardt. Both unions were advantageous, as both of her husbands were aristocrats and members of the inner circle at court. In 1919, with her family's encouragement, she wrote her memoirs. She told of the famous figures of the literary world she had met at her grandfather Olenin's home, the thrill of her first ball, and her passion for Jamal Eddin, whom she described as the love of her life. Over sixty years after the young man's death, he remained vivid in her mind, both as the man she had always dreamed of and a symbol of ideal happiness. He was the incarnation of human dignity, honor, and beauty. "He was tall, dark, and very well built," she often repeated, "and of royal bearing." She lived through the turmoil of the revolution and died in 1922 at the age of ninety.

PRINCESS ORBELIANI AND PRINCESS CHAVCHAVADZE

After eight months in captivity, the princesses were in a physically and psychologically fragile state, obliging them to return home across the Caucasus at a slow pace. Anna felt guilty about the death of the infant who had slipped from her arms during the wild cavalcade as they were being abducted. Of all the hostages, she suffered the most, taking ill while captive and losing her sumptuous tresses. She recovered from the ordeal with great difficulty. The two sisters then left for Moscow and Saint Petersburg to thank the Romanovs for having made their liberation possible by consenting to the return of Jamal Eddin. They spent nearly a week at the cottage of Peterhof-Alexandria, where the dowager empress gave a "country ball" for them, an event that belonged to other, happier times. The ransom payment had so depleted the Chavchavadze fortune that Czar Alexander II assumed the cost of rebuilding and restoring Sinandali. The family was granted use of the domain, which then became the property of Russia upon the death of Prince David. The manor is still there, in its tropical garden above the river.

Princess Varenka remarried late in life and died in 1884. George was her only child. Princess Anna died twenty years later, surrounded by her many children and grandchildren. They portrayed the imam Shamil as a great head of state. Their accounts and that of the French governess abducted with them—the first descriptions of the man from eyewitnesses—considerably changed public perception of the man's personality and moral character. They described him as a pious, loyal, and noble man of integrity, fighting for the independence of his people. The princesses' admiration and respect brought the imam renown and immense popularity in Russia and throughout Europe.

In France, the *Journal de Toulouse* even published a strange obituary notice, slipped in before the agricultural news, on October 19, 1858. The journal regretted to announce to its readers the death of "Djemmal-Eddin, son of Shamil," in Soul-Kadi, in the Caucasus, the result of an illness his doctor attributed to depression.

THE IMAM SHAMIL

In August 1859, scarcely a year after Jamal Eddin's death, the young man's prophecy came true.

Betrayed by his naïbs, abandoned by his people, robbed by the villagers, attacked on all fronts by the Russians, Shamil was forced to lay down his arms. He was beaten. Yunus, Mohammed Ghazi, and four hundred warriors followed him into his ultimate battle, fighting for their honor and the greater glory of God. All of them knew that their war against the invader was over. Shamil hoped only to die as a man of arms, in the village of Gunib that he was defending for the last time. However, he finally accepted the humiliation of giving himself up alive in order to spare his family, his wives and children. General Dmitri Alexeyevitch Milyutin, then aide-de-camp to Prince Bariatinsky, was present for his surrender. Shamil, Yunus, and the fifty surviving murids were certain that the infidels would execute them and send their sons into bondage. They were mistaken.

Exiled to Russia with Mohammed Ghazi, Shamil was treated with all the honor due a great warrior. The journey to the north that both expected to be a long trip to the scaffold turned out to be a triumphal tour. Shamil was welcomed as a hero in every city that crossed his path. Huge crowds greeted him and covered him with garlands of flowers. Parties were given in his honor, and everyone wanted to meet him. He was received by Czar Alexander II, later to be known as "Alexander the Liberator," who embraced him and called him his friend. Together they watched the Russian troops pass in review. At first wary, then surprised, and finally quite overwhelmed by such a welcome, Shamil observed the world around him. He remembered all that his son Jamal Eddin had told him, everything that he had refused to believe. The memory of his twice-sacrificed son was with him constantly. He walked in the footsteps of Jamal Eddin, meeting those who had loved him and visiting the places where he had lived. His third son, Mohammed Sheffi, his steward, his wives, and their households joined him at Kaluga, a small city south of Moscow. Shamil and his family lived there, under surveillance but widely honored and respected, for nearly ten years. In 1866, Shamil and his sons swore allegiance to the czar and took an oath of loyalty to Russia. The climate in Moscow proved fatal for several in his entourage, and those who remained were allowed to move farther south, to Kiev. Following his oath of loyalty, Shamil became a Russian citizen and was thus permitted to leave Russia to make a pilgrimage to Mecca.

He died in Medina on February 4, 1871, and was buried there according to his final wishes.

A few years after his surrender, the martyrdom of his people began once again in the Caucasus.

Entire populations were massacred, stripped of all their possessions, and deported. A series of crimes, more terrifyingly brutal than ever, followed.

The saga of Shamil was soon claimed by both camps, the Russians as well as the Chechens and Dagestanis.

At the National History Museum in Moscow, a permanent exhibit is devoted to his legend. His portrait and those of his children are on display, and an entire roomful of images tells the story of his exploits.

In Dagestan and in Chechnya, the imam Shamil is still regarded as the incarnation of the union of the Caucasian Muslims and the armed struggle for the triumph of God, the honor of men, and the liberty of the people.

Two of his sons shared this religious, political, and moral inheritance.

One of them, Mohammed Ghazi, never accepted the yoke of Russia and continued to fight for independence. He moved to Constantinople and later fought with the Turks.

The second, Mohammed Sheffi, served in the army of the czar.

The third son, born in captivity at Kaluga, would try to reconcile these two loyalties to Russia and to Dagestan. He named his own son after the legendary brother he never knew, Jamal Eddin.

This second Jamal Eddin Shamil also became a lieutenant in the Russian army. In 1911, Jamal Eddin II, then posted south of Tiflis, also fell in love with a Georgian princess, whom he kidnapped and married. He brought his Christian wife and their little boy to his family's native village, Ghimri, before disappearing into the maelstrom of the First World War.

But that, as they say, is another story…

Glossary

adat: law of the elders that governs daily life in the Caucasus
amanat: hostage given as a guarantee of good faith during peace negotiations in the Caucasus
aul: mountain village in the Caucasus
atalik: a sort of tutor who assists the parents in overseeing the education of a male child in the Caucasus
Avar: Caucasian tribe to which Jamal Eddin belonged
Bek: noble title
burka: a black, waterproof cape made of goat hair
cherkeska: Caucasian man's costume, typically buttoned and belted
Cherkess: Circassian. Also the main nation of the western Caucasus. Sometimes incorrectly used to describe a native of the Caucasus
cornet: lowest rank of officer in the Russian cavalry, equivalent of a second lieutenant
djighit: warrior horseman of the Caucasus
djighitovka: equestrian games of djighits
ghizir: cartridge belt worn across the chest of a cherkeska
giaour: pejorative term referring to infidels
Hakika: the truth
junker: Russian officer candidate, rank immediately inferior to a cornet
kanly: complex code of the law of blood and vengeance of the Caucasus
khan: aristocratic title in the Caucasus, a prince
kibitka: small Russian carriage that runs on wheels in the summer and sleigh blades in the winter
kinjal: long, straight-bladed dagger

kokoshnik: traditional Russian tiara, obligatory apparel of ladies at court at official balls, by order of Nicholas I during his reign

Lesghien: tribe of the Caucasus, close to the Avars and Chechens

madrassa: Islamic educational institution, place of study

Montagnard: general term applied to all the Muslims of the Caucasus by the Russians. The Montagnards included Circassians, Kabardians, Ossetians, Chechens, Inguche, Lesgheins, and Avars

murchide: spiritual guide of the Caucasus

murid: disciple of a Sufi sheik, warrior of Shamil

murtaghazet: combatant from an aul

naïb: war chief of Shamil, with powers over a specific region

Naqshbandi: Sufi fellowship to which Shamil belonged

padishah: title of the sultan of Constantinople, emperor

papakha: tall lambskin hat

qadi: Sharia-based religious authority with the power of a judiciary

ruble: unit of Russian currency worth about fifteen euros in 1850

saklia: house in a Montagnard village

seraglio: word used in the sense of a harem, part of a house reserved for women

Sharia: the law of God

shashka: a slightly curved saber, worn as a bandolier in the Caucasus

surat: chapter of the Koran

Tariqa: the path to God

ukase: edict pronounced by the czar

verst: distance corresponding to about seven-tenths of a mile

zikr: method of prayer leading to mystical ecstasy and direct union with God

List of Main Characters and Place Names

Abdul Aziz: surgeon in the Dagestani village of Untsukul, maternal grandfather of Jamal Eddin.

Akbirdil: one of Shamil's naïbs, who insulted General Klüge von Klugenau during the meeting at Chirquata in September 1837.

Akulgo: village of Dagestan that served as Shamil's fortress-headquarters from 1837 to 1839. The Russians besieged the village in the summer of 1839. Czar Nicholas considered its capitulation as a triumph that marked the end of the wars of the Caucasus. On September 5, 1839, he had a medal struck to commemorate the victory and awarded it to all officers, noncommissioned officers, and soldiers who had fought at Akulgo.

Alexandra Feodorovna (czarina, wife of Nicholas I) (July 1798–October 1860): married in July 1817. Their first son, the future Alexander II, was born on April 17, 1818, followed by three girls and three boys.

Alexandra Nicolaïevna (Adini): third daughter of Czar Nicholas I and Czarina Alexandra Feodorovna, born in 1825, married in 1843, died in 1844.

Alexander I (Pavlovitch): czar from 1801 to 1825, elder brother of Nicholas I, conqueror of Napoleon.

Alexander II: first son of Nicholas I, born at the Kremlin April 17, 1818, assassinated in 1881. Married Maria of Hesse-Darmstadt (Maria Alexandrovna) April 28, 1841. Assumed the throne upon the death of his father in February 1855. Was crowned after the Crimean War ended in 1856.

Alexandrovsky Cadet Corps of Tsarskoye Sielo (Christmas 1839–August 1841): elementary school for children ages six to nine, sons of poor or deceased officers. Their schooling was conducted by women under a male director. Jamal Eddin was transferred there after spending September to December 1839 with the First Cadet Corps of Moscow.

Ali Bek al-Kunzahki: naïb who defended the tower of Surkhaï at Akulgo.

Andi Koysu: river at the foot of Akulgo, one of whose tributaries is named Ashilta, like the village.

Ashilta: native fief of Shamil, where he was consecrated imam in 1834. Destroyed by General Fézé May 13, 1837.

Bahou-Messadou: Jamal Eddin's paternal grandmother.

Baratachvili, Nina (Princess Nina Baratov): Born in 1837, niece of Grigol and Elico Orbeliani. In 1854, at age seventeen, she was taken hostage with the entire household of Sinandali in a raid by Shamil's men.

Bariatinsky (Prince Alexander Ivanovitch): Caucasian viceroy who accepted the surrender of Shamil at Gunib in 1859.

Barti Khan: Shamil's maternal uncle, assisted Shamil at Akulgo.

Bashlik-Atslikar: battle near Oguzlu in Turkey, where Varenka's husband, Elico Orbeliani, was killed in 1854.

Buxhöwden, Count Sergei Petrovich (1828–1899): close friend of Jamal Eddin. They met in the First Cadet Corps. On

January 15, 1855, Buxhöwden was among those who accompanied him to the Caucasus.

Burnaya: "The Stormy," a Russian fort.

Chavchavadze, David Alexandrovitch (Tiflis, August 26, 1817–November 15, 1884): only son of Georgian poet Prince Alexander Garsevanovitch Chavchavadze and Princess Salomé Ivanova Orbeliani. His famous sister Ekaterina married Prince Dadiani and became sovereign of Mingrelia. His sister Nino married Griboledov, his sister Sonia, Baron Nicholas. David inherited the domain of Sinandali, from which his wife, Anna, and his entire family were kidnapped by Shamil July 4, 1854. He and Jamal Eddin became close friends during the few weeks they spent together at the Russian camp while negotiations for the exchange took place.

Chernychev, Alexander: became Nicholas I's minister of war, after Czar Alexander died in his arms. All administrative questions concerning Jamal Eddin were addressed to him.

Chechnya: Caucasian region bordering on Dagestan.

Chirquata: Dagestani village, dependent upon Shamil.

Chuanete: Shamil's fourth spouse, his favorite after Fatima's death. Born in 1825, she died in 1876.

Constantine Nicolaïevitch (1827–1892): grand duke, second son of Nicholas I and younger brother of Alexander II.

Constantine Pavlovitch: grand duke, one of Nicholas I's two older brothers, viceroy of Poland, who died of cholera during the Polish uprising of 1831. He should have succeeded Alexander I but abdicated the throne in favor of Nicholas I, a power vacuum that led to the Decembrist revolt.

Cooper, James Fenimore (1789–1851): one of Jamal Eddin's two favorite novelists (the other being Sir Walter Scott).

Cadet Corps of Moscow (September–December 1839): after his abduction, Jamal Eddin was placed in the primary school division of the Cadet Corps of Moscow. He stayed there only three months, since there was no mullah to provide him with religious training.

Cottage of Peterhof-Alexandria: domain of the imperial family overlooking the Gulf of Finland, where Czarina Alexandra gathered her family and intimate friends. Jamal Eddin spent his summer vacations there from 1846 to 1850.

Dagestan: region of the Caucasus bordering on Chechnya.

Daniyal Bek: sultan of Elisou, one of the pillars of the Russian alliance, who rallied to Shamil in 1844. His daughter married Jamal Eddin's younger brother, Mohammed Ghazi, in 1851.

Dargo-Veden: Shamil's headquarters in Chechnya, where he held the princesses captive in 1854–1855.

Dengan: father of Shamil, free man of Ghimri, in Dagestan.

Dmitriev-Mamonov, Hippolite Alexandrovitch: widower of Praskovia Nevedomskaya in 1860, remarried Jamal Eddin's former fiancée, Elizaveta Petrovna Olenina.

Engelhardt, Baron R. Antonovitch: married the widow of Dmitriev-Mamonov, Elizaveta Petrovna Olenina, former fiancée of Jamal Eddin.

Fézé, General Karl Karlovitch: butcher of Ashilta, Akulgo, and Tiliq in 1837.

Fatima: Jamal Eddin's mother, first wife of Shamil, born at Untsukul in 1810, died at Alusind in 1845.

First Cadet Corps of Saint Petersburg: military school where Jamal Eddin spent eight years, from August 25, 1841 to June 9, 1849. The school is located on Vassilievsky Island in Saint Petersburg, a short distance from Alexey Olenin's world at the Beaux-Arts Academy.

Garashkiti: village in greater Chechnya where Shamil and his family found refuge after their flight from Akulgo in 1839.

Ghimri: native town of Shamil and Jamal Eddin, besieged and razed in October 1832, then razed a second time after Shamil's election to imam in 1834, and a third time by Shamil himself, in reprisal for the complicity of the inhabitants during the siege of Akulgo in 1839.

Glinka, Mikhaïl Ivanovitch (1804–1857): composer whose operas glorified Nicholas I, in particular *A Life for the Czar,* written in 1836, and *Ruslan and Ludmilla* (Pushkin's heroes), in 1842.

Grabbe, Count Pavel Khristoforovitch (1789–1875): commander-in-chief of troops in the Caucasus in 1838, responsible for the abduction of Jamal Eddin at Akulgo in late August 1839. Recalled from the Caucasus, he was without a command for six years, then returned to service for the Hungarian uprising of 1849. He received a diamond-studded saber for his actions and ultimately became a member of the State Council.

Gramov, Isaac: Isaï Bey, Armenian, member of the general staff of Prince Grigol Orbeliani of Georgia. He served as interpreter during the exchange negotiations in 1855 and would again serve as Shamil's interpreter at Kaluga.

Griboyedov, Alexander Sergueïevitch (Moscow 1795–Tehran 1829): In 1824 he wrote his play *The Woes of Wit,* which was performed in 1831. He married Georgian Princess Nino Chavchavadze (1812–1857), Prince David's youngest sister, August 22, 1828, and was appointed Russian ambassador to Tehran, where he was subsequently assassinated.

Grosny: "The Terrifying," Russian fort built by General Yermolov in 1819, at the same time as the famous military road to Georgia.

Gruzinskaya, Anna Ilyinitchna (Anna Chavchavadze) (1828–1905): eldest daughter of Ilya Grigoriyevitch Gruzinsky and Anastasia Grigoryevna, née Obolensky. In 1848, she married Prince David Chavchavadze, eleven years her senior, in Moscow. On July 4, 1854, she was abducted by Shamil at her home of Sinandali.

Gruzinskaya, Varenka Ilyinitchna (Varenka Orbeliani) (1831–1884): second daughter of Ilya Grigoriyevitch Gruzinsky and Anastasia Grigoryevna, née Obolensky. In May 1852, she married Prince Elico Orbeliani. He was thirty-six, she just twenty-one. In 1853 she gave birth to twins, only one of whom, George, survived. Her husband was killed at Oguzlu December 8, 1853. Shamil kidnapped her, with George, July 4, 1854. She remained in his custody until March 10, 1855. She died March 30, 1884. George was her only child.

Gruzinski (of Georgia): family of the direct descendants of the last king of Georgia, George XII (born 1746, died 1800), who sought Russia's protection from Turkish and Persian invaders. Disregarding their pact, Russia simply annexed Georgia. His second wife, his widow Mariam Tsitsishvili (1768–1850), assassinated General Lazarev who had come to arrest her, in 1802. She was deported to Russia, then pardoned. She died at the age of eighty in 1850 and was buried at Tiflis with all the honors due her station.

Gruzinski, Colonel-Prince Elizbar (Ilya) (1790–1854): youngest son of George XII, last king of Georgia, and Queen Mariam. In 1827, at the age of thirty-seven, he married the daughter of Prince Gregory Petrovitch Obolensky, Princess Anastasia Grigoryevna Petrovitch Obolenskaya, who was born in Moscow September 25, 1805. The couple had five sons and eight daughters, including Anna Chavchavadze and Varenka Orbeliani.

Hadj Tasho al-Indiri: Chechen pretender to the imamat of Shamil in 1834, he would nonetheless join his ranks and participate in the battle of Akulgo.

Hadji Murat: foster brother of Omar, son of Pakkou-Bekkhe, queen of Kunzakh, assassinated by Shamil's partisans. He passed over to the service of the Russians, then left them to return in 1851. Hero immortalized by Tolstoy.

Hamzat Bek: second imam who served Shamil during the conquest of Kunzakh. He was assassinated in 1834 by Hadji Murat.

Hamzat: Shamil's nephew, offered as a hostage during the 1837 siege of Tiliq.

Ibrahim al-Husayn: Shamil's cousin, muezzin at Akulgo during the siege of 1839.

Jamal Eddin: Shamil's first son, born June 15, 1831, in Ghimri, died July 12, 1858, in Soul-Kadi.

Jamaluddin al-Ghumuqi al-Husayni: Shamil's mentor, who initially disagreed with the holy war but changed his position and placed all his influence behind Shamil during his election to imam in 1834.

Jawarat: second wife of Shamil, born in Ghimri in 1821, died at Akulgo in 1839.

Kaluga: city located about 100 miles south of Moscow, where Shamil and his family lived in exile from 1859 to 1869.

Karata: district given in 1851 to Shamil's son Mohammed Ghazi, where Jamal Eddin was kept under house arrest in 1858.

Karimat: daughter of Daniyal Bek, wife of Mohammed Ghazi.

Khadji: Shamil's house steward.

Khassav-Yurt: fort where Jamal Eddin stayed from January to March 1855, before the exchange. In 1858, one of Shamil's men would come here seeking the services of a doctor for Jamal Eddin.

Khazi Mullah: close friend and companion at arms of Shamil. First imam of Dagestan, born in Ghimri in 1793, died in Ghimri in 1832.

Kunzakh: capital of the khans of Avaria and of Queen Pakkou-Bekkhe. Shamil stole the city's treasure in 1834.

Kiselyev, Pavel Dmitrievitch (Moscow, July 8, 1788–Paris, November 14, 1872): friend of Czar Nicholas I, one of the only liberals at court and one of the most brilliant promoters of the emancipation of the serfs. Himself childless, he concerned himself with the education of his Milyutin nephews.

Klüge von Klugenau, General Franz Karlovitch: attacked Ghimri in 1832 and negotiated the peace of 1837. Participated in all the wars of the Caucasus.

Krasnoye Sielo: village located near Saint Petersburg where the grand military maneuvers took place in the summer. Jamal Eddin participated in them in 1849 and 1853.

Krestovaya: parade of the cross whose main feature is a huge crucifix installed by Yermolov on the military route to Georgia.

Lermontov, Mikhaïl Yurievitch (Moscow, 1814–Piatigorsk, Caucasus 1841): Russian writer exiled to the Caucasus for the publication of his poem on the death of Pushkin (*The Death of the Poet*, 1837). Frequent visitor at the Chavchavadze domain of Sinandali, he was killed in a duel July 15, 1841.

Machouk: home of Piotr Alexeyevitch Olenin (born in 1793, second son of Alexey Nicolaïevitch) and his wife, Maria (Macha Lvova, born in 1810), near Torjok in the province of Tver. Home where Elizaveta Petrovna Olenina (born February 26, 1832 at Torjok, known as Lisa or Lizok) grew up with her younger brothers and sisters, Alexis (born in 1833), Sergueï (1834), Tatiana (1836), and Nicholas (1838). Jamal Eddin spent all his free time at Machouk from 1852 to 1854.

Maria Nicolaïevna (1819–1879): grand duchess, eldest daughter of Nicholas I. Married the first time to Maximilian, Duke of Leuchtenberg in 1839, widowed in 1853. She was secretly engaged to Gregory Alexandrovitch Stroganov, without her father's knowledge and with the complicity of Tatiana Borissovna Potemkina, in the church at Gostilitsy, but married for the second time only in 1856, after her father's death.

Mikhaïl Nicolaïevitch (October 13, 1832–1909): fourth son and seventh child of Nicholas I, student at the First Cadet Corps of Saint Petersburg with Jamal Eddin. In September 1849, when the uncle for whom he was named, Mikhaïl Pavlovitch, died of a heart attack in Warsaw, he took over the command of all of his regiments, including the Vladimirsky Lancers, to which Jamal Eddin belonged. He became viceroy of the Caucasus in 1862.

Mikhaïl Pavlovitch: grand duke and younger brother of Nicholas I, born in 1798, died of a heart attack in September 1849, during maneuvers in Warsaw. Married Elena Pavlovna in February 1824. He was in charge of the administration of all the military schools of Moscow and Saint Petersburg and was inspector general of the First Cadet Corps and the Pages' Corps. Jamal Eddin chose to belong to the regiment of Grand Duke Mikhaïl Pavlovitch, whose ward he had been since his arrival in Russia. Thus he joined the Vladimirsky Lancers in 1849.

Milyutin, Dmitri Alexeyevitch (1816–1912): after various posts in the army, requested transfer to the Caucasus in 1839.

He served under General Grabbe, participated in the siege of Akulgo, and was wounded several times during the campaign. He took notes on all he saw and was the author of drawings of the mountain and the two plateaus used by the Russians. His journal gives a day-by-day account of the siege and does not fail to mention Russian atrocities. He returned in 1840 and spent three years in Saint Petersburg, leaving for the Caucasus once again in 1843. This tour was even more frustrating than the last, since his superiors ignored his suggestions for pacification. He thought of resigning from the army but found a post at the military academy. In 1848, he attracted the attention of the minister of war, with whom he became close. In November 1854, he presented a report on the wars of the Caucasus to Nicholas I. In 1856, Alexander II took his information into account before sending him back to combat Shamil for a third time. He followed Prince Bariatinsky, the new viceroy, in March 1856. He was present at Gunib when Shamil surrendered in 1859. He returned to Saint Petersburg in July 1860. A few years later, he became minister of war.

Mohammed al-Yaragli (Sheik): spiritual master of two of the imams of Dagestan, Khazi Mullah and Shamil. Partisan of the holy war.

Mohammed Ghazi: second son of Shamil, born in April 1833 in Ghimri, proclaimed heir to the imam, naïb of Karata, and married Kherimat, daughter of Daniyal Bek, in 1851. Died at Medina in 1902.

Mohammed Sheffi: third son of Shamil, born in 1839 in Baïan, died in 1904 in Piatigorsk.

Muraviev, General Count Nicholas Mikhaïlovitch (known as Muraviev-Karskii, to distinguish him from his son, "the hanger of Warsaw," and several others who shared his name,

"Karskii" meaning he who took the city of Kars, 1794–1866): general in charge of Russian troops in Warsaw in 1854. It was he who received the letter of Czarevitch Alexander, son of Nicholas I, describing the abduction of the Georgian princesses by Shamil and the necessity of informing Lieutenant Jamal Eddin. In his memoirs, he describes the young man's surprise and his reactions. He himself became general in chief of the Army of the Caucasus and made part of the trip to the mountains at the beginning of 1855 with Jamal Eddin. He reported regularly to the minister of war concerning Jamal Eddin's situation after the latter returned to his father.

Mohammed Mirza Khan: heir to Queen Pakkou-Bekkhe at Kunzakh, pro-Russian.

Naqshbandi: Sufi brotherhood to which Shamil belonged.

Neidhardt: general who replaced Grabbe and Golovine in 1843, whose vulgarity influenced the decision of Daniyal Bek, sultan of Elisou, to change sides and support Shamil.

Nicholas, Baron Leontine Pavlovitch: husband of Sophie Chavchavadze, brother-in-law of David and, by marriage, of Anna Chavchavadze. Commander of the fort at Khassav-Yurt, two days' ride from Dargo-Veden, Shamil's headquarters where the princesses were held, in 1854–1855. Jamal Eddin got along so well with him that he continued to request books from him during his detainment by his father.

Nicholas I (Gatchina, June 25, 1796–Saint Petersburg, February 18, 1855): third son of Paul Petrovitch Romanov and Maria Feodorovna. Married Charlotte of Prussia, known as Czarina Alexandra Feodorovna, in 1817. His reign began December 14, 1825.

Nicholas Nicolaïevitch (Tsarskoye Sielo, July 27, 1831–April 13, 1891): Third son of Nicholas I. Educated in the First Cadet Corps with Jamal Eddin, who was his age. Against his own wishes, he married Princess Alexandra Petrovna of Oldenburg February 6, 1856.

Olenin, Alexey Nicolaïevitch (1764–1843): illustrious grandfather of Elizaveta Petrovna Olenina, fiancée of Jamal Eddin. Member of the State Council, president of the Beaux-Arts Academy, director of the Public Library of Saint Petersburg, archaeologist, historian, the incarnation of Saint Petersburg intellectual life. At his country house in Priutino, he received his greatest contemporaries in the world of literature and art.

Olenin, Piotr Alexeyevitch (1793–1868): painter, second son of Alexey Nicolaïevitch Olenin. He and his older brother Nicholas Alexeyevitch fought at the Battle of Borodino in 1812. Father of Jamal Eddin's fiancée.

Olenina, Anna Alexeyvna (1808–1888): youngest daughter of Alexey Olenin and Elizaveta Marcovna, sister of Piotr and aunt of Elizaveta, Jamal Eddin's fiancée. Pushkin had proposed marriage to her at Priutino in 1829.

Olenina, Elizaveta Petrovna: born February 26, 1832, at Torjok, died in 1922 at the age of ninety. Fiancée of Jamal Eddin. She would marry several years after his death. Her family encouraged her to write her memoirs, and she described at length her tragic love affair with Jamal Eddin, whose memory she still worshipped.

Olga Nicolaïevna (1822–1892): second daughter of Nicholas I. Married Charles I of Wurttemburg in 1846.

Orbeliani, Elico (Prince Elizbar, Ilya Dmitrievitch Orbeliani, Elico) (1817–1853): married May 1, 1852, to Princess Varvara of Georgia. Ten years earlier, in 1842, he had been Shamil's prisoner in Dargo for eight months. Younger brother of the famous poet Grigol Orbeliani, he too was a career officer in the Russian army. He was a colonel when he died at Oguzlu December 8, 1853, killed by the Turks. Elico Orbeliani had only one son, born shortly before his death.

Orbeliani, Prince Grigol (1804–1883): renowned Georgian poet and older brother of Elico Orbeliani, husband of Varenka of Georgia. He was commander of the fort at Temir-Khan-Chura during the exchange of March 10, 1855.

Pakkou-Bekkhe: queen (khanum) of Kunzakh, in Avaria, assassinated with all her children by the second imam, Hamzat Bek, and Shamil, in August 1834.

Paskyevitch, Prince Ivan Fedorovitch (Warsaw, 1782–1856): victor of the Russo-Turkish war, in 1826 he replaced Yermolov as viceroy of the Caucasus. He was recalled in October 1831 to fight the Poles, whose resistance he crushed mercilessly. From this time on, he was always accompanied by his guard of Cossacks and Muslims. In 1849, he was in charge of repressing the Hungarian uprising. He was much loved by Nicholas I, who called him his "father colonel."

Patimat: Shamil's older sister, born around 1795, killed at Akulgo in 1839.

Piotrovsky: Russian physician who treated Jamal Eddin in Soul-Kadi in 1858.

Potemkina, Tatiana Borissovna (1797–1869): daughter of Boris Andreyevitch Golitzine. At eighteen she married Alexander Mikhaïlovitch Potemkin, a marshal of the Saint Petersburg aristocracy. She owned several properties, one of which, Gostilitsy, was located near Peterhof. In Saint Petersburg, she lived on the well-known Million Street. A mystic and proselytizer, she prided herself on her prison visits and on the thousands of Muslims and Jews she had supposedly converted. Her great-niece Elizaveta Petrovna Olenina spent much of her time with Jamal Eddin in La Potemkina's homes, at Gostilitsy, in Saint Petersburg, and at her property close to Torjok between 1850 and 1854.

Poullo, Colonel-General Nicholas: officer known for his cruelty, who met Shamil at Akulgo to attempt to open negotiations on August 16, 1839.

Preobrajensky Regiment: with the Chevaliers-Gardes and the Gardes-à-Cheval, the most prestigious regiment of the czar's army.

Priutino: Alexis Nicolaïevitch Olenin's family home hear Saint Petersburg, sold in 1838.

Pushkin, Alexander Sergueïevitch (Moscow, 1799–Saint Petersburg, 1837): Considered Russia's greatest poet, he wrote splendid texts about the Caucasus, notably the myth of *The Prisoner of the Caucasus*, published in 1821.

Saïd: Shamil's third son, killed by the Russians with his mother Jawarat as they fled from Akulgo in 1839.

Saïd al-Harakan: partisan of the Russians and mentor of the first imam of Dagestan, Khazi Mullah, who would eventually raze his home and burn all of his books.

Shamil: father of Jamal Eddin, third imam of Dagestan. Born in Ghimri in 1797, died at Medina in 1871.

Soul-Kadi: village where Jamal Eddin died July 12, 1858.

Shibshiev: Jamal Eddin's servant from 1849 to 1853.

Sinandali: Chavchavadze property in Georgia, from which the princesses were abducted in 1854.

Temir-Khan-Chura: Russian fort close to Ghimri and Akulgo from which Jamal Eddin was sent to Moscow in 1839.

Terek: Caucasian river celebrated by Pushkin, Lermontov, and Tolstoy.

Tiliq: city besieged by General Fézé in July 1837, from which Shamil was obliged to send his nephew Hamzat as a hostage.

Tolstoy, Leo Nicolaïevitch (1828–1910): one of the greatest Russian novelists of all time, who knew the Caucasus well and lauded it in his works. He fought there in 1854 and was haunted by the memory for the rest of his life. Author of *Cossacks* (1853) and *Hadj Murat* (1904).

Torjok: garrison town in the province of Tver, where Jamal Eddin's regiment of the Vladimirsky Lancers was stationed from 1851 to 1854.

Tsarskoye Sielo (the village of the czar): town outside of Saint Petersburg where Jamal Eddin first studied. Summer residence of the imperial family, where he was received between 1847 and 1853. One of the imperial parks housed the "Invalides," a home for horses put out to pasture and its cemetery.

Ulluh Bey: outlaw that General Grabbe commissioned to poison Shamil in 1840.

Untsukul: native village of Fatima, first wife of Shamil and mother of Jamal Eddin. The village was razed by the imam for having betrayed him.

Varenka: see Grunzinskaya, Varvara Ilyinitchna.

Vladikavkaz: Russian fort.

Vladimirsky Lancers or **Uhlans:** regiment under the command of the czar's brother, Mikhaïl Pavlovitch, which Jamal Eddin joined as a cornet June 9, 1849. At the death of Grand Duke Mikhaïl Pavlovitch on September 19, 1849, the regiment passed into the hands of Grand Duke Mikhaïl Nicolaïevitch, the seventeen-year-old son of Czar Nicholas and former classmate of Jamal Eddin. The Vladimirsky regiment became the thirty-eighth regiment of Vladikavkaz in 1862, when Grand Duke Mikhaïl Nicolaïevitch was named viceroy of the Caucasus and established his residence at Tiflis.

Vorontsov, Mikhaïl: named viceroy of the Caucasus in 1844. One of the Russian dignitaries who was remembered in Tiflis in a favorable light.

Yermolov, General Alexey Petrovitch: viceroy of the Caucasus known for his brutality, recalled after the revolt of the Decembrists. Shamil met him in Saint Petersburg in 1859.

Youssouf: classmate of Jamal Eddin in the First Cadet Corps of Saint Petersburg.

Yunus: the most faithful of Shamil's captains and Jamal Eddin's tutor, in charge of his education. He brought Jamal Eddin to the Russian fort of General Grabbe in 1839 and identified him sixteen years later upon his return, at Khassav-Yurt. He was in charge of negotiations between Shamil and Prince Bariatinsky and can be seen in all the depictions of the murid surrender at Gunib in August 1859.

Zaïdet: third wife of Shamil, born in Ghazikumuk in 1823, died at Medina in 1870. Daughter of Sheik Jamaluddin al-Ghumuqi al-Husayni, she married Shamil after the death of Fatima in 1845.

A Note on Sources

During my long quest in the footsteps of Jamal Eddin, six books were always with me. If they made my bags heavier, every time I read them I felt lighter, filled with renewed enthusiasm. They always revived my curiosity and gave me courage again in my moments of doubt. Over the years and on the paths of so many journeys, their authors have become my mentors, my partners, my traveling companions. I'd like to offer them a sentimental word of appreciation here.

First of all, a nineteenth-century Frenchwoman who traveled extensively, the first to have met some of the protagonists of Jamal Eddin's story, who wrote of her own adventures in the Caucasus. Anne Drancey opened a bookstore in the Georgian capital in 1853. When her business failed, she took a position as governess to the Chavchavadze princes.

During the attack the Tiflis press would call "the hostage taking of the century," she was abducted with the other women of the household by the Imam Shamil. The account of her life in captivity, magnificently edited by Claudine Herrmann at Mercure publishing house, in France, was reprinted in 2006, entitled *Captive des Tchéchènes* (*Captive of the Chechens*).

Some of Madame Drancey's anecdotes inspired one of Leo Tolstoy's masterpieces, *Hadji Murad*, as well as several chapters of Alexandre Dumas's *Voyage au Caucase*, two other works that have frequently accompanied my research. Dumas devoted about ten pages to the story of the sacrifice of Jamal Eddin, based upon his interviews with the Georgian princesses who owed the young Chechen their lives.

Following Dumas, English author John F. Baddeley did extensive research on Dagestan between 1879 and 1902, resulting in a veritable gold mine of information. He observed the ways and customs of the Caucasus with a rare degree of humility and questioned the Montagnards intelligently. He drew landscapes and photographed the countryside. The exhaustive works he then published, *The Russian Conquest of the Caucasus* and *The Rugged Flanks of the Caucasus,* are the invaluable product of his labor. Every biographer of the imam since then has used the collection of anecdotes and accounts in his books as an important source.

And last of all, the fascinating work of Lesley Blanch, *The Sabres of Paradise.* Published for the first time forty-eight years ago by John Murray Publishers in England, it was released in France three years later in a magnificent translation by Jean Lambert, *Les sabres du Paradis.* Editions Lattès published it then, and it was reprinted in 1990 and again in 2004 by Editions Denoël. Lesley Blanch's work remains, in my eyes, the most beautiful book ever written concerning this region of the world.

* * *

For readers who wish to explore further, I am providing here a short bibliography of works that have supported my work and added substance, including here only the texts relevant to history contemporary to the times of Jamal Eddin.

Dare I add, for a long time I was very skeptical of the rumor suggesting that Shamil's son had actually been about to marry a young Russian aristocrat. I simply thought it was too beautiful to be true, and I followed this lead with the greatest circumspection. I was wrong. Discovering his fiancée's memoirs was a great stroke of luck, and I shall start here by citing the references.

UNPUBLISHED MANUSCRIPT SOURCES

Most of the Olenin family collections are preserved in the archives of the city of Riazan, in Russia, in particular all the correspondence and several portraits. The manuscript of the Memoirs of Elizaveta Petrovna Olenina can be found in the state archives of literature and art in Moscow, under her married name:

ENGELHARDT, Elizaveta Petrovna, *Vospominania*, Rossiyskiy Gosudarstvennyi Arkhiv Literatury i Iskusstva. Fond 1124 (Olenin), opis' 1, delo 10.

SOURCES

Abd El-Kader, Emir. *Écrits Spirituels*. Paris: Le Seuil, 1982.

Aboulela, Leila. *The Lion of Chechnya*. BBC drama, June 26, 2005.

Akty Sobrannye Kavkazskoyu Arkheografitcheskoyu Komisseiyu, vol. X, XI. Tiflis, 1888.

Alexe, Dan. "Les Guerres des Soufis" in *Hérodote*, no. 81.

Ali Khan, Masood. Encyclopaedia of Sufism, Vol. XII, *Sufism and Naqshbandi Order*. New Delhi: Anmol Publications, 2003.

Ali-Shah, Omar. *Un Apprentissage du Soufisme.* Paris: G. Trédaniel, 2001.

Anderson, Tony. *Bread and Ashes, A Walk Through the Mountains of Georgia.* London: Vintage, 2004.

Anthology of Georgian Poetry, The, vol. I. Honolulu: University Press of the Pacific, 2002.

Anthologie des Voyageurs Français aux XVIIIe et XIXe Siècles, "Le Voyage en Russie." Paris: Robert Laffont, 1990.

Assatiani, Nodar and Bendianachvili, Alexandre. *Histoire de la Géorgie.* Paris: L'Harmattan, 1997.

Aucouturier, Michel. *Tolstoï.* Paris: Le Seuil, 1996.

——— *Le Caucase Dans la Culture Russe.* Paris: Institut d'études slaves, 1997.

——— Sémon, Marie. *Tolstoï vu par les Écrivains et les Penseurs Russes.* Paris: Institut d'Études Slaves, 1998.

——— *Tolstoï et l'Art.* Paris: Institut d'Études Slaves, 2003.

———Jurgenson, Luba. *Tolstoï et ses Adversaires.* Paris: Institut d'Études Slaves, 2008.

Baddeley, John F. *The Russian Conquest of the Caucasus.* London: Longmans, Green and Co., 1908.

——— *The Rugged Flanks of the Caucasus,* 2 vols. London: Oxford University Press, 1940.

Bagby, Lewis. *Alexander Bestuzhev-Marlinsky and Russian Byronism.* University Park: Penn State University Press, 1995.

Bell, James Stanislaus. *Journal of a Residence in Circassia During the Years 1837, 1838 and 1839.* London: Edward Moxon, 1840.

Benckendorff, Constantine. *Souvenirs Intimes d'une Campagne au Caucase Pendant l'Été de 1845.* Paris: Editions Grigorii Gagarin, 1858.

Bennigsen, Alexandre and Lemercier Quelquejay, Chantal. *La Presse et le Mouvement National Chez les Musulmans de Russie Avant 1920.* Paris: Ecole des Hautes Études en Sciences Sociales, 1964.

——— *Central Asia.* London: Weidenfeld & Nicolson, 1969.

——— *Les Musulmans Oubliés: l'Islam en URSS Aujourd'hui.* Paris: F. Maspero, 1981.

——— *Le Soufi et le Commissaire: les Confréries Musulmanes en URSS.* Paris: Le Seuil, 1986.

——— Wimbush, S. Enders. *Muslims of the Soviet Empire: A Guide.* Bloomington: Indiana University Press, 1986.

——— *L'Islam Parallelo, le Confraternite Musulmane in Unione Sovietica.* Genoa: Marietti, 1990.

Bennigsen, Marie and Avtorkhanov, Abdourakhman. *The North Caucasus Barrier: The Russian Advance Towards the Muslim World.* London: Hurst, 1992.

Berelowitch, Wladimir. *Le Grand Siècle Russe d'Alexandre Ier à Nicolas II.* Paris: Découvertes Gallimard, 2005.

Bérézine, Ilya Nikolaevitch. *Voyage au Daghestan et en Transcaucasie.* Paris: Geuthner, 2006.

Berry, Dr. Thomas E. *Memoirs of the Pages to the Tsars.* Calgary: Gilbert's Royal Books, 2001.

Bitov, Andrei. *A Captive of the Caucasus.* London: Harvill, 1993.

Blanch, Lesley. *Les sabres du paradis.* Paris: Denoël, 2004.

——— *The Sabres of Paradise.* London: Tauris Parke Paperbacks, 2004.

——— *Voyage au Cœur de l'esprit.* Paris: Denoël, 2003.

Bliev, Mark and Degoev, Vladimir. *Kavkazskaa Voïna.* Moscow: Roset, 1994.

Bloomfield, Georgiana L. *Reminiscences of Court and Diplomatic Life,* vol. I. London: Elibron Classics, 2006.

Brayley Hodgetts, E.A. *The Court of Russia in the Nineteenth Century*, vol. I and II. London: Elibron Classics, 2005.

Buxhöwden, Baroness Sophie. *Before the Storm.* London: Macmillan and Co., 1938.

Bzarov, G. *Russia and the Highlanders of the Greater Caucasus: On the Way to Civilization.* Moscow: Mysl Publishers, 2004.

Cahiers du Monde Russe et Soviétique, vol. VII, no. 4, (October-December 1965). Bennigsen, Alexandre, "Un Témoignage d'une Française sur Chamil et les Guerres du Caucase," 311–322.

——— *Ibid.*, vol. X, nos. 3 and 4, (July, December 1969). Boratav, Pertev. "La Russie dans les archives ottomanes, un dossier ottoman sur l'imam Chamil," 524–535.

——— *Ibid.*, vol. XIX, nos. 1 and 2, (January–June 1978). Lesure, Michel. "La France et le Caucase à l'Époque de Chamil à la Lumière des Dépêches des Consuls Français," 5–65.

——— *Ibid.*, vol. XXXIII, nos. 2 and 3, (April–September 1992). "Was General Klüge-von-Klugenau Shamil's Desmichels?" 207–221.

Canard, Marius. *Chamil et Abdelkader*, vol. XIV, 231–256. Paris: Annales de l'Institut d'Études Orientales, 1956.

——— *Les Reines de Géorgie dans l'Histoire et la Légende Musulmanes.* Paris: Geuthner, 1969.

Carrère d'Encausse, Hélène. *Réforme et Révolution Chez les Musulmans de l'Empire Russe.* Paris: Presses FNSP, 1966.

——— *La Politique Soviétique au Moyen-Orient.* Paris: Presses FNSP, 1976.

——— *L'Empire Éclaté.* Paris: Flammarion, 1978.

——— *L'Empire d'Eurasie, une Histoire de l'Empire Russe de 1552 à Nos Jours.* Paris: Fayard, 2005.

——— *Alexandre II.* Paris: Fayard, 2008.

Cazacu, Mateï. *Au Caucase: Russes et Tchéchènes, Récits d'une Guerre Sans Fin*. Geneva: Georg Éditeur, 1998.

Central Asian Survey, vol. II, no. 1 (July 1983). Henze, Paul. "Fire and Sword in the Caucasus: the 19th Century Resistance of the North Caucasian Mountaineers," 5–44.

——— *Ibid.*, vol. IV, no. 4 (autumn 1985) 7–45. (Three articles concerning Shamil by different authors).

——— *Ibid.*, vol. X, nos. 1 and 2 (1991). "Imam Shamil and Shah Mohammed: Two Unpublished Letters," 171–179; "Shamil and the Murid Movement, 1830–1959: An Attempt at a Comprehensive Bibliography," 189–247.

——— *Ibid.*, vol. XII, no. 3 (1993). "The Conqueror of Napoleon in the Caucasus," 253–265.

——— *Ibid.*, vol. XIII, no. 2 (1994). "Prince Bariatinskii, Conqueror of the Eastern Caucasus," 237–247.

——— *Ibid.*, vol. XVI, no. 3 (1997). "La Nouvelle 'Guerre du Caucase,' " 413–424.

——— *Ibid.*, vol. XVIII, no. 4 (December 1, 1999). "The Caucasus: Elites, Politics and Strategic Issues," (six articles).

——— *Ibid.*, vol. XXI, no. 3 (September 1, 2002). "Shamil and the Resistance to the Russian Conquest of the Caucasus." Special Issue in Memory of Dibir Mahomedov, 239–340 (ten different articles on Shamil).

——— *Ibid.*, vol. XXIII, no. 2 (2004). "Imagining a Chechen Military Aristocracy: The Story of the Georgian Princesses Held Hostage by Shamil," 183–203.

Council of American Islamic Relations. "Imam Shamyl, Ideal Muslim Warrior." September 2006.

Crankshaw, Edward. *The Shadow of the Winter Palace.* New York: Da Capo Press, 1976.

Crews, Robert D. *For Prophet and Tsar.* Boston: Harvard University Press, 2006.

Curtin, Jeremiah. *Memoirs.* Pioneering the Upper Midwest: Books from Michigan, Minnesota and Wisconsin, ca. 1820–1910.

Custine, Marquis de. *Lettres de Russie.* Paris: Gallimard, 1975.

——— *La Russie en 1839.* Arles: Actes Sud, 2005.

Delaveau, H. "Captivité de Deux Princesses Russes dans le Sérail de Shamil au Caucase en 1855, d'Après le Récit Russe de Monsieur Verderevskii," in *Revue des Deux Mondes* (May 1, 1856) 5–48.

Depping, Guillaume. *Schamyl, le Prophète du Caucase.* Paris: Librairie Nouvelle, 1854.

Dernovoï, Vladimir. "Soudba Amanatov," in *Krasnaya Zvezda* (November 18, 2000).

Des Cars, Jean. *La Saga des Romanov.* Paris: Plon, 2008.

Dourova, Nadejda. *Cavalière du Tsar.* Paris: Viviane Hamy, 1995.

Drancey, Anne. *Captive des Tchétchènes.* Paris: Mercure de France, 2006.

Ducamp, Emmanuel, and Walter, Marc. *Palais d'Été des Tsars.* Paris: Chêne-Hachette Livre, 2007.

Dumas, Alexandre. *Ammalat-Beg.* Paris: A. Cadot, 1859.

——— *La Boule de Neige.* Paris: Michel Lévy Frères, 1862.

——— *Chamil et la Résistance Tchétchène Contre les Russes.* Paris: Nautilus, 2001.

——— *Romans Caucasiens,* préface de Dominique Fernandez. Paris: Éd. des Syrtes, 2001.

——— *Voyage au Caucase.* Paris: Hermann, 2002.

——— *Voyage en Russia.* Paris: Hermann, 2002.

——— *En Russie, I. De Moscou à Tiflis.* Amiens: Encrage, 2006.

Dunlop, John B. *Russia Confronts Chechnya: Roots of a Separatist Conflict*, vol. I Cambridge: Cambridge University Press, 1998.

Edwards, H. Sutherland. *Captivity of Two Russian Princesses in the Caucasus.* London: Smith, Elder and Co., 1857.

Ein Besuch bei Schamyl: Brief eines Preussen. Berlin: F. Schneider und Comp., 1855.

Fernandez, Dominique. *St Pétersbourg; Le Rêve de Pierre.* Paris: Omnibus, 1995.

——— *La Magie Blanche de Saint-Pétersbourg.* Paris: Découvertes Gallimard, 1997.

——— *Dictionnaire Amoureux de la Russie.* Paris: Plon, 2004.

Franco Focherini, Isabella E. *Il Mistero del Profeta Al-Mansùr.* Rome: Datanews, 2001.

Gagarine, Grigori Grigorievitch. *Le Caucase Pittoresque Dessiné d'Après Nature par le Prince G.G. Gagarine, Texte par le Comte Ernest Stackelberg.* Paris, 1847.

Gagarine Grigori. Exhibition catalog. Saint Petersburg, 1996.

Gammer, Moshe. *The Lone Wolf and the Bear.* London: Hurst & Company, 2006.

——— *Muslim Resistance to the Tsar: Shamil and the Conquest of Chechnia and Daghestan.* Abingdon: Frank Cass & Co. Ltd., 2004.

Ganichev, I.A. and Davydov, B.B. "Prosto iz Gortsev," in *Prebyvanie v Rossii Djemal ad-Dina, Syna Imama Shamilya. Po Materialam Rossiyskogo Voenno-Istoritcheskogo Arkhiva. Ekho Kavkaza*, vol. I, 1994.

Gautier, Théophile. *Voyage en Russie.* Paris: Dentu, 1867.

Gobineau, Joseph Arthur de. *Les Religions et les Philosophies dans l'Asie Centrale.* Paris, 1865.

——— *Souvenirs de Voyage.* Paris, 1872.

Gogol, Nicolas. *Les Soirées du Hameau*, préface de Michel Aucouturier. Paris: Gallimard, 1989.

——— *Nouvelles de Pétersbourg.* Paris: Gallimard, 1998.

——— *Taras Boulba,* préface de Michel Aucouturier. Paris: Gallimard, 2000.

——— *Le Grand Guide de la Russie.* Paris: Gallimard, 2003.

Gouraud, Jean-Louis. *Russie des Chevaux, des Hommes et des Saints.* Paris: Belin, 2001.

Grève, Claude de. *Le Voyage en Russie.* Paris: Robert Laffont, 1990.

Griboïèdov. *Œuvres,* Bibliothèque de la Pléiade. Paris: Gallimard, 1973.

Griffin, Nicholas. *Caucasus, A Journey to the Land Between Christianity and Islam.* Chicago: University of Chicago Press, 2001.

Grigoriantz, Alexandre. *Etrange Caucase.* Paris: Fayard, 1978.

——— *La Montagne du Sang.* Geneva: Georg Éditeur, 1998.

——— *Les Damnés de la Russie.* Geneva: Georg Éditeur, 2002.

——— *Les Caucasiens.* Gollion: Infolio, 2006.

Grundwald, Constantin de. *Tsar Nicholas I.* London: Douglas Saunders, 1954.

Henze, Paul. "Daghestan in October 1997, Imam Shamil Lives!" Sweden: CA&CC Press AB, 1997.

Hertzig, Victor. "Dzemal-Eddin, Starchii syn Shamilia," in *Rousskii Arkhiv,* no. 9 (1890) 111–112.

Herzen, Alexandre. *Passé et Méditations,* 4 vols. Lausanne: L'Âge d'Homme, 1974–1981.

Hoesli, Éric. *À la Conquête du Caucase.* Paris: Éditions des Syrtes, 2006.

Hommaire de Hell, Adèle. *Voyage dans les Steppes de la Mer Caspienne.* Paris: Hachette, 1860.

Idries, Shah. *Cercatore di Verità, Il Sufismo e la Scienza Dell' uomo.* Rome: Ubaldini Editore, 1995.

Iordanidou, Maria. *Vacances dans le Caucase.* Arles: Actes Sud, 1997.

Isik, Hüseyin Hilmi. *Islam and How to be True Moslem.* Istanbul: Isik Kitabevi, 1980.

Jackman, S.W. *Romanov Relations.* London: Macmillan, 1969.

Kaziev, Shapi. *Imam Shamil.* Moscow: Molodaâ Gvardiâ, 2001.

Kelly, Catriona. *The Uses of Refinement, Etiquette and Uncertainty in the Autobiographical Writings of Anna Tyutcheva.* Oxford: New College, 1996.

Kelly, Laurence. *A Traveller's Companion to St Petersburg.* New York: Atheneum, 1983.

——— *Lermontov, Tragedy in the Caucasus.* London: Tauris Parke Paperbacks, 2003.

——— *Diplomacy and Murder in Tehran.* London: Tauris Parke Paperbacks, 2006.

King, Greg and Wilson, Penny. *Gilded Prism.* East Richmond Heights: Eurohistory.com, 2006.

Krylov, N.A. "Kadety Sorokovykh Godov (Litchnye Vospominaniya)," in *Istoritcheskiy Vestnik,* no. 9 (1901).

Lang, David Marshal. *The Last Years of the Georgian Monarchy, 1658–1832.* New York: Columbia University Press, 1957.

Layton, Susan. *Russian Literature and Empire, Conquest of the Caucasus from Pushkin to Tolstoy.* Cambridge: Cambridge University Press, 2005.

Lermontov, Michel. *Œuvres,* Bibliothèque de la Pléiade. Paris: Gallimard, 1973.

——— *Un Héros de Notre Temps,* préface de Dominique Fernandez. Paris: Gallimard, 1976.

——— *Œuvres Poétiques.* Lausanne: L'Âge d'Homme, 1985.

Leroy-Beaulieu, Anatole. *Un Homme d'État Russe (Nicolas Milutine).* Hattiesburg: Academic International, 1969.

Lieven, Anatol. *Chechnya, Tombstone of Russian Power.* New Haven: Yale University Press, 1998.

Lincoln, W. Bruce. *Romanovs, Autocrats of All the Russias.* New York: Anchor Books, 1981.

——— *Nicholas I, Emperor and Autocrat of All the Russias.* De Kalb: NIU Press Edition, 1989.

Londonderry, Lady. *Russian Journal of Lady Londonderry, 1836–1837.* London: Murray, 1973.

Mackie, J. Milton. *Life of Schamyl; A Narrative of the Circassian War of Independance Against Russia.* Cleveland: John P. Jewett and Company, 1856.

Maeda, H. "On the Ethno-Social Background of Four Gholâm Families from Georgia in Safavid Iran," in *Studia Iranica,* vol. XXXII, no. 2, (2003) 243–278.

Maistre, Xavier de. *Voyages Autour de ma Chambre: les Prisonniers du Caucase.* Paris: Flammarion, 1906.

Makanine, Vladimir. *Le Prisonnier du Caucase: Et Autres Nouvelles.* Paris: Gallimard, 2005.

McCarthy, Justin. *Death and Exile, The Ethnic Cleansing of Ottoman Muslims 1821–1822.* Princeton: The Darwin Press Inc., undated.

Meaux, Lorraine de. *Saint-Pétersbourg.* Paris: Robert Laffont, 2003.

——— *Récits d'Officiers Russes sur la Région Caucasienne et les États Voisins dans la Première Moitié du XIXe Siècle.* Institut Pierre Renouvin, April 2004.

Meurice, Paul. *Schamyl.* Paris: Théâtre de la Porte Saint Martin, June 26, 1854.

Miliyutin, Dmitri. "Gounib. Plenenie Shamilia," in *Rodina,* no. 1 (January 2000) Moscow.

Moser, Louis. *The Caucasus and its People.* London: D. Nutt, 1856.

Mossolov, A.A. *At the Court of the Last Tsar.* London: Methuen and Co., 1935.

Mouradian, Claire. "Le Caucase Entre les Empires, XVIe–XXe Siècles," in *Archives du Séminaire,* 1994–2006. CNRS, Paris.

Moynet, Jean-Pierre. *Le Volga et le Caucase avec Alexandre Dumas.* Amiens: Encrage, 2006.

Muller, Eugène. *Les Hôtes de Schamyl.* Paris: T. Lefèvre, undated.

Murphy, Paul J. *The Wolves of Islam.* Washington, DC: Brassey's, 2004.

Najjar, Alexandre. *Les Exilés du Caucase.* Paris: Grasset, 1995.

Nasr, Seyyed Hossein. *Il Sufismo.* Milan: Rusconi, 1975.

Nivat, Georges. *Les Sites de la Mémoire Russe, Tome 1, Géographie de la Mémoire Russe.* Paris: Fayard, 2007.

Osipov, Georgy. "Imam Shamil in Russia," in *New Times* (October 1, 1999).

Partchieva, Para and Guérin, Françoise. *Parlons Tchétchène Ingouche.* Paris: L'Harmattan, 1997.

Le Pays (September 9, 1854 and October 4, 1854).

Petin S. *Sobstvennyi Ego Imperatorskogo Velitchestva Konvoy, 1811–1911.* Saint Petersburg, 1911, no editor.

Pienkos, Angela T. *The Imperfect Autocrat Grand Duke Constantine Pavlovich and the Polish Congress Kingdom.* New York: Columbia University Press, 1987.

Piotrovskiy, S. "Poezdka v Gory," in *Kavkaz,* no. 70 (September 7, 1858), no. 71 (September 11, 1858).

Pope-Hennessy, Una. *A Czarina's Story.* London: Nicholson & Watson, 1948.

Pouchkine, Alexandre. *La Dame de Pique et Autres Nouvelles.* Paris: Garnier, 1970.

——— *Œuvres.* Bibliothèque de la Pléiade. Paris: Gallimard, 1973.

——— *Œuvres en Prose.* Lausanne: L'Âge d'Homme, 1973.

——— *Œuvres Poétiques,* 2 vols. Lausanne: L'Âge d'Homme, 1981.

——— *Lettres en Français.* Castelnau-le-Lez: Éditions Climats, 2004.

——— *La Fille du Capitaine,* preface by Michel Aucouturier. Paris: Gallimard, 2005.

Pronin, Alexandre. "Djamalouddin syn Chamilia," in *Argoumenty i Fakty,* no. 14, (July 18, 2003).

Przhetzlavski, P.G. *Shamyl ii Ego Semya v Kalougye 1863–1865* (*Shamyl and His Family in Kalouga*). Saint Petersburg: Rousskaia Starina, 1877.

Putnam, vol. X, no. 56, (August 1857). "Schamyl and His Harem."

Radzinsky, Edvard. *Alexander II, the Last Great Tsar.* New York: Free Press, 2005.

Ram, Harsha. *Prisoners of the Caucasus: Literary Myths and Media Representations of the Chechen Conflict.* Berkeley: University of California, 1999.

Reich, Rebecca. "Holding Court," in *The Moscow Times* (November 12 2004).

La Revue des Deux Mondes:

——— (November 1, 1853) 409–448.

——— (June 15, 1860 and April 15, 1860) 947–981.

——— (May 15, 1861) 297–335.

——— (December 15, 1865) 947–982.

——— (January 1, 1866) 41–62.

Revue du Monde Musulman, no. 10 (April 1910). "Chamyl, le Héros du Caucase, Jugé par les Siens," 533–541.

——— No. 11 (May 1910). "Hadj-Mourad, le naïb de Chamyl," 100–104.

Revue Littéraire Étrangère, January 1854.

Riasanovsky, Nicholas V. *Histoire de la Russie, des Origines à 1996.* Paris: Robert Laffont, 1994.

Rousskiy Invalid, "Vnutrennie Izvestiya," no. 77 (April 9, 1855).

——— "Podrobnoe Opisanie Razmena Plennykh Semeystv Fligel-Adjutanta Polkovnika Knyazya Thavtchadze General-Myora Knyazya Orbelyani," no. 85 (April 19, 1855).

Runovsky, A. "Apolon, Kanly v Nemirnom Krae (Blood Feuds in the Unpacified Country)," in *Voennyi Sbornik,* no. 7 (1860) unofficial part, 199–216.

——— *Zapicki Shamyla* (*Notes on Shamyl*). Saint Petersburg: Tipografiia Karla Vol'fa, 1860.

The Russian Review, Barrett, Thomas M. "The Remaking of the Lion of Daghestan: Shamil in Captivity," vol. LIII (July 1994) 353–366.

Sanders, Thomas and Tucker, Ernest. *Russian-Muslim Confrontation in the Caucasus.* London: Routledge Curzon, 2004.

Sava, George. *Valley of Forgotten People.* London: Faber and Faber, undated.

Seyyed, Hossein Nasr. *Il Sufismo.* Milan: Rusconi, 1975.

Shah, Idries. *Cercatore di Verità.* Rome: Ubaldini Editore, 1995.

Shamil, An Illustrated Encyclopedia. Moscow: Codroudjestvo, 2005.

Siddiqui, Mateen. *Sufism in the Caucasus.* Islamic Supreme Council of America, 1997–2005.

Silogava, Valéry and Sgengelia, Kakha. *History of Georgia.* Tbilisi: Caucasus University Publishing House, 2007.

Smith, Sebastian. *Allah's Mountains, Politics and War in the Russian Caucasus.* London: J.B. Tauris Publisher, 1998.

Sobolev, Boris. *Chtourm Boudet Stoit Dorogo...Kavkazskaya Voïna XIX Veka v Litsakh.* Moscow: Vinogradova, 2001.

Styazhkin, Nikolai. "Flowers to be Laid at the Tomb of Son of Imam Shamil," in *Itar-Tass Weekly News* (November 16, 1997).

Sutherland, Christine. *La Princesse de Sibérie.* Paris: Perrin, 1997.

Taylor, Brian. "Politics and the Russian Army," in *GB-Russia Society Reviews and Articles.* Cambridge: Cambridge University Press, 2003.

Tchitchagova, M. *Shamil na Kavkaze i v Rossii, Biografitcheskii Otcherk.* No editor. Saint Petersburg, 1889.

Timofeev, Lev. "Pushkin i P.A. Olenin," in *Vremennik Pushkinskoi Komissii* (1977). No editor. Moscow-Leningrad, 1980.

——— *V Krugu Druzei i Muz: Dom Oleninykh.* No editor. Leningrad, 1983.

Tioutcheva, Anna. *Vospominania.* Moscow: Zakarov, 2000.

Tolstoi, Léon. *Les Cosaques.* Paris: Gallimard, 1965.

——— *Enfance, Adolescence, Jeunesse,* préface de Michel Aucouturier. Paris: Gallimard, 1975.

——— *Journaux et Carnets,* préface de Michel Aucouturier, 3 vols. Paris: Gallimard, 1979–1985.

——— *Lettres I, 1828–1879.* Paris: Gallimard, 1986.

——— *Hadji Mourat,* édition annotée par Michel Aucouturier. Paris: Gallimard, 2004.

——— *Lettres aux Tsars.* Paris: Alban Éditions, 2005.

——— *Les Récits de Sébastopol.* Paris: Payot et Rivages, 2005.

Troyat, Henri. *Alexandre II.* Paris: Flammarion, 1990.

——— *Pouchkine.* Paris: Perrin, 1999.

——— *Nicolas Ier.* Paris: Perrin, 2000.

——— *La Vie Quotidienne en Russie au Temps du Dernier Tsar.* Paris: Hachette, 1959.

——— *L'Univers,* nos. 8, 10 and 11 (September 1854).

Tynianov, Iouri. *La Mort du Vazir-Moukhtar.* Paris: Gallimard, 1978.

Vambery, Armin. *Voyage d'un Faux Derviche en Asie Centrale.* Paris: Phébus, 1994.

Verderevskiy, E.A. *Kavkazskie Plennitsy ili Plen u Shamila.* No editor. Moscow, 1857.

Villari, Luigi. *Fire and Sword in the Caucasus.* London: T.F. Unwin, 1906.

Vitale, Serena. *Le Bouton de Pouchkine.* Paris: Editions Plon, 1998.

——— *L'imbroglio del Turbante.* Milan: Montadori, 2006.

Wagner, Friedrich. *Schamyl als Feldherr, Sultan and Prophet und der Kaukasus.* Leipzig: G. Remmelmann, 1854.

Ware, Robert Bruce and Kisriev, Enver. "Ethnic Parity and Democratic Pluralism in Dagestan: A Consociational Approach," in *Europe and Asia Studies,* no. 53 (January 1, 2001).

Warnes, David. *Chronicle of the Russian Tsars.* London: Thames and Hudson, 2004.

Wortman, Richard S. *Scenarios of Power, Myth and Ceremony in Russian Monarchy.* Princeton: Princeton University Press, 2006.

Yermolov, Alexey. *The Czar's General: The Memoirs of a Russian General in the Napoleonic Wars.* Welwyn Garden City: Ravenhall Books, 2005.

Zeepvat, Charlotte. *Romanov Autumn.* Stroud: Sutton Publishing, 2006.

Zelkina, Anna. *In Quest for God and Freedom.* London: Hurst & Company, undated.

About the Author

Photograph © 2010 Gamma Agency

French novelist and biographer Alexandra Lapierre is a graduate of the Sorbonne and the University of Southern California. Her best-selling books have been translated worldwide, including two titles in English, *Fanny Stevenson* and *Artemisia,* and have garnered her numerous awards, including the best book of the year by the readers of *Elle* magazine for her biography of American pioneer Fanny Stevenson. She was voted Woman of Culture by the city of Rome, Italy, and has been nominated Chevalier in the "Order of Arts and Letters" by the French government. Her most recent work, *L'Excessive,* was an immediate best seller in Europe and is being developed for a television series. Alexandra Lapierre lives in Paris.

About the Translator

Jane Lizop is a writer, journalist, and translator with a background in modern European history. She lives in Paris.

EXTRAORDINARY PRAISE FOR

aloft

"I appreciate a writer who's not overzealously committed to any one ideology or group, who likes to confound expectations, and who feels expansive enough in his spirit and ambitions to encompass not just his close kinsmen but the infamous Other. With *Aloft*, Chang-rae Lee proves himself just such a writer. . . . [A] master craftsman." —*The Washington Post*

"Lee's genius is this confidential voice, full of cultural analysis, ironic asides, sexual candor, and unconscious revelations, laced along through one breathless paragraph after another in improbably extended sentences, perpetually buoyed by wit and insight. He's perfectly captured the conflicted confidence of a man who knows he can be a jerk but hopes that knowing that might win him some consolation." —*The Christian Science Monitor*

"Like Richard Ford in *Independence Day*, Lee is extremely adept at satirizing this uniquely American and relentless obsession with real estate and home improvement, epitomized in *Aloft* by Battle's son and wife and their nouveaux riches friends. . . . Lee's writing is beautiful. . . . Lee is a master in developing Battle's narrative voice, one that is gentle, wistful, appealingly befuddled. There is great humor in the novel as well. . . . He has delivered an affecting portrait of a man trying to define his place as a father, son, and lover in America today. Looked at closely, Jerry Battle is not much different from Henry Park in *Native Speaker* and Franklin Hata in *A Gesture Life*. He has stoically avoided being vulnerable, all the while desperately wanting to belong to something larger than himself, to find the true meaning of citizenship and home. Really, what could be more American than that?" —*The Boston Globe*

continued . . .

"Accomplished, easygoing, gorgeously written . . . Like Richard Ford's *The Sportswriter* or Richard Russo's *Straight Man*, this wry, meditative novel relies entirely on Jerry's voice to bring alive a wide cast of characters." —*Entertainment Weekly*

"The prose is buoyant, as if, like Jerry, Lee himself feels liberated from the implacable laws of gravity governing American society. . . . *Aloft* ends up as a homily in praise of gravity, though the ride that Lee provides fulfills the continued promise of lift. . . . Prose that rises to heights above merely mundane sights and thoughts." —*Chicago Tribune*

"[A] majestic, moving novel. Lee isn't the first to point out that the suburbs hide uncharted depths of misery and discontentment—Updike, Rick Moody, and John Cheever, among many others, have been here before. But Lee's portrait feels somehow more up-to-date than anything else out there. . . . The glossy flawlessness of Lee's prose is itself a metaphor, a symbol of the superficial perfection of America's suburban splendor. Even though you can barely see the fault lines and stress fractures just below the surface, somehow it makes you feel them that much more keenly." —*Time*

"In *Aloft*, Chang-rae Lee's third novel, the author follows postwar giants like John Cheever, Walker Percy, John Updike, and, at moments, Richard Russo as he plumbs the soul of the 'not unhappy' man. . . . Lee writes with humor and acuity, swirling comic wit and subtlety into scenes so mundane and yet so poignant that the heart sighs in recognition. . . . In a series of deft moves and touching, often droll moments, Lee links Jerry inextricably to his family. He also lets Jerry speak directly to the reader, like some actor winking into the camera, revealing the pretend to be all the more real." —*USA Today*

"Slyly entertaining . . . Filled with passages of revelation about who we are and what we are becoming."
—*The San Jose Mercury News*

"Award-winning Korean-American novelist Chang-rae Lee writes about the complications of American life with a nuanced attention that is awesome. His third novel, *Aloft*, unfolds like a little origami box, each fold revealing yet another aspect of the complexities of aspirations, avocations, and ethnicities as they coalesce in the life of one Long Island family. . . . Lee illumines Jerry's thoughts in the best Cheeveresque manner. . . . In this rich, tragicomic and thoroughly engrossing novel of suburban American life, Lee puts a masterful and poetic touch on the interstices of fragile emotional lives." —*The Baltimore Sun*

"There's nothing streetwise or rough-and-tumble about Jerry Battle, the gentle, sweetly elegiac narrator of Chang-rae Lee's mesmerizing new novel. . . . Lee is a spellbinder. . . . When it comes to emotion, Lee is pitch-perfect. Like many Americans his age, Jerry is caught between generations, touched and changed by his relationship with his deteriorating father and his overextended son. . . . He pulls us inside Jerry's skin, and we share in all his love and confusion and his fully realized humanity."

—*The Hartford Courant*

"Elegant and surprising . . . [An] astonishing novel . . . Nearly every page of *Aloft* is full of surprises, of emotional land mines. . . . Chang-rae Lee designs beautifully meandering sentences that capture and pull a reader to the most unexpected of places. . . . Simply getting lost in the author's elegant and surprising prose is pleasure enough, but Lee is also a gifted storyteller, able to create scenes and images of profound emotional beauty. . . . Stunning, full of vivid, off-kilter details that both shock and resonate . . . The joy of *Aloft* is not only its brilliant depiction of a modern man's foundering attempt to keep his life perfectly manageable but also its deft ability to conjure up the most vibrant of feelings from a narrator who claims he has none. With this spectacular book, Chang-rae Lee proves himself one of our most riveting and remarkable novelists."

—*The Atlanta Journal-Constitution*

continued . . .

"*Aloft* is a traditional American novel in the best sense of the word *traditional*—a compelling plot, characters who change as the years pass, believable dialogue, a writing style that never perplexes, and turns of phrase that illuminate humanity in new ways. The same could be said about the two previous novels of Chang-rae Lee. *Aloft* is just more so, no small accomplishment. . . . Beguilingly insightful . . . Anybody who cares about contemporary literature must wonder after finishing *Aloft* what Lee will do with novel number four."

—*St. Louis Post-Dispatch*

"Chang-rae Lee's third novel looks like a simple story about how one man negotiates the emotional turbulence of family life. Its traditional structure eschews stylistic razzmatazz, but my bet is that *Aloft* will resonate with the same readers who loved Richard Russo's Pulitzer Prize–winning novel, *Empire Falls*. . . . The novel captures the 'now' and presents characters that buzz with life. . . . Lee invents narrators who, like the natural-born storyteller at a good cocktail party, can't help but draw and keep a crowd. . . . A fabulous storyteller."

—*The Cleveland Plain Dealer*

"This is a story that rises above the trials and tribulations of one family. It's a book about a vast slice of American society, its changing ethnicities and colors, its blurring of urban-suburban life, its ethical and moral choices, and its seemingly inherent optimism. In short, it's a terrific book."

—*Chicago Sun-Times*

"Lee's poetic prose sits well in the mouth of this aging Italian-American whose sentences turn unexpected corners. . . . Jerry's humble and skeptical voice and Lee's genuine compassion for his compromised characters make for a truly moving story about a modern family."

—*Publishers Weekly*

"In *Aloft*, [Lee] proves that he can evoke the desires and disappointments of the suburban territory mapped by Cheever, Yates, and Updike with similar artistry and compassion."

—*The Miami Herald*

"With the affecting, richly ruminative *Aloft*, Lee, further entrenched in the Updike and Cheever literary environment—and further establishing himself as a writer of nuanced expressiveness, force, and humanity—expands his scope beyond the confines of assimilation and identity. Instead of offering another study of an outsider looking in, Lee presents us with a well-crafted, beguiling study of an insider looking for an out. . . . By turns drolly incisive and elegiac, penetrating and poignant, *Aloft*, though a departure for Lee and more stylistically colloquial than *Native Speaker* and *A Gesture Life*, is as provocative as it is evocative. Wonderfully curmudgeonly at times, the novel is peppered throughout with keen social observations . . . [A] hot ticket of a novel."

—*The San Diego Union-Tribune*

"In his third novel, Lee applies his remarkable storytelling skills to create a monstrous first-person narrator. . . . A masterly portrait of a disaffected personality . . . Lee's radiant writing style will please fans of his earlier fiction, and the plot will interest readers who liked Louis Begley's *About Schmidt*."

—*Library Journal*

"Part of what makes the novel so successful is that Lee isn't intent on blowing sunshine at us when we know life brings its share of bad weather. He succeeds in portraying the emotional growth of a man in terms that fit his character and culture. . . . *Aloft* views suburban American life through the universal prism of a family growing up and growing old together. Without loop-the-loops or skywriting, Lee brings us quietly down to earth, engaging us in 'the mystery and majesty of our brief living.'"

—*Rocky Mountain News*

continued . . .

"A major step forward for Lee . . . Jerry's voice is raucous, silly, discursive, humorously profane, and entirely human."

—*Newsday*

"Out of this tangle of family crises and personal angst, Chang-rae Lee has spun a beautifully nuanced novel of alienation and reconciliation. The literary landscape has been plowed before, by the likes of John Updike and Richard Ford. But the sardonic humor of Lee's first-person narrative, his spirited characters, and his insights into the tug of memory on second- and third-generation immigrants are all his own. They, like Lee, who was born in Korea and came to the United States with his parents at the age of three, have melded into the multicultural crazy quilt of American life. . . . An exhilarating ride. As he showed in his two previous novels, *Native Speaker* and *A Gesture Life,* Lee is a shrewd, large-hearted observer of the human condition. He leaves his readers eager for the next chapter."

—*Milwaukee Journal Sentinel*

"Jerry Battle talks about Long Island in a funny, literate way that's a cross between John Cheever and Richard Ford, with a few Philip Roth rants thrown in for good measure."

—*The Sunday Oregonian*

"Chang-rae Lee's *Aloft* is a triumph of the human voice—the voice of Jerry Battle, a fly boy lost in the wild blue yonder, free as the breeze to indulge in ironies, erotic daydreams, and hilarious riffs, until mortality tugs him down to earth again, ground zero. There he learns at last how little distinction there is between 'falling and flying . . . fearing and fighting,' going on automatic pilot yet guiding and speaking for the race. A remarkable novel, full of humility, full of hope." —Robert Fagles

"Generously ruminative. . . . Beautiful writing, richly drawn characters, and a powerful sense of life enduring in spite of all. A fine and very moving performance." —*Kirkus Reviews*

PRAISE FOR

A Gesture Life

"What gives *A Gesture Life* its arresting pathos is the tone of Hata's voice: he tries to speak as he tries to live, with clarity and self-possession. . . . Hata is a fine, full-blooded creation, the kind of man who exists everywhere but far too seldom in literature. Lee brings him quietly to life. . . . The accretion of wisdom in Lee's novel is stunning. He expertly evokes the collision of unacceptable truth with the illusion of workaday serenity. . . . It's a beautiful, solitary, remarkably tender book."

—*The New York Times Book Review*

"Quietly stunning. . . . In an elegantly controlled narrative, Lee makes Hata's tortuous dilemma agonizingly real. . . . This is a wise, humane, fully rounded story, deeply but unsentimentally moving, and permeated with insights about the nature of human relationships. If Lee's first novel was an impressive debut, this one marks the solid establishment of a stellar literary career." —*Publishers Weekly* (starred, boxed review)

"[Lee] spin[s] his tale with the kind of deceptive ease often aspired to but seldom achieved . . . universal in its vision . . . A luminous novel of love, loss, and longing." —*People*

"Lee elegantly creates suspense out of the seemingly static story of a man trying hard not to feel. He has written a wise and humane novel that both amplifies the themes of identity and exile he addressed in *Native Speaker*, and creates a wonderfully resonant portrait of a man caught between two cultures and two lives." —Michiko Kakutani, *The New York Times*

"By rights, [*A Gesture Life*] should be depressing. But the writing is sure and convincing, the characters vivid, and the war story unforgettable. By the end of this masterly novel, all we are is exhilarated." —*Newsweek*

continued . . .

PRAISE FOR

Native Speaker

"*Native Speaker* brims with intrigue and political high jinks. . . . A tender meditation on love, loss, and family . . . A rapturous evocation of a past life, viewed across a great gap of time and culture." —*The New York Times Book Review*

"If there is such a thing as a genre of first novels, *Native Speaker* subverts the conventions of that genre. It takes as its subjects the things that often preoccupy novelists on their first outing—language, family, identity—and turns them inside out, making literal what is usually only metaphorical. . . . The prose Lee writes is elliptical, riddling, poetic, often beautifully made."

—*The New Yorker*

"Absorbing . . . Masterfully written—you can almost taste Lee's Manhattan. . . . Ultimately, *Native Speaker* is a broad reflection on the fragility of society's primal forces—marriage, blood, race, love. Lee writes with tremendous insight and respect for such forces, avoiding clichéd sentimentalism. And yet he leaves readers with a lingering hope, a faint smile, a new appreciation that there are native speakers from many countries, each with stories equally compelling. . . . Rarely are such stories so wonderfully rendered." —*USA Today*

"With echoes of Ralph Ellison, Chang-rae Lee's extraordinary debut speaks for another kind of invisible man: the Asian immigrant in America. . . . With lyrical prose and compelling explorations of language, culture, and identity, Lee rises above politically correct formulas, and the result is a revelatory work of fiction." —*Vogue*

ALSO BY CHANG-RAE LEE

Native Speaker

A Gesture Life

aloft

CHANG-RAE LEE

RIVERHEAD BOOKS

New York

The Berkley Publishing Group
Published by the Penguin Group
Penguin Group (USA) Inc.
375 Hudson Street, New York, New York 10014, USA
Penguin Group (Canada), 10 Alcorn Avenue, Toronto, Ontario M4V 3B2, Canada
(a division of Pearson Canada Inc.)
Penguin Books Ltd., 80 Strand, London WC2R 0RL, England
Penguin Group Ireland, 25 St. Stephen's Green, Dublin 2, Ireland (a division of Penguin Books Ltd.)
Penguin Group (Australia), 250 Camberwell Road, Camberwell, Victoria 3124, Australia
(a division of Pearson Australia Group Pty Ltd.)
Penguin Books India Pvt. Ltd., 11 Community Centre, Panchsheel Park, New Delhi—110 017, India
Penguin Books (N.Z.), cnr Airborne and Rosedale Roads, Albany, Auckland 1310, New Zealand
(a division of Pearson New Zealand Ltd.)
Penguin Books (South Africa) (Pty.) Ltd., 24 Sturdee Avenue, Rosebank, Johannesburg 2196,
South Africa

Penguin Books Ltd., Registered Offices: 80 Strand, London WC2R 0RL, England

Cover design by Honi Werner
Book design by Amanda Dewey

PRINTING HISTORY
First Riverhead hardcover edition: March 2004
First Riverhead trade paperback edition: March 2005
Riverhead trade paperback ISBN: 1-59448-070-2

The Library of Congress has catalogued the Riverhead hardcover edition as follows:

Lee, Chang-rae.
Aloft / Chang-rae Lee.
p. cm.
ISBN 1-57322-263-1
1. Middle class men—Fiction. 2. Suburban life—Fiction. I. Title.
PS3562.E3347A79 2004 2003058630
813'.54—dc22

PRINTED IN THE UNITED STATES OF AMERICA

10 9 8 7 6 5 4 3 2 1

To Michelle,

for all the love

one

FROM UP HERE, a half mile above the Earth, everything looks perfect to me.

I am in my nifty little Skyhawk, banking her back into the sun, having nearly completed my usual fair-weather loop. Below is the eastern end of Long Island, and I'm flying just now over that part of the land where the two gnarly forks shoot out into the Atlantic. The town directly ahead, which is nothing special when you're on foot, looks pretty magnificent now, the late-summer sun casting upon the macadam of the streets a soft, ebonized sheen, its orangey light reflecting back at me, matching my direction and speed in the windows and bumpers of the parked cars and swimming pools of the simple, square houses set snugly in rows. There is a mysterious, runelike cipher to the newer, larger homes wagoning in their cul-de-sac hoops, and then, too, in the flat roofs of the shopping mall buildings, with their shiny metal circuitry of HVAC housings and tubes.

From up here, all the trees seem ideally formed and

arranged, as if fretted over by a persnickety florist god, even the ones (no doubt volunteers) clumped along the fencing of the big scrap metal lot, their spindly, leggy uprush not just a pleasing garnish to the variegated piles of old hubcaps and washing machines, but then, for a stock guy like me, mere heartbeats shy of *sixty* (hard to even say that), the life signs of a positively priapic yearning. Just to the south, on the baseball diamond—our people's pattern supreme—the local Little League game is entering the late innings, the baby-blue-shirted players positioned straightaway and shallow, in the bleachers their parents only appearing to sit church-quiet and still, the sole perceivable movement a bounding golden-haired dog tracking down a Frisbee in deep, deep centerfield.

Go, boy, go.

And as I point my ship—*Donnie* is her name—to track alongside the broad arterial lanes of Route 495, the great and awful Long Island Expressway, and see the already-accrued jams of the Sunday Hamptons traffic inching back to the city, the grinding columns of which, from my seat, appear to constitute an orderly long march, I feel as if I'm going at a heady light speed, certainly moving too fast in relation to the rest, an imparity that should by any account invigorate but somehow unsettles all the same, and I veer a couple of degrees northwest to head over the remaining patchworks of farmland and scrubby forest and then soon enough the immense, uninterrupted stretch of older, densely built townships like mine, where beneath the obscuring canopy men like me are going about the last details of their weekend business, sweeping their front walks and dragging trash cans to the street and washing their cars just as they have since boyhood and youth, soaping from top to bottom and brushing the wheels of sooty brake dust, one spoke at a time.

And I know, too, from up here, that I can't see the messy rest, none of the pedestrian, sea-level flotsam that surely blemishes our good scene, the casually tossed super-size Slurpies and grubby confetti of a million cigarette butts, the ever-creeping sidewalk mosses and weeds; I can't see the tumbling faded newspaper circular page, or the dead, gassy possum beached at the foot of the curb, the why of its tight, yellow-toothed grin.

All of which, for the moment, is more than okay with me.

Is that okay?

Okay.

I bought this plane not for work or travel or the pure wondrous thrill of flight, which can and has, indeed, been scarily, transcendentally life-affirming and so on, but for the no doubt seriously unexamined reason of my just having to get out of the house.

That's certainly what my longtime (and recently ex-) girlfriend, Rita Reyes, was thinking about several years ago, when she gave me a flying lesson out at Islip for my birthday. Really, of course, she meant it as a diversionary excursion, just a hands-on plane ride, never intending it to lead to anything else.

At the time she was deeply worried about me, as I was a year into having early-retired from the family landscaping business and was by all indications mired in a black hole of a rut, basically moping around the house and snacking too much. On weekdays, after Rita left for her job as a home-care nurse (she now works the ER), I'd do my usual skim of the paper in front of the TV and then maybe watch a ladies' morning talk show and soon enough I'd feel this sharp nudge of ennui and I'd head to the nearby Walt Whitman Mall (the poet was born in a modest house right across the street, which is now something they call an "interpretive center" and is open for tours) for what I would always hope was the easeful company of like-minded people but would end up instead, depending on the selling season, to be frantic clawing hordes or else a ghost town of seniors sitting by the islands of potted ficus, depressing and diminishing instances both.

When Rita came back home, the breakfast dishes would still be clogging the table, and I'd be on the back patio nursing a third bottle of light beer or else napping in the den after leafing through my tattered *Baedeker's Italy* for the umpteenth time. She'd try to be helpful and patient but it was hard, as that's what she'd done all day long. More often than not we'd end up in a shouting match because she'd toss aside my guidebook a bit too casually and I'd say something loose and mean about her mother, and she'd retreat to the bedroom while I went to the car and revved the engine inside for a long minute before clicking open the garage door. I'd find myself at a run-down Chinese place on Jericho, chasing a too-sweet Mai Tai with wonton soup for dinner and then phoning Rita, to see if she wanted her usual pupu platter appetizer and shrimp with black beans, which she would, and which I'd bring back and duly serve to her, as the saying goes, with love and squalor.

All this began occurring too regularly and finally Rita told me I had better get into something to take up my time, even if it was totally useless and shallow. Immediately I thought maybe it was finally time I strapped myself into a convertible sports car or fast boat, some honeyed, wet-look motor that the neighbors would gape at and maybe snicker and whisper *micropenis* about and then pine after, too, but I wanted something else, not quite knowing what exactly until the moment I opened the gift certificate from Rita for Flaherty's Top Gun Flight School.

I must say I was nervous that day, even downright afraid, which was strange because I've flown in hundreds of planes, some of them single-engine like this one and certainly not as kept-up. I could hardly finish my breakfast toast and coffee. I kept trying and failing to pee, all the while thinking how it was that a person should die exactly on his birthday, how maudlin and rare, and so also a bit pathetic if it actually did happen, especially if you weren't someone famous, all of which Rita caught on to, fake eulogizing me all morning with hushed phrasings of "And he was *exactly* fifty-six. . . ."

But I could tell she was worried, too, for she wouldn't kiss me or even look me in the eye when I was leaving for the airfield, hardly glancing up from her cooking magazine as she murmured a casual, if all swallowed-up, goodbye. Sweet moment, potentially, as it should have been, with me supposed to drop my car keys back into the loose-change bowl and saunter over to Rita in my new aviator shades and cup her silky butterscotch breast through the opening of her robe and assure us both of the righteous tenure of our (then nearly twenty) years of devotion and love; but what did I do but mutter goodbye back and mention that I'd be home in time for lunch and could that osso buco she'd made two nights ago be heated up with extra orzo, or maybe even some couscous with snips of fresh mint? Rita, of course, responded with her usual "No problem," which anyone else even half-listening would think was a dirge of pure defeat and trouble but was long my favorite tune.

So I drove off with my sights set high again, for there's little else more inspiring to me than the promise of a hot savory meal prepared by a good woman. But the second I entered the private plane entrance at MacArthur Field and saw the spindly wing struts and narrow fuselages of the parked Pipers and Cessnas, my heart caved a little and I thought of my grown children, Theresa and Jack, and immediately speed-dialed them on my cell phone. I was ready to say to each the very same thing, that I was deeply proud of their accomplishments and their character and that I wished I could relive again those brief years of their infancy and childhood, and then add, too, that I would never burden them in my decline and that they should always call Rita on her birthday and holidays.

But then Theresa's English Department voice-mail picked up, not her voice but the ubiquitous female voice of Central Messaging, and all I could manage was to say I hadn't heard from her in a while and wondered if anything was wrong. Next I got Jack's voice-mail, this time Jack's voice, but he sounded so businesslike and remote that I left a message for him in the voice of Mr. T, all gruff and belligerent, threatening to open a big can of whoop-ass on him if he didn't lighten up.

This, too, didn't come out quite right, and as I was still early for the flying lesson, I called my father, who would certainly be in.

He answered, "Who the hell is this?"

"It's me, Pop. How you doing?"

"Oh. You. How do you think I'm doing?"

"Just fine, I'm betting."

"That's what you want to think. Anyway, come down and spring me out of here. I'm packed and ready to go."

"All right, Pop. The nurses treating you well?"

"They treat me like dog shit. But that's what I'm paying for. What I worked for all my stinking life, so I can wear a gown and eat airline food every meal and have a male nurse with tattooed palms wipe my ass."

"You don't need anybody to do that for you."

"You haven't been around lately, Jerome. You don't know. You don't know that this is the place where they make the world's boredom and isolation. This is where they purify it. It's monstrous. And what they're doing to Nonna over in the ladies' wing, I can't even mention."

Nonna was his wife, and my mother, and at that point she had been in the brass urn for five years. Pop is by most measures fine in the head, though it seemed around that period that anything having to do with mortality and time often got scrambled in the relevant lobes, a development that diminished only somewhat my feelings of filial betrayal and guilt for placing him via power of attorney into the Ivy Acres Life Care Center, where for $5500 per month he will live out the rest of his days in complete security and comfort and without a worldly care, which we know is simple solution and problem all in one, which we can do nothing about, which we do all to forget.

"I'm taking a flying lesson today, Pop."

"Oh yeah?"

"Have any words for me?"

"I never got to fly a plane," he growled, and not in response to me. "I never rode in a hot-air balloon. I never made love to two women at once."

"I'm sure that can be arranged."

"Aah, don't bother. I don't need any more examples of my sorry ass. Just do me one favor."

"You name it, Pop."

"If you're going down, try to make it over here. Top corner of the building, looking right over the parking lot. Aim at the old bag waving in the window."

"Forget it."

"You are not my son."

"Yeah, Pop. I'll see you."

"Whatever."

One of our usual goodbyes, from the thin catalogue of father-son biddings, thinner still for the time of life and circumstance and then, of course, for the players involved, who have never transgressed the terms of engagement, who have never even ridden the line. I then walked into the hangar office with a light-on-my-feet feeling, not like a giddiness or anxiety but an unnerving sense of being dangerously unmoored, as though I were some astronaut creeping out into the grand maw of space, eternities roiling in the background, with too much slack in my measly little line. And it occurred to me that in this new millennial life of instant and ubiquitous connection, you don't in fact communicate so much as leave messages for one another, these odd improvisational performances, often sorry bits and samplings of ourselves that can't help but seem out of context. And then when you do finally reach someone, everyone's so out of practice or too hopeful or else embittered that you wonder if it would be better not to attempt contact at all.

And yet I forgot all that when I finally got up off the deck, into the *Up here.* I won't go into the first blush of feelings and sensations but summarize to say only that my first thought when the instructor let me take the controls was that I wished he'd strapped a chute on himself, so he could jump the hell out. Nothing in the least was wrong with him—he was a nice, if alarmingly young, kid from an extended family of pilots, the Flahertys. But feeling the motor's buzz in my butt and legs, the shuddery lift of the wingtips in my hands, and gazing down just this middle distance on the world, this fetching, ever-mitigating length, I kept thinking that here was the little room, the little vessel, I was looking for, my private box seat in the world and completely outside of it, too.

After we landed and taxied toward the hangar I peppered the kid pilot for his opinion on what sort of plane I should buy and where I might find one. Through his big amber sunglasses (same as mine) he nodded to a three-seat Cessna with green stripes parked on the tarmac and told me it was for sale by a guy who had suffered a stroke on his last flight, though he had obviously weathered it and somehow brought himself in. It was an older plane, the kid said into his squawky microphone, in his clipped, mini–Chuck Yeager voice, but a reliable one and in good shape. It had been on the market for a while and I could probably get it at a good price. It wasn't the sort of plane I'd want if I was thinking about zipping back and forth across the country, but for shorter, leisure junkets it'd be ideal, which seemed just fine to me. Inside the hangar office the secretary gave me the guy's number, and it turned out he lived in the town next to mine, so on the drive back home I called and introduced myself to his friendly wife and we decided why shouldn't I come over right then and talk about it with her husband, Hal?

Their house was an attractive cedar-shingled colonial, built in the 1960s like a lot of houses in this part of Long Island, including mine, when the area was still mostly potato fields and duck farms and unsullied stretches of low-slung trees and good scrubby nothingness. Now the land is filled with established developments and newer ones from the '80s, and with the last boom having catapulted everyone over the ramparts there's still earthmoving equipment to be seen on either side of the Expressway (eight lanes wide now), clearing the remaining natural tracts for the instant office parks and upscale condos and assisted living centers, and then the McMansions where young families like my son Jack's live, with their vaulted great rooms and multimedia rooms and wine and cigar *caves.* I should say I'm not against any of these things, per se, because it seems to me only right that people should play and work as they please in this so-called democratic life, and even as I'm damn proud of my son Jack's wholly climate-controlled existence (despite the fact that we don't really talk much anymore), there is another part of me that naturally wonders how this rush of prosperity is ruining him and Eunice and the kids and then everybody else who has money enough not to have to really think so deeply about money but does all the time anyway, wherever they are.

A national demography of which, I suppose, I've been an integral part, though in the past few years—since getting this plane, in fact—I've realized I have more than plenty, if plenty means I can ride out the next twenty or so years of my life expectancy not having to eat dried soup noodles if I don't want to or call one of Jack's employees instead of a real plumber or always remember to press my driver's license against the ticket window for the senior citizen rate at the multiplex. And though I've never had enough real surplus or the balls to invest in the stock market (an unexpiable sin in recent years, though now I'm a certified financial genius for socking away everything I have in Treasuries), unless I'm struck down by some ruinous long-term disability, I'll be okay. Oh you poor-mouthing owner of a private plane, you might be thinking, and rightly, for the Cessna did cost nearly as much as a big Mercedes, and isn't cheap to maintain. But in my defense, I still live in the same modest starter house I bought just before Jack was born, and never wore clothes I didn't buy at Alexander's and Ward's (now at Costco and Target—my longtime patronage clearly no help to the former defunct), or dined if I could help it in any restaurant, no matter how good, with menu prices spelled out in greeting card script. And if this plane is indeed my life's folly, well, at least I found one before it's too late, when the only juiced feeling of the day will be yet another heartbreakingly tragic History Channel biography on a nineteenth-century explorer or the *ring-ring* of some not-quite-as-old coot at the door delivering my day's foil-wrapped meal-on-wheels.

When I got to the stricken pilot's house his friendly wife, Shari, greeted me and then suddenly gave me a quick hug in the foyer, and so I hugged her back, as if I were an old war buddy of his and she and I had had our flirtations through the years, transgressions which I would not have minded, given her sturdy nice shape and pretty mouth. She showed me into the big, dark faux-walnut-paneled den, where a man in a baseball cap and crisp button-down shirt was sitting in an uncomfortable-looking wooden armchair with a plaid blanket spread over his legs. The place was freezing, as though they had the air set to 62 degrees. The cable was on but he was faced more toward the sliding glass door than the TV set, looking out on the covered deck, where they had propped a trio of silky-looking cardinals on the rim of an ornate plastic birdbath. The birds were amazingly realistic in detail, with shiny yellow beaks and black-masked faces, except perhaps that they were way too big, but I'd never been that close to such birds and I figured most things in the natural world were bigger than you thought, brighter and more vibrant and more real than real. As we approached, it was clear that he was dozing, and for a long almost parental second we stood over him, Shari pulling up the blanket that was half slipping off.

"Hal, honey," she said. "Mr. Battle is here. About the plane."

"Uh-hum," he said, clearing his throat. He extended his hand and we shook.

"Well, I'll let you two boys talk," Shari said, excusing herself to fix us some iced tea.

Hal said, "Sit right down there, young fella," pointing to the leather couch with his one good arm.

Hal wasn't that much older than I was, if he was older at all, but I guess his condition gave him the right to address me so, which didn't bother me. He spoke out of the same good side of his mouth, with a whistley, spitty sound that was boyish and youthful. He asked what I did for a living and I told him it used to be landscaping, and he told me he was a private driver, or was until his stroke, the kind who drove around executives and VIPs in regular black sedans. He was a nice-looking fellow, with a neatly clipped salt-and-pepper mustache and beard. And I should probably not so parenthetically mention right now that Hal was black. This surprised me, first because Shari wasn't, being instead your typical Long Island white lady in tomato-red shorts and a stenciled designer T-shirt, and then because there aren't many minorities in this area, period, and even fewer who are hobbyist pilots, a fact since borne out in my three years of hanging out at scrubby airfields. Of course, my exceedingly literate, overeducated daughter Theresa (Stanford Ph.D.) would say as she has in the past that I have to mention all this because like most people in this country I'm hopelessly obsessed with race and difference and can't help but *privilege* the *normative* and *fetishize* what's not. And while I'm never fully certain of her terminology, I'd like to think that if I am indeed guilty of such things it's mostly because sometimes I worry for her and Jack, who, I should mention, too, aren't wholly normative of race themselves, being "mixed" from my first and only marriage to a woman named Daisy Han.

"What's your name again?"

"Jerry. Jerry Battle."

"So, Jerry Battle, you want to buy a plane."

"I believe so," I said. "There's nothing like the freedom of flight."

"You bet. But listen, friend. Let me be up front with you. A lot of guys have been by here who weren't really sure. Now, I'd love to chat but you won't be insulting me if you decided right now this wasn't right for you."

"I think it is."

"You sure?" he said, staring me straight in the eye. I nodded, though in fact I was starting to wonder.

"Because sometimes guys realize at the last second they don't want to buy a *used* plane. You know what I'm talking about, Jerry?"

He was looking at me queerly, and then suddenly I thought I did know what he was talking about. I remembered a client with a mansion in Old Westbury, beautiful place except they'd had a lot of diseased trees, and we'd come in and replaced all of them and did a lot of patio and pool work and redid the formal gardens. After that the place was mint. But the husband took a new job in California and they put it on the market, for whatever millions. They had lots of lookers, but no offers, so they lowered the price, twice in fact. But still nothing. So the listing agent suggested they consider "depersonalizing" the house, by which she meant taking down the family pictures, and anything else like it, as the owners were black. They were thoroughly offended, but no one was biting and so finally the husband said they would, but then only if they listed the house at the original price. They ended up getting several overbids, and eventually sold to a party who'd looked the first time around.

So I told Hal, looking right at him, that I didn't mind a good used plane.

"Okay, good. Now. How long have you been flying?"

"A good while now," I said, thinking of course of my many hundred hours at the helm in coach, tray table ready. I don't know why I felt the need to lie to the man. Normally I wouldn't care if he knew I'd just touched down from my very first lesson and he thought I was crazy, but I guess seeing him like that, sitting invalid-style, made me think it might somehow push him over the edge to know a complete beginner would be manning his plane.

"I'm looking forward to pride of ownership," I said, hoping this might sound suitably virtuous, to us both. "Take my interest to the next level. As it were."

Hal nodded, though I couldn't tell from the expression on his half-frozen face if he was agreeing or was now on to me.

He said, "I bought the plane ten years ago. This just after my son Donnie was killed. Donnie was going to start medical school at BU. Six-year program. You know about that?"

"I think one of my customers' kids is in it. He got a perfect score on his SATs."

"Donnie did, too."

"No kidding."

"Some people don't believe me when I tell them, but you don't lie about something like that. You can't pretend yourself into perfection."

"I guess not."

"No way," Hal said, shifting in the hard wooden chair. You'd think he'd have a cushy, blobby-layered TV recliner (like I have at home), something upholstered in a pastel-colored leather with a built-in telephone and cup holder and magazine caddy that he could fall into to vegetate until the next meal or when nature called, but you could gather from the showroom setup of the house that Hal was the sort of fellow who preferred the rigor of the bench, who always had a dozen needle-sharp pencils ready on his desk, who believed in the chi of spit-shined shoes and a classic, cherry motor humming with fresh amber oil.

"Before he died I was in your situation," he said, glancing at me, "just getting up when I could, renting planes wherever we went on vacation, you know, to get the overview."

"Exactly."

"I would've gone on like that. Been happy with it. But then Donnie had the head-on with the drunk driver. Son of a bitch has been out of jail for a few years now. On the anniversary day of the accident I go over to his place in Melville and sit out front with a picture of my son. Shari doesn't like me to do it but it's not like I have a choice. That man is not going to forget Donnie. Nobody is."

Just then Shari came back in, bearing a tray of three tall plastic tumblers of iced tea, each bobbed with a straw. She seemed to know what Hal was talking about, because she left her drink on the tray and without a word went outside on the deck, sliding the glass door closed behind her, and began culling the plants for withered blooms. Our clingy hug in the foyer should have clued me in to where this visit was headed, how every other stranger you bump into these days (or try to buy something from) has the compulsion to unfurl the precious old remnant of his life for you, his own tatter of a war story, which would be bad enough but for the companion fact that those closest to you seem to clam up at every chance of genuine kinship, with undue prejudice. But I was here now and still interested in buying the plane and this was probably the last wholly appropriate occasion Hal would have to tell his story, which no decent citizen of this world, and certainly not Jerry Battle, could rightly refuse to hear.

Hal took a long sip through his straw, nearly finishing his drink in one take. "After things got settled down I realized I had all this money set aside for him, for tuition and the rest of it. It wasn't going to cover the whole shot but it was enough to get him going, you know, so he wouldn't be pinned with all the debts when he was done."

"That's great."

"It *was* great. But now what? All of a sudden I'm looking at this big pile of cash." Hal laughed tightly, in the way he could laugh, which was like a form of strained, intense breathing. "What do you do with something like that?"

"I'm not sure, Hal."

"Well, Shari felt we ought to give the money to charity. Maybe to the medical school, for a scholarship in Donnie's name. A scholarship was fine with me, Jerry, because it's not like I didn't have a decent war chest going for our retirement, which thank God we have now. I'm not too proud to say we've always been set up right, in regard to our family. But Donnie was a good kid, bright and talented, but most of all just plain good, and I got to thinking he didn't need to be memorialized by us, at least in those usual ways. He never flew with me, because his mother didn't trust the rental planes, but he always wanted to, and I got to feeling that maybe he would think it was kind of neat that I bought a plane with his medical school money."

"I'm sure he's tickled."

"Thank you for saying that, Jerry," he said. "When I was having the stroke up there, I was thinking just that. Actually I wasn't thinking anything for a little while, because I was seizing. Lucky for me I was at 9500 feet when it hit. I must have spiraled down in a wide circle, who knows how many minutes of blind flying, because when I looked out again I was only at about 300 feet, and crossing right over the Expressway. I could see some kids slap-fighting in the back of a minivan, and the first thing that came to mind was that this was my son Donnie's ship, dammit, and I ought to be more careful with her. There was no way I wasn't going to bring her in. I knew it was the last real thing I was supposed to do."

"It's amazing you were able to land, using just one arm and one leg."

"It's hard to know for sure," Hal said, rubbing his face, "but I'm almost certain I still had use of my entire body. The doctors told me it's unlikely, even impossible, but I know they're wrong. There are mysteries, Jerry, when it comes to the body and mind. Take Donnie, for instance. He didn't die at the scene. He was in a coma for five days in the ICU. On the fifth day he sat right up in his bed and told me that he was already dead. Shari wasn't there, she was down in the cafeteria getting us fresh coffee. I was shocked that he was awake but I said, 'What do you mean, son, listen to yourself, you're alive.' And Donnie said, 'No, Dad, it just looks like I am. I died on that road, and you know it.' I decided to play along, because I didn't want to upset him, and because I was so happy to be talking to him, and I asked him what it was like, to be dead. And do you know what he told me, Jerry?"

I shook my head, because I didn't want to know, actually, death not being a state I've found myself terribly interested in, then or now or come any day in the future.

"He said it was nice and bright and chilly, like a supermarket. And that there was no one else around."

"He was alone?"

"You got it. Like he had the place all to himself. But he said it was okay, really fine. Then he got tired and lay back down. By the time Shari was back, he'd dropped back in the coma again. And he never woke up."

Shari came in from the deck and she saw Hal's face all screwed up, and instantly I could see she was trying her best to hold it together. I made the mistake of going over and gripping Hal's shoulder, and both he and Shari lost it. Before I knew it we were all huddled together, and Hal was wheezing like his windpipe was cracked and Shari's face was buried in my neck, her muted sobs alternating with what felt like delicate, open-mouthed kisses but were just her crying eyes. I glanced at Hal, who was covering his own face with his good arm, and as I stood up with Shari still draped on my shoulders, Hal mumbled, "If you two would please excuse me for a moment."

So I followed Shari into the kitchen, not unmoved by the display but also half-dreading an imminent Part II, HerStory, in which Jerry Battle would learn of the Turbulent Early Years, and the Cherub Donnie, and then of Waning Passions: A Late-Middle Passage, life chapters or what have you that I could certainly relate to and mourn and hallow with neighborly unction and sobriety, but that I would be wishing to decline, decline. But perhaps it was too late for all that, or simply that we were in her spotless kitchen, as Shari slipped into hausfrau mode and gave me a fresh glass of iced tea and a plate of oatmeal cookies and we were soon chatting about garbage pickup days and the recent spike in our property taxes, which would hurt retired folks and other people like them on fixed incomes. Apparently Hal had overstated their financial condition. They really had to sell the plane. Shari said they might even have to sell the house and move to a condo, though she said this almost matter-of-factly, without a hint of whine or anger, and for a moment she sounded just like my long-dead wife, Daisy, who, when not caught up in one of her hot blooms of madness, featured the casual and grave acceptance of someone who works outdoors and is once again caught in a lingering rain.

After a short while I told Shari I'd mail a check for the price they were asking, if that was all right.

"You're not going to bargain a little?"

"Should I?"

"I don't know," she said. "This seems too easy. We've been trying to sell it for half a year."

"I got that from Hal. Why it's been difficult."

"Oh that, that's poppycock," she said. "If anything, it's because they come and see him like he is, and they think the plane has bad luck."

"Does it?"

She paused, and then said, without looking at me, "No."

"Good," I said, though in fact for the first time since coming up with the whole headlong idea at the field I felt a little off-kilter, and scared. "Then it's settled, okay?"

"Okay, Jerry," she said, clasping my hand.

We went to tell Hal that the deal was done but he was fast asleep in his chair in the den, a wide slick of drool shimmying down his chin. Shari produced a hankie from her shorts pocket and wiped him with a deft stroke. He didn't budge. We tiptoed to the door and Shari thanked me for coming by and dealing with everything and helping them out, and I told her it was my privilege and honor to do so but that I certainly didn't believe I was helping them. And yet, all I could think of as we stepped out on the front stoop was that the rap sheet on me documented just this kind of thing, that I'm one to leap up from the mat to aid all manner of strangers and tourists and other wide-eyed foreigners but when it comes to loved ones and family I can hardly ungear myself from the La-Z-Boy, and want only succor and happy sufferance in return.

Shari and I hugged once more, but then she surprised me with a quick, dry peck on the mouth. On the mouth.

"I'm sorry," Shari said, stepping back. "I didn't mean that."

"Hey," I told her, my hands raised. "No harm done. See?"

Shari nodded, though I could tell she was feeling as if *something* was just done. She stood there on the stoop, self-horrified, trying to cover herself with her arms. Normally I would have begged off right then, made some lame excuse and neatly backslid to my car, but I couldn't bear to leave her hanging like that, so I wrapped my arms around her and closed my eyes and kissed her with whatever sweet force and tenderness I could muster, not even pretending she was my Rita, and not sorry about it either, except for the fact that I did enjoy it, too, at least macrocosmically, the notion of kissing a thoroughly decent and pretty woman who was another man's wife and not needing to push the moment a hair past its tolerances. And I think that it was in this spirit that Shari perhaps liked it, too, or appreciated the squareness of it, its gestural, third-person quality, whatever or whatever, for after we relented and let each other go she broke into this wide, wan, near-beatific smile, and then disappeared into the house. I waited a second, then got into my car and backed out of the driveway, when Shari came out again. She handed me two sets of keys to the plane.

"But I haven't paid you guys yet."

"I know you will," she said. "Just promise you'll look after it and keep it safe."

I told her I would. And then the awkwardness of the moment made me say that if she ever wanted to fly in the plane again, she could call me.

"I don't think so," she said. "But thank you. And don't forget what Hal always says."

"What's that?" I asked.

" 'There's no point in flying if you can't fly alone.' "

SOUND ADVICE, I believe, which I have tried to take to heart.

So here I am, afloat in the bright clear, surveying the open sky, measuring only what I fancy. I could go around again, which I sometimes do, swing back west past the spired city and over the leafy hillocks of northern Jersey, and if I desired make a quick landing at Teterboro and take a taxi to the taco stand in Little Ferry for an early dinner of chili verde and iced guava juice, then get up again and head south past the petro-industrial works of Elizabeth (not unbeautiful from up here), swing up the harbor and check the skyline for where the Twin Towers used to be, and then fly right along the pencil strip of Fire Island before I'd bank again, to head home for MacArthur. It's the grand tour of the metropolis I'd give if I ever did such things, or even fly with anyone else, which I rarely do anymore, and I doubt I will again. Indeed it turns out I'm a solo flyer, for a number of reasons I won't get into right now, but just say that it makes sense to me, and did right from the start.

Still, sometimes I wish I could bring Rita up here again, fly with her the way I used to on the clearest days to Maine or Nantucket, where we'd split a big lobster and bucket of steamer clams on the bleached sundeck of some harborside restaurant, browse the handicraft and junktique shops, maybe buy a bag of fudge or saltwater taffy, then fly back on buffets of just this kind of light, not talking much at all on our headsets save a name and then nod to whatever not-quite-wish-fulfilling town we happened to be passing over: *Providence. New Haven. Orient Point.* I'd land us as smooth as I could (touchdown the only part that scared her), then drive us back to the house with the top down in the old emerald Impala, our positions just the same, almost preternaturally so—man and woman in fast-moving conveyance—and we'd shower together and maybe make love and then nap like unweaned pups until the darkness fell, when we'd arise for a few hours to straighten up the house before the workweek began again the next day.

Now, I bring in my ship the usual way, making sure I fly over my house, which I can often spot without much trouble but is forever unmistakable now, ever since right after buying *Donnie* I had a roofing contractor lay in slightly darker-shaded shingles in the form of a wide, squat X. You can only see it clearly from up here, which is good because most of my neighbors would probably report me to the town if it were obvious from the street. I had it done for Rita, in fact, for she always asked me to point out our place from the air, which I did but to no use, as she could never quite find it anyway. I must say the sight still always warms me, not just for the raw-meat feeling that I've marked my spot, but for the idea that anyone flying or ballooning overhead might just wonder who was doing such a thing, this mystery man calling out from deep in the suburban wood.

Which would be somewhat ironic, because increasingly it seems I'm not a mystery to anyone, the very fact of which, as has been made more than clear to me on a number of occasions, is part of my so-called life problem. This from Theresa, mostly, though also from Jack (in Surround Sound silence), and from my once-loving Rita, each of whom holds to a private version of the notion, furious and true. The only one who seems unable to fathom my evidently patent, roughshod ways is my ailing father, who continues to misread my every motive and move, with the resulting accrual of enmity and suspicion steadily drowning out the few remaining vitalities of his mind (yet another mirthless progression to be considered and acted upon, and alarmingly soon). If anything, I'm afraid, he and I are long-steeped in a mystery without poetry, a father-son brew not just particular to us, of course, though ours is special recipe enough, and like the rest warrants further parsing, which I must try, try.

And as I aim my sweet ship in line with the field, I can just barely glimpse the X in the distance, faded enough from these brief seasons that it reads like a watermark on the broad, gently pitched roof of my ranch-style house, and the temptation is to interpret this muted-ness as muteness, my signage ever faint, and disappearing. This is probably true. I am disappearing. But let me reveal a secret. I have been disappearing for years.

two

FOR MOST OF MY LIFE I worked in the family business, Battle Brothers Brick & Mortar, a masonry company that my grandfather started in the Depression and that my father and uncles gradually turned into a landscaping company that I maintained and that Jack has plans for expanding into a publicly traded specialty home improvement enterprise to be renamed Battle Brothers Excalibur, L.L.C. (OTC ticker symbol: BBXS), replete with a glossy annual report and standby telephone operators and an Internet website.

The family name was originally Battaglia, but my father and uncles decided early on to change their name to Battle for the usual reasons immigrants and others like them will do, for the sake of familiarity and ease of use and to herald a new and optimistic beginning, which is anyone's God-given right, whether warranted or not.

Battle, too, is a nice name for a business, because it's simple and memorable, ethnically indistinct, and then squarely patriotic, though in a subtle sort of way. Customers—Jack says *clients*—have the sense we're fighters, that we have an inner resolve, that we'll soldier through all obstacles to get the job done, and done right (this last line can actually be found in the latest company brochure). My father insists that the idea for the name originated with him, and for just the connotations I've mentioned, which I don't doubt, as he was always the savviest businessman of his brothers, and talked incessantly through my youth about the awesome power of words, from Shakespeare to Hitler, though these days he mostly just brings up his favorite blabbermouths on the Fox News Channel. But it's not just marketing—for the most part the tag has been true, though certainly more so in my father's generation than my own, probably more in mine than in Jack's; but this is world history and I'm not going to rail on about the degradation of standards or the work ethic. My father and uncles did their work in their time, and I did mine, and Jack will do his at this post-turn-of-the-millennium moment, and who can say who will have had the hardest go?

Sometimes I think Jack's is a tough slot, given the never-ending onslaught of instant information and the general wisdom these days that if you don't continually "grow" your business at a certain heady rate it will wither and die. Good for him that for the last four years he has seemed to be practically printing money, what with all the trucks out every day and him needing to hire extra help literally off the street each morning in Farmingville, where the Hispanic men hang out. Now with the economy in the doldrums he probably wishes he hadn't built his mega-mini-mansion but he doesn't seem concerned. In fact, we're all meeting at his new house this weekend, both to celebrate Theresa's recent engagement to her boyfriend Paul (they're flying in from Oregon), and my father's eighty-fifth birthday, which of course he has forgotten about but will enjoy immensely, as he does whenever he is celebrated, which Jack and Eunice will do in high and grand style.

I do sometimes worry about Jack, and wonder if he's grinding too hard for the dollars. Just sit down with him to lunch sometime and you'll see all the digital hardware come unclipped from his belt and onto the table, the pager and cell phone and electronic notepad and memo-to-self recorder. At least my father and uncles had the twin angels of innocence and ignorance to guide them and the devil of hard times to keep working against. I merely inherited what they had already made fairly prosperous, and did what I could not to ruin anything, though Rita often pointed out that I had the least enviable position, given that I really had no choice in the matter, expected as I was to sustain something I never had a genuine interest in. This is mostly true. I had no great love for brick and mortar. When I was still young I was sure I wanted to become a fighter pilot; I sent away for information on the Air Force Academy, did focusing exercises to make sure my vision stayed sharp, tried not to sleep too much (you grew in your sleep, and I was afraid of exceeding the height limit). But when the time came I watched the application date come and go, applying only to regular colleges, my inaction not due to lack of interest or fear but what I would say was my disbelief in the real, or more like it, the real as it had to do with me. I suppose therapist types and self-actualizers would say I have difficulty with *visualization*, how you must see yourself doing and being—say, at the controls in the cockpit, or making love to a beautiful woman, or living in a grand beach house—but even though I can summon the requisite image and can get a little fanciful and dreamy, too, I can't seem to settle on any one picture of myself without feeling a companion negativity whose caption at the bottom reads, *Yeah, right.*

And if it's no surprise to those out there who are thinking that was probably my father's favorite line I would say it certainly was (and still is), not just to me but to everyone in the family and the business, with the exception of my little brother, Bobby, who surely would have benefited from a healthy dose of skepticism had he ever returned from his first and last tour in Vietnam. In all fairness, however, I'm Hank (The Tank) Battle's son, with the main difference between him and me being that I was never able to summon his first-strike arrogance, nor develop the necessary armature for the inevitable fallout from oneself. And while there will be more on this to follow, I will not complain now, and add that choices are a boon only to those who can make good on them. I made a fine living from Battle Brothers, and was able to raise my children in a safe town of decent families and give them every opportunity for self-betterment, in which I believe I succeeded. I always worked hard, if not passionately. I never took what was given to me for granted, or thought anything or anyone was below me. I was not a quitter. In these regards, at least, I have no regrets.

And I had more than my fair share of good times. Through all the work, I still took the time to travel the whole world twice over, going pretty much everywhere, including the North and South Pole (well, almost) and even a few "rogue" states in Africa and the Middle East, and slipped into those countries I wasn't easily allowed to enter, like Cuba and North Korea (if you count that conference table in the DMZ). Of course this was after the kids were in college, and most of the time Rita came along with me, though often enough she didn't have the vacation days left and I went alone. The only typical places I haven't been, oddly enough, are Canada and Mexico, not even their side of Niagara, not even Cancún, but these glaring omissions never bothered me much, and I doubt ever will. I like to think I make up for any intracontinental bigotry by sending planeloads of tourists to popular spots across both borders, as I've worked for a couple years now as a part-time travel agent at the local branch office of a huge travel conglomerate (which I'll call Parade) that runs full-page ads in the Sunday *Times*.

When I sold out my shares in Battle Brothers four years ago I hadn't fully realized that there was no place left for me to go, and decided, on the suggestion of Theresa, citing my extensive résumé as a "passenger," that I ought to try my hand at being a travel professional, which, it turns out, despite her snide deconstructive terminology, was just my calling. For long before I donned my red Parade travel agent's blazer I could speak to most every notable sight in every notable town in this shrinking touristical world, I knew the better ranks of inns and hotels and tour and cruise operators, and I knew which all-inclusives and play-and-stay packages offered good value or were just plain sorry and cheap.

Likewise, I'm not the man to call if you are looking for some cloistered, indigenous roost in a cliffside sweat-lodge-cum-spa or a suite in a designer hotel where the bellboys wear gunmetal suits and headsets and the rooms are decorated in eight shades of white. I am suspicious of the special. I have always believed in staying in vacation trappings that are just slightly nicer than what I have at home, and certainly not any worse, where at least breakfast is included (even if it's just coffee and a gelid danish in the lobby), and the cultural tour, whether by coach or by foot, is led by a cheerleading guy or gal with an old-fashioned and gently ironic sense of humor and a thick local accent and a soulful character suffused with a grand and romantic self-aspiration. I have always preferred wayfaring with such a group, exchanging our white-man *arigatos* and *auf wiedersehens* with jolly inanity while hitting all the trod-over sites and famous vistas, for the allure of traveling for me has never been in searching out the little-known *pieve* or backroad *auberge* but standing squint-eyed amidst the sunbaked rubble of some celebrated ruin like Taormina or Machu Picchu in the obliging company of just-minted acquaintances of strictly limited duration and knowing that wherever I go I'll be able to commune with fellow strangers over the glories of this world.

During her undergraduate years when she seemed angry about almost everything I did, and pretty much saw me, she once even said, as "the last living white man," my smart-as-heck daughter often felt compelled to expose my many travels for the rapacious, hegemonic colonialist "projects" that they were. At Thanksgiving or Christmas she'd idly ask where I'd been lately and I'd mention some island in the Caribbean or off the coast of Thailand and she'd start in on how my snorkeling was undoubtedly negatively impacting the coral reefs, and I'd swear I didn't touch anything except maybe an already dead starfish (which I brought home and had framed) and right there would be evidence of my integral part in the collective strip-mining of an indigenous culture and ecosystem. I'd answer that the locals seemed perfectly content to strip it themselves, given the number of shell and sponge and stuffed-bird shops lining the beachside streets, and then we'd get into the usual back-and-forth about the false-bottomed tourist economy (Theresa) and whether tourists should stay home so the natives could still weave their clothes out of coconut threads (JB) and the need for *indigenes* to control the mechanisms of capital and production (TB) and the question of who really cared as long as everyone was happy with the situation (JB) and the final retort of who could possibly be happy in this unthinking, unjust world (guess who)?

To which, when your once-sugar-sweet daughter, who used to hang on your shoulders and neck like a gibbon monkey, now just home from her impossibly liberal, impossibly expensive New Hampshire college, is glaring at you desperately with bloodshot all-nighter eyes from too much 3 A.M. espresso and clove cigarettes and badly recited Rimbaud (and other activities too gamy to think about), you're tempted to say, "I am," even knowing it would quite possibly put her over the edge. But then you don't, and hope you never do, just requesting instead that someone pass down the boiled brussels sprouts, which are as usual utterly miserable with neglect.

All this, it pleases me to report, has come full circle in our steady march toward maturation, as I'm now sitting at my desk at Parade Travel in Huntington comparing package prices for Theresa and her fiancé, the purportedly semi-famous (and only semi-successful) Asian-American writer Paul Pyun. I'm to say "Asian-American," partly because they always do, and not only because my usage of the old standby of "Oriental" offends them on many personal and theoretical levels, but also because I should begin to reenvision myself as a multicultural being, as my long-deceased wife, Daisy, was Asian herself and my children are of mixed blood, even though I have never thought of them that way. I must admit that I don't quite yet appreciate what all the fuss is about, but I've realized that words matter inordinately to Theresa and Paul, and far beyond any point I wish to take a stand on.

They're planning to get married sometime this coming fall or winter, right here on Long Island (Paul's parents, both medical doctors, live down the Expressway in Roslyn), and have asked me to look into a moderately priced one-week honeymoon in a tropical location. I assumed they wanted a *-que* holiday (*unique, boutique, exotique*), some far-flung stay with plenty of cultural sites and funky local flavor, but in fact Theresa told me herself that they were thinking something "spring breaky," maybe even a cruise. Apparently after endless backpacking forays into Third World sections of First World countries, they now desire the fun and the tacky, perhaps on the order of certain beachfront "huts" I can book them in Ixtapa, where they can roll out of bed and lie in the sand all day and get served strong, sweet drinks and only if they wish exert themselves with a paddleboat or parasail ride. No forced eco-hikes here. Theresa (and Paul, too, for that matter) can get her hair cornrowed and they'll have dinner at a "sumptuous international buffet" and then dance on a floating discotheque where they'll exchange tequila body shots and maybe even catch a wet T-shirt or naked belly-flop contest.

Here at Parade Travel we gladly enable much of this, as people would be surprised to find that it's not just college kids but young thirty-somethings like Theresa and Paul and then much older folks, too, getting into the act, more and more of our holidays geared to reflect what seems to be the wider cultural sentiment of the moment, which is basically that You and Everybody Else Can Kiss My Ass. No doubt you readily see this in play at your own office and while driving on the roads and almost every moment on sports and music television. I have to suppose this is the natural evolution of the general theme of self-permission featured in recent generations (mine foremost), but it's all become a little too hard and mean for me, which makes me wish to decline.

I wish to decline, even if I can't.

Still, I don't want to send my only daughter on such a trip, even if she thinks she wants to go. This is her honeymoon, for heaven's sake, and I won't let her spoil it with some folly of an ironic notion. For all her learning and smarts she has always had the ability from time to time to make the unfortunate life decision, plus the fact that she has much to learn about romance. Paul I don't know so well, but I suspect he can't be much different, or else totally cowed by her on this one. Luckily I've found them a tony plantation-style hotel in Mustique and have called the manager directly to request that he give them the best room whenever we know the exact dates (#8, according to knowledgeable colleagues). They'll get a champagne-and-tropical-fruit-basket welcome, and a special couples' massage, and though I know the antebellum trappings might initially speak to Theresa and Paul of subjugation and exploitation and death, I'm hoping they'll be spoiled and pampered into an amnesic state of bliss that they can hold on to for years (and if lucky, longer than that). This will be my secret wedding present to them, too, as their arts-and-humanities budget is barely a third of the final cost, even with my travel agent discounts.

Kelly Stearns, my coworker here at Parade, with whom I share a double desk, will tell me that I am a sweet and generous father any girl would be darn lucky to have. Each of us works three and a half days a week, overlapping for an hour on Fridays. Kelly is late again, however, as she has been quite often this summer. I'm worried about her, as it's not like her to take her responsibilities lightly.

Kelly is an attractive, big-boned blonde with a pixie, girlish face that makes her seem much younger than her mid-fortyish years, the only thing really giving away her age being her hands, which are strangely old-looking, the skin waxy and thin like my mother's once was. Kelly comes to us from the South, the Carolinas, which I mention only because it's obvious what an unlikelihood she is around the office, with her dug-deep accent and sprightly way of address and her can-do (and will-do) attitude, all reflected in the fact that her clients know exactly her days and hours. After the clock clicks 3, there's always a surge of call volume for "Miss Stearns," which I field as best as I can, though mostly they insist on working with her, even if it's just a simple matter of changing a flight time or booking a car. I suppose I come off like everybody else here on the Island, meaning that I'm useful to a point and then probably a waste of time. I completely understand this. Whenever I call a company or business and realize I've been routed to the Minneapolis or Chattanooga office, I feel a glow of assurance, as if I've been transported back to a calmer, simpler clime, and though I know it's surely all hogwash I can't help but fall in love just a little with the woman's voice on the other end, picturing us in an instant picnicking in the village square and holding hands and greeting passersby like any one of them might soon be a friend.

This is partly why I can talk to Kelly about almost everything, including the sticky subject of Rita, as she in fact has the stuff of kindness and generosity bundled right onto her gene strands, along with the other reason—namely, that she can summon the forgiveness of a freshly ordained priest. I should know, for she's forgiven me for certain transgressions, for which almost any other woman could only summon the blackest bile. You'd think she'd steer clear of me forever. This is not to suggest she's a pushover. I'll just say for now that we were intimate in the period after Rita decided to leave and did but then came back only to leave again, which Kelly always recognized as a difficult time, and she ultimately decided that whatever judgments were due me would be presided over not by her but by some more durable power, whose reckoning would be everlasting.

Another call comes in for Kelly but it's not a client. It's that tough guy again, the one sounding like Robert Mitchum, though even more diffident than that, and certainly charmless, and to whom I'm pretty much done showing patience. His sole name, as far as I know, is Jimbo (how he self-refers). I've had to field his calls the last few times she's been late, and was pleasant enough at first if only because I had the feeling he was her new boyfriend, which I don't think anymore, nor would I care about it if I did. Kelly introduced us once when he came to pick her up, Jimbo not even bothering to shake my hand, just offering a curt nod from behind his mirrored wraparounds. But the more I do think about it, I don't like the idea that Kelly has anything to do with him. There's a streak of the bully in his voice, a low whine that makes me think he's the sort of man who not so secretly fears and dislikes women.

"It's practically three-thirty," he complains. "She should be there."

"She's not."

"Did she call in?"

"No," I tell him. "Look, don't you have her number by now?"

"Hey, buddy, how about minding your own business, okay?"

"That's what I'm doing."

"Well, do yourself a big favor and shut your sassy mouth."

"Or what?"

"You'll know what," Jimbo says, all malice and mayhem.

"Why don't you come down here and show me, then."

He pauses, and I can almost hear his knuckle hair rising. "You're a real dumb fuck, you know that?" he says low and hard, and he hangs up.

I hang up, too, banging the handset back into the cradle. Where this will lead I don't know or care. These days every thick-necked monobrow in the tristate area likes to pretend he's a goodfella, some made guy, but having been in the brick-and-mortar and landscaping business I have plentiful experience with all varieties of blowhard, including the legitimate ones, who for the most part don't even hint at their affiliations.

I notice that the other people in the office have hardly looked away from their screens, except for Miles Quintana, our newest and youngest Parade travel professional, who *ack-acks* me a double machine gun thumbs-up, shouting, "Give 'em hell, Jerome!" He's young (and historically challenged) enough that he thinks I'm a member of the "Greatest Generation." He's seen *Saving Private Ryan* at least two dozen times and can describe every battle-scene amputation and beheading in digital frame-by-frame glory, and despite the fact that I've told him I was only born during that war he continues to see me as the reluctant hero, as if every graying American man has a Purple Heart (and Smith & Wesson .45 automatic) stashed away in a cigar box in his closet. Of course I'm sure he's playfully teasing, too, just slinging office shit with the old gringo, and if this is the way that a guy like me and a nineteen-year-old Dominican kid can get along, then it's fine by me.

Miles is the office's designated Spanish speaker (our office manager, Chuck, proudly taped up the *Se Habla Español* sign in the front window the day Miles joined up), and part of the company's efforts to attract more business from the large and growing

Hispanic community in the immediate area. The interesting thing is that Miles, though a perfectly capable travel agent, is actually not so hot at *habla*-ing, at least judging by the conversations he has with clients in the office and on the phone, when he uses at least as many English words and phrases as he does Spanish, if not more. In fact I can confidently say that one need not know any Spanish to understand him when he's in his translation mode, which employs gesture and posture more than speech. Still, he continues to get referrals from the Colombians and Salvadorans and Peruvians and whoever else they are waiting their turn at his desk, proving that it's not always the linguistical intricacies that people find assuring, but broader, deeper forms of communication. This jibes with my own sharpening feeling that I can hardly understand anybody anymore, at least as far as pure language goes, and that among the only real things left to us in this life if we're lucky is a shared condition of bemusement and sorrowful wonder that can maybe turn into something like joy.

My phone rings again and I'm ready to communicate with Jimbo once more, in whatever manner he'd like to take up. But it's Kelly on the line. She's calling from her little maroon econobox, which I notice double-parked across the street. I wave.

"Please don't do that, Jerry," she says, sniffling miserably. I can see her dabbing at her nose with a peony-sized bloom of tissues. She's wearing big sunglasses and a print scarf over her hair, like it's raining, or 1964. "I don't want anyone there to see me."

"Are you all right? You sound terrible."

"I don't have a cold, if that's what you mean."

"Do you want me to come out there?"

"Definitely not, Jerry. I'm looking pretty much a fright right now."

"I'm worried about you, Kel."

"Are you, Jerry?"

"Of course I am." Her tone is alarmingly knowing, even grim. I press on, not because I want an impromptu lecture (which I'm pretty sure I'll get), but because my friend Kelly Stearns does not talk this way, ever. I say, "I don't want to butt in because it's none of my business. But that guy called for you again, and I don't need to ask what you're doing with him to know that it can't be too happy."

"It's not, Jerry. I've told Jimbo that we won't be seeing each other for a while. He hasn't accepted it yet. But that's not the problem."

"So what's the matter?" I say, being as even as I can, given our very brief if not-so-ancient history. "What's wrong?"

"Everything's plain rotten," Kelly answers, enough Scout Finch still leavening her mature woman's voice to make my insides churn with a crush. Her old-fashioned idiom strikes me to the core, too, and I realize once again that I am a person who is taken much more by what people say than by what they do. I tend to overrecognize signifiers, to quote my daughter; I'm easily awestruck by symbol and tone. Apparently this is neither good nor bad. And right now it's easy to gather that this isn't our usual belle Kelly.

She says, "I just want to crawl beneath a rock and die."

"Did something happen?"

"Nothing *happened*," she says. "This is me living my life."

"This is definitely not your life, Kel."

"Oh yes it is," she says. "Of all people, Jerry, I'd hoped you'd not try to give me a line."

"I'm not. You're in a rut, that's all. I've seen you worse, which is still a hundred times better than anyone else on a good day."

"You certainly saw me in one way," she counters, to which I can't really reply. She's double-parked but badly, her back end sticking out too far into the street, right near the yellow line. A minor jam is building in both directions. She says, oblivious to the pepper of horns, "I don't blame you, Jerry. You were gentleman enough. Even though you dumped me no less than three times."

"Not to defend myself, but I'm pretty sure you dumped me the last time."

"You know very well that it was preemptive. My final effort at retaining some dignity. When I still thought I had some."

"You've still got plenty," I tell her, noticing that she's unscrewing the top from an orange prescription bottle. It's a slim, small bottle, definitely not the kind they give you vitamins in. She shakes out some pills and pops them into her mouth, chasing them with a long straw-sip from a massive Big Gulp, her signature drink. Though it's silly to say, the only thing about Kelly that really bothered me was her use of the 7-Eleven and the like as grocery stores, the result being her drive-thru diet of chili dogs and Hot Pockets and Doritos and aspartame-sweetened anything; nothing in the least natural ever entering her body. Really the opposite of Rita, who even made her own corn tortillas. This shouldn't have been the reason Kelly Stearns and I couldn't be together forever, and I never brought it up to her even though I understood so from the beginning, but it was.

"What's that you're taking, Kel?"

"Jimbo gives them to me," she says, shaking the bottle. "OxyContin. They say they're good for pain."

"I'm sure they are. Listen, why don't I come out there right now and sit with you. I'll tell Chuck you called in sick. It's real slow anyway, and I can take you back to my place and you can talk things out. We'll have an early dinner on the patio."

"I'm at my limit, Jerry. My outer limit. I know you don't feel that way because you've got it all together."

"You know that's not true."

"It is from where I'm sitting. You have your whole life accrued to you, and it's only getting better. You're a good-looking man who's going to be sixty but hardly looks a day over fifty. You have all your hair. You have your family nearby and enough money and you have Parade to pass the time with and you have your plane to go up in whenever you want to split. You can have all the girlfriends like me that you'd ever want."

"Kel . . ."

"I'm not criticizing. I'm a fairly nice girl but I'm not so special or unique and more times than not I get passed over. It's the truth and you know it. It turns out the only guy who wants to keep me forever is Jimbo."

"That's a load of bull."

"It's not. He makes love to me. Not very well, but he tries. He's not superbright or interesting or exceptionally kind. But he wants me. He needs me. It's as simple as that. Did you ever wonder about those women who get hitched to guys in jail? Why they would ever do that? Now I know. I'm forty-five years old today and . . ."

"Today?" I checked the desk blotter calendar, but I'd written nothing on it, today or any day.

"Yes, but I'm not giving you shit about that. I'm forty-five years old and never been married and I won't ever have children and I'm the only child of dead parents. I've got no pension fund to speak of. My furniture is rent-to-own. I color my own hair. I haven't done anything really terrible or wrong in my life but look, I've got next to nothing. All you have to worry about is keeping your health and not getting bored. I'm not criticizing. I'm happy for you. You're missing Rita, is all, but she's going to come back to you sometime, I'm sure of it. I talked to her yesterday. She asked how you were."

I'm not thinking much of anything for a moment, my heart clogging my throat. "You spoke to Rita?"

"I told her you were fine, but lonely, which is definitely the truth."

"How is she?" Kelly would know, as she and Rita have been friendly since the end of Kelly/Jerry II, meeting for Happy Hour at Chi-Chi's once a month or so, apparently jabbering about everything but me. I spied on them once, from the corner of the bar, tipping their waitress $20 to eavesdrop, which was not a good use of money, as the only thing she related was how they were joking about penis sizes.

"Same as you, Jerry, only not so lonely. She's still seeing Richard, on and off."

"Yeah." Richard as in Richie Coniglio, *coniglio* in Italian being the word for rabbit. Which he is—short, thin guy, kind who lives forever, fluffy in the hair, with prominent teeth, probably false. I've known him since middle school, when he followed me around the halls, as I was one of the few kids who didn't beat up on him daily. He was always smart, and he's become sort of a bigwig around here, with the charities and such. That's how he met Rita, at a hospital gala, where she was a volunteer hostess. He's divorced, exactly my age, though admittedly looks at least five years younger than me, Kelly's previous comment notwithstanding. He's a partner at a white-shoe New York law firm, collects Ferraris, and lives alone in a mansion in Muttontown. He takes Rita out east on the weekends, to his "cottage" in Southampton. I've actually spotted him out in public wearing jodhpurs, at the Bagel Bin with the Sunday *Times* tucked under his arm, his boots stuccoed with horse dung.

"I bet she's happy with him," I say.

"Don't beat yourself up, Romeo. Richard can be a peach but I think we all know where you and Rita are headed. I can hear it in your voices, and all around you. The tarantella has already started up."

"I wish."

"You better not just wish, Jerry Battle. You had better do. But why I'm bothering to tell you this right now astounds me."

"Because you're the sweetheart of Huntington Village," I tell her, already heartened immeasurably, though realizing that this has somehow become all about Me again, our chronic modality. So I say, "You should have told me it was your birthday. I'm going to hang up now and tell Chuck you called in sick and I'm going to take you out tonight. We'll go to the city. I'll get us a table at Smith & Wollensky. We'll get the double porterhouse."

"Don't you dare!" she shouts, the squawk almost hurting my ear. "Don't you even budge. I don't want to go to the city for dinner and I don't want you coming out here. I only stopped by to tell you I'm going away."

"What do you mean? Where?"

"I really don't know yet," she says, sounding high and tight like she's going to cry. "But I wouldn't tell you if I did. I'm not telling anyone. If you hear from me after today, it'll be from someplace far away."

"I don't like this word 'if,' Kel."

"Tough shit, Jerry!" she says, her emphasis more on my

name than the expletive. But she gathers herself. "Listen. I don't want to yell at you. Just tell Chuck I'm taking a leave of absence. If he doesn't like it, tell him I quit. And don't you worry about me. I'm going to be fine. I'm going on a trip all by myself. I'm superhappy about it. Don't worry."

But I'm deeply worried, this spiky scare rappelling down my spine, especially with her mentioning how happy she'll be, the image of her splayed out on a motel bed with a hand mirror snowy with crushed pills, a plastic garbage bag, a straight razor.

"I'm coming out now," I tell her firmly, "whether you want me to or not."

But just as I put down the phone and stand up I see Kelly wave, wave, and not really to me, like she's on the top deck of the *Queen Mary*, embarking on an around-the-world. Her blond hair spilling out of the scarf. (Why there is a glamour in all departures, I don't know.) Before I can even get outside she's speeding away, her dusty little car clattering down the main street of the village, being nearly broadsided as she drifts through a red light. There's another clamor of protesting horns, and then, momentarily veiled by a white puff of oil-burning acceleration, she's gone. I try her cell over and over but all I get is her outgoing message, whose molasses lilt always manages to upend me: "Hi y'all, Kelly here. I ain't home right now. But do say something nice."

WHICH I HAVE tried to do, at the time and then throughout this evening, but all I've been able to muster is to say I am here if she needs me, whatever hour of the night. It's nearing midnight now. All this sounds pretty good, like I'm on call for her, braced by the nightstand, wracked and sleepless. Of course if I were a wholly better person (and not just a former-lover-turned-friend) I'd be out searching the avenues for her, having already called her friends and maybe even Jimbo (number from the office Caller ID), having already gone by her apartment, instead of half dreading the *blee-dee-deet* of my cordless as I sit here on the patio beneath a starless Long Island sky, steadily drawing down an iced bottle of cut-rate pinot grigio. I'm worried about Kelly, of course, not quite admitting that part of me is scared stiff she might try to hurt herself, but here I am taking up space in my usual way, as if waiting for the news to come on, some defining word filtering down from the heavens to let me know what ought to be done next.

This is what Rita found most chronically difficult about me, and what Theresa has begun openly referring to as my "preternatural lazy-heartedness." Jack has to this point professed no corresponding view, which I suspect is because he's finally realized that in this regard the apple hasn't fallen very far from the tree (or off at all), and is perhaps an even more fully realized version of its predecessor. Kelly Stearns, if I may take the liberty to suppose, would probably identify this quality of mine as how I'm most like "a real jerk," which is what she called me after the last time we slept together, not for anything that happened (or didn't) between the sheets (I've always tried to be at least eager and attentive in love's physical labors, understanding I'm no expert), but for the solidly marvelous days leading up to that last passionate if cramped union, when I took her on a fancy Caribbean cruise despite my unswervable intent of breaking up with her once again, and for all.

In her opinion, I should have dumped her before the trip, which by any standard of decency and decorum makes good sense, though in my behalf I should say that I did want to treat her and spoil her one last time, not as reward or consolation but because I genuinely cared for her and wanted to make her plain happy and frankly saw no other way to accomplish it save for going on a carefree junket heading nowhere in our immediate world. Kelly et al. (the entire office, except for Miles, who surprisingly falls to my side of the ledger in most worldly matters) naturally saw my aims as self-serving and usurious in spirit, a sneaky final lust-grab and cruel deception, made even worse by the fact that Kelly and I had reached that certain juncture in our relationship when a romantic luxury cruise might seem an odds-on prelude to proposing a union unto death. Indeed, in anticipation of something special Kelly had brought along some of her more wicked boudoir getups, including a melt-away fruit-roll teddy burnished in edible gold that the Parade gals had slipped in her carry-on, as well as a distinctly matrimonial gown, complete with lace train, just in case I had arranged for the captain of the ship to perform a surprise wedding-at-sea. The first hint of trouble was when I unpacked my garment bag and only had a Permapress travel blazer to hang up, the sight of which momentarily arrested all her functions, as if she'd looked up to see a complete solar eclipse. I asked her what was wrong and she tried to ignore me but then broke into a sweet smile and said brightly, "Whatever could be wrong, my ever casual man?"

Kelly, like all the Southern women I've known (three total—the other two being the identical Cohen twins from Decatur, Georgia, Terri and Traci, who were lifeguards at the Catskills camp where I landscaped several summers of my youth), features an inborn lode of a chin-up, good sport reserve that I can tell you positively jazzes a guy like me, though eventually invites some ill use and taking advantage of, too, if unwitting and unintended. The Cohen twins, I remember, besides being splendid swimmers, were deadly rifle shots and archers, their identical carriage buxomly and erectly Aryan, which the young Jewish-American campers beheld with a hushed adoration and trembling. That last summer I dated Terri (I'm pretty sure), my buddy Lorne seeing her sister, and by the middle of the camp session we'd convinced them that losing their virginity with a couple of Gentiles was probably an ideal way to go, there being no strings or expectations. Ever reasonable, they agreed. So one night we paddled our canoes to the little foot-shaped island in the middle of Lake Kennonah, outfitted with sleeping bags and candles and condoms and a fifth of Southern Comfort. The four of us drank together and then Terri and I hiked to the other side of the island and spread our bedding atop a broad flat rock right by the water. We could still hear Traci and Lorne talking and laughing and then getting very quiet, and without even kissing much we took off our clothes and started making love. I say this not because I loved her or am uncomfortable using cruder terms but because I thought then and still do that no matter who it is you're with or whether it's the first and/or last time, there's always at least one verifiable moment when you can believe you're doing exactly that, literally trying to *make* love, build it up, whether by alchemy or chemistry or force of will. With Terri Cohen it was no difficult task, for she was ardent and mostly unafraid and steadfast beneath me on that absolutely ungiving rock, which made me feel like I was going straight through to the igneous, like we were plunging another axis for the world. (This is but one of many a young man's egoistic virginal follies—sentimental and ridiculous, I know.) Afterward, not unhappy, and both quite sore from the vigorous but clearly unclimactic-able sex, we hiked back in silence to where we'd put ashore. We weren't thinking about Traci and Lorne, or at least I wasn't, and suddenly we came upon them in the candlelight, in mid-engagement, her slender heels tapping out time on his back, and perhaps it was because they were twins that Terri didn't pull us away or try to hide us. We watched as they crescendoed and decrescendoed and crescendoed again, until they finally came (Traci before Lorne, amazingly), when Terri grabbed my hand and hustled us back to our spot on the rock and astraddle of me swiftly finished us both.

Now there's the definition of a good sport.

I'm long accustomed to the umbraged, oversensitive, volcanically eruptive type, firstly my good mother, who could shame a false confession out of Saint Francis and who, during her last moments on her deathbed, scolded us arrayed there to go wash our hands before leaning on her Belgian lace bedspread. When I was young she and my father had horrific arguments over his handling of the business and the periodic dalliances he'd have with his young bookkeepers fresh out of night school, the nastiest of their fights ending with my mother wielding a rusty fish-filleting knife, swearing that she'd gut them both if she ever caught them, and my father (recklessly quoting Sartre and Camus and *Reader's Digest*) taunting her with the then recently announced death of God. Hank Battle has always liked a rousing fight, especially with family, whether fair or not, and if I were constituted more like him I'm certain I'd have ended up with a woman who would burn the bed before letting me tread too long over her.

And so it's never been strange to me that I've gravitated toward women like Kelly Stearns, and then my Rita, who hardly said a word until the end and then coolly informed me, sotto voce, as we were driving home from the multiplex after having watched *Jurassic Park II*, that she had rented back her old studio apartment in Hauppauge and would be gone by the end of the week. I didn't say anything, because it was no great surprise; I didn't protest, because I had no arguments for her, the previous long years providing evidence enough of what we might expect (past performance, in the recent stock-crazed parlance, being in this case a bankable guarantee of future results), and I drove home feeling as if I'd been bitten clean through right at the sternum, my heart pumping fast but pumping nothing, my lower half already marinating in the gullet of a beast named Rue. Rita was by then more sorrowful than angry, though still plenty bitter, as the next morning she gave me back the diamond-and-ruby ring I'd given her to celebrate twenty-one years of living together, but then carefully packed for removal every last one of the expensive stockpots and sauté and cake pans I'd bought her over the years (despite the fact that she never cooked for just herself), understanding before I did the full measure of how this would pain me.

As I step inside the kitchen, the wall clock (shaped like the nose of a Sopwith Camel) mumbles "Contact" and fires up, the hands whizzing around until they stop back at the present hour, midnight. Still no word from Kelly, so I call her again, at her apartment and cell phone, but to no avail. My next move, I think now, is to call the police, to check if there has been any accident or report involving her, but then the phone in my hand rings and I know this is she, and something aberrant in me lets it go a few more bleats before I click it on.

I say, "Kelly . . ."

"Jerry?"

"Kelly, is that you?"

"No, Jerry. It's me. It's Rita."

I can't say anything, because of course I knew it was Rita,

almost before she even spoke, which makes no sense at all. And I have no sense now, the only feeling the clammy empty bottle in my other hand.

"Listen. I'm at work. I just got on shift and I really can't talk. Kelly is here. She came in about an hour ago. Actually she sort of crashed her car by the emergency entrance."

"Is she hurt?"

"Not from that," Rita says, and not casually. "She must have known she was in trouble and driven here, but couldn't quite make it. She took a lot of pills."

"Oxy-somethings," I say.

"That's right. How did you know?"

"She told me she was taking them," I say, realizing how not good this sounds, vis-à-vis me. "She's okay, though, right?"

"She'll be okay," Rita says grimly. "She didn't have enough to kill herself, but she could have really hurt herself. She's in a daze right now. She did ask me to call you. That's why I'm calling."

"I know."

"She said you might be looking for her."

"I was. I am."

There's an unsettling, sneaky long pause, the kind we got used to over the years, and then finally became sick of, though now I don't know that I'd refuse a great deal more of it, if this is all I'll ever have.

Rita says, nurselike, "She'll be okay, but she has to rest. She'll have been transferred to the main ward. You should go by there in the late morning."

"I'll come first thing," I say, knowing the night shift ends at 7 A.M., with a thirty-minute changeover, after which Rita will go back to Richie the Rabbit, snug in his baronial bedchamber.

"Let her sleep," Rita says, her tone riding somewhere between command and wish. "Listen, I've gotta go. Be kind to her."

"I'm always kind."

"Okay, Jerry. Okay. I'm hanging up now. Bye."

"Rita . . ."

But before I can say anything else she's clicked off. I punch ✶69 but it's the hospital operator, and by the time she connects me to the emergency room nursing station Rita's already unavailable, according to another nurse, as the paramedics are wheeling in a minivan's worth of teenagers from a nasty wreck on the Meadowbrook Parkway.

After this surprise brush with Rita, and then settling in with the increasingly sobering notion that Kelly may have really tried to hurt herself, I can't really sleep at all. I get up every other hour to satisfy my quick-trigger bladder and then poke around in the refrigerator and surf the late-night cable for anything remotely engaging (for me it's an infomercial for a rotisserie cooker, the chicken done to a perfect shade of polished cherry wood) and then sit in my old convertible out on the driveway, squinting in the scant moonlight at the just-getting-old guy in the parking mirrors. Not to worry, as this won't be that moment for a midstream self-appraisal heavy on deprecation and knowing charm, or a dark night of the soul's junket through the murk of a checkered, much remorsed-upon past. I won't suffer anyone bizarre fantasies or nightmares, as often happens in movies and books, because I'm not really capable of that sort of thing, being neither so weird nor smart enough. I'll simply relay what I can see, which is a man sitting alone at night in an open-air car, hands restless on the wheel, humming silently to himself, waiting for the sun to rise up so he can just get moving again.

Come morning, I'm already here, in the parking garage of the mid-county hospital. It's amazing how many cars are around at this hour, like it's the long-term lot at La Guardia during Thanksgiving week. You'd think that people (despite what they profess) in fact love hospitals, as they do everything they can (smoking, drug-taking, road-raging) to hurry themselves inside. Sometimes I used to pick Rita up from her shift (then the day shift) and they'd be practically lined up in the emergency waiting room in all manner of wreck and ruin, accidently poisoned, nearly drowned, stabbed and shot and burned, so that it seemed we were living nearer to Beirut than to Babylon, Long Island.

It's only just 7 A.M. and I'm determining exactly how I'm going to go about talking to Rita, or more to the point, have her talk to me. I've already visited Kelly Stearns in the adult ward, having told the nurses that I was her half-brother and had driven all night from Roanoke when I heard the news, leaving a couple of carnation-heavy bouquets of supermarket flowers (nothing else was open) and a surprisingly long and wholly loving note on her dresser, generally saying that I was sorry if I let her down and that I would never do so again. I was glad to leave the note, especially as she was asleep, and, strange to see but understandably, strapped down in restraints, and my one alarming thought was that she was going to wake up like that and might very well flip the hell out. So when the nurse left us alone I unfastened one of Kelly's hands, so that she could move a little bit, at least scratch an itch somewhere, if she needed to.

Concerning Rita, I know she'll exit the hospital from the ER entrance and come this way, past where I'm just idling, as her banana-yellow 1982 Mustang with the black racing stripes and fake chrome wheels is parked behind me, against the far wall.

She bought the car used, already in a dinged-up, rusty condition, and oddly enough it looks no worse than it ever was. She liked to say it was her PR Mobile (as in Puerto Rican), which I'm surprised Richie Coniglio allows her to drive into his estate area in Muttontown. Maybe he likes it, or maybe he has no choice. When she began living at the house with me I offered to buy her a new car, really anything she wanted, my heart breaking open with an uncharacteristic (back then) generosity, with only the smallest cell of me doing it for unsavory reasons. I never gave a damn what the neighbors thought, never really knowing them anyway, but I must admit, during those first few months of domiciling, to a certain twinge in my gut whenever she'd jounce up the driveway. These past six months I have been waiting for Rita to return just like that, with me staring out the kitchen window in the afternoons, waiting for her to step out in her white shoes and pad up the walk. For her to use her key.

I first met Rita almost twenty-five years ago, on a boat. It was one of those Friday sunset booze cruises they used to run out for two-hour sprees in the Sound in the summertime. A few years back (actually, probably more like fifteen or twenty) a Commack woman fell overboard and presumably drowned (the body was never retrieved), and the company promptly got sued and had to close down operations. I went only twice, meeting Rita the second time. They crammed about sixty or so of us single people onto an oversized cabin cruiser, charging $20 a head ($10 for women) for a cash bar, baked brie and crudités, and a DJ spinning funk and disco and some oldies (this is 1977, when oldies seemed more like oldies than they do today, maybe because they were played on records, and literally *sounded* old). I was working a lot then, this after Daisy died, with mostly my mother looking after the kids and then some neighborhood women pitching in when they could, and finally a string of nannies who never quite worked out.

One night I ran into an old high school classmate, Rick Steinitz, at the then brand-new cineplex on Route 110, both of us just coming out of *Close Encounters of the Third Kind.* Rick called out my name and somehow I knew who he was and though he was with a date (leggy, pretty brunette) he seemed to want to linger and chat, perhaps more so for it. He was a podiatrist, with an office in Huntington. We hadn't been friends in high school and in fact hardly knew each other. As I recalled we were both shy loners, neither popular nor reviled, though Rick would heartily disagree about my memory of him. The final truth here is unimportant. It's enough to say that ours was one of those midlife friendships between men that happen not because of a shared interest like liquor or golf or even the pleasure of each other's company but from a mutual, pointed need for a fresh association. Rick was just divorcing for the second time, clearly in a rut, and when he heard I'd been widowed for over a year and was still unattached he seemed inspired, as though I'd presented him with a particularly challenging case. When his date excused herself to go to the ladies' room, he insisted I go with him on this booze cruise that launched out of Northport.

Rick was something of a regular on the boat, part of a core group of guys and gals who hadn't yet found their match and for the most part tried each other out but ultimately weren't interested, which was okay by them. They got bombed in the first half hour and always started the dancing, and the rest of the boat seemed appreciative of their shake and roar, which in another venue would have certainly been boorish, embarrassing behavior but was just about the right speed here. Belowdecks there were a couple of spartan staterooms, which Rick had informed me could be "toured" for a twenty-spot gratuity to the captain's assistant, Rem or Kem, a beanstalky Eurotrash dude with a bleached ponytail who wore mauve silk blazers and snuck peeks at Kerouac paperbacks in the quieter moments of the trip. But I think stateroom visits were pretty rare, as most people preferred public displays that seemed risqué and full of possibilities but in fact were fairly chaste and thus ceremonial. For example, the night I met Rita, Dr. Rick had set up shop on the foredeck and was "reading" the soles of women's feet, offering extra rub therapy to anyone who wanted it, which was nearly all of them.

Rita wasn't one of the women who lined up for a foot consultation, nor was she a reveler or a party girl. To be perfectly honest she initially stood out to me and probably everyone else because she was the only one who wasn't white. It's no big news that in most places people tend to congregate with their own, or at least who they think is their own, and in this middle of the middle part of Long Island we're no different, nearly all of us on that boat descended from the clamoring waves of Irish and Italians and Poles and whoever else washed ashore a hundred or so years ago, but you're never quite conscious of such until somebody shows up and through no intention of her own throws a filter over the scene, altering the familiar effects. When she and her girlfriend walked up the gangplank I heard some idiot behind me mutter, "Hey, somebody invited their maid," but no one else minded save one older lady who made a face. He was focused on Rita. Anyone could see she was pretty much a knockout, Puerto Rican or not. She was wearing a crisply tailored cream-colored blazer and matching skirt cut well above the knee, her legs just full and rounded enough that you thought if you were her husband or boyfriend you'd always grip them firmly, with a purposeful appreciation. I was the first person to talk to Rita, not for any honorable reason except that I was standing next to her when the boat cast off, and we bon-voyaged the landlubbers on the dock, as seafaring people will. Later on, the guy who made the remark was standing right behind me at the bar in his white polyester suit, and when I got the order of strawberry daiquiris for me and Rita and her friend Susie I turned and fell into him, square and true, leaving a wide pinkish Rorschach of what looked just like a woman's mouth, and though I bought his drinks and gave him extra for dry cleaning I have to say the rest of his evening was a certified flop.

When I returned, Rita noticed a couple of drops of red on my shirt collar and thoughtfully blotted them with a wet wipe from her handbag, leaning quite close to me, which I liked immediately and Rick winked at but which I had to step back from—figuratively, at least. For just as suddenly I was aware of how I myself was viewing us, and especially viewing her, this lovely darker-skinned woman attending to some average white dude she'd just met, which should be, of course, a completely silly, waste-of-time consideration but one that I was spooling about nonetheless, even as I was trying to breathe in every last molecule of her perfumed, green appley-smelling hair.

Rick then suggested we dance and the four of us pretty much took over the small square of hardwood they'd laid down on the fat part of the boat, Rick and Susie getting kind of wild with the synchronized pelvic movements, Rita and I more grooving than moving, early '70s style. Rick brought Susie over and started a kick line with us, boy-girl-boy-girl, arms and shoulders linked, something that can be genuinely fun for about ten seconds. But then I felt Rick's hand start to grab at my neck, and then claw, and I looked over at him and his face was the color of concrete. Susie screamed and let go of us. I caught Rick before he collapsed and Rita went right into trauma mode, ordering Susie to tell the captain to turn around for port. He was having a heart attack. Rick's eyes were open but they didn't seem to be focusing on anything. Then they brightened. He said, "I'm okay, I'm okay," as if he truly meant it, and I swear I was sure he would be, because that's what we all wanted. But his eyes went dumb again and he didn't say anything after that.

Rita attempted CPR continuously, though by the time we got back to the dock twenty minutes later he was pretty much gone. I can say she was downright heroic, and then immeasurably composed throughout the ordeal, and simply held his hand at the end. The EMS crew that was waiting took Rick away, and the three of us followed the ambulance to the hospital. After a short time in the trauma room the ER doctor came out and told us he had died. Susie began crying, mostly because of the trauma of it, for she hadn't met him before. I was the only one who really knew him, but when the nurse asked me whom they could call (his ex-wife or siblings or parents), I had no idea who they were or where they lived. This was the truly sorry part. They basically had to treat him like any other DOA who was wheeled in alone, needing the police to look up his records and locate next of kin.

Rita's friend Susie was getting more and more upset, and so Rita told her that she should go home, and that she would stay with me until someone from Rick's family showed up. She lived close by and could easily take a taxi. I told her I was fine and that she'd done enough but she insisted, and I agreed only if I could at least give her a lift home. Rick's sister and most recent ex-wife showed up and promptly nose-dived as anyone would, and when they righted themselves a little, Rita and I took our leave as gracefully as we could, hugging the aggrieved and leaving our phone numbers and generally feeling shell-shocked ourselves. I drove her to her apartment and before she got out of the car she must have seen something wrong in my face because she asked if she could make me a cup of coffee.

We went inside her tiny but very tidy apartment and talked for an hour or so. She was just starting as a nurse's aide, going to nursing school at night, and sometimes doing child care for extra money. When I told her I had been having trouble finding the right person to watch my kids after they came home from school, we both sort of lit up and I swear I had no visions of romance when I asked if she might want to give us a try. It was only after a couple of weeks that I began to think about leaving early from work and then get this I-dropped-my-ice-cream feeling when it was time for her to go. Why shouldn't I have? When I'd get home she'd already be feeding the kids some delicious meal and for once since Daisy died they'd be eating all of it, and though it wasn't part of her duties she'd make plenty of extra and then pop open a bottle of beer and I'd take it to the shower with me and when I came back out dig in like Crusoe to the *carne* and dirty rice or whatever else she'd made (the gourmet cuisine she developed later). After she'd clean up the kitchen we'd all sit around and watch a sitcom or two until bedtime for the kids. Those were good times, as good as the few Daisy and I had when she was alive, and maybe even better, full as they were with a quiet pleasure that wouldn't be sullied by sudden implosions of crying or madness.

These days, I'm feeling shorn clean by time and event and circumstance, so much so that I'm not even so hungry anymore. But now here's Rita, in her white shoes, walking out of the ER doors. Her dark hair is straighter than before, a little shorter, devolumized of its natural kink. I have to believe this must be Counselor Coniglio's high-class influence, which I don't think in the least right, but none of it matters because she's a beautiful woman who's reached an age when her loveliness begins to haunt, in addition to the usual provoke and inspire.

Before I can wave she sees me. Halts for a beat. Finally comes forward, but not too close, staying near the front fender.

"I don't need a ride, you know."

"I know."

"Have you visited Kelly yet?" she says.

"She was asleep. I left her flowers. I'll come back later today."

"And where are you going now?"

"I was hoping to follow you somewhere. Maybe I can take you to breakfast?"

"I'm not eating breakfast anymore. Or lunch."

"What do you mean?"

"I'm on Slim-Fast."

"That shake stuff? You're kidding. You don't need to do that."

"I do. And don't be patronizing. You don't know, Jerry, what happens to a woman. How we age. You take everything for granted."

"You look great to me. Fantastic, even. Honest."

Rita just stares at me, I know rolling about that last word in her head. I am honest, certainly, and always am with her, but it's the doing more than professing that counts for the most, particularly in matters of love, especially when you've been long found out.

"I can sit with you, if you like. Just don't give me crap about my diet."

"I won't. Hop in."

"I'll follow you," she says, jangling her keys at me. "And don't try to take me anywhere near the house."

At a diner on Jericho Turnpike we take a window booth looking out onto the boulevard. It's backed up with the morning rush, as far as we can see, something that neither of us has ever had to deal with much, if at all, the sight of which makes our little square of space seem cozy and calm. Rita, looking better than great to me, her skin a summertime cocoa, orders just ice water and an extra glass. Out of sympathy I get a half grapefruit and toast and coffee, instead of my usual Mexican omelet. She takes a can of vanilla-flavored diet drink out of her bag and pours it, and it reminds me of those supplement formulas they give my father at the assisted living home, which he rails against but drinks anyway, mostly so he can complain how no one will ever again make the dishes for him that my mother did. Rita, as mentioned, is a gourmet cook, and it actually pleases me to think that she's having a shake for breakfast and for lunch and then a sensible (read boring) dinner with Richie, and not preparing him the scallop terrines and pepper-pork tenderloins and honey-glazed short ribs that made our years so thoroughly fine.

Or maybe she does, cooking just for him, serving it on fine china, in a sexy petite-sized uniform, nothing on underneath.

"Kelly told me you're still seeing Richie," I say, deciding that I probably don't have a lot of time (given our orders), or future chances. "How's it going?"

"I'm not sure it's any of your business. Especially since you know him."

"Only from a long time ago. Doesn't he ask about you and me? About all our history?"

"Actually he never has."

"Conceited little bastard. Even when he was a loudmouth runt who had nothing to be conceited about. That's why everyone picked on him. I was the only one who was nice to him, you know."

Rita doesn't defend him, or say anything else about it. She says, "How are the kids?"

"They're doing great," I say, for a second entertaining the fantasy that she is talking about ours, once little ones in jumpers with snot on their faces. "Theresa is engaged. To a writer. You never met Paul, did you?"

"Just once, briefly."

"You'll be there for the wedding, whenever it happens."

"I'm not sure yet."

"It would break Theresa's heart if you didn't show. You can bring Richie along, I don't mind. But I think you really can't miss it."

"I wouldn't bring Richie," she says, taking a sip from her drink. "What about Jack? How's his new house?"

"They've got space like you can't believe. It's about five times bigger than our place . . . I mean my place. They have refrigerated drawers in the kitchen, and a water tap right over the stove, for the pasta water. This is perfect for Eunice. She can only boil macaroni."

"She doesn't have time to cook. She's too busy with her decorating business."

"You mean too busy buying furniture and rugs. They're starting to buy art, and I don't mean poster reproductions. They went into the city last week for an auction at *Christie's.* I've got a feeling they brought back something grand."

"Sounds like Battle Brothers is doing well."

"Jack's expanding it like crazy. I never knew he could be such a mogul. He was always the shyest kid."

"He's like your father," Rita says. "Secret Mussolini."

"Oh God."

"Jack's not as confident as Hank. But he's a lot sweeter."

I say, "He cares too much what people think."

"Your opinion especially."

This is probably true, though I've never acknowledged it, for fear of making it forever stick. (Theresa has the opposite problem, by the way, which I have never minded, though often enough she can be a pain in the neck.) One thing I've learned as a parent is never to call a spade a spade when it comes to your offsprings' failings and defects, no matter their age. And now I remember, too, how well Rita knows my children, as she shepherded them through their adolescence when everything fell apart after Daisy died, and I was mostly absent to them and to much all else, save the business of shrubs and mulch.

"They love you, you know," I say, despite how completely low and unfair it is to bring up the kids like this. "They'll love you to death."

Rita of course instantly sees through all my stratagems but what I've said is undeniably true, and she can do little else but avert her gaze down into her foamy parfait glass and try not to relent. If I had the guts I'd follow with the coup de grace of how I feel about her, utter the words, or at least recite a few verses from the poet, to wonder if she might accept "The desire of the moth for the star/Of the night for the morrow, / The devotion to something afar/From the sphere of our sorrow."

But Rita doesn't wait for me, the great never-poet, to even try, and takes one last sip of her breakfast. She wipes her mouth and loops a hand through her bag handles, leaving a dollar for the tip.

"I'm leaving," she says, rising. "Goodbye."

"Wait a second."

"No."

"I haven't even finished my breakfast yet."

"You eat fast. You'll be done before I'm in my car."

"Can't you humor me just a little?"

Rita sits back down, eyes afire, and says in a whisper, "You have a lot of fucking nerve."

"I do?"

"Yes, you do," she says, leaning forward. "Because you don't even care how obvious it is, what you're doing. You have no clue what you're saying or what it might mean."

"That Jack and Theresa think the world of you? I don't have to hide what that means. It means you can't just up and leave their lives. You're almost their stepmother."

"Oh please," she says, gathering up her things again. "Do you know how silly that sounds? *Almost stepmother?* Anyway, they're not concerned. They know they'll see me again plenty. It's you, Jerry, like always. You're the one never budging from the center of the show. You're forever the star."

"If that's the guy who's got to do all the worrying, then so be it."

"Right," she says, with an unappreciative smirk. "Why don't you just say what you want to say. I know it's not that you're so worried about Kelly."

"Hey, you said yourself she'll be fine. At least she's in good hands," I say, though now I'm regretting how I unpadlocked her. "It's you I'm not so sure about."

"Me? You've got to be kidding."

"How can that guy be right for you? How do you stand him? He has no idea how ridiculous he looks. Sir Richard of Chukkah. Does he imagine that they'll let his dago ass into Piping Rock or Creek Club?"

Rita says, "He's a member of both, actually. Not that I find that impressive. So what else?"

"Okay, then. What's he do all by himself over there at Tara? And why did his wife leave him? I bet he screwed around on her, for years. And then worked some legal hoodoo to boot her and the kids out."

"She cheated on him, and ran off and married the guy. She didn't want the place. And his kids and grandkids stay with him for most of the summers. And for what he does around the house, he likes to garden and read. He practices tai chi. He's also a very good Asian cook, Thai and Japanese."

"I always took you to Benihana's."

"Yes, you did."

So I say, full of it, "He sounds like the ideal man."

"He certainly isn't!" Rita says, like she's tired of the idea. "But at least he's interested in things. He's still curious. He never complains about being bored. He's always searching, but not in a stupid or desperate way."

"Sounds sort of pathetic to me."

"That's not a surprise."

"So why don't you marry him, then?"

"I'm thinking about it," she answers, with a little oomph.

"He's asked you?"

Rita nods. "The other night."

"Christ. You've barely been seeing him six months."

"We're not young people."

"He give you a ring?"

She pauses, then takes a jewelry box from her bag, cracks it open. Voilà. It's huge, a rock and a half, the size of something that you get from a gumball machine tucked inside a plastic bubble. It's frankly amazing, its sheer objecthood, this token-become-totem. Having nothing to counter with, I feel ushered aside already, obsolete, biologically diminished just in the way I'm supposed to be by another man's splendid offering.

"Of course Richard wants me to take my time, really think it through."

What I'm thinking is, Richard is a dope.

I say, "Only fair and right."

Rita says, "But I don't want to linger with this. No way. I'm not going to do that."

"Listen," I tell her, bearing down now, "you're not someone who makes quick decisions. It's not in your nature. You shouldn't do so, especially now. It's no good."

"You think I should do what I did for the last twenty-one years? You think that was good for me?"

This is the part where I usually answered that our legal union wouldn't have made things better than they were, and where Rita would say that she'd have something now, after all she put into our relationship and my family, and where I'd point out that it was her unilateral decision to leave, to which she'd respond that of course it wasn't about money or property but respect, meaning my respect for her and for myself. This is the part that is hardest to speak about, because all along I'd thought I was treating her like a queen. Maybe I didn't shop at Tiffany or Harry Winston, but I always bought her very nice jewelry from Fortunoff's, and we took plenty of trips to sexy all-inclusive resorts, and I never expected her to keep working as a nurse, if she wanted instead to just stay home and garden and cook and read (all the things she's clearly doing with Richie). The aforementioned seems, at least from my view, to be as good as it gets with a guy like me, or maybe with anyone who isn't an emotionally available millionaire or professional masseur (the two life profiles of men women desire most, according to a magazine at my doctor's office). But I guess I'm dead wrong again because the sum reality of my efforts is that I'm sitting here trying desperately to say something she'll believe, or that at least will gain me a temporary stay.

"You can't marry Richie" is what I muster. "You just can't. Can't."

Rita waits for the reason, the angle or argument, though soon enough she realizes there is none coming, just this obtuse plea from her just freshly aging former lover, who is limply waving a serrated grapefruit spoon. *Can't.* She wants to scold me, throttle me, certainly say hell all and scram, but she doesn't yet move, God bless her, she doesn't bolt.

"You make me so tired," she says, slumping back a little. "You should leave me alone."

"I was trying."

"You have to try harder. Otherwise, I can't see you. I won't." Her meaning: *Ever.*

"Don't marry Richie," I say, though sounding funny to myself, like I'm a lamentable young man in an old summer-love movie, flesh-and-blood wreckage. "Marry me."

Rita giggles, then laughs, out loud, with enough hilarity that the jelly roll gang hunched at the lunch counter turn around half smiling, to see what the joke is all about.

"I'm serious, Rita. Marry me."

Rita stops laughing. She glares, then picks up her handbag

and walks out. I head outside after her, calling her, but she ignores me and quickly gets into her car, which she never locks. The windows are never rolled up either, and I stand right over her as she tries to get the old motor going, *karumph, karumph,* and if you didn't know any better you'd think I was a rapist or stalker or three-eyed space lizard, the way she's cranking that thing. I can tell she's flooding the engine, but I say nothing. Our waitress has followed me out, waving the check, but I'm not paying attention because this is a not-yet-depleted moment in what seems to be my increasingly depleted life, and I'm telling Rita to stop trying to leave as the waitress keeps saying, "Hey, buster," and tapping my arm, and finally Rita steps out of the car and whacks me hard on the chest, not quite open-handed.

"She's talking to you, Jerry! Listen!" Rita digs a ten-spot from her bag and gives it to the waitress, who shoots me a kick-in-the-shins smirk if there ever was one. Rita shouts, "What's the matter with you?"

"I'm serious," I say, feeling the stamp of her hand bloom hot on my skin. "I really am."

"Doesn't matter," she answers, now getting back in the driver's seat. She tries to roll up the window, but it only goes three-quarters of the way. "You think our not getting married is still the issue, don't you?"

"It's not not, is it?" I say, the idiot in me inappropriately focused on the unexpected palindrome. This is an excellent way to get into trouble. Though I rally. "I realize that it's not the whole problem."

"And what, in your mind, is that?"

"C'est moi," I say, though maybe a bit too eagerly. "It's me. It's all about me."

Of course this is accurate enough, though rather than

illuminate or chart a new course, this mostly deflates the moment, which seems to be a growing skill of mine.

Rita says, as if she's been holding her breath forever, "Fine, then."

"Can you come out of there now?"

Rita shakes her head. She looks down into her lap, slips her sunglasses on, and starts turning the engine over again, now going *badank ba-dank.* I'm sure it will soon quit entirely, but then somehow the damn thing rumbles to life, all muscle and smoke, spirit ghost of Dearborn. She clicks the car into reverse and tells me to watch my feet.

"Don't do anything yet," I say, "at least not until after the weekend. Theresa's flying in, and we're having a get-together at Jack's. Why don't you come? Everyone would love to see you."

"I'm sorry, Jerry."

"I'll pick you up on Saturday afternoon."

"Please don't," she says, backing it out.

"I'll call you!"

She mouths a big *No* and gives a tiny wave, like she's peering out the window from two thousand feet. Then she squeals rubber to accelerate out onto the jet flows of the Jericho Turnpike, and is gone.

three

THE HOUSE THAT Jack built is in a gated development called Haymarket Estates, a brand-new luxury "enclave" that sits on what was a patch of scrubby land a few exits east of where I live. From the Expressway you can actually catch a glimpse of the rooftops peeking out over the barrier wall, the covenant-defined cedar shake or slate tile shingles trimmed out with polished copper ice dams and gutters, the stone-faced chimneys and handcrafted lintel work fresh and gleaming, with the sole unglamorous detail being all the mini–satellite dishes looking up toward the southern sky with a strange kind of succor. When Jack bought the dusty .47-acre lot a few years ago for what seemed an inexcusable amount of money, he assured me that it'd be worth at least twice as much now, which has proven true despite the flagging economy, given what the last remaining parcels sold for in recent months. The heady rise in land values prompted him and Eunice to go ahead with plans for a much bigger house than they had originally wanted, not minding that the structure would take up most of their property, rendering it useless for any large-scale kids' play or a decent-sized pool. The proportion is really the opposite of my place, where my modest ranch house sits right smack in the middle of the property (just over an acre), so that I have plenty of trees and shrubs and lawn to buffer me from my good neighbors.

The side of Jack's house, on the other hand, is only about ten of my paces from the side wall of his neighbor's, which would be normal-looking in an old suburban neighborhood of row-type houses but feels as narrow as an olde London alleyway given the immensity of the houses. But as Jack has pointed out, who wants to be outside where it's buggy and noisy with the Expressway and in the summertime the rumble of the AC compressors (four for his house alone)? Jack's house is around 6500 square feet, not including the full-length basement or three-car garage, which is pretty typical of the development, or more than three times bigger than the house he grew up in. Eunice decorated the place herself, which continues to be a full-time job. You walk in to a vaulted two-and-a-half-story circular entryway with green marble floors inlaid with a multicolored sunburst, a double-landed soapstone stairwell rising up to the second floor. On the main level there's a media room with a widescreen television and every kind of audio component, including ones that seem not to do anything but monitor the sound, for frequency response and digital dropouts and some such. There's a separate rolling caddy for the army of remotes, which Jack has actually just replaced with a console-sized touch-screen unit that supposedly controls everything in the house, including the lights and HVAC and security system. There's of course the French country manor living room that no one ever uses and then the "library," which is in fact pretty gorgeous, lined as it is with panels of glass-smooth walnut and custom cabinetry and furnished with leather club chairs and sofas and antique Persian rugs. Jack even installed a special ventilation system in there, so he can smoke cigars with his golf buddies when they come back to play poker. The funny thing is that the bookshelves are mostly taken up by rows and rows of home and design magazines that Eunice gets each month, and then the big coffee-table art and design books, though Eunice says that they'll be getting some "shipments" of real books soon enough, as she's joined several book-of-the-month clubs, where you get twelve tomes for a penny. And there's a television, too, as there is in every room, though this one is regular-sized and discreetly tucked behind cabinet doors, maybe in deference to the dying world of letters.

The stainless-steel-and-granite kitchen is enormous, certainly, as it has to house two of everything, from refrigerators to dishwashers to trash compactors. Eunice and Jack like to entertain, as they are doing today, but on a wedding caterer's scale, which you can tell by the size of their baking sheets and stockpots, the latter being the kind you see in cartoons in which the natives are making soup of the hapless explorer. Off the kitchen is the plain two-room suite where the nanny/cook/housekeeper, Rosario, stays six nights a week, only leaving on Sunday morning to spend a day and night with her husband and two children and mother, who live somewhere deep in Queens. Eunice, in the parlance, doesn't work "outside the house," but as far as I can tell Rosario is doing all the heavy lifting inside, plus the light duty, too. I don't blame Eunice, as it's her prerogative and privilege to spend her days poring over her decorating books and taking yoga and not toasting a slice of bread unless it's a full-blown event (when she transforms into

Lady Sub-Zero, her tools and prep lists and chopped and measured ingredients c/o Rosario laid out on her island counter in military formation), but I wish sometimes she'd spend more casual, horsing-around time with the kids, just lollygagging, rather than scheduling the endless "enrichment" exercises and activities for them that are undoubtedly brain-expanding but must be as fun as memorizing pi to twenty-five places. At bedtime she or Jack will read them only library-recommended books and then retreat to their 1500-square-foot master bedroom suite featuring his and her tumbled-stone bathrooms fitted with steam shower/sauna and then the *lounge-in* closets that could make perfectly nice studio condos in Manhattan, Jack checking the company website and e-mail and Eunice surfing the six hundred channels for a movie she hasn't seen yet. (Once, in the downstairs media room, I browsed all the channels one by one, pausing long enough to get a good glimpse of each, and it took about thirty minutes to get back to where I started, which I realized was like watching a TV show in itself, and not in fact a half-bad one, relatively speaking.)

And as I drive past the gate (where the surly goateed guard still calls up the house to check if they're expecting me, this after about thirty visits) and turn onto the single long circular street of the development past the other not-so-mini mansions, I have to tell myself again that my son is doing more than all right, that I should be so lucky to have to worry that these bulwarks of his prosperity (not just the house but his German sedan, the luxury SUVs, the country club membership, the seasonal five-star vacations) are maybe too much for anyone to handle, and especially Jack, who's always been a bit impressionable and unsure of himself and sometimes too eager to please. Why he's like this I don't like to muse upon too much, as it more than likely has to do with what happened to Daisy when he was nine, though maybe this is not the whole story; Theresa (only a year younger) went through the same shitstorm of unhappiness and is totally different. Though again this may be her particular psychic response to misery and sadness, which made her become more like herself than she would have been had she been raised under neutrally pleasant laboratory conditions.

I suppose the Grandeur of Life does this to all of us, forging us into figures more like ourselves than we'd otherwise be, for better and/or worse, and so you wonder what ramifications in substance and detail there'd be, say, what kind of house Jack would be living in, had his mother never died, whether he would have married an altogether together woman like Eunice, whether he would have taken up the business of Battle Brothers at all. Naturally I think too of what might have become of me in that time line with Daisy still alive, if I'd be with her still, or else have gotten divorced and married Rita forthwith and had children with her. With the exception of the first six months and a few assorted days early on (the birth of the kids, a couple of anniversaries, that one Thanksgiving when Daisy practically carbonized the bird and we ended up in the city at Tavern on the Green, jaunting afterward down Fifty-ninth Street giddy with the Christmas lights and a bottle of Chablis, the kids riding high on our shoulders), there was rarely if ever joyousness or glee, with Daisy scuttled and sunk down in the troughs of her gray day moods. Probably I dug everything a bit deeper with my attitude, which back then was one of constant irritation and stress, as the economy was in the dumper and my father hadn't yet fully retired from Battle Brothers and the kids seemed only to speak the language of lament and whine, being generally neglected and cast aside, and then that episode of the $7000

Bloomingdale's charge. Still, I was a jerk, seriously unhappy as jerks often are, though this is no excuse for anything, and certainly not for what would become my chronic habit of abstaining from the familial activities of the house, in the evenings sitting alone in my study poring over the travel guides to places I wanted to go, highlighting the sights and restaurants like I was already on the tour charter, the little bottles of wine lined up on my tray.

Jack would sometimes come in and tell me Daisy wasn't in the house, and after a few times I'd stop asking where she'd gone to and just put him back to bed. Daisy would then come home at two or three in the morning wearing a fuck-me outfit smelling of cigarettes and Lancer's wine, and if we argued at all it was about her making too much noise when she came in. Jack would run out of his room crying for us to stop yelling, sometimes getting upset enough that he'd pee in his pants. It thus makes sense to me that Jack would end up being the one to feature this grand house (Theresa perfectly content with whatever post-doc-style housing she and Paul can flop in each academic autumn with their fold-up Ikea furniture), and then always gathering us for dinners and parties and taking "candid" black-and-white pictures, as if he and Eunice were trying to recast our family into one that might appear in a fashion magazine spread titled something like "The Spoils of Battle."

We'd probably be just right, too, for such a shoot, not only because we have a nice generational mix going (white-haired patriarch, sportive young parents, peach-cheeked toddlers) but also because we're an ethnically jumbled bunch, a grab bag miscegenation of Korean (Daisy) and Italian (us Battles) and English-German (Eunice) expressing itself in my and Jack's offspring with particularly handsome and even stunning results. As a group you can't really tell what the hell we are, though more and more these days the very question is apparently dubious, if not downright crass, at least to folks like Theresa and Paul, whose race-consciousness is clearly quite different from mine. I suppose what's critical to them is who's asking the question, for if it's an average white guy like me there's only awkwardness and embarrassment ahead, the assumption being I'm going to blindly buy into a whole raft of historical "typologies" and "antecedents" and turn around and plonk somebody with the label of Other. This, by the way, is and isn't a terrible thing. They inordinately fear and respect the power of the word, having steadily drawn down the distinctions between Life and Text. Let me say that when I was growing up the issues could be a lot heavier than that, a switchblade or Louisville Slugger being the *text* of choice, and one not so easily parsed or critiqued.

Jack, on the other hand, seems totally unconcerned about such matters, and always has been, but I can't say for certain, because we've never discussed the subject. He's never been what anybody would call a brainy kid, and not just in the test-taking academic sense (which was how smarts used to be measured), but I suppose none of that mattered much because he's done more than fine and seems happy enough and doesn't seem to wrestle with questions too big or medium or small. Maybe he has strong feelings and painful memories of awkward and searing experiences as to his identity and character but it's just as likely not. I've often thought it's because he's very fair and Anglo-looking, tall and long-legged and with barely a lilt to the angle of his eyes. Such as it is, I believe he's always *passed*, any lingering questions quickly squashed by his model-good looks and good-guy demeanor, which have always attracted plenty of the popular crowd to the house, to my eye at least. I can't remember his once dating a girl who wasn't your classic American blonde (from the bottle or not), Eunice (you-*NEECE*) Linzer Robeson being the most impressive of the bunch, and easily the sharpest. I see her now, outside on the massive slatestone front landing of her house, cordless phone ever in hand. She waves, and I pull into the semicircular part of the driveway already packed with cars. This surprises, as I thought the party was to be an intimate family affair, but then I should know that the Battles of Haymarket Estates can't do anything too downscale/downmarket, as if they'd ever really have a cookout of burgers and dogs.

"Where have you been, Jerry?" she says brightly, covering the mouth holes. "Jack's out getting more ice and juice boxes."

Eunice kisses me and sends me inside, signaling Rosario's teenage daughter, Nidia, as she's now getting into issues with the caterer about the flatware and wineglasses, which as usual aren't exactly what she requested. In these situations Eunice never yells or raises her voice, but rather speaks at the downward angle of a third-grade teacher, with a patient, if often chilly, enunciation. In the clickety marble rotunda Nidia, in a crisp white shirt and black skirt, greets me with a flute of Champagne, and I note that she's looking exceptionally womanly, particularly in the important parts, and I contrive to make her linger a little as I down the first glass and then take another. I've seen her perhaps once a year for the last four, each time appreciating more deeply the march of youth's time. She smiles (not unwickedly?), and trots off. In the rotunda I notice the walls have been stripped of the "old" wallpaper and freshly painted, and the windows newly shaded with a single panel of muted silken fabric, clearly redone to complement the quartet of abstract paintings that recently arrived from the auction house, which, at least to my Art History 101 eye, look like real Kandinskys (and I very much hope are not).

In the great room/media room, Jack's kids, Tyler (girl) and Pierce (boy), are watching a Britney Spears concert DVD on the widescreen with a handful of other slack-jawed toddlers and young children who I'm sure are also named for minor presidents, and when I kneel down to kiss them they do manage a faint grunt and smile. This is true love, given the circumstance, which I appreciate and don't question. Along my sight line from here through the kitchen I can see the score or so of grownups mingling outside on the back deck, friends of Jack's and Eunice's and old buddies of Theresa's, some of whom I recognize and could speak to of specific times way back when but whose names I could hardly remember then and have no clue to now. Theresa used to get furious at me whenever she'd bring friends home and I'd dance around having to address them and afterward I'd plead early Alzheimer's but she knew it was because I never quite paid full attention. Unfortunately she thought it was only her but really it was a much more global problem than that and something I'm not sure she's over yet, or will ever be. It's funny how my grandkids (and their playmates) are now the ones calling the shots, as they're endlessly fussed over by Rosario and their preschool teachers and by Eunice and Jack and then even by me. The only one not readily kowtowing is my father, whose firm and sometimes gruff stance with them is not so much about teaching deference or respect but reminding one and all of his own status as family patriarch/biggest boy.

He's nowhere to be found, though, and I head out onto the massive multilevel redwood deck, where Theresa and Paul are holding court by the buffet table. Paul sees me first and waves the big wave. Theresa glances over and nods, still talking to her friends, while Paul approaches. As mentioned, Paul grew up only a short distance from here, but after having spent a number of years on the West Coast he's no longer outwardly pushy and irritable like a lot of people on the Island. He talks softly, with an almost Western, cowboyish loll to his speech, which frankly is strange to hear from an Asian face. He wears his straight black hair quite long and somewhat ratty, though today he's gathered it in a ponytail, which is neater but still gives me the willies. From the back you'd swear he was a girl, with his short, slightish frame and periodic horsey tosses of the head, but from what I gather these days long tresses on a man usually indicate a hetero-supreme, a type, surprisingly, to which Theresa has always been drawn, and then to older ones, which Paul is (by eight years). I like him very much, despite his hemp-cloth-and-bead exterior, as deep down he's a thoroughly decent and affable fellow without a lot of that self-important artistic gaseousness that has to fill whatever room its owner finds himself in.

His parents, Dr. and Dr. Pyun, who aren't here today because this party was only recently planned and they had long booked (through me) an eighteen-day Bella Extravanganza tour to all the famous spots in Italy, are a sweet and always smiling couple, at least on the surface, though I can tell, too, like the few other Asians I've come into contact with over the years, that they are not so quietly tenacious about what they want. When they came into the office to set up their trip I got the distinct feeling that they were sure I was going to sell them the most expensive package, and were intent upon starting from the bargain-bin tours I'd normally only recommend for pensioners and Catholic school teachers. I'd heard from Paul that they were interested in going to Italy (for the first time), and I called them directly and urged them to come in to see me. Maybe my zeal was suspicious, plus the fact that they weren't sold on the idea that I was a travel agent for reasons other than the sorry pay and needling customers (they'd certainly never imagine passing their retirement that way). Mrs. Dr. Pyun even asked a few times what the trip would cost "not counting commissions." Undeterred, I took them through the whole range of offerings, noting what I thought were the best values and itineraries, and they decided to go with a great mid-priced tour called "Savors of the Past," which mixes art and ruins with food-and-wine-oriented excursions. When I informed them that I'd of course not only credit them my commission but also try to sneak them in at a special industry rate, they positively burst with happy refusals, saying there was absolutely no need, and Dr. Pyun said something to his wife in Korean and she said something back that somehow sounded to me like *Why not?* Soon enough they were insisting on taking the ultraluxe package I had only briefly mentioned, and only if they paid the regular price. Afterward we had a gyro lunch at the Greek place next door, where they basically told me that they believed Paul (much unlike their two other sons, who were Ivy League grads and established attorneys) had no real prospects and they would not be surprised if I was very upset, being Theresa's father. I told them I wasn't, and that I was confident Paul's career would soon take off, and that his talents would be fully appreciated, if not in financial terms. They both sort of laughed, which I took to be their way of throwing up their hands, and Dr. Pyun said with finality, "Ahh—he's never going to be famous."

But apparently Paul is somewhat famous, at least in certain rarefied academic/literary circles, which is great if true but also means that no one I've met on a train or plane or in a waiting room has ever heard of him, much less read his books. And I do always ask. *I've* read his books (three novels and a chapbook of poetry), and I can say with great confidence that he's the sort of writer who can put together a nice-sounding sentence or two and does it with feeling but never quite gets to the point. Not that I've figured out what his point might be, though I get the sense that the very fact I'm missing it means I'm sort of in on it, too. I guess if you put a gun to my head I'd say he writes about The Problem with Being Sort of Himself—namely, the terribly conflicted and complicated state of being Asian and American and thoughtful and male, which would be just dandy in a slightly different culture or society but in this one isn't the hottest ticket. I know, for example, that his big New York publisher just recently parted company with him, deciding not to publish his latest manuscript, which was also passed on by the other major houses and will be issued instead by a small outfit called Seven Tentacle Press near where they live in Florence, Oregon, in a softcover format.

"Hey there, Jerry," Paul says, giving me his usual lovechild hug, wiry and sneaky strong. "What's shaking?"

"Nothing much. Congratulations, by the way."

"Thank you," Paul says, his eyes checking me. "You truly okay with this?"

"Are you kidding? I'm thrilled. Theresa is lucky to have you."

"That's what you think. She's the one with regular employment."

"Of course she is," I say. "But you're the one everyone should support. You're the artist."

"The Artist Formerly Known as Publishable."

"Come on, now, you'll get this new one out and those editors in the city will come begging, checkbooks ready. There'll be piles of the book at Costco, right next to Crichton and Grisham."

"Sure," he says. "I bet there are remaindered copies at the All for $1 store, between bins of cheap nail polish and Spanish-labeled cat food."

"Well, you're wrong." But this makes me pause for a half second, as last year in fact I did find his second novel, *Drastic Alterations,* at such a place in the Walt Whitman Mall. I ended up buying all seventeen copies and giving them as Christmas gifts to the employees of Battle Brothers, only one of whom, my longtime foreman, Boots, e-mailed me with comments ("Kinda tough read for me, skip, but English wasn't my best subject. Also, I didn't get the small print at the bottom. Thanks, anyway"). I began to reply that the "small print" was *footnotes,* as in a research term paper, except that this was a story with *avant-garde features,* but then I realized Boots might not have finished high school, or even middle school for that matter, and I just commended him for trying. Of course I would never tell Paul about any of this, as I'm sure it would plainly depress the crap out of him, and further ratify his recent thinking about how his career was going, as he's put it, from "mid-list" to "no-list." In our last few conversations he's joked a bit too pointedly about self-publishing and getting into teaching or editing or even Hollywood screenwriting, perhaps trying to warn me that my daughter was marrying a fellow with ever-diminishing prospects. But that's the case with almost everyone in the broadening swath of middle age, isn't it, that we're all fatiguing in some critical way (sex, job, family), some prior area of happy vitality and self-definition that is now instead a source of anxiety and dread.

"Hey," I say, glancing over to Theresa, who's likewise been glancing over to me while talking to her friends, "I think it's high time you introduced me to your fiancée."

"Of course, of course," Paul says, and we slide over into the group, and Theresa steps forward and gives me a light hug.

"Hello, Jerry," she says, pecking me on the cheek. Theresa has called me Jerry pretty much since her mother died. I didn't correct her then, out of fear she'd be further traumatized or something like that, letting her do whatever she wanted, and we both grew accustomed to it. Right now I'm happy she's clearly not unhappy to see me, which is a welcomed happenstance, as more often than not she'd have been simmering about something I said or did since the last time we got together, gathering up this prickly potential energy to let loose on me when I was thinking all was perfectly fine. And she looks great to me, a little fuller everywhere, her skin warm with a summer glow.

"You remember Alice Woo and Jadie Srinivasan, don't you?"

"I certainly do," I say, shaking their smooth, petite hands. They address me as Mr. Battle, which fortunately jogs my memory of them, but not as being half as attractive and self-assured as they are now, more like gangly and foreign and shy. When they were young the three of them would sometimes play Charlie's Angels when they had slumber parties at our house, and they'd set up Jack's walkie-talkie, with me in the kitchen and them in the living room, and I'd say, "Hello, angels," which would delight them no end, and they'd act out whatever crazy story line they could come up with, and then vamp around a little bit, too, in sleazy makeup and clothes. But whenever I picked them up at the middle school after band practice or drama they slunk, as if trying to stay under the radar as they walked to the car, other girls running in from the fields in their team uniforms, ruddy-faced, hollering all, hair jouncing in shimmers of chestnut and strawberry and blond. I never drove them to the kinds of parties Jack was always invited to, mostly dropping them off for the train heading for New York or the art house cinema in Huntington Village. Of course I never said anything but wondered to myself what my daughter and her friends really thought of things, and of themselves, whether given a choice they'd remain just as they were or instead trade their black Edgar Allan Poe capes for field hockey skirts and Ray-Bans and the attentions of boys from Jack's crowd, the type who could swim (and soon enough drink) like fish and instinctively lace a pure backhand down the line. It turns out that Theresa and Alice and Jadie are exactly the sort of midnight-eyed young women you see increasingly in magazines and on billboards, which to me is a generally welcome development (being the father of such Diversity), though I'll not lie and say I'm at ease with most of the other attendant signs of our cultural march, one example being how youths from every quarter openly desire to dress as though they're either drug-addled whores or runaways or gangstas or just plain convicts, as though the whole society has embraced dereliction and criminality as its defining functions, with Theresa of course once pointing out to me that decades of governmental neglect and corporate corruption and pilfering have resulted in this hard-edged nihilistic street-level expression. At the risk of sounding like my father, I'll say that her reading of this doesn't really wash with me, though I have recently begun to accept her notions about the ineluctable creep in the realm, that the very ground beneath my feet is shifting with hardly my notice, to travel invisibly, with or without me. Though I did actually utter "My bad" the other day to Miles Quintana, after messing up a cruise reservation. So maybe I'm moving along, too.

"Do you remember," Theresa says to me, "how the three of us melted the top of the bathroom vanity with a curling iron, and you came home to all those fire engines in the driveway?"

"I don't. Did I get upset?"

"I thought you were going to have a coronary," Alice Woo says. "I'll admit right now that it was all my fault. I desperately wanted curls, just like these guys."

Jadie cries, "We practically fried your hair. But it wouldn't take."

"You needed Jeri-Curl," I say, trying my best. The girls chuckle, Paul laughing loud in his special way, a nasally yuck-yuck.

"You know, Mr. Battle, I was totally afraid of you," Jadie now says. She's very dark-complected, with immense brown eyes and a tiny silver stud piercing in her nose. Later on I'll learn that at merely thirty-one she's chief corporate counsel for a software company, where I suppose piercings and tattoos are a-okay, and maybe recommended issue, like French cuffs used to be. "Theresa can tell you. I'd always ask if you were going to be home. I thought you didn't like us coming over."

"That's not true," I say. "I was always happy for you guys to hang out."

Theresa says, matter-of-factly, "Jerry just didn't like it when people were having fun and he wasn't."

Alice offers, "That's understandable, isn't it?"

"You got that," I say.

"Sure," Theresa says, "but for a *parent*?"

This momentarily quells the moment, not to mention cutting me deep, because of course she's right in both principle and practice. I've never sat by well when others were at play, not when I was five, or fifteen, or fifty. I'd like to believe this was a question of my desiring involvement and connection, rather than of envy or selfishness. I'd like to blame my ever-indulging, spoiling, obliging mother (God bless her), or my wonderful brother Bobby for guiltlessly using up the years of his brief life;

I'd like to blame my father for giving me almost everything I required but really nothing I wanted, but that's the story of us all, isn't it, or of my particular American generation, or maybe just me, and nothing one really needs to hear about again.

"Though to be honest," my daughter now says, actually looping her arm into the crook of mine, "at least Jack and I were instructed by the master. Paul can tell you what an ornery bitch I can be, if I see he's doing a crossword when I'm washing the dishes."

"She once squirted me with the Palmolive," he says. "Right on my pajamas."

Jadie nods. "But our Theresa was like that from the beginning. When we played Barbies, Alice and I always had to keep our dolls in the camper, cleaning and making the beds, while Theresa's Barbie was outside tending the campfire, roasting hot dogs and marshmallows."

"My Barbie was chef de cuisine. You were my *femmes de chambre*. There had to be a clear order to things."

"This is sounding very sexy," Eunice says, flanked by Rosario, who is bearing a tray of canapés. Eunice explains they are "polenta blinis" topped with Sevruga caviar and lobster meat and chived crème fraîche. I'm sure Eunice did put together at least one or two model canapés, as I witnessed once at another party, with Rosario making the rest. Everybody takes one, Rosario nudging me with the tray edge to grab a couple more. I comply.

"Incredible. Did you really make these?" Alice asks, to which Eunice smiles modestly but distinctly. Rosario drifts across the massive deck, to offer them to the others.

"It wasn't so difficult. The key is good components."

"We would have been happy with carrot sticks and onion dip," Theresa says, "but I'm glad you went all out."

"Oh please, it's nothing special."

This is true. Ever since she and Jack got married I've never had so much Muscovy duck and Dungeness crab and Belon oysters coursing through the old iron pipes. Rita cooked fancy but always with modest ingredients, being loath to use anything that cost over $3 a pound. With Eunice it's only the rare and *cher*, artisanal meats and breads and cheeses, exotic flown-in fishes and fruits, wines from exclusive "garage" vintners, coffee from secret hillsides in Kenya and Nepal and Vermont. As she says, it's all about the components, which indeed are often wondrously tasty, reminding one of the fundamental goodness of the plain and natural; but there's still, I think, an even more satisfying gut-strum in what someone can magically do with a little herb and spice and heat, Rita's pulled-pork casserole being exquisite proof of that. Eunice can surely wow almost anybody with her deft arrangements, but I will swear there's a *love* to be found in your basic Crock-Pot alchemy, which even the sweetest lobster tail or dollop of sturgeon eggs cannot easily provide.

"I still cook the way Jerry taught me," Theresa says. "Remove pork chops from package, generously salt and pepper, bake at 375 degrees until there are no signs of moisture."

"Amazingly, it works with any meat or fish," Paul says. "Fowl, too."

"Now, I wasn't that bad," I say, mostly for the benefit of Eunice, for Alice and Jadie were sometimes actually there, watching me along with Theresa as I fumbled through the cabinets for the Shake 'n Bake and Hamburger Helper before Rita showed up. I couldn't afford a full-time nanny, and Battle Brothers was sinking fast, and I'd get home at six to cranky, hungry kids and burrow through the freezer for something that wasn't too brown-gray at the edges. "You have to realize I never had to cook until Theresa's mother died. Then it was every night I had to come up with something."

"At least until I took over," Theresa says.

"You were very advanced."

Eunice asks, "Why didn't you have Jack cook? He's older."

"I don't know. I guess Jack just didn't seem up to it."

"Jerry was afraid of feminizing him," Theresa says, right on cue. And here comes the rest. But she looks up at me and appears to wink—which is the tiniest thing but wholly a salve. What she says isn't quite right, though, which I can say with some surety because I wasn't completely unaware of what I was doing back then. The fact of the matter was I didn't want Jack to have to think of his dead mother every night, at least in a ritualized way, which in my thinking was sure to happen if he had to don an apron and fry up hamburgers. For a year or so after she died he hardly said a word, he was just a kid with eyes, and as Theresa seemed the sturdier of the two in almost all respects, I made an executive decision to have him do other chores like repainting the back fence and raking leaves and hosing out the garbage cans, which he never once complained about, and I like to think it was the bracing physical activity that eventually snapped him out of it, though I'm probably mistaken on that one.

Some of Theresa's college friends (retro eyeglasses, thrift-store chic clothes, goatees galore) come around, and the talk gets a bit too pop-cultural and swervy and superallusive for me, and so I wander about the deck, briefly mingling with couples who are obviously friends of the hosts. They're decent enough people, well-heeled youngish parents with stiff drinks padding about in upturned collars and Belgian driving loafers, crooning incessantly about the cost of beach houses and Jag convertibles and nannies, the basic tune being why all this good living should be so dear (though of course if it weren't, what would they take such fascination in, or not-so-sly pride?). One magnificently bronzed, lean-armed woman named Kit sits me down and practically goes stone by stone through the immense landscaping project she is having done on her North Fork property, the massive excavation and Teletubbies berming, the football-field-length retaining walls of Vermont slate, the 2000-square-foot limestone patio and the bluestone-decked and -bottomed pool, and the literally hundreds of mature shrubs and trees, the job (which Battle Brothers Excalibur is fortunately doing) to ring up at nearly three hundred grand alone. The recession is not of her world. Kit isn't complaining or angling for special treatment, but rather simply telling me her story, as if she is some Old Testament figure chosen to endure an epochal test from which she might someday emerge righteous and whole.

By the time Kit is all but strapping me into her Mercedes SUV to drive me out east to her place in Southold and show me the work-in-progress, Jack pats me on the shoulder, having returned from the store. Kit practically leaps into his arms, hugging him a bit too firmly for even a pleased and grateful customer, and I'm sure it's nothing even though you still hear stories these days of people offering more than loads of money to get good contractors to sign up for a job. In my day you had to dress nice and chat for as long as the customer wanted when you showed up to give an estimate, parking yourself for a long spell at a lady's kitchen table trying not to stare at the widening gap in her robe and listen to whatever she needed to tell you about her never-home husband or sick mother or super-rotten kids, knowing that nine times out of ten you wouldn't get the job. Jack chastely pecks her on the cheek and excuses us, saying that the Battle men are being requested inside, and Kit tugs at his hand, reflexively unwilling to let him go.

I trail Jack into the house. He's just a shade shorter than I am, 6'1" or so, and built a bit differently, being lower-slung than I am, his torso longer and thicker and his gait just like Daisy's was, meaning he moves in a slightly bowlegged fashion, knees pointing outward, a little bit like a pet iguana we once had, their similarities something I used to tease him about. He's got a hockey player's body, though he never played that, sticking to football and lacrosse, sports in which he excelled. As already mentioned, he's very good-looking, probably professionally so, and I can say with some pride that he's got my best features, which are a strong chin and a thick tousle of naturally wavy hair and those sparkly eyes that some people have, speckled (and in our case, hazel-colored) irises that certain folks not-so-brightly wonder aloud about—namely, whether they're bad for your vision. But it's flattering, anyway, and as Jack knows well enough is almost unfairly attractive to the opposite sex, for really all you need to do is just meet someone's gaze and hold for a moment, like the first time I met his mother, or when I met Rita, take a long, slow-shuttered picture, and watch the thing steadily develop. I go into all this mostly because I find myself admiring Jack and Theresa more and more, not so much for the people they are (they are fine people) but for their physical qualities, and I know you'll think I do so because ultimately it's all about me, my legacy and what I've bestowed upon them and so on, but it's just the opposite. Perhaps it's seeing them both here today, in full-blown adulthood, but the notion occurs that whatever I have given them is in fact very little, and diminishes with each day, and that it's already happened that they define me probably more now than I do them, which of course is just as well.

In the kitchen Nidia points us toward the powder room saying it's Pop, my father, who I didn't realize was already here but of course had to be the whole time. Eunice is talking to him through the locked door, Rosario standing by. When she sees us she steps back and says he's been moaning as though he's in pain but won't let anyone in. Just then Pop yells, "I don't need anybody. You people go away." He says *people* like we're a crowd on a subway platform, nobody he cares to know.

Jack tries the knob and says, "Come on, Pop. Let's open the door now."

"Everything stinks!" is his answer. For some reason this is my cue to make a try.

"We just want to know that you're not hurt, Pop. Are you hurt?"

"Is that you, Jerome?"

"Yeah."

"Where the hell have you been?"

"Outside on the deck."

"Well, then, everybody clear out. I only want Jerome to help me. I want my son."

"You still have to open the door for me."

"I can't," he says, weakly now. "I can't."

Jack pulls out his fat Swiss Army knife (which I taught him from early on to carry always) and plucks out its embedded plastic toothpick for me, so I can push in the lock.

"Okay, everybody scram," I say loudly. "I'll take it from here." Jack opens his hands and I wave him and Eunice and Rosario away, as well as the few kids—none from our clan—who've gathered in the hallway to rubberneck. When they've all gone back to the party I tell my father I'm coming in. He grunts, and I click out the tumbler.

My father's on the floor, his pants around his ankles. He tells me to lock the door again. I do. And then I realize that everything *does* stink, something fierce, like surly death itself, or maybe worse.

"All those damn goat cheese toasts gave me the runs," he says. Then more sheepishly, "I ran out of paper." The cabinet door to the vanity is ajar, a couple rolls of tissue spilled out onto the floor. He's made a mess of himself, soiling the edge of the seat and basin. His nose is bleeding. I try to sit him up but he groans hard when I lift him. I'm afraid it's his leg, or worse, his hip. He shrugs me off. "Goddammit, Jerome, just help clean me up first."

The stuff is all over his undershorts and slacks, riding up on his lower back and side. It's no great leap for me to think of the days when Jack and Theresa were swaddled babes, to remember carefully pinning tight their cloth diapers, holding the ends of the dirty ones and flushing them in the toilet, but this job is on another scale entirely, like in middle school when the science teacher brought out models of the Earth and Jupiter. Who could have imagined the actual difference? I know Pop has been having some control difficulty recently, enough so that the case nurse at Ivy Acres has recommended that he wear incontinence pants all the time, to prevent accidents and "needless embarrassment." I didn't bring it up with him, because I know where he'd tell me to stick it, though I note to myself that I'll soon try.

After taking off his soiled clothes I'm lucky to find a washcloth in the vanity, but it's awkward to use the bar of soap to clean him properly, and instantly understanding this Pop points to the spray bottle of Fantastik beneath the sink basin. I tell him it might burn his skin and would undoubtedly be unhealthy in any case but he says, annoyed, "You think I care about genetic damage or something? Go ahead."

The act of which is very strange, spraying him down like he's some mildewed vinyl couch brought up from the cellar. I can tell that the foam isn't sitting too well with him, his tough olive skin beginning to glimmer pink, but he doesn't wince or say a word. He just lies with his big squared head down on the tiled floor, like a sick horse or mule, not looking at me, which is a great mercy for us both. The sharp industrial scent of the solvent is an unlikely balm, too, and I clean him as quickly and thoroughly as I can. When I sit him up there's a huge grapey bruise on his upper thigh just below his hip. His wrist and elbow still sting from the short fall off the toilet but he says he can get up. I tuck my shoulder beneath his armpit and we rise. I feel the dense weight of his limbs, more of him now than there ever was, the last few years of sedentary living accruing to him like unpicked fruit, this useless bounty, and I think it's not only his body but his mind, ever cramming with unrequited notions and thoughts. As his clothes are ruined and I'm no doubt the closest in size, I take off my pants and give them to him, so he can get upstairs and shower off.

As I open the powder room door he says, "What the hell are you gonna do, walk around in your skivvies?"

"I'll get some sweatpants from Jack."

"Sounds like that's all that boy's going to be wearing, if things don't get better."

"What are you talking about?"

"What do you think? Some of us still call over there every day, you know, even though we retired a thousand years ago."

"And?"

"Sal said they've been having cash flow problems. They barely made payroll the last two weeks."

Sal is the bookkeeper for Battle Brothers, and has been since I was a kid. "Jack hasn't said anything to me."

"You ever talk shop with him?"

I don't offer an answer, and my father snorts knowingly. I still care about the business, though certainly not the way he does, and then never enough to shadow Jack all the time, nosing over his shoulder to armchair quarterback. In fact I'd say from the very beginning I tried not to mention Battle Brothers if I could help it, for just those reasons, and then partly in the hope that he would eventually pursue his own career. But I suppose such strategies are flawed and hubristic in the realm of family life and relations, that no matter what you do or don't do in the service of good intentions your aims will get turned about and around and furiously boomerang homeward. I don't doubt that one of the reasons Jack stayed on with Battle Brothers was that I exerted so little pressure on him, probably causing him to wonder why I wasn't bothering, and as a result eliciting in recent years his ever-redoubling efforts in expanding the enterprises of our family concern.

But what my father purports—and it is just that until proven true, given his mental state—deeply troubles me, as I've pondered how densely luxurious this house of Jack's has become, a veritable thicket of money-spending; I know for a fact that while there are still a handful of Eighth Wonder of the World jobs like Kit's, there aren't the ready scores of smaller, more modest projects that normally keep our manpower and machinery humming at near capacity. Jack is clearly a natural at broadening Battle Brothers' reach—unlike me, he's always been pretty fearless in exploring the unknown and untried, like the time when he was six or seven and without pause scrambled down a drainage pipe to retrieve a baseball I'd overthrown—but it's uncertain how or even if he'll understand that he needs to pull back in slow times, quickly beat a retreat, and if I've bestowed anything on him I hope it's my quick trigger for cutting one's losses, in business always and maybe also in life.

With my help Pop limps through the kitchen to go up the back stairwell, Eunice and Jack and Rosario standing by, just in case. Tyler, my sharp granddaughter of four, asks no one in particular why I'm wearing only my "panties," and why it stinks like poop.

"Your grandpa Jerome had an accident," Pop whispers to her, winking and paddling her behind. "But don't spread it around."

"Skanky," Tyler sneers, regarding me with what is already a distinctly teenage disdain. I note to myself that I must speak to Eunice about what the kids are watching all day and night.

"Help us upstairs," I say to Jack. He leans under Pop's other side and the three of us trudge upward trying to get our steps in sync. After we finally get Pop in the shower, Jack lends me a pair of Gore-Tex running pants, and we sit in the living area of the master bedroom, the double bathroom doors (of Jack's *toilette*) swept wide so we can keep an eye on Pop in the shower, who is the picture of old manhood as he lathers up behind the unfrosted safety glass: a hairy, saggy pear on legs. We offered to help but he growled, "You'll get plenty of me before I'm done," meaning not now but in the course of his remaining days. This is true, on many levels, though none I can really pause and think deeply about now. All I know is that today's episode is merely the beginning of the beginning, like the first intemperate days of winter, which always seem like mildest tonic later on.

While we wait, Jack's grabbed a couple beers for us from the under-counter refrigerator in the kitchenette section of the bedroom. There's a short run of cabinets and a microwave and an electric stovetop and even a mini-dishwasher, the effect being of a studio apartment, or grad student housing, though of course a lot nicer than that. Basically, he and Eunice wanted to be able to have a snack or make a cup of coffee without having to trek downstairs and to the other end of the house where the kitchen is, which seems reasonable enough until you realize that this is the kind of lifestyle detail that brought down the railroad barons and junk bond kings and dot-commers and whoever else will next rocket up and flame out in miserable infamy.

"You're good to throw Theresa and Paul this party." I say. "She seems pretty happy, don't you think?"

"For once in her life," Jack says.

"I suppose so," I reply, acknowledging the truth of his statement, but also caught off guard by its unexpected edge. "How's everything with you?"

"Couldn't be better."

"The house looks great."

"It's all good. It's all working."

"I guess business must have slowed down a bit."

Jack takes a long pull from his beer bottle. "Some."

"If you ever want me to come in it's no problem. I have all the time in the world."

"Okay."

"I'll ride along with the guys, if you want. Or I can even help Sal with the books."

Jack sits up. "You think Sal needs your help?"

"Why not? He's practically Pop's age. He's got to be making mistakes with that abacus of his. He's still using it, I bet."

"He does," Jack says. "But I check everything over, and everything's fine."

"I'm just saying, that's all."

"Sure you are."

"I am."

"Good, Dad. It's done. Really. It's all good."

There's nothing to counter with, mostly because Jack is a Battle and as a Battle is not unlike me, and thus endowed with a wide range of people-shedding skills, the foremost of which is how to curtail further talk when the talk gets most awkward, and so potentially perilous. Ask Rita, Kelly, maybe you could ask Daisy if she were here, ask Eunice about Jack, ask them all how difficult the footing becomes, how suddenly sheer the incline. Theresa, to be fair, manifests much of the same impassability, though her terrain features the periodic (and unaccidental) rock slide, an avalanche of obstructing analysis and critique and pure reason.

Pop curses from the shower, and we both nearly jump, though it's just him turning the handle the wrong way for a long second and getting all hot water instead of none. He's okay, if a bit scalded, and Jack gingerly helps him towel off, a splash of pink on one of his shoulders and upper chest. Pop tells us he's tired and wants to take a nap. Jack gives him a T-shirt and we walk him to the bed, tuck him in. Is this what growing old is about: another small though dangerous moment, somehow survived?

Downstairs the kitchen is crowded with people, as it appears everyone has come in from the deck, and Eunice, now seeing me and Jack, gently rings her Champagne glass with a spoon. The murmur and chatter subside. Rosario and Nidia are quickly going about offering fresh flutes and refilling others.

"We're so thrilled to welcome Theresa and Paul back home. And we are especially happy on this, the wonderful occasion of their wedding engagement." Eunice beams at Theresa and Paul, who seem tickled enough but also a shade uneasy, as academes and other intellectualized types sometimes are in real-life situations not squarely cast to be ironic.

"I'd like to propose a toast on the recent announcement of their nuptials, as well as offer our home as the place where Theresa and Paul and their guests can rendezvous whenever next year they'd like to celebrate the wedding. As all of us old married folks know, the time up through the wedding and honeymoon is the sweetest of all. Sad but true! So may you savor it! Cheers!"

A call of "Cheers!" goes around, and while everyone bottoms-up I notice that Theresa and Paul are more conferencing than celebrating, Paul shaking his head to whatever Theresa is insisting upon, which is what I imagine anyone dealing regularly and intimately with my daughter must learn to do. Theresa tries to get everyone's attention and Eunice, now seeing that she wants to speak, tinkles her glass again. Theresa nods.

"Paul and I want to thank my sister-in-law for the always luxurious party," Theresa says, her voice low, almost somber. "We thank Rosario and Nidia for their time and patience. And of course we thank Jack, too, for giving all three complete and total control." This elicits a laugh, and Jack, who's next to me, glumly raises his beer bottle.

"Paul and I wanted to let all of you know, too, that we're not going to get married next year. Don't worry. We're getting married this fall, probably in October."

"That's too soon!" Eunice cries. She's obviously been counting on producing the whole affair, as she does with everything having to do with our clan. (I should quickly note that Eunice is the only child of two very successful and prickly Bostonian parents, which for me is explanation enough for why she's such a zealous and tyrannical arranger.)

Theresa says, "On the plane we decided we didn't want to wait, and while we were never going to have a big wedding it'll be a very small ceremony now. But if I can take up Eunice's generous offer right here on the spot, I hope she'll have all of us back in a few months, for a little celebration."

"Certainly you can," Eunice says, doing her best not to sound curt. "We'd be thrilled."

Now Alice and Jadie and the rest of Theresa's friends pinch in on her and Paul for a new round of congratulatory hugs, and when I murmur to Jack about Theresa maybe being pregnant he responds with a blithe "Who knows?," which wouldn't normally bother me but does now with an unexpected sharpness. I shoot him a look but he's already drifted off, to help Nidia gather some used glasses and plates. Jack is considerate and generous like this and always has been, but if I have to tell the truth about him I would have to say he's never demonstrated the same feeling for me or Theresa that he does for his club buddies and employees or even strangers at the mall. And while I can try to accept our relationship as less than ideal (because of the usual father-son issues of superdefended masculinity and cycles of expectation/resentment and then the one of his mother suddenly dying when he was young, for which he squarely and silently blames yours truly), it pains me to the core to see how meager his expressions are for his younger sister, how bloodless and standard, as if she's merely a person jammed next to him in the middle seat on a plane, a reality and mild inconvenience to be affably addressed and elbow-jockeyed from time to time. Of course I'd always hoped and maybe too quickly assumed that they would cling for dear life to each other after what happened to their mother, but really just the opposite occurred, even as young as they were, both always heading to their rooms before and after supper, both always shutting the doors.

After the lifting hubbub of the news and the subsequent enervation, people start to leave. I walk by and see Paul sitting alone in the empty-shelved library, swirling a glass of white wine. I've already hugged and kissed Theresa, who hugged me quite vigorously back, whispering that we'd all talk later on, tomorrow maybe. Before I could ask what about, she begged off for a quick ride to the 7-Eleven with Jadie and Alice to buy bridal magazines, for what reason she wasn't sure, though citing her interest in cultural fodder and ritual. Yeah, yeah. She said she'd be back after dinner, as they were going to hang out for a while, and it struck me how pleased I was to see her acting so plainly girlish and silly.

Paul says, "Pull up a chair, Jerry. You want some?"

He pours me a glass of Eunice's "house" chardonnay, which it literally is, as a winery out on the North Fork sticks her own handmade labels on her annual ten-case order. We clink and sip and sit without talking, which is unusual for us. Paul is one of the few people who can always draw me out, and not just in a social, good-guy kind of way. I don't know why exactly, though perhaps it has something to do with the fact that he's not like me at all, that we come from dissimilar peoples and times and traditions and hold nearly opposite views on politics and the world, and so have neither the subtle pressure nor the dulling effect of instant concord, an ease and comfort I've enjoyed all my life but find increasingly wanting now. Maybe I'm a racialist (or racist?) and simply like the fact that he's different, that he's short and yellow and brainy (his words, originally), and that he makes *me* somehow different, whether I really wish to be or not.

"You're probably wondering what's going on with us," Paul says.

"Not really," I say. "You kids can get married whenever the hell you want, in my book. And I was going to tell Theresa but I might as well tell you. I'm going to give you twenty-five thousand for the wedding, which I set aside a while ago."

"You know we'll probably just go to a justice of the peace."

"Doesn't matter to me. The money's yours, to use as you please."

"Well, thanks. But it's not necessary."

"Listen. Maybe you want to use it for a down payment on a real house—you know, one that'll be big enough for all of you."

"We've never needed much room."

"Little ones take up a lot more space than you think," I say.

"I suppose that's so," he replies, though not in a way that inspires a load of confidence, and I'm reminded that these two have very narrow expertise, like probably only knowing how to prepare milk for cappuccinos.

"I'm just suggesting that you keep in mind where you two will be three or four years from now. What you might want. I'll always help you out, you know. Jack's doing better than fine, and so I figure I can give you and Theresa whatever you need, funds included. Kids are expensive, too."

Paul has a funny look on his face, a sort of smile if a smile weren't necessarily a wonderful thing, as though I've definitely said something awkward, and suddenly he's got his head in his hands, and barely shuddering with what must be joy, still holding his glass just now sloshing over with wine. I half expect this, given the combination of bardic and new age male sensitivity, and I reach over and pat him on the back, saying how eager I am to be a grandfather again, how happy, though wishing now that they weren't living clear on the other side of the country.

"Is it that obvious?" Paul says, looking up at me now, his eyes red.

"No, but this shotgun wedding announcement is a clue."

He chuckles, and we tip our glasses. I say, "You're welcome to stay with me until the wedding, if you like. Unless you have to go right back to Oregon."

"No, we're not doing that," Paul says, a bit uncomfortably. "We were hoping to hang around for a while, actually. Theresa has the fall term off, and she misses being back East."

"I'm happy to hear that."

"Eunice wants us to stay here but I know Theresa would prefer being back at your house."

"Really?"

"Sure," Paul says, "as long as it's all right with you."

"I said you're welcome, didn't I?"

"Just want to make sure."

"It'll be great, like summer vacation again," I say, warmed instantly by the idea that Theresa might ever choose to stay with me at 1 Cold Creek Lane. "Hey, the three of us can take an old-fashioned car trip somewhere."

"Okay," Paul says. "But can't we all fit in your plane?"

"It'd be a little tight. And I'm not sure I like the pressure, of piloting the next generations."

"I thought going by car was the most dangerous way to travel."

"Private planes are probably a close second."

"If there's anybody I'd trust, Jerry, it would be you."

"Oh yeah?" I say, steeling myself for the inevitable warm and fuzzy stage of our conversations, which I in fact have begun to half look forward to, and probably now nudge along, unconsciously and not.

"Certainly. You're the sort of fellow who's totally reliable, in the mechanical arts. I think you're an engineer in your soul. You have that beautiful machine expertise, that beautiful machine faith."

"I've just been a dirt-mover, Paul. But thank you."

He raises his glass, and we clink. Suddenly I realize that Paul may be a little drunk, or a lot drunk, I don't know, because he normally doesn't partake of more than a glass, for the reason that many of his brethren seem not to, as they turn beet red in the face after a couple of sips, looking as if they've played three sets of tennis in the tropics, teetering on some sweaty brink.

"Well, we don't have to fly," Paul says, brightly. "How about let's drive to D.C. You can give us the Jerry Battle special tour of the Air and Space."

Now he's talking, and I'm reminded yet again of one of the many reasons that I always enjoy his company: Paul is sensitive to what invigorates a guy like me, the kind of acknowledgment that really makes me levitate with a foursquare satisfaction, which is what you feel when you believe you've been thoroughly understood.

I say, "You know it's going to be great having you guys around for a little while. Just the idea makes me wish you didn't live so damn far away. Maybe you can move back. There are plenty of nice colleges around here. Stonybrook's just a short drive."

"Theresa just started her tenure track at Cascadia State. But we're not against coming back East, if there's an opening for her. It certainly doesn't matter where *I* live. I can write myself into obscurity just about anywhere."

"Hey, you have to stop talking like that, Paul," I say. "I know the literature-making business isn't the sort of thing where you have to be all rah-rah and gung-ho, but it can't help to run yourself down like that."

"You'd be surprised."

"But you're not the miserable angst-ridden writer type. At least not from where I'm sitting. You like the sunlight and kidding around and you genuinely like people. Everybody who knows you knows that. I'm not trying to give you advice, but it seems to me that you could put your easygoing nature to work for you."

"You mean write fluffy coffee-table books?"

"Don't ask me. But hey, come to think of it, Costco is full of them, and people snap them up like they do the twenty-four-count muffin packs. I know you're not in it for the money, but I have to assume the publishers are."

"You got that right. The one exception is my new publisher. The patron of my new press does it solely for vanity, so she can lord it over the rest of her Aspen circle that she cultivates boutique international writers."

"See, you're doing it again."

"I'm sorry, Jerry," Paul says, sliding deeper and deeper into the club chair. His face and neck are mottled several shades of lobster red-pink, a pretty clear sign that his genetically challenged liver has begun bucking this unusual overtime shift. I could gently chide him, but what the heck, for it's one of those seriously fortunate pleasures, is it not, to sit down with your (soon-to-be) son-in-law and a bottle of smooth, buttery vino and breezily tie one on and not have to swoop and dodge the baggage-strewn recriminations of a shared past (as you'd have with your own son), but rather wishfully opine on what joys the coming years might bring with unflinching sentimentality that says nothing is beyond our grasp, that the ceiling's limitless.

And in this spirit, I say, unqualified, "Hey, Theresa looks great, really great."

Paul takes a big quaffing gulp. Lets the medicine go down. He answers, "She does, doesn't she?"

"Her mother got just like that when she was pregnant. I think just before a woman is showing is when she's most beautiful. Like she's just stepped out of a hot shower. Lucky for me, Daisy showed very late. How far along is she? It can't be too much."

"She's not well, Jerry," Paul says. "I hate to tell you this. Theresa didn't really want to just yet. But I told her we had to tell you."

"Hold on. There's something wrong with the baby?"

"The baby is fine." Paul tries to smile, or not to, I can't tell. He says, "It's Theresa."

"Oh yeah? You better tell me."

"She has something."

I don't say anything. I don't want to say anything, but I say, as if I'm out on a job with the crew, "What the fuck are you talking about?"

Paul stares down into his wineglass. "It's a cancer, Jerry."

"Jesus, Paul. You're fucking kidding me. Where is it?"

"It's sort of not that kind. Besides, right now, she wouldn't want me to say."

"I don't care what she wants. You tell me now."

Paul takes another big gulp. He says, hardly saying it, "It's non-Hodgkin's lymphoma."

"What the hell is that?"

"It's cancer in the lymph nodes."

"But she'll get treatment, she's getting treatment."

He shakes his head. "We've been to every doctor in Oregon and Washington. We're seeing someone at Yale Medical School tomorrow. But I think it's going to be the same story. It's not something they can operate on, and the chemo and radiation would hurt the baby."

"So what the hell are you two doing? What the hell is this?"

"She doesn't want to hurt the baby, Jerry," he says. "We've fought over this and fought over this and I haven't been able to change her mind. She's going to try to wait until after the baby's born. It's due in December."

"She can have another baby!" I say. "She's only *thirty*, for heaven's sake! Am I missing something here? You can have a half dozen more, if you wanted."

"There's the problem of the chemo causing infertility. That's not certain, though. But really, it's that she's decided she wants this one. You talk to her tomorrow. Please talk to her. I can't anymore. Right now I just have to support her, Jerry, because there's no other way."

"Dammit, Paul, this is all fucking crazy. You're both fucking crazy!"

"Don't you think I know that?"

"Oh fuck it!"

We're suddenly shouting at one another, standing toe to toe, and I realize that I've gripped my wineglass so tight that it's snapped at the stem. One of the points is digging into my palm. I'm stuck and bleeding. I drop the two pieces onto the chair cushion. Paul reaches for a box of tissues and gathers me up a wad, and when I press it I get a sharp, ugly surge of that old feeling again, when Daisy was so lovely and so fragile, the feeling like I want to break or ruin something. Something I'll always need.

four

THE DAY THAT DAISY DIED was a lot like this one, early July, with the sun seeming stuck right at the top of the sky, casting the kind of light and heat that make all the neighborhood kids vault over themselves with pant and glee and then cows everyone else, moms and dads and us older folks and teenagers and the family pets. Daisy liked the heat, and though she didn't know how to swim she'd spend plenty of time in our backyard pool, tanning in her plaid one-piece in the floating lounger or else dog-paddling with an old-fashioned life ring looped under her arms. I tried to teach her how to swim a couple of times, but I'd end up cat-scratched about the neck and shoulders, and then half-drowned besides, Daisy lurching and pulling up on me whenever I let her go, yelling out if her face or scalp got wet. She wasn't so much dainty or persnickety but for some reason hated being submerged or drenched. She always showered with a cap and on alternate days shampooed her hair in the sink, the drain of which I'd have to unclog every couple weeks of the thick black strands, using a pair of chopsticks.

And I swear—I swear, I swear—that I never imagined for a second that the pool was dangerous, at least for her. Sure I jumped in a half-dozen times to pluck out one of my kids or their mangy, booger-streaked friends thrashing fitfully in the deep end, but Daisy was always careful and tentative, even after she started to change and began seeing our family doctor for meds. She always entered the water as if it were as hot as soup, then pushed off from the steps with her float tube and kicked, her taut chin just barely hovering above the surface.

Hey, honey, she'd say to me, the ends of her hair slicked to pencil points, I'm a mermaid.

Sexier than that, I'd say, through the Sunday paper, through the summer haze.

It was nice like that, a lot of the time. I remember how Theresa and Jack would spend pretty much every second between breakfast and dinner in our backyard pool, or else run about on the concrete surround and the lawn spraying each other and whatever friends were around with water pistols filled with Hi-C punch or sometimes even pee (I caught them once in the rickety little cabana I'd built, giggling and pissing all over their hands trying to fill-er-up). If it was the weekend I'd be out there for a good while, too, chuck the kids around in the water and play the monster or buffoon and do a belly flop or two for a finale, then dry off and wrap a towel around my waist and drag a chaise and a beer beneath the maples and snooze until one of the kids got hurt or fell or puked because they drank too much pool water, all of which in the heat and brightness and clamor made for a mighty decent time. This, of course, was dependent, too, on what mood Daisy was in, but in those early days she was pretty solid, she was pretty much herself, she was just like the girl I fell in love with.

In those days she would set up the patio table with all kinds of vittles, she'd have the soppressata and the sugar ham and the crock of port wine cheese and the Ritz and Triscuits and she'd have plenty of carrot and celery sticks and pimiento olives and then she'd have the electric fryer on the extension cords snaking back through the kitchen window, to fry up chicken wings or butterfly shrimp and french fries right there on the table, so it was hot and fresh. If my folks or other people were going to be over she made sure to put out her homemade egg rolls and some colorful seaweed and rice thing that we didn't yet know back then was sushi, which people couldn't *believe* she had made, and maybe some other Oriental-style dishes like spicy sweet ribs and a cold noodle dish she always told us the name of but that we could never remember but which everyone loved and always finished first. She had this way of arranging the food on the platters that made you think of formal gardens, with everything garnished by fans of sliced oranges or shrubs of kale or waterfowl she'd carve out of apples, giving them shiny red wings.

I was working a lot then, having just been made second-in-command at Battle Brothers by my father and uncles, and Daisy was like a lot of the young mothers around the neighborhood, meaning she took care of the house and the kids and the cooking and the bills and whatever else came up that I could have dealt with but somehow didn't, for the usual semi-acceptable reasons of men; but I will tell you Daisy didn't mind, that was never a problem between us, because when you got right down to it she was an old-fashioned girl in matters of family, not only because she wasn't so long removed from the old country, but also because her nature (if you can speak of someone's nature, before she changed and went a little crazy and ended up another person entirely) preferred order over almost all else, and certainly didn't want any lame hand Jerry Battle could provide.

In fact the first real signs of her troubles were the kinds of things you see whenever you go into most people's houses, stuff like piles of folded laundry to be put away, some dishes in the sink, toys loose underfoot, everything finding its own strewn place, but for Daisy, when it began to happen, it meant there was maybe a quiet disaster occurring, a cave-in somewhere deep in the core. One time, a day just like this, kids frolicking about, our guests arrayed as usual around the backyard and the spread of piquant goodies on the patio table, Daisy sort of lost it. I don't know what happened exactly but maybe one of the kids bumped the other table where she was working the deep fryer, and the hot oil lipped over the edge and splashed the table and then spilled down onto her sandaled foot. I knew it happened because I saw her jump a little and leap back, and it occurred to me only later that she didn't shout or scream or make any sound at all. I went over to see if she was burned but before I could get there Daisy did the oddest thing: she picked up the fryer by the handles and turned it over and sort of body-slammed it on the table, the oil and chicken wings gushing out sideways, luckily in nobody's direction. I ran up and quickly yanked the extension cords apart and asked her if she was all right and she had this sickened look on her face and she said it was an accident and that she was sorry. By this time our guests had descended and I'm sure no one saw what had really happened, as everyone was appropriately concerned, but I knew and I got angry (if only because I was confused and a little scared) and yelled at her about being more careful. She started crying and that pretty much brought an end to the afternoon, most of our guests deciding to leave, among them some neighbors who never called us again.

Of course somewhere not so deep down none of what happened with the fryer was a surprise to me. From the moment I met her on the main floor at Gimbel's in the city, where she was offering sample sprays of men's cologne (I think it was Pierre Cardin, a huge phallic bottle of which I bought that day and may still have in the bottom of the bathroom vanity), I knew Daisy was volatile, like the crazy girl who haunts every neighborhood, the one always climbing fences and trees and eating flower petals and terrorizing the boys with sudden kisses and crotch-grabs. At Gimbel's Daisy sprayed me before I consented and then sprayed me again, and I would have been really pissed except she was amazingly bright-eyed and pretty and she had these perfect little hands with which she smoothed down my coat collar. She had a heavy accent to her English but she wasn't a tentative talker like some who come to this country and seem just to linger in the scenery and either peep-peep or else have to bark to get your attention. Daisy just let it all spill out in her messy exuberant froth of semi-language, clueless and charming and quite sexy, at least in that *me Tarzan you Jane* mode I welcome, with its promise of most basic romance.

For I had no idea what real craziness meant. I thought people like my father and my mother and my brother Bobby were off-kilter and in need of professional help. I didn't know what it was to be DSM-certified, described in the literature, perhaps totally nuts. And it was a month or so after the deep fryer incident that the first genuine trouble reared itself, when Daisy went off to Bloomingdale's and charged $7000 for a leather living room set and a full-length chinchilla coat. We had a terrific fight, me rabid with disbelief and Daisy defiant and bitter, talking about how she "knew class people" and mocking me for "working in dirt" like some peasant or field hand. Her eyes were wild and she was practically spitting with hatred and I swear had she been wielding a knife I would be long in the grave.

I didn't know that the previous days in which she bought herself and the kids several new outfits and served us filet mignon and lobsters and repainted our bedroom a deep Persian crimson trimmed in gold leaf were indicative of a grandiose run-up to a truly alarming finale; in fact, I was pretty pleased, for Daisy seemed happy and even ecstatic for the first time in a long time. She was lively with the kids and once again we were making love nightly, and though she worried me a little with her insomnia and solo drinking and 2 A.M. neighborhood walks in her nightgown I figured I was still way ahead of a lot of other guys with young families I knew, who were already playing the field and spending most of their free time away from the house. I tell you if Daisy hadn't blitzkrieged our net worth at Bloomingdale's nothing much would have changed; probably I wouldn't have cared if she was only steadily depleting our bank account, a time-honored way in our civilized world. But this was 1975, when the economy was basically shitting the bed, and Jack and Theresa were seven and six and I was making $20,000 a year at Battle Brothers, which was a hell of a lot of money, actually, and much more than I deserved. But $7000 for anything was of course ruinous, so I had to beg the store manager to take everything back (with a 10 percent restocking fee, plus delivery), and then cut up her charge cards and take away her bank passbook and start giving her the minimum cash allowance for the week's groceries and sundries and gas.

As you can imagine, Daisy wasn't exactly pleased with the arrangement. It was a suggestion/directive from Pop, whom I hadn't consulted directly but who had overheard my mother telling Aunt Vicky what her daughter-in-law had done. The next day Pop barreled into the messy double office we shared at the shop and plunked his backside onto my desk blotter and asked me what the hell I was doing. I had no clue what he was talking about, and as usual in those days I just stared up at him with my mouth half-crooked, indolently probing my upper molars with my tongue.

"I'm talking about *Daisy*," he growled, as if he were the one who had married her, as if he were the one having the troubles. I should mention that Pop always adored Daisy. From the second he met her it was clear, he could never stop talking about how gorgeous she was and how sexy and whenever they met he'd corral her with a big hug and kiss and then twirl her in a little cha-cha move, all of which Daisy welcomed and totally played into like she was Audrey Hepburn in *Roman Holiday*, just the kind of humoring and ass-kissing that my father has always lived for and measured everyone by.

"I hear she went on a spree at the department store and damn near bankrupted you."

"Not near," I said. "It was seven grand."

"Holy Jesus."

"But it's fixed now. I'm making it go away."

"Damn it, Jerome, it's just going to happen again! Don't you know how to handle your wife yet?"

"I think I've learned something in these last eight years, yes."

"Bullshit. Listen to me. Are you listening, Jerome? This is what I'm telling you. You have to squash her every once in while, I mean completely flatten her. Otherwise a beautiful woman like Daisy gets big ideas, and those ideas get bigger every year. If she were a plain sedan like your mother you wouldn't have to worry, you'd only have to deal with a certain displacement, you know what I mean? But with a sleek machine, you've got to tool a governer onto the sucker, do something to cut her fuel."

"I have no idea what you're talking about, Pop."

"What I'm saying is you've got to be a little brutal. Not always, just every once in a while. Now is a good time. All this women's-libbing and bra burning is confusing everybody. Treat her badly, don't give her any money or attention or even a chance to bitch or argue. Don't let her leave the house for a week. Then when she's really down in the dumps bring her some diamond earrings or a string of pearls and take her out to a lobster dinner. After, screw her brains out, or whatever you can manage. Then everything will go back to normal, you'll see."

"And how do you know any of this works, if Ma isn't that kind of woman?"

"Trust your Pop, Jerome. I have wide experience. And if that doesn't do it, call Dr. Derricone."

Yeah, yeah, yeah, I must have said, to get him off my desk and case. But that very night when I got home Daisy was undertaking a complete overhaul of our house décor; she was going through a couple of hundred fabric swatches piled on the kitchen table, she had four or five different dining room chairs, some Persian rugs, several china and silver patterns, she had odd squares of linoleum and porcelain floor tile; she had even begun painting the dining and living room with sample swaths of paint, quart cans of which lay out still opened, used brushes left on the rims, dripping. For dinner she was heating up some leftover pasta on the stovetop. In the den the kids were watching TV, rolling popcorn in baloney slices for their predinner snack, and then spitting streams of Dr Pepper at each other through the gaps in their front teeth. When I asked her what the heck was going on Daisy simply looked up from her work and answered that she couldn't decide between a shiny or not-so-shiny silk for the living room curtains and what did I think?

She was grinning, though sort of painfully, like part of her could see and hear the miserable scene and understood that another part was taking over, and probably winning. I couldn't holler right then the way I wanted to, and instead just grumbled my usual "Whatever, dear" and went to the bedroom and stripped out of my dusty workclothes and turned on the water in the shower as hot as I could bear, because there's nothing like a good near-scald to set you right again, take you out of a time line, set you momentarily free. And suddenly I was even feeling a little chubby down there with the hot trickles in my crack and so gave myself a couple exploratory tugs but maybe I was still too pissed (which is usually plenty good reason), when Daisy opened the shower door and stepped inside, paint-splattered clothes and all.

"Jerry," she said, crying, I think, through the billowing steam, "Jerry, I'm sorry."

I didn't answer and she said it again, said my name again, with her rolling, singsong, messed up Rs, and I hugged her, clutching her beneath the spray.

"So hot!" she gasped, recoiling, and I let go, but she grabbed back on and held me tight, tighter and tighter until she got used to the temperature. Then she kissed me, and kissed me again, and when I kissed her back I thought I was tasting something mineral, like thinner or paint, but when we broke for air I could see the faded wash of pink on her chin, on her mouth, as she'd bitten her tongue trying to stand the hot water.

I pointed the shower head away from us and she took off her

wet clothes and she said "Make love to me" and we started to screw on the built-in bench of the shower stall, something we hadn't done since we first bought the house, before Jack was even born. I remember Daisy being five months pregnant and showing in a way I didn't expect to be so attractive (both our kids, by the way, were tiny when they born, barely six pounds full-term), the smooth, sheened bulge of her belly and her popped out belly-button and the changed size and color of her nipples, long like on baby bottles and the color of dark caramels. Daisy was not voluptuous, which I liked, her long, lean torso and shortish Asian legs (perfectly hairless) and her breasts that weren't so full and rounded but shaped rather in the form of gently pitched dunes, those delicate pale hillocks. I realize I may be waxing pathetic here, your basic sorry white dude afflicted with what Theresa refers to as "Saigon syndrome" (*Me so hor-ny, G.I. Joe!*) and fetishizing once again, but I'm not sorry because the fact is I found her desirable precisely because she was put together differently from what I was used to, as it were, totally unlike the wide-hipped Italian or leggy Irish girls or the broad-bottomed Polish chicks from Our Lady of Wherever I was raised on since youth, who compared to Daisy seemed pretty dreadful contraptions.

Unfair, I know, unfair.

Though that evening in the shower eight years into our marriage I wasn't so enamored of Daisy as I was hopeful for any break in her strange mood and behaviors. I thought (or so I thought later) that some good coarse sex might disturb the disturbance, shunt aside the offending system, and it might have worked had our little Theresa not opened the shower door and stood watching for God knows how long as I was engaging her mother in the doggie-style stance we tended to employ when things between us weren't perfectly fine. (Note: I've always suspected that it was this very scene that set Theresa on her lifelong disinclination for whatever I might say or do, and though she's never mentioned it and would reject the notion out of hand for being too reductionist/Freudian, I'm plain sorry for it and hate to think that knocking about somewhere in her memory is a grainy washed-out Polaroid of me starring as The Beast or The Rapist.) Daisy must have peered around and seen Theresa standing there sucking on her thumb and shoved me off so hard I slipped and fell onto my back, providing a second primal sighting of me in my engorgement that made Theresa actually step back. I covered myself and asked her what she wanted and she couldn't answer and then Daisy yelled at her to tell us.

Theresa said, "The macaroni is on fire, and Jack can't put it out."

"Take care of her!" I said to Daisy, and then I grabbed a towel to wrap myself with and ran down the long bedroom hall and then the next hall down to the kitchen, where Jack was tossing handfuls of water at the frying pan roaring up in flames. The steam and smoke were pooling at the ceiling, and I quickly pulled Jack away into the dining room; he impressively fought me a little, trying to go back, to fight the good fight. He was always a commendable kid, earnest and vigorous, and for a long time (right up through high school) I really thought he might become a cop or a fireman as most young boys say they want to be at one point or another; I could always see him donning a uniform, strapping on that studly *stuff*, charging hard with his mind unfettered into the maw of peril, "just doing his job." Sometimes it still surprises me how damn entrepreneurial he is now, what a *multitasking* guy he's become, as the term goes, though I wonder if being a CEO really suits him, even if it is heading a fundamentally working-class outfit like ours.

"Dad, it's burning the metal," he said, pointing to the steel hood above the stove, its painted surface blackening.

"Stay right here," I told him, tamping down on his shoulders, "okay?"

"Okay."

I rushed in and knelt below the range top and opened the bottom drawer of the stove, where Daisy kept the pot lids, searching for one large enough to cover the big skillet. I found one and tossed it on but it was about an inch shy all around and the flames only flickered low for a second, then vengefully leaped up again. Daisy always used a lot of butter or oil, and so I took off my bath towel and folded it and tried to smother the whole thing, the fire licking up where I wasn't pressing hard enough, singeing my forearm and chest hairs and making me instantly consider all things from the narrow, terrified view of my fast shrinking privates. Then Jack ran forward and tried to help by tugging down the edge of the towel. I picked him up and carried him to the living room and practically hurled him into one of the as-yet-unreturned sofas, shouting "Stay put!" and also warning him not to soil the upholstery, if he valued his life. But by then the towel had caught fire and instinctively I did exactly what Jack had already tried, splashing on water with my hands and then a coffee mug, which did no good at all. So I finally took the skillet by the handle and opened the sliding door to the deck and stepped out. The deck was cedar and I didn't know what else to do but maybe toss it over the edge onto the back lawn. The firelight caught the attention of our back neighbors, the Lipschers, who were throwing a small dinner party on their patio. I'd spoken to the husband maybe once or twice, the wife three or four times; we'd invited them over a couple of times for barbecues but they never actually made it over. They were into tony,

Manhattan-type gatherings, with candles and French wine and testy, clever conversations (you could hear every word from our deck) about Broadway plays or Israel or their favorite Caribbean islands, everyone constantly interrupting everyone else in their bid to impress, all in tones that said they weren't. Though the sight of me clearly got their attention. Someone at their table said, "Look at that!," and with the skillet in one hand I kind of waved with the other, the Lipschers and their guests limply waving back, and for some reason it didn't seem neighborly to chuck the frying pan and so I just held it out in full flambé, Daisy now stepping out in her towel with the kids in tow, all of us waiting for the fire to die out. It took a while. When it finally did Barry Lipscher said, "Hey there, Battle, you want to end the show now? We're still eating here, if you don't mind."

To this Daisy unhooked her bath sheet and wrapped it around my waist, then turned to the Lipschers and guests in all her foxy loveliness and gave them the finger. If I remember right, Theresa did the same, Jack and I grinning idiotically as we trailed our women inside the house.

But in truth, I'm afraid, it didn't quite end up as nicely as all that, young family Battle triumphant in solidarity, chuckling over the charred cabinetry and the toasty scent of burnt pasta.

"Clean this up," I said to Daisy, my voice nothing but a cold instrument. "We'll talk tomorrow."

The next day I instituted what Pop had suggested, basically placing Daisy under house arrest for the week (no car keys, no credit cards, $20 cash), and promising her that I'd never speak to her again unless she sent back all the samples and swatches and kept the house in an acceptable state and made proper meals for the kids and checked with me from that point on before she bought anything—I mean *anything*—other than staples like milk and bread or underwear or school supplies. Back in those days I could actually utter such a thing, threaten someone like that, even a loved one, and I have to say that I regularly did. I naturally got into the habit at Battle Brothers, hollering at the fellas all day and lecturing my subcontractors and sometimes even talking tough to my customers, if they became too clingy or whiny or just plain pains in the ass, which at some point in every job they all did. But maybe it wasn't so much the habit itself as it was its effectiveness that I kept returning to, how reliably I could get all sorts of people to move it or jump or shut the hell up. People say that I'm like Pop that way, that I'll get this expression on my face, this certain horrific look, like whatever you're saying or doing is the most sickening turn, this instant disease, and that for you not to desist seems purely contemptible, a veritable crime against humanity. And then I'll say what I want to have happen, what I want done, as I did that day to Daisy. She could hardly look at me as she sat on the edge of the tub as I shaved, her straight hair screening her face like those beaded curtains we all used to have, her palms pressed down against the porcelain, her elbows locked. I repeated myself and left for work and didn't call all day and when I got back (a little early, for I had the horrible thought that the house might be burning down) the whole place was peerlessly clean and quiet and the kids were in the den playing (Jack) and reading (Theresa) and there was a tuna casserole bubbling away in the oven, four place settings sparkling and ready on the kitchen table. The only thing missing was Daisy. I asked the kids where she was and they didn't know. I looked out back and in the street. Then I went into our bedroom to change, which was empty but trimmed out and neat, and when I walked into the bathroom, there Daisy was, still dressed in her pink robe with the baby blue piping, sitting on the edge of the tub exactly as she had been eight hours earlier, as if she'd been cast right into the cool porcelain.

"I fixed the house," she said, her voice husky, dried-out.

"Yeah," I said, just like I might to the guys, as though it was simply what I expected. It's always best, when you're trying to get things done, to utter the absolute minimum. You made it rain? Okay. You moved Heaven and Earth? Fine. This, too, was part of my general studies education à la Pop; he's the one who showed me how effective it can be to say grindingly little at the very moments you ought to say a lot, when you could easily be sappy and effusive and overgenerous with praise or forgiveness, when you could tender all you had and no one would ask for anything extra in return.

I know. I know about this. I do.

So when Daisy went on to say, "The other stuff, too. I got rid of it all. I did what you want, Jerry," what did I say back but simply, "Right," with a slight tip of the noggin, with a tough-guy grunt, which you'd think would be just what Daisy had had to deal with all her inscrutable Oriental/Asian life, and probably had, and was part of the reason she'd ended up with someone like me, some average American Guido she'd figure would have more than plenty to say, entreating every second with his hands and his hips and with his heart blithering on his sleeve.

Daisy didn't say anything and neither did I and for a moment our normally cramped en suite bath got very large in feeling, the only sound coming from the running toilet tank, this wasteful ever-wash I've always meant to fix but never actually have, even to this day. Daisy got up then and brushed past me and I could hear her walk out of our bedroom and down the hallway to the kitchen. I showered and changed and when I got to the table the kids were already eating their dinner, as usual furiously wolfing their food like a pair of street urchins who'd stolen into a cake shop. Daisy was making up my plate. As little kids, Jack and Theresa were forever hungry, a trait only parents must know to be peerlessly endearing, and the only time I can remember them not eating was after Daisy was buried and we had a gathering at the house, the two of them sitting glumly on the sofa, a plate of cold shrimp and capicola balanced between them on their legs.

Daisy set down my dinner and she sat, too, but wasn't eating. After serving all of us seconds she took our plates and began cleaning up. The kids chattered back and forth but Daisy and I didn't say a word to each other. In the morning, breakfast was the same, and it was like that for the rest of that week and the next. Finally I got tired of the whole thing and when he asked I told Pop his method was fine save for the rageful misery and silences. He told me to keep it in my pants a bit longer, that I'd break her and also break myself of "the need to please her all the time," and that he and Nonna would stop by on Saturday to run interference. I asked him to just come over and play with the kids, so I could patch things up with Daisy, maybe take a drive to Robert Moses and sit on the grassy dunes and tell/beg her that I wished for our life to be normal again, though in truth their visit would mean that Nonna would take the kids out to the playground or to a matinee and then somehow cobble together a gut-busting dinner of meatballs and sausages and pasta and a roast, with Pop haranguing me about the state of our business and then inevitably bringing up Bobby, which he did anytime we spent more than an hour together.

When my folks arrived Daisy was still in the bedroom getting dressed. No matter her state of mind or what was going on she always pulled herself together for them, and particularly for Pop. She'd wear her newest outfits and full evening makeup and jewelry and maybe she'd tie a little rolled silk scarf around her neck, which gave her a fetchingly game barmaid look. Pop of course lapped it up. He loved how she made silly mistakes with her English and always laughed at his jokes and patiently listened to all his stories and theories and opinions about the brutality of man and falsity of religion and the conspiring forces of a New World Order that would enslave all good men in a randy socialist vise-grip of eco-feminism and bisexuality and miscegenation (notwithstanding my and Daisy's lovely offspring). Daisy, I really have to say, always kissed his ass, and I don't really know why, as there was never anyone else but Pop who could elicit that kind of humoring and attention from her, no one I'm sure except for Bobby Battle, M.I.A. (the best degree, for Immortality), whom she met a couple of times only but I know would have loved.

Daisy floated out in a new hot-pink-with-white-polka-dot silk mini-dress and matching scarf tied around her throat as mentioned, with a white hair band holding up her black-as-black tresses. As annoyed as you might be with her you couldn't help but think she looked good enough to eat. She kissed my mother, who was already unloading the fridge of everything that we might possibly eat for dinner, culling as she went for mold and wilt and freezer burn. My mother, God bless her soul, was nothing if not dependable. It's a terrible thing to admit, but I used to think she wasn't the swiftest doe in the forest, because she rarely did anything else but keep house and feed everybody and try to make Pop's life run smoothly and comfortably, even as he was often a jerk to her and had several love affairs and was universally acknowledged to be a Hall of Fame jerk. She rarely read the newspaper and never read a book and wasn't even interested in movies or television, her main personal activity being shopping for clothes, not haute couture but sort of Queens Boulevard country club, bright bold colors and white patent leather bags and shoes and bugeye sunglasses. Every once in a while on no special occasion Pop would spring for a marble-sized diamond ring or a string of fat pearls, and I suspect it was my mother exacting tribute for his latest exposed dalliance. Lately I've been thinking that her lack was more emotional than intellectual; it wasn't because the gray matter didn't work well enough but that she preferred to keep her life as uncomplicated as possible, more thought and rumination leading only to misery and remorse and the realization that she could never leave him, that she could never really start over again.

Daisy twirled for my father and said, "What you think, Pop?"

"Gorgeous, doll, gorgeous." Pop used *doll* whenever they were together, *Your old lady* or *Your wife* when speaking about her to me.

"I got it at Macy's," she said, hardly glancing over. "It wasn't on sale price, but I couldn't wait."

"On you, it's a bargain at twice the price."

"You super guy, Pop."

"But I'm speechless at this moment," he said, smiling his Here's-how-to-handle-a-woman smile. "As Santayana once said, 'Beauty as we feel it is something indescribable; what it is or what it means can never be said.'"

"You too much, Pop!"

"Is this a liver or a beefsteak?" Nonna said, holding up a frozen brown slab.

No one answered, as no one knew.

Nonna, accustomed to the nonreply, said, "I hope it's a beefsteak."

"The dress looks real good," I said to Daisy, feeling I should utter something, bring at least some bread to the table, if not wine. And then I was all set to offer even more, maybe I was going to suggest running her right out to the department store and buying a bauble to go with the pretty dress, some earrings maybe, when Pop pulled a long dark blue velveteen jewelry case from his pocket and presented it to Daisy.

"For me?"

"Of course it's for you, doll. Open it."

She cracked the lid. It was a string of freshwater pearls, the beads small but delicate and dazzling in their iridescence. It was amazingly tasteful, even for Pop, who always surprised you with his eye for finish and detail, which somehow was more Park Avenue than Arthur Avenue.

"Look, Jerry, look what Pop got!" Daisy said.

"A customer of mine imports these from Japan, and he gave me a nice rate on them. They're just as good as Mikimotos."

"It's not my birthday even," Daisy said, hushed by the glitter in her hands. "This is so nice. This is so pretty."

"Call it a reward, for all the hardship of the last couple of weeks. Ask Nonna over there. It's no picnic, putting up with us Battle men. We're stubborn and prideful and we ask no less than the world of our women. The world. Your husband Jerome here is no different. We all know he can be sullen, but that's because he's always been too serious. Not like Bobby, who knew what real fun was. He was just like you. So you better learn patience, with this one."

Pop tousled my hair, and I let him, because incredulity freezes you, because I was like that back then, because Pop was Pop and I wasn't. Daisy was the one who stopped him, if only because she was hugging him, kissing him on the forehead and cheek, hooting a little, practically vibrating with glee and gratitude. Nonna had already ceased paying further attention to the scene, gone back to the daily calculus of how to make a meal from what was at hand. The kids ran in from outside and Pop had a handful of hard candies for them, as usual, toffees and sours and butterscotches. This was the minor parade my father always finessed for himself, wherever he went: my wife and kids, joyous with the old man. I drifted around the gleeful huddle and asked Nonna if she needed anything.

"I don't think so, honey," she said, never, ever ironical. She was scraping the freezer burn from the ice-hard meat, a little pile of root-beer-colored shavings collecting at the edge of her knife blade. "I think I have everything I need."

IN THE WEEKS AFTER Pop came bearing gifts, everything pretty much went to shit. It did, it really did, though not in the manner I thought it would. I figured I'd be the one generating the enmity, the one beaming out the negative vibes, the go-to-hell shine first thing in the morning and stay-on-your-side rays before clicking off the bedside lamp at night. I thought Pop's stunt (which I should have been ready for) and Daisy's giddy celebrations would lend me the pissy high ground, at least for a few days, long enough to keep Daisy on the defensive and not out there spending our future, long enough so I could figure out how to fix the problem without forever placing her under house arrest. But the fact was, Daisy was the one who took further umbrage. She wouldn't speak to me, not a word, her silence made that much more unpleasant by the fact that she seemed livelier and brighter in her dealings with everyone else.

Did the time mark a strange kind of renaissance for her? Was it, in language Theresa might employ, an epochal turn? I really don't know about that. What's clear to me is that Daisy pretty much exploded with life, and our life, as it went, exploded right along with her. Up to then, my basic conception of crazy was still the one I'd held since youth, the picture of a raven-haired Irish girl named Clara who climbed the trees in her pleated Catholic-school skirt not wearing underwear and lobbed Emily Dickinson down to me in a wraithlike voice (*I cannot be with You/It would be Life/and Life is over there/Behind the Shelf*), my trousers clingy with fear and arousal.

With Daisy, I didn't know, nor did anyone else, for that matter, including Dr. Derricone, the extent of her troubles, the ornate reach and complication. Those initial shopping sprees would in the end seem like the smallest indiscretions, filched candy from the drugstore, a lingering ass pat at a neighborhood cocktail party, nothing you couldn't slough off with a laugh, nothing you couldn't later recall with some fondness even, with wistful rue.

The first thing was, she would hardly sleep. If at all. After Pop *venit* and *vidit* and *vincit* that weekend and she stopped talking to me, Daisy's metabolism went into overdrive. We usually went to bed at 11 or so, after the news for me and maybe a bath for her, but she started getting up at 5 in the morning, and then 4 and 3 and 2, until it got to the point when she didn't even get *ready* for bed, not bothering to change into a nightgown or brush her teeth or even take a soak. A couple times in the middle of the night I awoke to the *plash-plash* of water, and I peered through the curtains to see, in lovely silhouette, Daisy paddling around in the pool with the inner tube hooped beneath her arms. She was naked, just going back and forth, back and forth, and I had the thought that I should go out there and keep her company. But I desperately needed my sleep back then (these days it's a different story, as I lie in wait for the muted *thwap* of the morning paper on the driveway) and rather than get up I know exactly what I did, which was to just fall back into the pillow and scratch at myself half-mast and maybe dream in sentimental hues of gorgeous black swans, who must always swim alone.

After a couple weeks I didn't even notice that Daisy was never in bed. She probably slept a couple of hours while the kids were watching TV, but I can't be sure of that. As for sex, it wasn't happening, and not just because of the fact that she decided not to talk to me. Pure talk was never that important to us anyway, even at the beginning, when it was mostly joking and flirting, for though her English was more than passable it was just rudimentary enough for us to stay clear of in-depth and nuanced discussions, which suited me fine. The truth was that while I was hungering for her I had an equally keen desire to hold out as long as I could stand, because if she had any power over me it was certainly sexual power, which, most other things being equal, is what all women should easily have over all men. Daisy could always, please forgive me, float my boat, top my prop, she could always crank up the generators at any moment and make me feel that every last cell in my body was overjuiced and soon-to-be-derelict if not immediately *launched* toward something warm and soft. In her own way she was a performer, as they say actors can be when they enter a room; something in them switches on and suddenly everybody is pointed right at them, abject with confused misery and love.

And this really happened, mostly while I was slumbering. I don't know how many times she did it, but one night the doorbell rang and roused me from a deep sleep and I trudged tingling in the limbs to the door to find my wife wrapped in a big blue poly tarp with a burly young officer of the local law standing behind her waving a long flashlight.

"Are you the head of this household, sir?" he asked, momentarily blinding me with the beam, and fully waking me up.

"You wanna kill the light, chief?"

"Sorry, sir," he said, slipping the flashlight into his belt. "Are you the head of household?"

"If you mean am I the owner, then yes."

"Is this your wife?"

I looked at Daisy, who just looked glum and down in the mouth, as if this whole thing was yet another chore of her unglamorous life.

"Yes. She's my wife."

"She was at the elementary school, in the playground there. There was a complaint."

"What? Is it illegal, to be over there?"

"I believe there's a school grounds curfew, sir, but that wasn't the whole problem."

"Oh yeah?"

Daisy then said, "Just cut it out, Jerry. Good night, officer. Thanks for the ride home." She tippy-toed and pecked him on the cheek, and then stepped inside. "Oh, this is yours."

She peeled the tarp from herself, and handed it to him. She was wearing only sneakers, white Keds with the blue pencil stripe on the rubber. The young cop thanked her and said good night, like it was a goddamned date or something. Daisy disappeared inside.

The cop said, "Sir, if you could please tell your wife I'll have to cite her the next time."

"There's not going to be a goddamn next time!"

"I'm just saying . . ."

"Good night," I said, and I slammed the door.

I found Daisy in the kitchen, making tuna-and-egg salad for a sandwich. She had the eggs going at furious boil in the stockpot, the bread in the toaster, she had the jars of mayonnaise and mustard and sweet pickle relish out on the counter, she had the celery and carrot and onion on the cutting board, and she had the ice blue German chef's knife in her hand, the one Pop had given her at Christmas. But the strange thing was that she did it all so casually, as if a nude woman in sneakers chopping vegetables at three in the morning after a neighborhood police sweep was *de rigueur* around here, our customary midsummer night's dream.

"What the hell are you doing?"

"I'm hungry. You want to eat, too?"

"No, I don't."

"You have trouble sleeping?"

"What do you think, Daisy?"

She didn't answer, engrossed as she was in the julienned stalks of carrot and celery. She was working carefully but fast, making perfect dices as she went, the crisp *chock-chock-chock* of the blade on the cutting board undoubtedly keeping time with her ever-quickening synaptic pulses. I didn't want to disturb her, I was going to wait until she was done, but maybe it was my state of angry half-sleep or the searingly bright fluorescent kitchen lights or the notion of my supple-bodied immigrant wife tooling around in a squad car with a wide-eyed cop, that I had to holler, "This is total shit!"

She looked around with unfeigned gravity and said, "Go back to sleep, Jerry."

"This is going to stop," I said. "You're going to see Dr. Derricone tomorrow. I'll go with you."

"Go to sleep, Jerry."

"You're going to see him about this, and I mean it this time. No more ranting at him. No more threats. No more scenes with his receptionist."

"He's a *complete fool*," she said, with a perfect, and faintly English, accent, as though she'd heard some actress say the phrase in a TV movie or soap. Daisy was a talented mimic, when she got the feeling. "*They are all complete and utter fools.*"

"I don't care if you think he's the King of Siam. Dr. Derricone has been around a long time and you'll show him respect. He's seen it all and he's going to help you. I made him promise, and though you treat him like dirt he's not giving up."

"I don't want help from him, or nobody!" she cried, confusingly, though of course I knew what she meant.

"That's it, now, Daisy! I mean it. I've had enough!"

"Me too!" she shouted, in fact really screamed, and I thought about the kids for a second, how they'd wake up to their mother's distressed cry and probably think I was doing something horrible to her, like flicking a backhand at her or grabbing at her throat, which I never, ever did. But the whole truth be told, in those days I let myself think about such things every now and then, I too easily imagined picking her petite body up and flinging her onto the bed like you might a cat, mostly because you thought she could handle it, and that the ugly pleasurable surge would somehow satisfy the moment and make everything good and right. Spoken like a veritable wife beater, I realize, and I really can't defend myself, except to say that Daisy was never a completely passive or feckless party in our troubles, she being ever ready to say or do whatever it took to make me feel the afflictions settled so insolvently within her.

"Quiet down," I told her. "You'll wake up the kids."

"I don't care!" she cried, and then that's when it happened.

She lunged at me, in her splendid nakedness, knife and all, her eyes dull with dark no-method, with the chill of empty space. And I will tell you that I froze, not so much with fear (of which there was plenty) as with a kind of abstention, for the horror of what was happening was too realistic to even begin to consider; it was actually enough to make me say, *I must depart, I must depart* (perhaps this the seed of my eventual interest in flight), and not mind whatever the rest. And the significant detail (of the rest) is not that Daisy missed my throat with the chef's knife by a mere thumb's-width, jabbing the point into the door of the refrigerator a good two inches beneath the vinyl skin (the perfect slit is still there, rusty around the pushed-in edges), but that when we both fully returned to the moment, our faces almost touching, we each saw in the other the same amazing wish that she'd not flinched and hit her mark.

Not that I didn't want to live.

I did want to live, just not that way.

Daisy, suddenly scared out of her craziness, broke down and collapsed in a naked heap on the linoleum floor, crying her eyes out.

So with the first light good Dr. Derricone appeared with his scuffed black visiting bag, and before the kids were even awake he gave Daisy a sample bottle of Valium with instructions to keep taking them as long as she felt, as he put it, "Too frisky." I don't know what a trained specialist would have said, what a psychiatrist or psychologist would diagnose as her particular state or behavior and duly prescribe; I wasn't even thinking of "the right thing to do," but was instead just needing to jam hard on the brakes, do whatever it took to stop the train, indeed, do just what Theresa would no doubt say was my only modality and like most lazy modern men compel the desired result with the most available and efficient measure on hand, which often, not surprisingly, takes the form of another lazy modern man but with better credentials. Frank Derricone was Ma and Pop's doctor; he'd delivered me and Bobby and dozens of my cousins and nephews and then Jack and Theresa, and he was indeed a general practitioner of the grand old school, in that he believed in his skills across the disciplines, that good doctoring, as in most professions, was a matter of common sense, empirically applied. This salty view had no doubt served him well for the thirty years up to that point, and for the twenty or so more years afterward, and I don't doubt that Daisy was but among a handful of his patients who didn't end up healthy and long-lived. And while I don't blame Frank Derricone in the least—I'm not the one who can, not in any scenario or space/time continuum or alternate universe I can come up with—I do naturally wonder what might have been, and can't ignore what the good doctor said to me at a party in honor of his retirement, that it probably wasn't the best thing to have kept Daisy on sedatives after she'd come down from her manic heights, in that period of trough. For who really imagined that there could be a state grayer than that for our mad, happy Daisy, lower than low, beneath the bottom, when suddenly it was all she could do to lift herself out of the bed in the morning and drag a brush through her tangled, unwashed hair? Who knew that while I was at work and the kids were at day camp she'd steadily medicate herself on the back patio with Valiums and a case of beer, and on one stifling summer afternoon in August go so far as to induce herself into a dream of buoyancy, such that she, unclothed as preferred, drifted floatless into the pool, perhaps paddling a calm yard or two, before flying, like a seabird, straight down to the bottom.

five

A STORY IN THE NEWS has caught my eye in recent days. It concerns a guy about my age who is trying to balloon around the world, solo. No surprise that he's a billionaire, some slightly daft and extra fit British entrepreneur with knighthood, Sir Harold Clarkson-Ickes, who's making his third attempt at spanning the globe. Of course he's not up there in his silvery high-altitude upside-down dewdrop float *absolutely* alone; he's got several laptops and a satellite linkup and digital cameras set up such that the whole world can check up on him via the Internet. You can track his flight path and the coming weather patterns and browse still pictures of him working his instruments and making himself hot cocoa in his mini-microwave and looking terribly brave, if cold. You can even send Sir Harold an e-mail, which the website says he promises to answer, if not in flight then afterward, *When the mission is complete.*

I wasn't planning to e-mail him, as I figured he had plenty to do and probably had thousands of e-mails jamming his in-box, but last night, driving back from Jack and Eunice's party, and not having talked to Theresa about *that* (she called Paul to say she was staying out late to go to the city with Jadie and Alice), I heard on the radio that Sir Harold had entered a massive storm somewhere over the Indian Ocean. After getting into bed and tossing restlessly for a couple hours I went to the study and turned on the computer. There was no new information on the website, only that his last verified position was some six hours old, the point at which he was likely to have entered the eye of the system and his GPS signal flickered out. I didn't know exactly what I was feeling about the situation, but I found myself typing out this message:

> Sir Harold! We go with you into the vortex! Stay the lofty course! Godspeed!
>
> —*an American friend*

I intentionally used the exclamation points, as I imagined the winds wickedly whipping and tossing him around, and wanted to convey the sense that our hearts and minds were truly with him, up there in his high-tech basket. As for the crusty tone, I figured what else comes naturally to such moments for explorers and their fans, and hoped, too, that he'd appreciate my lame attempt at speaking his language, as Kelly Stearns or Miles Quintana will do for me in their respective ways, and see as a note of goodwill. And all in all it was probably better than "Keep your head down, chief," which is the advice I generally dispense for most situations, no matter the weather, if I even bother to give it anymore.

My interest in Sir Harold is somewhat unusual, as there was never a time in my life when I was known to be a *fan,* of anyone or anything, even when I was still a bachelor and living on my own and not yet fully involved with Battle Brothers. You'd think a fairly sportive, not unconventional guy like me wouldn't mind hooking on to the fortunes of, say, a hometown team, to lend a little modulation to his days, a little virtual drama, and thereby connect with the necessary direness and commonality of this life. That and having a socially acceptable mode of publicly acting out, which is a form of pleasure that your sometimes overintellectualized types (perhaps like Theresa and Paul) and those others long cosseted by a tad too much safety and comfort (perhaps like yours truly) don't or can't quite appreciate anymore.

Sure, I tagged along a couple times with some guys on the crews to a Giants game at the Stadium, but I couldn't quite muster the flushed-neck hoorahs of my spittle-laced compadres, and I'd only rise halfway to the occasion, getting up on my toes for a big play and groaning in concert with the thousands and drinking maybe one jumbo brew too many. Afterward I'd just trudge down the banked exit ramp with only a syncopated tic in my gut, a half-lurch like nothing really got started, never quite feeling the pure sheer liberty that comes from stomping your feet and hollering out your lungs because some burly throwback with a digit sewn onto his shirt has just dived for and reached a certain chalk mark on the field.

I waited for another fifteen minutes, sifting through the cluttered nil of the Web, which to me feels like a flaky neighbor's junky attic, then checked my e-mail, but of course there was no answer, and I woke up this morning actually thinking first about Sir Harold rather than Theresa, wondering whether he had come out of the storm and was still floating, or else scuttled at the bottom of the seas. I then felt a grave jolt of guilt, though one I'm accustomed to, and I tried to think it was simply what Rita would deem my deeply lazy emotional response, but even I couldn't bear the thought that I could be that anemic, and so I called over to Jack's house when the hour at last seemed appropriate, meaning a couple ticks past 8 A.M.

Theresa answered the phone, catching me totally off-guard.

"What's up, Jerry?" she said, sounding fresh and snappy.

"You're up. You went out last night?"

"Yup. Alice and Jadie and I had dinner at a bistro in Tribeca, and then danced at a club. It was a blast. We got back at three in the morning."

"Should you be doing that?"

"Why not? I feel great."

"Come on, Theresa," I said, trying my best to be calm. "I had a conversation with Paul."

"Oh yeah. I heard."

"You heard."

"I was going to talk to you, but I'm kind of glad he went ahead."

"You mean about you being pregnant, or the fact that you're seriously ill?"

"Hey, Jerry," she said, that old unleavened tone instantly rising. "Take it easy."

"Are you serious? Those are two pretty damn big things. I wonder when the hell you were going to tell me what was going on."

"You're the first."

"Thanks, honey."

She paused. "Of course I was going to, about the pregnancy, but it was too early. And then when it wasn't, we found out about the other thing. It got complicated, and I thought we should wait."

"Wait for what, the 'other thing' to kill you?"

"I'm sorry you're so mad."

"How can I be mad?" I said, thinking that there were probably a thousand ways I could be, though none of them very useful. And all of a sudden I had the feeling that I was talking to a much younger version of myself, she being perhaps even more like me than her brother, whom I'd always considered the one who took after me.

I said, taking a breath, "I assume Jack doesn't know yet."

"I'm going to try to talk to him today. When we get back from the doctor."

"Who is this doctor?"

"She's the wife of a grad school friend, at Yale–New Haven. Don't worry, she's an expert."

"Look, I'm sorry I have to say this, but can you tell me what the hell you think you're doing?"

"I'm doing what I can."

"But what's the point of experts if you won't let them do anything?"

"You have to trust me, all right?" she said, quiet and serious. "Okay, Dad?"

I couldn't answer, as the *Dad* part unexpectedly knocked around inside my chest and throat for an extended beat.

"Paul's already outside. We were just leaving."

"Come pick me up. I'll go with you. I'll keep Paul company in the waiting room."

"I don't think so," she said, firmly, the way I do when I believe the conversation is over. "I promise, we'll come back with a full report."

"When will that be?"

"Dinnertime. Or maybe not. We'll call. Paul and I want to

shop a little in the city. But we're going to stay with you from now on, right?"

"What do you think? Of course you are. I'll get your room ready."

"Thanks. Gotta go."

"We're going to talk about this, Theresa. Really talk. I mean it."

"I know. See you later. Bye."

After we clicked off, though, I began to wonder what I'd really say to her and Paul, when they came back with nothing different, to thus continue with their Christian Scientist–style plan of waiting out the "other thing," which of course is pure unalloyed madness, and exactly *not* what I, or anyone else in my family line, would do, or so I'd hope; besides this, you'd think such a thoroughly hip and progressive postmodern/postcolonial type woman like Theresa, who marched on our nation's capital at least a half dozen times in her youth for a woman's right to choose and unionism and the environment and affirmative action et cetera, would do as any other liberal overeducated professional-class person would do in her situation, which is hand-wring and wallow in self-pitying angst and consult countless other liberal overeducated professionals before "finally" coming to the "difficult decision" to cut one's losses (you know what I'm talking about) and move on, which is what most other people (like me) would decide to do in about a half minute, underscoring the notion that most of us (at least in this centrist Western world) are pretty much of the same mind, though we believe in and require vastly different processes in the getting there.

Of course I spent several hours online doing all sorts of searches on the disease, there being an astounding amount of material and hot links and hospital and pharma company sponsored sites on Hodgkin's and non-Hodgkin's lymphoma, and soon enough realized that I could search within these for pregnancy issues. This second stage of Googling/Yahooing, however, yielded surprisingly few "results," and what there was only outlined predictably general recommendations for what a woman in Theresa's situation might do, the basic wisdom (no surprise) being that you treated the cancer as soon as the baby was born (or prematurely induced if the condition of the mother was serious), or the pregnancy was "terminated," either way trying to ensure the best "outcome" for both but then certainly favoring the health of the mother over that of the fetus, though of course this was never actually expressed. What seemed clear, though, was that the *time* of diagnosis would determine whether (if early) you would end things right away and move on and hope you could get pregnant after you were cured, or (if late) you would make the best of it, as long as that seemed prudent. Nowhere did I read any mention about an early diagnosis *and* riding it out, as if that scenario weren't the purview of medical professionals but some other more philosophically capable group.

So the question is, How, then, does our own Theresa Battle resolve to take the path of essentially a person of faith (or epochal stubbornness)? I don't know. Perhaps it's that I never introduced her to the ready comforts of institutionalized religion, even after her mother died, or that her intellectual studies were in good measure predicated upon the Impossibility of Meaning, or that our tidy post-Daisy troika has really been the loose association of three very separate, unconnected beings, who share only the minimum genetic material and the securely grounded belief that a full belly makes for a carefree, loafing soul (zealous eaters that we are). Maybe it shouldn't surprise me at all, then, that Theresa should take a whopping leap right here and choose for the moment her fetus's life over her own (despite the chances that neither might make it), and commit to something so wholly unreasonable that it would seem no other act in her days spent or to come would ever be as pure.

But I don't know. This is the sort of thinking often proffered in deadly serious novels full of nourishing grace and humanity, but which seems, served up in our famished real life, to be about as satisfying as a radish. Maybe this in turn explains my undue interest in and empathy for imperiled billionaire balloonists, whose public trials are patent and palpable and, as in the worst of our own ordeals, ultimately self-inflicted. And maybe Sir Harold, and Theresa, and the rest of us presumedly wracked agonistes, are in fact making very simple choices, dull to ramification, as we are unable to do much of anything else.

After eating a breakfast of plain live-culture yogurt and honey maple granola and bananas and black coffee, which I mention only because it's the exact breakfast Rita always had, every day, without fail, even when we were in Paris and the baguettes and café au lait were magnificent, and which she probably still eats with Marquis Richie in his wrought-iron-and-glass conservatory breakfast room, I tried to see what new news there was about Sir Harold. There was nothing in the paper and after futilely trying for thirty minutes to log on and sign in to my often balky Internet service, the popular one that every person I know under thirty-five tells me is for dodos and suckers, I gave up and drove over to the Battle Brothers "office" near Commack to use their computer. I sometimes do this when I can't connect, as Jack has of course installed a special connection line that is 10 or 100 or whatever times faster than what I have at home, and which is always on, and which I don't understand. At Parade our computers are solely travel reservation terminals, though that will soon change, I hear, and besides I don't like to go in when it's not my workday, as there's often a backup and I'm pressed into duty. I'm still not quite sure why Jack needs the fast line at Battle Brothers, unless he thinks keeping the guys on the crews hyped up and happy with the constant streams of electronic smut is a necessary and important company perk. Before the trucks get sent out at 7 A.M., you'll see a bunch of guys huddled around a computer in the back office checking out some website featuring Nasty Teens or Horny Housewives and making the age-old locker room comments about the gynecological wonders of this world. I've perused these sites myself, of course, as at least 90 percent of the e-mail I get each day is linking advertisements to sites for every sexual practice, taste, and persuasion imaginable and unimaginable (the computer guy voice should really say, "You've Got Porn!"), the rest being get-rich-quick schemes and second-mortgage offers and then every once in a while an e-mail from someone I actually know, usually not a personal message but a forwarded joke or humorous news item or, alas, some doctored nude picture of a celebrity.

When I drive in through the gate it's already past nine and so the yard has pretty much cleared out of trucks and equipment trailers. Jack's SUV isn't here, either, which dumb thing of dumb things gives me a welling of idiot pride, all because I imagine he's out directing his men, which he probably isn't, as he's probably doing estimates and yakking with suppliers or meeting with his bankers to discuss the possible IPO, which seems less likely every day. I must say the place looks pretty decent, despite the fact that the whole property is paved and fenced and should be nothing special to look at, if not a typical industrial zone eyesore. The three acres Pop and his brothers paid diddly-squat for after the war is probably worth at least a million now as long as there's not some huge environmental problem with it because of all the motor oils and fuels we keep around here, not to mention the fertilizers and lawn chemicals.

Down the road is a cluster of smallish houses from the 1950s where a girl I dated one summer named Rose lived with her mother and aunt and sad drunk of a stepfather who she said touched her once but never again because she practically bit the tip of his ear off and he got spooked and cried like a baby, and I mention her mostly because since then I've somehow always associated Battle Brothers with her, if in the smallest way; in fact there's not been a time I've come here that my thoughts haven't ranged to the Cahills' cramped, dusty house that always smelled of frying bacon and stale beer, and to Rose, who would tug down my undershorts back in the far bay of our garage with a wry sneaky smile and handle me so roughly with her short fingers I sometimes had to ask her to stop. We got along fine enough, but the funny thing was that Rose saw me as a rich kid and I suppose compared to her, with her big toe poking through her thirdhand Mary Janes, I definitely was; after necking we'd walk back to her house and sit on the front stoop, and more than once she said I had it made in the shade for the rest of my life. I knew even then that she was probably right, which made me feel equal parts pride and resentment for Pop and the family and a kind of unfair dominion over her that I've admittedly also felt with Daisy and Rita (and Kelly), who all came from pretty hardscrabble backgrounds and though generally not into money weren't exactly naïve about it either. And maybe they all partly fell for me because of the very inevitability of my future, which is the happy, lucky curse of much of my generation and the next but I'm not sure will be for Jack or his kids, despite these flush times. Sometimes I think Jack and Eunice subconsciously know this, too, and maybe that's why they tend to go overboard with the spending, as if they're not just suburban American well-to-do but jet-set wealthy, to get theirs while they still can.

As for the Battle Brothers building, Jack has changed quite a few things since I early-retired, including the old hand-painted script signage of "Battle Brothers," which he switched out for hefty three-foot-high stainless steel letters that were drilled into the building. Jack likes to refer to the place as "the firm," but to me it'll always be just a shop. A few months ago construction was finally finished on a new suite of offices that were built on the street side of the double-height eight-bay garage, a funny-looking free-form mass of an addition (based loosely after the style of some world-famous architect), which itself has three different kinds of façade claddings and colors and oddly placed windows cut into it like a badly done Halloween pumpkin. I guess it's interesting enough to somebody knowledgeable, for Eunice got a fancy design magazine to come out and take pictures of it outside and in, but to me it looks like the leavings of some giant robot dog, a freakish metallic pile of you-know-what. The new reception area is all Eunice's doing, outfitted with custom-hewn panels of Norwegian birch wood and a long two-inch-thick glass coffee table suspended by tungsten wires coming down from the ceiling, a banquette upholstered in graphite-hued crushed silk running along the walls, which are adorned with contemporary paintings, these changed out monthly to feature another avant-garde local artist (no impressionistic seascapes or boardwalk scenes here). If you didn't know any better you'd think you were in the lounge area of some trendy Asian-fusion restaurant in SoHo, as the receptionist behind the shoji-style console, a hot little multicultural number (like a young Rita but with some West Indian or Thai mixed in) always sporting a walkabout headset, with a tough set to her mouth and given to wearing clingy black T-shirts embroidered with sequins spelling out things like QUEEN BEE and PRECIOUS, will serve you with unexpected earnestness a freshly made espresso or cappuccino from the push-button automatic Italian coffee machine Eunice insisted upon, or else offer you a selection of juices and mineral waters or even steep you a personal pot of green or herbal tea.

"Hey, Mr. Battle," the girl says a little too brightly, as if it's a shock I'm really here. Her shirt today reads SWEET THANG. "Your son is out. We don't expect him back until the afternoon."

"I'm just here to use the computer," I say, liking the white-shoe sound of "we" but wondering who exactly that is, or might be.

"Sure thing," she says, and gets up to walk me back to where the "public" computer is. Eunice designed the main office space back here as well, continuing the theme of Chic Eastern Calm, though here there are additional touches of what Eunice informed me during renovations is Comfy Bauhaus, meaning lots of clean surfaces and lines, to inspire efficiency and high creative function. She even instituted a set of office rules about paper and knickknack clutter so that her design scheme wouldn't be sullied. She needn't have worried, though, because there aren't enough employees as yet to fill the space, just Sweet Thang there out front and Jack's assistant, Cheryl, a forty-something looker who normally sits outside Jack's private office but is out sick today, and then the bookkeeper Sal Mondello, who has been with Battle Brothers since pretty much the beginning and refuses to move out of his original office in the old part of the garage. Upstairs in this new wing is a showroom of the work Battle Brothers will soon be doing, mock-up designer kitchens and bathrooms and media rooms with real working appliances and big-screen TVs and furnished (or *appointed*) as luxuriously as Jack's own house, with antique rugs and heirloom cabinets and framed oil paintings and mirrors. The master plan as indicated by the empty desks is that the administrative and professional design staff will soon expand with the company's gradual shift to work in high-end home renovations, which seems to me to be a bit too gradual, as I haven't yet heard of any confirmed jobs or commissions. Right now Jack and Cheryl and the receptionist and Sal can handle the steady flow of the usual landscaping work and I'm glad to see that Jack hasn't gone ahead and already hired two or three more girls to sit around stripping off their nail polish.

I can't remember her name and so I'm hesitant to start any small talk, though with her clingy top and even clingier matching micro-skirt with no panty lines discernible and heel-to-toe catwalk lope, a springy internal automata makes me want to utter some-*thing*, some-*thang*, some-*thong*.

But nothing acceptable comes, and I give up.

"I'm really sorry, but would you please tell me your name again?"

"Maya."

"Of course. Hiya, Maya."

She giggles. "Hiya, Mr. Battle."

"Jerry."

"Okay, Jerry," Maya says, sitting down at the computer. She palms the mouse, and the screensaver (a group shot of the whole Battle Brothers gang, leaping in unison) instantly disappears, revealing the last image viewed, which is an overly exposed picture of a pasty-looking white couple doing it doggie-style on the polished deck of a powerboat. They're ordinary right-down-the-middle Heartland-type people you'd see at any shopping mall, both looking straight at the camera with an expression of the same prideful glee that fishermen have in photos when they've just hauled in a prize sailfish.

"Oops," she says, quickly clicking on the boxed X in the corner to get rid of it. But another nested picture of the same twosome takes its place; this time they're waving (the woman leaning on her elbows), like they're saying, *Look, no hands.*

"Sorry," I hear myself offering in an avuncular, sensitive-to-harassment-of-any-kind mode. "I'll have Jack talk to the fellas. They shouldn't be looking at this stuff here."

"It doesn't bother me," Maya says. "It's a free country. Anyway, I'd rather have to look at porn than some dumb chart of the stock market."

"Really?"

"Why not? As long as no one's forced into anything, I don't see why I have to freak about it. I'm a big girl. Most of the guys know that just because they look at this stuff here doesn't mean I'm available to them."

"Most? Who doesn't? I'll set them straight."

"It's actually just one, but it's all right. He's harmless."

"You can say. Who?"

Maya points to the door on the garage end of the room.

"Old Sal?"

"He leaves dirty notes on my desk. He thinks I don't know it's him but he handwrites them and I know his script."

"Really?"

"Wait a sec." She goes up front to her desk and returns with a full card hand of square yellow Post-it notes, indeed marked in thick lead pencil with Sal's distinct left-hand scribble, fat and squat and bent the wrong way: *Rock hard for you. Will lick you clean. Prime my love pump.*

"See? He sometimes leaves them for the temps, too."

I nod, certainly embarrassed for her, and for myself and Jack, and for the near-venerable institution of Battle Brothers, and although I'm ashamed of Sal and feel pity for him, I can't help but also admire the sweaty, slick-palmed adolescent tone, the undiminished gall and balls of an old dude whom I always thought of as randy from the waist-high stacks of skin magazines he openly kept in the wide, low washbasin of his grim, dank bookkeeper's office that Pop had converted from a janitor's closet, this when Pop didn't think Battle Brothers needed a full-time ledger man. When I was in high school I once caught him lying down on his desk with the secretary (named Roz) squatting on his face so you could just see his bushy head of hair poking out from her skirt as if she were sitting on a fuzzy pillow. Sal has to be pushing seventy-five now and I don't think he ever married, though he did have a long secretive affair with Pop's baby sister Georgette until she was killed in a car accident in 1965. After Pop handed over the reins to me everyone figured Sal might quit, given that I obviously didn't know or care too much about the business; when Sal came in my first day as head honcho he asked for a "meeting" after work, and I was expecting he'd demand a slice of the company and was all ready after consulting with Pop to offer him 12.5 percent and not a half point more. But all he asked me for was a $50-a-week raise and when I said I'd give him $45 he took it without another word.

"Sal is harmless," I say. "But I'll have a talk with him anyway."

"What talk do you want, there, Jer?"

"Hey, Sally."

It's Salvatore Mondello, just arriving to work. He's dressed as usual in his low-rent white-collar style: short-sleeve dress shirt, too-short stubby tie, trim-fit gabardine slacks, worn cordovan wing tips. He's one of those handsome lanky Northern Italian types who age magnificently. His skin has a clean-scrubbed light olive glow, his hair still thick and full and streaked with enough dark strands that it appears spun straight from silver. If he had been a slightly different man he could have enjoyed a long career as one of those duty-free international playboys jetting from the Côte d'Azur to Palm Beach with a wealthy mistress waiting desperately in each hotel suite for him to blindfold her with his silk ascot, fragrant of musk and Dunhill 100s, and do things to her with his tongue and lubed pinky finger that her inattentive jerk husband long gave up doing.

But fortunately or unfortunately Sal is not a slightly different man, and while he is plenty smart and has let his dick lead him through life like a lot of the rest of us, I would say he did so without a companion ambition for fame or money, and so is who he is, which is basically an old local stud who worked just hard enough to pay the rent and take out fresh pussy every Friday and Saturday night. This until maybe eight or ten years ago, when I think the high mileage on his purportedly horse-sized rig (this from one of the mechanics, who early on in Battle Brothers history caught him jerking off in the john and described Sal's action "like he was buffin' a toy baseball bat") finally caught up to him and broke down, relegating him to a retirement of titty bars and dirty Web chats and twice-a-year Caribbean cruises on a popular line on which he travels free for serving as a nightly dance partner for singles and widows, though with this new hard-on wonder drug they've invented, Sal might soon fly the flag high once again.

"What, Jer, they fire you over there at the agency?"

"Not yet. I'm just saying hello today."

"Hey there, Maya."

"Morning, Sal," she answers him, without a hint of umbrage. Though not with great warmth, either. "I gotta get to work."

"You do that, honey," Sal says. When she's back out front he says, "If I could just be sixty again."

"Yeah? What would you do?" I say, remembering as I do almost daily now that I'll be that very age in a matter of nothing, just when the world tips on its axis and our propitiously temperate part of it starts to die out again, wreathe itself in the dusty colors of mortality.

"Are you kidding? Me and that amazing piece of ass would be balling all day like those horny monkeys on the nature program. What do they call them, bonobos? Those monkeys just screw each other all day, and they'll even get into some dyke and fag action when nobody's looking."

"No kidding?"

"Saw it just last night. The girl monkeys, you know, with the bright red catcher's mitt twats, will squat back to back, rubbing themselves on each other. The boys will hang upside down and play swords with their skinny units. These monkeys are different than other ones who would rather fight viciously than fuck. I guess we're supposed to be more like the fighting monkeys."

"I guess you're a bonobo, huh, Sally?"

"You got that right. What about you?"

"Probably neither," I say, thinking that there must be a third kind of monkey, only slightly more advanced, who sits high up in the trees and collects his fruit pits, indolently noting how much he's eaten.

"How's Rita treating you?"

"You don't know?"

"Oh, Christ, Jer, don't tell me something's happened to her."

"No, no, nothing like that. She just left me. Almost a year ago, I guess."

"Oh. That's even worse. It means she's with someone else."

"Yeah."

"Do I know the guy?"

"Richie Coniglio. From the neighborhood. Hairy little guy."

"That pipsqueak? What's he do now?"

"He's a fancy-pants lawyer. Richer than God. He lives over in Muttontown."

"I guess we all knew that little wiseass was headed for loads of dough. But he has to end up with your girl, too?"

"I know. It's not good."

"And when that girl is somebody like Rita. Christ. I've always liked Puerto Rican chicks because they're like black chicks who aren't black, if you know what I mean. But when you started up with Rita I was especially jealous. She's a sweet lady and a great cook and then she's got those big chocolate eyes and the nice skin and that gorgeous shapely round . . ."

"Hey, hey, Sally. It's still pretty fresh, okay?"

"Sorry, Jer. I'm just telling you how good you had it with her. Did you fuck things up or did she just get sick of you?"

"Both, I think."

"Probably you weren't giving her enough head. These days women expect it."

"You're probably right," I tell him, reminded now why over all these years Sal and I never got to be closer, despite the fact that

I've always liked him well enough and even looked up to him like the older brother I sometimes wished I'd had. Sal has a way of making you agree with him not because he's a bully but because you don't really want to get into the full squalid array of details necessary to complete a typical conversation with him. I'd like to add here, too, that Rita didn't expect anything in the labial way, and while she clearly liked it plenty whenever I did do my oral duties, she was generally of the mind that men shouldn't get so right up close to a woman's petaled delicates, if they were to remain in the least secret and alluring and mysterious.

Or so she told me.

Sal adds, too: "Seems like these young ones like Maya up there don't even care for old-fashioned penetration anymore. They'd all just rather be lesbians, if they had it their way. If you don't believe me it's on the Internet."

"Whatever. But if you can do me a favor, Sally, just keep it in your pants here at the office."

"What," he says, looking up front. "Has there been a complaint?"

"No, no, nobody's said nothing. But you hear about what's going on these days with sexual harassment. Jack doesn't need anybody suing the company because the work environment is, you know, whatever they call it, 'predatory.'"

"Hey, I'm not the one wearing suggestive T-shirts."

"I'm just saying, Sal, let's keep it professional around here, okay? Keep the shop going like it is."

"No problem with me, Jer," he says. "It's Jack you should worry about."

"What? He's fucking around?"

"I wouldn't know about that," Sal says. "I just think he's running Battle Brothers into the ground."

"What are you talking about? It seems like we've got more work than we can handle. Seems like the trucks are always all out."

"Sure they are. We're doing nice business, just like we have the last five years. But that's the *old* work. The dirt work. We get decent margins there, but nothing fantastic. You know that."

"Sure."

"The new stuff is what's the problem. See all those new workstations and plotters?" he says, pointing to the six custom maple-wood desks with large flat-panel computer monitors and a huge plotter for making large-format prints. "That's Jack's design operation. He and Eunice spent top dollar on that equipment and software, almost seventy grand. We could probably design fighter jets on those things. But we've only been using one of the terminals, and half-time at that. The high-end construction and renovation work is out there, but we're not getting it. People know us as landscapers and stonemasons, not kitchen and bathroom designers. Jack's idea that he could become this supercontractor for the whole tristate region is an interesting idea, but he's spending all his hours driving to Cheesedick, Connecticut, to do an estimate and getting squat. I think he's finally landed a couple jobs, but I think he had to lowball to get them, and after looking at the bids I won't be surprised if we lose twenty-five or fifty grand on each. And do you know how much this new office and showroom wing is costing us? Five hundred grand, and counting."

"Jesus. I had no idea."

"But that's not the worst of it, Jer. I hate to tell you this, but I'm pretty sure Jack's been borrowing against the business. I think he's been trying to hide it from me but I got some statements by accident about interest payments on a big note against the property, and then another on the business itself."

"How big are they?"

"They add up to a million and a half."

"Anything else you want to tell me?"

"That's it. Though I can't promise that these aren't just the ones I've gotten wind of. I don't know what he's doing, Jer, but I think you better talk to him."

"Yeah. I will."

"Jer?"

"Yeah?"

"What's your line on me and Miss Curry Pot?"

"Way long. I'd keep it platonic for now. Okay, Sally?"

Sal smirks, and heads to his office through the frosted-glass door that is the partition between this expensive sleek new world and the grubby oil-streaked one of old. On the computer I type in the address of Sir Harold's site and actually have to pause before tapping the Enter key.

The news is good. He emerged from the storm shortly after I'd last looked, and is flying high again, his path only slightly altered, and just a few hours shy of schedule. The electronic message board for him is lit up with hundreds of emphatic postings, such as "Fly, Harold, Fly!" and "Tally Ho!" and "You Can't Keep A Good Man Down," and though I'd like to add my two cents to the feel-good kitty (mostly if not exclusively for the psychic benefit of us onlookers), I can't quell this steady pulsing dread that trouble still lies ahead for him. Because when you think of it, the truly depressing thing is that the trouble will probably not be a limitation of Sir Harold himself or his wondrous technology but just the fact of something as guileless as the winds, and the weather, these chance clouds that should determine a person's ultimate success or failure. This is why I fly my *Donnie* only when the sky is completely clear, with no threat of weather for at least another day, as I want no obstacle or impedance to a good afternoon's soar. Of course this also means I've never ranged too far from here, never hopped from small airfield to airfield the way most guys have on weeklong junkets to Florida or California, never flown after dusk in the watery blue light or through the scantest rains; I have to wonder what will happen if I ever do find myself in an unforecasted fog, how well if at all I'll work the controls and fly solely by instruments, if I'll be able to forge through the muck and break back into daylight.

And as I pad into Jack's plush office and sit in his broad leather desk chair that seems to promise only good fortune and prosperity, I feel somewhat bereft (and not because of any monies he's maybe lost or losing), for I don't quite know what I'll say to him, or more specifically, what I'll say that won't deeply cut or insult him or make him talk to me even less than he already does. If, as I've noted, the main problem with Jack is that he too much needs to impress, the very close second problem at this point is that he knows that's exactly what I'm thinking whenever I step into his cavernous home or visit one of his jobs or come calling around here. And perhaps over time it's this already anticipated turbulence that brings a family most harm, the knowledge unacknowledged, which at some point you can try and try but can't glide above.

six

NOW AND THEN, clear out of the blue, just as he did when I first arrived at Ivy Acres this afternoon for an early dinner visit, Pop will tell me, "Bobby was the one who should have married Daisy."

At the moment, he's dozing hard, his mouth laid open, unhinged, his eyes pinched up like something really, really hurts.

I shouldn't rouse him.

To be honest, I used to burn inside whenever Pop said that. Mostly because I know how dead wrong he'd be, if that had ever come to pass. Bobby met Daisy maybe twice before he left for basic training in the fall of 1968. That summer he was playing in the instructional league in Puerto Rico but got sick of the heat and the bugs and the food, and like a dope signed up for the Marines instead of seeing what might have come of his raw talent for the game. Bobby and Daisy got along instantly, Bobby taking her for a ride in the gleaming emerald green '67 Impala convertible that Pop had bought brand new for himself. I remember them coming back with ice cream cones, with both of them, ego-typically, sporting triple dips. After a brief stint at Camp Pendleton he was shipped to Vietnam, stationed who knows where, serving six months of duty until the night he was separated from his Marine platoon during a chaotic firefight and never heard from again. They searched for his body over the next few days and found his helmet and a bloody boot, but then the whole division had to quickly pull back under an intense VC counterattack and naturally the next thing that happened was a carpet bombing of the area, which obliterated everything living or dead. After the war he was on the long roster of MIAs submitted to the Vietnamese government during prisoner and bodily-remains exchanges, but even Pop knew that that was pretty much the end of the story for Robert Henry Battle of Whitestone, New York, and never fought the reality or was one of those people who made pilgrimage to Vietnam or agitated for more efforts from the government.

I think Pop made the best of the situation, at least for himself, for while he didn't have Bobby's body he could entertain the notion of Bobby Ongoing, which was unassailable and ever-evolving. Not that Pop was under any delusions that he was still alive somewhere, but he could imagine Bobby growing older, Bobby maturing and marrying, Bobby as a father and the scion of the family business, all this without interference from any Bobby Actual, whose presence, like all our presences, would have been an inglorious mitigation. Ma, of course, was inconsolable for a long time; she wouldn't talk much when she and Pop came over and just trudged about the kitchen wiping surfaces or occupied herself with pressing my shirts down in the basement or sweeping the patio. In her own house she wouldn't let anybody into Bobby's room, not even Pop, until a leak in his dormer after a bad storm eventually led to a smell that couldn't be ignored, and when Pop and I finally went in there, it was like a lab lesson in the varieties of fungi and molds, green-gray splotches on the walls, grayish shadings on the window panes, and then a cottony white fur growing in and out of his old sneakers and shoes. The room was so sharply musty that Pop had a contractor come in and tear it down to the studs and floor joists before building it back again.

Almost nothing of Bobby's was salvageable, none of his clothes or pennants or books. The only items Ma could keep were his many baseball trophies, which she soaked in a tub of bleach and then displayed on the mantel in their living room, where they remained until I moved Pop into Ivy Acres. They now sit atop the microwave in his quasi-efficiency suite, pedestaled brass Mickey Mantle–modeled figures, posed in their home run swings; these, by the way, are the only objects from the old house that Pop has kept for himself. It'd be squarely sad-sweet, for sure, except that Pop sometimes confuses whose trophies they are and will brandish one and compliment me on my glovework at the hot corner, or worse yet, talk about his own power to right center field, the bolting line drives that even Willie Mays couldn't have run down.

Bobby was by any account a memorable baseball player, and I won't go into it except to say that he was a speed demon on the bases and definitely the one with the flashy glove and power to the alleys and perhaps could have gone all the way, given the physique and skills he had. He was built like Jack but was more lithe than Jack could ever be, big and strong and flexible the way most of these extremely tuned and pumped up professional athletes are today but that back then was quite rare, especially as expressed (if you'll excuse my saying) in some neighborhood white kid. After the instructional league ball in Puerto Rico, he signed up at a Marine kiosk, leaving behind both a minor league contract and a full college scholarship, which would have put off his being drafted, and maybe changed his luck entirely. I'd already been a Coast Guard reservist, and during those years I spent every other weekend on a boat sailing mostly nowhere, which was perfect for me.

And like I've said—although I never said it to anyone—I thought Bobby was a fucking idiot, and on several important levels (and not because it was Vietnam, because Vietnam wasn't Vietnam yet, at least to us back here), but to my amazement nobody considered what he was doing to be a terrible idea, not even Ma, who seemed to think going into the service was like an extended sleepaway camp, and not even Pop, who thought Bobby should spend a year or two and take in the sights of Southeast Asia and just come back and lace up his old spikes for St. John's or the Columbus Clippers, no problem whatsoever. Like everybody in our neighborhood Bobby was patriotic enough but it wasn't love of country or sense of duty or anything else so fudgeably grand and romantic that made him do such a thing. For no matter how excellent he was at something (and there were many somethings besides baseball, like acting and singing and then drawing, which I remember all the girls adoring, because he'd sketch them to look as lovely as they'd ever be, accentuating their eyes or lips), Bobby had a habit of cutting short his involvement before anything really great could develop. He was what people these days would term a grazer, a browser, a gifted Renaissance kid who never quite wholly commits (one could maybe think ADD). But really, if I have to say it, Bobby was Bobby because he didn't ultimately care. It wasn't a nihilistic streak, nothing dark like that, but rather a long-ingrained insoluble indifference, which sprang from how easily he could do things, like pick up any instrument, or a new sport, or have a beautiful girl fall in love with him, with what was always this effortless sparkling performance of Himself, which he was mostly unconscious of, and thus why most people instantly championed and loved him. And so you could think his predraft enlistment was just another circumstance to be easily sailed through, but I have thought that what it really was was Bobby pushing the venue, pushing the parameters to include, finally, the chance of testing his mortality.

Which turns out is what many of us otherwise self-tucked in chronic safety will do, and with surprising regularity, whether we're aware of it or not.

If Bobby were still alive it is almost certain that he would have ended up running Battle Brothers; although we were seven years apart (Ma had two miscarriages between us), I would have simply put in a few years until Bobby was old enough and then gone off on my own and probably pursued something to do with flying. Although I always dreamed of being an ace of a P-47 Thunderbolt (long ago manufactured by Republic down the road in Farmingdale) or a Grumman F9F Panther like in *The Bridges at Toko-Ri*, I didn't end up applying to the service academies and thus had no genuine shot at being a fighter jock and having a subsequent career as a big-jet commercial captain. I do believe I would have been like a few guys you hear about around the hangar lounge who try to climb the ladder themselves, average Andys who just love flying so much that they wait for their chance to pilot commuter puddle-jumpers or regional mail runners or even just drag those message banners above the South Shore beaches that say MARRY ME ROSALIE or MAKE IT ABSOLUT. Or if I didn't quite do that maybe I'd have my own little travel business, by handle of My Way Tours, offering eight- and fifteen-day guided re-creations of all of Jerry Battle's favorite trips ("Serengeti Supreme," say, or "Blue Danube"), because anyone knows that the best way to make a living is to spend the workaday hours submitting to your obsessions and that everything else is just plain grubby labor. But that's the life of the charming and the lucky and the talented (i.e., people like Bobby), and for the rest of us perfectly acceptables and okays and competents it's a matter of persistence and numbness to actual if minor serial failure and a wholly unsubstantiated belief in the majesty of individual destiny, all of which is democracy's spell of The Possible on us.

Still, and though Pop would never agree, Bobby would have probably run Battle Brothers into the ground. I can say this because he was always too generous, and would have undoubtedly bid too low for jobs and been a soft touch with the crews and not cut enough corners when he could with the customers or the vendors and who/whatever else there was holding down our margins. I'm no natural business whiz and the worries never once kept me up at night but Battle Brothers was the whole of Pop's life and in the sum of it pretty much mine. I think my career-long effectiveness came from the fact that I could funnel all of my frustrations and exasperations and notions of self-misprision into just the right kind of fierce mercenary pressure, which I could reserve until called for and then unvalve on some poor sucker caught in the wrong place at the wrong time.

Christ I could holler. Mostly, though, I was just in a pissy mood. Some of the guys, I know, would kid around and refer to me as Jerry Not So Merry or Jerry Sour Berry (their other, non-public names for me I'm sure much more rank and vile). At the annual landscapers' association banquet (last year emceed by the dashing Jack Battle at the Brookville Country Club), I never particularly associated too well, always choosing to sit with the newer contractors on the periphery and pretend I didn't know anybody. The Pavones and Richters and Keenans and Ianuzzis would hold their royal blowhards court and roast each other and get fresh with the hired girls and undoubtedly scuff up the putting green with their drunken fisticuffs, these overtanned, blunt-fingered guys upon whom I would wish a horrid pox or blood plague but who in fact weren't unlike us Battles at all.

Bobby was the one who would have fit right in; he was ever willing to tolerate those he considered to be any kind of comrade in arms, and not at all for business reasons. I don't know where he got this need to be part of the crowd, part of the gang, as neither Pop nor I is so constituted, but then again he was universally adored, and after we had his memorial service there came together what amounted to a big block party for him in our old neighborhood, which wasn't thrown by us, as Ma for once in her life didn't much feel like putting out a spread for company and went right up to her bedroom to change into her nightgown and take a few pills for sleep. Pop trudged down into our finished basement and clicked on the talk radio extra loud, and though I don't like to think about it probably just played with his 1/175-scale USS *Arizona*, which took him at least three years to make, painting included. Daisy refused to come, as she despised funerals and cemeteries and was back in Long Island with the kids, and so I moped around the kitchen for a bit until I heard music coming from the street.

When I went out there I was amazed to see how large and festive the gathering was—it was more a celebration than a wake, some kind of commencement, like a demigod had been approved to ascend Mt. Olympus. Everybody was hauling out their extra card tables and chairs and setting out the Pyrex casseroles of baked ziti and lasagna and sausages and stuffed clams and bean salad that was probably just their family dinners. They had a keg of beer for the men and jugs of blush wine for the ladies, and the kids were playing Red Rover and Kick the Can at the end of our coned-off street, and even a couple of cops had stopped by for a cold one. Basically it was like one of those Saturday night city street fairs except there weren't any flashing string lights or cotton candy machines or necking couples, though I do remember seeing a kid puking on the Radoscias' garage door, probably having filched too much leftover Lambrusco.

Everybody was hugging me and friendly in a way I had never known them to be friendly, which, if I have to be honest, was clearly not so much about condolence or sympathy but rather whatever they might have sensed of Bobby as residually expressed in me (he had those sparkly eyes, too, and the same wavy dark hair). But none of it was unpleasant or even sad, and I can tell you that I felt more comfortable and at ease that evening on 149th Street than in all the years growing up there as a not unhappy youth, because when you're among others and don't have to be exactly in your own skin it can be the strangest blessing, not to mention the added effect of feeling an afterglow as warm-hued as Bobby Battle's. (Perhaps this explains my love of travel, because when you're walking along some quay or piazza or *allée* there's an openness and possibility and that certain intimacy with strangers which is near impossible on an American street or food court, the scale still hunched and human.) Guys were toasting me and making sentimental speeches about Bobby's honey singing voice and stunning bat speed, and the ladies were the ones who seemed to be putting on a serious buzz, as I'd be passed from one to another in a rope line of tangos, and then later that evening when almost everybody had folded up camp and gone inside for the night, a woman named Patricia Murphy came up to me and told me she had gone out with Bobby for a little while during middle school and asked if I would walk her to her car.

I actually remembered her, or thought I did, as she was one of those fourteen-year-old girls who are physically developed beyond anybody's capacity to handle too well (much less craven adolescents). She had a grown woman's hips and thighs and she had a bigger, fuller chest than any senior girl in the high school. She was certainly okay-looking but it probably wouldn't have mattered if she looked like Ernest Borgnine she was so built, and like too many girls in her position she probably ended up giving away a bit too much for popularity's or some other sake to those very boys in the school keen on taking as much as they could.

Bobby wasn't one of those, certainly, and I remember they were in a school production together, something called *A Medley of Shakespeare*, featuring bits from three or four of his plays, and maybe their romance lasted a couple weeks at most afterward, I'm sure ending with the requisite study hall dramatics and tears. That night after the funeral Patricia was in a funny kind of mood, which is odd for me to say given that I didn't know her at all. She was sort of laughing to herself and gently poking at my ribs and arms like my sexy cousin Wendy Battaglia used to do at those big Sunday family dinners that nobody ever throws anymore, and when we got to her car, which was parked right in front of our house, she announced she was too drunk to drive and could we maybe sit inside for a little while? I figured that made good sense and by that point I was feeling pretty valorous with all the back slaps and glad hands accrued to me during the evening. I figured my folks would be sound asleep, which they were, as I could hear Ma's high snoring titters, *wee-ha, wee-ha.*

So I went into the kitchen and put on a pot of coffee for her, but when I turned Patricia Murphy was right there, practically pressing up against me, her chest maybe not any bigger or fuller ten years later but still plenty magnanimous, with a kind of space-age uprightness and pomp that makes you think this is why you live in this confused post-Newtonian world. She asked if I could show her Bobby's room. I didn't think anything of her request, really, or her proximity, and we went up the tight stairs to the second door on the left with the old Polo Grounds poster tacked on it.

Bobby Battle's bedroom, pre-fungus, was as advertised, the picture of American Golden Boy-hood, festooned with pennants and posters of starlets and books on log cabin construction and model rocketry. I thought she'd maybe poke her head in the closet or sit on the bed or try his still supple third baseman's glove on for size, but she stood apart from me at an awkward distance and then said in a coquettish thespian whisper, "You are merry, my lord." I replied, confused, "Who me?" and before I knew it she fell upon me, down to her knees, swiftly unlatching my belt. And as she took me barely chubby in her dryish small mouth I finally for once that evening thought of my brother, lost somewhere back in Vietnam, his soul wandering the death fields, who would go on forever and ever, like any true titan, through all of our flawed enactments, whether he would wish to or not. And that's when I first really felt what must have been a pang of brotherly lacking, which for me wasn't so much an emptiness as this mysterious prosthetic groan, from down deep. And I was thinking of Daisy, too, of course, and how I'd ever begin to explain myself if she found out, and was just in fact planning a delicate extrication when Pop walked in and caught me and Patricia Murphy, duly arrayed. He could have been angry, certainly, or at least repelled, but he simply looked at her, and then at me, and said like it was quarter to four in the afternoon on a job already running a day behind, "Let's pick it up here, Jerome."

Pop has never mentioned that night, not even in these recent months when it's just that kind of best-forgotten off-color item exclusively crowding his memory, and which he'll tell you all about, over and over again: the time he was playing golf on the Costa del Sol and caught the future King of Spain hocking a loogey in the water cooler on the fourteenth tee, or when he got the clap from a hooker in Kansas City and was afraid to touch Ma for three months, or the time he was out on a big job in North Hills and saw the lady of the house naked in the kitchen, brushing her nipples with salad oil, for no reason he could fathom. He'll tell you his awkward stories of all of us, of his cousins and employees and people on television and especially the politicians he reads about in the stacks of ultraright and left-wing newsletters he subscribes to, the power plays and conspiracies to cover up what he believes runs through everything and everyone, which is corruption, total utter corruption, of heart and mind and of the soul. Only Bobby, no surprise, is not subject, which is fine by me, and maybe even appreciated, because if Pop were exposing him, too, I'd wonder what light or verity was left to him.

For Pop, unlike Bobby, isn't so unconcerned about dying. Sure he talks about having me dive-bomb *Donnie* into this place, or bribing the nurse's aide to sneak him a couple bottles of

Sominex, or dropping the next-door-suite lady friend's curling iron into his bathwater, but in fact he's as death-averse as any striving red-blooded man of his generation (or mine, for that matter), and would always prefer to cling to life forever, even if it meant constant physical misery and a near-vegetative mental state, not to mention the utter depletion of the Battle family reserves. The thing to remember about Pop is that despite the denuded superego and messy accidents there is nothing really too wrong with him; his blood pumps at more pacific pressures than mine and his bad cholesterol is lower and he still eats (and normally shits, he assures me) like a draft horse, and as long as he has someone helping him up and down steps and out of loungers and beds so he doesn't fall and break a hip, he might well preside at my funeral, part of me suspecting how it would give him a peculiarly twisted tingle of accomplishment, this last, last patriarchal mumble over his sole surviving issue, finally succumbed.

A soft triple tone goes off in a minor key, like you'll hear over the public address in many Asian airports, which immediately wakes Pop out of his slumber; it's the call for chow in the dining room for those who aren't otherwise being served a tray in bed. Pop points to his robe and I help him with it as he tucks his pontoon-like feet into his slippers. He's unshaven as usual and his oily silvery hair smells like warm beeswax, and though we're the same height he's seeming ever-shorter to me now, the hunch in his shoulders growing more and more vulturesque with each visit.

"How do I look?" Pop says to me, the one thing he'll always ask in earnest.

"Like a man with a plan."

"I'm seeing a woman, you know."

"You mentioned that last time. Who is she again?"

"A looker named Bea. But don't ask me anything else, because I don't know the first thing about her. It's just a lot of hot sex."

"That's great, Pop."

"Don't be such a wiseass, Jerome. At least your old man is getting his share in here. It's the only thing that makes this place bearable. That reminds me. Next time you come bring a bottle of that Astro Glide, and not a dinky-sized one, either. Get the one with the pump."

"Got it."

"That stuff is a miracle. They ought to make it taste better, you know."

"I said I got it, Pop."

"You'll see, when it's your turn. You'll want your whole life lubed up."

"I'm sure I will," I say, thinking how maybe I don't want to wait. "Listen, don't you want to throw on a shirt for dinner?"

"Bea's no uppity broad."

"All right. How about some real pants?"

"Forget it. Let's go, I'm starved."

Down the hallway we go, Pop holding tight on to my arm, and it shocks me to see how unsteady he is. Maybe it's that he's still somewhat sleepy, or it's just part of his well-honed act of late (Decrepitude on Ice), but it is frankly alarming to feel the dire vise-grip of his fingers on my elbow joint, the tremolos of each heaving step, and then to hear the wheezy cardiacal mouth breathing that is all too typical around here at Ivy Acres, these once exuberant smokers and whiskey drinkers and steak eaters now sitting down to three mostly color-free meals a day, easily eaten with a spoon.

The dining room is actually pretty nice, if you like pastelly framed harborside prints and bleached oak tables and chairs and piped in Lite FM (a Grateful Dead song actually came on once, freezing me and the staff, though only momentarily), the décor done right along the lines of Kissimmee Timeshare, which I'm sure is no accident. The ambience around here is meant to evoke the active vacationing life, which for most of these folks is exactly what they remember best and most fondly, not sweet youth so much as those first dizzying years of their retirements, twenty-five or thirty years ago, when all their spouses were still living or vital and they still could walk every side street of San Gimignano and dance all night in the cruise ship disco and didn't mind in the least a three-city routing on the way to the Marquesas Islands, so they could live (just a little) like Gauguin. (This is what Rita and I should be doing, rather than painting ourselves into recriminatory corners with love's labors lost, the fact of which depresses me all the more, knowing that I might not have such memories when it's my turn to be thoughtfully assisted into oblivion.)

It seems a good quarter of the folks here in the dining room are wheelchair-bound, maybe half of those requiring help from the nursing aides to put spoon to mouth, and Pop leads us to the back of the room, far from the entrance, where the more able-bodied (if not -minded) types take their accustomed chairs.

Bea, Pop's object of affection, if that's what she is, is already eating her dinner of cut green beans and roasted turkey and mashed potatoes, and says, "Good evening, Hank," to him as we sit down, sounding uncannily like my mother. He says hello back with no great passion, and introduces me to her again, for perhaps the fifth or sixth time. Bea has a little trouble with her short-term recall, which I don't mind because there's not much to talk about and so it's good to get acquainted over and over again. She is usually pulled together and face-painted for dinner or the evening movie, and then decked out in a strictly nautical/maritime style, with the sign of the anchor featured on every last piece of her clothing, even her little white socks, appliquéd and stitched in and printed on, repeated enough that it has begun to read like some ominous Occidental ideogram, this admonitory vision of the two-sided hook. I could go further into this imagery à la Theresa, how it suggests my own guilt about "placing" Pop here and my attendant anxiety about being dragged along with him (now in mind, later in body), but I won't, because despite the fact that this is the most socially acceptable means of getting back at him for all those years of his being a pigheaded domineering irascible bull in the china shop of life, your typical world-historical jerk, I still 110 percent respect the man, even if I can't love him, which I probably do anyway, though I would never ever say.

What Bea sees in him I'm not exactly sure, but maybe at this stage and locale it's enough for a man to have any bit of spirit left, any whiff of piss and vinegar, to make the ladies swoon. There is, as Pop purports, more action going on around here than anyone cares to imagine, and it's not what we'd like to think is just some smoochy doe-eyed cuddling in the dayroom. Bea isn't looking terribly right this evening (or afternoon, as 4:45 is the first dinner seating), for she's also wearing her bathrobe and slippers, and her shoulder-length hair, which I recall being thoroughly warmly blond, is now white for an inch at the roots (has it been that long since I last visited?), and not brushed. With no makeup on her face I can hardly recognize her, her eyes seeming that much sleepier, sunken, the unrouged skin of her cheeks so sheer as to seem transparent, her faintly purplish lips dried and cracked. Maybe I'm old-fashioned and don't mind being duped by a deft hand with the Maybelline, but I don't think I'm overstating things when I say that if she weren't otherwise eating with some gusto and sitting upright I might say poor Bea was about to kick the bucket.

"Jerry, are you Hank's brother or son?" Bea asks me, like she's asking for the very first time.

"He's my son, sweetheart," Pop tells her. "He's the one who put me in here."

"Then I should thank you," she says, "for sending me my sexy companion."

"Please don't use that word," Pop says.

"Sexy?"

"*Companion.*"

"Why not?"

"It sounds fruity."

"So? You are fruity. Fruity with me."

"Yeah, but I don't want my son to know."

Bea grins at me, with her perfect set of porcelain choppers, a speck of green bean clinging to her incisor.

The nursing-aide-posing-as-waiter approaches and tells us what's on the dinner menu, which is just what Bea is working through, save the option of fish instead of the turkey. Pop asks what kind of fish it is and the fellow says a *whitish fish,* of course meaning he doesn't know or care. Pop says we'll both have that, and I don't fight it. He's always ordered for everyone, even the guys on the crews when the lunch truck came by (he made a point of buying lunch whenever he was around), because he's proud and he's a bully, and he'll be buying dinner for as long as his triple-tax-free munis hold out. The other folks at the table, two men and a woman, appropriately clad, all order the turkey, and while we wait for our plates to be delivered I check out the rest of the room, now nearly filled up with most of the residents of Ivy Acres, whose mission is to serve those, according to its glossy brochure, "moving between self-sufficiency and a more needs-intensive lifestyle," meaning of course the heading-downhill-fast crowd. What strikes me is that there's never as much conversation as I think there will be, there's just this sedate bass-line murmur to accompany the piped-in easy-listening format, because as much as I'd like to believe that these old-timers can hardly contain their accrued store of tales and opinions and observations, the truth of the matter is they would rather talk to anybody else but their Ivy Acres brethren, wishing to be a part of the chance daily flow again, the messy unknown arrays of people and situations that you and I might consider bothersome or peculiar or annoying but to the institutionally captive are serendipitous events, like finding a ten-dollar bill in the street. So I feel it's part of my duty whenever I visit to eat with Pop and listen to whatever his tablemates have to say about their neglectful families or their lumbago, and nod agreeably to their shock at the price of a gallon of gasoline or a three-bedroom house in Centerport, and patiently discuss their views on abortion and the right to bear arms. Bea usually tells me about her divorced eldest daughter, the one who has a son who is a junkie and a daughter who is already a lesbian ("at the age of thirteen!") and who asks her for monthly counseling money for all three, which Bea knows she uses instead toward a lease on a new Infiniti sedan.

Across from us sit Daniel and his fraternal twin Dennis, who ran a family bakery in Deer Park, and are decent enough fellows, though one of them is hard of hearing and so they both talk way too loudly, and both spit a bit doing it. They like to argue with each other about the Middle East crisis, one of them approvingly Zionist in the conservative American Gentile tradition and the other something of an anti-Semite, inevitably bringing up the idea of Jewish conspiratorial influence in Washington and Hollywood and on Wall Street. They can sometimes get quite angry at each other—one of them might even slap the table with a big loafy hand and leave red-faced—but Pop assures me that they hardly speak when visitors aren't around, and just get up together at 3 A.M. out of lifelong habit and play Hearts to kill time until coffee is served in the Sunrise Room.

There are, of course, a number of residents that you never see, who are housed in a special wing of the complex called "Transitions" (though informally known as "The Morgue," as it is situated, in a somewhat unfortunate attempt at an expensive contemporary look, behind a massive pair of polished stainless steel sliding doors). This is the unit where the living isn't so much *assisted* as it is *sustained*, and while I've been invited multiple times of late by the executive administrator to take a tour of its specialized facilities and meet its staff I've not yet done so, the reason, I think, being not exactly denial of the coming reality but my feeling that I'd rather be cathartically jolted by shock and dismay and surprise by what Pop requires than have to ruminate too much now on all the grim complications and possibilities. Maybe that's a sneaky form of denial, too, but it's what I can do.

Our dinners are brought to us and it's no stretch to say that Pop gravely misordered. The fish on our plates is an unnaturally rectangular fillet of meat, grayish and bluish and not nearly whitish enough, with veiny streaks of brown running through the engineered block. A glum slice of lemon is steam-adhered on top. The fish has been poached in its own past-due juices, which are now infiltrating the green beans and mashed potatoes and the overfancy garnishes of carrot flowers and parsley. I can hardly stick my face over the plate, but Pop is digging right in, and nobody else at the table seems to notice, or cares if they do. I'll remind you that Ivy Acres is an upscale nursing facility, and it's amazing to think what they might be serving at some of the other homes I looked at, which were but half the price. What would it take to slap a decent piece of sirloin on the griddle and let it sear to medium-rare, and serve it the way Rita does with a pat of sweet herbed butter and maybe even a half glass of dry red wine? I've always thought that Ivy Acres spent too much dough on the glossy brochures and advertisements and then on landscaping the grounds, which I can say from my former professional point of view is clearly top-shelf, with the pea-stone pathways and English garden perennials and a high-end playground set for the visiting grandkids (who don't go outside but just sit in the dayroom watching whatever the residents are watching). In fact I've never seen any of the residents hanging out outside except when their families insist on "getting some air." Like everything else here the money is spent by management for the sake of us visitors, the same way pet food is designed to please the owners, to assure us in our wishful thinking that our folks are already, as it were, in a better place.

I used to joke to Rita about the idea of having assisted living centers for the perfectly able and independent, places where busy families and lazy empty-nesters and even single professionals could live in residence hotel–style accommodations and enjoy valet services and a modified American meal plan (no weekday lunch) and organized Club Med–type activities on the weekends. The notion isn't so far-fetched, if not already being developed, for it seems a lot of people of even historically modest means now demand a host of services simply to maintain a decent middle-class standard of living. They have their dry cleaning picked up and delivered and have bottled water contracts and lawn and pool service and the week's meals prepared and apportioned by a local caterer and delivered frozen in a tidy Styrofoam cooler every Friday night. The only real difference is that they still live in their own homes, but as any owner will tell you, the constant upkeep and maintenance (whether you're doing it yourself or paying someone else) can be a steady soul-wearying grind. I think a hell of a lot of our nation's people would give up some privacy and separateness (as they happily do on their vacations) in exchange for the ultimate luxuries of Ease and Convenience, which these days are everyone's favorites. I'd site my place in a semi-rural area with lots of covered parking and call it something like Concierge Farms, the hook being "Just bring your clothes."

Not that I would sign up myself, even if Rita were to agree to come back to me and were willing to live in such a place, which she never ever would. My hope for my years of degradation and demise is no different from any other guy's—namely, that I drop instantly dead at the Walt Whitman food court with Cinnabon in hand or in my (please, please, still conjugal) bed, and thus endure none of the despoiled lingering of contemporary death. And in this sense I very much feel for Pop, whose complaints about being here at Ivy Acres are fundamentally just surrogate grousings for what is addressable by only the greatest poets: the much bigger, hairier Here, which nobody but nobody can easily escape. I'll never admit it, but whenever Pop talks about offing himself I'll dismiss him with a sigh or impatient guffaw but also silently whisper *Go ahead*, not with any righteous ease or malice but with what would be humble grace and mercy if I were in any position to bestow such lovely things. But I know, too, that my inward bleatings carry as much resolve as I might twenty or thirty years from now, when Jerry Battle's the one dangling the hair dryer above the surface of the bath water, which is to say none whatsoever, as I'd cry up the water level another inch before ever letting go.

I'm still prodding at my rigid tile of fish when I see that everyone else is mostly done. Pop is a world-class stuffer and always has been and it is actually a semi-pleasing sight now, to watch him pack in the gizzard. It's like every bite is a necessary breath, an angry little war against extinguishment. Daniel and Dennis are already onto the dessert of cling peach crumble, which from here looks like dirt-topped soup, with the other woman at the table, Sarah May, trying to fish out a slippery peach slice with her fingers. Daniel jabs it for her with a fork and hands it to her, like she's his baby sister. I see Bea, on the other hand, sort of scratching at her throat, and I immediately think of how peaches and pineapples have some chemical that makes me sound hoarse. I ask if she'd like a fresh glass of water, but she doesn't answer, still idly scratching away with a faraway look on her face, the face of maybe five hundred peaches ago, that time coming home from the Jersey shore when her father stopped the car at a farm stand and bought a half bushel and they ate them all the way up to New York, a pile of wet peach stones collecting on the floorboards. But of course that's my memory, with Pop insisting that he stop again for another half bushel so my mother could put up some preserves, but when we got home most of the new ones turned out to be mushy and wormy and Ma put them out for the neighborhood raccoons. I'm sure Bea is having a similar recollection, because she's sort of grinning now and looking girlish and reaching out for Pop's hand, which he sweetly automatically takes, and I am noting to myself that I'll remind him of this the next time he starts in on a complaint about the grimness of this place when Bea stands up and without so much as a warning splash-retches her dinner on the table.

Pop lets go as he pushes back and cries, "What's the big idea, Bea?"

The others hardly move and I am looking for one of the staffers to clean up the mess that doesn't smell at all like vomit when I see that Bea has now fallen onto the floor. She's shaking, and her eyes have rolled up, and I realize she's been choking this whole time. Pop is already kneeling down beside her and he orders me to do something. I prop her up and try Heimlich-ing her a couple of times, to no use. A few staff people descend and practically throw me off and they try the same. But Bea is still down and now purple-faced, and though there's instantly a shouting crowd of medical people and staffers and curious residents pinching in upon poor Bea at the bottom, it's my father that I can hardly bear to see, for he is crying as I've never seen him cry before, not for Ma or Daisy or even for Bobby, with great shuddering gasps rippling the almost operatic costume of his billowy stained robe and polka-dot pajamas, and though I want to do something utterly basic like put a hand on his shoulder or nudge him or do anything else to bridge the widening gap, I really can't, not from any of the usual intimacy issues but because for once in my life, really for the very first time, I am scared for him.

seven

JACK CALLED ME EARLY this morning and said to turn on CNN. I asked him what for and he said, "It's your Englishman."

I thanked him and hung up, and after some tense moments of searching for the remote I was looking at a low-quality video of a helicopter surveying rough water somewhere in the South Pacific, with the caption at the bottom of the screen reading, Around-the-World Balloonist Feared Downed. The voice of the reporter spoke about Sir Harold Clarkson-Ickes's control team having made last contact with him some twelve hours before, but said that yet another intense weather system had developed directly in his path and engulfed him. It was hoped that Sir Harold would have emerged from the storm a couple of hours earlier, perhaps blown significantly off course but with his pod intact and communications still functioning. At the moment, though, they had no word and were considering him to be downed some 500 kilometers east of New Zealand. A desperate search-and-rescue mission was in progress, but as yet there had not been any sign of the floatable high-tech carriage or the silvery-skinned balloon.

I watched for another hour or so through a couple news cycles but the story wasn't changing and I decided to take a drive in the Impala. In fact I started to head out to MacArthur so I could get up in the nice weather and feel as though I was doing something for Sir Harold instead of just sitting there like snuff-show sleaze waiting for the gruesome signs of his death. But after I got to the field and took the tonneau cover off *Donnie,* and removed the cowl plug and pitot tube and wheel chocks, and climbed inside to check the electronics and test the play of the ailerons and rudder, I suddenly felt completely ridiculous, like I was some dopey kid pretending to be a salty air ace, dreamily preparing to set out and look for the poor bedraggled explorer himself (which I'm not sure I would do had Sir Harold splashed down right smack in the middle of the Sound, out of dread of actually spotting the deflated balloon floating forlornly in the water like a tossed condom, but also because I can't bear too much traffic anywhere, and especially up there), all of which seemed too utterly safe and symbolic even for yours truly. And I realized perhaps, perhaps, while taking off my headset, that the crucial difference between me and Sir Harold was not only a few extra zeroes in the bank account or that he possessed a genuine thrill-seeking Type-T personality (whereas mine, as Rita once snidely suggested, was really more Type-D—i.e., Down-filled-Seeking), but rather that one of us would always be peeking about while venturing forth, checking and rechecking for the field, no matter how fair the air. So for the first time ever I buttoned *Donnie* back up without flying her, and went about idly cruising around the county under the dusky-throated power of 327 cubic inches of prime American displacement, the sound of which can almost make you think you might actually be *accomplishing something,* if unfortunately these days in a selfish world-ruinous sort of way.

At one point I passed near enough to Ivy Acres to consider (and feel the obligation of) stopping in to check on Pop, but I knew he'd be in the same unsettled mood he's been in since what happened to Bea, and I decided to keep on rolling. Bea, I should report, has made it, but not in a good way. In fact I can say without hesitancy that it couldn't be worse. After I and the staff and then the actual licensed medical personnel took our turns not getting out what was lodged in Bea's throat, she was rushed to the hospital, where the ER doctors finally removed the foreign object from her airway (a diamond-shaped patch of renegade turkey sternum that had somehow slipped through the boneless-breast-roll machines) and got her heart pumping again. Soon thereafter they put her on a ventilator and apparently it was touch and go that night. But she is now, a week later, finally breathing on her own, though it seems that she is no longer saying or thinking or feeling very much, or at least showing any signs of doing so, now or in the near future.

The near future being all Bea—and a lot of the rest of us—has left.

What's a bit shocking is how thoroughly fine Pop seems to be with the whole thing, or how far he's already moved past it. I drove him over to the hospital and we had a decent enough visit with Bea but the next day before I was to pick him up again he called to tell me he didn't want to go. I said no problem, that I could take him whenever.

"Don't bother yourself," he said, his voice uncharacteristically hoarse, like a smoker's. "I don't want to see her anymore."

"You don't mean that," I said.

"Yeah, I do."

"You're just exhausted by all this. Sounds like you're coming down with something."

"Probably. I don't feel good."

"I'll come over and have someone take a look at you."

"Forget it."

"Let's talk tomorrow," I said. "You'll feel different I bet."

"I don't want to see her anymore, Jerome. I'm not kidding you. It's over between us."

I didn't quite know what to say to that last bit, which made it sound as though he and poor Bea had a falling out, a lovers' quarrel, rather than the atmosphere-obliterating airburst that it was, and is.

"Okay. Maybe in a few days."

"No way. She's not for me."

"She's not herself right now, Pop. You know?"

"Not herself? Did you take a good look at her, Jerome, with her arms and legs as stiff as pipes? Who else do you think she might be? Esther fucking Williams?"

"I'm sure she'll get physical therapy soon. Maybe when she gets out of the hospital and they bring her back here, to the Transitions ward."

"Hey, buddy boy, I know the whole story. The nurses' aides will have to cut her toenails and fingernails and sponge-bathe her, too, but probably won't do a good job of it, so she'll start to smell bad and they'll resent having to deal with her even more than they do now. So they'll treat her worse and worse until the last dignified remnants of the old Bea get so fed up that she won't open her mouth to eat or drink."

"You have to stop thinking like this, Pop."

"I'm not thinking!" he says, loudly enough that his voice distorts through the handset. "I don't have to *think*. I've got eyes. And I've seen enough of what happens to the dried-out hides around here to know none of it is pretty. So don't expect me to put on a brave face and make the best of it, because that's all horseshit. I'm not a pretender, Jerome, I think you know that. I've never run my life that way and I'm not going to do it now. So listen to me. Bea is gone, gone forever. You can do me a big favor and not mention her anymore. Because if she ever does come back here from the hospital I'm not going to talk to her or visit her or go hold her hand or do anything else like that. She's kaput, okay? Dead and buried. I'm done with it, I'm finished."

"So what are you going to do now?"

"Whatdya mean, what am I going to do? I'm busy as hell. I'm gonna sit here and grow my nose hair. I'm gonna grind down my corns. If I'm lucky I won't slip in the tub and break my ass. What's this I hear about Theresa maybe being pregnant?"

"Who told you that?"

"Jack. He visits me every week, you know."

"I didn't know that."

"He's no emotional deadbeat."

"She told him?"

"He thought she looked like she was showing at the party. And now they're getting hitched sooner, right?"

"I guess."

"So what else is there?"

"Not much," I said, though at that moment I surprised myself by nearly asking for his advice, which wouldn't be advice so much as an opinion on what he would do and the blanket idiocy of any other course, probably to the tune of me putting my foot down and telling her that if she didn't jettison the baby and start treatments asap, she and Paul would have to pack up and leave and expect no support from me because I wasn't the kind of guy who would stand by tapping out the inexorable countdown of life while his daughter was ensuring her own doom, or something like that.

So I said, "It's early. She's not due for a while."

"Well, I decided if it's a boy I'd like him to be named Henry. Or Hank. Tell her that. I don't care if he's got hardly any Battle in him. Jesus. How did our family get so damn Oriental? I guess you started it. Even Jack's kids—you'd think with that Nazi wife of his they wouldn't look like such little coolies."

As usual I didn't say anything to this, because there's no point, no point at all, though in truth I've thought the same basic thing countless times, if in somewhat more palatable terms, merely to muse upon the fact and not at all to judge, though whether that makes it generally acceptable or not I'll never be sure.

"I'll swing by later."

"Don't do anything on my account."

"Come on, Pop. Cut me a break, okay?"

"Yeah, yeah, whatever."

"Tell me you're going to be okay."

"Tell yourself," he growled, and he clicked off before I could say anything else—our customary truncation, which is necessarily fine with me.

But I am bothered, and worried. I'd like to think that part of Pop's swift turn of sentiment is just a self-defense stratagem, or that it's because he doesn't have a long history with Bea, but to be honest I know of course Pop is right, that he has already dug right down to the core of the matter, as he does, alarmingly, most all of the time, for Bea *as is*—her limbs wooden and immobile, her pupils coal blue and unfixed, completely speechless and soundless save for the feeble high-pitched wheeze she'll make when the nurse shifts her in the bed—is really nothing but precisely unequivocally herself, the same "ain't nobody else" that Pop and I and you and yours will turn into (if even by a senseless accident) and instantly, wholly, embody.

Naturally, by any standard, Bea deserves better from him (and certainly from her daughter and grandchildren, who just departed on a monthlong Maui vacation, according to the Ivy Acres scuttlebutt), not to mention the fact that none of us really knows the full extent of her sentience, what she might be taking in. But at the same time I can't blame Pop for moving on, if that's what he's really doing. What concerns me is that as distraught as he was when it happened he's definitely being a bit too dispassionate now. Right now, whether it was for Bea's sake or not, he would normally be railing against our society's urgent program to isolate its old folks in air-conditioned corporate concentration camps, to expunge all signs of disease and disability from public view, to sanitize not only death but the conspiracy to deny its existence, all his archly negative highfalutin notions that remind me where in fact Theresa comes from. Instead, he is sitting alone in his room with a dismal slump to his shoulders, his toenails hoof-like with neglect, not even bothering to watch the logorrheaists on the Fox News Channel.

In fact, I'd trade this lingering quietude for an angry jag or two of paranoid bombast, just to know he's still there. I'm worried about him as I've never worried about him. Not to mention that he's sounding slightly short of air, emphysemey, which is not like Pop at all, who has always been the free-breathing type, having spent most of his life outdoors in the superfertile waft of suburban gravel and loam. This last little detail had a sneaky effect on me, and when a little while later I called him and he answered again in the same existence-weary tone, I actually hung up on him. I couldn't quite bear to hear it, though I wanted to confirm, too, that he wasn't just doing it for me, the broken-down geezer act.

I almost called him again, given my habit/condition of disbelieving the Real. The fact is, I don't think I've ever seen him seriously sick or injured. Maybe once or twice, when I was a kid, he had a bad enough headache after work that my mother had to prepare a bowl of ice-cold compresses to place over his eyes as he lay down on the living room sofa, and another time at an extended-family picnic when his cousin Gus accused Pop of screwing his second wife (smoldering Aunt Frannie, of the perky sky-searching tits) and attacked him with a bat during the traditional softball game, knocking him out cold for ten scary minutes. Other than that, Pop has been as physically solid as the masonry work he and his brothers used to do at the big North Shore mansions, artisan-perfect brick walls and slate patios and Carrara marble pillars and stairs that will probably last five hundred years as long as there's no asteroid strike or polar ice cap melt or some other civilization-ending event. So perhaps it's also my disbelief in the Real that leads me to think and hope—and ultimately, truly, believe—that all this cruddy rime will soon slough off and that Bea will rise up from her broccoli dreams to once again give Pop tender dentureless head in the moonlit corners of the dayroom after everyone's been medicated for another passage through this world's turn. And that he himself will remain exactly as is, in his costume armor of crazy old titan, while the universe trembles through and beyond him in its darkly incessant expansion. And yet, voilà, *non* mirabile dictu (as Paul or Theresa will sometimes sigh, I think unironically), the Real insists, it heeds no time or other cosmic dimensionalities, brooks no terrestrial dissent, it ignores even the poignant majesty of our noblest human wishes, which are like ground mists to the hot morning sun, lingering as long as they can before being almost instantly transmogrified, dispatched, forgotten.

Ask Sir Harold how quickly things can fall apart.

Which is why, with no one to call, Theresa and Paul gone out on an errand somewhere, and Jack on the road to present another bid, and feeling distinctly outside of things, I have given in to what is my most accessible trouble and driven over to Muttontown, where I am now, parked outside of Richie Coniglio's brick Georgian-revival mansion. The house is from the 1920s or so, the last time in our history when they really did build it right, with its glossy black shutters and white window trim and tendrils of ivy curling up over the patinaed copper gutters, the muted, multihued slate roof a stolid, stately cap over it all, bespeaking (or bellowing, more like) a hushed rampart of the Establishment. The rest of the neighborhood is of similar scale and order, the houses and properties primped and manicured enough but not so much as to seem nouveau, and some aspects of me must look the part, as the private security guard drove past and slowed and then gave me a toadying salute. The gleaming car, no doubt, helped do the trick—it's just the kind of nostalgic set of wheels the salt-and-pepper neighborhood fellows (or a visiting friend) would tool around in on a fine summer Sunday.

I've guessed right, because Rita's yellow Mustang is parked in back by the five-bay carriage house (going back two cars deep), along with another dusty not-so-late-model coupe, which is probably the housekeeper's car, and one of Richie's

Ferraris, the other six or seven new and vintage no doubt tucked neatly inside. Richie is somewhat famous in the area as an avid collector (being featured in full-color spreads in local periodicals like *Island Lifestyle* and *Nassau Monthly*), and even races a couple of specially tuned models at rich-guy rallies in California and Italy. Out front, on the semicircular drive, are two BMW sedans and a Range Rover, and it's not hard to figure that the Rabbit is entertaining guests, which in another circumstance and time might have dissuaded me from inviting myself in, but today feels like no big thing at all.

At the door, a portly older black woman dressed not in a uniform but in a dark, severe housedress that might as well be one asks if she can help me.

"I'm a colleague of Rita's," I say, hoping that she'll assume I'm some kind of doctor or hospital administrator. "She asked me to drop by."

The woman nods, tight-lipped, impressive with her high-domestic manner, an utterly neutral bearing that still leaves everything about you in doubt. Her accent is faintly Caribbean. "Just a moment, sir. Your name, please?"

"Jerome Battle," I say, suddenly liking the way that sounds.

"You will wait in the foyer, please."

"No problem."

She regards me for an extra beat, as if she's telling me with her eyes that every wall hanging and knickknack in the room is now accounted for and catalogued, as are my height and hair and eye color. I fix/flash the ol' sparkle eyes, but no dice. The lady has a robot heart. She pads down the long hall in black orthopedic shoes and slides open a pair of pocket doors, glances at me once more, then disappears, closing the doors behind her. I'm listening for voices, but I can't hear a thing, not a single thing, as if all the rooms are hermetically sealed off from one another. This is not quite the case in my drafty ranch house, where (when I wasn't living alone) you could hear every footfall on the creaky floorboards, every middle-of-the-night toilet flush and throat-clearing. Luxury means privacy, to people like Richie, even inside your own home. To a somewhat lesser degree it's the same deal at Jack's house, though there the new construction is in fact shamefully light-duty, so that you'd hear everything, too, if the place weren't so huge and many-winged.

Here in the Rabbit's lair, after I glimpse into the parlor on one side of the foyer, and the library on the other, it's instantly obvious that we're talking all custom material, even beyond the ultra-high-end stuff Jack wants to peddle, the kind of prime antique furnishing and ornamentation that you would never be able to put together if you weren't bred in the life, or didn't handsomely pay someone who purported that he or she did, which was clearly Richie's route. I know where he grew up, the Coniglios living in the same nice but not great Atomic Age Italian neighborhood of Queens as we did, in a brick shoebox house on a ⅛-acre lot, where the single garage door below the living room was barely wide enough to squeeze a fat-ass Buick inside. Mr. Coniglio, like a lot of the dads, was some kind of mechanic or driver or municipal employee, a policeman or fireman or garbage man, a something-man with his name stitched on his workshirt or number stamped on a badge, a guy who didn't mind hitting you fungoes in the street after his shift in his tank undershirt, and afterward maybe letting the bunch of you split one of his fresh cold beers. Where he grew up, the smells drifting out from the houses weren't of sandalwood and myrrh, you were careful not to scuff the then-new Formica and Congoleum, and high art was a deep-shag wall rug of sailboats or wild horses your mother and aunts had hand-knotted, or else posters of hilly seaside villages in Italy and Sicily, every one of them brittle in the corners and fading too fast. And yet knowing all of the above makes me feel a little more generously inclined toward Richie than I otherwise would, given his station and current intimacy with Rita (which is another detail that speaks well for him, not caring that she's a brown person), because no matter what, you have to hand it to a guy who never peeked or looked down on his way up to the top, who never paused or wondered or else settled too readily into any of life's intermittent drafts of friction-free gliding.

After what seems like barely a ten-count (as if she sprinted here on hearing my name), Rita appears in the doorway of the library, where I'm poking through dusty, moldering leather-bound volumes of late-nineteenth-century English maritime law, just the sort of deductible decorative element white-shoe attorneys love to impress visitors (and interlopers) with, having bought out some law library annex. Rita, on the other hand, looks absolutely fresh, *phhht!*, right out of the can, as she's dressed in tennis whites, a tiny little skirt and sleeveless top, pom-pom peds, and brand-new Reeboks, and my first thought-picture is how the skirt must flip up to reveal the frilly white underbrief against her smooth mocha thighs, and suddenly I'm more than a bit piqued.

"You don't play tennis," I say, sounding maybe too much like Pop, that aggrieved, aggressive combo of knowing nothing and knowing-it-all.

"What are you doing here, Jerry?" she says, not moving any closer. "I swear, you're losing it. You have to leave, right now. Please leave now, Jerry."

"But you don't play tennis."

"Will you stop that? Anyway, I've started. I'm taking lessons."

"From Richie?"

"No. The pro at his club. Though Richard is a pretty good teacher. Listen, why do you care?"

"You never told me you were interested in tennis."

"I didn't know I was. I didn't know about a lot of things I might have enjoyed."

"You say that like it was my fault."

Rita shakes her head, her pinned-up hair making her look like a schoolgirl. I swear I would have fallen in love with her, at any age. Think of Jeanne Moreau, who looked good at every age, but with a darker complexion, a sweeter manner. She says, "Let's leave it alone. And anyway, that's not the issue. The issue is, What are you doing here? I asked you not to come around here, remember?"

"I wanted to talk."

"You could have called me at home. He's having guests today."

"Champagne brunch and tennis."

"That's right."

"You know I'm thrilled that you're not saying *'we.'*"

"This is Richard's house, not mine."

"And when you're married?"

"That's none of your business."

"He has you signing a prenuptial, right?"

"I'm not talking to you."

"I knew it. He's got it all spelled out, I bet. If you divorce or he dies, you don't get the house, or the cars, or the bearer bonds, or the Aspen ski lodge, or the bungalow in Boca. You just get whatever clothes or furs or jewelry he bought you, plus some parting gift, a check to cover six months' expenses."

"That would be a lot more than I got from you."

"Hey, you never asked. And I would have given you anything you wanted. Anything. I would have given you my house. My plane."

"What would I do with your plane, Jerry?"

"I'm just saying. Come on, Rita. Come back home with me. I'll build you a tennis court in the backyard. There's plenty of room, where the pool was. I'll make it whatever surface you like, concrete, clay. I'll even do grass. It's a bitch to maintain but I can get the special mowers. . . ."

"Will you please stop, Jerry? I just want you to leave, before Richard comes in and you embarrass me. I'm asking you nicely now but I swear if you don't listen to me I'll never talk to you again. Never, never, I swear. Are you hearing me?"

I am hearing her, hearing her good 'n' plenty, as my mother liked to be silly and sometimes say, but that doesn't seem to matter because I'm not moving in the direction she wants—namely, out the door—and instead I'm still just standing here in this mahogany-paneled purgatory and jabbering what is clear pure reason to me but obviously sheer bankrupt babble to this woman I have loved perhaps wisely but not too well (or maybe not even that). Rita is glaring at me and crossing her arms in the way she does and I've long known, which might appear like plain pissed-offness but is really, if you could touch her, a steady boa-like self-constriction, the kind of anal-retentive stress response that you'd think would never afflict a beautiful fiery Latina; but in fact Rita is neither too fiery nor too much of a Latina, and never was, which is in no small measure why she and yours truly could have any history at all. The last gasp end of said history, I can finally see, has long commenced.

And that is when I tell her, out of body, and amazed with every word, "Theresa's in trouble."

"What trouble?" she says, stepping toward me now. "What are you talking about?"

"She and Paul have seen a doctor."

"They're pregnant? Something's wrong?"

"Yeah."

"What's wrong? Is something wrong with their baby?"

"It's complicated."

"If you're pulling something here, Jerry. . . ."

But right then who pops in but Solicitor Coniglio, in his own shock-white tennis togs, looking tan and trim and not even that gray up top, an upmarket Jack La Lanne.

"I had a suspicion it was you, Jerry," Richie says, shaking my hand, all bluster and smile, like he's the fucking chair of the membership committee. "Have you eaten lunch yet?"

"Nope."

"Come outside, then, Alva's got her special buffet going. She's an amazing cook, you know. Rita can vouch for her. Her curried lobster salad is stupendous."

I glance at Rita; she's been thrown enough off balance, I can see, not to call me out on the kilim. And now I'm sorry that I brought up Theresa at all, because Rita has always loved both the kids, though naturally in different ways, tending to mother Jack and be girlfriendy with Theresa, which was just right for who they were.

But then she says weakly, "He was just going."

"Oh come on, Jerry, that's silly," he says to me, like I'm the one protesting. "You're already here. Besides, my doubles partner just pulled up lame, with a tight hammy. We'll all have a quick bite, and then you can fill in."

He says to Rita, "You know, Jerry used to play a lot."

"Not really," I say. This is mostly true, save for the summer before senior year in high school, when I decided to try something different from the Catskills camp and took care of a three-court tennis club up on the coast of Maine. I played with anyone needing a partner, and I found the game came naturally to me. By the end of the summer I was giving this small college-team player a run for his money, and when the school year started I lettered on the tennis team, at #2 singles, somehow making all-league honorable mention.

Rita's eyes plead no contest, and I plead the Fifth, so Richie ushers us through the kitchen and dining room to the back patio, where his colleagues are sitting around a large wrought-iron table with their drinks, a huge market umbrella shading them from the hot sun. The women are out on the court, playing Canadian doubles. I'm introduced by name only, and everyone tells me theirs, though I forget them instantly, as I'm sure they do mine. The men are attorneys in the firm, one of them younger than Richie and me by at least ten years, the other two quite a bit younger still, this clearly being the senior-partner-hosting-the-underlings sort of gathering, probably so that he can remind them again why they're billing 3000 hours this year and next year and every year after that.

But it's not an altogether typical crew (though probably I'm dead wrong), as the two young lawyers are minorities, black and Asian (their wives or girlfriends are both white, I should note), only the older one being more or less what you'd think, this vaguely Teddy Kennedy–looking fellow with a florid, Irishy face and a gut and obviously pushing fifty and a first bypass. He's the one who's strained a muscle, no doubt trying to hold up his end competing with Richie against the young-uns, who I'm certain feature assured, classy games groomed at Hotchkiss-Choate-Trinity-Williams. They're of completely different races, of course, but they look to me like they're very much the same, oddly identical in their cool, semi-affable carriage, that self-satisfied apprentice master of the universe demeanor with which they encounter everyone but red-phone Richie, who rates the alpha-wolf treatment of flattened ears and tucked tail and gleeful yelps of respect and gratitude, and not so metaphorically speaking. The Asian associate is a bit more brownnosing than the black one, in that he laughs too heartily at Richie's jokes and observations and talks just like him, too, in tenor and rhythm. The black kid is somewhat careful, superpolite, his tentativeness masking what is probably a world-shaking ambition. Lame Teddy K. over there comports himself with plenty of self-possession, but probably exactly as much as Richie will allow. You can't blame any of them, certainly, because it is, if you'll excuse me, pretty fucking incredible around here, even in my long experience working for the Island gentry. Richie's property stretches magnificently beyond us in this run of lawned space long enough that I could probably land *Donnie* on it in a pinch, the Har-Tru tennis court tastefully sited to one side and screened by a low boxwood hedge "fence," so as not to spoil any vista, trees and shrubs and paths like something you'd find in the Tuileries, the stonework weathered to just that seemly state of honorable decline. And then there is icy Alva's kitchen handiwork, an all-white tulip centerpiece accenting a buffet spread that would put any cruise ship's to shame, not just with its curried lobster and other pricey salads but also littlenecks on the half shell and gargantuan deep-fried prawns and fan-sliced tropical fruits and breads and a colorfully arrayed homemade dessert cart that includes my personal favorite, fresh coconut cream pie.

Richie flashes a china plate and asks what I'd like, apparently ready to serve, which I can't help but notice instantly warms his guests toward my surprise presence. It seems, though, to have an opposite effect on Rita, who suddenly excuses herself and heads inside. Richie, meanwhile, piles on the grub, and as I eat (Why not? It's here, and I like the idea of making my own minuscule ding in the ocean liner of his bank account) Richie, most surprising to me, tells his guests the story of how I once saved him from a certain beating by a greaser known as The Stank (from Stankiewicz). He's doing this to show his softer side, I have to guess, though the tale is conveniently set more than forty years in the past and thus is effectively about somebody else.

The Stank was a hulking kid, in that he'd been left back two or three times early on and by eighth grade was pretty much a man-child, with muscled forearms and full mustache and the armor-piercing b.o. of a plumbing contractor. They didn't know it then, but he had one of those rogue bacterial problems that no amount of washing can cure, which it was rumored he did at least two or three times a day, slipping off to the locker room to shower between classes. He wasn't so much mean or a bully as he was volatile—say, grabbing an earth science teacher's throat if he thought a question was meant to embarrass, which may or may not have happened but became part of school lore. I never had any problem with him, even though I was one of the bigger kids in the school, which can often mean in the eyes of the school that we'd have to square off, almost by default, like they do with top prizefighters.

Richie, as he tells it now, made some wiseass comment about the barnyard odor of the lunch selections; The Stank stood a couple kids ahead on the cafeteria line, and being extra-sensitive about his aroma, glared with rage.

"I saw The Stank's face," Richie says, "and to be perfectly honest I hadn't meant to insult him. I wasn't a complete fucking idiot."

His guests chuckle uneasily, throttling back in case this is just underling bait.

"But you guys know how I like to work."

"Balls on the block," the Asian associate croons, tipping his glass toward Richie. "Ass in the fire."

"You got it, Kim-ster," Richie replies, animated. "But I couldn't help myself, something came over me, and I kept talking shit, louder and louder. The Stank is about to explode, but he gets his food and walks off, and I think I'm home free. But when the bell rings he's waiting for me and drags me outside. I'm saying the Lord's Prayer, because I'm about eighty-five pounds, and The Stank's easily one seventy-five. He's got me literally pinned up against the school building, in a choke hold, my feet kicking. I was just about to black out when Jerry here happens by."

"You kicked The Stank's butt, Mr. Battle?" the other associate asks. I think his name is Kenton.

"No way," I try to reply, through a mouthful of smoked-trout frittata.

"My old friend Jerry here talked some sense to him. I don't remember now. What did you say, Jerry?"

"I think I told him he should probably reconsider, because he really might kill you, and then where would he be? He'd spend the rest of his life at Sing Sing, where they'd let him shower just once a week."

"In fact the same insult," Richie points out.

"I guess he let you go soon after that."

"I guess he did," Richie says, gazing off into his pastures.

"After that, Jerry was my hero. I think I bought you sodas for a week."

"I would say about that."

There's a bit of a lull then, just the soft pocks of the women's ground strokes, and it's clear that the story didn't quite entertain in the way Richie perhaps thought it might, though I can't see how it would, at least from the perspective of impressing his colleagues. But then among a certain class of people, tales of woe and near-ruin have a sneaky kind of honor, these badges of pathos that lend some necessary muck to otherwise wholly splendid, smashing lives. Although Richie and I both left out a few details of the conclusion of that incident—namely, that The Stank (who was not as dumb as people thought) insisted on exacting his own price for Richie's wising-off, such that Richie had to do all his homework for the rest of the year, and also submit to one small physical punishment, both of which, I guess, I brokered. And if you look real close at Richie now you can spot it, how he has the scantest hitch to his gait, this infinitesimal hop to the left foot, where all 175 pounds of The Stank jumped up and landed with his steel shank shitkicker boot, breaking the bones of Richie's foot into an extra dozen little pieces.

"Rat and I'll stomp your fucking head," The Stank said, and Richie, to his credit, just nodded through clenched teeth. I helped him to the nurse's office, where he told her a big rock had fallen on him. She was incredulous, but didn't care enough to pursue it.

The women come back from the tennis court, saying it's getting too hot and humid to play, which it is. We meet and greet. They're all elite professional types, two lawyers and a portfolio manager, as well as very attractive, though not in the way I prefer, meaning they're a bit too thin and sharply featured, like you might jab yourself if you hugged and kissed them with any real verve. Daisy was slim, but she had a round moon face and was unusually supple of body, and Rita, of course, is a lovely plenteous armful, legful, everything else, which I'm sure makes a man like me not really yearn to conquer or destroy or run my part of the world, but rather just dwell and loll and hope to float a little, relinquish the burdens.

And I'm wondering how long she'll remain inside, when Richie suggests the men play doubles; but the younger guys balk, saying they're too full with brunch, obviously just wanting to drink more beer, the older fellow still leaning on the table, trying to stretch out his leg, and Richie takes a racquet and hands it to me, practically supplanting my luncheon fork, and tells me I'm up.

"No way. I haven't played in more than twenty years," I tell him, not an untruth, the last time being at a divorced/widowed singles holiday mixer at an indoor tennis bubble, and only because I was bored to death.

"We'll just hit."

"I'm not dressed. Look at my shoes." I show him (and everybody else) my knockoff Top-Siders from Target. I'm wearing long shorts and an old polo shirt with a Battle Brothers logo on the breast, the head of a rake.

"What's your sneaker size?"

"Twelves. There's no way I'd fit into one of yours, what, you're an eight, nine?"

"We've got lots of extra pairs around here. Alva, if you can take a look, please."

"Yes, sir."

"Forget it. Anyway, I just ate."

"So did I."

"I haven't finished."

"Listen, Jerry," Richie says, irked, in his sharp conference table alto, "when are you going to figure out that there's no free lunch around here?"

Suddenly everyone's calling on me to play, except of course for Alva, who has just disappeared inside the house on her errand.

"Okay," I say, looking back to the house for Rita, my only ally, though thinking that perhaps she's been instructed to stay inside by Richie, so that she won't be a good health professional and dissuade this fifty-nine-year-old idiot from killing himself on the court.

We start hitting, or at least Richie does, as I blast his first three balls to me over the fence; after the third, Richie tells me to cut the bullshit. But I'm not playing games; it's my first time with these new titanium racquets, my last weapon being a lacquered wood model (Jack Kramer Flight) strung with natural gut that you could nicely spin the ball with but had to whip to get any decent pace. This feather-light shiny thing feels like a Ping-Pong paddle in my hand, its head seeming twice as big as it should be—yet another game-improvement technology that makes anyone instantly competent in a sport he should probably never pursue but will anyway, leading to a lifetime of further time/financial investment. But after a couple more moonshots and a few overspins that dive and hit the court on *my* side of the net, I start to get the old stroke back, my arm feeling like the twenty-year scaffolding around it has been dismantled, and soon enough I'm solidly striking my ground strokes, at least those I don't have to range too far for, as my footwork is shot and probably gone forever. And *Ah yes,* comes the revelation, *I have legs, I have knees.* Richie, on the other hand, appears to be playing a narrower court than mine. He's always hitting from the correct body position, knees flexed, shoulder to the target, weight moving forward, and though he doesn't hit for power he consistently places his balls deep, right inside the baseline, and periodically shaves a nasty cut backhand that skids low on the Har-Tru, making me bend that much more than I really can. He's good, for sure, obviously not self-taught, nothing natural about it, but thanks to hundreds of hours with his pro and a home ball machine and traveling tourneys with his club, he's got game.

"Not too shabby, Jerry," Richie calls out. "Not too shabby at all."

I can't really answer because it's taking all my energy to keep the rally going, and although I'm enjoying the action and its rhythms, the breezeless air suddenly seems unbearably humid, like I'm playing inside a dryer vent, and I just stop, letting his approach skip past me unharmed.

"What's the matter?" Richie says, poised at the net.

"I think I'm done."

"Not possible, Jerry," he says, chopping at the top of the white tape with his racquet. He's excited, though hardly breathing. "You gotta keep going. You're just getting into a groove. I think we're nicely matched. I usually play against guys who hit it pretty flat, but you have a lot of topspin on your shots, even your backhand."

"I'm done, Richie. Plus my feet are killing me."

I slip my sockless foot out of the deck shoe, half afraid to look. But it's not horrible, gone the color of watermelon, just that shade (white) skin turns just before the blisters puff out.

"Come on, it's nothing," he tells me, like his play date is being cut short. "Anyway, look, here comes Alva. Rita, too."

I turn around, and indeed the two of them are approaching the court, Alva holding an orange shoebox, Rita sporting an expression of extreme confusion and alarm, as if the sight of me holding a racquet near Richie were tantamount to wielding a machete, as in what is that lunatic Jerry doing now?

Alva flips the box top and hands me a pair of brand-new Nikes. "Twelve on the dot, Mr. Jerry," she says, it seems to me a bit gleefully. "I already laced them up for you. With fresh socks inside."

I say to Richie, "Where did you get these?"

"I told you," Richie says, coming on to my side of the court, "we keep tennis shoes around, for guests. You can keep them."

"He doesn't need them," Rita breaks in. "Jerry, I'll talk to you later, all right?"

"Hey, now, Rita," Richie says. "He's a big boy."

"Jerry!" she says, her voice firm and sharp enough that I reflexively begin handing the sneakers back to Alva.

Richie pushes the pair into my chest and says to Rita, "Hey, sweetheart, be a nice girl and sit down, okay?"

"Jerry was just going . . ."

"We're having *fun* here, Ri-ta," he says, more pronouncing her name than speaking it. "We'd like to focus on the business at hand. Please sit down and watch, or else join my friends and have something more to eat. Can I ask you to do that? Is that too much for me to ask? Because if it is, I'm confused. Maybe I'm dumb. But hey, if you insist, I'll do what you want."

Rita doesn't answer, because it's really not too much to ask but of course it is, especially when you ask that way, and I understand now why I never really liked Richie Coniglio too much, why I never really regretted standing by while the The Stank made a tortilla out of his foot, and why, too, maybe the worst kind of bullies are the ones who exert brain power rather than muscle power (as they can badly mistreat anyone they like, women and children, too, and still remain upstanding, for they leave no marks). Guys like Richie get pretty much 98 percent of whatever they want, that's their core talent, what they actually do for a living, the only thing slipping their grasp being that tiny sliver of unalloyed good feeling from friends and acolytes and lovers and other parties who should be celebrating but definitely are not. And maybe in a somewhat related manner, the people near and dear to me have perhaps decided that I'm not altogether different, that if I'm no rainmaker extraordinaire like Richie I'm a fellow who has enjoyed a bit too much calm flying for my (or anybody's) own good, and thus should suffer regular baleful storms of ill will to dash so unbuffeted a route. There's sense in this, for sure, but I'd say, too, that there's no other mode in this life of ours as sanctified as the one in which you glide to the finish, supine, reclined, as sleepy-eyed as a satyr.

"Let's play, Richie," I say, without pleasure or merriment. "One set."

"You got it. But what's the stake?"

"Whatever you like."

"Oh God," Rita says, starting back for the house.

"How about our wheels?" Richie says, straightening the strings of his racquet head. "What are you driving these days?"

"Impala convertible, '67."

"Yeah, I'll put up my '92 Testarossa. It's the one there by the garage. Four hundred original miles. It's worth at least eighty."

"Fine with me."

"Sure, but you'll have to do better. The Chevy's worth what, twenty at most? Don't you own a little plane?"

"You don't fly, Richie."

"You watch. I'll learn."

Rita has stopped, her posture and expression disbelieving that this has pretty much come to a pissing contest (though that would be a lot quicker and easier). She's waiting for my answer.

"Okay," I say, the sound of it harmless, not quite believing that this is for real, which is no doubt how chronic gamblers blithely invite utter ruin. Rita turns and immediately heads for the house. I tell everybody to wait a second, and follow her, at a respectful, cool distance, but once inside she goes right into a powder room next to the kitchen.

"Come on, now," I say through the walnut door. "We're just playing a game."

"You two are jerks."

"I still think he's worse than me."

"Just leave me alone, Jerry. Leave me alone."

I keep talking, but she doesn't answer, and soon just keeps flushing the can to drown out my words.

On the way back out I notice on the kitchen desk a laptop computer that's on, and hooked to the Web (the bastard has this same incredible fast line in his house that Jack does back at the shop), so I quickly tap in Sir Harold's address, and there it is, right on the big full-color flat screen, a grainy shot of Sir Harold's deflated silver balloon afloat in the water, signage of the party definitely being over, a skinny brown fisherman corralling it with a long-staffed hook. Another shot is of the damaged pod, its hatch missing, one side of it crushed in like a half-eaten whorl. The text is brief, and is addressed to Our Friends and Supporters:

> The Magellan III pod has been located. Sir Harold Clarkson-Ickes has not yet been found. Our search will continue.

One of the women knocks at the French doors and waves at me to come out. I click off the site and follow her to Richie's Centre Court, where the others are buzzing with talk of the wager.

But as I tie on my new sneakers I picture Sir Harold stiff-limbed and suspended in the dark water of the ocean, his hair streaming out in wildness, his gray-tipped beard fixed forever with its tragic explorer's-length growth, the shoes and socks knocked off his now bare feet, and his eyes, his eyes, gazing out at the terrible immensity of the deep. He surely loved to be alone, but not down there, submerged, caught in the wrong element. I feel suddenly sick to my stomach, and I step over behind the beautifully clipped boxwood and retch all of Alva's fine cold lobster curry. The shrub is tinseled in reds and greens. My eyes tear with the gagging, of course, but for a few seconds I really let go; I can't remember the last time I bawled like this (not even after Daisy), and it's only when I feel a hand on my shoulder do I suck it up.

"Maybe you ought to take a pass, Mr. Battle." It's Kenton, offering a napkin. "You look real sick."

"Oh, he'll be all right," Richie calls over. "Just game-day nerves. Come on, Jerry, let's get this show on the road."

Richie, being the lawyer, goes over the whole deal: one six-game set, 12-point tie breaker at 6–all, honor system for calls, and (this clause for me) any play-ending injury or other inability to continue resulting in the forfeiture of the match and the keys to his car and my plane, which we've placed in a wineglass on the courtside table, where everyone but Rita is sitting.

Not surprisingly, I start out slow, serving first and promptly losing the game love, dumping three of the points on double faults. Richie easily wins his serve, and in the next game I do better, though still lose, chunking one game-winning volley into the net, and then completely whiffing an easy overhead on an out, for an instant 3–0. No one is saying anything at the side change, least of all Richie, who simply micro-adjusts his wristbands and smiles the tidy smile of a man who knows the future. The fourth game looks bad for me, as Richie is working his big-kicking serves into my body, which I can't do much with save return harmlessly to him at the net, starting a predictable chain reaction of his crisp deep volley and my lame lob and his controlled smash and my desperate, futile get. But after those I sneak a couple skidding line jobs, and at 30–all he double-faults, I don't know how or why, but this squarely irritates him, I can see, because his whole game is not to commit any unforced errors, and on his ensuing serve (a bit flatter and wider) I go for broke and bust a forehand winner down the line. Game, Mr. Battle. I even pump a fist in the air, not just for me but also for Sir Harold, and while I'm mentally feting myself (because it sure feels to me as if I've already won), Richie breaks my serve again in a love game to go up 4–1; and as we change sides it dawns on me with a big fat *duh* that he's maybe eight lousy points away from taking my *Donnie*. But rather than inspire me, the circumstance paralyzes, I'm choked with dread, the picture of Richie soaring on high at the controls surveying the contour and line of his own earthly garden and then the rest of us gravity-stricken bipeds literally taking my breath away, and I have to clutch the net post to keep from falling down.

"Somebody give Mr. Battle there a drink," Richie says, already waiting at his baseline. "Nobody's going to croak here today."

Kenton comes and gives me a bottle of spring water, and says, with a hand on my shoulder, "You okay?"

I nod, finishing the bottle in one quick pull. He gives me another, this time advising me to drink it slow. When I look into his eyes I can see how he's seeing me, as a bedraggled pathetic heap, a veritable *old man*, which maybe I am but I'm not (but maybe I am?), and though *Donnie* is in jeopardy and I'm losing my ability to perspire, it's this that really shakes me, halts my breath.

Richie says, "What the fuck, Kenton, you nursing him now?"

"Jes bein a good water boy, boss," he says in a thick pickaninny accent, which gives them all a good laugh, including Richie.

"Well let's move it along, son."

Kenton yessuhs, and I mutter "Thanks, buddy" to him, and as he hands me my racquet in exchange for the empty bottle he says in a voice so low I can hardly hear him, "Play low to the forehand."

I don't acknowledge him, of course, because I can hardly manage anything more than the basics, but when play resumes I think about what he said and begin doing it, hitting short cut shots to Richie's forehand whenever he's well back, which normally wouldn't be recommended against a solid net player like Richie but is strangely effective, as he seems to have some trouble handling a shortish ball on that side, resulting in flabby groundstrokes that are long and out, or, if in, I can hit back hard. Maybe Kenton has played enough with Richie to have learned this tendency, but after yet another short ball that Richie has to scuttle forward for I realize perhaps the reason why: it's his left foot that leads that particular shot, his left foot broken in youth by The Stank. Maybe it plain hurts when he lunges on it, or maybe it's a phantom hurt (which can be just as disturbing, if not more), but the fact of the matter is, it's working for me, not just for cheap and easy points but also because he's at last clearly tiring, no longer trying to run down every ball. So I keep cutting and then pouncing, and somehow winning, and although I'm feeling a little wooden in the legs I'm really zipping my strokes with this newfangled racquet, hitting the ball with a ferocious pace Richie is obviously unaccustomed to, and not at all liking. With my mounting success his colleagues and their s.o.'s have begun to cheer each of his points, even Kenton barking for Richie with feeling (we can all act in a pinch), but it's no matter; eventually the score is 6–5, Richie still in the lead, but I've got him at triple break point and I step forward practically to the service line and Richie implodes, jerking both serves into the bottom half of the net.

"Fuck!" he shouts, tossing down and kicking his racquet, and then turns to his hushed gallery. "You can clap for him, for chrissake. He's goddamn playing well enough."

So they do, and with what I detect is an extra measure of appreciation for my helping to make this something other than your standard boss's brunch, not to mention the fact that they would always gladly pay good money to see Richie suffer a substantial hit to his ego, if not bottom line. But none of it matters, because in my game focus I just now notice that Rita has been watching at courtside, maybe for a whole game or two, her face still sour for this endless intrusion, for my once again (I can anticipate her now) thrusting myself in the center ring of everyone else's business and pleasure.

"Why don't you two call it quits now," Rita says. "You're tied and we've had our fun."

"The fun's not over," Richie says, testing his racquet strings against his heels. I'm sitting on the ground, trying to stretch my legs, which are feeling suddenly hollowed out but calcified, these toppled, petrified trunks. "Come on, Jerry, get up, let's do it."

"Why do you want to do this?" Rita says, to us both. Maybe only I can tell, for she's not yelling or gesticulating and her expression hasn't changed, but she's really very angry now, practically livid. I know because her chin is noticeably quivering, something that happens to most other people when they're on the brink of crying. But she's far from that.

"Don't you see how disgusting this is? You really have to take away each other's toys, don't you? It's vulgar, Richard. And Jerry, let's be honest, you can't afford to lose your plane."

"Hey now . . ."

"I'm not talking about just *money*. What would you do without it? What, Jerry? Come on, tell me. What are you going to do?"

It's an excellent question, exactly the kind of query I get all the time from my loved ones, thoroughly rhetorical but also half holding out for some shard of the substantive from yours truly, some blood-tinged nugget of circumspection and probity. But maybe just not right now, as I'm wondering myself how I'm going to unsticky this wicket I'm on, despite the 6–all tally I've worked, for my legs (are they mine?) feel absolutely inanimate, dumb, these knobby flesh logs that might as well be delicatessen fodder, glass-encased in the chill.

"I can't get up," I say to Rita. "I can't move."

"Cut the horseshit, Jerry," Richie says. "You've had enough rest. Come on. Your serve starts the tiebreak. Then we serve in twos. First one to seven."

"I really can't, Rita," I say. "I'm not kidding."

Rita quickly approaches, kneels down beside me.

"Are you serious?"

"Everything just froze up."

"Both legs?"

"Yeah. But in different parts."

Rita turns to Richie, who's now coming to inspect. She tells him, "Okay, that's it, Richard. He's all cramped up. He's probably totally dehydrated. Game's over."

"Hey, if that's what he wants."

"That's what's going to happen," Rita says, firm and nurselike.

"I guess I'll start taking flying lessons," Richie says.

"You can't do that," she says. "You can't take his plane because of this."

"I'd rather not, but I will. You were inside when we agreed to the rules."

Rita looks at me as though I've descended to yet another circle of stupid-hell, and I can only, lowly, nod.

She says to him, "Richard. Don't be a jerk. Just call it a tie and Jerry can go home and everybody will be happy."

"Listen, Rita, you're completely missing your own point about toys. That's exactly right. There's no purer pleasure. So would you butt out right now, okay? Jerry and I made an honest wager with clear guidelines, and Jerry himself will tell you that if I were in his shoes, or in my own, to be exact, he would be doing the same thing. Ain't it so, Jerry?"

Of course I don't want to, but I have to nod, because he's absolutely right, even Rita knows it, I'd be righteously slipping that fat Ferrari fob on my mini–Swiss Army knife keychain before even helping his skinny ass up off the deck.

"I can't stand this," Rita says, using my thighs as a support to stand. It hurts, but sort of helps, too. The cool touch of her hands. She doesn't say anything, but just picks up her straw handbag (the one I brought back for her from the Canary Islands, with a heart cross-sewn into the weave) and just walks away, traversing the lawn straight to the carriage house, where she rumbles her banana mobile to life. For the whole time we watch her, neither Richie nor I saying a word, though I wonder if what he wants to say to her is just what I want to say, which isn't at all original, or earthshaking, or even romantic; it's the most basic request, what a guy like me who always has plenty to say but never quite when it counts, wants to say most often: *Don't go.* And as I mouth it, she whirs her car backward on the driveway and into the street, and then, with a bad transmission jerk, rattles off.

Richie says, "Okay, Jerry, now that *that's* done, what the fuck are you going to do?"

I can't answer, angry as I am with his *that.*

"Come on, Battle, get up now. Or quit."

And I will tell you that Jerry Battle gets up on his feet then. And I make my legs work. And I make Richie pay for what we both should have done.

At least in that, I am magnificent.

eight

HERE AT MY SHARED DESK at Parade Travel, the foe is always inertia.

No one mentions it by name, certainly not me, but every trip or vacation I book for my customers is one more small victory for those of us who believe in the causes of motion and transit. This morning, for instance, I set up a December holiday for Nancy and Neil Plotkin, sending them first on a ten-day cruise of Southeast Asia, ports of call to include Bali, Singapore, and Phuket, where they will disembark and switch to overland on the Eastern Oriental Express for an escorted railway tour of the famous Silk Road, snaking up through Bangkok and to Chiang Mai, after which they'll fly back to Hong Kong for a two-night stay at the venerable Mandarin Oriental, to shop for trinkets and hike Victoria's Peak and take a junk ride across the harbor to the outdoor markets of Kowloon.

Pretty damn nice. The Plotkins, like me, are semi-retired, Nancy now periodically substituting at the middle school where she taught for thirty years, Neil actively managing their own retirement portfolio instead of the institutional mutual fund he ran since Johnson was president. They're pleasant enough people, which is to say typical New Yorkers, charming when they have to be and surprisingly generous and warm when they don't, though instantly skeptical and pit-bullish if in the least pushed or prodded. And they're easy customers to work with (this is the fourth big trip I've arranged for them), not just because they have plenty of time and disposable income and have varied touristical interests, but more that they seem to understand that a primary aspect of traveling is not just the destination and its native delights, but the actual process of *getting there*, the literal *travail*, which is innately difficult and laborious but also absolutely essential to create any true sense of journey. Unlike most customers, who naturally demand the shortest, most direct, pain-free routings, the Plotkins are willing to endure (and so savor, too) the periods of conveyance and transit, even when it's not a fancy ocean liner or antique train. For they don't dread the cramped quarters of capacity-filled coach, they don't mind arranging their own taxi transfers in unfamiliar ports, they don't balk at climbing aboard a rickety locals-only bus in some subtropical shanty-opolis, or an eight-hour layover at always grim Narita. Of course they needn't suffer any of the aforementioned, but rather, as I gather they have in the past, they could buy a package deal and take whatever direct charter to any number of esteemed beaches and deposit themselves on cushy towel-wrapped chaise longues and enjoy plenty enough seven no-brainer days of wincingly sweet piña coladas and a satchel of sexy paperbacks bought by the pound, choosing their own spiny lobsters for dinner and maybe on the last full day taking a back country four-wheeler ride to a secluded freshwater falls, where they might sneak a quick skinny dip beneath the lush canopy of jacaranda and apple palm, all of which I must say is perfectly laudable stuff, and nothing to be ashamed of.

And yet I feel especially eager to get Nancy and Neil's itinerary just right, not for the purpose of "challenging" them and making the trip strenuous for its own sake, but to remind them of what it is they're really doing as they jet and taxi about the world, let them feel that special speed and ennui and lag in the bones. In the future there will be no doubt some kind of Star Trek transporter device by which travelers will be beamed to their destinations, so that some Plotkin in the year 3035 might step into a light box in his own living room and appear a few seconds later in a hotel lobby in Osaka or Rome or the Sea of Tranquility, but I think that will be a shame for most save perhaps businesspeople and families with small children, as this instantaneous not-travel will effectively reduce the uncommon *out there* to the always *here,* to become like just another room in the house, nothing special at all, so that said Plotkin might not even bother going anywhere after a while.

Nancy and Neil, in the meantime, will indeed bother, arm themselves to the teeth with guidebooks and maps and travelogues of those who forged the paths before them, critiquing each other constantly (as they do whenever they show up at my desk) about what routing and accommodations and dining will prove most compelling, take them furthest and farthest, these two Dix Hills stratospheronauts by way of Delancey Street. They're plucky and sharp and understand at this most bemusing time in their lives that above all else they crave action, they need the chase as the thing, and when Neil handed me his credit card to pay for the trip he sighed presciently and moaned sweetly to his wife, "Ah, the miseries ahead."

Lucky you, I wanted to say.

Because in fact I don't know if I myself could manage any of these big trips anymore, as I used to do with (though mostly without) Rita tagging along, this when business at Battle Brothers was humming on autopilot and the kids were both in college and my wanderlust was at its brimming meniscal peak. Back then (not so many years, frighteningly), I would actually plan my next trip during the flights home, carrying along an extra folio of unrelated guidebooks and maps so that I could chart my next possible movements as if I'd already gone, play out scenarios of visited sites and cities, all the traversed topographies, basically string myself along, as it were, on my neon Highlighter felt-tip, to track, say, the Volga or the Yangtze or the Nile. Such planning quickened my heart, it offered the picture-to-be, and I can say with confidence that it was not because I dreaded being home or back in my life. This was not about dread, or regret, or some sickness of loathing. This was not about escape even, or some sentimentalist suppression. I simply wanted the continued promise of lift, this hope that I could in my own way challenge gravity's pull, and feel for whatever moments while touring the world's glories the mystery and majesty of our brief living.

A lot to ask, I admit, from a rough ferryboat ride from Dover to Calais.

And yet, even now, when I don't much travel anymore, and just get up top every so often in my not-so-fleet *Donnie* (who, I can try to believe now, was never in danger of being manned by Richie Coniglio, whose V-12 Ferrari sits with quiet menace in my garage, like a big cat in the zoo), I will still peer down on this my Island and the shimmering waters that surround and the plotted dots of houses and cars and the millions of people I can't see and marvel how genuinely intimate it all feels, a part of me like it never is on the ground.

And perhaps that's the awful, secret trouble of staying too well put, at least for those of us who live in too-well-put places like this, why we need to keep taking off and touch landing and then taking off again, that over the years the daily proximities (of your longtime girlfriend, or your kids, or your fellow suckers on the job) can grind down the connections to deadened nubs, when by any right and justice they ought only enhance and vitalize the bonds. It's why the recurring fantasy of my life (and maybe yours, and yours) is one of perfect continuous travel, this unending hop from one point to another, the pleasures found not in the singular marvels of any destination but in the constancy of serial arrivals and departures, and the comforting companion knowledge that you'll never quite get intimate enough for any trouble to start brewing, which makes you overflow with a beatific acceptance and love for all manner of humanity. On the other hand, the problem is you end up having all this gushing good feeling 10,000 feet from the nearest warm soul, the only person to talk to being the matter-of-fact guy or gal in the field tower, who might not mean to but whose tight-shorn tones of efficiency and control literally bring you back down.

Theresa, I wish to and should mention now, is in no imminent danger, at least as she characterizes the situation. Although of course I'm relieved, even thrilled, I'm not sure I 100 percent believe her, as she isn't at all willing to go into the same ornate levels of jargony detail that typically mark much of her and Paul's talk, their specialized language whose multihorned relativistic meanings I feel I should but don't much understand. Thus it worries me that all she'll say to me now, in referring to the neoplasms perhaps growing right along beside her developing child, is that "the whole thing" is "totally manageable," exactly the sort of linguistically lame and conversation-ending phrasing I myself instinctively revert to whenever I'm in a pinch.

Even more unsettling than this is that she has already named the baby (*Barthes*, after a famous literary critic), a step that clearly signifies her rather strict intention to push through, and to whatever end. Naturally I've tried to extract more detailed information out of Paul, but he, too, has been frustratingly vague and blocking. But I know *something* is askew. For instance: for the past month now that Theresa and Paul have been back at home I've found their company, though always a pleasure, oddly unstimulating (a modifier I never imagined applying to them), as they've been unusually antic and adolescent when together. When I got home from Parade Travel the other day they were actually wrestling in the family room (fully clothed and nonsexually, thank goodness), and when I wondered aloud whether such activity was advisable they paused for a second and then burst out laughing, as if they'd been smoking weed all afternoon.

But there's a deep seam of mopiness there, too, which becomes apparent whenever one of them is out, the other just heading for their bedroom and the stacks of novels and texts of literary criticism they've brought along and also buy almost daily, this play-fort made of other people's words. I've tried to remain on the periphery, not forcing any issues or criticizing, consciously conducting myself like any other happy soon-to-be-grandfather sporting a solicitous and mild demeanor, though I'm beginning to wonder if I'm doing us any good service, while we all let the time pass, and pass some more, everything swelling unseen. If nothing else I assumed that I would always be *included*, in the big matters at least, and not simply contracted to wait for my bit part to come up, a small supporting role that I've depended upon over the years for easy entrances and exits but seems awfully skimpy to me now.

Another odd happening is that Paul is cooking up a storm. Though I'm not complaining here. I never knew him to be a cook, at least not a fancy one. He could always throw together a decent pasta dish or some baked stuffed trout when I once visited them out in their ever-misty coastal Oregon town, but his tastes and skills have evolved impressively in these past few years he's been in the academic world with Theresa (lots of free time, enough money, discerning, always ravenous colleagues). Theresa, I should mention, has been eating like a grizzly bear during a salmon spawn, being absolutely insatiable whenever she's awake, though lately her hunger seems to have subsided. This is the one clue that makes me think she's all right, and so okay to be doing what they're doing. Each morning after a huge breakfast of oatmeal and eggs and fruit and pastries, she and Paul will roll out the Ferrari (why the hell not, as I don't like to drive it anyway; the sitting position is a bit too squat for my longish legs and it revs too hotly such that I can't make it do anything but jerk forward in ten-yard bursts) and lay down that fourteen-inch-wide rubber around the county in search of organic meats and vegetables and craft cheeses and breads, foodstuffs Eunice of course has FedExed in daily but that I had no idea could be had out here in Super Shopper land, where there are always nine brands of hot dogs available but only one kind of lettuce (guess which). They only buy what we'll be eating that evening, which works out because the Testarossa doesn't have any trunk space to speak of, only a tiny nook behind the two seats (which, by the way, is just enough room for a couple of tennis racquets). My sole complaint is the might-as-well-eat-at-a-restaurant cost of the supplies, not to mention the premium gasoline they're burning at the rate of a gallon every seven miles, but once you've had seared foie gras with caramelized-shallot-and-Calvados-glacé, or wild salmon tartare on homemade wasabi Ry-Krisps, and eaten it right at your own dreary suburban kitchen table where you've probably opened more bottles of ketchup than imported beer, you happily fan out the fresh twenties each morning and utter nary a word, counting yourself lucky that you can tag along, and in an odd way I feel as if we three are moving quite fast through the world, consuming whatever we can.

And yet the trouble pools on our plates. The other morning, while sitting at the kitchen table, with Theresa sleeping in, Paul at the counter mixing a whole-grain batter for pancakes with raspberries, I let down my mug with enough oomph to make the coffee splash up and over onto my *Newsday*, to which Paul said, "Just another minute, Jerry."

"It's not about the chow," I said.

Paul pretended not to hear me, decanting the oil into the skillet and lighting the burner beneath it.

Since they've moved in and Paul's been cooking with high heat like a pro, the house gets heavy with a savory smoke that makes me think Rita's been around, a redolence all the more dear and confusing and depressing at present, as she's not returned any of my phone messages since the brunch at Richie's two weeks ago. Maybe a guy like me has to figure he's got just a couple chances in this life for full-on love with a woman he's respected every bit as much as physically desired, and if I've really squandered my allotment I probably ought to be hauled off to the woods in back and shot in the name of every woman who was surely meant to enjoy more loving than she got but didn't, mostly because of some yea-saying bobblehead, who semi-tried as hard as he could but always came up short.

"Look, Paul," I said, "it's time to start clueing me in."

"I agree," he answered, carefully ladling in three pancakes. He put a ramekin of maple syrup in the above-range microwave to warm. "But you know, Jerry, I really don't know anything either."

"Gimme a break, huh?"

"I'm not kidding you," he said.

"Now you're pissing me off."

"Well that's *goddamn tough*," he said, bang-banging his ladle against the edge of the mixing bowl. The microwave stopped beeping and he popped the door button too hard and it flung open, hitting him in the face. He plucked out the syrup and slammed the door, which popped back out, and so he slammed it again. For a second I thought he might come over and jump me, as I could see him gripping and regripping the spatula; and to tell you the truth I would have been fine with it, not because I wanted a fight but simply to initiate something. I thought maybe his plonking me might loosen the clamps of all this goddamn Eastern restraint ratcheting in on us, which is no doubt an easy lazy pleasure to abide most of the time but is, of late, becoming a kind of torture to me.

But he didn't jump me, and I said, "You must have talked to the doctor, at least."

"Of course I have. A dozen times. But she's only telling me what Theresa allows her to."

"But you're her fiancé! It's *your* baby. This definitely can't be ethical, or Hippocratical, or whatever."

"It's Theresa's call, Jerry, whether I like it or not."

"Well, you can't just sit by. Don't you have *rights*?"

"What would you have me do, take her to court?"

"Maybe. You could sue her, over her treatment decisions. Or maybe I should do that. You could just threaten to leave her."

"She'd know I was just bluffing," he said. He flipped the pancakes, one by one by one. "Or else she might turn around and leave me."

I didn't answer, because it occurred to me that Theresa could very well do that, if only temporarily. When she was a teenager she only had one boyfriend (that I can remember), a lanky, melancholic, semi-creepy kid who wore a black scarf no matter the weather and wrote science-fictional love poems to her, a few of which I found in the pockets of my old letterman's jacket (which she liked to wear with the sleeves pushed up); for whatever inexplicable reason she was madly in love with the kid, as she'd spontaneously burst into tears at the mere mention of him, regularly enough that before I could even say anything she herself began refusing his phone calls, and because of nothing he did, which made her even more miserable for a while (and him as well, the poor goth neuralgic), but soon enough she'd cured herself of the crying jags and they went steady until she dropped him, she told me later, because she was really tiring of "his work."

"You know what the doctor finally said to me when I talked to her on Friday?" Paul said, handing me my plate of flapjacks, syrup on the side. "Theresa and I had a bad little fight, so after she went to take a nap, I called. They wouldn't put me through but I pretty much freaked out and the doctor came on. So I gave her a whole speech about responsibility and the benefits of shared knowledge but it was like she didn't hear a word."

"Some lady doctors, you know . . ."

"Well, whatever it was. She didn't have time to talk, so she just said that perhaps I ought to consider getting us to couples therapy, if our 'communication levels' weren't where they should be."

"What a superbitch! I hope you told her off."

"Unfortunately, I did. I told her she could go fuck herself."

"Really?"

"I shouldn't have."

"Good for you!"

"It was *stupid*. She's our *doctor*. But you know what, Jerry? She might be right, about our communication."

"What the hell are you talking about? All you two *do* is talk."

"Yeah," he said wearily, slumping down in the chair. He wasn't eating yet. "But maybe not in any way that counts."

"Let's not get ridiculous here. It's not a great situation, by any stretch. That, and you're someone who's definitely got a reserve of patience and faith in people that's larger than the next guy's."

"You don't have to sugarcoat it, Jerry. I know I'm a pushover."

"You're not!" I told him, firmly holding on to his arm, not letting go until I'd made my point. "You love her, and love her dearly. As her father, I couldn't be happier about how obvious that is. It's all I'd ever worried about for her, if you know what I mean. Theresa isn't the easiest gig around. Okay, okay, so maybe you could push back a little more, because people like Theresa respond to shoves more than nudges. But if you really can't it's only because you think the world of her. And maybe I'm not the guy who deserves to say it, but there's nothing else of any worth."

Paul then said, "I'm scared to death here, Jerry. You know, I'd give her up now if someone promised me that nothing would happen to her."

"Nothing will. And you're never going to give her up. Just keep busy, like you're doing."

"Me? I can't do anything."

"Is the writing still on pause?"

"It's full stop. I haven't even *thought* about one line of poetry since the diagnosis, much less written one. I've officially quit the novel I was already not writing. You'd think I'd have all this determination and energy left over to focus on this thing, but I seem to have less and less every minute."

"You're sure cooking a helluva lot."

"Theresa seems like she wants to eat, so it's easy."

He smiled, but then he looked stricken again. He got up. "You want more?"

"Maybe just one, if you're making some anyway."

"It's no problem."

Paul clicked on the burner, and just then Theresa came padding into the kitchen in her bare feet, wearing summer-weight men's pajamas, short-sleeve Black Watch plaid.

She crooned, "Morning, Jerry."

"Morning, dear."

She kissed Paul on the mouth, goosing him slightly in the butt. The tired pinch of his eyes seemed to soften. "Those for me?"

"Yeah," I said.

Paul asked, "How many you want?"

"Just two, today. I'm not feeling so hungry."

"I'll make you an extra, just in case."

"Okay."

And soon enough we were back to our customary places at

the kitchen table, Paul and I sitting on either side of Theresa, who's generally been settling down in yours truly's place at the head since they've moved in, the new array of which doesn't feel in the least awkward or wrong. Maybe it's even right, as Paul and I seem ever balanced in our need to glance over constantly at her, to keep a tab on how it's all going down, whether she's eating a little less today than yesterday, which in fact appears the case, though the gleaned quantities must be minuscule, in our inexact but somehow confident science.

I'm definitely on the warpath, eating everything that comes my way. Unbidden, Paul packs me a lunch on the days I come into the office here at Parade. Yesterday it was some vegetarian maki rolls, today a panini with prosciutto and mozzarella di bufala and a tub of roasted sweet peppers sprinkled with extra-virgin olive oil and fresh basil.

Miles Quintana now enters, carrying his own lunch of two bulging fast-food bags, and shoots me a "S' up, bro?"

I S'-up-bro him back. He's a little early for his 3 P.M. to 9 P.M. shift (I work until 5), and as is customary he'll eat one of his meals now before getting into the routine of checking fares for his clients and greeting the walk-in browsers and booking impulse vacations for the fed-up after-work crowd, then heat up the other bag later in the office microwave, for a quick break/snack. Being technically still a teenager Miles requires the triple-meat cheeseburger with ultrasized fries and chocolate milkshake value meal, 4000 calories of pure pleasure and doom, though of course none of it appears to be slowing him now, as he's maybe 150 pounds fully optioned in his slick Friday night dancing slacks and wine-red silk shirt and black-and-white bowling-style shoes. At the close of the evening his ever-silent baby-faced buddy Hector will pick him up in his low-riding hi-rev tuner Honda waxed to a mirror finish, and then they'll streak up and down the Northern Parkway dusting bored family men in their factory Audis and Saabs and afterward hit some under-twenty-one club, where they'll pick up unruly rich girls from Roslyn and Manhasset and ferry them to Manhattan for a couple of hours of real drinking and dancing before each taking (if the girls are willing, which they always are) a half-night room at a truckers' motel on the Jersey side of the Lincoln Tunnel. They'll stay until dawn and then eat steak and eggs at a diner before cruising back through the conquered city, to drop the girls off at their parked car before heading back for their mothers' row houses in Spanish Huntington Station. Not a bad life, if you ask me, and once Miles even suggested I tag along sometime, just for the hell of it, but I knew better than to take him up on it, as my presence would certainly obliterate his evening and probably our good working friendship, which depends in part on our mutual view that the other is somehow exotic and thus a little bit glorious.

There's no one here but us (it's slow in the summer, especially in the afternoons, and Chuck the manager is at a travel seminar in Mineola), and so Miles pulls up a chair to my desk and we eat together. I naturally filch a few sticks from his mountain of fries.

"So what's up with our gal Kelly?" Miles says, already halfway through his burger. "Is she ever coming back to work?"

"Maybe today. The plan is today."

"No shit. You talked to her? How is she?"

"She's doing all right," I say, though more wishful than sure. I had indeed talked to her, at the hospital and then at her place after I brought her back home, but I can't say we conversed, as Kelly was pretty much mum about everything, and after I fetched her some basic groceries she ushered me out with a weak embrace and promised that she would definitely be in touch, which she has not been. So a few days ago I went over to her apartment and spoke with her through her door, which she wouldn't open because she wasn't, as she said, her "pulled-together self," and when I reminded her that I'd seen her plenty of times in all her preablutionary glory she emphatically shouted, "Well, you're not going to see any more of that, Jerry Battle!" The sharp response unnerved me, and I literally stepped back from the door, for a second imagining Kelly with her hair on fire, carving knives in her hands, waiting for me to try something heroic.

Miles says, "I don't see why she tried to off herself."

"She didn't. She's just confused. It's a tough time in her life."

"Doesn't seem so tough to me," Miles says. "She's got a decent job and a nice place to live and she's still pretty good-looking, for an old lady."

"Forty-five isn't old, Miles."

"Sounds old to me."

"It isn't. She's a baby."

"Yeah, sure."

"She is," I say again, insistently enough that Miles actually stops chewing for a second. I tell him, "You have to understand something here, buddy. You've got another twenty-five years before you're that age, so it's hard for you to fathom. But it's going to go quick. Before you even know it, you'll look up and suddenly your buddies will have beer guts and will be getting gray all over and they'll be talking about sex but not in great anticipation, but with dread."

"Now that's some crazy-ass shit, Jerry. You're creeping me out, man."

"I'm not trying to scare you. That'll only be the surface. But what I'm really saying to you, Miles, is that, mostly, you won't change. At least not in the way you think of yourself. You'll stay in a dream, the Miles-dream."

"The what?"

"The Miles-dream. Maybe you'll have more than one. It's like this. You'll have an idea of yourself being a certain age, and for years and years when people ask you'll still think you're twenty-five, or thirty-five, or whatever age that seems right to you because of certain important reasons, because that will be the truth of your feeling inside."

"Oh yeah? So what's the Jerry-dream?"

"I don't know. Maybe I'm thirty-two, thirty-three, something like that."

"What, were you getting a lot of pussy back then?"

"I wouldn't put it that way, exactly."

"Yo, I was just kidding! I'm just fucking with you, man. But hey, you were happy, right?"

"Actually not really too happy, either."

Miles looks somewhat confused, as he should be, because I haven't explained myself very well. To do so I'd have to back up, tell him the whole messy story of Jerry Battle, for all he knows of me is that I work here a few days a week, and that I live in the area, and that I was dating our coworker Kelly for a couple of months before things fell apart; I'd have to tell him all about Rita, and about Theresa and Jack, and then of my marriage to Daisy, the time of which, at least in the beginning, was how I thought of myself for a long, long time, even after she died.

Miles revisits his burger, maybe thinking that the Ol' Gringo is finally losing it, and that he ought to just humor me while I'm on the loose out here in the world. Though often enough he hears this kind of midbrow poetic phooey from me, which he never appears to mind. Miles is in fact seriously bright and sensitive beneath his resplendent El Cojones exterior, always telling me about his classes at the community college where he's forever taking a part-time load and working toward no particular degree. He'll take whatever odd course or two strikes his fancy, from Topics in the Internal Combustion Engine to Feminist Archaeology to his current favorite, Greatest Hits of the Romantic Poets (I note that I should definitely hook him up with Theresa and Paul, as I'm sure they'd intrigue and delight one another with their varied approaches to all manner of Material and Text), where he says his professor gets downright weepy over "all that natural beauty and shit" in Keats and Byron and Wordsworth.

O there is blessing in this gentle breeze, I even overheard Miles say recently to a visiting client, in sealing the deal on a large corporate group trip to the Bahamas.

Miles asks, "So how 'bout now, man? Did the Jerry-dream ever change?"

"I guess not. I just felt that way when I was in my early thirties," I say. "That was it for me."

But of course that's not true. For I am sure, absolutely, that in twenty years (if I'm still around) I'll think of myself as being in this very time, the last Jerry-dream I'll probably ever have. The strange thing is that maybe I'm having the Jerry-dream right now, too, this prescient sense of the present, this unsettling prenostalgia whose primary effect is to lay down a waxen rime of both glimmer and murk upon everything that is happening with Theresa and Rita and probably very soon with Pop; this is why I'm suddenly hesitant to say anything more to my young friend Miles, because you can reach a point in your life when The Possible promises not so much heady change and opportunity but too frequent rounds of unlucky misery. We want action and intensity, we want the bracing scent of the acrid, but only if it's "totally manageable," which most times it's not.

Then it's just plain woe and trouble, which is apropos of the present moment, as who drives up and parks and now stands outside the office entrance but Kelly Stearns, with no less a personage in tow than the stout little guy and our mutual friend Jimbo, wearing a big gold necklace in the shape of his name and a shiny emerald-colored track suit and thus looking all in all very much like a steroidal leprechaun.

They appear to talk with happy animation, his hands bracing her shoulders, coachlike, though he only comes up to Kelly's chin, and Kelly is no towering Amazon. She nods meekly to his instructions, like they're going over a play at the time-out and she's his ungainly backup center. To my surprise she is all gussied up, in a toffee-colored skirt and blazer and white cotton blouse, and quite possibly looking more glamorous than I've ever seen her before, though not in an entirely fetching way, with her goldenrod locks glazed-tipped and pinned up and off her pale neck, her face powdered and painted more colorfully than usual, and today set off by glittery pendant earrings and a necklace that must surely be costume, given the sizes of the stones. There's also a fat, multiclustered ring, also not in the least keeping with her style, and I realize that this may prove yet one more instance in which I'll have to partake in a testy social challenge/display with a rival du jour.

I should be perfectly happy for Kelly, as I desperately want to be, but there's something about this new guy that irks me, nothing innately to do with him but whatever he is/does that makes Kelly not quite herself. Maybe our brief love affair wasn't exactly ideal but I know that she never had to change her spots for me, inside or out, I never once asked her to be anything else but who she was, a decorously sweet, affable Southern lady with honey eyes and a broad firm bottom and just enough pluck to soldier through the big messes. She is not someone, I still think, who would take too much OxyContin and try to crash her car into an ER entrance. She is not, I think, someone who would shout and holler through closed doors. She is not, I still hope, a woman who would relinquish her strength and will to anyone, me included, but especially to some Micro-Mafioso (with both a neck and trouser inseam size of 21) who will probably just get harder and meaner the longer they're together. But what do I really know, because the two of them are now kissing in the parking lot like it's VE Day on the Place Charles-de-Gaulle, Jimbo practically dipping her to the ground and laying one on her so long and wet that even Miles has to say, "The little dude's going deep."

When they finally come up for air Jimbo walks her to the entrance and opens the door for her, casting me a scathing look, as if I'm the one who gave her the "pain" pills, and as ridiculous as it is I can't help but glare back at him like we're on WWF Smackdown or some such, both of us madly flexing the small muscles of the face, The Little Green Giant versus Jerome "The Bulge" Battle. But it stops there, as he heads back toward his car and makes a call on his cell phone while Kelly walks in, bearing along her usual tutti-frutti scent of hard candies but then, too, more than a hint of his musky aftershave, which sours me. She plunks down her handbag on her side of our double desk.

"Okay, Jerry, I'm here. You can go home now. Please just wait a minute for Jimbo to leave."

"I still have another two hours."

"I'll cover for you."

Miles gives me the bug eyes and mutters, "Got to get to work," and ferries the remains of his lunch back to his desk. His phone rings and he picks it up but he keeps an eye on us as he talks.

"Listen, Kel," I say. "Just hold on. Why don't you sit down and let's talk."

"Let's not bother, please?"

"I know I should have come by your place more, after you left the hospital. I was feeling that way, but then the other day, I guess, you pretty much suggested you wanted privacy."

"That's a real funny way to look at it."

"Maybe it is. Anyway, I'm sorry. I really am."

"Oh, Jerry!" she says. "You don't even know what you're sorry about!"

"Sure I am. I'm sorry about all that's happened."

"And what do you think has happened?"

"Well, for starters, how about the pills, or crashing into the ER, or that ham hock standing out there by the car . . ."

"Don't you say a word about him, Jerry. You of all people don't deserve to."

"Okay, fair enough," I say. "But just because you're deciding again that I didn't do right by you last year, doesn't mean we can't talk like we always have, does it? You can despise me a little, but you don't have to hate me forever."

Kelly groans. "You just think everything's your fault, don't you? Well, let me tell you buster, I'm sick of it. Sick of it." She leans over the desk and starts to push at my shoulder and chest. "I didn't try to hurt myself because of you. I wouldn't do that. Never ever."

"Fine. Then for God sakes, why?"

"I did it for *me*, you big dope. Me and me alone."

"That makes no sense at all! Attempting suicide isn't exactly *therapy*, Kel."

"Maybe it is, when Jerry Battle's involved."

This one stings, and certainly more deeply than she intended, one of those special heavy metal–tipped rounds that penetrate the armor and wickedly bounce around inside, for maximal flesh damage.

"I'm sorry, Jerry. See? You better just lay off."

"I'm not going to lay off, because you're my friend," I say, adding, "Maybe my only friend."

"An ex-girlfriend who can hardly stand the sight of you is your only friend?"

"I know it's pathetic."

"Oh, Jerry," she sighs, heavily, terribly. "I love you sort of and I hope I will always love you sort of but I definitely can't stand you anymore."

This almost soothes, but really it's no great news, for yours truly, and after a brief moment I take gentle hold of her arm and say, "Come on. What do you think things would be like for all of us if you really went through with it?"

"Not so different. And I'm not being sorry for myself. Everyone would be suitably upset. Maybe Chuck would have to find another agent and Jimbo another girlfriend and you'd be down in the dumps for a few days. But like all the bad weather in your life, Jerry, it would quickly pass. Or if it didn't, you'd take up that plane of yours and just fly right above it."

"It's not like that."

"Yes it is."

She looks away from me but I see her eyes are shimmery and

as she gasps a little I bring her close, and she hugs me, with Miles flashing a "go for it" hand signal as he jabbers Spanglish into the handset; and although I have to admit that it feels squarely, preternaturally good to hold Kelly once again in all her big-framed honey biscuit-smelling glory, I remind myself not to cling too long or too tightly, lest one (or both) of us gets what would certainly end up being the wrong idea of trying to do something right, which would be emotionally lethal for us, or worse. But Kelly apparently has the same notion, as she pinches me very hard where she was holding me on the love handles, holding and pinching before pushing away. This hurts, and not so good. But just then the metal-framed glass door bangs open and it's Jimbo, still clutching his cell, his pixie face all pinched up and flushed, like he's been holding his breath out there this whole time, and now heading toward me like I was the one clamping off his airway, this mad, mad little missile. A funny sound comes out of Kelly, an airy bleat, and for a nanosecond I can't help but think of a night in Phuket when I was almost killed on a side street by one of those crazy-looking pickup-truck taxis called *tuk-tuks,* the thing screaming to a stop about three inches from me, and then innocently honking: *bleat-bleat.* And perhaps that is why I don't, or can't, now move, this false sense of déjà vu, for when Jimbo's pointed shoulder hits me in the gut I am practically giddy with astonishment and wonder for this unusual world, and I am ready to decline.

I decline, Mini-Jim. I really do.

But the next thing I know, Miles and Kelly are pulling the homunculus off me, though not quite in time to spare me a serious new-fashioned "bitch slapping," at least according to Miles. Apparently Jimbo stunned me with the tackle to the solar plexus, knocking the breath out of me, and as he wailed away with his cub paws while straddling my chest, all yours truly was able to manage was to cover up his overrated mug and plead a misunderstanding. After what seemed to me a lethal fifteen rounds but was probably a quarter minute at most, Miles finally got him to desist and drive off (with Kelly) by wielding a Parade Travel paperweight, an etched, solid-glass globe the size of a grapefruit that we sometimes present to our best customers (the Plotkins have one), and yelling in a puffed-up, profanity-laced Spanish. It was as good a language display as I ever heard from him, though probably it was all in the delivery, the ornate hormonal tone, and I must say I felt a warm rush of what was almost parental pride and gratitude from down in my sorry horizontal position, hearing his flashy street defense of me. And while I'm sure Jack would have pummeled my assailant silly, I'm pretty certain he would have done so with little of Miles's relish or animation.

WHICH IS NOW PART of what I'm noodling about, as I drive slowly home from Parade, my face tingling and raw, my gut muscles tightly balled and sore, acridity abounding, because when anything squarely intense happens these days I get to thinking about *la famiglia*, as most people might, though in my case it's not just to count heads and commune in absentia but to wonder in a blood-historical mode about how we got to be the way we are, whether okay or messed-up or deluded or, as usual, just gently gliding by. In this sense maybe I should thank Jimbo for providing some contour to the day, though of course I should ultimately thank myself for being an utterly serviceable, companionable boyfriend to a more-fragile-than-it-appears woman like Kelly caught in an eddy of middle life, a combination that meant I was mostly useless and lame. And as I cross over the ceaselessly roaring Expressway and turn into my aging postwar development just now beginning to look and feel like a genuine neighborhood, the trees finally grown up in a vaulted loom over the weathered ranches and colonials, I wish I could have certain countless moments back again, not for the purpose of doing or fixing or righting anything but instead to be simply there once more, present again, like watching a favorite movie for a third or fourth time, when you focus on different though important things, like that stirring, electric moment in *To Kill a Mockingbird* when the upstairs gallery of black folk stand up to honor Atticus Finch after the verdict goes against Tom Robinson, their expressions of epic suffering and dignity laying me low and then more generally instructing me that there are few things in this life as heartbreaking as unexpected solidarity.

A chance for which I'll maybe have once more today, for as I coast down the driveway I see Jack's Death Star–style luxury Blackwood pickup parked to one side of the turnaround, which is a surprise in itself, and boosts my spirits. He rarely comes by like this during the workweek, if ever, and when the garage door curls open I see the Ferrari parked inside, Theresa's and Paul's driving caps tossed on the seats. I tuck the broad-fendered old Chevy snugly in the other bay, the family gas guzzlers at rest, the clan all here except for Rita Reyes, who should have long been Rita Battle, and may yet be Rita Coniglio if yours truly doesn't conjure up some serious voodoo very soon.

The sound of familiar voices echoes from the backyard. I pause for a long moment before stepping around the corner of the house, to listen, I suppose, though I'm not sure for what or why, and I hear Jack explaining something about the prime rate and the state of the economy in the dry unmodulated way he talks about everything having to do with business. Paul asks about home mortgages, whether the rates will be lower in the fall; this is good to hear—they're still planning ahead. While Jack responds I don't hear a peep from Theresa, though, which deflates me a little, for maybe what I was hoping for was to happen upon some easeful sibling exchange, some cheery, smart-alecky shorthand that they'd pepper each other with, to no harm. And I even hoped she wasn't present, but when I step into the back I see that the three of them are there, sitting out beneath the umbrellaed patio table with soft drinks and salsa and chips.

"Hey, what happened to you?" Theresa says, in mid-dip.

"Nothing," I say, all of them examining me. "Why?"

"Looks like you just had an all-day facial," she says, patting her cheeks. "I think maybe I should try that."

"You don't need a thing, sweetheart," Paul tells her. "You're perfect."

"I just never had one, you know."

Jack is the only one drinking a beer, and I murmur that I could use a cold one, to which he dutifully rises and steps inside to the kitchen.

"You do look a little puffy, Jerry," Paul now says, looking at me with concern. Paul can feature the unruffled manner of a seasoned doctor sometimes, a mien he clearly gets from his parents. "You may be allergic to something."

"Dad's allergic to workplaces," Jack says as he returns, with uncharacteristic sharpness, I might add, sounding like his sister in her youth. He hands me an icy bottle, holding two others that must be for him.

"Here you go, old fella. The swelling should go down soon enough."

I look into Jack's eyes and they seem to laugh a little, and suddenly I realize he may in fact be inebriated. This is not at all the usual. I glance at Theresa and she gives the slightest shrug.

I say, "Jack's half right. It's probably all the dust kicked up by the power blowers. I guess after all these years I've finally developed a sensitivity. In our day, we used to rake and then sweep up with gym brooms."

"You mean you had me and the guys raking," Jack says.

"I guess that's true, too. But I did my fair share."

"The noise of those blowers is incredible," Theresa says. "I never realized how loud it is in the suburbs. Paul and I are the only ones here all day, and it seems like the landscapers never quit. Not to mention all the renovation and construction crews. You're practically the only one on the block not doing work to the house, Jerry."

"Cheers to all the work," Jack says, finishing up his bottle and opening a fresh one. "Every one of those remodels needs new lighting and plumbing fixtures and tiles and cabinetry. And it's all high-end stuff, exactly our Battle Brothers Excalibur products. How do you think I keep Eunice living in the style to which she's accustomed?"

"I thought it was your style, too."

"It's fine," he answers her, "but I don't need it to be that way."

"I've never seen a house like yours," Paul says. "The kitchen is amazing. I love that folding faucet over the stove, so you can fill the pots right there."

"Eunice got the idea from a show on HGTV. That particular fixture is triple-nickel-plated, from a maker in Northern England. It retails for eighteen hundred. We just won the bid to be the exclusive dealer in the metro area. They supply all the European royalty, including Monaco."

"And now the whole North Shore of the Island," Theresa adds. "Just perfect."

"Hey, if people can afford it, they have a right to whatever they like."

"Well, I don't quite know about that," Theresa autoresponds, but then she somehow thinks better of it, and quickly recasts. "But hey, Jack, it's no big deal."

"Yeah it is," he says, with an edge. There's a tenor to his voice I don't like, like he's not speaking to his baby sister, like he's never even had one. "I thought everything's a big deal with you. Isn't that what you do for a living? You criticize—excuse me, *critique.* Every little thing is so critiqued, so critical and important, life or death or purgatory. Everything can mean everything."

Theresa says, "That's in fact a good way of looking at it, though context is also everything. . . ."

"Whatever. I believe someone can pay his hard-earned money and buy a faucet he likes and it's perfectly okay if he doesn't think about all the possible injustices and implications of doing so. He doesn't have to think about anything."

"You must really believe that."

"Yeah, I do."

"Okay, then."

Jack says, "Okay what?"

"I said *okay,*" she says, sounding suddenly weary, and not just of the conversation. She has sunglasses on, so I can't see her eyes, but there's a hunch to her shoulders that seems more pronounced than it should in anyone so young.

Jack says, "It's not like you to agree. Why are you agreeing?"

"Hey, hey, guys," Paul says, "we were enjoying the early evening sun here."

“That’s right,” I say, “let’s cut it out now.”

Jack says, “I’m in ‘the sun’ all day, okay, so I don’t exactly need to enjoy it like all you people who are retired or might as well be. I came over to talk. But suddenly all the talkers don’t want to talk.”

Silence, except for the sound of the neighbor’s electric waterfall, this blocked old-pisser trickle none of us noticed before.

“I think I need to lie down,” Theresa says, getting up. Paul gets up, too, and holds her arm as they step into the house.

“See you later, Jack,” Paul says. “We’ll be by.”

Jack mutters *Yeah, Paul,* like it’s a Scandinavian language, and then downs the rest of his beer in one clean, long gulp.

He rises to leave, too, but I tell him to sit and stay awhile. He does, which is good, but this is again indicative of what sometimes irks me about him, his too-quick compliance, at least to me, no matter the situation. He’s definitely been drinking before he got here, being a bit flushed about the cheek and ears and neck, a reaction he doesn’t derive from me (I tend to get paler with every glass of jug-decanted Soave), and I wonder if he’s doing this every afternoon at 4 o’clock, in some skanky out-of-the-way lounge or the polished wood-paneled men’s grill room of his country club. Though this in itself would be neither surprising nor worrisome. In our business you can have a lot of empty time on your hands no matter how numerous and busy the jobs are, especially toward the end of the day when the guys are slowing down and just about to gather the tools and roll everything up into the backs of the trucks, and the clients are no longer so anxious and clingy, when there’s just enough of a reason not to go straight home because after a long day of ordering and hollering and assuring and brownnosing you want to talk to someone (including your wife) without having to convince or sell them on anything. Sometimes this means you mostly choose to just sink deeper in the captain's chair of your smoked-glass truck, with not even the radio on. In my prime years with Battle Brothers I'd tell the guys I was going to do an estimate but instead I'd park my work truck in some random neighborhood off Jericho Turnpike and spread a Michelin map on the passenger seat, mentally tracing a slow route from Nice to Turin, every switchback like a sip of a cold one.

But Jack Battle really isn't Jerry Battle, which I should be glad for but am not, at least right now, because if he were perhaps it would be easier to say something to him that I could be sure was tidy and effective, an impartial communication, like a patriarchal Post-it note with simple, useful information (how to make a noose, how to pile up charcoal briquettes), or else something slightly chewier, some charming Taoist-accented aphorism bespeaking the endlessly curious circumstance and befuddlement of our lives.

But like everybody else around here (save maybe Paul) I can't quite help myself, and I say, without any delight, "What the hell is going on with you? I don't get it. With what your sister is going through right now?"

Jack twists the cap off another beer.

"Are you hearing me, Jack?"

He says, "To tell you the truth, Dad, I really shouldn't know. I should know nothing. Because no one told me."

"Theresa didn't tell you?"

"No, she didn't," he says, roughly setting down the bottle, hard enough that it splashes and foams and spills through the metal mesh of the table. He stands up and shakes his workboots. "Do you know how I know? I had to hear it from Rosario, who

I suppose heard it from Paul. Come on, Dad, what the fuck is that?"

"It's not like them . . ."

"You mean it's not like Paul. Your daughter is another story. Eunice, if you care to know the truth, is furious. The worst part is she really feels like dirt, and I don't blame her. She went all out and threw a big party and offered to throw the wedding reception and now she feels like we're goddamn nobodies in this family."

"I thought they told you, or I would have, right away."

"Well, they didn't. You should have, automatically. Automatically. Paul is one thing, but you."

"I'm sorry," I say. "This won't make you feel any better but I found out mostly by accident, too. And I don't really know what's going on now, because she refuses to go into details. But I think we should give your sister some room here. She's no dummy, and we have to trust her to make the right calls."

"Would you be saying that if I were in her place?"

The question surprises me, both in its sharpness and implied self-criticism, and in the face of it I say (too automatically, perhaps), "Of course I would."

Jack mutters, "Yeah," and drinks some more of his beer.

"You don't think so?"

"Forget it," he says. He gazes out over the backyard, and though I feel like telling him he's being childish, I don't, not just because I only ever get dangerously close to doing such a thing but also because nothing he's saying is off the mark. And for the first time in a very long time I can see he might be genuinely hurt, this indicated by the pursed curl in his lower lip, the slight underbite that he would often feature when he was a boy, when his mother wasn't doing well, and then after she was gone.

"You should let me send the guys over and redo this place," Jack suddenly says. "It's getting to be a real dump, you know."

"I wouldn't say that."

"I would," he says, but not harshly, and he's already up out of his chair and out on the lawn. He's standing on the spot where the pool used to be, now just another unruly patch of grass, splotchy and scrubby, the erstwhile beds bordering the pool now unrecognizable as such, with the sod grown over so that they look like ski moguls in the middle of the lawn. All the surrounding trees and shrubs are in need of serious pruning, the brick patio having sunk in several spots and gone weedy in the seams, the yard appearing not at all like a former professional landscaper's property but rather what a realtor might charitably appraise as "tired" or "in need of updating" or, in fact, if you were really looking hard at the place, a plain old dump.

"Listen," Jack says, gesturing with his long-necked beer, his tone unconsciously clicking into just the right register for what he does, what I call contractor matter-of-fact, assured and fraternal and with just enough of a promise of prickly umbrage to keep most customers at bay. "It wouldn't be a big deal. I'd shave these mounds flat and scrape away the whole surface and lay down fresh sod. Then we'd get into the trees and cull the undergrowth and prune up top as well. I'd want to replace all the shrubs by the patio and maybe put in a few ornamental fruit trees over by the driveway, to create a little glade. The patio we'll do in bluestone, finished out with an antique brick apron, to match the siding of the house."

"Sounds pretty nice. But I wouldn't want to tie up a whole crew," I tell him, as I know Battle Brothers would never charge me a dime. "Especially when it seems there's so much work out there."

"It's actually slowed down a bit," he says, sipping his beer. "Don't worry, we're at a good level now. We can spare a couple guys."

"Maybe I will have you do some work. I've been kicking around the idea of moving to a condo the last couple years, but I don't seem to be doing anything about it."

"Why should you?" Jack says. "The house is paid for, isn't it? Pop is tucked away and taken care of. You're on Easy Street, Dad. I'd just enjoy the air, if I were you, and make this place nice for yourself. Nothing's in your way."

"Nothing's in your way, either," I tell him.

Jack says, "Nothing but a jumbo mortgage and two kids to send to private day school and a wife with exceptional taste."

"Eunice does like nice things," I say. "But you do, too."

"I go along."

By now I've joined him, and we walk around the inside perimeter of the property, bordered by those overgrown trees, Jack making suggestions to me and jotting notes on the screen of his electronic organizer. He doesn't seem even mildly drunk anymore; it pleases me to think that maybe the work mode enlivens him.

"What about there," I say, referring to the expansive swath in the center of the property. "Just leave it as lawn?"

"I don't know. Maybe you ought to put a pool back in."

"A pool? I don't need to swim anymore."

"Sure, but the kids would love it. Lately I've been wanting to put one in, but there's not enough room at my house for a nice-sized one. If you had a pool back here again, you'd see the kids all the time."

I nod and say, "That'd be good," even though I've already worried that I might not *like* his kids if I spent a lot of time with them (even if I'll always love them).

"Plus," he says, "maybe Theresa and Paul will move back to Long Island someday, with their kid, or kids."

"I was thinking of that, too."

"Sure. If you wanted, my pool guy could drop in an integrated hot tub for you, right alongside the regular pool. I'd have him install a slide instead of a diving board, though."

"Kids like slides."

"Definitely," Jack says. "I always wanted one."

"Really?" I say. "I never knew that. You should have asked me. I would have gotten you one, no problem."

"I know. I don't know why, but it never occurred to me to ask you. But then, I suppose, it was too late."

"I guess it was," I say, not quite understanding that we're all of a sudden talking about *this,* about which there's never been any great family prohibition or denial, any great family taboo, but still.

"I bet Mom would have had a blast with a slide," Jack says.

"Maybe," I answer, "but she'd have had to go down with her ring float on."

Jack looks at me like I'm crazy.

"You think?" he says.

"I guess not," I answer, realizing how stupid I must sound, talking about her *float.* So I say, "Your mother would have done whatever she liked."

"That's why we loved her, right?" Jack says brightly, with just the scantest tinge of edge and irony.

I can only nod, and just stand there with him in the middle of the big patch of messy lawn, and I don't have to try hard to recall how he and Theresa spent most of their time right here (at least up to a certain age), especially in the summer, turning as brown as coconuts as they hopped and raced and climbed atop everything in sight. Every parent says it, but they really were like those tiny tree monkeys you see at the zoo, their faces all eyes and their fingers and limbs impossibly narrow and lithe. They'd be crawling onto and off you and tugging at your shoulders, your ears, then (unlike most primates) leaping with abandon into the pool, even before they learned how to swim, thrashing about half-drowning before I'd pull them out.

And I'll say right now it really was a very decent pool, just what you'd imagine for a solidly middle-class postwar family house, a 20-by-40 inground with a meter-high diving board and nice porcelain tile work around the lip, though after what happened to Daisy and with no one around during the work hours to supervise I decided to have the guys fill it in, which in fact none of us seemed to regret, not even Jack, who was a natural swimmer and the star of the neighborhood club swim team. In fact it amazed me how quickly he got past it all, how intensely he threw himself into his other sports, and to astounding success, in turn becoming socially confident and popular, the tight busy orbits of which allowed him, I suppose, to recover fully, even if these days everyone even half-witted thinks that to be a spurious notion or concept. But I'm not so sure. Maybe the key to returning to normalcy was my quick response, my instant renewal of our little landscape, that I filled in and bulldozed over the offending site and rolled out perfect new sod that they could at least play upon without a care or thought, if never really frolic in the same way again.

"Tell Theresa I'm sorry," Jack finally says, gathering his things on the patio table, to head out. "I'll call her later, too."

"That would be good," I say, as I walk him to the driveway.

"So what about it?" he says, nodding back to the yard. "I'll send the guys around. But what about the pool?"

We'll see, I say to him, or I think I do anyway, and before he steps up into the saddle of his impossibly high-riding vehicle I give him a healthy pat or two on the back, to which my son grunts something satisfyingly low and approving, a clipped rumbling *yyup*, and I think of how good it is to have both of them here again, regardless of the terms, because (and you know who you are) you can reach a point in your life when it almost doesn't matter whether people love you in the way you'd want, but are simply here, nearby enough, that they just bother at all.

nine

JERRY BATTLE hereby declines the Real.

I really do.

Or maybe, on the contrary, I'm inviting it in. An example is how I now find myself here in my dimly lighted two-car garage, the grimy windows never once cleaned, sitting in the firm leather driver's seat of the Ferrari, its twelve cylinders warbling like an orchestra of imprisoned Sirens, and only when the scent becomes a bit too cloying do I reach up and press the remote controller hooked on the visor to crank up the door, the fresh air rushing in just like when you open a coffee can.

"What the hell are you doing?" Theresa shouts from the wheel of the Impala. She's idling on the driveway, staring out at me from behind Daisy's old Jackie O sunglasses, which she found in a night table I'd put down in the basement probably twenty years ago.

I back out the machine, in two awkward, revvy lurches. I sidle up to her. "I sometimes forget to open the door first."

"You big dummy. Are you sure you want to do this?"

"I'm sure. I'll buy you guys another car."

"Forget it. We don't really need one. We'll use this one, when you're not working. Hey, I want to stop at the Dairy Queen on the way out."

"Didn't we just have breakfast?"

"I need a milkshake and fries, Jerry. Right now."

"Okay, okay, that's good."

It's amazing how quickly she'll get her back up these days, not for the conventional reasons of my political and cultural illiteracy/idiocy, but for any kind of roadblock to calories sweet and fatty and salty. I'm glad that she's ornery, still feeling hungry, for with this thing looming she seems extra vulnerable, like an antelope calf with a hitch in its stride. We thumbs-up each other, like pilots and comrades will do, and I lead us out, remembering there's a Dairy Queen just off Richie's exit.

I've continued to be respectful and am hanging back, willing in my lazy-love (as opposed to tough-love) manner to leave the navigation to her, but something about the status of the status quo has set off a sharp alarm in my viscera, this clang from the lower instruments that we're pitched all wrong here. And so a good part of the reason I've decided to return Richie's car to him, no gloating, no strings, is not just that I'm a wonderful guy, or that it's an inherently hazardous machine for Theresa and Paul to be tooling around in among all the sport-utes riding high and mighty, or that I will never be able to make the car really feel like mine (even though I know Richie would have had *Donnie* already repainted and the seats reupholstered, if he didn't immediately sell her for a month's share of an executive jet), but to try to simplify, simplify, what seems to be our increasingly worrisome matters of family. I should probably be effecting this by gathering all my loved ones and doing something like passing out index cards and having everyone write down for candid discussion three “challenges” that face us (as I saw suggested in a women’s magazine at the supermarket checkout the other day), but it’s easier to begin by clearing out whatever collateral stuff is crowding what appears to be our increasingly mutual near future, a category in which the Rabbitmobile neatly fits. As much as Theresa and Paul like using the car, I’ve been feeling that it’s literally a foreign object, plus the fact that it reminds me too much of Rita’s disdainful regard.

So here we are, Theresa and I, in our convertible caravan of two. I glance back in the rearview every ten seconds, and wave. She waves back, glamorous in the gleaming chariot. It gives me pleasure to see her at the wheel, reminding me of the days when she and Jack used to sit up front with me and take turns sitting in my lap and driving. Of course you’d probably get arrested these days for doing such a thing, charged with child endangerment, but back then Jack would even press the horn when a patrol car passed, the officer answering Jack with a little *whirrup* from his siren.

We have a decent ways to go before we get to Richie’s town, which I’m not minding, as it’s midafternoon, everyone still at the beach, with the Expressway moving along at a fine smooth clip that feels even headier from the open cockpit of this High Wop machine supreme. As I pass the cars on my left and right, their drivers, I notice, can’t help but take a good long look at me, men and women both, but especially the men, younger guys and middle-aged guys and guys who shouldn’t still be driving, and I know exactly how they’re thinking what a detestable lucky-ass piece of shit I am, the respect begrudged but running deep as they unconsciously bank to the far edge of their lanes, to give me room. The younger chicks are the ones who drift closer, closer, maybe to see if the hair is a rug or weave, if I've got a flappy gobble to my neck, this one saucer-eyed blondie jouncing alongside in a Jeep Wrangler even raising her sunglasses up on her head to wink at me and mouth what I'm sure is a smoky *Follow me home.* Maybe Jerry Battle should reconsider. The wider shot here is pretty okay, too, the broad roadway not seeming half as awful as I think I know it to be, and I have to wonder what else—for our kind, at least—really makes a place a place, save for the path or road running straight through it, ultimately built for neither travel nor speed?

At the Dairy Queen we're pretty much alone, given that they haven't officially opened. Theresa got the two teenage employees to open early for us by telling the somewhat older assistant manager that she'd let them try out the Ferrari after they filled her order. They're both husky and greasy-faced, your basic big-pore, semi-washed, blank-eyed youth who in fact run almost everything in our world-dominating culture, but you've never seen soda jerks in this day and age move as fast as these two do now; they've got the fries bubbling in the hopper and the ice cream in the blenders and they're even filling a squeeze bottle with fresh catsup. I've joined Theresa in the front seat of my antique wheels. Like carhops they bring out our snack on a clean tray and I throw the assistant manager the keys and ask him not to maim or kill anyone, and before Theresa can even pop her straw into her shake he is smoking the fat rear rubber, wildly fishtailing down the avenue.

"Have some fries, Jerry."

I help myself, though I'm completely not hungry, something I've been a lot lately, no doubt inspired in some latent biological way by the sight of pregnant kin. Or maybe I shouldn't be eating at all, to leave more of the kill for her. In any case Paul, who is enabling this behavior, is back at the house dry-rubbing Moroccan spices on a hormone-free leg of lamb he'll grill for dinner and serve with herbed couscous and butter-braised *spargel,* German white asparagus he found on special at Fresh Fields for a mere $5.99 a pound. He's been cooking even more furiously than ever, preparing at least four or five meals for every three we eat, so that we're building up enough surplus inventory to last us a couple of weeks, in case there's some threat of a late-summer hurricane and a run on the supermarkets. Last week I made Paul quite happy by cleaning out an old freezer in the basement and plugging it in and then buying him one of those vacuum sealer machines so his lovely dishes wouldn't get freezer-burned. Every day since it seems he's vacuum-packing not just hot food and leftovers but dry goods like roasted cashews and Asian party mix and banana chips and Peanut M&M's, apportioning and shrink-wrapping whatever he finds bulk-packaged at Costco that catches his eye. No one's said it, for of course these are meals that would certainly come in handy after the baby is born, but that's many months off and then maybe not quite appropriate, as it doesn't seem quite right that you'd be heating up a maple pinot noir glazed loin of veal or halibut medallions in aioli-lemongrass sauce between breast feedings or diaper changes. Or maybe you would.

While I'm pleased that Paul is thusly keeping busy with what one hopes are therapeutic activities, I'm growing increasingly worried that he's maybe starting to sink in his soup, that he's getting too engrossed in work that seems worthwhile and positive but is in fact the culinary equivalent of obsessively washing one's hands. Yesterday as he was coming up from one of his nearly hourly descents to the basement freezer I asked him again (casually, gently, as if accidently) if any writing was going on. He weakly chuckled and muttered, "What?" and then in the next breath asked me in a serious tone if I thought he had what it took to sell Saturns at the new dealership just opened up on Jericho. When I realized he wasn't kidding I told him yes, he'd probably be great at it, for Paul with his gentle, trustworthy, liberal carriage is no doubt just right for those haggling-averse academic-type customers (though he still probably ought to lose the ponytail and hemp huaraches), and after leaving him to roll up some pounded chicken breasts with a spinach chevre pignolinut stuffing I wandered off thinking how utterly disturbing this whole mess must be for him, despite what has been since his first disclosure to me an otherwise thoroughly affable Paul Pyun performance. People say that Asians don't show as much feeling as whites or blacks or Hispanics, and maybe on average that's not completely untrue, but I'll say, too, from my long if narrow experience (and I'm sure zero expertise), that the ones I've known and raised and loved have been each completely a surprise in their emotive characters, confounding me no end. This is not my way of proclaiming "We're all individuals" or "We're all the same" or any other smarmy notion about our species' solidarity, just that if a guy like me is always having to think twice when he'd rather not do so at all, what must that say about this existence of ours but that it restlessly defies our attempts at its capture, time and time again.

Richie's car streaks by in a red candy flash, the shearing whine of the motor indicating that the assistant manager is driving in too low a gear. He leaps back and forth between the two lanes, weaving in and out of the slow-moving traffic with surprising skill, and turns down a side road, to disappear again. His coworker, shaking his fist in the air, is shouting at the top of his lungs expletives of high praise.

"I forget, how old is Pop again?" Theresa asks out of the blue, between slurps of her vanilla shake. I'd wanted to bring up the Big Issue, but Theresa is now tolerating no talk whatsoever of her pregnancy or the non-Hodgkin's (the *non* always throwing me off, like it's nonlethal, nonimportant, nonreal), and then practicing deft avoidance maneuvers whenever I try to pry.

"He was eighty-five, around the time of the party."

"And you're fifty-nine."

"Yup," I say, thinking how that number sounds better than it ever has before. "Sixty, on Labor Day. You're probably thinking, 'How ironic.' "

"Gee, Jerry, you must think I'm the most horrible person."

"No way. But you can be honest."

"Okay, so maybe I had a flash of a thought. But nobody would say you haven't worked hard all your life. Not even Pop."

"Only because he's not saying much." Though this is not quite true. Pop's actually been in a decent mood since the immediate aftermath of the incident with Bea, generally behaving well during my visits, being soft-spoken and circumspect and displaying what for him is an astoundingly modest demeanor, even pleasant, the unvolubility of which should be frightening me to death but that I'm simply glad for whenever I'm there, the two of us slouched in his mauve-and-beige-accented room for a couple uneventful hours (with him propped up in the power bed, and me in the recliner, likewise angled) staring up at the Learning Channel or the Food Network. This might sound dismally defeatist, but when you can't pretend anything else but that your pop is in the home for life and his former main lady is now permanently featuring a bib and diaper, you tend not to want to examine the issues too rigorously, you tend to want to keep it *Un*-real, keep the thinking *small* because the issues in fact aren't issues anymore but have suddenly become the all-enveloping condition.

Theresa says, "Would you like a party for the big one?"

"Definitely not."

"Why not?" she says. "It'll be great fun. We'll have a birthday roast. We'll invite all of your friends."

"I don't have any friends."

"That can't be true. What about all the Battle Brothers guys?"

"We're still friendly, but we're not friends. Never were."

"Then some other group, neighbors, people from the neighborhood. School chums. Don't you have buddies from your Coast Guard days?"

"I told you, I don't have friends. I never really have. I just have friendlies."

"Then we'll invite all your friendlies. It doesn't have to be a huge thing. I'm sure Paul will be happy to cater it."

"It seems like he's already started."

"Isn't he great? Actually, Paul's the one who mentioned doing something special for your birthday. I didn't know, of course, because I'm so damn assimilated, but in Korea the sixtieth is a real milestone. I guess numerologically it's significant, plus the fact that in the old days it was quite a feat to live that long."

"It still is," I say. "It's just that these days nobody really wants you to."

"Oh, stop whining. In my mind it's settled. We'll throw you a sixtieth birthday party. That will be our present, as we have no money. I'm sure Jack and Eunice will get you something huge, like a new plane."

"That's just what I'm afraid of." I'm trying to tune in an oldies station on the radio, as the ones that I've always liked to listen to (in this car especially) have somewhere along the line fiddled with their programming, shifting from '50s and '60s songs to mostly '70s and '80s pop, which are of course now oldies to Theresa and often completely new to me. Finally I have to switch to cruddy lo-fidelity AM to find the mix I want, which is no mix at all, just Platters and Spinners and Chuck Berry and James Brown, though it comes out scratchy and tinny like from the other end of a can-and-string telephone. This, of course, is part of the ever-rolling parade of life, slow-moving enough that you never think you'll miss something glittery and nice, but then not stopping, either, for much anyone or anything. And by extension you can see how folks can begin to feel left behind or ushered out, how maybe you yourself come in a format like an LP or Super 8mm that would play perfectly fine if ever cued up, if the right machines were still around.

But they're gone, gone forever.

And I say, unavoidably, hoping not desperately, "I've got some time."

"Sure you do. But you never know, do you, Jerry?"

Theresa, bless her soul, can always bring it on.

I say, "You never do. I could have a bad stroke right now, not be able to brush my teeth, and you'd have to put me in Ivy Acres."

"You could be roommates with Pop," she says, almost brightly. "I wonder how often that happens."

"I'm sure it's rare."

This is a prospect I haven't yet considered, but one I probably need to; not that it will actually happen or that I would let it, but I should realize that this is how people my daughter's age might naturally see me, and not even because they wish to.

"But you wouldn't really want that, would you?"

"To live with Pop in the home?"

"No," she says. "Just the home part."

"Is there an alternative?"

"Sure there is."

"Like what?"

"You know."

"I do?"

"Sure you do."

Or I *think* I do, but I'm afraid to say it first, the idea instantly replenishing the abandoned gravel pit of my heart. I think she's talking about what all of us not-for-a-while-middle-aged folks would love to hear whenever we get together with our grown kids, which I'll unofficially call The Invitation. Since they moved into their big house I've been secretly waiting for Jack and Eunice to float the idea that I eventually sell my house and move in with them, maybe agreeing to give them half the equity for my future maintenance by an attractive home nurse, the other half going to the kids' education or an inground pool or whatever else they deem to be worth the misery and trouble. I've hoped this even despite the fact that Jack and I aren't close in any demonstrable way, or that I'm undeniably only so-so with the kids, being willing to take them to a carnival or the zoo but otherwise unable to sit with them for more than a few minutes in their great room amid the ten thousand plastic toys and gadgets. I admit even to murmuring admiration over recent years for Jack's half-Asian blood, periodically extolling the virtues of filial piety (which Daisy once accused me of knowing nothing about, after forbidding her to call long-distance anymore to Korea, as she was running up bills of $200 a month), hoping that he'd someday put aside our thoroughly unspectacular relations and decide to honor some vague natal charge I'd slyly beckoned, some old-time Confucian burden that wouldn't depend (lucky for me) on anything private and personal. On this score I think us old white people (and black people, and any others too long in our strident self-making civilization) are way down in the game, and it wouldn't surprise me at all if the legions of my brethren about to overwhelm the ranks of assisted buttressed life prove to be among history's most disappointed generations.

As for Theresa, I never imagined she would ask me to join her crew, even if she were in a position to do so. But perhaps the current circumstance has initiated in her what is proving a sentimental bloom of hope and generosity, and in the sweet light of this I can't say much now, except to burble, genuinely and gratefully, "You've got plenty to think about with yourself and Paul."

"I know, I know. But so it's even more important to talk about it."

"Absolutely right," I say.

The Dairy Queen boys switch, the second one a bit more tentative than the first, as he seems to have little experience driving a stick, a video game probably the extent of it. The first customer presently turns in to the parking lot, and the kid at the wheel nearly hits him as he pulls out onto the road. We watch him as he bolts down to the next light, stalls, U-turns at the signal, stalls, and then hustles back.

Theresa finishes the milkshake, drilling about with the straw to draw up every last drop. Over the past couple weeks she's gained weight from Paul's four-star training table, as have I, with her cheeks and neck and shoulders looking fleshy and sturdy in her crème-colored cotton tank top. As she sits coolly at the wheel of my Impala wearing the Jackie O sunglasses, I can't help but wonder how close the two of them might be, she and Daisy, how they'd be plotting the family milestones, how, if I were a very lucky man, they'd be endlessly teasing me and causing me troubles and generally giving me a constant run of heartbreak.

"I'm glad to hear that from you, Jerry," Theresa says. "I was discussing it with Paul last night. About me."

"You?"

"Of course me. We decided that if things got horrific and the baby was already out and there was nothing left but blind faith, that he would help me take the necessary measures."

"Necessary measures? What the hell are you talking about?"

"What we're talking about."

"I thought we were talking about our *future*."

"Exactly," she says. "I don't want Paul and you and maybe Jack, if he even cares, to carry me beyond what's reasonable. I'm not going to go for anything heroic here. I'm not interested in lingering. Besides, I think it's appalling, the level of resources our society puts toward sustaining life, no matter the costs or quality."

"I don't care," I say, doing my best to switch gears unnoticed. "I think it's noble."

"Noble? It's craven and egotistical. This when thousands of children are born each day into miserable conditions, when our public schools are crumbling, when the environment is threatened at every turn. Really, it's ridiculous, how antideath our society is."

"Look, honey, I don't know what you want me to say, but I'm definitely antideath. Especially yours."

"You may think that now. But if I were down to eighty

pounds and I couldn't hear or see, and the pain were so great I couldn't stop moaning, all of it costing you and everyone else two thousand dollars a day, would you want me to endure every last breath?"

"I don't like talking about this."

"You're a big boy, Jerry."

"Okay. All right, then. I think you deserve your turn."

"My *turn*? You think Pop is enjoying his turn?"

"You're missing my point," I tell her. "Pop is where he is because there's no better choice. I put him there for his own good but he's not locked up. He doesn't like Ivy Acres, but in fact he doesn't want to live with me or Jack or anybody else. He can walk out anytime. What he really wants is his old life back, which he can't have. So he's doing what everybody does, which is just to ride it out for the sake of his family, so Jack and his kids can go over there and sit with him for an hour and fiddle with the bed controls and watch *The Simpsons*."

"It doesn't matter that nobody's really enjoying themselves?"

"Nope. It's just part of what we have to do, and Pop's job now is to be Pop-as-is. I'm not talking about heroics here, because there's no way that I would want you to suffer. But if things don't go so well I hope you don't do something sudden. There's a certain natural run to these things and I think we'll all know if it's really time. But I don't think it truly ever is."

"Don't you think Mom did something *sudden*?" Theresa says, the scantest edge in her tone.

"Of course not. She didn't commit suicide."

"But it wasn't purely an accident either, right? If she hadn't been so miserably unhappy, maybe she'd have been more careful."

"Could be," I say, focusing on the *miserably unhappy*, not so much the truth of it but the fact of Theresa, as a young girl, knowing her mother in such unequivocal terms. This not even getting into all her possible views on my contributions to that unhappiness, the broad intense feelings probably swamping her back then and the thousands of chilly extrapolations she's made since, all of which, coming from her, are liable to scare me straight unto death.

"I've been thinking, Jerry," she says, looking serious now. "I want to ask you to promise something."

"Whatever you say."

"I want you to promise you'll take care of Paul and the baby."

"Theresa . . ."

"And when I say Paul, I mean even if the baby isn't around."

"Jesus, I don't like you talking like this."

"I mean it. I want you to look after him. Maybe he can stay at the house with you a little while. My life insurance from the college is lame and would only hold him for six months, tops. He won't ask his parents for a dime."

"Would he ask me?"

"No, but if you offered he might accept your help. He's too messed up by what his parents think of his career choice to ask them for anything."

"Good thing he doesn't care what I think."

"It is," Theresa says. "Paul's an excellent person and a fine writer but he's sometimes too much of a good boy. He has this need to please them and by extension most everybody else, which is okay day to day but in the long run is going to get him into trouble. I haven't yet said anything to him but I think it's become a problem as he's gotten older, especially with his work. He hasn't really sloughed them off yet. I don't need to get into this with you, but he's sometimes too fair in his treatment of things, too just—like he's afraid or unwilling to disappoint or offend. An artist can't be averse to being disagreeable, even tyrannical."

"Hey, I like that Paul is nice to me."

"And he always will be. But you don't quite make the father-mentor-master pantheon for him, if you don't mind my saying. Paul can just hang out with you, exemplify nothing extraordinary or special, which is why I think you're good for him. He can be one of the guys with you, Jerry, a part of the wider male world."

"Why am I not feeling so complimented?"

"Oh, relax. All I'm saying is that he'd be most comfortable with you, in a way he certainly couldn't be comfortable with his father or mother or even, for that matter, a lot of our friends and colleagues back at the college. Sometimes I think that if I weren't around they'd all prove too strong for him, overwhelm him, and he'd end up just sitting there at his desk doodling in the margins."

"It's a good thing Jerry Battle is just filler."

"But you're fine filler, Jerry. You're always just there, taking it in. Like tofu in soup."

"Wonderful."

"It is. I always thought you were just right, especially as a dad. Maybe not for Jack but for me. You were never in the least pushy or overbearing, even when I was getting totally out of hand."

"When was that?"

"You know, that one summer, my biker-slut period. When I basically ran away and you and Jack had to drive out to Sturgis and bring me back. You didn't even yell at me. You were pissed, but only because you'd just lost your Chevron card. Jack was the one who was genuinely angry, about having to miss a few lacrosse matches."

"We stopped at the Corn Palace, didn't we? You and I taste-tested BLTs and chocolate milkshakes, state by state."

"See? You were enjoying yourself."

"I guess so," I say, though I'm not as tickled by the memory as I'm making it sound. For despite the obvious satisfaction I might have from hearing that my ever-skeptical daughter has generally approved of my parenting style, the notion of being Daddy Tofu seriously mitigates any lasting appeal. And the now insistent implication—something Theresa always seems to evoke for me—is not that Rita might view my years of boyfriending in a similar metaphorical light (which she no doubt does), or that there might be anything I can do to reform her perspective (save the usual dumb and desperate measures, like asking her, now, after all these years, and when she's no longer mine, to marry me), but rather that I should be addressing right now, posthaste, chop-chop, what I should not have let slide for hours much less weeks, which is to demand to know what the hell we're (not) talking about, to be part of what's going on with her, and how we are to proceed.

To not, yet again, profess my desire to decline, which I so wish to.

So I say, with as much resoluteness as I can muster, "Listen. The question isn't about me and it's not about Paul. You can be certain I'll keep an eye on him. I'll do whatever it takes. He can live with me as long as he can bear. But what I'm having great difficulty with is that you're not including me."

"I'm saving you the trouble. Remember, Jerry, you don't like trouble?"

"Dammit, Theresa! This isn't *trouble.* Trouble is what I have with Rita. At this point, trouble is still what I have with Pop, which I suppose I should be grateful for. But this is way past that. Let me tell you, I appreciate that you're trying to make this a nice extended summer visit to your dad, where we eat like gourmands and go to the movies at night and plan a modest little wedding for you. But I can't just allow myself to just sit by any longer, if that's what you're hoping for."

"I'm not hoping for anything," she answers, without tenor. "But fine. What do you want to be included in?"

"I don't know yet! You have to tell me!"

"Okay," she says, staring me right in the eye. "Do you want to be included in the fact that my red blood cell count is falling like crazy right now? Or that my doctor is warning me that my placenta might be seriously weakened? Or do you want to be included in my morning sickness ritual, which is to vomit right before and after breakfast, this morning's being bloody for the first time?"

"Bloody? What does that mean?"

"I don't really know, Jerry."

"Shouldn't you call your doctor?"

"I don't want to. We're seeing her next week anyway."

"Call her now," I say, handing her my cell phone. "I'll drive you tomorrow."

"No."

"What do you mean, no?"

"It'll just give her more reason to bring up termination, which I don't want to hear about anymore."

"Maybe you should hear it."

"Hey, Jerry, just because you're included doesn't mean you have a say."

"I think I do."

"I don't see why."

"I'm your *father*, Theresa. That still means something."

"Doesn't matter. Paul is mad all the time now, but he's heeding me, so you should, too."

"We don't have to be quiet about it."

"Sure. And *we* don't have to stay with you any longer, either."

We both shut up for a second, not a little surprised at how quickly things can reach an uncomfortable limit, which often happens when you start playing chicken with a loved one. My first (obtuse) impulse is to just say hell with this and drive over to the field and crank up ol' *Donnie*, fly her as high as I can get her. But I can't help but marvel at my daughter's hissy don't-tread-on-me attitude, courtesy of Daisy, and then wonder, too, in a flash that scares and deflates me, how bad the situation might really be, for her to be so darn immovable. She's hands down—along with Jack—the very best thing I've brought about in my life, the true-to-life sentiment of which I trust and hope is what every half-decent person thinks when he or she becomes a parent. But the slight twist here is that I am pretty sure Theresa has always known this to be the case as well, not because she's particularly high on herself, but from what has been, I suppose, my lifelong demonstration of readily accepting whatever's on offer, which I'm sure hasn't escaped her notice. From her angle, I could see, I haven't been much of a producer or founder, nothing at all like Pop, or millions of other guys in and between our generations, rather just caretaking what I've been left and/or given, and consuming my fair share of the bright and new, and shirking almost all civic duties save paying the property taxes and sorting the recycling, basically steering clear of *trouble*, the mode of which undoubtedly places me right in the vast dawdling heart of our unturbulent plurality but does me little good now, when I need to be exerting a little tough love back.

But then Theresa says first, "I'm sorry, Jerry. I can be such an ornery fucking bitch."

"Don't you say that," I tell her, as firm as I've ever been. "You're Theresa Battle, and you should be like nobody else, and you're perfectly great as you are."

"You think so?"

"I've never not."

She leans over and gives me a quick kiss on the cheek, stamp-like and tiny the way it felt when she was a kid, before Daisy died, and she would kiss me all the time.

"You know you're a pretty silly Mr. Empowerment."

"I don't care. If you don't."

"Of course not. Hey, are you going to finish your milk-shake?"

"Go ahead."

More customers have pulled in, enough so that the assistant manager steps out near the road and waves his hands, to get his partner to come back. The kid finally does, swerving in neatly right next to us. He gives me the keys, trying to thank me but unable to say anything but an awestruck *fuckin' hot!*, over and over again, and the thought occurs to me that I should just give the damn car to these two soft-serve-for-brains, fodder for a nice feature on the local news, *Old dude just gave us the keys!*, they'd be saying, but they'd probably kill themselves in it or worse hurt somebody else like a pregnant sick young woman out for a cone. But they're decent enough, because as we're pulling out the younger one sprints to Theresa's car and hands her another large shake for the road.

As we near Richie's place there's a discernible hush, a lurking prosperity, the oaks and maples ascendant. The only sounds are the throaty low-gear gurgles of the Ferrari, and I still can't help but make the back tires squeal as I sling and lurch around these generous mansion-scale streets. Theresa, trailing half a block behind, gently rudders the old boat down the lanes. I've called Richie's house but only the machine answered and I didn't leave a message, and anyway I'm thinking it's best if I just park the car out on the semicircular driveway and drop the keys through the mail slot, with not even a note. Let Richie figure it out.

And that's exactly what I do, though giving his machine a last few screaming redline revs in neutral before shutting it down right at the front entrance. But after I shove the keys through the slot (cut into the brick façade rather than the door), and turn around to leave, the front door opens and who's there but Richie, in a dingy off-white bathrobe, Saturday afternoon unshaven, his half-height reading specs perched on the end of his narrow nose. Really, he looks sort of terrible, not in the least Waspy and upmarket, suddenly bent over and darkish like any other of us newly aging New York Guidos, and for the first time since he was a kid I feel as though someone (if not Jerry Battle) ought to cut him a break.

"What's the big idea?" he says, holding out the keys to me. "I don't welch on my bets."

"Relax, Richie," I say, standing on his pea-stone driveway. "I just don't want it anymore."

"That car was the bet. You can't have a different one."

"I don't want a different one. I'm not trying to trade it in here. I'm giving it back to you."

"Why don't you sell it, then? Sell it and pocket the cash. It won't bother me. Who's that in your car?"

"My daughter."

"Your daughter?" Richie waves, and Theresa waves back. "She's a beautiful woman."

"She's pregnant, and engaged."

"Well good for her. Congratulations, Jerry."

"Look, I'm giving back the car. I'm not going to sell it."

"Well, I can't take it back," he answers, suddenly sounding not in the least like he's from the old neighborhood.

"Why the hell not?"

"My colleagues all witnessed the match. They verified the terms. I entertain them and others in the firm here regularly. If they saw the car around I couldn't possibly explain to them why you'd ever give it back."

"You can hide it in the garage."

"I'm not hiding anything."

"Tell them I'm a nice guy."

"Nobody's a nice guy."

"Tell them I was trying to trade it back to you for Rita."

This stops Richie for a second, as he absently jiggles the keys. "That they might believe. Anyway, it doesn't matter. Rita's not mine to trade."

"I know that."

"No, you don't," Richie says. "We broke up last week. She was here earlier this morning, to pick up the last of her things."

"You're kidding."

"I'm not."

"I don't believe you."

"Well, what the fuck do you think this is?" He reaches into his robe pocket and shows the diamond ring, the one with the stone as big as a hazelnut.

"What happened?"

"I don't know. After you came by that day it all went to shit. But I'm not blaming you. Maybe she got sick of me. Maybe she didn't like my friends. Maybe she still loves you."

Something Jerry Battle can always hear. And I can't help but ask, "Did she say that?"

Richie's smarting, which I've never quite seen from him, and before I can mercifully retract the question he says, "Not exactly. I'll say one thing. It's amazing what certain guys can get away with. I don't see why she'd even speak to you, with how you strung her along and wasted her youth. But maybe the long-term dodge is the most effective kind."

"She never said one word about wanting to get married."

"Well, even I know that doesn't mean a damn thing," he says, shaking his head. "You have no idea how lucky you are, do you, Jerry? You've always had steady attention from the girls, and I'll be honest and say you're also not a terrible guy, and so it's no surprise you got plenty of ass. With me, I always knew I'd have to make a shitload of dough to get a pretty woman to share my bed."

"Hey, Rich . . ."

"That's okay, I know what I look like. It got me focused early. I've taken nothing for granted, women or money or anything else. I'm not bragging here, I'm just saying how these things don't come easily to guys like me, and maybe people assume I wouldn't want to be anyone else but a partner at a top law firm with a big house in Muttontown and five Ferraris."

"Six, now."

"Okay, six. I'm not saying I want to trade places, but I'm not early-retired like you, I'll still be working seventy hours a week five years from now. I'll croak in the saddle, looking right over Park Avenue. And I'll grant you there's always some hot ambitious broad wanting to have a wealthy guy for a boyfriend but it's no guarantee of having the love of a beautiful, good woman like Rita."

"Which I don't have either," I remind him, "plus no big bank account."

"You got Rita still thinking about you, you big dumb fuck. That counts for a lot right there. Don't try to say anything or pretend you're insulted. You're going over there now, I already can see it in your eyes. So when you see her tell her I'm not about to keep this with me. I don't need something around to pull out and depress me."

Richie takes my hand and slaps the engagement ring into it. I try to give it back to him, because I can already see Rita's face when she sees me with it, here's Jerry up to something low-down and dirty, some sly scheme whereby she'll be finessed into opening up a half inch too much and he'll instantly squinch himself in and inhabit the gap, but Richie steps back inside and closes the door on me, and when I tell him to open up he says, with heartache and defeat, "You already bought the ring with the car, Jerry. Now go away. She's all yours."

ALL YOURS, Jerome, all yours. I keep thinking this as Theresa drives away, to do some last-minute ingredient errands for Paul, leaving me on the sidewalk in front of the deep, narrow row house Rita rents the back half of so she can have her summer vegetable garden. This is a risky strategy, I know, to have yourself left seven miles from home at the doorstep of your ex-girlfriend's without a way to get back under your own power, but at the last second before begging Theresa to stand at the door with me I decide to play this one as straight as I can, for reasons not altogether clear. Perhaps I'm realizing that I've been too willing to share my life's loads with loved ones, never having the stomach to endure anything alone, how after Daisy died even given the tough circumstance I leaned way too hard on my mother and her sisters for help with the kids, and on Pop, too (at least as far as my livelihood went), and then soon thereafter on Rita, especially Rita, who never said a word and soldiered on raising Jack and Theresa through the hairy messes of adolescence, despite their lukewarm attitudes and provisionally stanced love and amazing chronic underappreciation of her cooking (at least until they returned home, respectively, after a couple months of college dining). But none of this was as bad as my daily, hourly, by-the-minute want of her total participation in all things me, her Jerry Husbandry, finding expression in even the most insignificant details I somehow got her to take care of, literally right down to the level spoon of sugar she'd stir into my morning coffee, the pat of butter she'd leave melting on my toast. Certainly I'd do any heavy lifting she asked for, but after our first couple years there really wasn't much of it, as the lawn care and hedging and the gutters and the snowblowing were contracted out, and though I could afford a housekeeper Rita ended up looking after the kitchen and bathrooms and the laundry and pressing, the only thing I did for her diligently being the food shopping, enjoying the early Saturday morning stroll down the aisles, ticking off items on the list she'd written out on the back of an old utility bill, rapt in the specter of that week's glorious meals.

One morning late in our relationship and maybe the thing that finally did us in, I returned from the supermarket to find her still in bed with her night shades on and aired some vague jackass comment about maybe getting something *done* today.

She popped up like a viper and laid into me like she'd been itching to do daily for a decade at least, saying how the only time I ever did something for her or anyone else without grousing or complaining or with a sour puss on was when there was a distinct possibility of some benefit to me, how in that way I was maybe—no, definitely—the most trivially needy, self-centered person she had ever met, that if she were verily on her deathbed and it was the lunch hour I probably couldn't help but ask her how she prepared her special egg salad with the diced black olives and sweet pickles and then bring the mixing bowl into the bedroom for a full-on demonstration.

That kind of smarted, to be sure, and as I went into a tortured and convoluted defense about trickle-down beneficiaries of a person's self-interest (I'm no Reaganite, being rabid about nothing, but still the theory has a natural attraction for me, given that the trickling aspect is just my sort of "work"), she stepped out of bed and came up from behind, tapping my shoulder, and whacked me square in the face with her pillow as I turned to make a point. It didn't hurt so much, of course, being more a shock than anything else, but this suddenly bloodthirsty look in her usually nurturing huge brown eyes did stun me into silence, and I'm not so sure she wouldn't have wielded whatever she grabbed first that morning, be it a pillow or a bat.

And even though there's probably no better time to go kissing up to her than now, when she's just cut loose from Richie and knocking about the house alone and maybe against all good judgment thinking fuzzily about us, this present near future of me standing here on the rickety back stoop of Rita's shotgun house holds a potentially dangerous outcome, and not because I think she might haul off and bonk me again. The reason is that she might just be tempted enough to let me have another taste, the circumstance of which, if it can't sustain, will certainly leave me in a desolated state. Theresa in her own stubborn manner has allowed me to remain in the rare air of some seriously aromatic denial (for which My Declining Self has been grateful, every day and every minute), but there's another part of me that doesn't care anymore if I can't help but see the loose grit and grub of this life, and risk something more intense than irritation or annoyance. It's the question of participation, again, though this time I'm slotted to practice it in a form wholly singular, unbolstered, which you'd think would be the highest manifest pride of a full-blooded American guy like me but has long been my greatest dread, save final extinguishment itself.

I can barely press hard enough to ring the bell.

Nothing happens, and I'm going to ring again, but in the next moment I find myself mincing down the steps to flee before any flak bursts erupt, already thinking of how I'm going to be walking all night to get back home, when I hear Rita say in her loamy autumnal voice, "I'm here, Jerry, I'm here."

She is wearing a loose white cotton dress, with a pretty lace pattern at the neck, sort of South-of-the-Border style, the sight of this and her dark-hued beauty reminding me of those raven-haired señoritas in the westerns, not the lusty barmaid or wizened hooker but the starry-eyed young village woman who endlessly carries jugs of water and wears a big silver cross and though captivated by the stoic gringo gunslinger come to save the town remains loyal in the end to her long-suffering peasant husband. But I'm no hero, and neither she nor her people ever needed any help, and if I had a hat I'd be holding it out for whatever lowly alms might be given, a ladle of water, a crust of bread, a slip of time beneath the shade tree out back, to gather myself before at last moving on.

"I don't mean to bother you," I say, suddenly feeling ashamed of myself. "I don't know what I'm doing. I'll leave you alone."

"How did you get here? I don't see your car."

"Theresa dropped me off."

"But she's gone," she says, her voice riding a hard edge.

"I know. It's my fault. It was stupid and I'm going."

"I'll call Theresa at the house."

"She's gone on errands. She won't be home for a couple hours, at least."

"I can call you a taxi, then. I can do that for you."

"You don't have to."

"What, Jerry, are you really going to walk home along the Expressway? You'll get hit. You're not going to put that one on me. I'll call a cab now. You can wait right there if you want."

"Okay, then."

She steps inside for what seems a long time, and enough for me to look around and notice that her garden is overgrown, the ground-hugging tomatoes spidery and wild for not having been regularly pinched back, the string beans and squashes too big for good eating, the basil and parsley long bolted and flowery, what almost everyone else's plot looks like late in the season but never Rita's, who kept her patch in the far western corner of my property looking like one of those serene, ultramanicured Japanese gardens, a miniaturized Eden of gently tended plants with their ripened issue gorgeously shining and pendant. Every summer but this one I waded daily through those rows, eating the vegetables right there, my roving live salad, Rita hardly able to make a full dish for my culling, though never in the least minding. She enjoyed the plain hard work of it (like with everything else she does), which is why the present sight disturbs me so, as if having to deal with guys like me and Richie has steadily depleted her hardihood and forced her to run too long on low battery; in fact as I look around it's all a bit forlorn, the small paint-flaked stoop unswept of dead bugs and leaves, the flowerpots empty save for hardened, white-speckled dirt, and I can't help but peer through the screen door to the counter of the tiny kitchen, weedy with mugs and plates, and mourn for her a little, knowing that this should be the golden period of Rita's life, being fifty and still beautiful, when she ought to be tasting the not-so-proverbial fruit of her good character and labors with a man she loves and who loves her back and is wise and generous enough not to waste another moment of her precious time.

"There's no cab available," she tells me, through the screen. "One's going to come, but not for an hour."

"Thanks. I'll wait out front."

"You don't have to do that, Jerry. I don't despise you, you know."

"I know."

"Besides, you can help me pack up some things."

"Pack up?"

"My lease is up this month, and I don't want to live here anymore."

I can't believe it's been a year, though at times it's seemed like ten. "What are you going to do?" I ask, stepping inside the kitchen. It's dark and cramped but still smells good, of mint and lemons. She's just made supersweet iced tea (her sole addiction, in every season) and unconsciously pours me a glass, the small automation of which would be enough to break my heart, if there weren't the uncertainty of where she might now go.

"I've looked at a couple places. They need experienced RNs pretty much everywhere, especially in the South and the West."

"You like Long Island."

"I thought I did. But why should I? I certainly don't like the crowds, or the roads. The people aren't very nice. I don't like to boat or fish. I'm starting to think it's the worst of all worlds, pushy, suburban, built-up, only shopping to do."

"But this is our world."

"Maybe yours, Jerry. I don't know. Kelly told me about Portland."

"In Maine?"

"Oregon. She said it's a nice small city, with friendly people, mild weather, mossy and woodsy. I checked. I could pack my clothes and throw a garage sale for the rest and get on a plane next week."

"You don't know a soul out there."

"Maybe that's better."

"Everybody is white."

"Everybody is white everywhere."

"But you have *family* here."

This stops her, for a moment, because of course she doesn't have anyone around in terms of blood relations, which has never seemed to bother her, but I think really has.

"I wish Theresa had stayed and visited," she says.

"It's my fault. She wanted to, but I told her I needed to see you alone."

"You said at Richie's she was in trouble. You never told me any details. Or was it just another Jerry story?"

"Maybe it was," I say, thinking how present matters (and the larger scheme, too) demand less complication, and not more. "But you should talk to her anyway."

"I will. How is Jack? I thought I saw him last week in that big black truck of his, driving out of the Lion's Den."

"That bar in Huntington?"

"I was meeting Kelly for lunch. I was parking, and I waved, and I thought he saw me, but he just drove off. Sort of wildly, in fact. He almost got into an accident."

"He's been out of whack, of late. Things haven't been so hot at Battle Brothers. You should really call him, too. But only if you want to."

"Of course I want to, Jerry!" she says, with due exasperation. "Don't you think it makes me unhappy, not to see them as much as I'm used to?"

"No one's keeping you away. I've never not asked you to come to something. Maybe I should have made sure I wasn't there."

"That would have helped."

"Okay, I got it. But Jack really needs you, I'm sure of it. He talks less and less to me. The last time he came by he was sort of drunk, so he said a few things, we yakked, it was pretty decent stuff. Maybe alarming, but decent. Otherwise it's pretty much hello and goodbye. Soon he's not even going to grunt at me, it'll just be all nods."

"What do you want him to say?" she says, though not in an accusatory tone.

"Maybe he could tell me how the business is falling apart. Or he could lie, give me a big cotton candy story. I don't care. Maybe he could tell me what those spoiled brats of his are up to, or what *objet* Eunice just bought for the house. He could tell me about my yard, which is what he did last time. Now, that was nice."

"Why am I not surprised to hear nothing about what you told or asked him?"

"That's not my job! And even if it were, what do I have to talk about? Nothing's ever different in my life, except for you and me, which he definitely does not want to discuss. He's the one who's young and in the thick of it. I had my turn of trouble. Or so I thought."

"You're always saying that, Jerry. Like you already had a lifetime of it with what happened to Daisy."

"I think that counts for a damn big share."

"Of course it does," she says, sitting down next to me at the half-sized corner breakfast table, close enough that our wrists almost touch. "But somehow you think nobody else has ever had similar difficulties."

"That's not true. And hey, I've never whined or gone on about it, have I?"

"No," Rita agrees. "You haven't mentioned Daisy more than a dozen times since I've known you, and maybe just once or twice referred to *that.* But everything you do—or don't want to do, more like—has an origin in what happened to Daisy, which at this point is really what happened to *you.*"

"It did happen to me!"

"But it's never ceased for you, Jerry. You look to spread the burden all the time. Everybody is a potential codependant, though with you they hardly know it. You're sneaky, that way. When I wanted to have a baby, what did you say to me?"

"That was a long time ago, sweetie. Who can remember?"

"I'll refresh your memory. It was my thirty-seventh birthday, and we were having dinner at The Blue Schooner."

"Gee, that was a fancy place. Huge shrimps in the shrimp cocktail."

"Of course you remember that."

"Okay. I don't know. Probably something about my being too old and tired to raise another kid."

"Not quite," she says icily. "You said *I* was too old and tired."

"Not a chance. I'm not that stupid."

"Actually you were trying to be helpful. It was your way of saying I should be enjoying my youth instead. Traveling a lot and dancing and staying out late. The thing was that I was already raising Jack and Theresa, which I was happy for and never felt bad about or regretted. I loved those kids even if they didn't quite love me."

"They loved you, and they love you now."

"Oh, I know, I know. The thing that makes me crazy is that I knew then that you weren't thinking of me, of my potentially lost youth. You just naturally wanted to ensure you had me available to go places with."

"Look, if you had insisted on having a baby, I would have agreed."

"Right! You might have said okay but you would have pissed and moaned all through the pregnancy and after the baby arrived been a total grouch every time it peeped. I should have left you then, because I really did want a baby, but for some reason I'll never understand I thought I would only have it with you. I'm a total bimbo fool."

"Don't say that."

"It's the truth."

"Maybe you loved me a little, too."

"Maybe."

"I'll make it up to you."

"What, Jerry, you're offering to knock me up?"

"Sure. Right now, if you want."

Rita laughs, though wearily, like it's the thousandth time from me she's heard it all. "Well you know how old I am, Jerry. And you're sixty."

"Nearly sixty."

"Nearly sixty. Together that's a lot of mileage on my eggs, and your sperm."

"A woman older than you just had a kid, she was, like, fifty-seven. They can work miracles now with the hormone drugs."

"That's a crime, not a miracle. Anyway, ours would definitely come out with three heads."

"As long as it's happy."

"Do you think that's remotely possible?"

"I think it's very possible."

Rita quietly sips her iced tea, as do I, the window fan around the corner in the living room sounding like a monk droning on in the misty, craggy-hilled distance. It's his only song, and he's telling me to keep still, to shut my mouth, to be bodiless and pure, to not spoil this moment with the usual spoutings of ruinous want and craving, my lifelong mode of consumption, to sit before this lovely woman of epic-scaled decency whom I desperately love and let the bloom just simply tilt there before me, leave it be in the light, undisturbed, unplucked. And if ever I could manage such a thing (if there be Mercy), it should by all rights be at the present moment, when I'm as conscious as I'll ever be of what Rita means (and not solely to me). But what do I do but corral her shoulder and supple neck and deeply kiss her, kiss her, like I've been imagining I would do for the last dim colorless half year, taste the soft pad of her lips, her perennially lemony breath, while in parallel process steeling myself for the next second's indubitable turn, the repulsed insulted shove-off. What happens, though, is exactly not that, for while she's not pressing into me she's also not quite pulling back, and when I sneak a peek through my bliss-shut eyes I see that she's closed hers extra tight, like someone who's about to get a flu shot, and maybe her heart's thinking is that she'll endure this unpleasant but soon invaluable inoculation, the little sickness that wards off the permanently crippling disease.

"Oh, Jerry, what are we doing?"

"We're making love."

"I don't think so."

"Give it a chance."

"I don't want to."

But she lets me kiss her again, and I don't have to be loony to think that she's kissing me the tiniest bit in return, reversing the flow, and then just like that we're standing back in the living room, her arms hanging straight down in a fast-diminishing wish of neutrality, with me holding on to her sides just north of where her hips jut out, my favorite spot no doubt because it was the first patch of her I ever touched; and who but all regular fellows like me (and the occasional Sapphist gal, too) can understand the achy bottoming-out feeling in your variety meats as I glean the gauzy cotton dress for the stringy banding of her panty, this bare narrow line of everyperson's dreams.

Rita turns her face away and buries it in my neck, as if she can't bear to meet my eyes out of shame and self-disbelief, such that I can almost hear her mind going *Idiot I am he's such a slime,* and so it occurs to me that I should hug her as tightly and chastely as I know how, which I do, and in mid-clutch she sort of cracks, literally, her spine aligning with the sudden gravity, and I pretty much carry her to the sofa before I ease her up onto it, hands cupping her thighs, head in her throat, rubbing my face in the heat-heavy spot of her wishbone, the tiny redolent dugout I've tasted thousands of times. And if I could remake myself into just that shape and size it's right here I think I would forever reside.

After a while she says, breathless, "The taxi's going to come."

"I'm on it," I answer, stumbling back into the kitchen. I pull a $20 bill from my wallet and flag it with a stickup note (*Sorry buddy!!*) and close it in the door.

"Let's stop now," she says, when I return.

"All right," I say, but already I'm all over her, making her lie back, her dress nicely crumpling, and after another while she's all over me, roughly, almost angrily, like a woman possessed. I know she's missed me some, too, because she's liberally using her mouth, the diverse songs of which of course I preternaturally love but which always ultimately lend for me a somewhat sorrowful undertone to the production (besides the depraved one instilled early on by my nun-based education), and I pull her up to kiss her and we wrestle out of our clothes. Soon we're in the familiar saddling of our bodies, girl on top but not yet conjoined, hers still amazingly youthful if definitely fleshier than I recall, thicker around the middle and the upper arms and thighs, while I, looking down at myself, am this odd-sectioned hide of pale and tan, flabby and skinny except for my gut, the only remotely vital thing being my thing itself, darkly hued, though only decently angled, in truth looking a bit like something trapped under plastic wrap, reduced for quick sale. Rita maybe senses this, for she grasps it like an old airplane stick, arcing us into a slow and steady climb, and I can't help but wonder aloud, "How was he?"

"Richard?"

"Yeah."

"What are you asking?"

I nod. "You know."

"Jesus, Jerry."

"I can ask."

"No, you can't."

"But you can tell me."

"Richard was twice the gentleman you are," she says, a spiteful cast in her eyes.

"And?"

"Okay," she says, gripping down hard. "Maybe only half the man."

I'm pretty sure she's lying, but it doesn't matter in the least, for this is an instance when it really is the thought that counts, and it shows, for suddenly I feel as if I'm giant, as if I have a one-and-only axis, ruddering me blindly to a star, and I whisper, "Do you want to?"

"A-hum," she barely whispers back. She kneels up and lifts herself, her breast sway more pronounced than I remember, showing a bit more travel, which is no awful thing at all. I take a heft of each as she guides us toward the cloistered inlet, our trusty craft hugging the shore, and it's no surprise I feel like I'm encapsulated in the moment, in this module of my dreams, knowing it's of little use or consequence to be still doggedly working the controls. For Rita is the one who's in command, suspending us now in an eddy, for which I'm actually glad, for even at my age I don't know if I can withstand that first quick plunge (it's been a long time, dammit), and it's telling that I wouldn't mind if we simply stayed in this most intimate contiguity, just hugging, which perhaps reveals the truth of what they say happens even to guys like me, that you go soft first and foremost in the mind, long before the rigging ever fails.

Rita stares me in the eyes. She doesn't want to know whether it'll be another story this time around, because of course in fact it won't be, and rather than some set of hard questions for me is what basic thing she sees she needs that I, in my chronic lack of empathy and wisdom, still somehow manage to provide; I fear

I'm now present at the moment of some sober mutual recognition, which in my late reckoning is perhaps the surest sign of any lasting love. Rita grabs the back of my neck and lowers herself down, down, our fit familiarly cosseted and snug, and for a few seconds neither of us really tries to shift or move or start a rhythm. But then the doorbell rings, somebody's at the back, and this gets us going in a nicely syncopated time; it *ring-rings* again and I call out that I left some money and don't need the cab. The voice that I hear calling back sounds much like Theresa's, which I don't expect and so ignore. But she calls again and Rita, realizing who it is, quickly climbs off.

"It's your daughter, Jerry, go let her in."

I get up, but given my indecent state (the situation reminding me of those mornings when I had to wait out my wake-up wood beneath the covers while the kids jumped all over me and Daisy in our bed), I shake my head, and so Rita tosses my trousers onto me and quickly pulls on her cotton dress. As they greet one another with warm cheer and chuckles, my situation naturally wanes, and by the time they walk back to the living room I'm mostly dressed, tucking in the tail of my Battle Brothers logo polo shirt.

"Sorry to crash the party, guys," Theresa says.

"Of course you're not," Rita offers, almost motherly in her abashedness. "You want some iced tea, honey?"

"That'd be great, I'm parched."

Rita heads to the kitchen.

"What's the matter?" I say, searching Theresa's face. "You feeling okay?"

"I'm perfect," she answers. "But there is a problem."

"Okay."

"It's Pop," she says, a bit too softly. "I called on the way home and spoke to Paul. He said that Ivy Acres was trying to reach you, and after a little work he convinced them to tell him what was wrong."

"Okay."

Rita comes back and hands Theresa a glass. We stand there, waiting.

"It seems that Pop has run away."

"What do you mean, *run away*?"

"He's AWOL, I guess. They think since yesterday at dinner."

"They think? They haven't seen him for nearly a whole day?"

"I was wondering that myself," Theresa says. "I called them while I was driving back here, but nobody would talk to me, since they only have you as the stated guardian. But I know from Paul that they haven't yet called the police."

"I'm calling now," Rita says, standing at the hall phone. "I have a friend at the county sheriff's office. He'll know what to do."

"Where the hell could he have gone?" I say. "He doesn't even have a wallet anymore. How did he get anywhere? He can't walk more than a few blocks."

Theresa says, "Maybe there's a mall bus that leaves from there. If we're lucky, he's probably just sitting in a Banana Republic."

"Jesus, let's hope. We better go to the nursing home right now."

I stop and kiss Rita as we leave. I tell her, "Please don't pack. Please don't move. Don't do anything. At least not until I sort this out. Okay? Okay?"

Rita nods, not quite looking me in the eyes, and then gives Theresa a quick deep hug. Then she gives me one, too, with a little extra, and while this should do nothing but hearten and calm, I have the awful flash of an idea that this is the last I'll ever see her. Here we are, just brushed by passion, certainly back on my plotted-out course, and all I can think to do is take one mind-picture after another of her brown sugar eyes, and her brown sugar cheeks, and the uncertain tumbles of her thick, coally hair. Yes, here's a beautiful woman. And when soon thereafter my daughter and I are back in the front bench of the softtop, though now with me at the wheel, opening up the big-chambered engine, the old rumble so bold and booming you'd think we could fly, I have to ask, Why should this be? Why now? But there's no answer to that. Just this: here is the Real, all Jerry's, all mine.

ten

I USED TO HAVE NEIGHBORS down the street named Guggenheimer, George and Janine, a couple right around my age with a bunch of kids and longhaired dogs. They moved in just after Daisy died and lived there for eight or so years. From my point of view they were a happy, sprawly, boisterous lot, always playing lawn darts or Wiffle ball, the hounds racing around and almost knocking over the kids, George and Janine constantly attending to their house (the same ranch model as mine), either sweeping up or landscaping. Despite what seemed their constant activity, the yard front and back (they had a corner lot) was always kind of a mess, pocked with plastic toys and dropped rakes and bags of Bark-O-Mulch and lime. It really didn't bother me at all, because after a while as a professional landscaper you get sick of the totally clipped and manicured look, and don't mind a guy who looks after his property himself, even if he does it half-assed and badly, which is how George Guggenheimer did it, though with obvious ambition for the place, given all the projects he'd start. There was the new paver brick walkway, and the hedge of arborvitae, and then undoubtedly the most difficult thing he tried, which was the koi pond in the backyard, spanned by a miniature Japanese-style bridge.

The paver brick walkway turned out okay, if you wanted to be charitable, mostly because you couldn't see it from the street. Up close it was completely uneven and buckled, some spots so high or low that you could hardly go the length without stubbing your toe and tripping. The arborvitae hedge lasted about three weeks after he put it in, about thirty ten-gallon plants, the victim of both too shallow planting and overwatering.

Naturally I'd given him some neighborly advice about both projects and he even wrote down some of the finer points but I suppose in the end it's about execution and attention to detail and George wasn't the kind of guy you'd let hammer a nail you were holding, or maybe even dig you a hole. This last skill was part of the problem with the koi pond, which looked great to start, with fat orange and pearl-colored koi and blooming water lilies and a faux-rock waterfall that played Hawaiian-style music whenever someone approached. It was George's finest hour, but only for about a week. The pond began to drain after one of his older boys tried to guillotine a koi with a garden spade, missing of course and slicing through the liner. I advised George to completely empty the thing and patch the liner when it was totally dry but he went ahead with some supposedly special underwater "glue" he found at a pool supply store and proceeded to kill all the fish (they bloated up and turned black in the face). This would have been okay had he stopped right there, but the younger kids were crying all day about the poor dead fish and Janine was pissy and probably withholding sex because of the moody kids, and George decided next in his know-nothing homeowner wisdom to cut out the part he'd glued. He ended up punching a hole in the underlying concrete shell he'd laid in too thin to begin with, discovering in the process a large sinkhole right next to the pond hole, where the old septic system had been and mostly still was. He would have done something about that had he not had the egregious fortune of having a wicked summer storm surge in that night, raging with lightning and thunder and three inches of rain. In the morning the sky was perfectly clear, the ceiling unlimited, though I knew something was awry because when I picked up the paper at the end of the driveway I could smell an epic rot, like some dirt of prehistory, and when I walked over there after breakfast a crowd of neighbors had already gathered at the back of George's house, all holding their noses, peering into what had been a smooth back lawn but was now a huge jagged trench running from where the koi pond had been all the way to the street, the Japanese bridge smashed in half and lying mud-soaked in the trench. Really, you could have filmed *All Quiet on the Western Front* right there at the Guggenheimers'.

George was down about it certainly but with extra mopiness, and after the crowd thinned out and the sewer guys told him the ballpark figure for the job he took me aside and said he might not survive this one. I told him to laugh it off and just write the check (just the way you would blithely say in any "nice" neighborhood with a bit of resignation and no veiled pride), that he'd fix the mess and get another koi pond, this one bigger, but he just shook his head and sat down on the wet lawn and in a real breach of suburban decorum began to bawl like a baby. I crouched down beside him and held his shoulder for a half minute until he piped down a little, and I told him the way I used to tell all my worried, scared clients (and there wasn't anybody who wasn't), in my laconic captain-of-the-squad way to pull it together because this was one we were going to win. I immediately regretted using "we" because he hugged me with his sloppy face and I think he assumed that maybe I'd get the guys from Battle Brothers over with a couple of earthmovers and backhoes and roll out fresh sod. Before I could say anything else or backpedal he said they were financially shot. I asked him what he meant by that because like everybody else it seemed the Guggenheimers were spending what they pleased and on what they wanted and so that automatically meant they were making the money, too, but he said it again, they were shot, fucking shot, the directness of which surprised me, as you never hear in neighborhoods like this how everything was about to fall apart.

I felt bad about it, which automatically meant that I would call him the next day to "check in" and commiserate from a distance and then promptly make myself scarce for two or three weeks, which is exactly what I did, your basic poor-fuck-but-damn-glad-it-ain't-me routine, but then it happened that the very night after the koi pond debacle George stopped for a gallon of milk at the Dairy Barn and bought a lottery ticket and won, won pretty big, not one of those mega-million games but a kind of jackpot they don't seem to offer anymore, where you get a set amount of money each year for as long as you live. It was promoted with a slogan like "Salary for Life," and was $100,000 a year paid with a wink every Labor Day, an amount that in those days wasn't just plain vanilla upper-middle-class living, and for the Guggenheimers it was a ticket to ride high. Like me, George had inherited his livelihood from his parents, in his case a couple of long-established dry-cleaning stores in Kissena Park, Queens, but he'd done a thorough job of running them into the ground, not to mention ignoring the new competition from all the Korean and Chinese owners coming in. The truth of the matter, as he told me the day before, was he'd been planning to sell the businesses and get into some other line (what that was going to be he didn't say), because he was out of equity and cash and was carrying a hefty debt on his ranch house and the cleaners, and was just about to step into the crosshairs of the collection agencies and banks, which is exactly the appropriate time in our good culture to throw away your last few bucks on a 20-million-to-1 shot.

There was a short segment about the Guggenheimers on the *Eyewitness News,* George and Janine looking sweaty and stunned as they held either end of a big cardboard check, the amount for which I noticed wasn't a number but a question mark followed by a lot of zeroes, the point being the sky was the limit. Right away they sold the dry-cleaning stores (to Koreans, of course) and did the smart thing and paid off their most pressing debts, consolidating the others through one of those sketchy New Jersey mortgage outfits, and then setting about to fix the sinkhole in their backyard. But soon enough the spending geared up. They hired Battle Brothers to bulldoze and clear-cut the property and plant and lay everything in totally fresh. George traded in his old cars for a couple of brand-new Mercedes convertibles, his (silver) and hers (red), and when they went out as a family they had to take both cars and jam the kids in each.

Janine it turned out was very much into modern art and design and began buying a lot of stuff from local galleries, sculptures of figures either really skinny or really fat as well as Cubist-style and Abstract-ed paintings featuring the same kind of figures, and furniture from Maurice Villency and Roche-Bobois that was sleek in form and always cold and uncomfortable, the program in fact not so dissimilar to what Eunice has done over at Château Battle. The house itself was completely razed and done over and in the end not so strangely it was almost an exact replica of the Guggenheim Museum, ⅕ scale, with a big circular parking garage–inspired turret dominating the massing and hardly any windows. The concurrences didn't in the least occur to Janine or George, as neither had been to the museum, nor by extension any surname irony, the facts of which made you pull for them all the more, as they were simply enjoying the found fruits of their good luck.

And maybe it would have all gone swimmingly, had George not been involved in a frightening little car accident just before another year had passed. While driving on the Southern State Parkway he was rear-ended, the front of his convertible accordioned in, too, when he was thrust into the car in front. George was banged up pretty badly and got forty stitches in his face and hands and spent a night at the hospital for observation of his concussion. After a few days he was fine but I suppose he got to thinking about his brush with death and what that would mean for his Salary for Life, and pretty soon you hardly saw him driving and then even walking in the neighborhood. He called me up one day and asked if Battle Brothers could put up an eight-foot chain-link fence around the entire property, which we did, and he had house alarms and cameras rigged up, and before long he was hardly ever outside in his own yard, fearing that he'd catch some deadly virus like AIDS, which was just coming into the news then and was still mysterious enough to keep you wondering. George even began to stay airlocked in his private bedroom suite (he'd moved out of the master because Janine was naturally venturing out to shop and ferry the kids around and see friends, and was thus a ready importer of contagion), and grew more and more distrusting and fearful of anything having to do with the outside world. So it came as no surprise that after a year of this Janine divorced him, taking the kids to what I hear is a nice gated golf community in North Carolina, where Janine looks after the central clubhouse. George still owns the house, I believe, though he moved out long ago, to where nobody knows.

Of course, I'm thinking about George at the present moment not because I had so much feeling for him (which I did, aplenty, in a knowing, down-the-street neighborly way that had to do with our shared existence of familial and realty responsibilities), but because I, perhaps like George Guggenheimer, am beginning to see this sprawly little realm as laden with situations not simply dangerous and baleful; it's the fact that no matter how fast or high you might keep moving, the full array of those potentialities are constantly targeting your exact coordinates, and with extreme prejudice. And while this is self-absorption in the classical mode, I must admit Rita was right, I did think I'd banked a life's worth of slings and arrows after Daisy, maybe even enough to safeguard the next generation, maybe to wash back, too, on the one previous. But Theresa's illness and now my father's almost magical disappearance are new instructions from above (or below or beyond), telling me in no uncertain terms that I cannot stay at altitude much longer, even though I have fuel to burn, that I cannot keep marking this middle distance.

I am not even mentioning the latest turns in Jack's financial totterings, which compared to these other potential calamities would seem downright welcome if they were the only things we had to consider and deal with, but, to be honest, something about his trouble pushes me right up to the very limits of my tolerances for what life can sometimes unsparingly orchestrate. With Jack it has to do certainly with the issue of legacy, namely the fucking-up of said thing, which if we come right down to it is what we secretly find most compelling about legacies (yes, even our own), not the pleasures of bestowal or some rite cycle of being, but rather the surprise diminution that in the not-so-fetching opera of our lives comes in the inglorious rushed finale, the wondrous aria by a brash new tenor, who can hit every soaring note except the one that counts. For there's nothing as deeply stirring as familial failure, cast across time.

And the skinny of that failure is this: Jack has sunk the ship. If I may be business-channel-like about it, let me say that he is accomplishing it with a highly effective one-pronged strategy of capital overinvestment. Namely, everything he has been buying for the company, from the new cube vans to the five-ton haulers to the mini-backhoes (equipment we always leased per job or week or perhaps for the season at most), he has been buying outright with the idea that Battle Brothers would be subleasing to itself (in the form of paper subsidiaries) in a complicated (and no doubt semilegal) cash flow optimization/accelerated depreciation scheme that he did not bother to vet with crusty old Sal, dealing directly instead with an offshore banking firm registered in the Caymans or Nigeria or Uzbekistan or some other such "republic" where generally accepted accounting principles are held in an esteem equal to whatever national constitution was drawn up for them by do-gooding wonks at the IMF. Not that I understand exactly what's happened, but the result is that with the long-anticipated slowdown in work (due to the sluggish economy, plus the intense competition of late, as every hammerhead and his ADD-afflicted, Dremel-wielding brother have gotten into the home improvement business in the last ten years), he's no longer able to pay off the debt service on the machines and getting no real or even "accounting" profit back, meaning he's sinking in shit both ways. This would not be so big a problem if he could sell the rigs anywhere near cost but everybody demands a huge discount these days and it's almost not worth bothering, except that there's a whole bunch of office equipment and technology and software and other high-priced gizmos that become obsolete a few seconds after you plug them in, which it turns out nobody wants at any price, and that Battle Brothers seems to own enough of to open our very own Staples store.

The other day, for a minor example, when secretly called in by Sal to look over the ledgers for myself, I happened to stub my toe on what I figured was a funky coffee table Eunice had ordered up at full suggested retail but was actually a gross case of five or ten thousand floppy disks, brand-new and still in the shrink-wrap, meant originally for backing up every last transaction of our business. They now have been superseded of course by compact disks that hold many multiples the data and will be cheaper eventually though not soon enough for us. Predictably I happened upon in the supply room gathering dust the floppy disk drives that were recently changed out, piled forlornly with their cables hanging out and tangled like the viscera you used to see troughs of at the butcher's, though all those sloppy kibbles and bits were turned into something somebody somewhere wanted, and duly *got*, eventually, whether they knew it or not. All of which makes you sort of worry if our wondrous civilization has evolved to the point that we've somehow abrogated that particular law of thermodynamics concerning the conservation of all energy and matter, as it seems that what we're coming up with now is made so that it can't possibly be used or reintegrated after the initial burn. It's pure by-product from the start, slickly marketed and apotheosized as essential for mass sale to a well-meaning guy like Jack Battle, and finally reposed as mere foot fodder.

I've already detailed the extensive corporate headquarters–style renovations to our once humble garage, costs that surprisingly were not mortgaged and amortized as they normally should have been but instead (for the purpose of a discount negotiated by Eunice) outlayed in cold hard cash, cold hard cash something the business is quite low on in reserves, so low in fact that our usually cuddly banker at Suffolk National has begun sending chilly missives concerning our insufficient and recently missed payments on the seven-figure note Jack took out shortly after I stepped down from the helm. Apparently Jack has been attempting to refinance this hefty note (okay, it's $3 million, twice as much as Sal suspected), but even in this age of before-you-even-ask-for-it credit he hasn't yet found any takers, partly because he spent way too much for a nicely treed four-acre parcel of land directly behind our property (he was itchy for a major expansion right from the get-go), though mostly because the property itself has come under suspicion of being an environmental hazard.

I'd always feared it was our original property that might go afoul certain green regulations and standards, but it seems the previous owner of the new plot had a big-time commercial photofinishing business in Hicksville. For the past twenty-five years he dumped the chemicals and other liquid unsavories from interests he had in a string of instant-lube centers into an old well on the property, which he neatly bulldozed over and sealed and covered with fill and fresh sod. This would be bad enough except that the local homeowners whose properties abut in a ring this new one of ours are now filing a lawsuit claiming health problems (one of whom not so ironically being that girlfriend of mine from youth, Rose Cahill, who actually lives in that same house now with *not one but two* supposedly autistic adult sons), their experts and also now county and state and probably soon federal environmental safety inspectors drilling for soil samples and testing surrounding well water for heavy metals and radicalized chemicals and oils, such that our nice big little family business with its surfeit of plant and equipment is now, given the potential liabilities, worth pretty much zilch.

Though Sal, bless his randy old soul, insists this isn't quite as bad as it sounds.

Apparently there are certain protections having to do with declaring bankruptcy that will shield us for a while from legal action and foreclosure, plus we now have our own representation, too, serving notice to both Mr. Mercury Water and our alarmist neighbors, namely (this time), mirabile dictu, Richard Anthony Coniglio, Esq., who was completely gentlemanly when I (ready to grovel, ready to beg) phoned him. Richie instantly conferenced me in on a call to his underlings, scrambling those fast jet associates Kim-ster and Kenton from the deck of the Fortune 50 multinational they've been defending (against the outrageous claims of some greedy supposedly ruined Micronesian fishing village) and vectored them screaming into our own modest fray.

The key now, of course, is to delay and delay and delay, and delay some more, let everything and everyone stew in the procedural stays that we litigious Americans have perfected into high performance art. Richie has even been so generous as to offer to bill us only for his associates' hours, and not his own, and though it's unclear *pro* exactly what/whose *bono* is inspiring him into such magnanimousness, I would like to think it's a feeling that we're alumni of sorts, brothers from the old neighborhood and even linked via Rita in that way men are when they do all they can to crush each other and only then intimately glimpse the reflection of their own vulnerability. Probably closer to the truth is that we're at the general point in our lives when almost all the heaviest lifting has been done, and you can finally begin to measure yourself not solely by the usual units of accomplishment but by the plain stupid luck of your draw in a macrocosm rigged with absolutely nothing particular about you in mind.

One might be wondering how it is that I've learned about these goings-on, given that I haven't talked at all to Jack since he came by the house last, which is certainly the case, and I could say that Sal has been the mostly disinterested informer and go-between and facilitator, which is also the case; but it should be no surprise to anyone who has been a father or a son, or for that matter born into any kind of real family at all, to hear that Jack and I haven't discussed said huge subject, or endured any lingeringly awkward moments because of it, or even plied each other with subtle, passive aggressions that would steadily accrue on the cellular level until one or both of us up and burst in a cascade of recrimination and vitriol. For all I can see, he's continued to show at work each day at 6 A.M. sharp and gone about addressing Total Dissolution with some help from Sal while making no attempt to hide from me what's been happening, knowing full well that I know full well, and not agonizing (at least publicly) about what any of us might think. Of course, I don't know what's going on in his head, or in his household (though I'm almost certain Eunice has no inkling, as she'd have been all over me with directives from her command-and-control center of a pearlescent white Range Rover); whatever he's thinking or feeling I do have to say, gotta say, that I'm kind of proud of the boy, goddammit, not for fucking everything up of course but for soldiering on as he has, for just trudging ahead with old-fashioned head-down dignity, plowing forward like one of those ice-breaking ships in the Arctic, whose prow is harder than it is sharp.

Too bad that what lies ahead in the visible horizon are just floes and more floes, with ice fields re-forming in his wake, supplies and fuel running dangerously low, and morale undoubtedly dwindling besides (the Discovery Channel, it turns out, does indeed corroborate with life on the ground); and although I've said I'm at a limit as to what I can stand to witness, the first question for yours truly must be why I'm not doing more to bear necessary heat upon this situation. Pop, in my place, would certainly rain fear and misery upon Jack's suppliers, and lay off half the crews and the entire office staff (except Sal, who would have to answer the phones, too), fire-sell anything that couldn't otherwise be used to dig a ditch or lay in brick or fix one of the machines, and then force-feed the Suffolk National guy and his wife double porterhouses and vanilla-y merlot at Ruth's Chris, instead of perching here as I am in my God seat and bemoaning, bemoaning. Truth is, Pop would be referring to this as Our Problem, Our Mutual Assured Destruction, Our Shit Sundae, and he'd be digging in with the same gusto he'd have for my mother's self-admittedly mediocre cooking (*"You're welcome to make the sauce"*), which he groused about nightly but always accepted seconds of, and even thirds; vis-à-vis Jack, even at his age he would have thundered with disbelief and anger but then stood by him and taken on whatever load needed bearing and generally gotten hopped up on the disaster of it all, because, unlike me, he could never stop believing in the significance of the enterprise, he could never look on that stolid grimy box of a four-bay garage and see anything but the shape of a glorious lifework which the Fratelli Battaglia literally put up one brick at a time.

Jerry Battle, it must appear, can let the mortar pit and crumble. He can stand by and watch the gutters overflow, the water pooling against the foundation. He can gaze yet a thousandth time upon the buckles becoming waves in the asphalt yard, only to pick up the phone and speed-dial ahead for his three-soft-taco lunch. And though all of this (semi-) metaphorical illustration is pretty much the bare fact of it, and frankly how I had always wanted it to be, duly punched out for the very last time, *no matter what*, I can't now loll around and let Jack sink lower in the icy water, and not because I give a hoot about Battle Brothers. I don't. I never did. Pop always knew that, but he didn't mind, because through luck and happenstance and my sagely ever-passive hand, business tended to get done. So it squarely depresses me now to think that Jack might have thought I *did* care, which has to be my fault entirely, and perhaps explains the lengths he's gone to trying to make the business worth more than it ever possibly could be worth. No doubt that I should have derided his interest when he was in college and asked to work summers for us; I should have mocked it as dummy's work, an idiot's errands, said anything that might have plumbed his core anxiety about himself, which he has always harbored, instead of letting him join and then eventually become foreman of one of the landscaping crews, and then hang out after they rolled back in at the end of the day and drink beer with the mechanics, when he was the boss's son but a regular guy and so maybe too readily accepted and admired.

And while I know Jack was never headed for a fancy law associate's position like Richie's Ivy League minions, or was an intellectual sort like his sister, I'm damn sure that he could have made a perfectly fine sales rep for one of those big pharmaceutical companies, or a valued young executive in some corporate human resources department, taken full advantage of his athlete's natural poise and fealty to the team for the cause of genteel and estimable profit. That would have been good by me, for sure, though I must acknowledge, too, that I never pushed Jack away from Battle Brothers too assiduously, namely because—surprise, surprise—I actually didn't mind the idea of his taking over someday, if that somehow meant Pop would get and stay off my back about The Future, thereby committing the sin of tendering one generation's dreams for the illusory expectations of another, which is no doubt a practice wretched, and shameful, if time-honored.

I'M NOODLING all this about at the moment, or trying not to and failing, sitting here on Pop's made-up bed in his room at Ivy Acres. I'm waiting for the head administrator to drive back in from his home in Cold Spring Harbor after normal business hours and explain to me how an eighty-five-year-old man with limited mobility walks off a twenty-acre campus without a trace and then isn't missed for an entire night and day. He's going to do so because I've threatened his assistant that otherwise he'll be speaking exclusively to a jodhpur-clad partner of Whitehead Bates in the morning, and the duly confused/impressed assistant immediately slipped off to a secure phone and called his boss.

Jack, meanwhile, has gotten it into his head that he's going to drive around the county checking the bus depots and diners and the dozen or so local Starbucks shops because Pop had their coffee once and thought it was a revelation and might now make some kind of crazy coot pilgrimage there, as if he were going to hire on as a barista before he kicked off, which after I considered for a second didn't seem that far-fetched a notion.

Paul has accompanied me to Ivy Acres for moral support, but after an hour of waiting here in Pop's room he's all but talked out on the incompetence of institutional structures and systems and turned on the television instead, switching with the jump button at the commercials between the Discovery Channel (Wild Predators) and HGTV (Before and After renovations). The combination, as you might expect, proves remarkably soothing to yours truly, as all I need to forget everything else is a good meaty nature channel show where the ants and the termites are about to wage total arthropodan war.

"I only like the Before," Paul says. "At least the old place had some wool to it. Some shagginess. Now everything looks as if it's been bikini-waxed."

"Most people like that."

"I guess. What bugs me even more is how they had no qualms about destroying everything, even the good stuff, like that great fireplace."

"That was a beauty."

"Sure it was. You know better than anybody that you can't buy that old brick anymore. And the newel posts of the staircase. Did you see how that guy took his sledgehammer to those? He found that pleasurable."

"He *was* loving it."

"No kidding," Paul says, getting excited, maybe even agitated. "There's no respect anymore. People want what they want and they want it now. Nothing comes before them, literally or in time. Everyone is Client Zero."

"Numero Uno," I say.

"Chairman Me."

"A Solo Flyer."

"Exactly," Paul says. "They think they can go anywhere and do anything, as if none of their actions has any bearing except on themselves, like they're in their own mini-biosphere, all needs self-providing, everything self-contained, setting it up like God would do himself. It doesn't matter that there are people on the outside tapping at the glass, saying, 'Hey, hey, I'm here. Look out here.'"

This stops me for a second, as he's striking closer to home than I'd prefer. Then I realize why Paul isn't quite acting like himself, which I assumed had to do with Pop being missing and all of us feeling anxious and moody. He's talking not about me but about his wife, Theresa, who, if you think about it, has done a pretty spiffy job of shutting out any chance of real inquiry, any real debate, who hasn't let by more than a few loose atoms of dissent, the only surprise here being that you'd think her seriously empathic prose-poet husband would have been asked to help steer from the beginning.

Theresa was feeling a bit tired, and so despite her wanting to come along I'd somewhat forcefully suggested she remain back at the house, just in case Pop managed to make his way there. In fact I scolded her, finally getting sick of her merely humoring my opinions. This I feel bad about, as she's looking washed-out of late, as though the blood isn't being fully pumped to all parts of her body. Her coloring is all wrong, her face appearing as if it were lighted from within by an old fluorescent tube, an unsteady flicker in her usually bright eyes. And I should really say she's been feeling tired all the time, though of course not breathing a word of complaint; I've just noticed her lingering a bit, in whatever armchair she's sitting in, or leaning with discernible purpose against the kitchen counter, or sometimes not showing up at all for breakfast, even after Paul goes back to their bedroom to let her know the herbed omelets are ready. In fact I would say she's not eating half the food she normally would, with Paul and me taking up the slack, as evidenced by our sudden fullness of gut and cheek.

Sometime last week I went into their bedroom after they'd gone out to shop for maternity clothes, as I was searching for some of the Cessna manuals in the closet, and noticed crumpled in the wastepaper basket a threefold informational booklet like the kind you see in plastic holders beside the magazines in the doctor's office, though this one you probably got from the doctor himself in the privacy of the exam room. It was a general introduction and overview of symptoms and treatment of non-Hodgkin's disease, which is among the most treatable of cancers, assuming, of course, that it *is* treated, with some combination of surgery and radiation and chemotherapy, depending on the particular stage and expression of the disease. But the thing that got me was a single-sheet insert that was also crumpled up inside the booklet, titled "Non-Hodgkin's and Pregnancy." This basically outlined what a pregnant woman would normally do, with those in the first trimester advised to terminate the pregnancy and pursue treatment, with those others postponing treatment—and only if the disease were slow-developing—delivering early (32nd to 36th week) by cesarean, then immediately employing a vigorous regimen to attack the disease. Theresa is just now into her 22nd week, obviously making no plans for anything other than a full-term delivery. It isn't hard to figure out that she's doing none of the recommended above (no matter the progression of the cancer, which might be spreading to who knows where), and judging by how tightly the literature was balled up, is not about to stray from her self-charted course. If I think about it, this episode with Pop has at its best provided a diversion from my children's troubles, diversion being perhaps the most ideal state of existence.

"Perhaps the best thing," Paul says, looking nearly angry now, his fleshy cheeks ruddy with vim, "is that pretty soon we won't have any true Befores, only Afters, shiny and virtual Afters. This host won't have one decent thing left to destroy, and he'll have no choice but to cancel the show."

"Maybe it'll be called After the After," I say.

"After the After doesn't exist," Paul says grimly. "Not for me anyway."

"Sure it does," I say, instantly sounding a bit too much like I'm trying to convince myself of something. "Look at me. I've had a whole life of After."

"Is this when Theresa's mother died?"

"Sure. When it happened I thought everything else would fall apart. I had no idea how I was going to raise the kids and still run Battle Brothers. For a couple months there nobody wanted to get out of bed. We'd get wake-up calls from the principal's office at the kids' school. Then I met Rita, and she saved our lives. Rita was After the After."

"You were lucky, Jerry," Paul says. "My life's going to be too sorry to save."

"Look, son," I say, in the gravest in-all-seriousness mode I can muster, "she's not going to die."

For a second Paul's eyes desperately search me, as if I might know something he doesn't. But then he sees that of course I don't.

He says, "It's good of you to say that. You should keep saying that."

"You ought to, as well."

"I know. Keep reminding me."

"Okay."

"You're not exactly like Theresa always said you were." Paul says, "She's always complained about you a lot."

"Hey, hey, a lot?"

"Well, much less these days. Actually not at all, lately."

"But before."

"Yes. She griped regularly how you'd run roughshod over anybody whenever things got troublesome for you, or something got in your way or made you work harder than you had to. That you had this supernatural ability to short-circuit dealing with the needs of others, so well in fact that people generally avoided any attempts to involve you."

"She couldn't just say I was 'lazy'?"

"Theresa has her way. There was also the usual complaint about how you could never bear doing anything purely for someone else, unless there was at least some modicum of benefit to you, but that's not relevant, because what I was going to say is that Theresa is so much like the person she makes you out to be, really just the same except she's perhaps more forthright and aggressive in her stance than you are, which you'd think would invite more discourse and interplay but shuts it down all the same, and even more finally in fact. And I'll admit to you now this is pissing me off, Jerry. I'm sorry, but it really is. It makes me feel a lot of anger toward her that I certainly can't express to her but that I can hardly deal with anymore. Yesterday I made a whole spinach lasagna with this nice béchamel and I browned the top of it a bit too much. Normally that would be acceptable but you know what I did? I took it out of the oven and walked to the back of your yard and I just chucked the whole thing, glass casserole and all, as far and high as I could, and it cracked into at least fifty pieces on a pile of logs."

"I was wondering why we ordered in."

"I went to clean it up this morning, but some animal had eaten the whole thing. I just collected glass, and the episode made me angry enough again that I cut myself picking up the shards. I bought you a new dish today, just so you know."

He shows me a bandaged finger, and says, "I'm losing my grip here, Jerry."

"That's okay."

He says, "Maybe the truth is I don't want to know anything."

Here's surely something I can relate to, but it's not the moment to let him give in to the Jerry Battle mode of familial involvement, that ready faculty of declining, my very worst strength, and I have to say, "You're not built like that, Paul. Whatever you're thinking of late about your writing, I know you can't accept being in the dark or on the 'periphery.' I've read every word you've published and even if I haven't really understood the half of them I'm pretty certain you're a guy who can't stand not being part of what's happening. I don't need a Ph.D. or square-framed glasses to see that it's killing you to just stand by and let Theresa make all the decisions about what's going to happen. It's her body and I'm sure she's got all kinds of rationales and constructs about that to throw at you, but it's your life, too, and you probably can fling some funky constructs right back at her, plus the fact that you're miserable. Let her know that—show her. Lose your shit if you have to. We Battles only really respond to fits and tears and tantrums, the more melodramatic the better."

"Theresa sometimes talks about how bad her mother got, which I think really scared her. She sometimes still has nightmares."

"Really?"

"She had one last night, in fact. Her mother was a very intense woman, huh?"

"Really only at the end," I say, realizing that I'm instantly defending myself, and trying to forget the picture of my daughter at the tender age of five, sitting at the dinner table with cheesy macaroni in her mouth, too fearful to even chew as Daisy chopped cucumbers for the salad furiously at the counter, white-and-green log rounds bouncing all over the floor.

"I'm sorry I'm so focused on myself, Jerry," Paul says. "Here I am talking to you about your not-so-well daughter, and now your father is missing."

"I'm doing all right."

"It must seem as though things have taken a strange turn."

"They're both going to be fine."

"Yup." Paul smiles, nodding with hollow vigor and optimism, all welcomed, and I join in as well, and it's enough good gloss between us to make me feel that I can believe whatever either of us might say, or propose. For while Pop is presently MIA, I have this strong conviction that he's not in any real trouble, that the old gray cat isn't so much wounded or confused or fighting back feral youth in whatever cul-de-sac or strip mall he's lost in, but rather delighting in the open possibility of the range, perhaps in fact sitting in a coffeehouse lounge, chatting up some willowy chai-sipping widow. The only detail gumming up the works is that it doesn't seem that he left with anything but the clothes he was wearing, save for his Velcro-strap black orthopedic walkers, his last outfit being his polka-dot pajamas, which you'd think the sight of in public on an unwashed and unshaven old man would prompt any number of citizens to alert the authorities.

The home show ends and I browse channels. Paul excuses himself to get some tea from the dining room. I find an animal program that I've seen before, about the lions of the Serengeti: the "story" is of a crusty old male lion they (the producers, the native bush-beaters, the cinematographer?) named Red for the color of his mane, which, apropos of nothing, is exactly the hennaed hue of Kelly Stearns's last self-dye job. Red has long been the dominant male of the pride, showing his appreciation of the hunting prowess of his lionesses by serving them sexually whenever they are in heat and then spending the rest of his time power-dozing and snapping at flies and sometimes chasing off the younger upstarts or killing some death-wishing hubristic hyena who thought he could carry off a cute cub and get away with it. Red has apparently ruled this lair for a long time, but is now being challenged by a very large mature young male newly arrived on the scene, named Nero (for no specific reason), who is making forays into Red's territory, sniffing at the females, and generally making a show of himself as an electable new king.

Red, of course, hitches himself up and out from the sorry shade of his acacia and charges the interloper, driving him off, but only temporarily. Nero comes back that night, and although there's no footage of the battle, the next morning we see that Red has been badly mauled, his right hindquarter slashed nearly to the bone, his mane matted with his own blood, a deep gash in his jowl. He's limping off to an old den, maybe the one where he was born. Nero, meanwhile, is holding court by the tree, spraying it liberally with his stud juice, receiving unctuous groveling licks from the males and females, and brusquely mounting most of the latter. The King is dead. Long live the King. The last we see of Red, he's lying on his side, slowly panting in near-death, too weak to even shoo the multitude of flies who swarm about the huge hind wound in a teeming shiny quilt of black. Before nightfall the pack of vengeful hyenas picks up his scent, and by the morning Red is but a rickety boat-shell of ribs and hide; he's not even an appetizer for the scrawny young jackal who's scampered by too late, and later on birds will take the scattered tufts of that arrogant hennaed mane as thatching for their nests.

Maybe Pop really is in trouble.

Maybe he really is lying face down in a roadside ditch.

But if he is, I have a feeling he's only doing so because he's hiding from state troopers patrolling the roads for him, which they're presently doing (this definitely not the standard operating procedure for missing persons but courtesy of Rita's highly placed sheriff friend), Pop ducking at each spray of headlights so he might enjoy a few more hours on the lam. And instead of feeling sorry for himself as I expected he would (as I no doubt would be feeling for myself), at least he's goddamn doing something about it, even if it is completely stupid and dangerous; at least he's taken hold of the moment angling away from him and typically wrenched it back his way.

I used to hear stories from my uncles about him when they were young, how they'd get into some serious rumbles where they lived up in Harlem against marauding gangs of micks and kikes and niggers, everybody using whatever was at hand, broomsticks and chains and tops of garbage cans as shields. My uncle Joe said it was like a fucking Wop Coliseum in the alleyways up there around 135th Street, these barbaric knock-down brawls where it seemed somebody was definitely going to get killed but the worst thing that ever happened was when Big Anthony Colacello slipped on a pile of horseshit as he was about to clock some poor Irish kid and hit his head on the curb and didn't wake up for two whole days. When he did he was exactly the same except he'd lost his sense of smell, and they'd play pranks on him like spreading limburger cheese on the back of his collar as they were on their way to skipping school.

Apparently Pop was the best fighter of their gang because he didn't mind getting hurt and had no fear of anyone. He would just lower his head (thus becoming Hank the Tank) and take whatever punishment he had to as he pushed in and waited for the guy to tire before counterattacking with a viciousness that surprised the crew every time. Pop I guess was a lot angrier then inside and out for the usual reasons of privation and poverty and general mistreatment by family members and people in the street and at school and by the authorities, which these days you'd call racism and discrimination but then was known as the breaks, how it was, your miserable fucking life. No doubt these days they'd have identified him and his brothers and cousins and the rest of their street-clinging crew as "at risk" youth and placed them in special programs with teams of sociologists and educators and therapists evaluating their intelligence and home life and probably diagnosing them with all kinds of learning and emotional disorders and prescribing medicines and skills-building regimens, finally buoying them up with grand balloons of self-esteem that they might float high above the rank fog of their scrounging dago circumstance, to land somewhere in the sweet-smelling prosperous beyond.

Pop certainly did, as did almost every last one of his generation's Battaglias, with the exception of his cousin Frankie, who died of a freak heart attack at nineteen, and then another named Valerie, who from the age of eleven smoked like an iron smelter and came down with lung (and liver and brain) cancer a month after her nuptials and was in the grave before she could even conceive a child. For if you took an accounting of all who proceed us, our alive and semi-alive relations from Forest Hills to Thousand Oaks to Amelia Island and to everywhere else they've rooted themselves with a vengeance, you'd have some kind of portfolio of golden twentieth-century self-made American living, all those spic-and-span houses and Gunite pools and porcelain- and crystal-filled curio cabinets and full-mouth braces for the kids and the double wall ovens set on timers to bring the roast rosemary chicken and casserole of sweet-sausage lasagna to just the right crisp on top as Dad pulled the white Lincoln up the driveway, their contribution to our Great Society being the straight full trickle-down to my generation of Battaglias and Battles and Battapaglias and the rest of us with the sweetheart deal of a Set-It-and-Forget-It existence. Like everybody halfway decent and useful I of course recognize that one's character should rightly derive from privation, crucibles, pains in the ass, and so I guess my only semi-rhetorical question is from what else does it come, if there's always been a steady wind at your back, a full buffet as your table, and the always cosseted parachuted airbagged feeling of your bubbleness, which can never brook a real fear?

Pop's pop was one of those stumpy, big-handed, gray-haired

fellas in coveralls you still spot every once in a while shimmying up on a neighbor's roof to repoint the top of the fireplace chimney, because guys like Pop and then me didn't want to learn the skill and they could never retire because there was no one else who knew how to do the job and they could never not take the call. In fact maybe Pop and I have more in common than I know, because really he had little interest in building garden walls and cladding Manhattan townhouses in limestone or doing anything like what Nonno was doing, whom I know he loved like a God but considered not a little backward and ignorant and lucky that he had him as a son. Growing up, Pop was smart enough to see how everybody was moving to the suburbs into their own houses with big yards and patios and pools and paved driveways, and he knew that the owners would be working too hard in their regular jobs to come home on the weekends and want to take care of it all. So against Nonno's wishes he moved the business out here to the suburbs, mostly dropping the bricklaying part (only stick-built, clapboarded houses out here) and shifting the focus to landscaping and yard care, which for a good many years was a veritable gold mine for the Battles, because he kept his early clients and moved along with them to bigger and bigger places right up until they died.

Pop was pretty magnificent then, this when I was a kid tagging along in the summers and he was in his prime (Bobby was just an infant). He'd stand there at the start of the day on the bed of his truck, hands spread atop the roof of the cab, calling out the jobs and saying who'd be working on them and with what foreman, exhorting the guys to do the job right (because if you do it right you don't have to remember to be honest) and then giving out a few loose bucks to those who were making the grade, cracking jokes the whole time and praising everybody and being the studly captain of the crew. When everybody had their marching orders he'd slap the cab and say, "All right, fellas, let's roll 'em out." The trucks would start up in a sweet dieselly cloud and he'd lead them out of the yard in a column like he was fucking Field Marshal Rommel. On the job I'd watch as he glad-handed the customers and was tough on them, too, and I'd have to say that whatever I know about common commerce and people I know from him, how he'd convince some guy to line his pool with real tiles instead of the cheaper rubber liner for the sake of standards and posterity, appealing to what pushed the guy out here in the first place, which was an idea about the destiny of the good American life and how each of us had a place in it, guiding it along. If George Guggenheimer had been his neighbor he would have been his best customer; Pop would have had him put in two koi ponds instead of one, with a waterfall in between, and then maybe an entire authentic Japanese garden, with a Zen sand pit and a manicured bamboo "fence" and a couple of those baby red maples that look so delicate and weepy, never for a second allowing George to entertain the idea of doing anything himself but feeding the fish (and maybe not even that), and definitely going over there after the lottery win and slapping some sense into him about not being such a pathetic, fearful, neurotic twitch of a man.

With the women he dealt with Pop was a natural charmer. He'd always compliment them on their clothes or hair even if they were just standing there in their housesmocks, and they'd often offer him coffee or if late in the day a cold can of beer. He'd always—always—accept, and if he felt particularly good or if there had been a problem with the job he might sing a few bars from Puccini or Verdi for them, his brassy tenor voice reaching me outside as I waited on the stoop or in the truck if it was raining. Sometimes, of course, I'd have to wait a very long time. Once I wandered around the back of one property to see if there was a swing set or basketball hoop and I saw Pop and the lady of the house balling away on the deck lounger by the pool Pop had just put in with Spanish blue tiles laid on the bottom in the shape of a schooner, Pop's big pale ass bobbing up and down between her doughy, stippled thighs and her heels (she was wearing brown spikes) digging holes into the cushion, where she was trying to get some traction. I was too young to think too much about it, and to be honest it never bothered me as it might have. I wasn't angry for my mother's sake, because she seemed as though she knew, and maybe because Pop didn't make a big deal of it or try to sell me a story. All he did was buy me a special high-flying kite I'd been asking for, The Big Bombardier, which I flew whenever the wind kicked up the littlest bit or a summer storm was blowing in.

I sure loved that Big Bombardier.

And maybe if you asked him Pop would proudly say he was the colonist, the pioneer, the one who had to clear-cut the land and fight tooth and nail with the natives, and that I'm the settler, the follower, the guy who grooved the first ruts in the road, the one who finally overflowed the outhouse shithole, who has presided over the steady downward trend of our civilization perhaps just now begun its penultimate phase of entropy and depletion. And if you're Theresa or Jack or Rita or anybody else (or even me for that matter), you could easily extend the argument to include the other collations between us, our frank father/son successions, that he's the racist to my apologist, the sexist and womanizer where I'm the teaser, canonist to popularist, stand-and-deliverer to recliner. And if I'm obliged to bring in the customary automotive metaphors, Pop must be one of the last of the great American sedans, those wide-body behemoths, possessed of egregiously wasteful power, overarmored, fuel-hungry (ever-desirous), picking off on his way to the store every doe and dog and rabbit and squirrel without showing as much as a dent, when I'm doing everything I can to prove that I'm something other than an early '80s model from a fallen Detroit, something big and bulky on the outside but alarmingly cramped within, with scandalously poor gas mileage and rickety suspension, though trimmed in buttery leather throughout, and with an AC system that could cool Hades. And in this sense, maybe Jack is the last hurrah of our golden Pax Battaglia, the burly all-terrain multitasking machine that will go anywhere it pleases, but it looks more and more as if he'll soon have to retrofit himself with fuel cells and narrow bicycle tires, shrink down the sheet metal into one of those pint-sized helmet-on-wheels jobs that are sadly the norm in London and Paris and Rome.

And if I may for a moment jump back to the previous metaphor and the (de-) moralizing story of Red I will say it is not Pop's story and in fact probably not even mine, but rather Jack's and Theresa's and Paul's and maybe yours, because it's the jackal and birds with whom we departed, skittering over the dust-dry plains after the great lion has roared and we hyenas and buzzards have split up the rest, and what is there left but the merest shaving of the splendid, just enough of a taste to pang the knowing belly?

Paul returns with his tea, as well as with the Ivy Acres administrator, whom I met on the first day I deposited Pop and have seen in the parking lot a couple of times since, a guy named Patterson. Patterson is a sleepy-eyed, semi-balding, mid-forties white guy in no-wrinkle khaki trousers who could pass for a lot of us out here, fed a bit too well on big Australian shiraz and rotisserie chickens and super-premium ice cream, who buys shelled pistachios only and snacks on them in his big Audi out of sheer crushing boredom, who'll go down on his wife as long as she's just bideted, who is easygoing except when it comes to the bottom-line expediency of his life, which, to nobody's credit, he can usually find in peril everywhere, at home or at the mall or here at work.

"Good evening, Mr. Battle."

"What the hell is going on here, Patterson?"

Patterson makes as if he can't hear that particular register, and just stands there a second waiting for the air to clear. "It's good that you and your son-in-law have come in."

"Good? I want to know how you let this happen, and what you're doing about finding my father."

"Why don't we sit down, Mr. Battle. If you please," he says, ushering Paul and me into chairs, while he sits at the foot of the bed. "Let me inform you of what's transpired so far, and the actions being implemented."

I'm annoyed by his sneaky tactic of cutting out any culpability in this mess, keeping it all in the passive, and then backing up the conversation, which is of course what I myself would do with a customer whose job we'd maybe messed up. But despite recognizing this I don't call Patterson on it, mostly because I understand that Pop's run is not Patterson's fault exactly (if at all), and that he's had to drag his flabby ass out of the lounger and tape the rest of whatever jackass-glorifying TV show he wasn't closely watching. I even almost feel sorry for him because his is just the dicey situation our litigious scapegoating civilization tends to put you in, when you've been installed at the big controls just long enough to absorb the most serious trouble, while bearing no real power at all.

Still, some chump's got to *represent*, and be punching bag for the rest, and so I say, to get the discussion snapped back on terms of my liking, "Look, Patterson. You had better start doing more than some good informing, or you're going to have a major action on your hands. My attorney's Richard Coniglio, senior partner at Whitehead Bates, who has constant wood for this kind of thing."

This seems to freeze up Patterson, like he's actually heard of the firm, for he breaks into a wide why-me smile and clears his throat and kind of hitches himself up, balls to gut, like some pitcher down 3–0 in the count.

"There's room for calm here," Patterson says, collecting himself. "Our experience leads us to believe that your father is likely fine, if what he's done is just wander off."

"Your *experience*? How often does this happen?"

"Almost monthly, Mr. Battle. Ivy Acres is not a holding facility, a prison. Sometimes people forget that fact. We consider our community members to be adults, and as adults they're free to move about, come and go on the shopping shuttle, take outings with friends and relatives, really do as they please. We're talking, of course, about our members housed in the main part of the facility, and not those in Transitions, who aren't as independent or mobile."

"I thought you had a pass system."

"We do. But it's only so we know where members are and how long they'll be out. When people don't come back we wait twenty-four hours and almost always they were at a niece's house and stayed over after dinner, or they just lost track of the time and missed the last shuttle and checked into a hotel. It has been very rare during the time I've been here that there have been *issues*."

"I think you should tell us about those," Paul says. "Just so we're aware."

"That's privileged information, I'm afraid."

"Well, everyone tells me I'm a privileged guy," I say, without the scantest levity or irony.

This doesn't intimidate Patterson, certainly, but I can tell he is beginning to plot out the best course for himself, trying to calculate whether he ought to toe the company line and say nothing more or maybe turn a little state's evidence right here and now, see if he can't ride the fine middle course and slip through this thing without any serious damage. I'm wondering, too, whether this might be one of those moments that I as an American of obvious Southern Italian descent might take advantage of (given the cultural bigotry/celebration concerning certain of our neighborhood associations), and suggest to Patterson that he'd do well to tell us whatever we want to know, lest the firm of Whack, Rig & Pinch arrange a special late-night deposition for him, dockside or alleyside or maybe right in the garage of his Cold Spring Harbor colonial, when he's just about to roll out the garbage container to the street. I really shouldn't, in deference to Pop, who can't stand any such talk, despite and perhaps because of the well-known fact that the Battaglia brothers got their start paving and walling the properties of certain connected guys at their second-home mansions in Brookville and Lake Success, but I warn Patterson he'd better start plain "wising up," and "stop being such a punk." Patterson now clears his throat again and says, "Unfortunately the two people involved clearly intended to leave the campus. They took specific measures."

"Like what?"

Patterson ahems. "One of them ground up three bottles of sleeping pills and mixed them into a milkshake at a diner, where he was found dead in the men's room. The other was a woman who took our shuttle to the mall and shopped for most of the day. But instead of returning on the bus she somehow made her way up to the roof and jumped off the top of Saks."

"Christ . . ."

"Besides those instances, Mr. Battle, we've had only success. Now, you wanted to know what we're doing about finding your father. The police have been notified, of course, and we've also hired two private investigators, who are out searching for Mr. Battle right now. The lead investigator called me as I drove in, and so far they can confirm a sighting of an older man of his description."

"Where?"

"At the Walt Whitman Mall. In fact this very morning. A security guard apparently escorted him out, as he wasn't appropriately dressed."

"Escorted him out where?"

"Just out. I asked this, too, but the guard didn't note where the man went."

"Did he say what *the man* was wearing?"

"I believe it was trousers and a pajama top."

"Fucking great. That was Pop."

Paul says, "At least he was fine as of this morning, which means he got through last night on his own."

"It's a whole other night tonight," I say, thinking how good it is that Jack is driving up and down the Nassau-Suffolk border scouring every park and playground and strip mall for his grandfather. As I've noted, the thing about Jack is that he has never been in the least lazy in his life; I can't remember an instance when I asked him to clean the gutters or shovel the driveway or set the dinner table and had him groan or shuffle his feet or do anything but get on the job, the same as if I'd suggested that we throw a football around, or maybe go to Shea Stadium, which we did only once, when a customer of mine gave me a couple of playoff tickets in 1973 (Jack was thrilled because he got Rusty Staub's autograph). Jack's trouble has been of course that he tends to respond not wisely but too well, like a cricket that jumps whenever you touch him; it doesn't matter that he might be perched on the edge of some chasm. This is not my way of intimating once again that I think Jack isn't the brightest bulb on the tree, because even if that were true it doesn't matter in the least. Let's face it, for most of us in this more-than-okay postbellum Western life, smarts really don't count for a tenth as much as placement and birth, the particular trajectory of one's parturition, and if there's a genuine flaw to Jack's character it's no secret he gets too focused and purposeful for anybody's good, and especially his own, for it would never occur to him to lift the hatch and just bail out before the groundrush stops everything dead.

"Maybe Jack will find him," Paul says, as usual reading my mind. "I'll call and let him know about Pop being sighted at the mall."

He doesn't know Jack's cell number (nor do I), so he takes my phone outside the building to speed-dial him while I reacquire Patterson, who appears a bit sodden all of a sudden, like he's just come off a chartered fishing boat on a chilly, mist-spritzed day, like he'd pretty much give anything to get back home and pull on his flannel pajamas and crawl into bed. And though in fact I have zero interest in suing anybody ever, and can't think of what else to have him do save piss away his time keeping me company while I fret about Pop in my backslidingly diffuse and scattered manner, I say, anyway, "You're going to make this come out right, Patterson, or I swear once my attorney gets busy you'll be lucky to run the nut-and-candy cart at Roosevelt Field."

To this Patterson is mum, his lower lip pressed up tight against his half-exposed top teeth, so that he looks like a big bald, worried rodent, and I'm ready for whatever sweet load of sunshine he's going to try to blow up my ass, thank you very much. But presently Paul appears in the doorway, and then Jack, bearing what looks like a pile of dirty laundry in his arms, laundry with sneakered feet. I realize he is carrying Pop, wrapped up in a soiled—and very smelly—bedsheet.

"Pop . . ."

"He's not dead," Jack pronounces, evidently responding to my expression.

Pop moans with trenchant exasperation, as he always does. He's alive.

"He's pretty out of it," Jack says, laying him down on the bed. The top of the sheet flops down, revealing Pop's face, which is sunburned and badly peeling. "He told me he didn't sleep for two days."

"Where did you find him? At a mall? A park? Not at *Starbucks* . . ."

"Right outside here," Jack says. "I was parking the truck and I saw something move in the pachysandra by the duck pond."

"What the hell do you mean?" I turn to give Patterson a look, but he's already gone, yodeling something from the hallway about finding the house doctor.

"He was back over there, where that other section of the home is."

"*Transitions,*" I say, picturing him grimly looking in at Bea from the window.

"He's probably very dehydrated," Paul says. "And in shock."

Jack says, "I pinched his skin, and it's pretty bad. I asked him and he said he had been drinking water. But I didn't see any bottles. Maybe from the sprinklers. Or the duck pond."

"Oh Jesus," I say. "Is Patterson getting a doctor?"

"I'll go find him," Paul offers. He runs out, leaving the three of us in the room, posed like in one of those neo-Classical deathbed paintings, the acolytes deferentially arrayed at the great man's torso, his mouth twisted in the last mortal coils of agony, his eyes cast upward to the Maker . . .

"Can you two give a guy a little room here?" Pop hoarsely blurts out, hacking up some very gluey spit. Jack cups his chin with a tissue and Pop spews it out. "And instead of trading all your medical theories, how about a goddamn glass of water?"

While Jack fetches one from the bathroom, I try to take the dirty sheet from him, but he won't let me.

"Come on, Pop, it's filthy. And so are you."

"I like it this way."

"You smell like cat piss. And other things."

"I don't care. It makes me feel alive."

Jack gives him two glasses, and he bolts both down, which is probably not ideal, and hands them back to him for more.

"What the hell did you do these past two days?"

"I walked by day," he says, intoning not a little prophet-like. In fact he seems too tranquil, and steady, for what he's obviously weathered.

"I guess you didn't get very far, with your legs bothering you."

"Just to the gate," he says. "I was just going to take a short walk at first. But then some kid drove by and asked if I needed a ride, and I told him I did. He dropped me off out in East-hampton."

"You went out that far?"

"That's where the kid was going."

"Didn't he wonder why you were wearing a pajama top?"

"Hey, he was wearing a shirt with cuts all over it, like it got run over by a combine. Plus he wasn't too swift."

Jack brings the glasses back full and hands them to Pop. "So what did you do out there?"

He bolts them down, again. "Like I said, I walked. I walked on the beach, all the way out to Montauk Point."

"That's got to be fifteen or twenty miles at least. You really walked all the way?"

"Well, I almost got there. I could see it, that's for sure."

I ask, "Did you have any money? What did you eat?"

"Of course I didn't have money. I was just going out for a little walk, remember? Plus I'm kept a pauper, so I have no freedom. And if you want to know, I panhandled."

"You begged?" Jack says, crinkling his forehead, like his mother sometimes did.

"It's not below me," Pop replies, glancing at yours truly. "Nothing's below me."

I say, "So you begged on the beach in the Hamptons."

"Yeah," he says. "Most people wouldn't part with any dough, but they were decently generous with the food, which I ate but didn't like. Sushi, some other rolled thing they called a 'wrap.' This is what people bring to the beach. And how come everything has to have smoked salmon in it? Nobody appreciates an honest ham sandwich anymore."

Jack asks, "Did you sleep on the beach?"

"Oh yeah. It was real nice, sleeping outside. It wasn't too cold either. In the morning some cops gave me a ride to town. After I got together enough for a doughnut and coffee, I hitched a ride back from a guy in a Jaguar. I think he thought I was some nutso billionaire like Howard Hughes. When I got back here I didn't want to go inside right away, so I lifted a sheet from the laundry service truck and camped out."

"You could have told somebody, you know."

"What, that I was going to sack out with the ducks? The jerks here would have called you, and you would have called some shrink, and all of you would have gotten together and sent me to a place where they have metal grating on the windows."

"I wouldn't have," Jack says, most unhelpfully. "Next time, you can come stay with us. I'll set you up on the deck with a pup tent."

"I need the open air."

"Fine, then, anyway you want it. Better yet, you can come stay with us now if you like."

"Oh yeah? You mean it?"

"Why not? You have a month-to-month lease, right?"

"Ask Mr. Power-of-Attorney. Hold on, I gotta use the head." We help Pop out of bed, but he bats away our buttressing and goes into the bathroom.

"Of course it's month-to-month," I say to Jack. "But shouldn't you talk about this with Eunice?"

"What makes you so sure I haven't?"

"I know you."

"You think you do."

"Well, have you?"

Jack says firmly, "She'll be fine with it."

"But you ought to make sure, don't you think, before getting him all excited? Besides, I don't know if it would be the best thing for him."

Pop calls out, "I'll take the guest room with the big TV, okay, Jack?"

"Sure thing, Pop."

"Are you hearing me, Jack?"

He stares right in my eyes. "The best thing for Pop, or for you?"

"For me? For him to stay at *your* house? Christ. I don't know what that means. I really don't. And I'm thinking about you, kid, especially you. You've got a wife, and kids, and a big house to run, and a business to . . ."

". . . You know, the one with the big *tube* TV . . ."

"Sure, Pop, sure," he says, and then to me, "To what?"

"What?"

"*To what.* A business to what?"

"You know what."

"Tell me, Dad."

"Forget it."

"Come on, let's hear it."

"I said forget it."

Jack gives me a look—or actually, he doesn't, which is a look in itself—and for a scant moment I feel myself tensing my neck and jaw for what I'm intuiting will be a straight overhand right, popped clean and quick, and I actually shut my eyes for a breath. Of course nothing comes, nothing at all, and when life flips back it's just Jack gazing straight at me, his mouth slightly open in his way, with that resigned enervation, like he's waiting for a train that always runs late.

"Well, don't worry about it," he says. "It's going to be okay."

"I won't," I say. This sounds as empty as it is untrue, but like most men we accept the minor noise of it and try to move on.

But presently we don't have to, as Paul and Patterson and a light-brown-skinned guy with his head wrapped in a bright purple cloth—presumably the doc—enter the room in a rush, though they're momentarily frozen by the sight of the empty bed; Jack points to the bathroom, where we converge, Jack first. He knocks, calling for Pop, and then opens the door. Pop is sitting hunched on the edge of the tub, grasping his arm.

"What's the matter?" I ask.

"My arm hurts. And my neck. It's like clamped inside."

"Please let me in," the doc says, pushing through. But just as he does, Pop sharply groans and pitches forward with sheer dead weight, and it's only because of Jack's quick reflexes that he doesn't smack his face on the hard tile floor. He and the doc gently turn him onto his back, and the doc gets to work, 100 percent business (definitely a welcome change of pace), checking his vitals, trying to track the pain, with Pop wincing as fiercely as I've ever seen him, tiny tears pushing out of the corners of his eyes.

"What's wrong with him?" I ask, all of it in sum beginning to spook me. "Shouldn't we call an ambulance?"

Paul says, "It's already coming."

The doc tells Patterson to alert the hospital to ready a cardiac team.

"He's having a heart attack?" Jack says.

"Possibly," the doc answers. "But we won't know how bad it is, or even what it is, until we get him to the hospital." He asks Pop if he thinks he can swallow some aspirin, and Pop nods. Patterson is sent to get some. When he returns with them, Pop takes two, crunching on them like children's tablets, and lies back. The doc now regards him more generally.

"Why is he in such a miserable condition?"

Patterson says, "This is the gentleman who left the premises."

"I see."

"Can't you do something for him?" I say.

"There's nothing else I can do. We simply have to wait for the ambulance."

But now Pop sort of yelps, and claws angrily at his neck, like there's something ditch-witching its way out of him. Jack holds him steady and then eases him back down, and for a moment he seems to calm, but then all at once his whole body becomes sort of warped and rigid, like a sheet of plywood that's been soaked and then too quickly dried. He rests again, his eyes shut. And then it starts again.

"Steady him now," the doc says, he and Jack quelling the new tremor. "Steady him. Steady. He'll make it through."

Paul is nodding in assent, but in fact it looks to me like Pop's going, really going. Going now for good.

eleven

I REMEMBER, from the time I was old enough not to care so much, Pop liked to say to me, with a put-on twang, "You're okay, Jerome, but I'd like you a whole lot better as a nephew than a son."

And I'd say to him, "Likewise, Uncle Hank."

We'd have a chuckle about it, our little hick routine, and often we'd play along that way for a while, through whatever we happened to be doing, driving in the car or painting the fence, and talk about stuff that we normally wouldn't talk about, which was pretty much everything, though this was of course only when Bobby didn't happen to be with us. When the three of us did go out together I was happy to sit in the back and let them shoot the shit and razz each other and just focus on my books on flying aces of WWII. It's no great shock that after Bobby went to Vietnam we didn't play the game anymore, and not because I was getting too old. But it was sort of fun while it lasted. Maybe we'd be driving out east to buy shrubs for a job and Pop would ask me about my girl and whether I'd finally gotten my fingers stinky, to which I'd make like I was hoisting my rig and say, *If my big one counts,* and we'd stupidly yuck it up like that all the way to the nursery, yakking like nimrods about women in the street and the latest car models and the merits and demerits of certain brands of beer. It was all a dumb joke but it was easy and comfortable and it doesn't take an advanced degree in psychology to figure out what we were doing, or why, or that those times were probably in fact when we felt closest to one another, most like a father and son.

I recount this with less nostalgia than a kind of wonder that we played the game at all, though at that moment in the jostling ambulance with the sirens *wop-wopping* and the sturdy EMS gal barking in Brooklynese his sorry vitals ahead to the ER, when it was clear that this was Pop's last careen on our side of oblivion, I thought for sure that I heard him try to drawl some avuncular sobriquet to me through the misty oxygen mask, some snigger to ol' Jerry-boy to check out the lushly ample hindquarters of the lady paramedic. But it wasn't that, of course, rather the muffled gasp of a death throe, in equal parts pissed and terrified, punctuated by his grasping my hand so tightly that I had to squeeze back as hard as I could to make him relent, actually crackling the little bones in his hand. Pop then kind of wailed and the butch paramedic possessed of these huge caramel-brown eyes noticed us holding hands and said with a fatalism and tenderness that walloped me deep in the chest, "It's really all we got, huh?"

I guess I blurted a yeah, not thinking much about what she was referring to, and it's only now, a few weeks later, when things have settled down and I'm finally up here again in sleek *Donnie,* Theresa serving as my copilot, cruising at a smooth altitude above this familiar patch of planet, that I'm able to peel away to the fuller meanings.

I should note without further delay that Pop has not been lowered into the ground, or sifted into an urn, or shelved away in a granite wall cabinet, nor is he otherwise in any way closer to the netherworld than he was when rescued from the Ivy Acres ground cover, but ensconced in the lap of Jack and Eunice Battle luxury, *bain en suite*, satellite TV clicker and walkie-talkie in hand, so he can squawk down to Rosario and order up a Bloomin' Onion or other microwave treat whenever he feels a lonely hollow in his gut. He is convalescing in style after the combination heart attack and mild stroke (an extremely rare occurrence, we're told, both to experience and then survive, particularly with no extreme ill effects). Eunice I hear has been especially solicitous, turning down his bed herself while he receives his daily bath from the hired home nurse (female, untattooed), and then fans out the dozen or so journals and magazines she replenishes weekly for him on the west end of the king bed, pillows fluffed and propped, the forever-blab of Fox News on the big tube awaiting his scrubbed pink return. Jack, too, is being extra helpful, keeping Pop up at night with a special subscription to an adult channel, his favorite program being the *Midnight Amateur Hour*, in which we are introduced to the porn star aspirations of excruciatingly ordinary middle-class folks, one couple Pop swears featuring the head cook at Ivy Acres. Even I have been going over there every other day, bearing gifts of guilt-larded fruit like biscotti and Sambuca and twine-wrapped soppressata or other such items that might bolster his memory of another time in his life when things weren't any better or worse but when at least most of his family and friends were still alive. Maybe it should be no surprise that it takes a serious brush with death to really land oneself in Nirvana, which in this case for Pop—and soon enough me, soon enough you—is a convening of family predicated not so much upon either obligation or love as on a final mutual veto of any further abandonment.

And if *family* is the "it" the ambulance gal was talking about, the all-purpose F-word for our times, *really all we got*, like anybody else I'm not sure whether that's an ultimately heartening or depressing proposition, though perhaps that's not the point. I will confess that at the very moment I thought Pop was a goner, kicking the bucket, croaking for good, I didn't much *feel* love for him, even as I *had* love; I felt intellectually sure, is what I'm saying, which is no excuse. What this might suggest about families in general or ours in particular or just sorry old me is that while prophets tell us we're innately bestowed with enough grace to convey righteousness and bliss to entire worlds (much less one person), we mostly don't, at all, just pure potential that we are, just pure possibility. And the people who most often witness and thus endure the chasm between our exalted possible and our dreary actual are the ones we in fact love, or should love.

This is why Pop is in fact so lucky now, so very lucky, which has nothing to do with his being alive. (We're all alive, aren't we?) And for a host of reasons I doubt this attention lavished on Pop will be duly lavished on me when my time comes due, the primary one being that unlike Pop I'll probably be pushing hard for special treatment, and thus receive none in return. I should wise up and probably start getting chummier with Jack's (and eventually Theresa's) kids, besides just appearing in the doorway of their double-height foyer with the Disney videotape of the week, waving it like Fagan might a piece of bread above the dancing urchins. In addition I can't bear to tell Pop that his only grandson and bearer of the Battle Brothers torch will soon have to relinquish several lifetimes of accrued capital for a final grand blowout liquidation sale, which even then won't cover the various notes come due. I can't bear to tell him that our sole recent investment in the property is a fix for the section of cyclone fence that one of the guys accidentally ran through a few years ago with a backhoe, and only because Suffolk National Bank ordered us to secure the grounds and garage. Richie Coniglio tells me that Battle Brothers will be pretty much stripped, but assures that Jack himself will be safe, if safe means still owning the big house and big cars but no longer possessed of the salary to maintain it for too long.

Lately Theresa has been accompanying me on my visits to her brother's, and to my happiness has been exceedingly warm toward him and Pop and also toward Eunice, who has taken the news of Battle Brothers' demise quite hard. After Pop had his trouble Jack suddenly came clean and opened the books to her, and apparently for a week or so she didn't do anything different, quarterbacking the household offense as always with Rosario blocking upfield, picking through the various ladies' lunches and kids' pool parties with that austere English-German efficiency, even audible-izing an impromptu single-malt scotch tasting at the country club followed by a raclette party back at the house. But then the next day while waiting to pay at Saks, somebody allegedly nudged her and she pretty much freaked and actually started singing a pop song, quite loudly, all of which she couldn't remember, and then bent all her credit cards in two and had to be escorted out to her Range Rover by mall security. She's been seeing a counselor twice a week since, and appears to me to be calmly, perfectly okay, though perhaps calmly, perfectly okay is a worrisome drop-off for someone accustomed to rolling forth at full throttle and being all-time 4WD-engaged. Though we don't know whether she is on medication, Theresa has recognized the imbalance as potentially serious, and has taken her, without a whiff of irony, on a couple let's-just-be-girls outings, including a longish session at the fancy new Korean nail salon on Deer Park Avenue and an even longer one at the all-you-care-to-eat Brazilian meat palace, where at least Eunice thoroughly ruined her manicure clawing and gnawing on char-grilled short ribs and baby backs.

Theresa, I'm sure, practiced her current form of all-you-care-to-eat, as she did earlier this afternoon at the marina restaurant near Bar Harbor where I ordered us each a two-and-a-half-pounder with drawn butter and dinner rolls, she barely touching her meal. We're heading back now along the seaboard, our flight path taking us past the southern beach suburbs of Boston and over Buzzards Bay, to cross the Sound at its wide mouth and then follow the northern shoreline of the Island, until the final turn to MacArthur Field. Having Theresa along is an unusual circumstance, and one she initiated. In fact, I'd normally never fly on a day like this, when the weather, although supremely fine on the journey up, holds the chance for an inclement change. At present, we're approaching the start of the Cape and I can see far off in the distance and probably still southwest of New York City the broad white cottony mass of the approaching system, nothing like dark thunderheads fortunately but to this exclusively fair-weather flyer material stuff all the same, and a sight I've never seen, at least from up here.

At breakfast this morning Theresa was in an expansive mood and talking about how she was starving. Paul instantly whipped together some French toast from day-old challah bread, which was excellent but she couldn't eat, and then after Paul sort of slunk away deflated she expressed an intense hankering for lobster and asked me if we could fly to Maine. I called the weather service for the forecast and told her probably not, as a low front was moving rapidly up from D.C. and could make for uncertain conditions on the return. I offered to pick up some lobsters at the fish market instead but she insisted and said she was finally feeling hungry for *something* and I figured who was I to say no to her. Paul thought it would do her (and clearly himself) some good to get her out of the house, and so we drove to Islip and went through our checks and got *Donnie* right up, riding a strong tailwind to Maine in what had to be record time.

On the bleached-cedar dining deck of The Peeling Skiff the sun was undiffuse and brilliant, both of us sporting baseball caps and sunglasses, Theresa's hand aglitter with the ring Richie bought for Rita and that I attempted to give back to her and that she and I quickly agreed to put to better use, by bequeathing it to the next generation. With the fat candy-store rock on her finger and her Yankees cap, Theresa was looking particularly girlish, and for a moment I felt a strange blush of accomplishment, for no other reason than that I had known her for the entirety of her years, now not so few, which is no great feat, of course, but still the sort of stirring that can make you almost believe that there might not be any more crucibles ahead, just this perennial interlude of melody and ease. When our plates arrived she got all excited and quickly tied on her white plastic bib and took the cracker right to a meaty claw, but after forking out the chubby little mitt she just sort of nibbled on it like it was her second or third lobster and after putting it down chewed idly on a couple of the small legs before neglecting it altogether. I didn't say anything because I wasn't that mad and really what was there to say that wouldn't be completely fake or depressing. After I finished mine, she pushed her plate over and I ate her lobster, too, even though I was already full, solely because I couldn't bear it slumped there unrequited between its lemon wedge pillows, staring up at us one-armed, thoroughly wronged.

"Hey, what's that?" she now says over the headset, pointing ahead to a strip of small islands off the Cape. "Is that the Vineyard or Nantucket?"

"No, no, they're over there," I say, motioning farther out. "You're looking at Naushon, I think. Or Pasque. Those are old-money hideouts, where I think they choose not to have electricity. They boat in ice and candles."

"Ice and candles?"

"That's what I hear."

"Sounds kind of kinky."

"Definitely not."

"I guess that's class."

"Yeah. Class."

We nod to each other, for emphasis, though neither of us is caring to make much of a point. This is how we talked on the way up, too, with her asking about a certain geographic or urban feature, to which I'd offer a bit of trivia about the nuclear submarine yards at New London or the history of Portuguese immigration to Providence or mention a surprisingly excellent fish-and-chips place in Buzzards Bay, where they brew their own malt vinegar. Conversing over the headsets is never like a real conversation, the overlaps and separations and pauses and canned feeling of the sound making for brief information exchanges at best, not to mention the constant pulse of the motor buzzing every nook of your being, which is not a bad thing at all if you want to feel as if you're busy just sitting there. This used to frustrate Rita sometimes, that we'd spend a whole day in the plane and seemed to have chatted nonstop but not about anything remotely personal, which suited me okay and in the end perhaps suited her as well. And why shouldn't it? Because when you're up here and aloft and all you're really trying to do is figure a word for the exact color of the sky, or count the whitecaps risen in a certain square of sea, or make sense of the almost infinite distance between yourself and the person driving his car on the lonely dead-straight road below, you don't want to engage in the familiar lingering intimations, allusions, narratives, all that compacted striated terra-firma consideration, but instead simply stir with this special velocity that is in itself worth the whole of any voyage, this alternating tug and weightlessness of your constant departure.

"What do you think is going to happen with Jack?" Theresa says, speaking of terra-infirma.

"Jack? At some point he's going to have to sell that house. And probably a lot of that stuff they have."

"Eunice does love that house."

"I don't think Jack does, or ever did."

"Where will they go? They have so much stuff. Not to mention Pop."

"I don't know," I say, instantly picturing the movers bubble-wrapping and crating him right there in the bed, propped up with clicker and Hot Pocket in hand.

"I can't see Jack and Eunice in a rental."

"You can get a real nice condo these days. They'll do fine."

"But there's no more Battle Brothers."

"Jack will get something going again."

"Are you going to help him?"

A loud rasp of noise squelches the end of her question, and I pretend it got lost in the wires.

After a moment, she says, "Well, are you?"

"Am I what?"

"Are you going to help Jack?"

"I'm retired, remember? And I'm not rich. At least not enough to start a new business."

"You should still *help,*" she says, with clear alarm, her emphasis actually squawking the sound. "You have to."

"Of course I will," I say. "It's just not yet clear how."

"I can tell you how, Jerry."

"Okay."

"Why don't you invite them to live with us?"

"Are you nuts?"

"We have plenty of room."

"Plenty of room? There are three bedrooms, last time I looked. Jack and Eunice would need one, the kids another, and unless Pop is willing to go back to Ivy Acres, which I doubt, then one for him. That still leaves you and Paul, and then me, the owner of the house."

"You can convert the study to another bedroom for yourself, and Paul and I can move downstairs."

"Downstairs? That's the basement!"

"Maybe Jack can build some walls. There's already a half-bath down there. Besides, we're not going to stay with you forever."

"What are you talking about?"

"You forget I'm on leave. I'm going to have to teach again."

"What about extra maternity leave?" I say. "Isn't that the *law* these days?"

Theresa says, "I suppose so," though without much conviction, and not because she's someone who doesn't keep up on her worker rights and benefits. There's not been much pessimism in the house, if at all, the only indication of worry and trouble being that Paul sometimes has to excuse himself from the room or take a stroll around the neighborhood, probably so his heart doesn't suddenly shatter into a thousand jagged pieces; but by the same token there hasn't been any talk whatsoever of the future, or of any future past a few days out, which I can say over the last couple months we've been together has been a pretty liberally bestowed mercy among us, and judging from the sudden panicky hollow pinging in my gut, one I haven't appreciated near deeply enough.

I say, "You should take unpaid leave and stay longer. Paul can finally finish his book. When you have the baby you can take the master bedroom. There's an old crib in the basement that I'll clean and move up for you."

"That sounds nice."

"No problem."

"But what about the others?"

"What about them?"

"Come on, Jerry."

With the light shining from behind her sunglasses I can see her eyes searching me, perhaps not so much looking for the desired answer but rather the glimmer of a character somehow more wise and generous and self-sacrificing than the one that I for some fifty-nine and fifteen-sixteenths years have come to possess. Being who she is, Theresa would never have cared for the kind of father with whom she could discuss fuzzy intimacies, talk interspersed with full-on hugs and remembrances of previous challenges righteously met and overcome, all at a pitch of loving confirmation muted only by the wistful minor-key note that we couldn't always be together every moment of our lives. Then again, I don't know if she would have even wished we were that rare pair who could take turns riffing, say, on the Lacanian imbrications of contemporary family life (another few words I've learned this summer), or talk fast and loose in slick jump cuts between our favorite neo-Realist films and hip-hop marketing and the sinister global triumph of capitalism. No doubt things could have been different between us, much different, and maybe there's no actual alternative reality that would have proven any better than what we have now, or at least that we could practically abide. We are consigned to one another, left in one another's hands whether we like it or not, and perhaps the sole thing asked of us is that we never simply let go.

Still I say, "Jack won't want to come back to the old house."

"That's not what Eunice tells me," Theresa answers. "She's ready, too. All you have to do is call."

"You're kidding, right?"

"Nope."

This confounds me, even thrills me, but still, I say, "What about Rosario? There's definitely no room for her."

"She could come three times a week, to help tidy up, until she finds another full-time job."

"Who's figured this out already?"

"Take a guess."

I look at my daughter, lightly touching her controls. I say, "The house will be a zoo."

"We'll all have to pitch in. Including you. Including me."

"Myself I can see," I say. "But you're doing fine."

"Come on. I let Paul do everything."

"Which he's pretty damn good at, if you ask me."

"Doesn't make it right."

"It does at the moment. Besides, if he didn't work so hard, he'd go crazy."

Theresa starts to say something, though her mouth must have come too close to the headset microphone, because the reply is distorted with noise. We're quiet now, just the steady blenderizing of the 150-horsepower Lycoming engine. She's gazing off to the northwest, over toward Hartford, or Albany, where there's still clear sky overhead. To the southwest, where we're headed, it's definitely going to be a bit soupy, which is plenty alarming, and it's probably good that I've already decided to fly back on a pretty direct route, in the hope that we'd somehow cut a few minutes off the trip, a few minutes maybe proving the difference between a cloudy or clear touchdown. The specter of not seeing the field for the landing is one I've often imagined, nosing down into the murk and trusting only the instruments, hoping for enough daylight between the mist and the field to get a comfortable sighting before the final approach, for which I have some practice but not enough to make me happy. This is no pleasing challenge for a guy like me, who likes very much to see where he's going to step next, especially when life is a Paris street, fresh piles of it everywhere.

"Pop is going to be tough. But I suppose I have to heat and cool the whole house anyway," I say, disbelieving the Real as now embodied in myself. Which must always be a sign of deep trouble. "We can try it for as long as people can stand it."

"Okay, Jerry," she says without a note of congratulation. "Maybe you can call Jack when we get home."

"Can't you call him? You could just tell Eunice, couldn't you?"

She waves me off with a flit of the hand as a mother might a too-old child begging for a nostalgic piggyback. I want to tell her that she's not quite understanding this one, that even though she thinks it's about my laziness and long-practiced avoidance of appearing tender and loving before my son, it's really about Jack himself, that he should be spared the ignominy of having to hear and acknowledge such an offer, which, as modestly as I might play it, and I will, naturally abounds with all sorts of subtle and excruciating indications of shame and failure. Or maybe I'm not giving Theresa enough credit, maybe she knows this to be the case and thinks Jack should face the paternal demonhead straight on, just accept whatever that minor if terrible god will extract of his vital masculine juices and afterward get on with the quotidian work of replenishing.

"You two have plenty to talk about anyway," Theresa says. "The business notwithstanding."

"What now? Is he having trouble with Eunice?"

"There's tension, but only because of the money troubles. They're actually pretty devoted to each other, beneath all the nickel plate and granite."

"That's good," I say, "because it's only Formica and chrome from here on in."

"It's just time to call him, okay? He's shaky."

"Yeah, okay, but he seems the same to me." This is mostly true, at least to my perception, everything about his manner and dress unchanged, save for the odd sight of his unwashed black truck, the alloy wheels grimy and the usually mirror-shined body splattered with dried work site mud and dull all over with a toffee-hued grunge. He's cutting back, which is necessary, as I know he always had the truck washed once a week on Saturday mornings for $22.95 (the #4 Executive, with double polycoat and tire dressing), for I'd meet him every other month (and spring for the #1 Commuter, at $8.95) and have a big breakfast at the Pit Stop Diner next door. And yet on this one I kind of wish he weren't economizing, because at certain times you really do want your loved ones to keep up appearances, and for all the worst truth-blunting reasons. If I had a personal voice recorder I'd note to myself that when I do call as Theresa recommends I'll offer to treat him to the #4 Executive, plus blueberry pancakes, this very weekend.

"He even mentioned Mom the other day."

"Daisy?"

Theresa nods, taking off her sunglasses, as the sun has now dipped behind a high bank of clouds, many miles in the distance. "Actually, he was talking about the day she drowned."

"Oh yeah?"

"Yeah," she says, squarely looking at me, and not in the least somberly. "It's amazing. It turns out he was around when it happened."

"What are you talking about?" I say. "You were both at your day camps. When I got home there wasn't anybody but Daisy."

"I guess that's true," she says, "but Jack was there before."

"He was at lacrosse camp. You were at music camp."

"Drama camp," she corrects. "I was at mine, but Jack told me he turned his ankle and got an early ride home. Do you remember that he was limping?"

"No."

"It's funny, but I don't either," she says. "I really don't remember anything, which I'm happy about. But Jack says he was there. He has no reason to lie."

"Why didn't he say something then?"

"I guess he was upset, and scared. Besides being a little boy."

"So what else did he say?"

"Just as he got dropped off, someone was coming out of the house. A delivery man or something. Except this guy was drinking from a bottle of beer, and Jack remembers feeling angry toward him, though it was nobody he knew."

I don't answer her, because I don't know how much Theresa recalls of that part of Daisy's life and I'm certainly not interested in educating her here and now, but she says, "I assume he was there to see Mom. That's right, isn't it?"

"Probably so," I say. I suddenly remember all the empties in the house that afternoon, almost a whole case in all. Of course it wasn't the first time I'd come home to find that she'd been drinking heavily, though she mostly drank her sweet plum wine when she drank and the party-like litter of beer bottles had seemed unusual. I'd figured she'd been entertaining, a fact that wasn't so terribly hurtful to me at that point, the literal mess of the house more pissing me off, which really says it all, and after finding her suspended near the bottom of the pool the likely fact of some random guy having been there simply dissolved away among the thousand other details and duties that follow any death, and it never seemed important to mention to the cops who came around later that day that Daisy hadn't been drinking alone. But still the flashes of that day quicken my breath, and all at once I feel as though I'm flying at 50,000 feet, or maybe 150,000; it's like the air is thinning so rapidly we're in danger of floating up into the exosphere, right out into the black.

"Anyway," Theresa goes on, "Jack went inside and saw a lot of beer bottles in the kitchen, but not Mom. She wasn't in your bedroom, either, but while he was there he saw the bed all messed up and her underclothes on the floor. And more empty bottles. That's when he saw her out in the back. Jack was going to step out the sliding door of your bedroom and say he was there but I guess he didn't. He just watched her for a while. She was standing naked on the edge of the diving board, drinking a beer. He told me she looked very beautiful. Like a Roman statue, before any ruin."

"Jack said that?"

"I'm quoting verbatim," she says, unwistfully. "But he said he was scared, too. And I guess still angry, though he didn't really understand why. You can imagine what a bizarre and sexual sight it was for him. So he's just standing there watching her, and he realizes all the pool floats have been taken out of the water. The tubes and the swan raft and then that big pink doughnut she always used."

This was true, and something I didn't really think about when I got home. I'd assumed the pool had been cleared out by the cops or ambulance people, though it was an odd sight to see all the floats neatly lined up on the concrete deck, like the audience for a swim meet.

"So what did he do?" I ask.

"He said he ran," Theresa answers. "He just ran out of the house, as fast as he could. He went to the playground, he was so scared, and went on the swings, for like an hour."

"Oh, Jesus, Jack."

"So when he finally comes home it's all over. He knows exactly what's happened. The driveway's full of police cars and fire trucks and the ambulance, with its lights going. That's what I remember."

"Why didn't he say something?"

"I'm sure he thought he was responsible."

"I guess so," I say, remembering now how he kept asking if little kids were ever sent to jail.

"But of course nothing happened to him. And then you were so efficient afterward."

"What? Because I had her cremated? That's what Daisy wanted, you know."

"I didn't know, no," she says, finally a little bitterly. "And I'm not talking about cremation. I'm talking about how you managed everything so quickly after that. I mean, come on, Jerry. It was a world speed record for goodbyes. I didn't think it then but it was like a freak snowstorm and you shoveled the driveway and front walk all night and the next day the sun comes out and it's all clear, all gone. And then the fact of our not even being allowed inside the funeral parlor."

"You were there, but Nonna kept you two in another room."

"Yeah, Jerry, I know. We sat in the back of an open-casket wake."

"Jesus. I didn't know that."

"I'm sure you ordered her to keep us away."

"I didn't say to go to somebody else's funeral! Anyway, don't you think that was the best way? You were little kids, for chrissake. I don't care what anyone says. Kids don't have to mourn. And now that I know what Jack saw and had to deal with, all the better."

Theresa turns to her window. "You're probably right," she says, after a while, and tries to smile. Genuinely. I try to smile back. But none of it's any real solace to me. For I could say that I'm still reeling, that I've not yet begun to process all this new information, but that would pretty much be an outright lie. Wouldn't it? Not because I had any knowledge that Daisy's death wasn't wholly an accident, because I didn't, but you'd have to be a complete innocent (or maybe a kid) to imagine such a thing *not* happening, that her drowning in the pool wasn't somehow foreseeable, given the way she was raging and downfalling and the way I was mostly suspended, up here before I was ever up here. And if any part of what I'm saying is confessional, it's not *re:* Daisy but rather the kids, who I knew years earlier would almost certainly end up witnessing some excruciatingly awful moment.

Outside the air is getting a bit choppy, the *d-dump d-dump* as if we're cruising in a speedboat on a rippled-surface lake, the meter even and steady. I can see the weather coming together maybe 50 miles directly ahead of us, not thunderstorms, thank goodness, but odd high-hung batons of cottony haze, odd because you'd normally encounter such a thing in the early morning before the sun rose and burned it off but rarely if ever now, in midafternoon in late summer. Because of the change in weather I've called MacArthur for an instrument approach, the new routing duly given, and taken us down to 5000 feet, and we've just flown over Westerly, R.I., passing over the mouth of the Pawcatuck River, and are now approaching Mystic and Noank and will fly along the northern shore of Fishers Island right down the line to Plum Island and then Orient Point, tracking in along old Route 25, hitting Southold and Cutchogue and Mattituck before buzzing the big outlet mall at Riverhead, where I'll pick up the Expressway and take it on in before banking south for my home field, the route so ingrained in my head and hands that I could probably fly it at night with shot gauges, just the long ropes of the car lights to serve as my guide.

But now the turbulence ramps up, the invisible pockets hitting us hard and fast (like speed bumps in midair), the up and down severe enough that I tell Theresa to tighten her seat belt and brace herself, just not on her control wheel. It's raining on us now, or better we're in it, and I hope like heck that we're not heading into a so-called embedded thunderstorm, surprise shit that no pilot wants ever to see. I glance over and Theresa's curled up a bit, and I can see she's already a little green about the gills, that sloe-eyed open-mouthed pant. I reach back behind her seat to where I keep the coffee bags for getting sick in and hand one to her. To my surprise she immediately retches into it, not a lot, because she didn't eat any lunch, but enough to make me worry that it's not solely airsickness. She folds it up and wipes her mouth with the back of her hand.

"You okay?"

"Yeah," she answers, leaning her head against the window. "I'll be fine."

"We don't have long to go," I say, "but it might get rougher."

She half-smiles and gives me a thumbs-up full of irony and goofiness and cool, and for a mostly happy instant I think I can see almost every one of us in her, Battles and Daisy both. But suddenly I feel she's very young and I'm very old and I can't believe I've ever allowed her to come up here. For a while I considered keeping a parachute in the back for Rita but she hated the idea and now I'm wishing like crazy I had, so I could strap it on Theresa just in case one of the wing struts now fails, before she's trapped with me in the metal-heavy groundrush. And no sooner than I finish the thought does *Donnie* get a deep frontal wallop, *Whomp!*, and then another, *Whomp!*, the force of each rocking us in our hard cockpit seats, violently enough that my sunglasses fall off and land somewhere down near the pedals. The rain is fearsome. Theresa's headset has rotated forward on her head such that the band is in front of her eyes, and I reach over and pull it back into place. She's wincing, and suddenly there's a blot of blood glossing her lower lip.

"Theresa!"

She touches her mouth and inspects the smear. "It's okay, I just bit my . . ."

Whomp-Whomp!

Donnie bucks, then feels like she's yawing straight sideways, and for a long, long second I lose hold of the wheel and accidently push the rudder pedal, and we dip hard to starboard like we're on a bombing run, diving to 4 o'clock, the airspeed indicator boinging inside the crystal like a fat man stepped on the scale; *Donnie*'s motor screams, the wings shuddering right down to the rivets, the airframe racked to its outer tolerances from pulling a G or two more than it was designed to pull, and you finally understand in that continuous pregnant second what people are talking about when they hold there's a nano-fine and mostly philosophical distinction between falling and flying. Or fearing and fighting, which perhaps explains how despite my overwhelming impulse to curl into a single cell I not-too-consciously manage to right her, get her level and steady, only to see we've lost 1000 feet, an entire skyscraper, which is absolutely fine as long as there's no more funny business.

"Are you okay?" I ask Theresa, who is canted forward a bit awkwardly. "Hey, talk to me."

"Yeah," she says weakly. "I've had enough of this, though. I want it to stop. Okay, Jerry? Make it stop."

"Okay, honey. We just . . ."

Whomp!

". . . we just have to get out of this damn pocket!"

Whomp-Whomp!

"Shit!"

Whomp-Whomp-WHOMP!

This set is nearly concussive, and produces in me what must be the dream of a boxer as his clock is being supremely cleaned, the wash of giddy relief that this is not yours truly but some other chump caught in the klieg lights of ignominy. As the beautiful dream dissipates, though, I can feel that my neck is already stiffening, the little bones fusing, with everything else that's jointed, hips and above, feeling distinctly unhinged.

"Theresa, honey," I hear myself say, my eyes probably open but not really working, unwilling to witness what will no doubt be the *coup de grace,* "hold on, honey, hold on!"

But the final wallop doesn't come. The *whomp* just doesn't *whomp.* The rain has stopped. And all we have is the alto hum of *Donnie*'s prop, the rpms in the key of A, a drone that's as sweet as any Verdi tenor crooning of a singularly misguided love.

"Theresa, baby, we're clear, we're clear."

She nods to me and even smiles but there's a look she's manifesting that I have seen plenty in the mirror, and on Jack, and Paul, and even Pop of late, but never on Theresa Battle—namely, this face of deferral—and I say, "What the hell is wrong?"

She glances down to her lap. And there, between her tanned legs in black Bermuda shorts, on the red vinyl seat, is a shiny pool of wet. She lifts a knee and the clear liquid dribbles over the white-piped edge.

"Please tell me you peed."

She shakes her head.

"Oh shit."

"It's too early," she says. "The baby's much too young to be born. We're only at twenty-five weeks."

"Do you know how much time you have, before it gets dangerous?"

"No." And then, with the alarm of a hard fact, "I have to get to the hospital. Now."

"It's going to be twenty minutes to the field, maybe more."

"To what field?"

"The field we came from! The only one."

"You have to fly me to New Haven, Jerry," she says. "That's where my doctor is, at Yale–New Haven. I can't go anywhere else. Not now. Please!"

"I don't know. I've never flown there."

"Does it really matter?"

"It shouldn't. But this doesn't seem the time to experiment."

"Can't you use your chart?"

She reaches back and hands it to me, and I don't want to waste any time looking, but now that I'm really flying again I can see we've strayed from our flight path in just the direction she wants. This fact isn't material; even though I can't see much for the thickening haze, I know we're in fact much closer to New Haven than we are to Islip, which is probably twice the distance from here and definitely shrouded with the same weather. So I flip through the charts as quickly as I can while we remain on our due-east heading. And I see that there in fact is a field, which of course I knew some time before in a normal frame of mind, called Tweed, in East Haven, just a few miles from her hospital.

"All right," I tell her, "we'll go where you want. How you doing?"

"I feel okay I think."

"Are you sure?"

"Owwww . . . !"

"What the hell is wrong?"

"Something hurts," she says, suddenly breathing short and fast. "Oh shit . . . shit . . . owwww!"

"We should be there in ten minutes, if I can do it in one run. Let me try to call the tower now so I can ask for an approach, and an ambulance."

She nods, her eyes closed tight with the pain. When I get on the tower frequency for Tweed and explain the situation to the controller he rogers me for an instrument clearance for immediate landing on a south approach, runway 2-0, and places the other traffic in a holding pattern. At least the airspace and field will be exclusively ours. I'll head west over the Sound for a minute and then veer northwest overland before banking back for the landing. The problem is that it's now cotton candy up here, the visibility diminishing fast, and the guy in the tower warns me that it'll probably be a few feet as I'm approaching, which means I won't be able to see any landing strip lights until just before the wheels touch down. I know Theresa can hear all this but between the rapid lingo-laden technical instructions and sketchy audio quality and the astoundingly equable tones of our aeronautical exchange she probably isn't fathoming the potential peril ahead of us. When I finish talking with the tower and give her a thumbs-up I'm heartened to see that she shoots me one right back, no matter what she really knows.

But as I make the turn inland the vapor steadily thickens, puffy batts of mist moving quickly past the windscreen and thus reflecting what seems our now inhuman speed, the ground wholly invisible below, the last blue patches of sky fatefully receding above, and I'm seriously beginning to wonder why this should be the moment of payback for my years of exclusively fair-weather flying, why I couldn't have simply been torn apart all by my lonesome in a nasty gray-black thunderhead à la Sir Harold. Why I couldn't enjoy your basic heroic romantic disappearance from the radar and been interred and eulogized *in absentia*, which really ought to be my fitting end.

Theresa says weakly, "Thanks, Jerry. For taking me flying."

"Are you kidding? I can't believe I let this happen. It's all my fault."

"I'm the one who wanted lobster."

"Doesn't matter. I'm your father."

"So?"

"I should have said no."

"Maybe you're right."

Theresa laughs, or screams, quite volubly, I don't know which.

"Are you comfortable?" I ask her. "What can I do? Are you cold?"

"I'll be okay," she says, tightly cradling her still gently mounded belly. "Just fly, Jerry, okay? Just fly."

So I do. The tower takes me over what must be land, and then has me turn 180 degrees for the runway, adjusting my heading as he lines me up with the field, and I check my airspeed, my altitude, my localizer, my glide slope, every indicator a go, and I take us in. And the air down here isn't rough, not rough at all, in fact it's the lightest meringue and we're a clean, sparkly knife, which is exactly what I'd hoped, for Theresa's sake. But what it is also is totally blanking, we've been swallowed up whole, the world outside gone completely opaque; I can't see the wings, or the struts, I can't see the damn nose. It's pure whiteout. I could be flying us upside down, or on our side, or pointing us straight toward the ground, and despite what the gauges posit my surging instinct is to pull up sharply and break off what is surely a doomed course, for whoever these days can fly blind and still so faithfully true?

Not Jerry Battle, for sure. But as we descend the floating crosshairs in the crystal magically align, literally right on the dot, and I take a hand off the wheel and grab hold of my daughter's unperturbedly cool fingers and palm, and at the last moment I actually shut my eyes, clamp them as tight as the engine housing, because what does it matter when there's nothing to see anyway, no real corroborative signs? And in the strangely comforting darkness I see not some instant flashing slide show of my finally examined and thus remorseful life but the simply framed picture of Theresa's suggested grouping not in the least difficult to delimit or define, all our gentle players arrayed, with scant or even nothing of me in mind.

I'll go solo no more, no more.

A skidding bump, the back-tug of the flaps, and we're here, running at neighborhood street speed on the field. To the port side, parked next to the terminal, an old-time ambulance is waiting in the fog, its lights silently spinning.

"We're here, baby," I say, my eyes giddy with tears. "We're here!"

But when I let go of her hand to turn and taxi *Donnie* back to the terminal it falls limply between us. I look over and her head is thrown back, her eyes closed, the band of her headset scraping at the side window, and for a second it feels just like that one summer when I was taking us home at the end of her failed runaway junket, when after the first couple of hours I truly wasn't angry at all, and was even secretly pleased, in fact, to be driving down the straight-shot highway as I watched her sleep the beautiful sleep of her at-last-exhausted adolescence, the bronzed arid palettes of the Dakotas rushing by at eighty-five.

"Baby?"

And when I look once again, I'm confused, for her face and throat, I think, are surely not cast in such a light-shaded stone, or wan papier-mâché; they can't be that null newsprint color. When I undo the seat belt and pull her over she slumps sideways on me with such a natural drape that I'm almost sure everything will be perfectly fine, my girl's just tired, and as we jounce along the paneled tarmac, it's like both of us are now guiding this little ship in, both of us at the controls.

twelve

LIFE STAYS THICK AND BUSY, on the ground.

Rita, my sweet never-at-rest, stands at the stove making today's lunch of grilled ham-and-cheese sandwiches (and ones without ham for the kids) while I set the dining room table with plastic utensils and cups and paper napkins and plates. She's already prepared the cucumber and tomato salad, and a tray of homemade brownies for dessert, and for my contribution to the meal I've emptied a bag of rippled potato chips into a bowl and opened a fresh warm jar of gherkins (the pantry closet, unfortunately, run through with hot-water pipes). Along with the brats' juice boxes and raspberry seltzer for Rita and Eunice, and because it's an unusually mild October Saturday, and because I simply wish to, I'll put out a six-pack of light beer for us guys, which I'll have stowed in the freezer for a short stretch before, so that the first sip feels almost crystalline, like tiny ice pops on the tongue.

Pop, not amazing to report, wasn't wild about this at first, but he's grown into a fan. He puts in cans for himself now, though half the time he forgets and plucks one out of the nonfreezer section of the fridge and instead I have to throw away the burst ones regularly. But I don't mind. You could say we've all had to come around in the last few weeks, dealing with one another's daily (and especially nightly) functions and manners and habits and quirks, which in themselves of course are thoroughly inconsequential, and one hopes not half as telling of our characters as are our capacities for tolerance and change. Perhaps from this perspective we blood, relational, and honorary Battles should be considered a pretty decent lot, for we've been mutually permissive and decorous and even downright nice, if nice means being mostly willing, mostly communicative. This doesn't preclude of course the periodically pointed communication, as Eunice aired earlier today after breakfast while she was cleaning the bathrooms, her self-appointed Saturday chore. As the kids were settling in to a solid four-hour block of *Nick Jr.* on the tube and Jack was showing Pop the work going on outside, with me heading down to the basement to finish constructing the wings on a balsa-framed model of *Donnie* (a hobby I haven't taken up since youth), Eunice marched out to the kitchen wielding a wet toilet brush in her yellow rubber-gloved hands and called for a conference on the Problem of Hair. Apparently with just two bathrooms for the seven of us we are steadily shedding enough of it to weave a hallway runner, which, though not as disgusting as dried pee on the toilet seat (a snuck glance by her at Pop), has resulted not just in a furry feeling underfoot but a serious clog in the sink and tub drains. Jack piped in about people not winding up the water hoses, and I added a note on the strange desire to illuminate empty rooms, and it was only when Rita arrived bearing grocery bags of foodstuffs and asking if she'd just missed Paul (Yes, ma'am) did we all clam up and retire to our respective tidier-than-thou corners.

Paul, who despite my protests insists on sleeping in the basement behind a sheet pinned to a clothesline and so tends to stay out of our hair, as it were, would probably not partake in the colloquium anyway, as he has more serious things on his mind than prickly domesticities. Just before Rita arrived for her Saturday visit to cook and clean a bit and then take me away for a night, he departed as he does each morning for St. Jude's Hospital, where in the preemie unit his son and my grandson, Barthes Tae-jon Battle, all 4 pounds 8 ounces of him, sleeps inside a clear plastic boxed crib. Twice a week I'll make the trip with him, but of course he goes every day, sometimes returning home and going back at night, and from what I can see and hear talking to the nurses, he has the same routine each day. He'll stop by the cafeteria first and get a large tea, and if the baby is sleeping or in a state of "quiet alert" he'll read aloud from the pile of books he brings in his knapsack, hours and hours from volumes of poetry or novels or the literature-studies journals containing critical essays of Theresa's, these last of which I can hardly understand but like to listen to anyhow in the same way I suspect the baby is not knowing but still listening intently, the purely plucked tones of Paul's calm writerly voice like an incantation, like a spoken dream. He'll read until the baby wakes, and then rock him and play with his unworldly tiny fingers and toes, small and tender enough to appear nearly transparent, hardly seeming to qualify as bone, and then get the boy suckling from an equally diminutive bottle, which the kid has always taken to quite well, voraciously in fact (indication enough that he's ready for Battle).

Whenever I'm accompanying, Paul will hand him over to me for a stint, and though without fail I'll play the ham-handed dolt for the cute, hefty nurses there's zero chance that I don't know what I'm doing. When I cradle his body in hardly two hands it seems to me I'm holding a refinement rather than something premature, too young or too small, a perfection of our kind that needs no more special handling than an unwavering attention, which might be object lesson enough. Each time I'll examine him closely, and I'll note that his pixie face is distinctively un-Caucasian, not much of a beak to speak of, the eyes almost like stripes in the skin, and the only thing that makes me pause for a half second is not that he doesn't look anything like me, which is how it has to be, but that I can't quite see his mother in him either, not yet, anyway, as he is an exact replica of the infant Paul's parents have shown us in pictures from his baby album. But maybe it's better this way for Paul and the rest of us, and that she's somewhere there, but not there, maybe mercifully good that in this one expression she's presently demurring.

But then the sweet runt will cry out (more like intensely mewl), or loudly crap in his diaper, and I'll know some opinion's afoot. For some weeks now the baby has no longer been aided by any breathing apparatus or fed intravenously, but for another couple weeks will still be monitored round-the-clock for steady vitals and the right mix of blood gases and sugars. Then, if all looks cheery and flush, and he puts on weight with the formula, Paul will finally bring him home.

Naturally, the all-agreed-upon plan is to ensconce Paul and the baby in the master, Jack and Eunice to sleep on the pullout in the family room for however long it takes for the second master bedroom addition to be completed, which by then should be close. Jack has been directing the construction, the final project in the books for the venerable firm of Battle Brothers Inc., est. 1938, and which promises to be a sizable loss. But no mind. I told Jack to build it the way he wants, with the grade of finishes that will make him and Eunice happy and comfortable, and that whatever Richie Coniglio couldn't slush into the larger write-off of the business, I'd absorb. Jack, however, has done the whole job straight off the shelves at Home Depot and Lowe's, Eunice ordering the sale fabrics and furnishings from Calico Corners and Pottery Barn, the sort of floor-sample fancy just about anyone should be able to appreciate, and certainly counts as deluxe for me.

On this score I'm damn proud of Eunice, for it seemed like she was constantly wincing at the start of construction as she flipped through the catalogues of mass-produced and marketed items but is now (perhaps with regular bathroom duty on her mind) celebrating availability and easy-care use as her primary design considerations. She was pretty depressed to have to move out of their house at Haymarket Estates (Jack found a Danish corporate executive on assignment to take a three-year lease on the place for $6000 a month, fully furnished, which will cover the mortgage and taxes plus), but she's no dummy and as Theresa said is genuinely devoted to Jack, duly remaking her bed minus all the silk shams and throws. The plan, I suppose, is that they'll use the time to regroup and reload and maybe in three years return to the château, assuming Jack is back earning. But I'm hoping things will go well enough here at our busy little ranch and maybe they'll have refigured their aims and priorities and decide to stay on longer, just renting their mini-mansion out again. The truth (which I'm sure Jack and Eunice already know) is that the chances of Jack's making the kind of dough he was paying himself are as slim as some homeowner adding a 20 percent tip to a Battle Brothers contracting invoice, and why I was the one first championing the bedroom addition, to make it as easy as possible on them to stay, my secret plan being that not too far down the road Jack will take over the house permanently and still have room for their kids and Pop and Paul and Barthes, and that I, with whatever luck is left to me, will find my closing digs elsewhere, such as Rita might desire.

Slim chances there again, champ.

At least this is what Pop tells me after lights out. With the kids in the third bedroom, we're bunking together, the space between our twin beds just wide enough that we can't simply reach over and nudge/hit each other. This is a good thing, I suppose. The other night he was snoring again with such a tortured, bestial rage, as though his body were trying to force his tonsils out through his nose, the wracked growls alternating with nearly minute-long cessations of breathing (Rita says it's sleep apnea), that I had to toss a slipper at his hulking mass, and wake him.

"Do you know what time it is?" he said, like I was the one who'd been sawing away.

"It's late."

"What do you want, Jerome?"

"You think I should put up another headstone out there?"

"What?"

"You know, out there."

"There *are* stones out at the cemetery."

"I mean one for Daisy."

"Oh," he said, scratching at himself down low. "I was wondering why there was that space in between your mother and Theresa."

"I think it all looks pretty good. But Daisy's spot just seemed kind of lonely."

"Maybe to you."

"Still. I should put another one up."

Pop rolled back away from me, onto his side. “Well, I thought that from the day she died. So did your mother.”

“Really? Why didn’t you say something?”

“She was your wife.”

“But you both loved her. You had a say.”

“You think you would have listened to us?”

“Yeah,” I said. “I probably would have.”

“Well, maybe that’s why we didn’t say anything. Now let’s get some shut-eye.”

I thought about that for a while, as Pop almost immediately started rattling the windowpanes with his two-stroke, how in fact after what happened Pop didn’t seem to bother much with me as he’d always bothered before, instruct me to do exactly this or that with the customers or the business or the kids. He just kind of receded in an un-Pop-like way, which I attributed to my mother telling him to back off for a while and just lend me whatever hand I might need. Which they both did, my mother especially helpful around the house and Pop, too, at the garage, where he came by a couple of times a week to keep the mechanics in line by replenishing their dented metal cooler with cold beer and sandwiches. It never occurred to me back then as a presumably long-minted adult that he might have finally decided it was time to let me stew in a holding tank of my own, be it eye-high with shit or honey, and not, as was his wont (born out of ego-fied generosity and expedience), to keep giving me things anymore, foremost opinions and advice. I suppose this would normally be my moment to be expressing gratitude to him, for the usual (if tardy, extra-subtle) parental relinquishment, but I still wish he’d naturally intruded and called me a cowardly coldhearted fool and went ahead and ordered up a customary funeral and headstone for Daisy, as I wouldn't now be staring at an oddly unbalanced plot of sod whenever I visit the cemetery with Paul, following a day at St. Jude's.

At the gathering at our house after Theresa's funeral, in fact, among the countless other miserable happenings of that day, Sal Mondello (who is officially retired now, after the bankruptcy filing) came up to me afterward and extended his condolences and then added, "It's a shame her mother can't be with her." If the randy old geezer hadn't actually looked so brittle about the chops I'd have busted him one solid and wrung his neck with his own Major Johnson. But I didn't, and just nodded and accepted his old-country gesture of an envelope, then received the scores of her friends and relatives and other sundry people who came out, some of whom I didn't even recognize. But of course her high school friends, Alice Woo and Jadie Srinivasan, were there, in black-on-black dresses and hose, clinging to each other like there was a fierce ill wind blowing, crying their eyes out from the pew to the grave, and then those who obviously came out for us bereaved, like Richie and his associates, and Kelly Stearns and Miles Quintana, who despite showing no such indication were clearly there *together* (the Movietone story of how this happened I later learned from Miles, and it involved a final Parade parking lot altercation with Jimbo and the subsequent mutual realization by a maturing white Southern woman and her young brown urban knight that they had more in common than simply a love of enabling their respective constituencies to temporarily exit the dreariness of life through mid-budget holidays). The supporting presence of these friends and associates didn't comfort so much as reveal for me a surprisingly pernicious secondary gloom over the already near-suffocating pall of woe, the knowledge of collective mourning initially soothing but soon enough all the more depressing, such is the idea that no one completely escapes.

Paul, to his credit, didn't try to keep it together for anybody's sake. He lost it at the house that morning, and on the car ride to the church, and literally a few words into his remarks at the pulpit he simply stopped and stepped down and sat down next to us and bawled as loudly as he could. I was proud of him. At the lowering of the casket Jack had to hold him up, lest he stumble and fall into the hole, and back at the house afterward he had an attack of sharp pains in his belly and chest, which Rita and one of our doctor friends attended to, successfully treating with a dose of Pop's antigas tablets. That night, after everyone else had gone to sleep, while sharing the last $150 bottle of a boutique cabernet that Jack had brought over and opened unbidden and somewhat oddly insisted the two of us drink, Paul thanked me for getting up and finishing his eulogy. I said it was no problem, an honor and a privilege. So we drank to those, and to a few other puffed up et ceteras, even chuckling a bit, and soon thereafter we polished off the plump, inky wine. Because he naturally couldn't handle it and was completely grief-exhausted besides, I had to walk him to his bed, where I'm sure for the first time in days—certainly then and perhaps since—he slept an intractable, unfettered sleep.

I didn't, quite, and lay in bed for a long while staring up at the ceiling, tracing paths along the mottles and cracks, of course only inviting a dreadful circularity. I began to feel as if I were lying in a box and naturally didn't want to continue on that line and so I stepped outside onto the patio in the cooling night air and sat slumped in a deck chair beneath the moonlit sky, the distant, big-hearted-river sound of the Expressway filtering through the dry leaves of the trees. The sky, despite the half-moon, was still brilliant with celestial lights, and when I looked back over the roof I thought I saw a glinting streak fall to the horizon. There was another, and another, though appearing lower in the sky each time, and to see the next ones better I went around to the side yard, where I kept the gutter-cleaning ladder, and quietly leaned it against the gutter. Then I climbed up onto the roof, walked atop the house back over the kitchen, and sat down and waited.

There was nothing then. And I was trying my best not to remember the day but kept thinking anyway how I had finished up reading Paul's speech, which came right after Pop's, and then Jack's. It was beautifully somber, serious, elegantly lyrical stuff, and not just heady with its quotations from Heine and the Bible and the I Ching and Blake but also marked by earthy and detailed remembrances of her and their life, and even though they knew it had been written by Paul a number of people complimented *me* on the moving, heartrending words.

Though I'd told him he could take a pass, Pop insisted he was fine, and was clearly bent on saying a few words; but he only spoke off the cuff for a minute or two at most, coughing between words to suppress any burgeoning gasping or tears, and talked respectfully of her tough spirit and independent views, though he ended somewhat gruffly and inappropriately, mumbling that he hadn't seen her much of late at "the home." Jack, on the other hand, left little unmentioned in his sheaf of prepared remarks, moving quite slowly and for some reason nonchronologically through this or that scene from their childhood and teen years, noting in most every instance how his brawn had been neatly trumped by her brains. At one point he had to pause for an awkwardly long time because he was physically shuddering at what seemed surely the end of his talk, but then held it together and continued some more and didn't quite arrive to any concerted finish but instead mostly just stopped.

I was supposed to speak next, Paul slated to go last, all this outlined in the printed program. But after Pop and Jack went, Paul turned and nodded to me and then just popped up from the front. And while it wouldn't be right or fair to say that Pop's and Jack's speeches were failures exactly, because nothing expressed (or not) in such a circumstance can be anything but painfully singularly real and thus in its own profound way absolutely truthful and worthy, there hung in the silence of the church after Jack said his piece a distinctly off-kilter note that seemed desperately in need of some harmonizing response, which automatically summoned the poet in Paul to rise from the bench.

When Paul then took his turn and thereby preempted me I wasn't in the least offended or upset. I was feeling lucky, even glad. Even though I surely had in mind a thousand modest, authentic things I could have said, among them how I'd always liked the loose windblown way she wore her all-black clothes, or didn't dig how she'd often hug the yellow line when she drove, or could mention, too, if it were the least okay to do so, that while she never did regain consciousness in the ambulance after her placenta detached and bled out in a manner that, I swear, I swear, I would not describe if even my life depended on it, I was almost certain that her hand's grasp on mine kept tightening with purposeful assurance and not that she was dying or already dead. No, no, I didn't have any words, lofty or not, to offer the broken-faced throng.

No, none.

And why not? I don't know. Maybe it was old-time unreconstructed denial, or that oft-documented lazy-heartedness of mine, or else what might simply be a pathological fear of sadness. None of these of course is any good excuse, which I can mostly handle, except what does disturb is the thought that somewhere up there (I hope and pray, *up there*) Theresa Battle has had to pause in free mid-soar and grant pardon to an utter terrestrial like me.

That night I sat for some time on top of the house, and then, seeing nothing else falling in the sky, stood up to go back down. But when I checked my footing on the shingles I noticed it, the faint shade of the wide X I had inlaid, which strangely glimmered now more vividly in the moonlight than it ever had in the day. And after I locked the sliding door inside and checked on Paul and Jack's kids and climbed back into my empty bed, I thought no matter how much I wished to disappear sometimes, to fly far off and away, I really couldn't, and maybe never did. Or will.

Rita says, "The sandwiches are almost ready, Jerry. You better call everybody."

"Maybe I won't just yet," I say, my fingers tapping on her hip the first few bars of a majestic unknown song of love. "Maybe I'd just like to stay here with you."

She leans back into me. "It's a lot of sandwiches."

"We can manage it."

She kisses me, but quick and light. "Just go."

In the den I inform the kids that lunch is ready. They hardly nod at me as they momentarily stop sucking with fury on their thumbs, their action cartoon at full-bore climax, worlds exploding in a cataclysm of galaxial smoke and fire. They wait in silent, fearful awe until the hunky robot hero reappears and then cackle like the damned. I tell them again, and with their free hands they wave me on to the adjoining laundry room, where Eunice is plucking clothes from the dryer.

"Thank god for Rita!" she says when I mention lunch, handing me a stack of folded dish towels. "Take these back to the kitchen, will you? And please put them *away*, okay?"

After I comply I head outside and see Pop coming from around the side of the house, where the bedroom addition is going up. He's wearing a ratty sweatshirt and jeans, a leather tool belt loosely wound around his ample waist. He's been eating well since leaving Ivy Acres, and he's been pretty energetic besides, walking daily around the neighborhood and even helping Jack with the construction, only superlight-duty stuff of course, like measuring and cutting pieces of cedar siding.

"How's it going today?"

"Like always," he says, patting his tape measure. "Guns blazing."

"Is Jack back there?"

"Tell me it's chow time."

"A-huh."

"Good, I'm starving. Where are you going?"

"To get Jack."

"He's not over there."

I stop. "So where is he?"

Pop says, "Look in the hole."

What Pop is calling the hole, of course, is not quite that. It's a 20-by-40-foot pool trench, dug by Jack himself a couple of days last week with a backhoe from one of our former competitors, who was more than happy to rent him the machine at half the regular rate as a going-out-of-business present (Pop later told me, as it was being loaded on the truck for return, that he'd taken a nice long whiz in the gas tank). Jack figured that with all they'd given up, the kids could at least have a pool, and I wasn't one to argue. He's done a pretty nice job, given that he probably only had fifteen or twenty hours on such equipment before this, and the only associated mishaps were a couple crushed terra-cotta planters and a deep gash in the corner of the garage from the shovel, damage that looks truly horrid but definitely isn't structural. Jack pretty much dug out what had been filled in all those years ago, and the excavation proved to be unexpectedly archaeological, as we uncovered some of his and Theresa's rusty yard toys and some rotted sneakers and dolls amid the fill and gravel, and as he plumbed each side of the old pool you could sift about and find a few of the original decorative tiles, like it was some ghostly ruin of Pompeii.

I now see that Jack is indeed just climbing out, having probably made some final checks of the depth and grade. It's crazy, but we're going to try to do the finish lining ourselves. I tell him lunch is on and he gives me a nod.

"Is it ready?" I ask.

"Ready as ever," he tells me. "Maybe Monday, we'll give it a go?"

"Okay."

He shows me the soiled palms of his hands and heads for the side door to the laundry room, where the utility sink is. But instead of going in too, I step down the ladder to the bottom of the hole. Unlined as yet with concrete and tiles, it's a huge dark shoebox, the earth cool and still moist in the corners and along the deep end. And as scary and unnervingly quiet as it is to be even this far below ground, I do like the smell, which is loamy and fat and sweetly vernal, not at all of extinction, and I breathe in as deeply as I can bear. I've found myself coming down here at least once or twice a day, standing and sitting and then leaning back against the steeply ramped dirt, gazing up at a perfect frame of firmament for flights endless, unseen.

Now where's Jerry? somebody says, the barely audible sound traveling just above and far enough away from me that I don't immediately answer. It's okay. No problem. They'll start without me, you'll see.

acknowledgments

I would like to thank the John Simon Guggenheim Memorial Foundation and the Hunter College Research Foundation, for support during the writing of this book.

I also wish to thank Frank and Richard Branca for the helpful aeronautical consults, Richard Purington and Ann Dickinson for the quiet, cool writing cottage, and my colleagues in the Council of Humanities at Princeton for their friendship and inspiration.

I am indebted, as ever, to Cindy Spiegel and Amanda Urban.

And to my sweethearts, Annika and Eva, for being just as they are.

BY CHANG-RAE LEE

Readers Guide

For more information on ALOFT and Chang-rae Lee, please visit www.riverheadbooks.com.

DISCUSSION QUESTIONS

1. Jerry's relationships with the three women in his life are complicated and interrelated. What were the happiest moments of the life he shared with Daisy? Why did Rita help Jerry raise Jack and Theresa when he denied her the opportunity to have children of her own? Why doesn't Jerry do more to help Kelly in her most desperate moment of need?

2. On the surface, Paul and Jack are completely different: Paul is a small, wiry bookworm, an out-of-work writer, while Jack is a natural-born athlete and manager of the Battle family business. But while the differences are apparent, both men practice a form of denial with regard to their relationships with their wives. How are both men governed by the demands of these relationships? Discuss the differences and similarities between Jack and Paul as they try to cope with the conflicts of their married lives.

3. Why is Theresa determined to have her baby—even at the cost of her own life?

4. When Jerry goes to Richie's house to look for Rita and is reluctantly drawn into a high-wager tennis match, he allows his plane, *Donnie,* to be the collateral with which he will play. *Donnie* is Jerry's favorite escape. Is his potentially sacrificing it enough to show Rita that he wants her back? Why does Rita decide to stay and help Jerry put his family back together again?

5. Discuss the metaphor of flight as it relates to Jerry's propensity for escapism and for distancing himself from the problems that arise in the world.

6. How does Jerry deal with Theresa's illness differently from Daisy's?

7. When Hank sounds sick over the phone, Jerry admits to his disbelief in "the Real." Jerry continually tries to ignore "the Real," to float beyond it until the trouble has passed and someone else has dealt with it. How does this attitude affect his ability to raise Jack and Theresa? Theresa later praises Jerry for his parenting skills. Do you think Jack feels the same way toward his father?

8. When Paul and Jerry are in Pop's bedroom watching TV, Paul explains that the problem with the world is that everyone is too self-absorbed: "They think they can go anywhere and do anything, as if none of their actions has any bearing except on themselves." Jerry often characterizes himself in much the same way. Does he avoid feeling guilty by believing his problems originate with Daisy's death? Does he excuse all his family members of their faults with the same justification? How, if at all, does learning more about Daisy's last few hours change Jerry's opinions about himself?

9. How do you think Jerry characterizes Theresa's death? Was it his fault? Hers? How would Jerry view Daisy's death in contrast? What is your interpretation of the circumstances that lead to each woman's passing?

10. The novel begins with Jerry flying in his plane and ends with him stepping into a rectangular hole in the ground that will later be a pool, lying down, and looking up at the sky. Discuss the symbolism of the book's final image and how it relates to the metaphor of flight throughout the rest of the novel.

Chang-rae Lee is the author of *A Gesture Life*, winner of an Anisfield-Wolf Book Award, a Gustavus Myers Outstanding Book Award, an NAIBA Book Award for fiction, and an Asian-American Literary Award, and *Native Speaker*, winner of the Hemingway Foundation/PEN Award for first fiction, an American Book Award from the Before Columbus Foundation, the Oregon Book Award, a Barnes & Noble Discover Great New Writers Award, and QPB's New Voices Award. Selected by *The New Yorker* as one of the twenty best writers under forty, Chang-rae Lee teaches writing at Princeton University.